STEPHEN JONES lives in London, England. A Hugo Award nominee, he is the winner of four World Fantasy Awards, three International Horror Guild Awards, five Bram Stoker Awards, twenty-one British Fantasy Awards and a Lifetime Achievement Award from the Horror Writers Association. One of Britain's most acclaimed horror and dark fantasy writers and editors, he has more than 155 books to his credit, including *The Art of Pulp Horror: An Illustrated History*; the film books of Neil Gaiman's *Coraline* and *Stardust*; *The Illustrated Monster Movie Guide* and *The Hellraiser Chronicles*; the non-fiction studies *Horror: 100 Best Books* and *Horror: Another 100 Best Books* (both with Kim Newman); the single-author collections *Necronomicon* and *Eldritch Tales* by H.P. Lovecraft; *The Complete Chronicles of Conan* and *Conan's Brethren* by Robert E. Howard, and *Curious Warnings: The Great Ghost Stories of M.R. James*; plus such anthologies as *Horrorology: The Lexicon of Fear, Fearie Tales: Stories of the Grimm and Gruesome, A Book of Horrors, The Mammoth Book of Halloween, The Lovecraft Squad* and *Zombie Apocalypse!* series, and thirty volumes of *Best New Horror*. You can visit his web site at *www.stephenjoneseditor.com* or follow him on Facebook at *Stephen Jones-Editor*.

ALSO FROM PS PUBLISHING

Edited by Stephen Jones and Ramsey Campbell

Best New Horror #1
Best New Horror #2
Best New Horror #3

Edited by Stephen Jones

The Best of Best New Horror Volume One
The Best of Best New Horror Volume Two
Best New Horror #25
Best New Horror #26
Best New Horror #27
Best New Horror #28
Best New Horror #29
Best New Horror #30

BEST NEW HORROR

#30

BEST NEW HORROR

#30

EDITED AND WITH AN INTRODUCTION BY

STEPHEN JONES

DIP

BEST NEW HORROR
Volume №30

Collection and editorial material copyright © Stephen Jones 2020.

Front cover illustration by Warren Kremer.
Originally published on *Black Cat Mystery* #37, July 1952.
Back cover illustration attributed to Al Avison.
Originally published in *Witches Tales*.

This trade paperback edition published in November 2020
by Drugstore Indian Press, an imprint of PS Publishing Ltd.,
by arrangement with Stephen Jones.

2 4 6 8 10 9 7 5 3 1

ISBN 978-1-786366-91-7

Design and Layout by Michael Smith
Cover design by Smith & Jones

Printed and bound in England by TJ Books Limited

PS PUBLISHING
Grosvenor House, 1 New Road
Hornsea HU18 1PG, England

editor@pspublishing.co.uk
www.pspublishing.co.uk

CONTENTS

ACKNOWLEDGEMENTS

THE EDITOR WOULD like to thank Kim Newman, David Barraclough, Mandy Slater, Jo Fletcher, Amanda Foubister, Andrew I. Porter, David A. Sutton, Ellen Datlow, Gordon Van Gelder, Robert Morgan, Jim Gerlach (ERB, Inc.), Lydia Gittins (Titan Books), Rosemary Pardoe, R.B. Russell, Andy Cox, Michael Kelly, David Longhorn and, especially, Peter and Nicky Crowther, Mike Smith, Marie O'Regan and Michael Marshall Smith for all their help and support. Special thanks are also due to *Locus*, *Ansible*, *Classic Images*, *Entertainment Weekly*, *ISFDB* and all the other sources that were used for reference in the Introduction and the Necrology.

THE KEEPERS OF THE LIGHTHOUSE copyright © Ken Mackenzie 2018. Originally published in *The Keepers of the Lighthouse*. Reprinted by permission of the author.

THE HUNGRY GRASS copyright © Tracy Fahey 2018. Originally published in *New Music for Old Rituals*. Reprinted by permission of the author.

GHOSTLY STUDIES, DR. GRACE, AND THE DIODATI SOCIETY copyright © Daniel McGachey 2018. Originally published in *By No Mortal Hand*. Reprinted by permission of the author.

IT NEVER LOOKS LIKE DROWNING copyright © Damien Angelica Walters 2018. Originally published in *Great British Horror 3: For Those in Peril*. Reprinted by permission of the author.

THE WINDOW OF ERICH ZANN copyright © Michael Marshall Smith 2018. Originally published in *The Lovecraft Squad: Dreaming*. Reprinted by permission of the author.

POSTERITY copyright © Mark Samuels 2018. Originally privately distributed on Patreon. Reprinted by permission of the author.

OCTOBERLAND copyright © Thana Niveau 2018. Originally published in *Octoberland*. Reprinted by permission of the author.

PORSON'S PIECE copyright © Reggie Oliver 2018. Originally published in *The Ballet of Dr Caligari and Madder Mysteries*. Reprinted by permission of the author.

HE SINGS OF SALT AND WORMWOOD copyright © Brian Hodge 2018. Originally published in *The Devil and the Deep: Horror Stories of the Sea*. Reprinted by permission of the author.

Remembering old friends and colleagues

Paul Dale Anderson
David Bischoff
David Case
Maurine Dorris
Gardner Dozois
Dave Duncan
Harlan Ellison
Pat Lupoff
Peter Nicholls
Dave Reeder
Walter Velez
David J. Willoughby

INTRODUCTION

HORROR IN 2018

ACCORDING TO STATISTICS released for 2018, book sales in the US were up slightly, but at the smallest rate of growth seen over the previous five years. Especially notable was that YA and juvenile sales only increased by a fraction of a per cent.

In the UK, sales increased £34 million above the previous year, while Canadian book sales basically flattened thanks to a small decrease in fiction but an increase in non-fiction.

Meanwhile, according to a survey conducted by The Authors Guild, the average annual income for American authors had declined by some 42% since 2009 and stood at around just $6,000. The drop was blamed on declining royalties, publishing companies only interested in "blockbusters" and the business practices of Amazon.com.

Publisher Marc Gascoigne announced that he would be leaving Angry Robot Books, the imprint he founded in 2008 and won a World Fantasy Award for, at the end of the year in search of "a new challenge". Gascoigne's position was not directly replaced, while Angry Robot's editorial co-ordinator and publicity director did not relocate from the company's Nottingham office to its new headquarters in Islington, London.

Nick Wells' Flame Tree Publishing launched its new genre trade fiction imprint, Flame Tree Press, in September with twelve titles. Don D'Auria was the executive editor, and it was planned that the imprint would publish up to thirty books a year, by both established and up-and-coming writers.

Susan Moldow retired from her position as president of Scribner Publishing Group at the end of the year, which resulted in the closing of the Touchstone imprint, which she was also president of, while Prometheus Books sold its SF imprint Pyr, founded in 2005, to Start Publications.

In October, Medallion Press filed for Chapter 7 bankruptcy liquidation in the US Bankruptcy Court of Northern District of Illinois, blaming its financial problems on "difficulties facing the publishing industry". In its filing, the publisher listed assets of $100,001 to $500,000 and liabilities in the same range. It cited between 200 to 999 creditors.

In Britain, Alexander Mamut of Lynwood Investments sold his majority stake in booksellers Waterstones to Paul Singer's Elliott Management hedge fund. James Daunt stayed on as CEO, a role he had held since 2011. Meanwhile, Waterstones acquired the Foyles chain of family-owned bookshops, which had a 115-year history.

Stephen King's 58th novel, *The Outsider*, marked the return of obsessive-compulsive investigator Holly Gibney, as she teamed up with detective Ralph Anderson to look deeper into a series of gruesome child-murders committed by "*El Cucu*", a supernatural doppelgänger that took the identities of those it came into contact with. At least the author credited Edgar Allan Poe's 'William Wilson' as inspiration. The May 25 issue of *Entertainment Weekly* carried an exclusive excerpt.

Scott Carey had problems with his decreasing weight and his lesbian next-door neighbours in King's short novel, *Elevation*, which was set in the Maine town of Castle Rock and illustrated by Mark Edward Geyer. The lead character's name was a nice tribute to Richard Matheson's most famous book.

The vampire Lestat recalled how he came to rule over the world of the undead in Anne Rice's latest entry in "The Vampire Chronicles" series, *Blood Communion: A Tale of Prince Lestat*, also illustrated by Mark Edward Geyer, while *Serpentine* was the twenty-sixth volume in Laurell K. Hamilton's erotic "Anita Blake" series.

Past Tense, the twenty-third volume in Lee Child's best-selling "Jack Reacher" series, strayed into horror territory with a sub-plot set in a motel in the woods.

The world was threatened by a man-made respiratory virus on the anniversary of the 1918 influenza epidemic in Robin Cook's precedent medical thriller *Pandemic.*

Dean Koontz's *The Crooked Staircase* and *The Forbidden Door* were the third and fourth volumes in the author's "Jane Hawk" series. A Barnes & Noble exclusive edition of *The Crooked Staircase* included an additional essay, while *The Forbidden Door* was available as a signed hardcover.

Originally published in Sweden in 2014 and 2015, John Ajvide Lindqvist's *I Am Behind You* and *I Always Find You* were the first two volumes in the "Locations" trilogy, set in a world transformed into an endless plain of grass.

The Woman in the Woods was the sixteenth volume in John Connolly's "Charlie Parker" series, while *House of Secrets* and *Echoes in the Walls* were the first two volumes in a new Gothic series credited to the long-dead V.C. Andrews'.

Editor Christopher Tolkien promised that J.R.R. Tolkien's *The Fall of Gondolin* (a compilation of various story-drafts in the late author's series of "Lost Tales" of Middle-earth) really would be "indubitably the last" of his father's unpublished writings. Alan Lee supplied the sumptuous artwork.

Amy Thomsett, the girl who flies on moth wings, was back in Kim Newman's *The Haunting of Drearcliff Grange School*, a sequel to the author's 2015 novel *The Secrets of Drearcliff Grange School*. This time Amy and her super-powered school friends in the Moth Club travelled to London to compete in a contest and found themselves haunted by a limping ghost.

A rogue archaeologist and the crew of his reality TV show were following in the footsteps of an explorer from 1909 when they investigated a mysterious cavern hidden high up in the Grand Canyon. They didn't like what they found in *The Anomaly* by "Michael Rutger" (Michael Marshall Smith).

Second-hand clothing turned Londoners homicidal in Graham

Masterton's *Ghost Virus*, while a mother and daughter found their apparently normal lives unravelling in Sarah Pinborough's *Cross Her Heart*.

Phantom vehicles and car lanes suddenly appeared on the Los Angeles freeway in Tim Powers' *Alternate Routes*, and M.R. Carey's *Someone Like Me* was about a teenager who could see both of her mother's violent split-personalities.

A married gay couple and their adopted seven-year-old daughter were menaced by four strangers who claimed that one of them would have to be willingly sacrificed to avert the coming Apocalypse in Paul Tremblay's home-invasion thriller *The Cabin at the End of the World*, which came with a glowing endorsement from Stephen King.

Set in the mid-1840s, Alma Katsu's historical horror *The Hunger* added a neat supernatural twist to the true story of the cannibalistic Donner Party.

After her hand was amputated, Rachel Cooper started dreaming about a woman imprisoned in a tree-trunk who eventually crossed over into her world in James Brogden's *The Hollow Tree*, which was based on a real-life urban legend.

A batch of bootleg moonshine distilled by a cult of diabolists resulted in those who drank it experiencing demonic visions of decay and destruction in *Creatures of Want and Ruin*, the follow-up to Molly Tanzer's *Creatures of Will and Temper*.

When a couple moved to the wife's ancestral home in England, they started having visions and dreams connected to their dead daughter and a creepy Victorian children's book in Dale Bailey's haunted house novel, *In the Night Wood*.

The third and final book in Angela Slatter's "Verity Fassbinder" trilogy, *Restoration*, found the tough heroine working for a psychotic fallen angel.

The Folded Land was the second volume in Tim Lebbon's "Relics" trilogy, in which Angela Gough continued to explore the world's dark underbelly as she struggled to save her niece during an uprising of mythical creatures.

A mother searched for her missing daughter in a realm outside reality in Tim Waggoner's *The Mouth of the Dark*, and a strange creature stole siblings' toys in *The Toy Thief* by D.W. Gillespie.

Psychic Angela Constantine encountered a group of terrorists in Terry Goodkind's supernatural thriller *The Girl in the Moon*, while Rio Youers' *Halcyon* was about a psychic ten-year-old girl and her family who ended up as part of a strange cult on the eponymous island.

A newly-divorced woman returned to her childhood home and discovered that a recent drowning victim was a woman she had been dreaming about in Wendy Webb's *Daughters of the Lake*, while a carpenter's plans to fix up an old house as a Halloween attraction were interrupted by a real ghost in Brian Everson's *The House by the Cemetery*.

Inspired by Charles Maturin's 1820 Gothic novel *Melmoth the Wanderer*, Sarah Perry's *Melmoth* was about a translator in Prague who was apparently being menaced by a female monster that had been haunting those who do bad deeds for centuries.

A pair of film composers looking for inspiration stayed at a haunted Californian castle, the site of a series of unexplained murders in 1925, in *The Sorrows* by Jonathan Janz, while a sceptic agreed to spend a month in a haunted house in *The Siren and the Specter* from the same author.

Zero Day was the third and final volume in Ezekiel Boone's "The Hatching" trilogy about an ancient species of deadly spiders taking over the planet. From the same author, *The Mansion* was a high-tech haunted house novel set in the near future.

A band discovered that their lead singer may have bargained their souls in return for success in Grady Hendrix's heavy metal horror novel *We Sold Our Souls*.

John Hart's *The Hush* was set a decade after *The Last Child*, and found Johnny Merrimon hiding from his fans in the woods.

A couple spending the summer in a Maine cottage discovered there was something in the woods in Hunter Shea's *Creature*, while David Tallerman's *The Bad Neighbours* had basically the same plot.

When a pair of New York millenials were forced to move to a house in the suburbs, they discovered a monster in the basement in *The Chrysalis* by Brendan Deneen.

A new subway line revived an ancient horror beneath New York City in *Awakened* by James S. Murray and Darren Wearmouth, and a newly engaged couple became the live-in caretakers of a haunted house-turned-museum in Ben Dolnick's *The Ghost Notebooks*.

In Afghanistan, the Cerberus Unit encountered creatures that inspired the vampire legend in Richard Jeffries' *Blood Demons*, while a group of soldiers returning from Afghanistan all shared the same disturbing dream in *Burning Sky* by Weston Ochse.

Forsaken was the second book in Michael McBride's "Unit 51" series, and Simon Green wrapped up his "Secret Histories", "Nightside" and a few other series with an epic confrontation in *Night Fall*.

With the Landry agency disbanded, the British Prime Minister turned out to be a narcissistic Elder God in *The Labyrinth Index*, in the ninth volume of Charles Stross' Lovecraftian "Landry Files" series.

Set in a dystopian world dominated by H.P. Lovecraft's Mythos monsters, Ruthanna Emrys' *Deep Roots* was the second book in the "Innsmouth Legacy" series, which began with *Winter Tide*.

After going missing for four years, a boy returned with strange powers in Caroline Kepnes' Lovecraftian novel *Providence*. Peter Levenda's *Dunwich* was a sequel to the author's *The Lovecraft Code*.

Seanan McGuire's *The Girl in the Green Silk Gown* was a sequel to the author's *Sparrow Hill Road*, as legendary hitchhiking ghost Rose Marshall was still pursued by the immortal killer who murdered her on her prom night.

Joseph Fink's *Alice Isn't Dead* was based on the author's horror podcast series about a trucker searching for her long presumed-dead wife in a world of serial killers and zombies. Cote Smith's *Limetown* was a prequel to the podcast created by Zack Akers and Skip Bronkie, about the mysterious disappearance of all the inhabitants of a small Tennessee town.

Originally published in Sweden in 2015, Mats Strandberg's *Blood*

Cruise was a gory romp set on an old ship travelling between Sweden and Finland that was cut off from the outside world, while Icelandic author Snorri Kristjánsson's *Kin* was the first novel in a new series of Viking murder mysteries featuring the character "Helga Finnsdottir".

Still trading on his great-grand-uncle Bram's legacy, Dacre Stoker's *Dracul*, co-written with J.D. Parker, was a re-imagined prequel to *Dracula*, which purported to fill in some of the gaps in the original novel caused by cuts made at the behest of the publisher.

Dracula's daughter, Lucy Harker, was assigned to protect Winston Churchill during the First World War in Cynthia Ward's novella *The Adventure of the Dux Bellorum*, the second volume in the "Blood Thirsty Agent" series.

Dreadful Company, the second novel in Vivian Shaw's series about "Greta Helsing", found the doctor to the undead travelling from London to attend a medical conference and encountering a coven of vampires, ghost-hunters, a werewolf, a demon and such characters as Oscar Wilde, Lord Ruthven and Varney the Vampire.

The Last Wolf was the first book in the "Legend of All Wolves", a new werewolf romance series by Maria Vale.

Justina Ireland's *Dread Nation* was an alternate history novel set in a world in which the dead ("shamblers") revived during the battle of Gettysburg, towards the end of the American Civil War.

The Valley of Shadows by John Ringo and Mike Massa was a spin-off zombie novel set in Ringo's "Black Tide Rising" universe.

Published under Riverdale Avenue Books' Afraid imprint, *Rabid Heart* was expanded from a short story by death-metal musician Jeremy Wagner into a rom-zom road-trip by a woman and her undead fiancé, set six months after a "Necro Rabies" pandemic had ravaged the world.

In John Kessel's *Pride and Prometheus*, an expansion of his award-winning novelette, Lizzie Bennet's younger sister Mary encountered Victor Frankenstein and his sympathetic Creature.

Jonathan Wright translated Ahmed Saadawi's 2013 Arabian allegory *Frankenstein in Baghdad*, in which a local peddler assembled a creature from body parts he picked up during the Iraq War.

Mary Jekyll and her group of mad scientists' daughters travelled across Europe to rescue Lucinda Van Helsing in *European Travel for the Monstrous Gentlewoman*, the second in Theodora Goss' "Extraordinary Adventures of the Athena Club" series.

Author Edgar Allan Poe teamed up with his detective character C. Auguste Dupin to investigate a woman being visited by her lover's ghost in *Edgar Allan Poe and the Jewel of Peru*, the second in a series by Karen Lee Street.

When a female explorer returned to 1895 London with a strange Carpathian box, author Bram Stoker got involved in Robert Masello's *The Night Crossing*.

Lois H. Gresh's *Sherlock Holmes vs. Cthulhu: The Adventure of the Neural Psychoses* was the second volume in another dispiriting mash-up series.

Nick Setchfield's debut thriller, *The War in the Dark*, was the first in a supernatural spy series from the features editor of *SFX* magazine.

L.L. McKinney's first novel, *A Blade So Black*, was like a trippy mash-up between *Alice in Wonderland* and *Buffy the Vampire Slayer*, as African-American teenager Alice learned to become a "Dream-walker" and cross over into the Wonderland, which was populated by Nightmares.

When one of their number went missing, a group of old school friends began investigating and discovered the strange volume of the title in *The Book of Hidden Things*, a first novel written in English by Italian author Francesco Dimitri.

A truck-driving serial killer selected a pregnant woman as his next victim in Marcelle Perks' debut novel, *Night Driver*, while a washed-up journalist started getting violent visions from a series of mysterious tattoos in Gary Kemble's first novel, *Strange Ink*.

A former dancer's nightmares started coming true in *The Dark Beneath the Ice*, a first novel by Amelinda Bérubé.

A mother killed supernatural creatures and sold their body-parts on the Internet in Rebecca Schaeffer's debut, *Not Even Bones*, the first in a trilogy about a supernatural teenager who rejected her monstrous heritage.

A teenage girl in 1877 Texas battled the walking dead in Emma Berquist's YA zombie Western, *Devils Unto Dust*, and a pair of sisters, drowned as witches centuries before, returned each summer to possess new bodies and lure boys to their doom in Shea Ernshaw's debut YA novel *The Wicked Deep*.

A teenager living in the South wanted her exorcised demon back in Jimmy Cajoleas' *The Good Demon*, illustrated by Michael Hoeweler.

A woman uncovered the secrets of her childhood home in Katya de Becerra's debut novel *What the Woods Keep*, and scary tales told around a campfire started coming true in Shawn Saries' first novel, *Campfire*, which came with a Foreword by James Patterson.

The "British Library Tales of the Weird" series of classic reprint anthologies included *From the Depths and Other Strange Stories of the Sea* and *Glimpses of the Unknown: Lost Ghost Stories*, both edited by Mike Ashley, along with *Spirits of the Season: Christmas Hauntings* edited by Tanya Kirk.

From Oxford University Press, *The Great God Pan and Other Horror Stories* edited with an Introduction and notes by Aaron Worth collected nineteen stories by Arthur Machen. The same publisher also issued a new edition of Mary Shelley's *Frankenstein* edited with an Introduction and notes by Nick Groom. It followed the 1818 text, but added the author's 1831 Introduction and Percy Bysshe Shelley's essay 'On Frankenstein'.

Penguin's reprint of Shelley's 1831 version added Douglas Clegg's 2013 Introduction and an Afterword by Harold Bloom from 1965.

The Promise of Air/The Garden of Survival from Stark House reprinted two longer works from 1918 by Algernon Blackwood with an Introduction by Mike Ashley.

Night Shade Books' superb series of hardcovers chronologically collecting Seabury Quinn's *The Complete Tales of Jules de Grandin* continued with *Volume Three: The Dark Angel* (1931–33) and *Volume Four: A Rival from the Grave* (1933–38). Along with an Introduction by editor George Vanderburgh and the late Robert Weinberg, Darrell Schweitzer and Mike Ashley supplied the respective Forewords.

Edgar Rice Burroughs, Inc. reissued the author's 1944 novel of savage Pellucidar, *Land of Terror*, in two attractive hardcover editions in slipcases. Featuring alternate dust-jacket art and fold-out frontispieces by Bob Eggleton and John Coleman Burroughs, the books also boasted a new Foreword by Dr. Robert B. Zeuschner, interior colour artwork by Frank Frazetta and Roy G. Krenkel, endpaper maps and unique die-cut bookmarks. The special Grosset & Dunlap and ERB, Inc. editions of *Land of Terror* were limited to 200 numbered and fifty-two lettered copies apiece, all signed by artist Bob Eggleton.

ERB, Inc. also published *Savage Pellucidar*, the seventh and final novel in Burroughs' series, in a matching format. The two slipcased volumes were available in a signed and numbered set of 248 copies, with a new Foreword by Richard Lupoff and Preface by Phil Burger, and dust-jacket paintings by Bob Eggleton and Thomas Grindberg. The set also included more than thirty illustrations by J. Allen St. John, Larry Ivie, Frank Frazetta, Bob Eagleton, Thomas Grindberg, Joe Jusko and Shuji Yanagi.

Edited with an Introduction by Victoria Nelson for the New York Review Books Classics, *Compulsory Games* collected fifteen of Robert Aickman's lesser-known "strange stories".

Scholastic's new 20th Anniversary Editions of J.K. Rowling's *Harry Potter* series featured cover art by Brian Selznick.

Return to Fear Street: You May Now Kill the Bride and *Return to Fear Street: The Wrong Girl* were the first two titles in a new young adult series by R.L. Stine.

Alisa Kwitney's Victorian steampunk novel *Cadaver & Queen* was inspired by *Frankenstein*, while Kiersten White's *The Dark Descent of Elizabeth Frankenstein* reimagined Mary Shelley's novel from the point-of-view of Victor Frankenstein's adopted sister.

Chandler Baker's *Teen Hyde*, a contemporary reworking of Robert Louis Stevenson's classic novel, was the second volume in the "High School Horror" series.

Set in Edinburgh, the twelve-year-old protagonist of Victoria Schwab's *City of Ghosts* tried to hide the fact that she could see dead people.

On an island in the Pacific Northwest, a teenage girl was forced to protect her family, friends and the other townsfolk from her monstrous mother in Leslye Walton's *The Price Guide to the Occult*.

A trio of teenagers investigated an island with a dark history, where girls had been disappearing for decades, in *Sawkill Girls* by Claire Legrand.

Five teenagers were trapped in a cave where something was hunting them in Kim Liggett's *The Unfortunates*, while another five friends discovered an ancient stone box in the forest and made a deadly pact in Martin Stewart's *The Sacrifice Box*.

A creepy old book caused chaos during a field trip in Katherine Arden's *Small Spaces*, and a young tutor discovered that there was something wrong with the wealthy family she was working for in Liana Liu's *Shadow Girl*.

A young girl confronted her worst fears while hunting the shape-shifting "grabbers" that haunted the woods around her village in Charlotte Salter's *Where the Woods End*, while a teenage wiccan brought some dead girls back to life to investugate their deaths in Lily Anderson's *Undead Girl Gang*.

Kim Liggett's *Heart of Ash* was a sequel to the author's *Blood and Salt*, *Neverwake* was a sequel to Amy Plum's *Dreamfall*, and *Court of Shadows* was the second volume in Madeleine Roux's "House of Furies" Gothic horror series, illustrated by Iris Compiet.

A Map of Days was the fourth volume in Ransom Riggs' "Miss Peregrine's Home for Peculiar Children" series. Illustrated with vintage photographs, a Barnes & Noble exclusive edition added nineteen pages of deleted material.

Lost was the second in the "House of Night Other World" vampire series by P.C. Cast and Kristin Cast.

Broken Lands was the first in a new YA series set in Jonathan Maberry's "Rot & Ruin" post-apocalyptic zombie world, and a young girl battled zombies in Justina Ireland's historical horror novel *Dread Nation*.

Lauren Baratz-Logsted's *Zombie Abbey* was everything you would expect from a YA mash-up of *The Walking Dead* and *Downton Abbey*.

Scream and Scream Again!: Spooky Stories from Mystery Writers of America included twenty stories by Heather Graham, Wendy Corsi Straub and others, including editor R.L. Stine.

Once again edited and introduced by Mark Morris, *New Fears 2: More New Horror Stories by Masters of the Macabre* featured twenty original stories from an impressive line-up of authors, including Priya Sharma, Stephen Volk, Robert Shearman, Gemma Files, Tim Lebbon, Ray Cluley, Brian Hodge, Catriona Ward, V.H. Leslie, Rio Youers, John Langan, Paul Tremblay, Alison Moore and others.

Ellen Datlow's new anthology *The Devil and the Deep: Horror Stories of the Sea* contained fifteen all-new tales by, amongst others, Christopher Golden, Terry Dowling, Ray Cluley, Stephen Graham Jones, Steve Rasnic Tem, A.C. Wise, John Langan, Brian Hodge and Michael Marshall Smith, along with an Introduction by the editor.

Phantoms: Haunting Tales from the Masters of the Genre edited with an Introduction by Marie O'Regan featured eighteen stories (four reprints) by Angela Slatter, Robert Shearman, Joe Hill, Tim Lebbon, Muriel Gray, John Connolly, M.R. Carey, Paul Tremblay, Gemma Files, Alison Littlewood and others.

Edited with an Introduction by Stephen Jones, *The Mammoth Book of Halloween Stories: Terrifying Tales Set On the Scariest Night of the Year!* brought together twenty-six stories (seventeen original) and a poem by, amongst others, Neil Gaiman, Alison Littlewood, Storm Constantine, Marie O'Regan, Ramsey Campbell, Lisa Morton, Joe R. Lansdale, Eygló Karlsdóttir, Robert Silverberg, Michael Marshall Smith, Sharon Gosling, Scott Bradfield, Robert Shearman and Jane Yolen.

The Lovecraft Squad: Dreaming was the second volume in the shared-world Lovecraftian series from the same editor. It contained eleven "Chapters" about the exploits of the super-secret organization dedicated to battling eldritch monstrosities by Reggie Oliver, Lisa Morton, Brian Hodge, Michael Marshall Smith, John Llewellyn Probert, Stephen Baxter, Angela Slatter, Kim Newman, Peter Atkins, and Sean Hogan and Lynda E. Rucker.

Edited by Alex Shvartsman, *The Cackle of Cthulhu* contained twenty-two humorous Lovecraftian stories (nine reprints) by Neil Gaiman, Lucy A. Snyder, Nick Mamatas and others.

Dracula: Rise of the Beast was an epistolary anthology of five stories chronicling the secret history of the vampire Count. Edited by David Thomas Moore, contributing authors included Adrian Tchaikovsky and Emil Minchev. From the same editor, *Creatures: The Legacy of Frankenstein* contained five stories about scientists following in Frankenstein's footsteps by Paul Meloy, Emma Newman, Kaaron Warren and others.

Edited by Emily Hockaday and Jackie Sherbow, *Terror at the Crossroads* contained twenty-one horror stories originally published in *Analog, Asimov's, Alfred Hitchcock's Mystery Magazine* and *Ellery Queen's Mystery Magazine*.

As part of Flame Tree Publishing's series of attractive "Gothic Fantasy" hardcover anthologies of new and classic tales, *Lost Souls Short Stories* came with a Foreword by Roger Luckhurst. It featured fifty-three stories and excepts (eleven original) by, amongst others, E.F. Benson, Ambrose Bierce, Mary Elizabeth Braddon, M. Marion Crawford, Charles Dickens, Amelia B. Edwards, Sheridan le Fanu, Mary E. Wilkins Freeman, W.F. Harvey, William Hope Hodgson, E.T.A. Hoffman, James Hogg, Washington Irving, Henry James, M.R. James, Jerome K. Jerome, H.P. Lovecraft, Arthur Machen, Charles Maturin, E. Nesbit, Margaret Oliphant, Edgar Allan Poe, Walter Scott, Lucy A. Snyder and Edith Wharton.

Two new titles in Flame Tree's series of "Thrilling Tales" anthologies were *Alien Invasion Short Stories* (twenty-eight stories, seven original) and *Endless Apocalypse Short Stories* (thirty-one stories, thirteen original). Patrick Parrinder supplied the Foreword to the former and Florian Mussgnug to the latter, while amongst those authors included were Steven Vincent Benét, Lord Byron, Arthur Conan Doyle, Austin Hall, William Hope Hodgson, H.P. Lovecraft, A. Merritt, Edgar Allan Poe, M.P. Shiel, Jonathan Swift, Lucy Taylor, Jules Verne, Voltaire and H.G. Wells.

Hark! The Herald Angels Scream was a Christmas anthology of eighteen original stories by Kelley Armstrong, Tim Lebbon, Seanan McGuire and others, edited by Christopher Golden.

From Night Shade Books, *The Best of the Best Horror of the Year: 10 Years of Essential Short Horror Fiction* contained twenty-eight stories culled from the past decade of editor Ellen Datlow's annual "Year's Best" series by, amongst others, Suzy McKee Charnas, Glen Hirshberg, Tanith Lee, Steve Rasnic Tem, Stephen Gallagher, Neil Gaiman, John Langan, Nathan Ballingrud, Ramsey Campbell, Brian Hodge, Gemma Files, Peter Straub, Adam L.G. Nevill and Carole Johnstone.

Edited by Datlow and from the same imprint, *The Best Horror of the Year Volume Ten* contained twenty-one stories by, amongst others, Mark Morris, A.C. Wise, Brian Hodge, Stephen Gallagher, Tim Major and John Langan, along with a summation of the year by the editor.

From Prime Books, *The Year's Best Dark Fantasy & Horror: 2018* edited and introduced by Paula Guran reprinted twenty-nine stories from 2017 by Priya Sharma, Helen Marshall, Robert Shearman, Steve Rasnic Tem, Angela Slatter, Stephen Graham Jones, Caitlín R. Kiernan, Jeffrey Ford, Lisa L. Hannett, Conrad Williams, Mark Samuels, M. Rickert and others.

The new Datlow and Guran volumes shared two authors (Carole Johnstone and Kaaron Warren) with different stories.

Co-edited by Robert Shearman and Michael Kelly, *Year's Best Weird Fiction Volume Five* was the final book in the series from Canadian imprint Undertow Publications. It collected twenty-four stories by Kurt Fawver, Kristi DeMeester, Helen Marshall, Alison Littlewood, Adam-Troy Castro, Paul Tremblay and others. The book shared one author (Carmen Maria Machado) with the Datlow volume and one (Helen Marshall) with the Guran volume. Lack of sales was blamed for the series' cancellation.

Having once again slipped in the schedule, *Best New Horror #28* edited by Stephen Jones contained twenty-two stories by twenty-one authors from 2016. These included Angela Slatter (with two contributions), Maura McHugh, Glen Hirshberg, Peter Bell, Darren Speegle, Reggie Oliver, Lynda E. Rucker, Dennis Etchison, Lisa Tuttle, Mark Valentine, Alison Littlewood, Michael Marshall Smith, Kristi DeMeester and others.

Stephen King released a free short story entitled 'Laurie' to his website as an "appetiser" to his new novel, *The Outsider*, which was published a week later.

As part of a research project known as "Ambient Literature", Kate Pullinger's *Breathe* was a fifteen-minute ghost story delivered through a smartphone app. The difference was that, after you gave it access to your camera and location, it knew where you were reading it, when you were reading it and how you were reading it, and adapted the story to incorporate those variables. As a result, the story changed every time you returned to it.

Issued by Open Road as e-books, *The Monster Novels: Stinger, The Wolf's Hour and Mine* and *The Southern Novels: Boy's Life, Mystery Walk, Gone South and Usher's Passing* were two omnibus editions of Robert McCammon's books from the 1980s and '90s.

Writer and film-maker Frazer Lee's *The Daniel Gates Adventures Vol.2: The Lilyth Mirror/The Lucifer Gate* was the second in a series of e-books published under the Crossroad Press imprint Macabre Ink.

John Joseph Adams' free monthly online publication, *Nightmare Magazine*, included new stories by Adam Troy Castro, Nalo Hopkinson, Alison Littlewood, Weston Ochse, M. Rickert, Halli Villegas, Usman Malik, Adam-Troy Castro and Carrie Vaughn. Halli Villegas, Lynda E. Rucker, Laura Anne Gilman, Joe McKinney, M. Rickert, Stephen Graham Jones, Priya Sharma, Ray Cluley, Kelley Armstrong, Terry Dowling, Gary McMahon, Barbara Roden, Conrad Williams, John Langan, Lucy Taylor, Gemma Files and Paul Tremblay all contributed reprint fiction. There were also interviews with S.P. Miskowski and Linda D. Addison, essays by Lisa Morton, Lucy Taylor, Halli Villegas, Nadia Bulkin, Grady Hendrix and A.C. Wise, and book reviews. Each month's contents were also serialised on the website.

Edited by Sean Wallace and Silvia Moreno-Garcia, the free monthly online magazine *The Dark* featured original fiction by Steve Rasnic Tem and reprints from Kristi DeMeester, Ray Cluley, Mark Morris, Stephen Graham Jones, Angela Slatter, Priya Sharma and Chaz Brenchley, amongst others.

Jeani Rector's monthly e-zine *The Horror Show* contained stories by Joe McKinney, Ramsey Campbell (in a special double-issue devoted to the author), P.D. Cacek, Graham Masterton, Jeff Strand, Nancy Kilpatrick, Lisa Morton and Tim Waggoner, amongst others. A print compilation of some of *The Horror Zine*'s original fiction, poetry and artwork was also available.

Graeme Hurry's *Kzine* was published three times a year as an e-book and in a PoD edition via Amazon websites. Issues included horror fiction by Nathan Driscoll, Ken McGrath, Ryan Fitzpatrick and others.

Contributors of original fiction to Tor.com included Dale Bailey, Carrie Vaughn, Victor Milán and Jonathan Carroll.

Robert Lloyd Parry perfomed a live broadcast on M.R. James' 'The Stalls of Barchester Cathedral' on the Nunkie Facebook page on February 26th.

Possibly one of the most important genre books of the year came from David A. Sutton's print-on-demand imprint, Shadow Publishing: *Such Things May Be: Collected Writings* was a bumper 300-page retrospective of the work of Arkham House author James Wade (1930–83), edited by Edward P. Berglund. With a Foreword by Fritz Leiber, the trade paperback not only included all of the author's weird fiction (much of it set in the "Cthulhu Mythos"), but also poetry, essays, reviews, a film treatment and even a music composition based on three sonnets by H.P. Lovecraft.

Edited by Peter Coleborn and Jan Edwards, *The Alchemy Press Book of Horrors* was a welcome anthology of twenty-five original stories by Ramsey Campbell, Storm Constantine, Samantha Lee, Marie O'Regan, Mike Chinn, Tina Rath, Tony Richards, Stephen Laws, Adrian Cole, Ray Cluley and others, with heading illustrations by Jim Pitts.

From Dark Regions Press, *Nightmare's Realm: New Tales of the Weird and Fantastic* edited with an Introduction by S.T. Joshi was an oversized PoD trade paperback containing seventeen original stories centred around dreams by an impressive line-up of authors, including Ramsey Campbell, Nancy Kilpatrick, Richard Gavin, Steve

Rasnic Tem, Caitlín R. Kiernan, John Langan, Gemma Files, Simon Strantzas, Reggie Oliver and others. The anthology also included two reprint poems on the theme, by H.P. Lovecraft and Edgar Allan Poe.

From the same imprint, Michael Bailey and Darren Speegle edited *Adam's Ladder*, an anthology of eighteen original dark SF stories by Ramsey Campbell, Chaz Brenchley and others. It was also available in a deluxe, signed edition limited to 100 copies.

Available in both hardcover and trade paperback from Written Backwards, *Chiral Mad 4* was an anthology of collaborations, co-edited by Michael Bailey and Lucy A. Snyder and featuring four short stories, four novelettes, four novellas, four graphic adaptations and an Introduction by Gary A. Braunbeck and Janet Harriett. Contributing authors included Brian Keene, Kristi DeMeester, Elizabeth Massie, Marge Simon, Erinn L. Kemper, F. Paul Wilson, Maurice Broaddus and the late Jack Ketchum. The novella by Sarah Monette and Elizabeth Bear was the only reprint.

Edited by Kenneth W. Cain, *Tales from the Lake Volume 5* from Crystal Lake Publishing contained twenty-two apparently original stories and three poems by, amongst others, Lucy Taylor, Jason Sizemore, Bruce Boston, Gene O'Neill, Lucy A. Snyder, Tim Waggoner, Gemma Files, Marge Simon and others.

From the same PoD imprint, *Darker Days: A Collection of Dark Fiction* contained twenty-six stories (eight reprints) by Cain, while *Varying Distances* was a collection of twelve stories (one reprint) by Darren Speegle with an Introduction by Jeffrey Thomas.

Figures Unseen from Valancourt Books collected thirty-five stories by Steve Rasnic Tem with an Introduction by Simon Strantzas, while *All I Ever Dreamed* featured eighteen stories from 1993–2016 by Michael Blumlein, with notes by the author.

From PM Press, *Thoreau's Microscope* collected the newly revised title essay and four stories by Blumlein, along with an interview with the author by Terry Bisson.

Lisa Morton's *The Samhanach and Other Halloween Treats* from JournalStone/Trepidatio collected fourteen stories, with an Introduction by Nancy Holder.

Dan Coxon edited *This Dreaming Isle* for Unsung Stories. A Kickstarter-sponsored anthology of seventeen supernatural stories (one reprint) set around the British Isles, it included all-new fiction by Catriona Ward, Tim Lebbon, Stephen Volk, Robert Shearman, Alison Moore, Alison Littlewood, Ramsey Campbell and others.

Coxon also edited *Tales from the Shadow Booth Vol.2*, which featured twelve original stories from, amongst others, Mark Morris, Kirsty Logan and Ralph Robert Moore.

From Nightscape Press, *Ashes and Entropy* edited by Robert S. Wilson was another Kickstarter anthology, featuring twenty-two original stories by, amongst others, Tim Waggoner, Erinn L. Kemper, Damien Angelica Walters, Lynne Jamneck, John Langan, Kristi DeMeester and Lucy A. Snyder. The PoD trade paperback also included many effective black and white illustrations by Luke Spooner.

With a Foreword by John Gilbert, *Phantasmagoria Book 2: Danse Macabre* collected eleven short stories by Trevor Kennedy.

A Heart in the Right Place was a self-published comedy werewolf novel under the Pigeon Park Press imprint from the writing team of Heide Goody and Iain Grant.

A young boy encountered the ghost of Mark Twain in a library in *The Phantom Files: Twain's Treasure* by William B. Wolfe, published by Dreaming Robot Press.

Edited with a Foreword by Dean M. Drinkel under the Lycopolis Press imprint, *Into the Night Eternal: Tales of French Folk Horror* consisted of four original novellas by Romain Collier, Jan Edwards, Phil Sloman and the editor.

Issued under the Sad Mannequin Press imprint, *Sweet Chuckling Morbidity* collected seventeen stories (six reprints) by Californian writer Jeremy Thompson.

Selected and edited by Robert M. Price, *Lin Carter's Simrana Cycle* from Celaeno Press collected eleven reprints of Carter's fantastical "Dreamland" stories, inspired by the work of Lord Dunsany and others, along with two new "posthumous collaborations" (with Robert M. Price and Glynn Owen Barrass). As a bonus, the PoD paperback also featured eight reprint stories by Dunsany and another by Henry Kuttner, along with new work by Adrian Cole, Darrell Schweitzer, Gary Myers, Charles Garofalo and editor Price, interior illustrations by Roy G. Krenkel, and a specially-commissioned cover by Stephen Hickman.

Inspired by the works of H.P. Lovecraft and the Petersen Games tabletop game *Cthulhu Wars, In the Belly of the Beast and Other Tales of Cthulhu Wars* collected eight short stories and the titular novel by Ben Monroe.

Horrors & Abominations: 24 Tales of the Cthulhu Mythos was a self-published volume collecting twenty-four Lovecraftian fantasy and horror stories by Mark McLaughlin and Michael Sheehan, Jr. The book originally appeared on Kindle as *The Testament of Cthulhu: Tales of Weird Fantasy and Horror,* and all but three of the stories had appeared in previous electronic collections by the two authors.

From editor Eric J. Guignard's Dark Moon Books, the second volume in the "Modern Masters Presents...Exploring Dark Short Fiction" series was *A Primer to Kaaron Warren.* The trade paperback included six stories (one original) and a new essay by the Australian author, along with an interview and a bibliography, plus academic commentary by Michael Arnzen and illustrations by Michelle Prebich.

A subsequent primer volume devoted to the work of American author Nisi Shawl followed a similar format.

Also from Dark Moon, *A World of Horror* edited by Guignard and illustrated by Steve Lines described itself as "an anthology of new dark and speculative fiction stories from authors around the world". It included twenty-two new stories from South Africa, Singapore, Indonesia, Japan, Philippines, Nigeria, Uganda, Ukraine, Jamaica and other countries by David Nickle, Billie Sue Mosiman, Kaaron Warren, Ray Cluley and others.

The Horror Hiding in Plain Sight was a collection of seventeen apparently new stories by Rebecca Rowland, from Dark Ink Books.

A portal to another world deep in the Alaskan wilderness was at the centre of a reality TV show in Nick Kibri's debut novel *Death Game,* issued by KGHH Publishing.

From the same imprint, *But Worse Will Come* was a novella by C.C. Adams about a man pursued by something from his past. It was a sequel to the author's 2014 short story 'Sunset is Just the Beginning'.

Edited by Douglas Draa, *What October Brings* from Celaeno Press contained seventeen Halloween stories inspired by H.P. Lovecraft. Contributors included Nancy Holder, Darrell Schweitzer, Storm Constantine and Lovecraft himself, who was represented with a reprinted poem.

Although the first book was issued by PS Publishing, the charity anthology *Dark Places, Evil Faces Volume II* appeared as a PoD edition under the Dark Terror Publications banner. Compiled by Mark Lumby and edited by Lisa Lee Tone, the hardcover featured stories donated by such authors as Clive Barker, Joe R. Lansdale, Graham Masterton, Stephen Laws, Ramsey Campbell and other, less well-known names, along with tributes to Draven Ames and Jack Ketchum. Twenty-one of the thirty-two stories were original, and all proceeds from the book went to Rethink Mental Illness.

Sha'Daa: Toys from MoonDream Press was an original anthology edited by Edward F. McKeown. The sixth and possibly final volume set in the apocalyptic shared world created by Michael H. Hanson, it apparently featured the final story by C.J. Henderson which Hanson "transcribed from memory" after the author narrated it to him two weeks before his death in 2014.

With an Introduction by Theresa Derwin (who originated the project to benefit breast cancer organisations), *Dark Voices: A Lycan Valley Charity Anthology* featured thirty-eight stories and poems (ten reprints) by female authors, including Linda D. Addison, Lynn M. Cochrane, Pauline E. Dungate, Penny Jones, Nancy Kilpatrick, Billie Sue Mosiman, Anne Nicholls, Marie O'Regan, Angela Slatter and others. Lycan Valley Press Publications also issued copies of the hefty PoD trade paperback with a tipped-in sheet signed by some of the contributors.

Published by Hippocampus Press, *A New York State of Fright: Horror Stories from the Empire State* was an anthology edited by James Chambers, April Grey and Robert Masterson that featured twenty-three stories and a poem (eight reprints) by such New York authors as Monica O'Rourke, Patrick Freivald, Amy Grech, J.G. Faherty, Lisa Mannetti, Grady Hendrix, and Jack Ketchum and Edward Lee. All the proceeds from the book went to New York City's Girls Write Now, a non-profit organisation that pairs at-risk teenage women with professional writers and career mentors.

British author Priya Sharma's debut collection, *All the Fabulous Beasts*, from Canadian imprint Undertow Publications, included sixteen stories (two original), while *Nothing is Everything* from the same publisher featured ten stories (five original) by Simon Strantzas.

Also from Undertow, the first proposed annual volume of *The Silent Garden: A Journal of Esoteric Fabulism* was an attractive, full-colour hardcover compiled by the ever-changing "Silent Garden Collective" that included original, translated and reprinted fiction, poetry, artwork and essays on the weird and *avant-garde* by, amongst others, D.P. Watt, Brian Everson, Ron Weighell, Nick Mamatas, Helen Marshall, V.H. Leslie and Reggie Oliver.

Edited by Rhonda Parrish, *E is for Evil* was subtitled *Book 5 of the Alphabet Anthologies*. Issued by Canada's Poise and Pen Publishing, it featured twenty-six new stories (each titled after a letter of the alphabet) by, amongst others, Michael Fosburg, Stephanie A. Cain, Sara Cleto, Cory Cone, Beth Cato and Michael M. Jones.

From Australian PoD imprint Broken Puppet Books, Brian Craddock's *The Dalziel Files* was a fun collection of six stories (one original) featuring globe-trotting photojournalist Richard Dalziel and his encounters with the supernatural around the world.

Editor Steve Dillon's Things in the Well/Oz Horror Con imprint from Australia produced two substantial anthologies during the year. *Beneath the Waves: Tales from the Deep* boasted a cover painting by Bob Eggleton and fifteen original tales about the sea, along with a poem by Alfred Lord Tennyson and reprints from Clive Barker, Brian Lumley, H.P. Lovecraft, Jules Verne (a chapter from *Twenty Thousand Leagues Under the Sea*), H.G. Wells and the editor. Will Jacques supplied most of the interior illustrations.

Behind the Mask: Tales from the Id contained twenty-two macabre tales of masks, menace, murder and mythology. Along with the seventeen original stories, there were reprints this time by Clive Barker, Ramsey Campbell, Paul Kane, Edgar Allan Poe and Algernon Blackwood.

Steve Dillon's own collection, *The Beard and Other Weirdness*, was also published as a PoD volume by Things in the Well. It contained thirty-one short, scary, hairy horror stories and poems (four reprints).

Alessandro Manzetti's *Naraka* was a reprint science fiction horror novel set on a lunar prison, released in English by the author's Italian imprint Independent Legions Publishing. Stefano Cardoselli and Enrico D'Elia supplied the interior illustrations.

The same publisher also issued *Tribal Screams*, a collection of eleven reprint stories and a novel preview by Owl Goingback, while *Knowing When to Die* contained eleven previously uncollected stories by Mort Castle.

Monsters of Any Kind, introduced and edited by Manzetti and Daniele Bonfanti, contained eighteen stories (twelve original) by Cody Goodfellow, David J. Schow, Lucy Taylor, Michael Bailey, Ramsey Campbell, Bruce Boston, Damien Angelica Walters, Edward Lee, Monica J. O'Rourke, Erinn L. Kemper and others.

The Italian imprint also published the novels *A Winter Sleep* by Greg F. Gifune and *Dark Mary* by Paolo Di Orazio, along with the collections *Spree and Other Stories* by Lucy Taylor and *Knowing When to Die* by Mort Castle, while *Artifacts* was a poetry volume by Bruce Boston.

Recovering from an accident, a Welsh teenager received a bizarre present in the form of a baby black-backed seagull that turned everybody against him in *Plague of Gulls* by Stephen Gregory, published by Peter and Nicky Crowther's PS Publishing.

The Way of the Worm was the third and final volume of Ramsey Campbell's Brichester Mythos trilogy, "The Three Births of Daoloth", and set more than thirty years after the events in *Born to the Dark*.

Although most mainstream publishers appeared to have finally given up on single-author collections of horror, they continued to appear and, indeed, flourish from independent imprints such as PS.

By the Light of My Skull was a welcome reprint collection of fifteen of Ramey Campbell's recent supernatural and psychological horror stories. The book was illustrated by J.K. Potter and featured a new Afterword by the author.

Walking with Ghosts was Brian James Freeman's first full-length fiction collection. It contained thirty stories (four original) split into four sections, along with an Introduction by William Peter Blatty and a Foreword and Story Notes by the author.

The Long Way Home was a large collection of Richard Chizmar's recent writing. It included seventeen stories (one original), two essays and Story Notes by the author.

Issued under the PS Australia imprint, *Phantom Limbs* was a collection of fifteen stories (one original) by Margo Lanagan, along with Story Notes by the author, while *Uncommon Miracles* contained eighteen offbeat stories (three original) by Julie C. Day.

Just in time for Hallowe'en, Thana Niveau's *Octoberland* collected twenty-five stories (four original), along with an Introduction by Alison Littlewood.

Stephen Volk's *The Dark Masters Trilogy* reprinted slightly revised versions of the novellas 'Whitstable' and 'Leytonstone'—featuring Peter Cushing and Alfred Hitchcock, respectively—and added a third, 'Netherwood', in which black magic novelist Dennis Wheatley was summoned to the aid of Aleister Crowley in 1947.

All the above PS titles were published in signed and numbered limited editions, along with regular trade editions.

PS Publishing's reprint of Stephen King's 1987 novel *The Tommyknockers* was issued in a three-volume slipcased edition. Illustrated by Daniele Serra and introduced by Angela Slatter, it was available in a 1,000-copy limited edition signed by both Serra and Slatter.

PS's hardcover reprint of *The Colorado Kid* by Stephen King included a 2006 Introduction by Hard Case Crime publisher Charles Ardai, a 2005 Afterword by the author, and illustrations by Dave McKean. A signed, slipcased edition was also available.

Edited by Paul Kane and originally intended to have been published by Spectral Press, *Dark Mirages: Film & TV Vol.1* collected unmade or rare TV/film treatments and scripts from Stephen Jones and Michael Marshall Smith, Stephen Gallagher, Axelle Carolyn, Peter Crowther, Muriel Gray and Stephen Laws.

From the PS trade paperback imprint Drugstore Indian Press (DIP), *To Charles Fort with Love* and *The Ammonite Violin & Others* were two reprint collections from Caitlín R. Kiernan, from 2005 and 2009, respectively.

Ramsey Campbell's *Visions from Brichester* was a companion volume to the author's previous collection from DIP, *The Inhabitant of the Lake and Other Unwelcome Tenants*. It collected all of the author's remaining Lovecraftian stories and non-fiction, along with the first drafts of 'Cold Print' and 'The Franklyn Paragraphs' and the limerick sequence 'Mushrooms from Merseyside'. Like its companion, the trade paperback was illustrated by Randy Broecker.

The Curse of Yig and Selected Ghastly Ghostwritings was the seventeenth volume in the "Lovecraft Illustrated" series from yet another PS imprint, The Pulps Library. Featuring a number of full-colour illustrations by Pete Von Sholly, it also contained five "collaborations" between H.P. Lovecraft and Zelia Bishop, Hazel Heald and William Lumley, along with a useful Introduction by S.T. Joshi and essays by Von Sholly, W.H. Pugmire and Robert M. Price.

From Cemetery Dance Publications, *The Ones Who Are Waving: Tales of the Strange, Sad, and Wondrous* by Glen Hirshberg collected eleven stories and was limited to 600 signed and numbered copies, while Bentley Little's *Walking Alone* was published as a trade hardcover and contained twenty-seven short stories and flash fictions.

Glenn Chadbourne illustrated Richard and Billy Chizmar's novella *Widow's Point*, also from Cemetery Dance, and Brian James Freeman's *Lost and Lonely* was a collection of five stories (one original).

Freeman also edited *Detours* from the same publisher, containing seventeen pieces that were written but never used by Stephen King, Clive Barker, Dean Koontz and others, illustrated by ten artists. It was published in a 1,000-copy hardcover edition signed by the editor, artists and Owen King, and a $300 leather-bound lettered edition.

Edited by Stephen King and Bev Vincent, *Flight or Fright* was an anthology of sixteen stories (two original) plus a poem about flying by, amongst others Joe Hill, Ray Bradbury, Dan Simmons, Roald Dahl, David J. Schow, Arthur Conan Doyle and the two editors. A 1,000-copy slipcased "artist edition" from Cemetery Dance featured additional illustrations by Cortney Skinner and was signed by Vincent and the artist, while a traycased lettered edition signed by King, Vincent and Skinner was available for $1,500 per copy.

Edited by Hans-Åke Lija, *Shining in the Dark: Celebrating Twenty Years of Lija's Library* was an anthology celebrating the titular website devoted to news about Stephen King. It featured twelve stories (five original) by Clive Barker, John Ajvide Lindqvist, Ramsey Campbell and others, along with a chapbook of black and white illustrations by Erin S. Wells. The limited edition of 1,250 copies from Cemetery Dance was signed by Lija and cover artist Vincent Chong.

With a cover by Richard Corben, Harlan Ellison's *Blood's a Rover* from Subterranean Press included three stories and a previously unpublished teleplay in the author's dystopian "Vic and Blood" series. Editor Jason Davis supplied an Introduction, along with a chronology of Ellison's books. A signed, traycased, lettered edition of twenty-six copies was available for $500.

Mark Alan Miller's *Hellraiser: The Toll* was a "Pinhead" novella, based on Clive Barker's unfinished story 'Heaven's Reply'. Set between the events in *The Hellbound Heart* and *The Scarlet Gospels*, the book was illustrated by Barker and was available in a deluxe hardcover edition limited to 724 copies signed by just Miller, and a twenty-six copy leather-bound, traycased edition signed by both Miller and Barker ($250.00).

DJS Stories: The Best of David J. Schow collected twenty-nine stories and an introductory poem chosen by the author from his almost forty-year career. It was available in a 1,000-copy signed edition from Subterranean Press.

The Ballet of Dr Caligari and Madder Mysteries was Reggie Oliver's seventh collection of stories for Tartarus Press. It contained thirteen tales (two original), including a posthumous collaboration with M.R. James. The book was limited to 400 signed and numbered hardcover copies, while the author's accompanying pen-and-ink illustrations were also available as limited-edition prints.

A new 200-copy signed, numbered paperback edition of Reggie Oliver's *Holidays from Hell* contained fourteen stories, each featuring an illustration by the author, along with an Introduction by Robert Shearman.

Limited to 300 copies, *Figurehead*, the debut collection from Welsh author Carly Holmes, included twenty-six stories (twelve original), while *The Clockworm and Other Strange Stories* included nineteen stories (seven original) by Karen Heuler.

Michael Eisele's second collection of short stories, *Tree Spirit and Other Strange Tales*, contained fifteen stories, and *Inner Europe* by John Howard and Mark Valentine collected thirteen stories (eleven original).

Pauliska, or, Modern Perversity was the first-ever English translation of the 1798 French Gothic novel by Jacques-Antoine Révéroni, baron de Saint-Cyr (1767–1829). Translated by Erik Butler, it was limited to 300 copies.

A reworking of the author's classic *Tales of Horror and Imagination*, Tartarus' *The Macabre Tales of Edgar Allan Poe* included a number of additional stories, an Introduction by Brian Stableford, and eight tipped-in colour plates, twenty-three full-page illustrations and numerous ornaments by Harry Clarke. The book featured a reinstated illustration for 'Morella' and a variant illustration for 'The Facts in the Case of M. Valdemar' and was limited to 400 numbered copies.

Tartarus also reprinted *Arthur Machen's 1890s Notebook*, which is now kept at the Harry Ransom Center at the University of Texas, edited by The Friends of Arthur Machen. The paperback edition contained notes and abandoned ideas for the novel that was to become *The Hill of Dreams*, along with ideas for other novels and stories, some of which were never finished.

The Tartarus edition of *The Quest for Corvo: An Experiment in Biography* by A.J.A. Symons was limited to 300 copies. This 1934 biography of English author and eccentric Frederick Rolfe ("Baron Corvo", 1860–1913) was augmented with more than sixty photographs of the people discussed by Symons, and reproductions of the letters he received and sent while conducting his research. Mark Valentine supplied a new Introduction.

The book was launched in May at a bookstore in London where there was a small exhibition of material relating to A.J.A. Symons and Rolfe/"Corvo".

From German imprint Zagava, *The Uncertainty of All Earthly Things* was Mark Valentine's first short story collection in five years. It contained twelve previously uncollected tales and an unpublished journal of story ideas and reading notes. It was available as a 199-copy illustrated hardcover and in a signed, lettered deluxe edition of twenty-six copies bound in handmade marbled paper.

The debut collection *It's Not the End and Other Lies* from Canadian publisher ChiZine featured twenty-one stories (three original) by Matt Moore, with an Introduction by David Nickle.

From the same imprint, only a young boy could see what was wrong with the "perfect" village of Touchstone in Tim Major's YA novel *Machineries of Mercy*.

Set in a besieged Bruges of 1328, a group of disparate female warriors battled the Chatelaine of Hell in *Armed in Her Fashion* by Kate Heartfield.

A man believed that he was listening to a demon trying to teach him how to become one himself in *Mutilation Song* by Jason Hrivnak.

Brian Hodge's *The Immaculate Void* was a cosmic serial killer novel from ChiZine, while *Graveyard Mind* by Chadwick Ginther was about a necromancer who watched over the unquiet dead.

Issued in a slim and attractive limited hardcover edition by Sarob Press with dust-jacket art by Paul Lowe, *Revenants & Maledictions: Ten Tales of the Uncanny* collected a selection of superior supernatural stories (four reprints) by Peter Bell.

A Ghost & Scholars Book of Folk Horror edited and introduced by Rosemary Pardoe featured seventeen Jamesian folk horror stories (seven original) by, amongst others, Michael Chislett, Chico Kidd, Ramsey Campbell, C.E. Ward, Terry Lamsley, Gail Nina Anderson, Tom Johnstone, John Llewellyn Probert and David A. Sutton.

Another fine volume from Sarob was Daniel McGachey's second collection, *By No Mortal Hand*. Containing eleven stories (five original), it included three sequels and prequels to the ghost stories of M.R. James, five tales featuring the author's character Dr.

Lawrence, and three stories pertaining to the obscure author "Dr. H.S. Grace".

Limited to 300 copies, *The Dummy & Other Uncanny Stories* was a welcome new hardcover collection of eighteen stories (two original) by Nicholas Royle from Ireland's The Swan River Press.

Sparks from the Fire collected nineteen subtle strange tales (seventeen original) by Rosalie Parker and was also available in a numbered edition of 100 copies, while, from the same classy imprint and limited to 300 copies, *Death Makes Strangers of Us All* collected ten stories (six original) by R.B. Russell. Some Swan River titles came with a postcard signed by the author laid in.

Lynda E. Rucker took over the editorship of *Uncertainties Volume III* for the publisher. It contained twelve "strange tales" by, amongst others, S.P. Miskowski, Adam L.G. Nevill, Joyce Carol Oates, Robert Shearman, Lisa Tuttle and Ralph Robert Moore. It was limited to 400 hardcover copies, and also came with a postcard.

Initially set up by author Stephen Gallagher to issue his own titles in paperback, The Brooligan Press expanded to publish a restored edition of Laurence Staig's YA novel *The Companion* (aka *Shapeshifter*, 1992) and a reprint of Tim Lees' *Frankenstein's Prescription* (2010).

Stories about the sea seemed to be a recurring theme in 2018, and the anthology *A Book of the Sea* from Egaeus Press was another addition to that niche nautical market. Edited by Mark Beech and split into four sections, it was limited to 400 copies and contained twenty-one original stories and poems by, amongst others, Rosalie Parker, Tom Johnstone and D.F. Lewis.

Strange Island Stories from Stark House Press was edited by Jonathan E. Lewis and contained twenty stories (one original) by H.P. Lovecraft, Arthur Conan Doyle, Algernon Blackwood, M.P. Shiel and others.

Set in a 1907 where H.G. Wells' Martians had returned and taken over the Earth, Sherlock Holmes was invited to the red planet to solve a murder in Eric Brown's novella *The Martian Simulacra* from NewCon Press.

From TTA Press and edited by Andy Cox, the trade paperback anthology *Crimewave 13: Bad Light* included twelve stories by Mat

Coward, Steve Rasnic Tem, Ralph Robert Moore, Andrew Hook, Mike O'Driscoll, Ray Cluley and others.

Dawn G. Harris' debut novel *Diviner* from Telos Publishing was compared by the publisher to the work of M.R. James, while Soloman Strange's *The Hauntings of Gospall* was another first novel from the same imprint.

Telos also reprinted Graham Masterton's political horror novel *The Hell Candidate*, originally published in 1980 under the pseudonym "Thomas Luke", while *Tanith Lee A-Z* collected twenty-six reprint stories by the late author, one for each letter of the alphabet, selected by her husband, John Kaiine.

Edited by publisher Steve J. Shaw for his Black Shuck Books imprint, *Great British Horror 3: For Those in Peril* included eleven stories once again inspired by the sea from, amongst others, Stephen Bacon, Paul Meloy, Thana Niveau, Rosalie Parker, Damien Angelica Walters and veteran Guy N. Smith.

Published in aid of Birmingham Dogs Home, *In Dog We Trust* edited by Anthony Cowin contained eleven stories about our canine companions no longer being man's best friend by Ray Cluley, Gary Fry, William Meikle, Phil Sloman and others, along with a Foreword by Emma Green.

New Music for Old Rituals collected nineteen atmospheric folk horror stories (ten reprints) by Irish writer Tracy Fahey.

Following on from the previous year's *A Suggestion of Ghosts: Supernatural Fiction by Women 1854-1900*, *An Obscurity of Ghosts: Further Tales of the Supernatural by Women 1859-1903* featured sixteen rare Victorian reprints along with a Foreword by Professor Melissa Edmundson. It was limited to just fifty numbered hardcover copies signed by editor J.A. Mains and cover artist Les Edwards.

Despite being published as the seventh volume in the publisher's "Black Shuck Shadows" series of pocket-sized paperbacks, Simon Kurt Unsworth's *The Martledge Variations* was an excellent mini-collection of four original linked stories.

Other new volumes in the series included Gary Fry's *The Death of Boys* (three new stories), Phil Sloman's debut collection *Broken on the Inside* (five stories, one original), and Simon Bestwick's *Singing Back the Dead* (five new stories).

The "Black Shuck Signature" series of novellas was launched in March with Paul StJohn Mackintosh's *The Three Books* and Rich Hawkins' *Black Star, Black Sun*.

Spectral Evidence from Trepidatio Publishing collected nine stories from the past decade by Gemma Files, while companion volume *Drawn Up from Deep Places* collected ten tales from the past fifteen years.

Translated with a biographical Introduction by Brian Stableford for Black Coat Press, Etienne-Léon de Lamothe-Langon's 1816 French novel *The Mysterious Hermit of the Tomb* (*L'Hermite de la tombe mystérieuse, ou Le Fantome du vieux château*) was originally ascribed wrongly to English Gothic novelist Anne Radcliffe.

From the same imprint, Frank Schildiner's historical novel *The Devil Plague of Naples* was a sequel to *Napoleon's Vampire Hunters* and incorporated characters created by J. Sheridan Le Fanu, Paul Féval and others.

Published in an edition of just 100 numbered copies under the Newell & Newell imprint, *The Ghost of the Private Theatricals: A True Story* was an attractive chapbook reprinting of a "lost" tale from the Christmas issue of *The Keepsake for 1844*. Originally credited to "M.S.", Adam Newell made a credible argument in his Afterword for the author to actually be Mary Shelley. The attractive booklet also included a hand-printed linocut frontispiece by Sharon Newell and reproductions of an engraving by Charles Heath and *The Keepsake*'s original title page.

Nicholas Royle's series of signed chapbooks from Nightjar Press continued with *Living Together* by Matt Thomas, *The Hook* by Florence Sunnen, *The Message* by Philippa Holloway and *The Violet Eye* by Mike Fox. Each booklet was limited to 200 copies.

Published in a smaller chapbook format by Midnight Press and limited to seventy copies, *The Bride's Hand* was a traditional ghost story set in the Yorkshire Dales by Ken and Avril Mackenzie. *The Keepers of the Lighthouse* by Ken Mackenzie alone was a clever ghost story set in a remote Scottish lighthouse during World War II. Published in the same format, it was limited to only sixty copies, ten of which were signed by the author.

The latest chapbook ("O") from the enigmatic Sidecar Preservation Society, *Three Tales of Madness*, featured a trio of reprint stories and interior artwork by Cincinnati author Robert James Collas Lowry (1919–94). The chapbook was limited to 120 numbered copies, some of which were bound in hardcover.

Inspired in equal parts by H.P. Lovecraft, Thomas Ligotti and David Cronenberg, Todd Keisling's NECON chapbook *The Smile Factory* from Precipice Books was a novelette of corporate horror.

A Season in Hell was a self-published chapbook by Kenneth W. Cain based around the game of baseball, while Marlena Frank's werewolf novella *The She-Wolf of Kanta* was published by Radiant Crown Publishing. The e-book version of the latter contained exclusive content.

The chapbook *This Ae Nighte, Every Nighte and Alle: 33 Poems of the Weird, Horrific, and Supernatural* was A Mind's Eye Publication showcasing the work of "formalist" poet Frank Coffman.

Jon Padgett's *The Broker of Nightmares* was an attractive chapbook from Nightscape Press with full-colour illustrations by Luke Spooner.

Andy Cox's *Black Static* only managed five bi-monthly issues in 2018. Along with new fiction by Kristi DeMeester, Nicholas Kaufmann, Simon Avery and Cody Goodfellow, there were interviews with Anna Tambour, Priya Sharma, Catriona Ward, Georgina Bruce and Stephen Volk, regular opinion columns by Lynda E. Rucker and Ralph Robert Moore, and movie reviews by Gary Couzens. With issue #64, Peter Tennant gave up his his book column after more than a decade, and his place was taken by a number of different reviewers.

Companion magazine *Interzone* also only turned out five issues, featuring fiction from James Sallis, Julie C. Day, Tim Major, Fiona Moore and others, along with the usual columns, interviews and book and film reviews.

Edited by C.C. Finlay for publisher Gordon Van Gelder, *The Magazine of Fantasy & Science Fiction* entered its 69th year of publication with six bi-monthly issues featuring fiction and poetry by Dale Bailey, Gardner Dozois, Susan Palwick, Marc Laidlaw, Mary Soon Lee, Albert E. Cowdrey, Nina Kiriki Hoffman, Rachel Pollack, Mary Robinette Kowal, James Sallis, Harry Turtledove, Geoff Ryman and Jeffrey Ford. Charles de Lint, Elizabeth Hand, Kathi Maio, Michelle West, David J. Skal, James Sallis and Tim Pratt supplied the review columns, while unusual or forgotten books were spotlighted on the always-interesting 'Curiosities' page by Graham Andrews, Robert Eldridge, Phoenix Alexander, Paul Di Filippo, Mike Ashley and David Langford.

The July issue of Arthur B. Evans' academic journal *Science Fiction Studies* was a *Frankenstein* special guest-edited by Michael Griffin and Nicole Lobdell.

The Ghastling was a beautifully-designed magazine from Cardiff, Wales, devoted to "Tales of the Macabre, Ghosts and the oh-so Strange". Edited by Rebecca Parfitt, Book No.VII was devoted to "monsters" and featured fiction by Tina Rath and others.

Doug Draa's *Weirdbook* from Wildside Press put out three PoD issues featuring fiction and poetry from Darrell Schweitzer, Adrian Cole (a "Nick Nightmare" story), Franklyn Searight, W.H. Pugmire, Cynthia Ward, Frederick J. Mayer, Kyla Lee Ward, Jessica Amanda Salmonson, Lucy Snyder, Kurt Newton, Mike Chinn, Paul StJohn Mackintosh, John Linwood Grant, Andrew Darlington, Clint Smith and many others. As usual, Allen Koszowski supplied the interior artwork, and there were striking covers by Alexandra Petruk, Vukkostic and J. Florêncio.

Before going on hiatus, *Dark Discoveries* produced a new issue featuring original fiction by Ramsey Campbell, Tananarive Due, Jeffrey Thomas, Philip Fracassi and others.

Cemetery Dance magazine managed just one belated issue in 2018. Along with regular columns by Bev Vincent (about Stephen King), Thomas F. Monteleone, Ellen Datlow, Peter Straub, Michael Marano and Mark Sieber, there were interviews with Stephen King and Richard Chizmar, Joe R. Lansdale, and movie director Mike Flanagan, original fiction from Danny Rhodes, Ray Garton, Gerard Houarner and others, and a selection of book reviews.

Having been relaunched in 2012 in an electronic format after publisher Steve Davidson acquired the lapsed trademark, *Amazing Stories* returned to a print format after a successful crowd-funding campaign. Originally debuting in 1926, the first new issue under managing editor Ira Nayman was launched at the World Science Fiction convention in San Jose and included a historical introduction by Robert Silverberg and new fiction by Allen Steele, Lawrence Watt-Evans, Rudy Rucker and others.

Issues of *Fortean Times* included a two-part article on the ghost stories of author Russell Kirk, the making of *Witchfinder General*, and a look at how H.P. Lovecraft's fiction was influenced by history and archeology, along with an interview with Guillermo Del Toro.

After fifty-two years of continuous publication, editor-in-chief Hildy Silverman announced that *Space and Time* was set to close in 2019 because the magazine no longer had enough subscribers to remain viable.

From Tartarus Press, the two issues of Mark Valentine's *Wormwood*, subtitled "Writings about fantasy, supernatural and decadent literature", included critical essays on the fiction of Caitlín R. Kiernan and Algernon Blackwood's 'The Fruit Stoners', along with regular review columns by Reggie Oliver, Douglas A. Anderson and John Howard.

The two issues of the British Fantasy Society's *BFS Horizons* underwent another editorial change and featured original fiction and poetry by, amongst others, Allen Ashley, Malcolm Devlin, M.M. Lewis, Cardinal Cox, Becca Miles and Allen Stroud. The latter was also the editor of two issues of the *BFS Journal*, which amongst the dry academic articles and reviews did at least include the conclusion of David Sutton's three-part history of the first fifteen years of the Society, Mike Barrett's look at the fiction of Richard Malden, and a short interview with Stephen Volk.

Locus celebrated its 50th anniversary with the April issue. Along with the usual news, reviews and listings, the monthly publication also included interviews with, amongst others, John Crowley, Angela

Slatter, Jeffrey Ford, Laura Anne Gilman, Andy Duncan and Kim Stanley Robinson. Following the death of regular contributor Gardner Dozois, the magazine revised its short fiction reviews, splitting the columns between Rich Horton (print magazines and anthologies), Karen Burnham (online sources) and Paula Guran (dark fiction). The November issue included a spotlight on "SF in Israel".

The twelfth issue of editor Katsushi Makihara's attractive Japanese horror and dark fantasy magazine *Night Land Quarterly* was devoted to "The Unfathomable Zone" and featured translated stories by Kim Newman, Pete Rawlik, Richard Gavin, Simon Strantzas, Nathan Ballingrud, Mearle Prout and Jean Ray, along with an interview with comics artist Daijiro Morohoshi.

The usual six bi-monthly issues Canada's *Rue Morgue* magazine featured interviews with directors Ari Aster, David Gordon Green, Anthony C. Ferrante, Panos Cosmatos and Luca Guadagnino, actors Jamie Lee Curtis, Joe Bob Briggs and Jessica Harper, playwrights Jeremy Dyson and Andy Nyman, author Maria Alexander and Valancourt Books publisher James D. Jenkins. The 21st Anniversary Halloween double-issue was a special *Night of the Living Dead* edition, with commentary by John Landis, Joe Dante, Ken Foree, Judith O'Dea, Patricia Tallman, John A. Russo and others.

The January issue of *Classic Images* featured a fascinating article by *Carnival of Souls* actress Candace Hilligoss, extracted from her autobiography *The Odyssey and the Idiocy: Marriage to an Actor: A Memoir*, about an encounter she had with legendary Hollywood star Veronica Lake in the late 1950s.

The March edition included a piece by Tom Weaver on Universal's proposed 1944 remake of *The Old Dark House* starring Rondo Hatton, and the Korean giant monster movie *Pulgasari* (1985). The monthly newsprint magazine also featured profiles of actors Hatton, Beverly Garland, Richard Denning, Dick Foran, Richard Anderson, Joi Lansing, Paul Cavanagh and Frank Moran, as well as film producer Alex Gordon.

Issue #33 of Rosemary Pardoe's *The Ghosts & Scholars M.R. James Newsletter* featured fiction by Michael Chislett (inspired by James' story 'Oh, Whistle, and I'll Come to You, My Lad') and Mark Nicholls. With the following issue, the small press magazine reverted to its original title of just *Ghosts & Scholars*, with the usual mix of news and reviews, along with two pieces of short fiction by Elsa Wallace and a story by Paul StJohn Mackintosh. There were also interesting articles about "James Gang" member H.F.W. Tatham by Joseph Hinton, and a comparison between the work of M.R. James and Elliott O'Donnell by Peter Bell.

The seventh issue of Trevor Kennedy's *Phantasmagoria Magazine* was a first-year anniversary Hallowe'en special. It contained fiction and poetry by the editor, Dean M. Drinkel, David A. Sutton, Eoin Murphy and Helen Scott, interviews with Stephen Volk and Karina Sims, and articles and reviews of books, films and television. Consultant editor John Gilbert supplied the guest Editorial.

The regular two issues of David Longhorn's *Supernatural Tales* included fiction by C.M. Muller, Helen Grant, Mark Valentine, John Howard, Michael Chislett and others, along with book and movie reviews by the editor.

Twilight Echoes: Tales of Swords & Dark Magic was an attractive new sword & sorcery publication from editor Steve Dilks. The first issue, dated Summer 2018, featured reprint stories by Charles Gramlich, Davide Mana, Steve Lines and Robert E. Howard ('The Vale of Lost Women'), along with illustrations by Jim Pitts, Régis Moulun, Kurt Brugel, Tony Gleeson and Yanis Rubus Rubulias.

The June issue of *Disturbed Digest* was a "6th Anniversary Double Issue" edited by Tyree Campbell. It featured fiction and poetry by, amongst others, Josh Schlossberg, Bruce Boston and Marge Simon, the latter also contributing two illustrations.

It was perhaps unfortunate that #55 of *Rabbit Hole*, the always-fascinating newsletter of The Harlan Ellison Recording Collection, was mailed out to subscribers on the same day that its subject died. Editor Jason Davis managed to get three issues out in 2018, containg all the usual Ellison news and updates.

John Locke's revealing non-fiction study *The Thing's Incredible! The Secret Origins of Weird Tales* was a history of the seminal pulp magazine's origin from late 1922 through to its near-collapse two years later.

Meanwhile, Alec Nevala-Lee used previously unpublished material to explore how one editor changed the landscape of science fiction in *Astounding: John W. Campbell, Isaac Asimov, Robert A. Heinlein, L. Ron Hubbard, and the Golden Age of Science Fiction*.

From Shadow Publishing, *The Black Pilgrimage & Other Explorations: Essays on Supernatural Fiction* reprinted twenty-nine essays about M.R. James by editor and foremost James scholar Rosemary Pardoe. The trade paperback also included a further eight essays on other authors, such as Fritz Leiber, Arthur Machen, E.G. Swain and Manly Wade Wellman, along with a miscellany of nine additional pieces on a variety of topics.

Edited by Sidney Perkowitz and Eddy von Mueller, the critical study *Frankenstein: How a Monster Became an Icon: The Science and Enduring Allure of Mary Shelley's Creation* included an interview with film-maker Mel Brooks. Meanwhile, Paul Ruditis' *Vault of Frankenstein* not only explored how Shelley's creation became a pop-culture icon, but also included such extras as a glued-in envelope, copies of the original manuscript pages, two reproduction movie posters, a playbill and a photo of Boris Karloff on set.

Mary Shelley: The Strange True Tale of Frankenstein's Creator was an illustrated young-adult biography of the author by Catherine Reef.

Published by New York University Press, Douglas E. Cowan's *America's Dark Theologian: The Religious Imagination of Stephen King* explored the use of religion in King's fiction.

Mark Dery used recently discovered correspondence and interviews with authors influenced by the artist for his biography *Born to Be Posthumous: The Eccentric Life and Mysterious Genius of Edward Gorey*.

From McFarland & Company, *Once Upon a Time in a Dark and Scary Book: The Messages of Horror Literature for Children* by K. Shryock Hood focussed on more recent examples horror for younger people in books and the media.

Ruth Bienstock Anolik's *American Gothic Literature: A Thematic*

Study from Mary Rowlandson to Colson Whitehead looked at how American Gothic literature diverged from its British roots.

In *Growing Up with Vampires: Essays on the Undead in Children's Media*, editors Simon Bacon and Katarzyna Bronk compiled a dozen essays about the undead in books, comics and movies, while *The Bite, the Beast, and the Blood: Why Modern Vampire Stories Suck Us In* was a critical look at the attraction of vampires by Amy Williams Wilson.

As part of McFarland's "Zombie Studies" series, *The Politics of Race, Gender and Sexuality in The Walking Dead: Essays on the Television Series and Comics* was edited by Elizabeth Erwin and Dawn Keetley and included twelve critical essays. Christopher M. Moreman's *Dharma and the Dead: Zombies Mortality and Buddhist Philosophy* explored how the walking dead related to the Buddhist religion.

Edited with a preface and commentary by Leverett Butts, *H.P. Lovecraft: Selected Works, Critical Perspectives, and Interviews on His Influence* contained five stories, two poems and two essays by Lovecraft, critical essays by S.T. Joshi, Robert M. Price and others, and interviews with Caitlín R. Kiernan, Richard Monaco and Cherie Priest.

Originally initiated as a Kickstarter project by Century Guild, Phil and Sarah Stokes' The Clive Barker Archive took over the publishing of the *Imaginer: The Visionary Art of Clive Barker* series in 2016 with the third volume. The latest two volumes, *5: Paintings 1993–2012* and *6: Paintings 1985–2017*, contained the usual superb colour reproductions of Barker's often surreal artwork (some as fold-out pages), along with complimentary text by the artist. Both volumes were available in limited editions of 1,000 copies, along with deluxe signed, numbered and slipcased editions of 100 copies apiece.

From Centipede Press, Scott Connors edited and introduced *In the Realms of Mystery and Wonder: Collected Prose Poems and Artwork of Clark Ashton Smith*, which contained forty-six poems illustrated with more than 200 examples of Smith's sculptures, paintings and drawings. It was available in a slipcased edition of 300 copies signed by the editor.

Neil Gaiman's 2013 novella *The Sleeper and the Spindle*, which combined the fairy stories of Sleeping Beauty and Snow White, was reissued in a single edition with illustrations by Chris Riddell.

From Jayde Design, *James Cawthorn: The Man and His Art*, written and compiled by the late British artist's sister, Maureen Cawthorn Bell, featured almost 1,000 pieces of art along with a Foreword by Alan Moore, an Afterword by Michael Moorcock, and contributions from David Britton, Michael Butterworth, John Coulthart, John Davey, Jon Farmer, Burne Hogarth, George Locke, D. Peter Ogden, Charles Partington, John Picacio and Frank Westwood.

Despite having S.T. Joshi as consultant editor, a Foreword by Ramsey Campbell, and Mike Ashley, Matt Cardin and Rosie Fletcher amongst its contributors, Flame Tree Publishing's *The Astounding Illustrated History of Fantasy & Horror* was a complete mess, not helped by the oversized volume's appalling layout and design.

David Plunkert illustrated *Frankenstein: The 200th Anniversary Edition*, which reprinted the 1818 text by Mary Shelley.

Innsmouth: The Lost Drawings of Mannish Sycovia from Alaxis Press featured portraits of the ichthyoid inhabitants of H.P. Lovecraft's cursed seaport by Mark A. Nelson and Stephen D. Smith.

From Flesk Publications, *The Illustrated Call of Cthulhu* was an attractive hardcover edition of H.P. Lovecraft's 1928 novella, nicely designed by Maecelo Anciano and profusely illustrated with black and white pencil sketches by Gary Gianni. As a bonus, the book also included H.G. Wells' 1898 short story 'The Sea Raiders', also illuminated by the artist. However, the volume would have benefited from the inclusion of some historical context.

From the same publisher, *Spectrum 25: The Best in Contemporary Fantastic Art* edited by John Fleskes contained 450 works by more than 250 artists from 2017. Arnie Fenner contributed a profile of Grand Master Award winner Claire Wendling.

The Douglas Klauba 2018 Adventure Calendar was a Kickstarter project featuring the work of the Chicago artist.

American Gods Vol.1: Shadows from Dark Horse Books collected the first nine issues of the comic book series scripted and designed by P. Craig Russell with artwork by Scott Hampton and others, based on the novel by Neil Gaiman.

Edited by the film-maker and his wife Sandy King, *John Carpenter's Tales for a Halloween Night Volume 4* was the latest volume in the annual full-colour, graphic anthology series from Storm King Comics. Bringing together storytellers from the worlds of movies, novels and comics, it included stories by Capenter and David J. Schow, along with an Introduction by Steve Niles.

Adapted and illustrated by the legendary Esteban Maroto, *Lovecraft: The Myth of Cthulhu* from IDW Publishing was a black and white graphic adaptation of three of H.P. Lovecraft's stories, originally done in the 1980s. Newly translated by Anna Rosenwong from *Los mitos de Cthulhu de Lovecraft* (2016), the hardcover was introduced by José Villarrubia.

Along similar lines from Pegasus, *H.P. Lovecraft: He Who Wrote in the Darkness* was a graphic novel/biography of the author by Alex Nikolavitch, illustrated by Marco Gervasio, Carlos Aon and Lara Lee. With a Preface by David Camus, it was originally published in France as *Howard P. Lovecraft: Celui qui écrivait dans les ténèbres*.

The first volume in Archie Comic Publications' *Chilling Adventures in Sorcery* included classic reprints from the 1970s by artists Steve Ditko, Gray Morrow, Alex Toth and Howard Chaykin, along with new stories by Roberto Aguirre-Sacasa.

The first issue of *Mary Shelley Presents*, a new series from Kymera Press presenting fiction by Victorian-era women horror writers, featured a graphic adaptation of Elizabeth Gaskell's obscure 1852 story 'The Old Nurse's Story', scripted by Nancy Holder and illustrated by Amelia Woo.

From Kevin M. Glover's indie horror comic label Scary Tales Publications, *Lady Frankenstein and the Mummy's Brain* was a six-book limited series with artwork by Mexican artist Manuel Martin.

Babayka Land was a follow-up to British writer and artist Andrew Reed's series of self-published horror graphic novels that began with *Brides of Babyka*.

Anthony Bourdain's last published work was, of all things, a graphic novel in which chefs from around the world told supernatural stories to a greedy billionaire. *Hungry Ghosts* even included five new recipes from the late celebrity chef, who committed suicide in France in June.

Movie tie-ins in 2018 included *The Predator* by Christopher Golden and Mark Morris, and *The Shape of Water* by Guillermo del Toro and Daniel Kraus, which included artwork by James Jean. The epistolary novelisation of *Slender Man* wasn't credited to anyone so as to lend the Internet myth greater verisimilitude, while Katharine Turner and Barry Waldo's *Anna and the Apocalypse* was a YA tie-in to the teen zombie musical set at Christmas.

Barnes & Noble's exclusive "Expanded Edition" of Jason Fry's *Star Wars: The Last Jedi* included scenes from alternative versions of the script and other additional material, along with sixteen pages of colour stills. A similarly "Expanded" edition of Mur Lafferty's *Star Wars: Solo* was also available.

Ernest Cline's 2011 novel *Ready Player One* was reissued in a movie tie-in edition, and Neil Gaiman's 2006 collection *Fragile Things: Short Fictions and Wonders* was reissued to tie in with *How to Talk to Girls at Parties*.

Greg Keyes' *Pacific Rim Uprising: Ascension* was a prequel to the 2018 movie sequel, and other tie-ins/prequels/sequels to movie series included *Alien: The Cold Forge* by Alex White and *The Predator: Hunters and Hunted* by James A. Moore.

To celebrate the 50th anniversary of *Planet of the Apes* (1968), *Planet of the Apes: Caesar's Story* by Maurice and Greg Keyes recounted the plots of the three new movies in the form of a biography of the ape leader. Zachary Baldus supplied the illustrations.

Death of the Planet of the Apes by Andrew E.C. Gaska was based on the original series of movies, revealing what happened when stranded astronaut Colonel George Taylor disappeared into the Forbidden Zone.

A.W. Jantha's *Hocus Pocus and The All-New Sequel* was not only a novelisation of the 1993 movie, but also a continuation featuring a new generation of Salem teenagers.

TV shows that got the tie-in treatment included *Supernatural:*

Joyride by John Passarella, while *Once Upon a Time: Regina Rising* by Wendy Toliver and *Once Upon a Time: Henry and Violet* by Michelle Zink were young adult novels based on the ABC-TV series.

Written by James Lovegrove, *Firefly: Big Damn Hero* was based on an idea by Nancy Holder, and *The Librarians and the Mother Goose Chase* and *The Librarians and the Pot of Gold* were both by Greg Cox.

Following the BBC's revival of Target, the imprint that first published the *Doctor Who* novelisations in the 1970s, a new batch of titles included former showrunner Steven Moffat's 50th anniversary special *The Day of the Doctor*; Russell T. Davies' *Rose*, an adaptation of his first-ever episode of the revived 2005 show; *The Christmas Invasion* by Jenny Colgan, which marked David Tennant's first appearance as the Doctor, and Paul Cornell's *Twice Upon a Time*, which marked Peter Capaldi's final outing as the Time Lord.

Despite being prominently billed on the cover as "The Lost Aventure by Douglas Adams", *Doctor Who and the Krikkitmen* by James Goss was actually based on an Adams script featuring Tom Baker's fourth Doctor that had been rejected by the BBC in 1976.

Doctor Who: The Missy Chronicles collected six original stories by Paul Magrs and others about the Time Lord's likeable foe, while *The Triple Knife and Other Doctor Who Stories* contained five tales by Jenny T. Colgan about women who knew the Doctor.

Doctor Who: Twelve Angels: Twelve Stories of the Villains from Doctor Who featured a dozen stories by Dave Rudden, and the spin-off novels continued with *Doctor Who: The Good Doctor* by Juno Dawson, *Doctor Who: Combat Magicks* by Steve Cole and *Doctor Who: Molten Heart* by Una McCormack.

Dan Simmons' 2007 novel *The Terror* was reissued in a TV tie-in edition.

James R. Tuck and Marc Guggenheim's *Arrow: Fatal Legacies* and Richard Knaak's *Flash: Climate Change* were both based on The CW television series featuring DC characters.

The Quotable Negan featured quotes by the villain from the comics and TV show *The Walking Dead*, with a Foreword by creator Robert Kirkman and artwork by Charlie Adlard and others.

Planet of the Apes Omnibus: Volume 3 collected four novelisations of the 1974 TV series by the late George Alec Effinger—*Planet of the Apes: Man the Fugitive, Planet of the Apes: Escape to Tomorrow, Planet of the Apes: Journey Into Terror* and *Planet of the Apes: Lord of the Apes.*

Marvel's Spider-Man: Hostile Takeover by David Liss was based on a video game, as was S.D. Perry's *Shadow of the Tomb Raider: Path of the Apocalypse.*

Beautifully published by Titan Books and The Ray and Diana Harryhausen Foundation, Richard Holliss' *Harryhausen: The Movie Posters* was a sumptuous oversized volume covering the legendary stop-motion animator's career from 1949 to 1981. John Landis contributed a very brief Foreword.

Neil Snowdon's excellent Midnight Movie Monographs series under PS Publishing's Electric Dreamhouse imprint continued with John Connolly's fascinating assessment of *Horror Express* (aka *Panico en el Transiberiano,* 1972), *Les Vampires* (1915) by Tim Major and *Spirits of the Dead* (aka *Histoires Extraordinaires,* 1968) by Tim Lucas.

From Centipede Press, *Joe Dante's The Howling: Studies in the Horror Film* by Lee Gambin was a look at the cult 1981 werewolf movie, with a Foreword by Dee Wallace.

Simon Brown's *Screening Stephen King: Adaptation and the Horror Genre in Film and Television* from the University of Texas Press was a critical examination of how the author's fiction had been treated on both the big and small screens.

From the University Press of Mississippi, Nicholas Parisi's *Rod Serling: His Life His Work and Imagination* was a biography of the creator of *The Twilight Zone* with a Foreword by Anne Serling.

Ryan Frost's *Transform and Roll Out* from Telos Publishing was a guide to the origins and development of the original *Transformers* franchise, including the 1980s toys, comics and TV cartoons.

From the same publisher, Alistair Hughes' *Infogothic: An Unauthorised Graphic Guide to Hammer Horror* explored the history of the British film studio through graphics, diagrams, illustrations and maps. Caroline Munro supplied the Introduction.

Tom Weaver's "Scripts from the Crypt" series from BearManor Media continued with a volume dedicated to the 1959 movie *The Atomic Submarine*, which featured an Introduction by co-star Brett Halsey and a memoir of producer Alex Gordon by Karen Latham Everson.

Ron Palumbo continued Philip J. Riley's "The Universal Filmscript Series" from BearManor with Abbott and Costello's *Hold That Ghost* (1941). Robert Rinaldo supplied the Introduction.

As usual, McFarland & Company, Inc. turned out a number of film-related titles. *The Creature Chronicles: Exploring the Black Lagoon Trilogy* by Tom Weaver, David Schecter and Steve Kronenberg looked at the trilogy of 1950s movies featuring Universal's Gill-Man.

In *Good Versus Evil in the Films of Christopher Lee*, Presbyterian pastor Paul Leggatt explored the British actor's legacy, while Dean Conrad looked at female actresses in *Space Sirens, Scientists and Princesses: The Portrayal of Women in Science Fiction Cinema*.

Amy J. Ransom's *I Am Legend as American Myth: Race and Masculinity in the Novel and Its Film Adaptations* explored the movie versions of Richard Matheson's classic novel starring Vincent Price, Charlton Heston and Will Smith.

Bryan Senn's *"Twice the Thrills! Twice the Chills!"* was a study of horror and science fiction double features, between 1955–74, while Rolf Giesen investigated the influences on the making of F.W. Murnau's 1921 vampire movie in *The Nosferatu Story: The Seminal Horror Film, Its Predecessors and Its Enduring Legacy*.

Editors Cynthia J. Miller and A. Bowdoin Van Riper selected twenty-one critical essays for the niche study of *Terrifying Texts: Essays on Books of Good and Evil in Horror Cinema*, also from McFarland.

The Archive of Magic: The Film Wizardry of Fantastic Beasts: The Crimes of Grindelwald by Signe Bergstrom was just one of a number of tie-ins to the new J.K. Rowling movie adaptation. It included a Foreword by Jude Law and inserted items such as glued-in envelopes, documents and a bookmark. Ian Nathan's *Lights Camera Magic!: The Making of Fantastic Beasts: The Crimes of Grindelwald* featured a Foreword by Eddie Redmayne, while *Fantastic Beasts: The Crimes of Grindelwald: The Original Screenplay* reprinted Rowling's script with illustrations by MinaLima.

Gina McIntyre's *The Art of Ready Player One* showcased the concept art for the movie, with a Foreword by director Steven Spielberg and an Introduction by Ernest Cline, whose novel the movie was based on.

Designed to look like a beat-up hardcover from the 1980s with a worn and torn dust-jacket, *Stranger Things: Worlds Turned Upside Down: The Official Behind-the-Scenes Companion* carried the odd byline "Written with Gina McIntyre". Featuring a Foreword by Matt and Ross Duffer and an Afterword by Shawn Levy, the book came with a glued-in map and a Morse code signal disc.

Emily Haynes' *Inside American Gods* was an extensively illustrated look behind-the-scenes at the first season of the TV show. The book featured two interviews with creator Neil Gaiman, while *Inside Black Mirror: The Illustrated Oral History* by Charlie Brooker, Annabel Jones and Jason Arnopp contained various interviews about the Netflix anthology series.

Monsters of the Week: The Complete Critical Companion to The X-Files was an episode-by-episode guide by Zack Handlen and Todd VanDerWerff that apparently couldn't even get the title of the show correct!

Dispiritingly, Marvel Studios had half of the ten highest-grossing films in the US in 2018.

Set in the super-scientific African nation of Wakanda, Disney and Marvel's *Black Panther* didn't bring much that was original to its tale of rival brothers (Chadwick Boseman and Michael B. Jordan) wanting to be crowned king beyond an impressive supporting cast that included Lupita Nyong'o, Martin Freeman, Angela Bassett, Forest Whitaker, Andy Serkis and yet another cameo by Stan Lee.

That didn't stop it from delivering the second biggest four-day opening in box-office history with a domestic take of $242 million, just trailing the $288 million made by *Star Wars: The Force Awakens* in 2015. The cumulative worldwide gross for *Black Panther* was almost $1.347 billion, making it the #1 movie of 2018.

Chadwick Boseman's T'Challa/Black Panther returned in the #2 movie of the year, Joe and Anthony Russo's *Avengers: Infinity War*.

The first in a genuinely epic two-part culmination to the decade-long build-up of the "Marvel Cinematic Universe", a vast cast of superheroes—along with the Guardians of the Galaxy, various side-kicks and Stan Lee driving a bus—teamed up in an attempt to prevent Thanos (Josh Brolin beneath the CGI) from obtaining all six "Infinity Stones" and wiping half of the universe out of existence. The ending was genuinely shocking.

Avengers: Infinity War had the biggest opening weekend in America, beating *Star Wars: The Force Awakens* by nearly $10 million with a $257.7 million debut, and closed-out its domestic gross with $678.8 million, making it the fourth highest-earning movie of all time. A cumulative worldwide gross of more than $2 billion also ranked it all-time fourth.

Ryan Reynolds was back as Marvel's potty-mouthed mutant in David Leitch's irreverent sequel *Deadpool 2*, the #5 movie of the year, as the reluctant hero brought together an unlikely team to defeat "Cable" (Josh Brolin again, in his second Marvel movie of the year), a time-travelling warrior cyborg from the future. Brad Pitt, Matt Damon, Fred Savage, Nicholas Hoult, Evan Peters and James McAvoy all turned up in surprise cameos. A "Super Duper Cut" of the movie released on home video featured an additional fifteen minutes of added footage, while a PG-13-rated version was re-released in November containing all-new footage.

In Peyton Reed's *Ant-Man and the Wasp* (#7), an entertaining sequel to the 2015 original, Marvel's pair of miniaturised heroes (Paul Rudd and Evangeline Lilly) once again teamed up with scientist Hank Pym (Michael Douglas) to rescue the latter's wife Janet (Michelle Pfeiffer) from the Quantum Realm.

At #9, Ruben Fleischer's better-than-expected *Venom* was a spin-off from the *Spider-Man* movies, as Tom Hardy's investigative journalist Eddie Brock found himself possessed by the titular alien symbiote.

The trend for studios churning out even more sequels, prequels, spin-offs, remakes and reboots continued in 2018.

Chris Pratt and Bryce Dallas Howard still lacked any screen chemistry together in J.A. Bayona's bloated *Jurassic World: Fallen Kingdom*, as they returned to Isla Nublar to rescue the remaining dinosaurs from an erupting volcano. Even a classy supporting cast that included Rafe Spall, James Cromwell, Toby Jones, Ted Levine, Geraldine Chaplin, Jeff Goldblum and B.D. Wong (the latter two recreating their characters from the original movies) couldn't save this by-the-numbers sequel, although a post-credits scene hinted at a much more interesting continuation of the series.

Ron Howard replaced original directors Phil Lord and Christopher Miller on the bland prequel, *Solo: A Star Wars Story*. It starred Alden Ehrenreich as a young Han Solo (taking over the role from a much more charismatic Harrison Ford), who met up with his future co-pilot Chewbacca (Joonas Suotamo) and Lando Calrissian (Donald Glover) years before he reluctantly joined the Rebellion.

Despite having a script co-written by Lawrence Kasdan and a supporting cast that included Woody Harrelson, Emilia Clarke, Thandie Newton, Paul Bettany, Warwick Davis, Clint Howard, Anthony Daniels, Ray Park and the voices of Phoebe Waller-Bridge, John Favreau and Linda Hunt, domestic audiences were down 65% the second week, and Disney closed out the US run of the movie—which fell well short of expectations—at $213.7 million. It grossed $392.8 million worldwide.

Scripted by J.K. Rowling, David Yates' *Fantastic Beasts: The Crimes of Grindelwald* was that rare thing—a sequel that was actually better than the original. Eddie Redmayne's magician, Newt Scamander, travelled to 1920s Paris to track down Johnny Depp's escaped criminal, Gellert Grindelwald. Katherine Waterston, Dan Fogler and Alison Sudol all reprised their roles from the first film, and there was fine support from Jude Law as a young Albus Dumbledore.

Steven S. DeKnight's *Pacific Rim: Uprising* was another breezy sequel that was more fun than its 2013 predecessor, thanks to stars John Boyega and Scott Eastwood as a new generation of Jaeger pilots, forced to battle another invasion of Kaiju monsters from within their giant robot suits.

Despite reuniting a grizzled Jamie Lee Curtis' Laurie Strode and Nick Castle as "The Shape" from John Carpenter's 1978 original, David Gordon Green's 40th Anniversay *Halloween* was yet another unnecessary sequel, which simply ignored the previous nine sequels and reboots. Despite that, it enjoyed the second highest-ever opening for a 'R'-rated horror movie in the US and eventually scored more than $255 million worldwide against a budget of just $10 million, becoming the highest-grossing film of the franchise by far.

Julius Onah's *The Cloverfield Paradox*, the third installments in producer J.J. Abrams' *Cloverfield* series, received a surprise digital release on Netflix in early February to make it "immediately profitable," according to industry sources. Set on an orbiting space station, experiments with a particle accelerator opened the door to a dark alternate reality. The cast included Gugu Mbatha-Raw, David Oyelowo, Chris O'Dowd and Donal Logue.

The third and supposedly final film in the Blumhouse trilogy, Adam Robitel's *Insidious: The Last Key*, saw Lin Shaye's troubled ghost whisperer return to her childhood home in New Mexico, where both disturbing childhood memories and a demon awaited her. The cast also included Bruce Davison, Patrick Wilson and Barbara Hershey.

Children were reportedly "left terrified" after an advert for the movie was shown on YouTube just before a video of songs from Disney's *Frozen* and other children's programming.

Gerard McMurray's tired fourth film in another Blumhouse franchise, *The First Purge*, was a prequel that explored the first time America's authoritarian government experimented with a law-free night on Staten Island. Marisa Tomei played the nïave psychologist who came up with the homicidal idea.

The fifth movie in New Line Cinema's "The Conjuring Universe", Corin Hardy's *The Nun* starred Taissa Farmiga as a novitiate in early-1950s Romania investigating the origin of the demonic nun Valak (Bonnie Aarons), seen in two of the previous instalments. Despite being no better than many direct-to-video releases, the movie had a franchise-record opening of $53.8 million and went on to gross more than $460 million around the world in its first month, making *The Nun* the second-largest domestic release in the "Conjuring" franchise and the largest worldwide release in the series to date.

A belated follow-up to the decade-old original, Johannes Roberts' *The Strangers: Prey at Night* was about a family menaced by a trio of masked psychopaths in a deserted trailer park.

After appearing in the original 1987 movie, Shane Black returned as director of *The Predator*, as two alien predators battled it out across a small town over Halloween. The movie's release was repeatedly delayed, and the entire climax had to be re-shot due to poor test-screenings.

Original star Jack Black's "R.L. Stine" was mostly sidelined in favour of the teenage cast of Ari Sanfdel's disappointing sequel, *Goosebumps 2: Haunted Halloween*, which involved a demonic ventriloquist's dummy. At least it included a neat Stephen King gag.

A teenager discovered he was under surveillance from a laptop's previous owner in the low-budget sequel *Unfriended: Dark Web*, which replaced the 2014 movie's original supernatural theme with psychological techno-terror.

Maze Runner: The Death Cure was the third—and thankfully—final movie in the trilogy based on James Dashner's popular series of post-apocalyptic YA books, as Dylan O'Brien's teen hero and his group of "Gladers" set out to break into WCKD's last city and find a cure to the disease known as "The Flare".

Set in 1987, *Bumblebee* found the eponymous Autobot taking refuge from a pair of Decepticon trackers (voiced by Angela Bassett and Justin Theroux) with Californian teenage mechanic Charlie Watson (Hailee Steinfield). Michael Bay and Steven Spielberg were amongst the producers of this likeable prequel, which turned out to be the best-reviewed but worst-opening movie yet in the *Transformers* series.

As good as Emily Blunt was as a darker version of P.L. Travers' title character in Disney's belated (fifty-four years!) sequel *Mary Poppins Returns*, Rob Marshall's movie was nothing more than a re-tread of the original. The supporting cast included Julie Walters, Meryl Streep, Colin Firth, 93-year-old Dick Van Dyke (playing the son of one of his characters from the first film), Angela Lansbury and David Warner, along with a brief cameo by the original "Jane Banks", Karen Dotrice.

Emily Blunt was also one of the voices in the animated sequel *Sherlock Gnomes*. Elton John's involvement as executive producer may explain the involvement of Mary J. Blige, Michael Caine, Chiwetel Ejiofor, Dexter Fletcher, James Hong, Matt Lucas, James McAvoy, Stephen Merchant, Ozzy Ozbourne, Maggie Smith, Julie Walters, Richard Wilson, and Johnny Depp as the voice the garden-ornament detective investigating the mysterious disappearance of other gnomes.

After a wait of fourteen years, Disney and Pixar's *Incredibles 2* not only shattered the previous opening weekend record for an animated film in the US, but finished with one of the top ten openings of all-time for a film of any genre, with a take of around $180 million. Brad Bird's convoluted sequel picked up immediately after the first movie, as the super-powered family tried to change public opinion after they were banned.

Adam Sandler's lonely Count Dracula and his friends and family found themselves on an exotic cruise captained by the descendent of the vampire's sworn enemy in *Hotel Transylvania 3: Summer Vacation* (aka *Hotel Transylvania 3: A Monster Vacation*), the third in the animated series.

In Luca Guadagnino's pointless 1970s-set rehash of Dario Argento's far superior *Suspiria*, Dakota Johnson's aspiring dancer travelled to Berlin to enroll in a mysterious academy run by Tilda Swinton and her coven of witches. Original star Jessica Harper had a cameo.

Alicia Vikander took on the mantle of archaeologist/adventurer Lara Croft, searching for her missing father (Dominic West), in Roar Uthaug's ho-hum remake/reboot of *Tomb Raider*, based on the popular video game. Kristin Scott Thomas and Derek Jacobi needed to have a chat with their agents.

Produced by J.J. Abrams, Julius Avery's *Overlord* was a terrific, low-key World War II horror movie, as a group of American paratroopers trapped behind enemy lines on the eve of D-Day uncovered a Nazi plot to create a zombie army. It was reputedly supposed to be the fourth movie in the *Cloverfield* series.

Rafe Spall and his three friends fell foul of a monstrous legend while hiking in the Swedish mountains in David Bruckner's accomplished slice of folk horror, *The Ritual*, based on the novel by Adam L.G. Nevill. Andy Serkis was an executive producer.

Jason Statham's apparently indestructable salvage specialist set out to save the crew of Rainn Wilson's deep-sea research facility from a seventy-five-foot-long prehistoric shark in Jon Turteltaub's fun but ludicrous *The Meg*, based on Steve Alten's 1997 debut novel.

In *Mandy*, Panos Cosmatos' trippy homage to David Lynch set in 1983, Nicolas Cage's lumberjack went full gonzo on the religious cult and demonic bikers that murdered his artist wife (Andrea Riseborough). The always-busy Cage was back, co-starring with Selma Blair as worn-out suburban parents inexplicably driven to kill their self-obsessed kids in Brian Taylor's equally crazy comedy *Mom and Dad*, which also featured Lance Henriksen.

British-born actor Dean S. Jagger portrayed the eponymous rogue police detective, murdered and brought back from the dead as the ultimate vampire-killer, in his brother Ben's *Corbin Nash*. The supporting cast included Corey Feldman, Malcolm McDowell, Rutger Hauer, Bruce Davison and Courtney Gains.

In Steven Sonderbergh's *Unsane*, Claire Foy's fragile stalker victim was committed to a mental institution because she was mad—or was she? Reportedly shot on an iPhone 7 in just ten days, the supporting cast included Amy Irving, Juno Temple and an uncredited Matt Damon.

Following the death of her reclusive mother, model-maker Annie (Toni Collette, who seemed to have wandered in from a different, frankly better movie) and her family found themselves beset by various supernatural terrors in writer-director Ari Aster's haunted house debut *Hereditary*, which also starred Gabriel Byrne.

Helen Mirren brought a much-needed touch of class to the role of Sarah Winchester, the widow of a the rifle manufacturer, who believed her Californian mansion to be haunted by the vengeful souls of the weapon's victims in The Spierig Brothers' *Winchester*, an odd blend of biography and horror inspired by the real-life, multi-room tourist attraction in San José.

Kelsey Grammer turned out to be the surprise villain of *7 Guardians of the Tomb* (aka *Guardians of the Tomb*), a pulpy,

Australian-made adventure about a 2,000-year-old Chinese tomb protected by a species of giant mutant spider.

John McPhail's low-budget *Anna and the Apocalypse* was a Christmas musical with zombies, shot in Scotland. Teenager Anna (Ella Hunt) and her schoolfriends found themselves in the middle of an undead apocalypse during the holiday season. The film was re-edited and shortened for its American release.

Tyler Posey and her fellow college students ended up playing the eponymous game with a deadly supernatural twist in Jeff Wadlow's *Truth or Dare*.

A girl (AnnaSophia Robb) discovered that the headmistress (Uma Thurman) at her new boarding school was meddling with the supernatural in *Down a Dark Hall*, which was based on the novel by Lois Duncan and had been sitting on the shelf for a couple of years.

A sleep doctor (Maggie Q) tried to protect her family from a demon that fed on their night terrors in *Slumber*, which also featured Sam Troughton, Sylvester McCoy and William Hope.

Domhnall Gleason's doctor was called to an apparently haunted house from his past in *The Little Stranger*, Lenny Abrahamson's slow and muddled adaptation of Sarah Waters' best-selling psychological ghost story set during the summer of 1948. Ruth Wilson, Will Poulter and Charlotte Rampling portrayed the family with secrets.

Despite being based on a successful West End stage play written by co-directors Jeremy Dyson and Andy Nyman, and featuring a cast that included Nyman, Martin Freeman and Paul Whitehouse, *Ghost Stories* was a dull and disappointing homage to the kind of much better anthology horror movies that Amicus used to produce.

A group of friends summoned an urban bogeyman in *Slender Man*, while a masked serial killer used a travelling Halloween amusement park as a cover to find his victims in the low-budget slasher *Hell Fest*.

In Clay Staub's low-key debut *Devil's Gate*, Amanda Schull's FBI agent teamed up with a local sheriff's deputy (Shawn Ashmore) to find a missing woman and ended up uncovering a very different kind of alien abduction.

Chloë Sevigny and Kristen Stewart starred in *Lizzie*, which reimagined the alleged 19th century axe-murderess' lesbian relation-ship with her Irish maid.

Elle Fanning was cast in the title role of Haifaa Al-Mansour's feminist biopic *Mary Shelley*, which charted the *Frankenstein* author's insipid romance with poet Percy Bysshe Shelley (Douglas Booth). Tom Sturridge was Lord Byron, Ben Hardy played Dr. John Polidori, and Mary's stepsister Claire Clairmont was portrayed by Bel Powley.

A woman (Matilda Lutz) hunted down the three men who raped her in the desert in Coralie Fargeat's French-Belgium debut *Revenge*.

Recalling the plot of Jack Clayton's 1967 film *Our Mother's House*, Spanish writer and director Sergio G. Sánchez's debut *Marrowbone* (aka *The Secret of Marrowbone*) found four motherless siblings hiding out in a creepy abandoned Maine farmhouse. The "twist" ending borrowed heavily from a well-known supernatural movie.

Lars von Trier's nihilistic *The House That Jack Built* followed the life of Matt Dillon's clever 1970s serial killer over twelve years. The supporting cast included Bruno Ganz and Uma Thurman. When the film premiered at the Cannes International Film Festival in May, more than 100 audience-members—including some critics—report-edly walked out. When released in America the movie was cut by five minutes.

The animated *Spider-Man: Into the Spider-Verse* combined 2-D and 3-D graphics and was about teenage Afro-Latino webslinger Miles Morales (voiced by Shameik Moore) teaming up with half-a-dozen Spider-People from alternate universes—including an ageing Peter Parker (Jake Johnson), Spider-Man Noir (Nicolas Cage), Spider-Woman (Hailee Steinfeld) and the anthropomorphic pig Spider-Ham (John Mulaney)—to battle Liev Shrieber's Wilson Fisk/Kingpin. Stan Lee, who died a month before the movie came out, had a number of cameo roles.

Despite being, well, a bit wet, James Wan's version of DC's *Aquaman* took more than $1 billion worldwide thanks to Jason Momoa's likeable turn as the titular half-Atlantean hero, Arthur Curry, searching for the Trident of Neptune to defeat his evil half-brother Orm (Patrick Wilson). Also featuring Amber Heard, Willem

DaFoe, Dolph Lundgren, Nicole Kidman, and Julie Andrews as the voice of a sea monster, the movie took $246 million in just twenty days in China, where it opened first.

A hardworking Emily Blunt and her husband/director John Krasinski played parents living in a post-apocalyptic world where the slightest sound attracted the attention of blind insectoid monsters with super-sensitive hearing in *A Quiet Place*, which made a lot of noise at the box-office.

The Rock's former-special-forces-soldier-turned-primatologist (yes, really) used his pet giant albino gorilla to stop a genetically-mutated wolf and crocodile from destroying Chicago in the video-game inspired *Rampage*.

Following the reappearance of her missing husband (Oscar Isaac), Natalie Portman's ex-army biologist led an all-female team into a mysterious meteor zone known as "The Shimmer", where the rules of nature didn't apply, in *Annihilation*. Alex Garland's follow-up to *Ex Machina*, based on the novel by Jeff VanderMeer, went straight to Netflix in the UK after audiences at test-screenings found it "too intellectual".

Based on the YA novel by Ernest Cline, *Ready Player One* was Steven Spielberg on auto-pilot as Tye Sheridan's futuristic young video gamer entered a virtual reality game to solve a puzzle left behind by its deceased inventor (Mark Rylance). Ben Mendelsohn was the evil corporate boss trying to stop him, and there were numerous references to pop-culture icons (including the Overlook Hotel from *The Shining*, the DeLorean time machine, The Iron Giant, the Batmobile, Chucky, the 1933 King Kong and the Tyrannosaurus rex from *Jurassic Park*) to keep you awake during the interminable running time.

Despite being produced and co-written by Peter Jackson and based on the best-selling series of YA steampunk fantasies by Philip Reeve set in a ludicrous post-apocalyptic world of cities on wheels, Christian Rivers' $100 million *Mortal Engines* was a justifiable 3-D flop at the box-office, debuting in North America with a gross of just $7.5 million.

The Darkest Minds was based on yet another trilogy of YA books, this time by Alexandra Bracken. Set in a dystopian future world where a pandemic had killed most of the children, those that survived developed superpowers and were locked-up in internment camps by the nasty adults. It also flopped at the box-office, so don't expect to see a sequel anytime soon.

Co-produced and co-scripted by James Cameron, Robert Rodriguez's 3-D *Alita: Battle Angel* was based on Yukito Kishiro's manga comic series, as Rosa Salazar's amnesiac cyborg was reactivated by Christoph Waltz's "Dr. Ido" to save the world. It also featured Jennifer Connelly, Jackie Earle Haley, Jeff Fahey, Casper Van Dien and an uncredited Edward Norton and Michelle Rodriguez.

Elle Fanning's visiting alien tourist ended up in 1977 partying with Alex Sharp's South London teenager in writer/director John Cameron Mitchell's nostalgic indie comedy *How to Talk to Girls at Parties*, based on the 2006 short story by Neil Gaiman. The supporting cast included Matt Lucas, Ruth Wilson, and Nicole Kidman as an outrageous punk rocker.

The busy Fanning also turned up to ruin the post-apocalypse solitude of fellow survivor Peter Dinklage's recluse in Reed Morano's *I Think We're Alone Now*, which also featured Charlotte Gainsbourgh and Paul Giamatti.

Forest Whitaker attempted to return to his pregnant wife in a post-apcalyptic world in *How It Ends*, while an alien spacecraft crash-landed in Moscow in the 3-D Russian-made *Attraction*.

Set in the near-future, Leigh Whannell's *Upgrade* starred Logan Marshall-Green as a quadriplegic given an experimental computer-chip implant that allowed him to hunt down the gang that murdered his wife and left him for dead.

Set in a riot-torn, near-future Los Angeles, Jodie Foster's no-nonsense nurse ran a secret hospital for criminals in Drew Pearce's directorial debut *Hotel Artemis*, and a boy (Alex Neustaedter) bonded with the top-secret military robot-dog of the title in *A-X-L* (which stood for "Attack, Exploration, Logistics").

Finally released three years after it was first screened at festivals, Mathew Cullen's *London Fields*, based on the dystopian novel by Martin Amis, was about a clairvoyant woman (Amber Heard) who began affairs with three different men (played by Theo James, Jim Sturgess and Billy Bob Thornton), one of whom she knew would eventually murder her.

In 2015, director Cullen filed a lawsuit against the producers, accusing them of tampering with his final cut. Meanwhile, the following year, the producers sued Heard for $10 million for breach of contract, claiming she refused to do nude scenes for the film despite knowing that her role would require them. They also accused Heard of violating her contract by refusing to show up at the film's planned premiere at the 2015 Toronto International Film Festival.

The dispute was finally settled, and although it was Cullen's preferred cut released in cinemas, the film set a new record as the second worst wide-release opening in box-office history. Released in the US on 613 screens, the film only grossed around $160,000, for a per-screen average of just $262.

London Fields also featured Gemma Chan, Jason Isaacs, Cara Delevigne, Lily Cole, and an uncredited Johnny Depp, who appeared as a favour to his then-wife, Heard, who subsequently accused him of domestic violence and divorced him.

Melissa McCarthy's hardboiled detective teamed up with her former partner, a foul-mouthed PI puppet (voiced by Bill Barretta), to find out why the puppet cast of a hit 1990s TV show were being murdered one-by-one in Brian Henson's lowbrow R-rated comedy *The Happytime Murders*. Elizabeth Banks, Maya Rudolph and Joel McHale portrayed other humans living in a world where they co-existed with puppets.

When a sinkhole opened up near an English boarding school, it unleashed an army of monsters in Crispian Mills' hit-and-miss comedy/horror *Slaughterhouse Rulez*, starring Simon Pegg, Nick Frost, Michael Sheen and Margot Robbie.

Will Ferrell and John C. Reilly starred as the eponymous detectives in the comedy *Holmes & Watson*, which was as dumb as you would expect, despite a supporting cast that included Rob Brydon, Billy Zane, an uncredited Steve Coogan and Hugh Laurie, and Ralph Fiennes as "Professor Moriarty".

Eli Roth (*Hostel*) was the surprise choice to direct *The House with a Clock in Its Walls,* based on the classic 1973 children's book by John Bellairs. The delightfully dark children's movie featured Owen Vaccaro as a ten-year-old orphan who helped his eccentric warlock uncle (Jack Black, in full flow) and their witchy neighbour (Cate Blanchett) prevent Kyle MacLachlan's resurrected wizard from bringing about the end of the world through black magic.

Inspired by the real-life Mafia kidnapping of a thirteen-year-old boy in 1993, a young girl (Julia Jedlikowska) set out on a journey through a magical landscape to find her missing classmate (Gaetana Fernandez) in Fabio Grassadonia and Antonia Piazza's *Sicilian Ghost Story.*

Oprah Winfrey, Reese Witherspoon and Mindy Kaling starred as three celestial travellers who helped a troubled young girl (Storm Reid) search for her scientist father (Chris Pine) in Ava DuVernay's $100-million misfire adaptation of Madeleine L'Engle's much-loved 1962 fantasy novel *A Wrinkle in Time* for Disney. The studio had previously adapted the book for television back in 2004.

Disney's $132 million *The Nutcracker and the Four Realms* was based on E.T.A. Hoffman's 1816 story and Tchaikovsky's ballet about a grieving young girl (Mackenzie Foy) who found herself transported from Victorian London to a fantasy world where she encountered gingerbread soldiers, an army of mice and Keira Knightley's Sugar Plum Fairy. The starry supporting cast included Morgan Freeman and such Brit actors as Meera Syal, Matthew Macfadyen, Omid Djalili, Jack Whitehall, Richard E. Grant, and Helen Mirren as the creepy "Mother Ginger". Joe Johnston was called in for a month of re-shoots when original director Lasse Hallstrom was not available.

In a reversal of the usual plot, Warner Bros.' animated 3-D *Smallfoot* was about a Himalayan yeti, Migo (voiced by Channing Tatum), who befriended a TV host (James Corden) and thereby proved that the legendary "smallfoots" (humans) actually existed.

Benedict Cumberbatch voiced the title character in yet another version of *Dr. Seuss' The Grinch.* The new animated version also featured the voice talents of Rashida Jones, Angela Lansbury, and Pharrell Williams as the narrator.

Monster Family was a German-made animated comedy about a family transformed into the classic monsters by a witch. The British voice cast included Emily Watson, Jason Isaacs, Nick Frost, Celia Imrie and Catherine Tate.

The French-made cartoon *Zombillénium* was set in the eponymous struggling theme park, where real monsters could hide in plain sight.

Jim Carter and Alice Krige voiced their roles from the 2000 live-action adaptation of Angela Sommer-Bodenburg's *The Little Vampire* for a Dutch/German-made animated version in 3-D.

Robin and the other super-kids from the Cartoon Network TV show made the jump to the big-screen in *Teen Titans Go! to the Movies*, as they encountered Will Arnett's masked villain "Slade" while trying to travel across Hollywood. In a nice piece of stunt casting, Nicolas Cage voiced Superman.

Wes Anderson's stop-motion *Isle of Dogs* was set in a futuristic Japan, where a canine flu had resulted in man's best friend being banished to a junk-heap island. The impressive voice cast included Bryan Cranston, Edward Norton, Bob Balaban, Jeff Goldblum, Bill Murray, Frances McDormand, Scarlett Johanson, Harvey Keitel, F. Murray Abraham, Yoko Ono, Tilda Swinton, Liev Schreiber and Angelica Huston.

A young boy was visited by his sister from the future in Mamoru Hosoda's *Mirai*, an *anime* which was set in a world where different periods of time co-existed.

Christopher Nolan supervised a 70mm photochemical restoration of Stanley Kubrick's *2001: A Space Odyssey* for a 50th Anniversary theatrical reissue. Nolan was born two years after the film was first released.

Guillermo del Toro's *The Shape of Water* received thirteen Oscar nominations, winning Academy Awards for Best Original Score, Best Production Design, Best Director and Best Picture.

In July a US District Court dismissed a lawsuit by the family of playwright Paul Zindel (1936–2003), claiming that del Toro's movie was "in many ways identical" to the Pulitzer-winner's 1969 play *Let Me Hear You Whisper*, which was also set in a 1960s secret laboratory and featured a woman's relationship with a talking dolphin.

Other 2018 Oscar-winners included 'Remember Me' from *Coco* for Best Original Song, and that movie also picked up the statue for Best Animated Feature Film. Jordan Peele's *Get Out* won the Oscar for Best Original Screenplay, while the awards for Best Cinematography and Best Visual Effects went to *Blade Runner 2049*.

Udo Kier took over the role of "Andre Toulon", now an evil Nazi puppet-maker, in the direct-to-video sequel *Puppet Master: The Littlest Reich*, which also featured genre stalwarts Michael Paré and Barbara Crampton.

Inspired by a 1980s video game, the Spanish-made *It Came from the Desert* was supposed to be a homage to 1950s creature-features, as tedious teenagers were menaced by giant ants.

Frank Grillo's tough LA cop tracked down the aliens who had captured his estranged teenage son in *Beyond Skyline*, a belated sequel to the 2010 original, filmed in Indonesia and featuring actor Antonio Fargas.

Peter Stray's low budget horror-comedy *Canaries* (aka *Alien Party Crashers*) was set during a Welsh New Year's Eve party interrupted by an alien invasion.

Spike Lee again executive produced *Tales from the Hood 2*, a belated direct-to-video sequel to the 1995 original, in which Keith David's mysterious "Mr. Simms" related stories about demonic dolls, possessed psychics, vengeful vixens and historical ghosts.

All the Creatures Were Stirring was another anthology movie, this time set at Christmas and starring Constance Wu, while the British-made *Why Me?* (aka *Christmas Presence*) was set in a remote lodge over the festive season.

Markie Post starred in Lou and Dave Elsey's short film *Keep the Gaslight Burning*, based on a Victorian ghost story by R. Chetwynd-Hayes.

Just in case there was anybody on the planet who didn't yet own Universal's Legacy Collection of horror movies in their various home video permutations, the studio added the 1943 version of *The Phantom of the Opera*, some associated Abbott & Costello movies and a 48-page booklet to the Blu-rays to create *Universal Classic Monsters—Complete 30-Film Collection*.

Presented in a new 4K restoration in both Blu-ray and DVD editions, Eureka! Entertainment's release of Universal's *Old Dark House* (1932) starring Boris Karloff, Melvyn Douglas, Charles Laughton, Gloria Stuart and Ernest Thesiger featured a video essay by David Cairns, commentary tracks from Kim Newman and Stephen Jones, Gloria Stuart, and director James Whale's biographer James Curtis, a conversation with Sara Karloff and an archival interview with Curtis Harrington, all in a beautifully illustrated slipcase by Graham Humphreys. The movie received a welcome theatrical re-release in the UK in April to tie-in with the Blu-ray.

Jones and Newman were also represented with a new commentary track on Hammer's 1963 remake of *The Old Dark House*, which was part of Powerhouse Films/Indicator's *William Castle at Columbia Volume Two* Blu-ray set. Limited to 6,000 units, it also included remastered versions of *Zotz!* (1962), *13 Frightened Girls* (1963) and *Straight-Jacket* (1964).

Tim Lucas supplied the commentary for Kino-Lorber's *Jack the Giant Killer: Special Edition*, which not only included the original 1961 movie, but also a re-envisioned musical version!

A new 2K restoration of Mario Bava's classic *giallo Blood and Black Lace* (1964) from Kino included a commentary *by Diabolique Magazine's* Kat Ellinger and an archival video interview with star Cameron Mitchell.

Criterion's Blu-ray and DVD of George A. Romero's *Night of the Living Dead* (1968) featured a restored print by the Museum of Modern Art and The Film Foundation, along with *Night of Anubis*, a previously unreleased work-print of the movie, plus never-before-seen 16mm dailies reels.

The 1970 TV movie *The House That Would Not Die* starring Barbara Stanwyck was issued by Kino-Lorber with an interview with dirrector John Llewellyn Moxey and commentary by film historian Richard Harland Smith.

Kino's *The Outer Limits: Season One (1963–64)* featured thirty-two episodes of the classic TV show, newly re-mastered in HD and featuring audio commentaries by David J. Schow, Tim Lucas, Gary Gerani and others. Schow also contributed a forty-page booklet to set.

Also from Kino-Lorber, *The Ghost of Sierra De Cobre* was a 1964 pilot episode for *The Haunted*, intended to be a companion horror series to *The Outer Limits*. Starring Martin Landau, Diane Baker and Judith Anderson, the Blu-ray and DVD included an alternate cut of the show with audio commentary by film historian Eric Grayson.

Writer and director Darin Coehlo Spring's documentary *Clark Ashton Smith: The Emperor of Dreams* was hosted by the poet Donald Sidney-Fryer and included interviews with Harlan Ellison, Scott Connors, S.T. Joshi and others.

Filmed in one take at Hemingford Grey Manor by Nunkie and ThomThom Productions, the DVD of *Oh, Whistle, and I'll Come to you, my Lad* featured Robert Lloyd Parry performing M.R. James' classic ghost story by the light of a single candle. The disc came in a specially designed "greetings" card, and the bonus material included a forty-minute documentary, *Wits in Felixstowe*, a rehearsed reading of MRJ's short story 'Rats', and Patricia Hammond performing Robert Burns' poem 'Whistle an' I'll Come to Ye, Me Lad'.

A man who had picked up a reel of 16mm film in the bargain bin of a junk shop in Brighton, England, in 1984 discovered that it was a lost twenty-minute version of Edgar Allan Poe's *The Tell-Tale Heart*, starring Stanley Baker and made by Adelphi Films in 1953. The film was restored and digitised by the British Film Institute, who put it up online for two weeks for free as part of a season of Hallowe'en "horror curios".

A blindfolded mother (Sandra Bullock) and her two children had to negotiate their way through a suicide-inflicting alien apocalypse in Susanne Bier's *Bird Box*, a sort of sight-centric riff on *A Quiet Place* on Netflix, based on the 2014 novel by Josh Malerman. John Malkovich and Sarah Paulson co-starred in the film, which was watched by 45 million subscribers—a third of the platform's customer base worldwide—in its first seven days. However, after footage appeared on social media of the "#BirdBoxChallenge", featuring idiots injuring themselves while walking around blindfolded, Netflix was forced to issue a warning to viewers!

Infected by a pandemic that turned people into shambling, flesh-eating "virals", Martin Freeman's father tried to find sanctuary for his infant daughter (Simone Landers) in the post-apocalyptic Australian outback in *Cargo*.

When Sam Worthington's military pilot volunteered for a programme to help him survive on Saturn's moon, he didn't expect them to mess around with his DNA in Netflix's *The Titan*, which also featured Taylor Schilling, Tom Wilkinson and Agyness Deyn.

A mysterious videotape drew two grown-up orphaned brothers (directors Aaron Moorhead and Justin Benson) back to a creepy UFO doomsday cult in the cosmic horror movie *The Endless* on Netflix.

The episodic *The Ballad of Buster Scruggs* was about as offbeat a Western as you might expect from writers/directors Ethan and Joel Coen. The final segment, 'The Mortal Remains', was all-out horror, featuring Brendan Gleeson, Jonjo O'Neill, Saul Rubinek and Tyne Daly.

Dan Stevens' prodigal son searched for his sister, abducted by an isolated island's strange religious cult led by Michael Sheen's charismatic prophet, as director Gareth Evans wandered into Welsh *Wicker Man* territory with *Apostle*.

Jeffery Wright's naturalist searched the Alaskan wilderness for a missing seven-year-old boy taken by wolves in Jeremy Saulnier's *Hold the Dark*, while a pair of fake paranormal researchers (Florence Pugh and Ben Lloyd-Hughes) encountered the real thing in a haunted orphanage in Netflix's *Malevolent*.

Although the Wachowski's *Sense8* was cancelled by Netflix after just two seasons, the network came up with a special two-hour finale in June, which replaced the planned Season 3.

Black Mirror: Bandersnatch was a special "interactive" movie-length episode of Charlie Brooker's series on Netflix, as Fionn

Whitehead's 1980s games programmer adapted an insane writer's novel into a video game. The viewer could remotely choose how the plot developed.

An erotic webcam dancer (Madeline Brewer) found she had been replaced by an online doppelgänger in Netflix's *Cam*.

The same streaming platform's pick-up of the J.J. Abrams-produced *The Cloverfield Paradox* notched up just 2.8 million US viewers in its first three days, following a surprise post-Super Bowl release in February.

Based on *The Jungle Book* by Rudyard Kipling, Andy Serkis' long-delayed *Mowgli: Legend of the Jungle* went to Netflix. Rohan Chand played the boy raised by wolves, while the motion-capture animals were voiced by Christian Bale, Cate Blanchett, Benedict Cumberbatch, Eddie Marsan, Tom Hollander, director Serkis and others.

Kurt Russell portrayed a soul-singing Santa in Netflix's *The Christmas Chronicles*.

In the Sky/Netflix co-production *Anon*, Clive Owen played a digital detective in a near-future world free of anonymity and crime. While investigating a series of unsolved murders, he encountered a mysterious woman (Amanda Seyfried) linked to the victims who had erased her digital footprint so that the authorities could not track her.

HBO's dreadful remake of Ray Bradbury's novel *Fahrenheit 451* starred Michael B. Jordan as futuristic fireman "Guy Montag", who questioned his job of burning books after meeting a young woman.

Demián Rugna's Argentinian-made *Terrified* (aka *Aterrados*) on the streaming service Shudder involved a paranormal outbreak in a suburb of Buenos Aires.

One could only hope that Syfy's *The Last Sharknado: It's About Time*, as usual directed by Anthony C. Ferrante, lived up to its title, as Fin Shepard (Ian Ziering, still giving it his best) travelled through time to prevent the first Sharknado. Alongside regular cast members Tara Reid and Cassandra Scerbo, the list of guest "stars" included Vivica A. Fox, Marina Sirtis, Dee Snider, Gilbert Gottfried, Tori Spelling, Bernie Kopell, La Toya Jackson, James Hong, Bo Derek,

Gary Busey (whose name was misspelled on the credits) and Al Roker.

In December, Tara Reid filed a $100 million lawsuit over the use of her face on *Sharknado* slot machines. She accused Syfy and the movies' producers of using her likeness without her consent. The actress later dropped the suit.

Broadcast the same month as *The Meg* was released in movie theatres, Syfy's low budget knock-off, *Megalodon*, starred a slumming Michael Masden as an Admiral on board a military vessel searching for a US Navy rescue submersible that encountered a giant prehistoric shark. As if that wasn't a bad enough career choice, Masden also turned up in Jim Wynorski's *CobraGator*, which had been executive produced by Roger Corman back in 2015 and was so bad that it was deemed unreleasable for three years!

Surviving characters from Syfy's *Atomic Shark* (2016) and *Trailer Park Shark* (2017) were hunted in their dreams(!) by a supernatural shark in The Brothers Furst's *Nightmare Shark*, which was confusingly retitled *Curse of the Dream Witch* in the UK.

Syfy's South Africa-filmed *Leprechaun Returns* was supposedly a direct sequel to the original 1993 movie, as an evil leprechaun menaced a group of teenage students planning to build a new Sorority House in North Dakota.

Cucuy: The Boogeyman on Syfy was just another variation of the "Krampus" legend, as the eponymous monster kidnapped children and put them in its sack to eat later. Jearnest Corchado was the rebellious teenager who broke house arrest to hunt it down.

The Asylum's *Tomb Invader*, starring Gina Vitori as adventurous archaeologist "Alabama 'Ally' Channing" searching for an ancient Chinese relic, was clearly "inspired" by *Tomb Raider*.

Another obvious knock-off was *Avengers Grimm: Time Wars*, a belated sequel to the 2015 original, in which the band of storybook heroes had to travel through time to prevent Rumpelstiltskin (Eric Feltes) taking over the Earth.

Neatly ripping-off two successful film franchises in one go, *The Jurassic Games* was set in the near-future, as ten death-row convicts were forced to compete in a virtual-reality game in which they were pitted against dinosaurs, while dinosaurs were being used to grow human organs for transplant in The Asylum's *Triassic World*.

Zombie at 17 was a Lifetime Network movie about a teenager (Celeste Desjardins) slowly turning into one of the undead, while Angie Patterson's single mother found that her plans to open a Victorian bed-and-breakfast didn't go as planned in Lifetime's *Home Invaders* (aka *Deadly Inn/Deadly B&B*).

Jodie Whittaker's irritating incarnation of the Time Lord crashed through the roof of a stranded train and on to TV screens in early October in new showrunner Chris Chibnall's much-hyped reboot of the BBC's *Doctor Who*. Picking up a new set of companions— Graham (Bradley Walsh, the best thing in the show), Ryan (Tosin Cole) and Yasmin (Mandip Gill)—she embarked on a series of overly preachy adventures through time and space. This meant that for every episode that featured mutated spiders in Sheffield or 17th-century witch trials, there were unfortunately too many others set on dull alien planets or hammering home some politically-correct polemic, as during an encounter with civil rights champion Rosa Parks (Vinette Robinson) in 1955 Alabama. Guest stars included Art Malik, Chris Noth, Lee Mack, Alan Cumming, Mark Addy and Phyllis Logan.

The ten episodes of *Doctor Who* attracted an average domestic audience of 7.7 million, which was the show's highest average TV rating for almost a decade, although the numbers dropped from 10.54 million for Whittaker's debut to a low of 6.24 million for the penultimate episode.

Five estranged siblings were forced back together to face (literally) the ghosts of their past in creator Mike Flanagan's dismal re-imagining of Shirley Jackson's 1959 novel *The Haunting of Hill House* (previously filmed twice before). Despite a cast that included Henry Thomas, Carla Gugino, Timothy Hutton, Annabeth Gish and a cameo by Russ Tamblyn (who was in the 1963 version), the whole thing was unfortunately dragged out over ten stupefyingly dull episodes on Netflix.

Netfilix's three-part *Ghoul* was set in a near-future India, where a new military interrogator (Radhika Apte) discovered that an eerie prisoner had unleashed a demon from Arabic folklore upon his captors. Executive produced by Jason Blum, it was originally supposed to be a stand-alone feature film.

Blumhouse Television also teamed up with Hulu for *Into the Dark*, a twelve-part horror anthology series released in monthly installments. Hulu's *Castle Rock* was an attempt to pull the Stephen King multi-verse of characters and locations together in a weekly J.J. Abrams-produced show set in the eponymous small town in Maine. Troubled defence attorney Henry Deaver (André Holland) returned home after the mysterious death of his father decades earlier and discovered an unknown prisoner (Bill Skarsgård) locked in a cage in the depths of Shawshank Prison. The ensemble cast included Sissy Spacek, Tim Robbins, Scott Glenn, Terry O'Quinn and Frances Conroy.

Despite being executive-produced by Robert Zemeckis, NBC's *Manifest* might have seemed familiar to anyone who remembered King's *The Tommyknockers*, as a plane that disappeared in 2013 with 191 people on board mysteriously returned after five years and the passengers started hearing voices.

Jared Harris, Ciarán Hinds and Tobias Menzies starred in AMC's grim ten-part series *The Terror*, about two ships trapped in the Arctic ice and beset by madness, cannibalism and a mythical Inuit god while trying to cross the Northwest Passage in 1847. It was based on the novel by Dan Simmons, who was an excecutive producer along with Ridley Scott and numerous others.

The third and final series of Sky's *Fortitude* was wrapped up in just four episodes that left viewers asking more questions than were answered.

Natalie Dormer's disgraced turn-of-the-century headmistress became increasingly paranoid about the mysterious Valentine's Day disappearance of three Australian schoolgirls and their governess in Amazon/Foxtel's overheated six-part adaptation of Joan Lindsay's 1967 novel *Picnic at Hanging Rock*.

As misjudged as the Fox Network's previous revival of *The X Files* was two years earlier, a further ten episodes were even worse as

Mulder and Scully (David Duchovny and Gillian Anderson, still completely lacking any on-screen chemistry) continued to search for their missing son with the help of some unlikely allies (including Dean Haglund's long-dead "Richard 'Ringo' Langly"). Nobody cared.

'Wayward Sisters', a Season 13 episode of *Supernatural*, was a back-door pilot for a potential spin-off series of all-female hunters led by Kim Rhodes' semi-regular character "Sheriff Jody Mills". The CW eventually passed on the concept.

Meanwhile, having allowed himself to be possessed by Michael so that he could defeat Lucifer (Mark Pellegrino) at the end of the previous season, Dean Winchester (Jensen Ackles) was still MIA at the beginning of the fourteenth(!) season of *Supernatural*, as Sam (Jared Padalecki), Castiel (Misha Collins) and the Apocalypse World hunters teamed up with some familiar allies, and Jack almost died after being drained of his grace by the evil Archangel.

The CW's culturally diverse reboot of *Charmed* (1998–2006) featured three new "Charmed Ones"—Macy (Madeleine Mantock), Mel (Melonie Diaz) and Maggie (Sarah Jeffery)—who, following the death of their mother, discovered they were witches. The sisters soon found themselves dealing with magical demons and their own relationship problems.

Another, quite different, reboot from Netflix was the ten-episode *Chilling Adventures of Sabrina*, a much darker than expected spin-off from The CW's *Riverdale*, which was nothing like the 1996–2003 series starring Melissa Joan Hart, and also based on the Archie Comics series. Kieran Shipka's half-mortal, half-teenage witch Sabrina Spellman had to choose on her sixteenth birthday between a normal human life and a magical one as part of the Church of Night. Unfortunately, the latter involved her signing her soul over to the "Dark Lord".

The show received some unexpected publicity in November when an egalitarian religious group, The Satanic Temple (also known as the United Federation of Churches), filed a $50 million lawsuit for alleged violation of copyright against Netflix and Warner Bros. over a statue of "Baphomet" seen in The Academy of Unseen Arts that Sabrina attends.

The Satanic Temple claimed that "Baphomet is a historical deity which has a complex history, having been associated with accusations of devil-worship against the Knights Templar." The plaintiff went on to state that its version of Baphomet was designed "... to be a central part of its efforts to promote First Amendment values of separation of church and state and equal protection" and that the statue seen in the show not only infringed their copyright but also defamed the deity by featuring it in an unflattering light.

An agreement was reached later the same month, with the unique elements of The Satanic Temple's Baphomet statue being acknowledged in the credits of episodes that had already been filmed. Meanwhile, the remaining terms of the settlement were subject to a confidentiality agreement.

In the special Christmas finale of *Chilling Adventures of Sabrina*, the young witch hosted a séance as the winter solstice approached.

Meanwhile, following on from an uneven Season 2, which included an episode centred around *Carrie: The Musical*, Jughead (Cole Sprouse) and Betty (Lili Reinhart) teamed up to investigate the role-playing game "Griffins and Gargoyles" and an arcane cult known as "The Farm" in the third season of The CW's *Riverdale*, also loosely based on an Archie Comics property.

The final season of *The Originals* kicked off with a seven-year time jump as the Mikaelson family came back together to save New Orleans from a new evil. Following the end of both *The Vampire Diaries* and *The Originals*, the small Virginia town of Mystic Falls lived on in The CW's spin-off series *Legacies*, when a bunch of supernatural teenagers from the Salvatore School for the Young & Gifted took on a monster-of-the-week.

Based on the 2011 novel by Deborah Harkness, the first in her best-selling "All Souls" trilogy, Sky's eight-part *A Discovery of Witches* featured Matthew Goode as a weary, centuries-old French vampire who fell in love with Teresa Palmer's American academic-witch when her discovery of a missing magical manuscript in Oxford's Bodleian Library put her in danger from all kinds of otherworldly enemies. The supernatural soap's classy supporting cast included Alex Kingston, Trevor Eve, Owen Teale, Lindsay Duncan and Sorcha Cusack.

Steve Pemberton and Reece Shearsmith's offbeat anthology show, *Inside No.9*, returned for a fourth, six-part series on BBC2 in early January. Although only one episode ('Bernie Clifton's Dressing Room') was a stand-out, guest stars such as Rory Kinnear, Bill Paterson, Emilia Fox, Nicola Walker, Kenneth Cranham, Zoë Wanamaker and Nigel Planer kept it watchable.

Broadcast a few days before Hallowe'en, the *Inside No.9 Live Special* was about a man (Pemberton) who discovered a discarded mobile phone in a graveyard and made the mistake of trying to find its owner. Unfortunately, the show involved a scripted "technical glitch" that not only revealed what was really happening, but also resulted in many viewers mistakenly switching off early.

Mark Gatiss' attempts to revive *A Ghost Story for Christmas* on BBC4 continued with *The Dead Room* on Christmas Eve. Unfortunately, the half-hour drama, written and directed by Gatiss and featuring Simon Callow and Susan Penhaligon, was hampered by a lack of budget and an obvious twist. It was followed by repeats of Lawrence Gordon Clark's classic adaptations of M.R. James' *Lost Hearts* and *The Ash Tree*, both of which showed how to do it properly.

The BBC's six-part ghost story *Requiem*, written by Kris Mrksa, starred Lydia Wilson as a talented concert cellist who, after her mother committed suicide in front of her, discovered that her family was somehow linked to the mysterious disappearance of a four-year-old girl from a small Welsh town back in 1994.

Did the world really need yet another five-part adaptation of Wilkie Collins' gloomy 1859 Gothic mystery *The Woman in White*—especially one refracted through a contemporary prism? Well, the BBC obviously thought so, and it threw in a cast that included Jessica Buckley, Olivia Vinall, Art Malik, Dougray Scott, Charles Dance, and Riccardo Scamarcio as the dastardly "Count Fosco".

Brendan Gleeson returned as "Bill Hodges" in the second season of the AT&T/Audience Network's *Mr. Mercedes*, based on the 2014 novel by Stephen King. The retired detective was once again on the trail of manipulative serial killer Brady Hartsfield (Harry Treadaway), who was now under the care of an ambitious but morally ambiguous neurosurgeon (Jack Huston). In mid-July, the city of San Diego hosted a *Mr. Mercedes* Immersive Experience for three days.

The FX Network's improved eighth season of *American Horror Story*, entitled *Apocalypse*, included crossover characters from *Murder House* (Season 1) and *Coven* (Season 3). Set during the aftermath of a nuclear attack, the witches had to prevent Antichrist Michael Langdon (Cody Firth) from bringing about the End of Days. As usual, a number of regular cast members returned in new and recurring roles, and there were surprise guest appearances from Joan Collins, Stevie Nicks, Dylan McDermott, Jessica Lange, Lily Rabe and Angela Bassett.

After being on hiatus for more than a year, NBC finally pulled the plug on *Midnight, Texas* after a nine-episode second and final season. Based on the book series by Charlaine Harris, a new hotel opened up in the titular town, while the surviving Midnighters united against the Dark Witches in the series finale.

The 100th episode of *Teen Wolf* ended the MTV show's sixth and final season. Very loosely based on the 1985 movie, some familiar faces showed up to help Scott and Stiles in their war against an army of hunters.

Season 3 of *Lucifer* ended on a cliff-hanger, with the titular character (Tom Ellis) killing the no-longer-immortal Captain Pierce/Cain (Tom Welling) for murdering Charlotte (Tricia Helfer), and Detective Decker (Lauren German) finally seeing her partner's true face.

To the surprise of fans, Fox then cancelled the popular series, but the network did show two extra episodes from the abandoned fourth season on a double-bill. These featured LAPD forensic scientist Ella Lopez (Aimee Garcia) being haunted by an apparent "ghost", and a "What if?" episode set in an alternate reality and narrated by the character's creator, Neil Gaiman, playing "God". The fans were still not placated, so Netflix stepped in to pick up the next season.

A second series of the Scandinavian show *Black Lake* came as a surprise, as a group of people found themselves trapped on the creepy remote-island retreat of Kallskar, historically plagued by mysterious disappearances.

Channel 4's short-lived docudrama series *True Horror* was

supposedly based on actual witness testimonies that involved a haunted farmhouse, a controlling ghost and a spooky churchyard. Michelle Ryan starred in special Hallowe'en episode, *True Horror: The Witches' Prison*.

Based on Aaron Mahnke's popular true-life horror podcasts, and executive produced by Gale Anne Hurd, the second season of Amazon Studios' *Lore* included episodes about Burke and Hare (Emmett J. Scanlan and Emmett Byrne), with Doug Bradley as Dr. Robert Knox; Countess Elizabeth Bathory (Maimie McCoy), and four further episodes featuring Jürgen Prochnow, Thomas Kretschmann, Steven Berkoff and Alicia Witt.

The Syfy channel continued to churn out numerous genre series that mostly flew below the radar and somehow kept getting renewed, although they did cancel *Superstition*, about the owners of a mysterious family-run funeral parlour battling the occult, after just one season.

Melanie Scrofano returned as Wyatt Earp's great-great-granddaughter, battling the demonic spirits of the outlaws her ancestor killed, for the third and final season of *Wynonna Earp*, which was based on Beau Smith's IDW comic-book series.

Meanwhile, the third season of Neil LaBute's *Van Helsing* found the vampire-hunter's descendant, Vanessa Van Helsing (Kelly Overton), and her companions attempting to track down the remaining undead Elders in a dystopian future.

Based on George R.R. Martin's 1980 novella (previously filmed in 1987), a team of scientists who travelled into space hoping to make contact with alien life discovered horrors closer to home in Syfy's ten-part *Nightflyers*.

The fourth season of the ten-part *Killjoys* found the trio of interpanetary bounty hunters trying to save D'av's newborn son.

As Season 3 of *The Expanse* opened, the crew of the *Rocinante* found themselves caught in a war between Earth and Mars. It ended with the Ring gates being opened, allowing access to more than a thousand inhabitable systems. Having been cancelled by Syfy, the series was quickly picked up by Amazon for a fourth season.

Syfy basically dumped the fourth and final season of its trippy

12 Monkeys, which was centred around a war across time as Cole (Aaron Stanford) and Cassie (Amanda Schull) finally confronted the Witness, and the time-loop was closed in a two-part finale.

Season 3 of Syfy's anthology series *Channel Zero* was about two sisters (Holland Roden and Olivia Luccardi) confronting the creepy Peach family headed by Rutger Hauer's patriarch in 'Butcher's Block', while in the fourth season's 'The Dream Door', a pair of newlyweds (Maria Sten and Brandon Scott) discovered a mysterious door in the basement of their home. The latter featured guest-stars Gregg Henry, Barbara Crampton and Steve Weber, and characters named "Hodgson" and "Carnacki".

The Syfy's post-apocalyptic zombie drama *Z Nation* was abruptly cancelled after the fifth season, with the final episode serving as the series finale.

With a new showrunner and a distinct lightening of tone, apparently nothing could stop the ninth season of AMC's *The Walking Dead*—not even the loss of two of its stars or a steep plunge in ratings. Andrew Lincoln, who had been with the show since the beginning as "Rick Grimes", decided to spend more time with his family in the UK, while Lauren Cohan ("Maggie") moved across to another network.

Despite still being the top drama on US cable TV, viewing figures for *The Walking Dead* fell by more than 60% in adults 18–49, with two episodes (including the season premier) reaching an all-time low.

In the episode 'What Comes After', a seriously-injured Grimes hallucinated such departed characters as Shane Walsh (Jon Bernthal), Sasha Williams (Sonequa Martin-Greene) and Hershel Green (Scott Wilson, who died a month before the episode aired) prior to another series time-jump of six months.

Meanwhile, the plot of AMC's companion show, *Fear the Walking Dead*, jumped ahead enough to sync up with *The Walking Dead*, as Season 4's new band of Texas survivors (including the original series' Lennie James as crossover character "Morgan") couldn't catch a break as they were forced to confront a hurricane during the zombie apocalypse.

Nathan Fillion was back as a decapitated zombie head in the second season of Netflix's enjoyable *The Santa Clarita Diet*, as the clueless Sheila and Joel Hammond (Drew Barrymore and Timothy Olyphant, perfect) and their daughter Abby (Liv Hewson) continued to search for a cure to Sheila's undead condition while trying to track down the source of some infected clams. There was solid support from Andy Richter, Maggie Lawson, Joel McHale and Gerald McRaney.

The USA Network decided someone wanted a TV series based on *The Purge* movie franchise, set in a totalitarian United States where for twelve hours a year all crimes—including murder—are legal.

The second and final six-part series of the Australian *Wolf Creek* found outback serial killer Mick Taylor (John Jarratt) preying on a coach full of international tourists.

Caleb Carr's 1994 serial-killer novel *The Alienist* was adapted by Netflix as a ten-part series, starring Dakota Fanning as New York's only female police officer in 1896, along with Daniel Brühl and Luke Evans.

The mysterious girl (Eline Powell) who turned up in the coastal town of Bristol Cove happened to be a seductive mermaid in Freeform's ten-episode *Siren*. More fish-people followed her.

The same network also aired the special *Hocus Pocus 25th Anniversary Halloween Bash* in October, executive-produced by original director Kenny Ortega and featuring exclusive cast and crew interviews.

Having been pulled mid-season by Fox, *Ghosted* returned in June with its final seven episodes and a new showrunner, as Max (Adam Scott) and Leroy (Craig Robinson) tried to discover who had bugged The Bureau Underground. They shouldn't have bothered.

Having thwarted the time-space continuum in Season 2, Stan (John C. McGinley) and Evie (Janet Varney) had to deal with a caterpillar monster, a murderous hitchhiker, an evil puppet, a demonic hospital and a fictional vampire world before finally managing to free the small town of Willard's Mill from Constable Eccles' curse at the end of the third and final season of IFC's *Stan Against Evil*.

After a slightly rocky start, Bryan Fuller and Alex Kurtzman's reboot *Star Trek: Discovery* for CBS All Access quickly settled down to be the best *Star Trek* series since *The Next Generation*. Set ten years before the original 1960s TV series, the crew of the *U.S.S. Discovery* had to avert an all-out war with the Klingons.

After a sixteen-month hiatus, the second season of HBO's *Westworld* was as baffling as ever, thanks to events occuring in different time-lines, as Ed Harris' mysterious Man in Black survived the robot massacre from the previous season and went searching for "the Door". Bernard (Jeffrey Wright), having discovered that he was a "host", washed up on a beach and was rescued by the troops from Delos Inc., while having sparked the revolution, the psychopathic Dolores (Evan Rachel Wood) and her gang rode around, killing as many human guests as they could find. Meanwhile, Maeve (Thandie Newton) kidnapped Delos' head writer (Simon Quarterman) and set off to find her daughter, ending up in Shogun World, and Anthony Hopkins was back as the theme-park's creator.

Along similar lines, the third and final series of Channel 4's *Humans* was set a year after the dawning of the synth consciousness, as the original "synthetic humans" fought for their rights in a world that feared them.

Hulu's smash-hit *The Handmaid's Tale* returned for a second uncomfortable season that moved beyond Margaret Atwood's source materal as it was revealed how Offred/June (Elisabeth Moss) and the rest of the world sleep-walked into the theocracy of Gilead. Following a devastating suicide attack on the ruling regime, Greg Bryk's creepy Commander Cushing took brutal revenge.

The third season of Amazon's *The Man in the High Castle* used elements of Philip K. Dick's planned, but never completed, sequel to his novel, as the resistance uncovered plans by the Nazis to travel to alternate worlds.

Executive produced by actor Bryan Cranston, the delayed final four episodes of *Electric Dreams*, inspired by Dick's short stories, finally aired on Channel 4 early in the 2018. Again, they were the usual mixed bag, of which 'The Father Thing' was probably the best.

Greg Kinnear, Juno Temple, Maura Tierney, Mel Rodriquez and Vera Farmiga guest-starred.

Having finally realised that their time-travel series *Timeless* suffered from all the same problems that *The Time Tunnel* did five decades earlier, NBC wisely pulled the plug (for a second time!) at the end of Season 2, which included episodes set in 1941 Hollywood and the Salem Witch Trials. Unfortunately, the network once again caved to fan pressure and agreed to air a two-part finale at Christmas. They really shouldn't have bothered.

Following a partial reboot at the end of the previous series, the third and final season of Netflix's *Travelers*, about visitors from the future requisitioning the bodies of people who were about to die, ended on an unresolved cliffhanger.

Traumatised refugees from a future war turned up seeking asylum in a small Oregon town in *The Crossing*, which starred Steve Zahn as the community's troubled sheriff. ABC cancelled the show after just eleven episodes.

Based on a 2014 Norwegian show, Netflix's limited series *Maniac* starred Jonah Hill and Emma Stone as two strangers who signed up for a pharmaceutical test programme run by Justin Theroux and Sally Field's mysterious doctors that targeted their subconscious. Predictably, things did not go quite as expected.

Set in a dystopian "cyberpunk *noir*" future where human minds can be transferred into new bodies, a prisoner (Joel Kinnaman) was revived 250 years after his death to investigate the murder of a wealthy industrialist (James Purefoy) in Netflix's ten-part *Altered Carbon*, based on the 2002 novel by Richard K. Morgan.

Sarah Shahi starred as a former hostage negotiator who rescued people from a highly advanced virtual reality programme in NBC's *Reverie*, and Tallulah Haddon's lonely outsider found herself drawn into a mysterious virtual reality game in Channel 4's six-part *Kiss Me First*.

The third and final season of the USA Network's alien-invasion series *Colony* saw Will and Katie Bowman (Josh Holloway and Sarah Wayne Callies) joining up with the Resistance and settling down in the troubled Seattle refugee colony.

The eight-part Danish series *The Rain* on Netflix was set in a post-apocalyptic world where a deadly virus had wiped out most of the population six years earlier, while the third and final season of AMC's sci-fi samurai show *Into the Badlands* found bad-ass warrior Sunny (Daniel Wu) protecting his infant son from Babou Ceesay's fanatical warlord.

Set five years after overcoming the global famine, TNT's post-apocalyptic *The Last Ship* finally ended after five seasons as the *Nathan James* set sail on a final voyage when a crisis sparked a global war and Commander Tom Chandler (Eric Dane) was forced to confront his own visions.

Neil Cross' clichéd cop show *Hard Sun* involved Jim Sturgess and former model Agyness Deyn's glum London detectives investigating crimes and being pressurised by Nikki Amuka-Bird's ruthless MI5 agent, against the background of a cover-up conspiracy involving the end of the world. The six-part BBC/Hulu series wasn't anywhere near as interesting as it sounds, although the mad-doctor finale (which included a brief nod to H.P. Lovecraft) ended with the global extinction event apparently turning up four years earlier than it was due.

The fifth season of The CW's *The 100* staggered on, as the show resumed six years after the end-of-the-world revealed at the climax of the previous season.

Despite changing the scheming Dr. Smith to a woman (the excellent Parker Posey), Netflix's humourless ten-part *Lost in Space* wasn't a patch on Irwin Allen's original 1965–68 series, as Molly Parker and Toby Stephens' dull colonists and their annoying children crash-landed on an unexplored planet.

Tom Felton and Natalia Tena were amongst a group of strangers struggling for survival on board the eponymous abandoned space-ship over ten episodes of the South African-shot *Origin* on YouTube Premium.

Sean Penn and Natascha McElhone starred in the eight-part Channel 4/Hulu series *The First*, which was set in the near future and succeeded in making the efforts to send the first human mission to Mars seem exceedingly dull.

The ten-part French series *Missions* covered much the same sombre ground, as two rival tech billionaires were locked in a race to send the first human mission to the red planet.

Stargate Origins was a digital series released exclusively to the dedicated subscription-based platform Stargate Command. Ellie Gall's young Catherine Langford travelled to a world beyond the Stargate portal to stop the Nazis conquering the world in ten ten-minute episodes.

The sixth season of The CW's increasingly grim and violent *Arrow* ended with the death of a major supporting character and Oliver (Stephen Amell) finally admitting in public he was the Green Arrow before being incarcerated in prison (without due process!) by the FBI.

With Clifford DeVoe/The Thinker (Neil Sandilands) finally defeated by Team Flash at the end of Season 4 of *The Flash*, the fifth season kicked off with the surprise appearance of Nora West-Allen (Jessica Parker Kennedy), Barry and Iris' daughter from the future, and introduced a new villain, Cicada (Chris Klein), who was determined to exterminate all metahumans.

Having beaten Selena (Anjali Jay) and the Worldkillers with the help of some members of the Legion of Superheroes at the end of Season 3, the fourth season of The CW's *Supergirl* found the Woman of Steel (Melissa Benoist) and her friends attempting to protect National City from the xenophobic Children of Liberty.

Stephen Amell's Green Arrow and Grant Gustin's The Flash found themselves inhabiting each other's bodies in 'Elseworlds', the annual crossover between *Arrow*, *The Flash* and *Supergirl*. The three-night mini-series featured the return of Tyler Hoechlin's Clark Kent/Superman and John Wesley Shipp's 1990s TV Flash, while introducing Elizabeth Tulloch's Lois Lane and Ruby Rose's LGBTQ Batwoman.

Having turned up (from his eponymous cancelled series on NBC) earlier in Season 3, Matt Ryan's "John Constantine" joined The CW's fourth season of *DC's Legends of Tomorrow* as a welcome regular. While the Legends battled new magical threats and attempted to elude the Time Bureau, Arthur Darvill was back for one episode as "Captain Rip Hunter".

Ryan also recreated his character (in voice only) in the ten-part stylised animated series *Constantine: City of Demons* on the CW Seed, as the occult detective investigated the possession of an old friend's young daughter.

Based on another DC character, The CW's *Black Lightning* played like *The Cosby Show*'s Huxtable family—if Cliff was an African-American inner-city high school teacher (Cress Williams) who decided to revive his vigilante superhero career, and one of his daughters (Nafessa Williams) was a lesbian who had inherited his power to control electricity.

The fourth, penultimate, series of Fox's *Gotham*, entitled *A Dark Knight*, ended with James Gordon (Ben McKenzie) and a group of unlikely allies trying to prevent Jeremiah Valeska/The Joker (Cameron Monaghan) and his fellow Arkham Asylum escapees from reducing the city to complete anarchy. Alexander Siddig returned as "Ra's al Ghul", while young Bruce Wayne (David Mazouz) prepared to accept his destiny.

As the title indicated, the Syfy's ten-episode *Krypton* was set on Superman's home planet centuries before it exploded. Too bad it was so dull, despite Shaun Sipos turning up as a time-travelling "Adam Strange", Blake Ritson as "Brainiac" and Colin Salmon as "General Zod".

DC Universe's inaugural series *Titans* was a gritty take on the *New Teen Titans* comic series, as Detective Dick Grayson/Robin (Brenton Thwaites) and moody teenagers Rachel Roth/Raven (Teagan Croft), Koriand'r/Starfire (Anna Diop) and Gar Logan/Beast Boy (Ryan Potter) teamed up to prevent an occult apocalypse. Along the way, the superheroes also ran into the Doom Patrol in a back-door pilot that featured the voice of Brendan Fraser as "Cliff Steele" and the team of Hawk and Dove (Alan Ritchson and Minka Kelly).

The third season of AMC's increasingly bonkers *Preacher* began with Jesse (Dominic Cooper) returning to his creepy old home of Angelville to magically resurrect Tulip (Ruth Negga), and ended with eveyone battling neo-Nazis and the Devil. Meanwhile, vampire Cassidy (Joseph Gilgun) made new friends in New Orleans as the end of the world approached.

Unfortunately for Phil Coulson (Clark Gregg) and the rest of his team in Marvel's *Agents of S.H.I.E.L.D.*, much of Season 5 found them stuck in the future on a Kree spaceship, until they finally returned to their own timeline and unwisely teamed up with Adrian Pasdar's General Talbot in an attempt to prevent the destruction of the Earth by the "Destroyer of Worlds". At the end, Coulson apparently walked off into the sunset to die in what was supposed to be the series conclusion. However, ABC subsequently renewed the show for another, truncated season.

Presumed dead after a building fell on him in *The Defenders*, a broken Matt Murdock (Charlie Cox) returned as the Devil of Hell's Kitchen in the third season of Marvel's *Daredevil*. Also back was Vincent D'Onofrio's villain "Wilson Fisk", who was bolder and more calculating than ever. In November, Netflix announced that the show would not be returning for a fourth season.

The fabulous Krysten Ritter returned as the eponymous misanthropic private eye in the second season of the Netflix's *Jessica Jones*, as she searched for the answer to her superpowers. Carrie-Anne Moss and Rebecca De Mornay offered solid support, while David Tennant's evil "Kilgrave" returned for a brief flashback.

In Netflix's second season of Marvel's *Luke Cage*, Mike Colter's indestructible celebrity hero tried to protect Harlem from a new strain of heroin, while Finn Jones was back for a second and final series of Marvel's *Iron Fist*, as the man with the knockout punch went up against Alice Eve's "Typhoid Mary".

Following a six-month time jump, the second season of Fox's *X-Men* spin-off, *The Gifted*, opened with the Mutant Underground having to contend with rival factions like the Hellfire Club's Inner Circle, the Purifiers hate-group and the sewage-dwelling Morlocks, while in Season 2 of the FX Network's increasingly mind-bending *Legion*, David (Dan Stevens) finally confronted "The Shadow King" as he battled Farouk (Navid Negahban) for the future.

After a group of teenagers with special powers discovered that their parents were supervillains, they got their own underground lair and received an ultimatum in Season 2 of Marvel's *Runaways* on Hulu.

Meanwhile, over on Freeform, another pair of tragic teens, Tandy Bowen (Olivia Holt) and Ty Johnson (Aubrey Joseph), found themselves imbued with the powers of light and darkness, which brought them together in Marvel's *Cloak & Dagger*.

The conclusion to the first season of Amazon's revival of the 2001 superhero spoof *The Tick*, based on the 1980s comic book by Ben Edlund, found the blue spandex hero (Peter Serafinowicz) and his friends facing a final showdown with "The Terror" (Jackie Earle Haley).

A busy Neil Gaiman appeared as himself in a self-deprecating cameo in an episode of *The Big Bang Theory*, in which a tweet from the writer put Stewart's comic store on the map.

An equally busy Nathan Fillion turned up as Lemony Snicket's brother, Jacques, in the second season of Netflix's *A Series of Unfortunate Events*, as the Baudelaire orphans found themselves in a creepy circus run by the evil Count Olaf (Neil Patrick Harris).

Three young boys discovered the guidebook that their late inventor father left behind for them led to some fantastical adventures in Amazon's *The Dangerous Book for Boys*. It lasted for just six episodes.

Harry Clayton (James Nesbitt) had to prevent rogue MI6 agent Samuel Blake (Rupert Penry-Jones) from destroying his magical lucky Chinese bracelet in the third and final ten-part series of *Stan Lee's Lucky Man* on Sky 1. Stan Lee himself had a brief cameo in the first episode.

The lone survivor of a massacre that killed her family, Blackblood warrior Talon (Jessica Green) set out on a quest for revenge and discovered her own supernatural powers in The CW's ten-part fantasy series *The Outpost*.

A runaway teenager (Sorcha Groundsell) learned she was able to shape-shift in Netflix's eight-episode *The Innocents*, a British-Norwegian series that also starred Guy Pearce.

As a result of a reboot which saw six major cast members leave at the end of the sixth season, ABC's *Once Upon a Time* ended happily ever after for Lana Parrilla's "Regina" as she was finally crowned "The Good Queen".

Kevin Williamson's ten-episode *Tell Me a Story* on CBS All Access relocated a trio of classic fairy tales to modern-day New York City.

After discovering at the end of Season 1 that "The Good Place" was actually "The Bad Place" (aka Hell) and having their minds wiped and returned to Earth at the end of Season 2, the third season of NBC's *The Good Place* found Eleanor (Kristen Bell), Chidi (William Jackson Harper), Tahani (Jameela Jamil) and Jason (Manny Jacinto) all getting a second chance at life, thanks to an interfering Michael (Ted Danson), before they ended up hiding in Janet's (D'Arcy Carden) endless void.

Brian Weaver (James Buckley) found himself trapped in a "travelling Amazematorium" run by Steve Coogan's cruel circus ringmaster in the fantasy-land of Munty, while Sylvester McCoy turned up as the mighty "Protector" halfway through the third and final silly six-part series of *Zapped* on the Dave channel.

HBO's *Game of Thrones*, which skipped a year ahead of its final season, won nine Emmy Awards in September, including one for Outstanding Drama Series.

David Morrissey played a cop investigating a murder between two separate worlds in *The City and the City*, based on the dystopian *noir* novel by China Miéville. After showing the first episode on BBC1, the remaining three episodes were only available on iPlayer.

After twenty particularly downbeat episodes—including a possibly occult killer, a murder linked to research into teleportation and a dead man who predicted the future—the sixth (and supposedly final) season of CBS-TV's *Elementary* ended on a near-perfect note as Sherlock (Jonny Lee Miller) and Joan (Lucy Liu) were forced to leave New York and return to London to solve crimes together.

Neil Dudgeon's DCI John Barnaby investigated the murder of a musician and a "curse" surrounding a symphony in the ITV *Midsomer Murders* episode 'The Curse of the Ninth', guest-starring Simon Callow.

Jack Reynor starred as real-life 1940s rocket engineer Jack Parsons, who was a secret disciple of occultist Aleister Crowley's sex-magic cult, in CBS All Access' ten-episode *Strange Angel*, executive produced by Ridley Scott.

The twelve-episode Spanish series *The Plague* (*La peste*) starred Pablo Molinero as a heretical ex-soldier investigating a series of messianic murders—an omen of the end of the world—in a 16th century Seville gripped by an outbreak of bubonic plague.

Over nine episodes, Veerle Baetens' amnesiac had to reconstruct her life in order to discover the fate of a missing man in the Belgian series *Tabula Rasa*.

The now-traditional Hallowe'en episode of the BBC's daytime soap opera *Doctors* involved a scary story told during a power-cut at the Birmingham medical practice, a creepy costume party that took an unexpected turn, and a man who arrived at the police station claiming he had a head in a bag.

For the first time in fifteen years, Robert Englund donned the striped sweater and claws as he reprised his role of "Freddy Krueger" in the Halloween episode of the ABC sit-com *The Goldbergs*.

During an Innsmouth-inspired opening sequence, Cthulhu and Homer got into an eating contest in *The Simpsons Treehouse of Horror XXIX* on Fox, which also included parodies *of Invasion of the Body Snatchers*, *Split* and *Jurassic Park*. Another episode of the animated comedy series included a spoof on Stephen King's *IT*.

Matt Groenig's new animated series *Disenchantment* on Netflix was set in fantasy kingdom where a rogue princess (Abbi Jacobson) teamed up with an elf and her personal demon to escape an arranged marriage.

Stewie and Brian teamed up Sherlock Holmes and Dr. Watson to investigate a series of murders in Victorian London, Stewie's body-swapping machine malfunctioned with chaotic consequences, Peter came face-to-face with God, and Stewie's shrinking machine shrunk him and Brian down to microscopic size in episodes of Seth MacFarlane's animated *Family Guy*, which entered its seventeenth season on the Fox Network. Guest voices included Patrick Stewart, Gilbert Gottfried and Tom Ellis as Oscar Wilde.

Three teenagers awakened in a strange fantasy world with no memory in Netflix's animated series *The Hollow*, and the network also relaunched a more empowered version of the titular 1980s cartoon character in the thirteen-episode *She-Ra and the Princess of Power*.

The new BBC/Netflix animated adaptation of Richard Adams' *Watership Down* may have been overlong, but it featured an impressive line-up of celebrity voice actors that included James McAvoy, Peter Capaldi, Rosamund Pike, John Boyega, Gemma Arterton, Olivia Coleman, Taron Egerton, Mackenzie Crook, Gemma Chan, Ben Kingsley, Rory Kinnear, Tom Wilkinson and Anne-Marie Duff, amongst many others.

Despite being hosted by the *Hostel* director and featuring on-screen commentary by some big names—Rob Zombie, Mick Garris, Quentin Tarantino, Joe Hill, Stephen King, John Landis, Jack Black, Tananarive Due, David J. Skal, Bruce Campbell, Joe Dante, Tom Savini, Linda Blair and many more—*Eli Roth's History of Horror* on AMC offered little that was new over seven episodes devoted to 'Zombies', 'Slashers', 'Vampires', 'Ghost Stories' and other generic themes.

To kick off a season of related movies and TV shows, in late September the UK's Paramount Network showed *Stephen King: Master of Horror*, an hour-long biographical profile of the best-selling author narrated by Mariella Frostrup and featuring contributions from biographer George Beahm and illustrator Glenn Chadbourne, amongst others.

Although co-scripted by the knowledgeable Kim Newman, the deconstruction of various film genres by British critic Mark Kermode made each episode of the BBC4's documentary series *Mark Kermode's Secrets of Cinema* feel more like a university lecture than a reason to further explore the titles discussed. The penultimate episode looked at 'Science Fiction', while the fifth and final episode was devoted to 'Horror' and featured clips from *The Exorcist*, *Psycho*, *Texas Chain Saw Massacre* and *Get Out*. There was also a Christmas special that spotlighted movies for the Holiday Season.

Hattie Morahan portrayed a young Angela Carter in BBC2's *Angela Carter: Of Wolves and Women*, an hour-long drama-documentary that included commentary by Salman Rushdie, Jeanette Winterson and Margaret Atwood. Maureen Lipman, Kelly Macdonald and Laura Fraser read extracts from the author's work.

Broadcast on BBC4 in November, *Golem* was a filmed performance of the acclaimed multi-media stage production from theatre group 1927, loosely based on Gustav Meyrunk's 1915 novel.

In January, BBC Radio 4's *Archive on 4: Frankenstein Lives!* marked the bi-centenary of Mary Shelley's novel, as Christopher Frayling considered how the story had been repeatedly adapted into the media.

To celebrate fifty years since it was first released, Frayling also hosted a look back at the making of *2001: A Space Odyssey* in another hour-long *Archive on 4: The Ultimate Trip: Stanley Kubrick's Space Odyssey.*

On April 21, BBC Radio 3 presented the world premiere of composer Mark-Anthony Turnage's *Coraline*, an operatic version of Neil Gaiman's novel, directed by Aletta Collins with a libretto by Rory Mullarkey. The two-act Royal Opera House production was staged at the Barbican, London. Soprano Mary Bevan played "Coraline", while mezzo Kitty Whately was her evil "Other Mother".

Sunday Feature: Supernatural Japan, presented by Christopher Harding on the same station, explored how the country used ghost stories to make sense of themselves and their place in the world.

For a week at the end of September, BBC Radio 3 and 4 presented a series of programmes honouring Angela Carter under the umbrella "Get Carter" banner (see what they did there?), with actress Fiona Shaw as the voice of the author (who died in 1992). These included *An Evening with Angela Carter* on Radio 3, which featured new productions of Carter's first radio play, 'Vampirella' (1976) starring Jessica Raine and Anton Lesser in a story about Countess Dracula, and her second, 'Come Unto These Yellow Sands' (1979), about the life of Victorian painter Richard Dadd (1817–86), portayed by James Anthony Rose.

Lucy Catherine adapted Carter's 1984 novel *Nights at the Circus* as two hour-long dramas on Radio 4, while Olivia Hetreed drama-tised the author's 1979 collection of revisionist fairy stories, *The Bloody Chamber*, over five daily fifteen-minute episodes.

Written by Neil Brand and broadcast daily during the week up to Christmas, BBC Radio 4's *The Haunting of M.R. James* featured fifteen-minute dramatisations of five of the author's more familiar stories ('The Mezzotint', 'Casting the Runes', 'The Stalls of Barchester Cathedral', 'A Warning to the Curious' and 'Rats'), with John Bowler playing James.

Mark Gatiss took over the role of MRJ for Brand's original hour-long drama, also called *The Haunting of M.R. James*, which debuted on December 22, in which the author believed that he was being haunted by a murderous and malevolent spirit linked to his past stories.

Written by Sara Davies and Abigail Youngman, *Talk to Me; H.P. Lovecraft* explored the story behind the author's (John MacKay) two-year marriage to Sonia Greene (Tracy Wiles). Carl Ptekopp portrayed Samuel Loveman.

Sean Grundy's hour-long drama *Tolkien in Love* explored the real-life events that affected J.R.R. Tolkien (Will Merrick) and the love of his life, Edith (Claudia Jessie), and how their relationship would inspire events in *The Lord of the Rings* and *The Silmarillion*.

Having introduced government secret agent and 16th century ghost Mary Lairre (Nicola Walker) in 2017's *Mythos*, Julian Simpson's paranormal investigator returned for two new episodes in April. Phoebe Fox, Tim McInnerny and Ewan Bailey co-starred in stories about a haunted castle ('Glamis') and a mysterious sinkhole in London ('Albion').

As part of Radio 4's series of hour-long classic tales of adventure and peril, *To the Ends of the Earth*, Mike Walker adapted Rudyard Kipling's 1888 novella *The Man Who Would Be King*, while Sagar Arya portrayed "Captain Nemo" in *20,000 Leagues Under the Sea*, a dramatisation of Jules Verne's 1870 novel by Gregory Evans.

Broadcast in early October on Radio 4, *When the Pips Stop: The Dweller in the Darkness* was a forty-five minute remake of the1920s haunted house drama written by Reginald Berkeley (1890–1935) and originally performed for the BBC Home Service.

Broadcast daily during Hallowe'en week, *The Second Pan Book of Horror Stories* comprised five fifteen-minute dramatisations, adapted by Anita Sullivan from the 1962 anthology edited by Herbert Van Thal. Featuring an ensemble cast, the stories were 'The Vertical Ladder' by William Sansom, 'The Speciality of the House' by Stanley Ellin, 'The Black Cat' by Edgar Allan Poe, 'Leiningen v the Ants' by Carl Stephenson and Bram Stoker's 'The Judge's House'.

Over nine episodes of the third series of Matthew Broughton's conspiracy thriller, *Tracks: Chimera*, Hattie Morahan's Dr. Helen Ash discovered that she was pregnant with an impossible embryo.

Toby Hadoke adapted Nigel Kneale's lost 1963 TV play *The Road* for Radio 4, with Mark Gatiss' philosopher Gideon Cobb and Adrian Scarborough's scientist Sir Timothy Hassall investigating ghostly hauntings in a country wood during the 18th century. It also featured the busy Hattie Morahan, who played Hassall's wife, Lady Lavinia.

Hattie Naylor's hour-long adaptation of Ann Radcliffe's 1794 Gothic novel *The Mysteries of Udolpho* starred Georgia Groome and John Dougall, while *Curious, If True* featured Sally Hedges' dramatisation of Elizabeth Gaskell's 1861 short story 'The Grey Woman', featuring Elizabeth Spriggs, Stella Gonet and Adjoa Andoh, from 1998.

Love Henry James: The Turn of the Screw was an hour-long dramatisation of the author's ghostly 1898 novella narrated by John Lynch as James and featuring Kate Phillips as "The Governess" and Jake Ferretti as "Peter Quint".

An abridged ten-part serialisation of Sarah Perry's novel *Melmoth* by Jeremy Osborne for Radio 4's *Book at Bedtime* was read by Greta Scacchi and Anton Lesser, while Henry Goodman read Peter Benchley's 1974 novel *Jaws* over an equal number of episodes.

Broadcast in two one-hour episodes in early January, *Graeae's Midwich Cuckoos* was adapted from John Wyndham's 1957 novel by Roy Williams for the Graeae theatre company of disabled performers.

Toby Stephens returned as "James Bond" for Archie Scottney's ninety-minute Radio 4 adaptation of Ian Fleming's 1955 novel *Moonraker*, the third novel to feature the British spy. Director Martin Jarvis once again assembled a starry supporting cast that included John Baddeley as Sir Winston Churchill, John Standing as "M", Julian Sands as "Q", plus Jared Harris, Patricia Hodge, Jon Glover and Ian Ogilvy.

BBC Radio 4's annual "Dangerous Visions" stream in June included the SF dramas *Speak* by Philip Palmer, *Forward Presence* by Hugh Costello, *Freedom* by Gary Owens, Jonathan Holloway's reimagining of Dostoyevsky, *The Double*, and Anita Sullivan's adaptation of Steve Erickson's 2017 novel *Shadowbahn*, in which the Twin Towers mysteriously reappeared in South Dakota.

As part of the same dystopian series, *First World Problems* was a five-part dramatisation by Martin Jameson set in a UK on the brink of civil war, while Louise Erdrich's *Future Home of the Living God*, about an escape from a high-security maternity hospital, was read over ten episodes by Cherrelle Skeete.

Sebastian Baczkiewicz's cursed immortal wanderer "William Palmer" (Paul Hilton) returned for the two-part dark fantasy *Pilgrim—The Winter Queen* in early December.

On Boxing Day, Radio 4 broadcast Lucy Catherine's hour-and-a-half adaptation of *Neil Gaiman's Norse Mythology*, featuring the voices of Diana Rigg, Natalie Dormer, Colin Morgan and Derek Jacobi as "Odin".

In *The Hauntening*, writer and performer Tom Neenan explored the horrors that lurked in people's apps and electronic devices through three modern ghost stories, while James Fleet starred as "Professor Quanderhorn" in Rob Grant and Andrew Marshall's six-part 1950s SF spoof *The Quanderhorn Xperimentations*.

To commemorate the 40th anniversary of the first broadcast on Radio 4 of *The Hitchhiker's Guide to the Galaxy*, Douglas Adams' friend and collaborator John Lloyd presented the one-hour tribute *Don't Panic! It's the Douglas Adams Papers*, which explored the author's private papers held at Cambridge University and included contributions by Richard Dawkins and Stephen Hawking.

Based on Eoin Colfer's 2009 novel *And Another Thing…*, the six-part *The Hitchhiker's Guide to the Galaxy: Hexagonal Phase* was adapted and directed by Dirk Maggs with additional material by creator Douglas Adams. Simon Jones, Geoff McGivern, Mark Wing-Davey and Susan Sheridan all recreated their roles from the original 1978 series, with support from Sandra Dickinson, Jane Horrocks, Professor Stephen Hawking and Lenny Henry, with Jim Broadbent as the voice of "paranoid android" Marvin and Jon Culshaw as "Cthulu" (*sic*).

Scripted by Barry Cryer and his son Bob Cryer, and based on their 2012 book, the two-part comedy *Mrs. Hudson's Radio Show* focussed on the eponymous landlady (Patricia Hodge) of Sherlock Holmes (Orlando Wells) and Doctor Watson (Stephen Critchlow).

The ninety-minute drama *Night of the Wolf* was an early Hallowe'en treat for listeners to BBC Radio 4 Extra in October. Written by Victor Pemberton and originally broadcast in 1975, it starred the husband and wife team of Vincent Price and Coral Browne in a werewolf story set during the late 19th century in the Cambridge Fenlands.

First broadcast on the BBC World Service in the early 1970s, *The Price of Fear* was introduced by Vincent Price and featured half-hour adaptations of Jack Ritchie's 'Remains to Be Seen', Bram Stoker's 'Cat's Cradle' (aka 'The Squaw'), Charles Birkin's 'Meeting in Athens' (aka 'So Pale, So Cold, So Fair'), Robert Arthur's 'The Man Who Hated Scenes', Elizabeth Morgan's 'Lot 132', A.M. Burrage's 'The Waxwork', René Basilico's 'Fish', William Ingram's 'Soul Music' and Richard Davis' 'Guy Fawkes Night'. Mervyn Johns, Kenneth J. Warren, Charles Birkin(!), Peter Cushing, Douglas Blackwell, Peter Barkworth, Bill Kerr, Coral Browne and Adrienne Corri were amongst the actors involved.

Edward de Souza's mysterious "Man in Black" introduced Gregor Grice and John Ducquemin's 'Vicious Fish' for *Fear on Four*, and the series continued with Vincent Price introducing half-hour drama-tisations of John Graham's 'Playing God', Paul Sirett's 'Hellhound on My Tail', Aubrey Woods' 'Hearing is Believing' and Stephen Gallagher's 'Life Line', all from 1993. Price was back later in the year with Colin Haydn Evans' 'Tapping', Nick Fisher's 'The Chimes of Midnight' and Nick Warburton's 'Making Sacrifices', all from 1997, while de Souza returned to introduce 'Tissue Memory' by Judy Upton.

There was a vampire weekend on Radio 4 Extra at the end of May. First broadcast in 1974, Brian Hayles' feature-length drama *Lord Dracula* starred Kenneth Haig as "Vlad Dracula" and Nigel

Stock as the priest who knew him. Rebecca Lenkiewic's two-part radio adaptation of *Dracula* starred Nicky Henson as Bram Stoker's Count. Don McCamphill's version of Sheridan Le Fanu's *Carmilla* featured the voices of David Warner, Celia Imrie and Kenneth Cranham, while J.C.W. Brook's tale *The Bognor Regis Vampire* was from 1979.

Also repeated from the same year, Wally K. Daly's *The Silent Scream* was a three-part alien invasion thriller with James Laurenson, Hannah Gordon and Donald Hewlett.

From 1997, *Ray Bradbury's Tales of the Bizarre* featured dramatisations of the author's early stories, including 'The Man Upstairs', 'Jack-in-the-Box', 'The Scythe', 'The Wind', 'And So Died Riabouchinsk' and 'The Day it Rained Forever'.

Originally broadcast on the BBC Third Programme in September 1962, Nesta Pain's adaptation of Ray Bradbury's 1950 short story *There Will Come Soft Rains* starred Joan Miller and David King-Wood.

The Golden Apples of the Sun was first broadcast on BBC Radio 5 in 1991 and featured adaptations of Bradbury's title story, plus 'Hail and Farewell', 'The Flying Machine', 'The Fruit at the Bottom of the Bowl', 'A Sound of Thunder', 'The Murderer', 'The Witch' and 'The Foghorn'. The voice cast consisted of Don Fellows, Ed Bishop, Simon Treves and Judy Bennett.

The Female Ghost, also re-broadcast from 1997, included half-hour adaptations of Mary Elizabeth Braddon's 'The Cold Embrace', E. Nesbit's 'Man Sized in Marble', Edith Wharton's 'Afterward' and Elizabeth Bowen's 'The Demon Lover'.

As part of a series called *Just Before Midnight*, Radio 4 Extra broadcast Ted Willis' 'And No Birds Sing' from 1979, E. Nesbit's 'No.17' from 1963 and Philip Levene's 'The Invader' and Rosemary Timperley's 'The Dare Game', both from 1964. *The Strange and the Sinister* featured William Croft Dickinson's 'The Sweet Singers', 'Let the Dead Bury the Dead', 'Return at Dusk' and 'The Work of Evil' from 1961.

Originally broadcast in the late 1980s, *Ghost Story* featured Joss Ackland reading Alfred Noyes' 'Midnight Express', Ray Bradbury's

'The Crowd', Graham Greene's 'A Little Place Off the Edgware Road', Robert Aickman's 'Laura' and Marghanita Laski's 1955 story 'The Tower'.

From May 1978, Jill Hyem's *Remember Me* involved a remote guest house in the Peak District, a haunting music-box tune and an insane craving for revenge. Jill Balcon, Juilian Glover and Sarah Badel starrcd.

First broadcast in 1987, Bob Couttie's ninety-minute *The House on Spook Corner* starred Frank Windsor as a sceptical scientist investigating a ten-year-old poltergeist case.

Repeated from 1994, Gareth Armstrong read Oliver Reynolds' five-part dramatisation of Susan Hill's supernatural novel *The Mist in the Mirror* (1992), narrated by John Moffatt. George Parsons read Nigel Kneale's short story *The Pond*, repeated from 1988, and Judy Bridgland read a fifteen-minute adaptation of Vernon Lee's macabre story *The Doll*.

At the end of August, Radio 4 Extra broadcast a rare revival of *A Mass of Cobwebs*, Brian Batchelor's half-hour radio drama from 1959 based on M.R. James' story 'The Tractate Middoth'. It featured Peter Howell, Edgar Norfolk, Sheila Keith and Norman Bird.

In early October, the same station also re-broadcast a 1986 reading of M.R. James' 'Rats' by James Aubrey, and for a week in December *Ghost Stories by M.R. James* featured Benjamin Whitrow reading daily fifteen-minute adaptations of 'Canon Alberic's Scrapbook', 'Lost Hearts', 'A School Story' and 'The Haunted Dolls' House', all from 2008. However, Whitrow's reading of 'Rats' from the original series was oddly missing.

Also broadcast over Christmas week, *Haunting Women* repeated five fifteen-minute supernatural dramas written by Dermot Bolder from 2011.

From two decades earlier than that, Wally K. Daly's adaptation of Douglas Hill's 1987 novel *The Blade of the Poisoner* was re-broadcast on BBC Radio 4 Extra in four parts, while James McArdle, Aysha Kala and Shaun Dooley starred in *Earthsea*, Judith Adams' six-part adaptation of the first three novels in Ursula K. Le Guin's classic fantasy saga.

First broadcast in 1984, Brian Sibley's dramatisations of Mervyn Peake's *Titus Groan* and *Gormenghast* featured all-star casts that included Freddie Jones, Bernard Hepton, Judy Parfitt, David Warner, Eleanor Bron, Sheila Hancock, Maurice Denham and singer Sting as the manipulative "Steerpike".

Bert Coules' two-part adaptation of *Sherlock Holmes: The Hound of the Baskervilles* from 1998 starred Clive Merrison as Holmes, Michael Williams as Dr. Watson, Judi Dench as Mrs. Hudson and Donald Sinden as Sir Charles Baskerville.

Introduced by creator B.D. Chapman and originally broadcast on the BBC Light Programme in 1959, a space station's construction was halted by aliens in *Orbiter X*, starring John Carson. The fourteen-part serial was presumed to have been wiped until a set of transcription discs were recovered and restored.

From 1985, the second, six-part series of Charles Chilton's *Space Force* starred Barry Foster, Nigel Stock and Nicky Henson.

First released as an audio box-set in 2016, Mark Elstob starred as "Number Six" in six hour-long re-imaginings of the cult 1967 TV series *The Prisoner*, which originally featured Patrick McGoohan in the role.

Ed Stoddard starred as the square-jawed "Pilot of the Future" in the two-part SF dramas *Dan Dare: The Voyage to Venus*, *Dan Dare: The Red Moon Mystery* and *Dan Dare: Marooned on Mercury*, based on the space adventures of the *Eagle* comic character.

Once described as "the scariest programme ever made for children," comedian Stewart Lee looked back at the cult 1977 supernatural TV drama in Radio 4 Extra's *Happy Days: The Children of the Stones*, with the help of co-creator Jeremy Burnham, original cast member Katharine Levy and musician Julian Cope.

HarperAudio, the audio book division of HarperCollins, launched a series of vinyl recordings alongside its digital editions, including works by Joe Hill and Lemony Snicket.

Having premiered in Australia in 2013, director-choreographer Drew McOnie's production of the meta-musical *King Kong on Broadway* opened at New York's Broadway Theatre in November. It ran for just nine months. Based on the 1932 novel, it starred Christiani Pitts as farm girl "Ann Darrow", Eric William Morris as film director "Carl Denham", and a twenty-foot tall animatronic puppet as the "Eighth Wonder of the World".

The book for *King Kong* was written by Jack Thorne, the Tony and Olivier Award-winning writer of *Harry Potter and the Cursed Child*, and seven lead members of the original London West End cast of that two-part production—including Noma Dumezweni's Olivier Award-winning grown-up "Hermione", Jamie Parker's "Harry" and Paul Thornley's "Ron"—transferred with the show to Broadway's Lyric Theatre in March. New York fans were required to register their interest in purchasing tickets in a bid to stop touts from buying-up the sold-out shows.

Based on the book by Neil Gaiman, Aletta Collins' opera of *Coraline* received its world premiere at London's Royal Opera House at the Barbican, running from March 29 to April 7. With music by Mark-Anthony Turnage and libretto by Rory Mullarkey, Mary Bevan starred in the title role, while magic consultants Richard Wiseman and David Britland created the often-remarkable special effects.

Star Wars' Mark Hamill briefly turned up as the voice of a robot in the British 1980s-set sci-fi musical *Eugenius!*, written by Ben Adams and Chris Wilkins, and produced by actor Warwick Davis.

Tom Morris' musical production of *The Grinning Man* was based on Victor Hugo's 1869 novel *The Man Who Laughs*. It tranferred to the Trafalgar Studios in London's West End for a limited run following its premiere at the Bristol Old Vic.

As part of the Aldeburgh Festival 2018 in Suffolk, Emily Howard's chamber opera *To See the Invisible* was freely adapted by playwright Selma Dimitrijevic from the 1963 short story by Robert Silverberg.

A young couple (Tom Mothersdale and Anneika Rose) found themselves staying at a very strange B&B in Gettysburg, Pennsylvania, run by Marylouise Burke's witchy landlady in a revival of Pulitzer-winning playwright Annie Baker's 2015 slice of American Gothic, *John*, at the National Theatre, Dorfman in London.

London's Open Air Theatre in Regent's Park mounted a summer revival of Howard Ashman and Alan Menken's 1982 musical *Little*

Shop of Horrors, starring Jemima Rooper as the put-upon "Audrey" and Marc Antolin as the lovelorn "Seymour". The latter's tinkering with exotic plants resulted in the colourful creation of "Audrey II" (American drag queen Vicky Vox).

In September, *The League of Gentlemen Live Again! 2018* travelled around the UK over August and September, as the grotesque inhabitants of Royston Vasey (variously portrayed by Reece Shearsmith, Steve Pemberton and Mark Gatiss) went about their bizarre lives on stage for the first time in twelve years.

Anthony Neilson's contemporary re-telling of Edgar Allan Poe's 1843 story *The Tell-Tale Heart* at the National's Dorfman in December featured Tamara Lawrance as "Celeste Allen", who was having problems writing her second play. Imogen Doel played her creepy, one-eyed landlady and David Carlyle was a suspicious detective.

Adapted for the stage by Philip Wilson, *Phillip Pullman's Grimm Tales* played South London's Unicorn theatre over Christmas.

Sherlock: The Game is Now was a 100-minute "immersive escape experience" created by the producers of the BBC show, Steven Moffat and Mark Gatiss, along with the escape room game company Time Run. Situated in a West London shopping centre, tickets started at £54.00 per person as players solved mysteries with the help of video clips of the TV show's actors, including Benedict Cumberbatch, Martin Freeman, Andrew Scott and Gatiss himself.

Thunderbirds: Beyond the Horizon—a "live interactive theatrical event" based on the 1960s puppet TV series and due to open at a brand-new London venue in November—was postponed by the producers due to "technical reasons".

In America, *SpongeBob SqaurePants: The Musical* tied for the year's most nominated productions at the 72nd annual Tony Awards.

From The Clive Barker Archive came the first two volumes in "The Clive Barker Playscripts" series in attractive trade paperback editions with cover artwork by Barker himself. Edited by Phil and Sarah Stokes, *Hunters in the Snow* (1973) and *Crazyface: A Comedy (with Lions)* (1982) not only featured Barker's original playscripts, but also the original production cast and credits, historical Afterwords by the editors, and bonus visual material.

It was announced in January that during the half-year to November 2017, Games Workshop was the best-performing share on the London stock market, as sales increased from £71 million to £109 million, and profits rose from £14 million to £39 million.

Dontnod Entertainment's delayed RPG *Vampyr* was set in a plague-ridden post-First World War London, in which the player was a recently undead renowned expert in haematology.

State of Decay 2 from Undead Labs returned players to the same old zombie apocalypse, while Next Games' free-to-play *The Walking Dead: Our World* was an augmented reality game in which players were hunted by zombies in the real world, thanks to Google Maps.

Released in September, *Marvel's Spider-Man* for PS4 became the fastest-selling game of the year in the UK and took superhero RPGs to a new level. It featured a movie-style score by composer John Paesano and a cameo from Stan Lee. A three-part downloadable content pack, *Spider-Man: The City That Never Sleeps*, appeared monthly from October to December.

Square Enix's Lara Croft prequel/reboot game *Shadow of the Tomb Raider* was based around the Mayan apocalypse, as the theft of an ancient dagger set in motion the death of the sun.

The Finnish twin-stick shooter game *Tesla vs. Lovecraft* did exactly what the title said, as inventor Nikola Tesla attempted to stop a possessed H.P. Lovecraft's army of monstrosities from invading the world.

The *Harry Potter: Hogwarts Mystery* app was an RPG designed by Jam City for iOS and Android mobile devices. Warwick Davis, Michael Gambon, Maggie Smith, Gemma Jones, Zoë Wanamaker and Sally Mortemore voiced characters they had portrayed in the movie series.

In January, Britain's Royal Mail issued an attractive collection of fifteen First Class postage stamps based around the HBO TV series of *Game of Thrones*, supposedly to highlight "British contributions" to the show. Each stamp featured a major character, including Emilia Clarke's "Daenerys Targaryen", Peter Dinklage's "Tyrion Lannister" and Kit Harington's "Jon Snow". Perhaps more interestingly, there was also a five-stamp sheet that featured the "Night King", white walkers, direwolves, dragons and the Iron Throne.

The UK's Royal Mint produced a new £2 coin to celebrate the 200th anniversary of the publication of Mary Shelley's *Frankenstein*. Although the coin did not use an image of the creature, it did feature the word "Frankenstein" in the centre and "The Modern Prometheus" in the outer gold ring.

In October, Ireland's Central Bank launched a commemorative €15 Bram Stoker Dracula silver proof collector coin. Designed by David Rooney, the limited-edition coin went on sale for €60 and had an issue limit of 3,000 pieces.

Meanwhile, The London Library claimed it had located a number of the actual books used by Bram Stoker in researching *Dracula*. Stoker's notebooks list of a wide range of sources for the novel, including hundreds of references to individual lines and phrases in volumes that he consulted. Stoker was a member of the historical members' lending library, based in London's St. James' Square, for seven years during 1890–97, and a search of the Library's bookshelves revealed original copies of twenty-six of those titles, with many carrying detailed markings and notations that closely match Stoker's own notebook references.

Some of the most heavily-marked books included Sabine Baring-Gould's *Book of Were-Wolves*, Thomas Browne's *Necromancy–Divination of the Dead*, A.F. Crosse's *Round About the Carpathians* and Charles Boner's *Transylvania: Its Products and Its People*.

A new incarnation of Mego issued licensed eight-inch figures of Bela Lugosi's Count Dracula and Lon Chaney, Jr.'s wolf man from the Mexican-made *Face of the Screaming Werewolf*, along with the Frankenstein Monster and various figures from the *Bewitched* TV series. Each figure was limited to just 10,000 units.

A series of ceramic Universal Monsters-inspired tiki mugs featured stylised likenesses of Dracula, the Wolf Man, the Mummy, the Gill Man, and the Frankenstein Monster and his Bride.

Through January, the Mondo Art Gallery in Austin, Texas, put on an exhibition of new posters of the classic Universal Monsters, including Dracula, Frankenstein, the Wolf Man, the Mummy and the Creature from the Black Lagoon. Some of the artists contributing to the exhibition included Jonathan Burton, Sam Wolfe Connelly, Francesco Francavilla, Ken Garduno, Brandon Holt, Matthew Peak, Phantom City Creative, Eric Powell, Gary Pullin, Greg Ruth, Jessica Seamans, Stan & Vince, Ken Taylor, Matt Ryan Tobin and Bruce White.

Mezco Toyz's "Lament Configuration Puzzler" was a *Hellraiser*-inspired Rubik's Cube with reportedly 43,252,003,274,489,856,000 possible combinations.

Mattel announced the release of a new "Doctor Who Barbie" doll in honour of Jodie Whittaker's incarnation as the thirteenth Doctor, "with her signature suspenders, lace-up boots and sonic screwdriver". Unfortunately, the American manufacturer failed to realise that "suspenders" meant something very different in the UK, where they are known as "braces".

Britain's popular theme park, Alton Towers in Staffordshire, opened a £16 million "Wicker Man" rollercoaster ride in the spring, which was inspired by the 1973 film featuring Christopher Lee.

The *Stranger Things* Monopoly game allowed players to navigate the Upside-Down and buy houses in The Void.

In April, one of only two known six-sheet posters for the 1948 Columbia serial *Superman* sold at auction for $35,850, while a rare one-sheet for Republic's serial *Captain Marvel* (1941) nearly equalled it by realising $31,070. An oversized Swedish poster for *King Kong* (1933) sold for $26,290 and a one-sheet for Universal's *Creature from the Black Lagoon* (1954) went for $23,900.

A six-sheet poster for the same movie, with artwork by Reynold Brown, sold at auction in November for $19,200. At the same auction, a British Royal Charity World Premiere double-crown poster for *The Empire Strikes Back*, with art by Ralph McQuarrie, sold for $15,600, and a 1947 reissue one-sheet for *Frankenstein* (1931) went for $13,200.

William Hartnell's forty-three page script for the first *Doctor Who* episode ('An Unearthly Child', 1963), with the actor's original annotations in blue pencil, went under the hammer in early May and exceeded the top estimate, selling at auction for £7,500 (including fees).

That same month, Frank Frazetta's 1990 painting *Death Dealer 6* sold at auction for a record-breaking $1.79 million. The seller bought it in 2003 for $50,000.

Another Frazetta painting, *Escape from Venus*, used on the cover of the eponymous Edgar Rice Burroughs novel in 1974, went under the auction hammer in August. It sold for $660,000, the third-highest price paid for the artist's work in the US.

A Wonka Bar (made of cardboard, not chocolate) and a Golden Ticket from the 1971 film *Willy Wonka & the Chocolate Factory* sold at auction in July for £15,000. The prop had originally belonged to child actress Julie Dawn Cole, who played the spoiled "Verruca Salt".

Two months later, another Wonka Bar went for £9,840. At the same London auction, an Indiana Jones fedora sold for £320,000, Anakin Skywalker's lightsaber reached £110,000, and Marty McFly's hoverboard realised £30,000. Unfortunately, Indiana Jones' leather jacket—which was estimated at between £500,000–£1 million—failed to find a buyer.

In early December, a signed first edition of J.K. Rowling's *Harry Potter and the Philosopher's Stone* sold for £126,750—double the estimate and a record for the series. Only 500 copies were printed in 1997, with 300 of those going to libraries.

At the same sale at Christie's, a collection of original printing blocks for the first edition of Lewis Carroll's *Alice's Adventures in Wonderland* fetched £63,375.

A growing interest in Day of the Dead (*Dia de los Muertos*) found the traditional Mexican holiday to honour the dead over October 31–November 2 transformed into a multi-million dollar merchandising industry in the US. It included everything from a collection of associational items available in Target and Walgreens stores to a Day of the Dead Mariachi food storage container from Pyrex. In 2013, Disney faced a backlash when it attempted to trademark the term "Dia de los Muertos".

∽

Stephen King received the 2018 PEN America Literary Service Award at a gala presentation in New York on May 22 for a body of work that "helps us understand and interpret the human condition." Andrew Solomon, the president of PEN America, said King had "inspired us to stand up to sinister forces through his rich prose, his generous philanthropy and his outspoken defence of free expression." Carolyn Reidy, president and chief executive officer of Simon & Schuster, was also honoured as "an icon for a generation of women in the publishing industry".

Neil Gaiman, Frances Hardinge, Anthony Horowitz, Adam Roberts and Bryan Talbot were amongst a number of writers inducted as Fellows into the Royal Society of Literature in London on July 4. They signed the RSL roll-book with a fountain pen that once belonged to Lord Byron, George Eliot and T.S. Eliot.

On March 3, The Horror Writers Association (HWA) announced the recipients of the Bram Stoker Awards® at a ceremony held at the historic Biltmore Hotel in downtown Providence, Rhode Island.

The winner of Superior Achievement in a Novel was Christopher Golden for *Ararat*, while Robert Payne Cabeen's *Cold Cuts* was awarded Superior Achievement in a First Novel, and Superior Achievement in a Young Adult Novel went to Kim Liggett for *The Last Harvest*.

Damian Duffy and Octavia E. Butler won Superior Achievement in a Graphic Novel for *Kindred: A Graphic Novel Adaptation*. The Bram Stoker Award for Superior Achievement in Long Fiction went to Stephen Graham Jones for his novella *Mapping the Interior*, while Lisa Mannetti's 'Apocalypse Then' from *Never Fear: The Apocalypse*, won for Superior Achievement in Short Fiction.

Joe Hill's *Strange Weather* received Superior Achievement in a Fiction Collection, Jordan Peele's *Get Out* won Superior Achievement in a Screenplay, and Doug Murano's *Behold!: Oddities, Curiosities & Undefinable Wonders* picked up the award for Superior Achievement in an Anthology.

Superior Achievement in Non-Fiction was won by Grady Hendrix's *Paperbacks from Hell: The Twisted History of '70s and '80s Horror Fiction*, and Christina Sng's *A Collection of Nightmares* received the Superior Achievement in a Poetry Collection award. The Horror Writers Association Specialty Press Award went to Eraserhead Press.

As if all those were not enough, the HWA Board of Trustees, working in conjunction with Bram Stoker Awards chairs James Chambers and Rena Mason, approved the creation of a new Bram Stoker Award category for Superior Achievement in Short Non-fiction, to recognise works from 2,000–39,999 words.

The winners of the juried British Fantasy Awards were announced at FantasyCon 2018, held over October 19–21 at the Queen Hotel in Chester, England. *The Ninth Rain* by Jen Williams won the award for Best Fantasy Novel (the Robert Holdstock Award), while the winner for Best Horror Novel (the August Derleth Award) was *The Changeling* by Victor LaValle.

Best Novella went to *Passing Strange* by Ellen Klages, and 'Looking for Laika' by Laura Mauro (from *Interzone*) picked up Best Short Story. Joe Hill's *Strange Weather* was voted Best Collection, and the Best Anthology Award went to *New Fears* edited by Mark Morris.

Unsung Stories was recognised as Best Independent Press, *Gender Identity and Sexuality in Science Fiction and Fantasy* edited by Francesca T. Barbini was considered Best Non-Fiction, and *Shoreline of Infinity* collected the award for Best Magazine/Periodical.

Jeffrey Alan Love received the Best Artist Award. Best Comic/Graphic Novel went to *Monstress Vol. 2* by Marjorie Liu and Sana Takeda. Neil Gaiman's *Anansi Boys*, adapted by Dirk Maggs, won Best Audio, and Best Film/Television Production was Jordan Peele's *Get Out*.

The Sydney J. Bounds Award for Best Newcomer went to Jeanette Ng for *Under the Pendulum Sun*, while N.K. Jemisin was the recipient of the Karl Edward Wagner Special Award, chosen by the British Fantasy Society Committee.

The FantasyCon "Legends of FantasyCon" Award was jointly awarded to Alasdair Stuart and Marguerite Kenner.

The World Fantasy Awards are also juried. The 2018 awards were presented at the 44th World Fantasy Convention, held in Baltimore over November 1–4.

Lifetime Achievement Awards went to artist Charles de Lint and publisher Elizabeth Wollheim. *The Changeling* by Victor LaValle tied with *Jade City* by Fonda Lee in the Novel category, while *Passing Strange* by Ellen Klages won Novella, and the Short Fiction Award went to 'The Birding: A Fairy Tale' by Natalia Theodoridou (from *Strange Horizons*).

The New Voices of Fantasy edited by Peter S. Beagle and Jacob Weisman won the award for Anthology, Jane Yolen's *The Emerald Circus* was given Collection, and Gregory Manchess won for Artist.

The Special Award—Professional was awarded to Harry Brockway, Patrick McGrath and Danel Olson for *Writing Madness*, while Justina Ireland and Troy L. Wiggins won the Special Award—Non-Professional for *FIYAH: Magazine of Black Speculative Fiction*.

Well, that was some weird shit, to quote a former president of the United States.

My usual "end thought" for this volume was going to be about Patreon, GoFundMe, Kickstarter and all the other crowd-funding sources that many professional authors and publishers are increasingly turning to to raise money for specific projects or just give themselves a regular income—either because they are not producing a product that enough people want or are willing to pay a reasonable price for, or they just can't be bothered to go through the more traditional method of actually earning an income in return for putting in the work.

For the record, I'm mostly against it (as I am also against so-called "charity anthologies", but that's an argument for another day) and regard it—as Blanche DuBois so aptly put it—as depending on "the kindness of strangers". Maybe I'm old-fashioned, but it seems like nice "work" if you can get it...

But then something happened.

This volume of *Best New Horror* was always going to be late. Through no fault of the publishers, the annual schedule has been slipping over the past few years. This is due to a number of reasons, beginning with a family illness a few years ago that monopolised much of my time and resulted in unforeseen delays in a number of projects that I was working on. This has had something of a knock-on effect ever since.

On top of that, there is just so much *stuff* out there now—novels, collections, short stories, magazines, movies, television shows and god-knows-what-else related to horror—that it has become a full-time job just trying to keep up with everything being released on a multitude of different platforms and in various different formats.

And then COVID-19 happened earlier this year. That didn't help. It certainly slowed things down even more—I never expected to be compiling this 30th Anniversary volume in the middle of a real-life horror story!

To be honest, it has sometimes been a struggle. The publishers have been wonderfully supportive and understanding, as have the authors. The coronavirus pandemic has probably changed the world we are living in for the rest of our lives, and at this point it certainly looks like publishing will never quite be the same again.

So maybe I was wrong to dismiss those crowd-funding schemes earlier. Perhaps that is how publishing will make its way through these dark times, and emerge leaner but stronger?

I really don't know the answer. Only time—as is always the case with these things—will tell.

But for now, here is *Best New Horror* #30. Probably one of the biggest volumes we've ever produced, and certainly one of the most difficult. I hope you think it was worth the effort.

What the future holds for us—and for the horror genre specifically—I have no idea. But for now, all I hope is that you stay safe and well, and keep supporting publishers—both large and small—if you are able to.

And I trust we will all be here again when the next volume appears. Whenever that might be.

Until then, please take care of yourselves and each other.

The Editor
July, 2020

PETER BELL

THE HOUSE

PETER BELL has written numerous stories and essays for various journals and publishers. A member of The Friends of Arthur Machen, his article comparing Buchan's and Machen's mystical vision appears in *The Secret Ceremonies: Critical Essays on Arthur Machen* (Hippocampus Press, 2019). His most recent book, from which originate the two stories he has in this volume of *Best New Horror*, is *Revenants & Maledictions: Ten Tales of the Uncanny* (Sarob Press, 2018).

"'The House' was inspired by a visit to Oxford," recalls Bell, "where my friends and I went in search of a house known to have been inhabited by a deceased author of weird fiction."

Thankfully, that trip didn't end in the same way as the story that follows...

> The fabled incorruptibility of the peacock's flesh
> caused the bird to be adopted as a type of the
> Resurrection.
> —*Brewers Dictionary of Phrase and Fable*

ONE SULTRY SUMMER evening towards the end of August three gentlemen of indeterminate middle age made their uncertain way through the labyrinth of leafy streets that lie roughly between the Banbury Road and Jericho in the City of Oxford. Their quest was twofold: to visit a public house that appeared, unusually, in both the *Best Beer Guide* and the *Gazetteer of Historic Inns*; and, more improbably, to seek out the house where, for much of her life, dwelt a little known writer of supernatural tales, deceased these past fifty years, by the name of Isadora Wilde.

The three were attending a conference at an esteemed college of Oxford University on "The Gothic Novel". That learned forum, however, was proving less than stimulating. Dr. Allan, Dr. Chappell and Professor Stevenson, wearied of Freudian subtexts and the feeble contributions of graduate students, were skipping the evening plenary, not least because it would mean further imbibing of the college's watery claret and partaking of its deplorable "cuisine", beside which pie and peas at the Bridge Inn seemed the Food of the Gods.

The trio, had there been anyone in the vacant streets to observe, cut a strange sight—if anything in Oxford might be regarded as strange. Professor Stevenson, tall, broad-shouldered, in a tweed sports jacket, forever checking his gold pocket-watch, might have been lumbering from a meeting of the Chit-Chat Society. Dapper Dr. Allan, never seen without a bow-tie and a pin-stripe strutted confidently ahead; while Dr. Chappell, peering through horn-rimmed spectacles, strolled behind in a crumpled suit.

Their street map was unhelpful. Like that of Olaus Magnus, marking *Terra Incognita* beyond the confines of the known world, the university cartographer had sketched a northern perimeter beyond which the land of Gown faded into the blank wastes of Town.

"What's the address?" asked the professor.

"Ninety-seven North Bank Road," replied Dr. Allan. "North Bank is off St. Clement's Road—and here's St. Clement's now."

They left the roar of the Banbury Road down a leafy avenue of small terraces, with tiny gardens in various stages of benign neglect. Heavy-scented buddleia dangled straggly purple blooms; tall hollyhocks leaned, impeding the sidewalk. St. Clement's Road, curving sharply, extended endlessly. There was not a soul in sight. There was about the neighbourhood—neither genteel nor seedy—a touch of the mysterious, even sinister.

"This... Isadora Wilde?" Professor Stevenson queried, "it was her pen-name, you say?"

"Yes. Her real name was Rosalind Hayes," said Dr. Chappell. "Never married. Lived with a sister who predeceased her in the 1950s. Miss Hayes remained at North Bank Road until she died at the age of eighty-nine. Hadn't written a thing for half a century—so far as we know."

Dr. Chappell was author of a new book: *Phantoms, Fantasies and Class: A Study of the English Ghost Story.*

"What *did* she write—apart from this book of... ghost stories?" asked the professor.

"Not much—a couple of romances. Of course, when a writer uses a pseudonym one always wonders whether they wrote more—under yet another name... Oh, and a magazine article for *Blackwoods*— 'The Etiology of the Peacock.'"

"Romances?" queried the professor.

"Oh—for adolescent girls," replied Chappell. "You know the sort... fancy gilt bindings, ponies, jolly hockey sticks and all that... School prize stuff—supposed to be 'improving'—only these weren't. A bit racy, they said—probably ahead of her time!"

"Ever read them?" asked the professor with a raffish smile.

"Never seen them!" said Chappell. "I looked for them when I was writing my book. They contain supernatural content, I believe— séances, that kind of thing; she was into all that. She believed in the transmutation of souls. The only person I know who'd read them was the late Roger Freeman; and they were British Library copies...

"But they're not there now," he sighed. "Curiously, they're still listed in the catalogue—but so is the ghost story book, and that's not there either..."

"What were the titles of these romances?" inquired Dr. Allan.

"Oh, very exciting! *Poor Pamela* and *Teresa, Terror of the Fifth Form.* The latter was reprinted in an abridged version—that's the one Freeman saw; he'd never set eyes on a first."

"The expurgated version!" laughed the professor.

"Tell me," he added, "this chap Freeman? An Oxford man was he? I...er, I think I've heard of him. What college?"

"No, no," Chappell replied, "he was freelance. But he knew more about the subject than everyone at this conference! All we know about Isadora Wilde is thanks to Freeman. It was he who traced her identity—going through old wills, letters, publishers' records and so on..."

"Remind me," Stevenson interrupted, "the title of her ghost story book?"

"*The House: Seven Eerie Tales*," responded Chappell. "The peculiar thing is there's no story in the book called 'The House'. One of the tales does feature a house, true—but an odd title, one of the many enigmas surrounding Isadora Wilde."

"Quite a puzzle," mumbled the professor.

"Well it *is* a puzzle," said Chappell, "because there are only six stories. Freeman's theory was that she'd withdrawn the title story at the last minute. Maybe because she hadn't finished it to her satisfaction; she was a perfectionist. Freeman speculated a draft might still exist—or *have* existed. Hayes told her publisher she never threw anything away, but no one knows what happened to her papers, or who owns the estate...

"She was a school-mistress, by the way—taught biology—at a girls' private school here in Oxford."

"No wonder she took a pseudonym!" laughed the professor.

The walkers had reached a junction. They scrutinised the map's clues, eventually detecting North Bank Road.

"There's number one," Allan indicated, "on the left—we've still got a fair old trudge."

The road stretched ahead, dispiritingly steep. Faraway in the Land of Gown bells tolled in uneasy unison from the dreaming spires. Already, it was seven.

"See—up that alley!" Stevenson pointed.

A narrow lane snaked left, where they espied a cosy pub—a Shangri-La for the real-ale fetishist? Or a rough tavern of the Town which devotees of the Gown would do well to avoid?

"Well, it's in the book!" crowed the professor. "The Plantation... and it does food... Shall we eat here, do you think?"

"No, let's stick to the plan," insisted Dr. Allan. "We can come here for a last pint."

The properties on North Bank Road were substantial red-brick Victorian terraces. Though by no means run-down, they wore an air of faded gentility, tarnished elegance—the kind of dwellings built for the upper middle class a century ago, now expensive flats, or the homes of those with a penchant for a chic Bohemian antiquity.

Number 97 was an imposing three-storey house, an end terrace, entered by a porch to the side, its door open. Red roses hung over the garden wall, scenting the air. The downstairs curtains were drawn back, the room softly lit by a standard-lamp. Bookcases lined the walls; there were gilt-framed portraits and a bronze statuette in the bay—a domain of culture and good taste. Nobody was visible...

Chappell stepped over the road. Furtively, he snapped the house from many angles. As he composed the final shot, framing the gable against the sunset, he caught a brief movement at its sash-window— a face, he thought, peering through a veil of net-curtains—a thin, bird-like face. Hastily, he hid the camera, and with feigned casualness stepped back to re-join his impatient colleagues.

"Look! It's for sale!" observed Dr. Allan.

"I bet that's a pretty penny!" declared Stevenson.

"I wonder if they know who lived there?" opined Chappell.

"I doubt it," declared Allan. "Now, come on!"

A restless mood possessed Dr. Chappell as they proceeded. The house was for sale... If only he had known, he could have arranged to have a look round inside...

To walk where Isadora walked... To wander the rooms where she wrote her eerie tales... To view the prospect from the windows that accompanied her flights into fantasy... Dr. Chappell was something of an obsessive regarding literary shrines; this quest, from being a diverting evening stroll, had assumed the character of a sacred pilgrimage...

He had to see inside...

What if he knocked on the door?...Householders were notoriously reluctant to countenance such visits...

And yet...Was there anything to be lost trying?

His companions looked askance—or worse—when Chappell announced his plan; he was going back to the house forthwith while not too late to make an unsolicited call; if he had not joined them at the inn within the hour, he would catch them later at The Plantation.

The food at the Bridge Inn proved as good as foretold in the beer guide, as did the bitter, of which they had consumed two pints before wondering where their colleague had got to.

"He ought to have been back by now," remarked Stevenson, scrutinising his pocket watch. "He's been gone well over an hour. He said see us at the other pub—didn't he?"

"I'm not sure what we arranged," sighed Allan. "It was all a bit vague for my liking...What if he's on his way back here?"

"Then our paths would cross, of course."

"Not if he's in the house...Don't you think one of us should nip down first and see where he is?"

"Right," said the professor, "you stay here, and I'll whiz down to The Plantation. If he's not there, I'll come right back; if he is—well, we'll stay...

"Shouldn't you look at the house first, to see if he's there?"

"Well—I'll pass it on the way."

Dr. Allan ordered another pint.

Fed and refreshed, he wondered if he should have joined Chappell—he'd have liked to see inside himself—but the idea had sounded preposterous...And probably he had not been admitted, and was even now imbibing whatever fine ales The Plantation had to offer...

Professor Stevenson, stumping down North Bank Road, almost missed number 97. Retracing his steps, he glanced over the property. What a performance! If Isadora what's-her-name was so important, why hadn't they put up a blue plaque! Though darkness was gathering, the front room was now unlit, yet the curtains remained open. A dim glow came from the gable window. The middle-floor window was brightly lit, veiled by thin net curtains not quite drawn, showing a gap...

And there, with his back to him, was Dr. Chappell—still here after all this time while they dithered in the pub! His colleague appeared to have settled in; he had removed his jacket... And yet he looked anything but relaxed; it was as if he shrank as far as possible from the room, his back pressed against the window, arms stretched before him. Then Professor Stevenson realised: here he was—keen as any estate agent for a wide-angled shot—busy taking his blasted photos! Meanwhile, drinking time was diminishing. A wave of irritation suffused the professor.

It seemed undignified to shout from the road. He entered the porch; it was still lit, the outer door still ajar. He knocked on the inner door, half-paned with an Art Nouveau design depicting a peacock. There being no reply, he tried the handle—the door opened...

He stepped inside...

Dr. Allan turned in frustration from the crossword—forty-five minutes had elapsed since Stevenson's departure; nor had Dr. Chappell materialised. Draining his pint, he left.

It soon dawned on him he had made a wrong turn; but blundering on, he eventually came to The Plantation. Entering, he encountered the brouhaha of student life.

"No one's been 'ere all night," said the youthful barman. "No one your age, like."

As Allan reached number 97, all was in darkness—except for a glimmer, as from a small lamp, in the gable, and the light in the porch, its door still ajar despite the lateness of the hour. The inner door, too, surprisingly, was wide open.

Tentatively, he entered, bidding a hallo... He stood in a black-and-white chequer-tiled hallway, full of *bric-à-brac*, dimly lit. He called up the stairs... still without response... He wondered what to do; this was turning into an absurd game of chase—could his friends now be in the pub...but which pub? Had he, taking the wrong road, missed them on their way back?

Where shadow met the light from the porch he noticed, scattered over the floor, several peacock feathers...

Beside them lay their map and the professor's beer guide—it was as if they had been torn to pieces...At the top of the stairs something glinted—the professor's old-fashioned pocket-watch...shattered and eviscerated...

Warily he ascended...

There on the landing were still more peacock feathers, dozens of them...

And Dr. Chappell's horn-rimmed spectacles, smashed to smithereens...

A narrow stair led to the third floor. It was only a sense of unreality—a nightmare from which he must awaken—that, with the crazy compulsion of a dream, caused him to carry on...

He found himself in a spacious garret running the length of the house, a window at either end. It was empty, yet with a sense of recent occupation. An antique lamp rested on a green-baized desk at the front window, in the gable. Bookshelves lined every inch of wall, except where embers glowed in an iron fireplace. On a shelf near the desk, his eyes were drawn to a pair of books, one gold and red, the other gold and green, shining in the pool of light cast by the lamp...

Dr. Allan read the titles. He knew he must be dreaming: *Poor Pamela* and *Teresa, Terror of the Fifth Form*...First editions—the latter being the true, unabridged first...And here was *The House: Seven Eerie Tales*—in its dust-jacket, missing even from the British Library copy. No one, not even Freeman, knew what it was like, Chappell had said...It was pretty unremarkable, really, simply a picture of a house...*this house*...The rear displayed a photograph of the author—a slim, bird-like woman, with a feathered hat and a smile that was not quite pleasant...

Upon the desk was a quarto-sized notebook open at a half-blank page, where the bold, cursive script ended in a smudge of black ink...He turned to the cover...

There, inscribed in Isadora Wilde's beautiful, copperplate hand-writing, was the title: 'The House'...

Dr. Allan opened the first page and read:

One sultry summer evening towards the end of August three gentlemen of indeterminate middle age made their uncertain way through the labyrinth of leafy streets that lie roughly between the Banbury Road and Jericho in the City of Oxford.

Dr. Allan feverishly scanned ahead—the narrative ended in mid-flow, terminated by three dots...

It was not quite finished...

The footfall coming up the stairs was not the ebullient tread of Professor Stevenson, nor the languid trudge of Dr. Chappell; it was delicate—a light, scrabbling step—almost like a bird...

SIMON KURT UNSWORTH

THE SMILING MAN

S IMON KURT UNSWORTH is the author of two thrillers set in
Hell—*The Devil's Detective* and *The Devil's Evidence*—and six
short story collections (*Lost Places, Quiet Houses, Strange Gateways,
Diseases of the Teeth, The Martledge Variations* and *The Compleat
Nakata*). His is also the co-author, with his son Benjamin, of the
collection *Uneasy Beginnings*.

He lives by a river in the north of England with his wife, the writer
Rosie Seymour, and various children and animals, writing whatever
comes into his head, for which pursuit he was once, a near lifetime
ago, nominated for a World Fantasy Award.

He despairs of ever finding that there were mysterious signs and
portents across the world the night that he was born, and feels the
universe has let him down over this.

About 'The Smiling Man', he says: "My second collection of
stories, *Quiet Houses*, was a portmanteau linked by a central
character, a paranormal researcher called Richard Nakata. I liked
Nakata a lot, so revisited him a couple of years after *Quiet Houses* in
a standalone story and, further down the line, again in the mini-
collection *The Martledge Variations*.

"Martledge is a town based mostly on Chorlton-cum-Hardy
where I grew up, with a salting from the histories of other places I
know well, and that Nakata has ended up there is probably right
because it's very, *very* haunted.

"In 'The Smiling Man', most of the details about the over-filled ground of the churchyard and of bones being washed free every time it rained are true, lifted from Chorlton's history and deposited unceremoniously here, but it also sucks in another piece of history (or myth, or mythic history)—that of the 'Dent Vampire'. Dent is a small village about seventy-five miles north of Chorlton, and in its churchyard is a grave with a stake through it which was done to pin a local vampire to the soil and stop him walking. I wanted to blend these two disparate histories—make them into a single Martledge event—and this is the result."

"**I**T WON'T DO, van Hewson, it won't do at all."
The chair of the local Board of Health peered at the sexton over the glittering lowers of his half-moon spectacles and tapped the report on the table in front of him for emphasis. "St. Clements' graveyard is full, you admit it yourself?"

"Yes," replied van Hewson, agreeably enough. There was little point in denying what the Ratepayers Association's report said.

"There is, I am told, scarcely inches between burial plots and barely two feet of earth between the air and the faces of the dead, or at least, the tops of their coffins?"

"Yes," again because really, what was the point in denying it? The other board members variously shook their heads or mumbled in disapproval. Beside van Hewson, the Reverend Booth shifted uncomfortably.

"And when new burials are required? What do you do?" asked the chair, a small, round fellow called Bassett, whose hangdog face resembled the dog he was presumably named after. His jowls were edged by a fearsome pair of mutton-chops and the cord of his glasses kept tangling in the wiry hair in front of his ears and needed pulling free.

"Well, what can we do?" asked Booth, a touch of plaintiveness creeping in to his voice. Van Hewson tried not to let his irritation show as Booth carried on.

"The graveyard has been extended three times, but the last request for an extension was refused by the Parish. Our burial records go back to 1762, but there are gravestones with dates as far back as 1590, so we know that there are more dead than we have numbers for. We have no space, but the dead keep knocking on our doors. The crypts under the church are full, the bones of the dead are packed four or five deep in some places, and when the parishioners kneel Sunday after Sunday to pray, they do so in the dust of their ancestors."

"And we sympathise," Bassett said, "but there can be no more burials in the ground, except for those that can go in family plots with at least five feet of earth between coffin and air, or where you have made space. The Home Office has already agreed to a review of the situation in light of public health concerns, and when that review is concluded I'm sure an effective long-term solution will be found, but until then find a way, gentlemen, to prevent the current closeness of the dead to the living."

"But the dead are *always* close to the living in God," said Booth, quite spoiling the oratorical flow he had built up in his earlier, surprisingly accurate and impassioned comment. Besides, thought van Hewson, the board didn't know the half of it; if they had done, they'd have been far more worried.

Everyone knew that the St. Clements' graveyard was full, of course. Every time it rained the surface of the path washed away to reveal jaw-bones and finger-bones and once, the dome of a skull, although who the brain-pan had once belonged to was never ascertained. In particularly heavy storms, the bones themselves would escape the earth and wash down the paths, and be found scattered through Martledge's streets. These were always gathered and cast into a midden grave beyond the rear of the churchyard; although it was technically in unconsecrated ground, Booth always blessed the offerings as they were covered in their thin scrub of soil.

Following the instruction from the Health Board, the first thing they did was hire a pair of local labourers to remove all the old, unreadable gravestones, to smash them and to use the rubble to line a bigger midden grave dug specially for the purpose next to the existing one. That gave the churchyard an appearance of greater space, which pleased most people, and the fact that van Hewson had instructed the men to leave any newer stones also meant that no one living complained about barbarous treatment of their dead relatives.

The next stage was to dig new graves earlier than usual, before dawn by the light of lanterns, and to remove any coffin remnants and bones that appeared in the dig at an inconveniently shallow depth. These were buried under the church floor, below the congregation's unsuspecting feet, or in the midden if the remains had rotted down enough—the labourers paid for their silence as well as their muscle. It meant that the church could still carry out burials, take the interment fee; and if rains washed away topsoil from the paths in the churchyards to reveal pale glimmers of old bone, silver buckles and buttons, occasional leather edges or strips of material, then that was surely a small price to pay.

"We are," said Booth to van Hewson while in one of his ruminative moods, "a church built on the dead. It is our tradition, and our burden."

Everyone was used to it, and it had been this way for years, and no one would really have bothered except for the pokings of a nosy assessor who had raised the issue with the Ratepayer's Association, who had raised it with the Health Board who had, in turn, raised it with the Home Office, while also handing the issue's responsibility lock-stock-and-barrel back to Booth and his sexton.

George Dent had been buried in the churchyard only twenty years previously, and although he had no family, he had a hefty, solid gravestone that he had left provision for in his will. The engraving on the stone simply gave the dates of Dent's life and death and said below, HE SLEEPS IN SOLITARY DEPTHS. Dent's grave had been put at the back of the consecrated ground, near the wall, as it was popularly and correctly assumed that few people would visit the grave after the service.

Over the intervening years the stone weathered, moss growing in the grooves of the chiselled lettering and obscuring them, but in truth no one minded because George Dent hadn't been popular in

Martledge. It wasn't that he was a miser or a curmudgeon; he gave regularly to church funds and would join in the various events on the green—including the yearly pace-egging celebration during which he cheered on the children dressed as The Bold Slasher, the Black Morocco King and the Devil—and gave generously to the Tosspot, a boy dressed in girl's clothing carrying a bucket for donations. He was quiet and worked hard at the gunpowder works outside Martledge as their chief accountant, and was always dressed correctly but never ostentatiously. No, Dent's lack of popularity was because he *looked*.

Dent looked at the girls before they came to their menses, when they were flat and skinny like saplings; he looked at their sisters when their breasts were in bud like spring flowers; he looked at their mothers and their aunts when they were in full bloom, and his eyes were on their faces but also somehow crawling over their skin and taking delight in the way it made the looked-upon feel; and everyone knew Dent delighted in this because, when he looked, he smiled. It was a half-smile, always, a curl to the lips as though he knew something that no one else did; had a secret that he might share if only he was asked the right way. When Dent looked at the Martledge girls and women and smiled, they felt unclean, as though he had touched them in private places with secret fingers.

Dent's remains were moved one rainy night as more bone fragments were harried free from the swollen ground and carried out into Martledge. Booth ordered his body removed from his allotted grave and re-buried on the far side of the church wall, in the common unconsecrated ground, but away from the middens, while the bodies that had been buried over the years on top of Dent's were dropped into the middens and cursorily blessed. His stone was left where it stood, for appearances' sake, and because the man had left a bequest to the church and deserved to be shown some respect.

That had been in early spring, nearly two months after the Health Board meeting. The trouble didn't start until a few weeks later.

Florence Holt was late. Not so late that Pa would be furious, but late enough that he'd be stern; and stern was the road to furious if the situation wasn't handled right. So she walked fast. Not too fast, though, because she didn't want to be flustered when she arrived home, because flustered might make Pa think about what her and Peter had been doing, and if he came to the right conclusion about that, then everything would deteriorate from there. Instead, she walked fast, making sure her clothes didn't get messy, drawing her cape around her to keep the worst of the rain out. She'd pinned her hair back up under her cap before she'd left, thank God, and the rain had only just started, so she wasn't too messy. She would, she thought, get away with it.

It was only a few minutes to home now; she simply had to cross the green and then walk several streets back to the tiny terrace she shared with Pa and the others, her sisters and brothers. Until recently, Ma had been there too, always ready to smile when she came in, always putting herself between Florence and Pa, but now she was gone and Florence's world seemed much smaller. Martledge seemed smaller, hemming her in, pressing down on her, and she hoped that Peter would expand her world's horizons again, take her away from it all to somewhere she could call her own.

Through the lych-gate now, the Sutton Gate she supposed she should think of it as, its arched passage dark and echoing, only a few steps away now, and then someone stepped out from the shadows at the side of the gate as she emerged into the green and drew a cold finger across the back of her neck.

Florence started, turned, but there was no one there, just an impression of someone slipping through the rain around the gate to disappear along its side. "Hello," she called, hurrying to the corner and looking along the outer wall of the lych-gate. The side of the structure was deserted.

"Peter?" she called, but not too loudly. She didn't want anyone in the nearby houses to hear her. Glancing over, she saw that both pubs' lights were still on, which increased the chance of being seen by drinkers leaving either establishment. "Peter," she said again, this time hissing it so that he might hear how little she was amused. The rain pattered against her cap and shoulders, drizzling down her cape and dripping to the ground below. No reply.

"Peter," one last time, kinder now in case he had wanted simply a last kiss, but still nothing. She turned again, and the man standing immediately behind her reached up and trailed his fingers across her cheek. Florence screamed and the man darted away, merging with the shadows on the far side of the green.

Everyone thought it was Lewis Guthrie who had attacked Florence, although "attacked" was probably too strong a word for it, and the Reverend Booth went to visit Guthrie and his mother and gave the man a stern talking to. Guthrie wept and howled during the reverend's visit, claiming he had not left the house all night, and his mother confirmed this, but what could you expect of a simpleton and his mother?

Booth said his piece and left, and the next day he and van Hewson decided on the last set of graves to dig up while labourers collected the bone fragments, including a jaw-bone with teeth still attached, that now littered the roads around the church and green. They had bought themselves a few months' more burials, he supposed, but probably not much more. Every little helped.

Alice Moreby woke because someone had spoken. What had they said? Nothing complicated, she knew, and now there was silence. A single word, perhaps two at most. She rolled over in her bed and looked at the ceiling, trying to listen. Was one of the children awake? Kayleigh fretted at night in the rain, not liking the sound it made against the window of her room, and Samuel was teething. But no, neither child was audible. Had Joe spoken in his sleep? He'd done it before, a half-formed broth of words and sound in which phrases could sometimes be made out, but he slept next to her, breathing slow and easy. Then what? Someone in the street?

"Hello, Alice," said a voice. Alice tried to scream and couldn't. Fear had her by the throat—was squeezing just enough to prevent words forming, was turning her head towards the window from where the sound had come. *Joe*, she wanted to cry, *Joe*, but nothing would emerge. The voice spoke again, a single foul word as she rose from the bed, and now there was a kind of sullen anger mixing with the fear, driving her on because this was her home, her bedroom, and she would not be frightened in her own bedroom, the sanctuary in her house. Her hands came up as she reached the window, taking hold of the drapes' edges as the voice said her name a last time, low and silvery and somehow wet and rank. Breath heaving in and out of her chest, her body shaking and still unable to speak, Alice pulled apart the curtains.

George Dent smiled at her. Alice and Joe's bedroom was on the upper floor of the house, yet Dent appeared to be holding on to nothing—just hanging in the air, smiling that slow half-smile—and then dropping away, vanishing into the night as Alice Moreby found her voice and managed, at last, to scream Joe's name.

It went on.

Grace Cole was walking back along the top of the flood-bank by the river one dusk-time a week or so later—the river below her to one side, and the fields below her to the other. The sounds of tiny flies darting hither and yon, and the flop and spit of the river's surface breaking as fish went after the flies that were her companion on her walk. She had been delivering new cloths and curtains made by her mother to the landlord at The Spearman's Boat and had stayed to help the landlord's wife, the sweet, simple Elise, hang them. They made the dining area seem much brighter, Grace thought, and liked the way her mother's delicate weaving had helped the Spearman (as everyone in Martledge called it) seem a better place. The bargees no longer travelled the river in the numbers they once had, so the Spearman was setting itself as a gentleman's rest on the journey between towns, and was hoping to host cattle and farm auctions soon. Her mother's mark in the dining area was helping the Spearman on its way.

As she walked, enjoying the day's transition into night and the warmth of the air, Grace heard something behind her. She turned, looking first at the river in case something had broken the water—there were eels here, and rats that the labourers would bring ratting-dogs to catch on sunny days—but nothing appeared to have disturbed the water's surface, except for the tiny flies and the less-tiny fish below. The other way was the fields, and they seemed empty. At the base of the flood-bank was a thick fringe of high, waving grass that gave way to the fields after a few feet, the grass higher than a man at this time of the year.

Someone was in the fringe.

Grace couldn't see them, but she could see the trail they were creating as a kind of ruffle in the grass' surface—a narrow strip of stems bending and swaying in patterns different from the rest of the grass' wind movement. The nearest end of the trail was perhaps twenty feet back from her, and she watched as it crept closer. There was something stealthy about the way she could see the trail, but not its creator, as though they were crouching low and trying to remain unseen. The hair on her arms prickled, her scalp tightening slightly. She debated calling out, even opened her mouth, and then the trail stopped moving.

Even though Grace could not see anyone in the grass, which was dark like the sea at night, she felt she was being watched by whoever was in the shadows below her. She started walking again, slowly, looking back over her shoulder as she did so, and there was a face peering at her from the top of the grass.

It was insipid, the face, the eyes featureless below an expanse of forehead the colour of old whey. The nose was long and thin, and the mouth below it was smiling a little half-smile and Grace screamed because two hands were rising out of the grass in front of the face, the arms bare, and the figure was rising behind the hands, naked and pale as it leapt up, and then she was running.

Grace ran along the top of the flood-bank listening to the sound of the grass thrashing from behind—and was it getting closer? Yes, it was—closer and closer—and her breath was ragged in her throat now, knives scouring the inside of her chest every time she inhaled.

She risked a look over her shoulder, saw something pinkish-white arrowing through the fringe of grass, still behind her but gaining, and then she was angling down the side of the bank and into the high grass herself, feeling it slap and scratch at her, hearing the dull thud of her pursuer's feet hitting the earth but not their breathing, no words, and then Grace was out of the grass and onto the path that curved away from the river and would lead her back to Martledge. She looked around again, kicking her legs out so that they wouldn't tangle in her skirts and bring her down, and the pale pink thing was running almost out of the grass now, close behind her, almost close enough to reach out and touch, and she wanted to scream but needed all the air she had for her flight and the man, because it was a man, was looking at her as they ran and smiling, smiling a secret little smile as the grass striped his naked chest and legs.

Grace tried to run faster, but there was no more left in her, and as the path cut away from the river and started back to the town between two of the fields, she knew that her time had come; the man behind her would pounce any second, and that would be her done and gone. She didn't give up, though, she ran and ran until her vision was spotting black as though she had blood in her eyes, until her belly was clenching and spasming like a knotting thing, until her throat burned with pain and nausea, and her arms ached from pumping and grasping at air to try to keep pulling herself forwards, and then she tripped and was falling.

Grace hit the ground hard, jolting her head against the earth and making her teeth click together. Her hands immediately started burning where they had scraped through the dirt, and she waited for the man to land on her back.

It didn't happen. Eventually, feeling sick, feeling so frightened that her heart seemed to be bolting loose inside her, Grace had little choice but to roll over and sit up. She looked back down the path and saw the man, now little more than a pink and ivory blur, still standing in the grass at the base of the flood-bank. Grace stood, keeping the man in her sight while trying to glance around for a rock or something else to throw at him if he approached her. There was nothing, but it didn't matter because the man, instead of following, faded back into the shadows behind him.

Grace looked down at her dirty dress, at her scratched and punctured hands, remembered the smile on the man's face, and started to cry.

∼∽∼

Three nights later, Mary James was jerked awake by her blankets being yanked off her. Startled, she watched as the various sheets and linens wafted into the air above her and then fell down. Several of them fell over the man standing at the end of her bed, obscuring him, but when Mary's father, brought by her screams, punched at the shape it collapsed to nothing. Mary swore to everyone the next day that the falling sheets had formed the shape of Dent, although when she was asked how blankets could look like a man, let alone a specific man, she had no proper answer.

Ben Carter saw Dent creeping along Martledge's main street late one night, but as Carter was a thief and a drunk most people dismissed him without much thought. Grace Cole did not; nor did Mary James or Alice Moreby, and when the Manningham baby vanished from its cot in the kitchen in the middle of the day, everyone started to mention Dent's name. It was though a dam had broken, the various stories told recently about sightings of the smiling man swirling and coalescing around the vanished child until, as the police and volunteers searched Martledge and the surrounding areas for any clue as to what might have happened, they formed a patchwork whole that then generated its own reality.

Dent was seen by Emily Cooper skulking in the back garden one along from hers, peering at the upper windows of the houses about him, and her screams brought neighbours and light—it turned out to be a huddled cloth thrown carelessly onto a compost heap and leaning garden-fork. He was seen by the river, and the resulting cry brought a small mob of Martledge's concerned citizens to surround a labourer making his innocent way home after a day in the fields, the man narrowly escaping a beating or worse. The resulting furore reached the ears of both police and the clergy, with Reverend Booth preaching about tolerance and the lack of panic from the pulpit the following Sunday, while van Hewson, impassive, watched him from the side of the altar and the police made their presence known by standing at the back of the church and looking around, without accusation but stern nonetheless.

No trace of the Manningham child was ever found, though, and sightings of the dead man continued, some of them less easy to explain. He was seen several times in the churchyard, once by a group of people including a visiting land assessor, who described the odd, smiling man who had watched him as he marked out the cemetery and took various depth samples, to a fault, the description recognisable to those who remembered him as Dent. Other people saw him on the green at night, by the lych-gate, where he was seen to move around the structure to ensure he kept in sight an unsuspecting female passer-by, but vanished when people came closer.

By now even the normally unflappable van Hewson was beginning to wonder about the situation and the safety of the people of Martledge, and Booth was panicking because if too much publicity ensued, then their actions in making the cemetery a fit space for burial again might be studied in more than cursory detail. "I am happy I have acted within God's grace," said Booth to van Hewson, but he didn't sound convinced, and van Hewson shared his misgivings. What had seemed an easy solution was becoming a problem. George Dent was becoming a problem.

Some of the sightings of Dent van Hewson dismissed as hysteria, the thoughtless prattling of flighty girls or feeble men, but others were less inclined to be washed away so easily. As much as he trusted anyone, van Hewson trusted some of the people telling about their sightings of Dent. Grace Cole was sensible and steady, not given to sillinesses of nature or imagination, and even Ben Carter had been sober when he claimed to have seen the dead man. The Manningham child he thought was in the river, having been too sickly to live, put there by a father given to rages and impetuosity, but now the rumours of Dent's involvement were creating something new, something unwieldy and dangerous. Something, van Hewson decided, had to be done.

"I never met him," said Booth later that night. Under the guise of a perfectly normal parish business meeting between sexton and vicar, they were discussing the troublesome, dead Dent. Booth's wife had been sent from the room, as she always was, after providing them with refreshments, and the two men had begun to talk.

"There are always rumours, though," replied van Hewson. "Tell me about them."

"I don't listen to gossip or rumour," said Booth pompously, bristling.

"Perhaps you should," said van Hewson. "It might help you understand your parish a little better." It was true; Booth had come here around six years previously from a city parish, and never really fitted in. He seemed to understand little of the natural cycle that the farmers had to exploit, and his fondness for life's niceties had left him open to manipulation by van Hewson in a myriad ways. Both men had done well out of Martledge, though, by accident in Booth's case and design in van Hewson's, and their self-interest meant they had to protect the growing village. The church's coffers needed to stay fat if the two of them were to stay so comfortable.

"I know my predecessor wouldn't bury the man," said Booth suddenly. "I can't remember who told me, but old Scarrow brought someone in from a neighbouring parish to carry out the rites when Dent was buried, although he never explained to anyone why. When they asked, he'd just shake his head and turn away. Scarrow believed in the old ways though, I do remember that. He was always following some nonsensical superstition or other—saluting magpies to ward off bad luck, putting eggshells on the top of his chicken-coop to stop the chickens dying, believing that chewing wood from a tree that had been struck by lightning could cure toothache—that sort of thing. He wouldn't marry anyone in May either, nor bury people on the last day in October. I always thought whatever he had against Dent was just another part of that silliness."

Silliness. The folk myths and old wives' tales of an area dismissed wholesale as *silliness*, which was why Booth would never fit in anywhere like this. Van Hewson sighed, and tried to think. "So Scarrow didn't like him enough to refuse to bury him, but still let him be buried in the church grounds. Odd, don't you think? Either Scarrow and Dent had some personal furies with each other, or something else was going on for Scarrow to refuse and then to go to the trouble of bringing another vicar in. He'd risk a diocesan enquiry at the very least, wouldn't he?"

"Yes," said Booth after a moment.

"Yet Dent seems to have rested peaceful until only recently?"

"Yes," said Booth, more warily. He was like that, van Hewson knew, not wanting to talk about things in the past that were murky in case they were dragged out into the light, making him look bad. "But there's no connection, surely? Dent can't really be back from the dead, not as spirit nor a flesh-and-blood thing. Can he?"

"Our Lord came back from the dead, and we pray to the Holy Ghost," said van Hewson quietly. "If they can do it, who's to say someone else can't as well? The question is, how to make Dent rest again?"

Van Hewson spent some time researching the problem while Booth dithered. He encouraged Booth to pray each night in the cemetery, not because he thought it would work, but because it gave the man a focus, something to do; and while Booth bowed his head over his Bible, van Hewson bowed his head over the church records.

Scarrow had left a thick box of papers in his will which no one had ever gone through, and with good reason, van Hewson thought after perusing them; they were the dullest diary entries and accounts he had ever read. Scarrow had listed what he had eaten, the weather each day, the notes for his tedious-sounding sermons and his incomings and outgoings, but there was nothing about his parishioners, and nothing about Dent. The man had obviously taken seriously the notion that what he and parishioners spoke about was between the two of them and God. Scarrow, thought van Hewson, had been about as high as you could get without becoming Catholic, and clearly treated conversations like his Papist counterparts did confessions. *Damn him*, thought van Hewson, who had hoped some simple solution to the growing problem would be found in the papers.

If Scarrow believed in the old ways, maybe the answer was there? So thinking, van Hewson turned to folklore.

There were a bewildering variety of ways to lay the supernatural, he discovered. Apparently, you could whip ghosts out of places by chasing them and flailing at them with a leather strap, or drive them away by burning feathers at night in the places they haunted, or by talking at the ghost until it left through sheer boredom, but he couldn't see these activities going unnoticed in an already on-edge Martledge. Similarly, there was no spilled blood of a murdered man to drive a nail through to prevent the ghost walking. Besides, who knew what Dent actually was? Grace Cole had been very clear that her pursuer, the smiling Dent, had been corporeal, had affected and been affected by the grasses he pushed through. So, ghost or something more?

Did it matter? Dent had been quiet before his bones were moved, and what did his stone say? *He sleeps in solitary depths.* Was it as simple as that? Had they simply woken him by moving him? And if so, could they send him back aslumber by simply undoing their error? Was it that easy?

He thought it might be, and made plans to find out.

Van Hewson wouldn't let Booth hire labourers to do the job, reasoning that although their silence could be relied upon by the application of coin for the simple job of moving old bones, the atmosphere in Martledge now might unstitch their lips immediately; or failing that, the first time after the task they took a drink, and this needed to stay quiet and hidden. Instead, he and Booth did the deed—first opening Dent's old grave in readiness, and then going beyond the wall and digging down through the recently-turned and thankfully loose earth of Dent's new resting place, and reaching his bones without too much effort. Digging at night was a problem, but the moon was bright enough to see by and the trees around the graveyard shielded them from prying eyes. They worked in silence as far as possible, although van Hewson did have a cover story for if they were discovered. *We're digging up his remains to sanctify them,* he'd say, *because we discovered in the old records that Scarrow refused to let him be buried in consecrated ground. His stone is a marker with no bones beneath.* It wouldn't stand up to close scrutiny, but most of Martledge would accept it without question, he thought, if it meant Martledge's resident spook was laid away.

Van Hewson saw the figure as they carried the bones around the cemetery wall to the gate. It was over on the green, by the lych-gate, and although it was little more than a dark blur in the night, featureless and vague, he knew immediately that it was staring at them.

And smiling.

Van Hewson urged Booth on. Dent's dirty bones, now collected in an old leather satchel, clinked slightly as they went, van Hewson trying to keep Booth's attention away from the figure in case he went to jelly and started screaming. Van Hewson felt like screaming himself because the figure was moving towards them now, fast, loping across the green, and he was reminded of Grace's story about the way it moved through the grass and the speed it had attained, and he recognised it now from the descriptions he'd heard of the man and his smile.

George Dent was chasing them.

He thought they might be safe in the graveyard, it being holy ground, before remembering that Dent's ghost or spirit or restless soul or whatever it was had already been seen in there and, sure enough, as they darted along the path to the open grave before Dent's headstone, the shape entered the church grounds behind them with no hesitation. Booth, who still had not seen Dent, resisted van Hewson's pushing, wheezing from the effort of digging, but he pushed the man on. Looking back, he saw that Dent had left the path and was weaving through the graves, darting from one to the other, his shadow a streak across the silvered grass. Van Hewson tried to move faster but he, too, was unhealthy after years of good living, and his legs seemed too slow, too stolid. Dent slipped from one stone to the other, gaining, creeping closer, and now he looked somehow less than human, something angular and distorted yet still smiling that odd little half-smile that revealed just a flash of teeth. Van Hewson moaned as the dead man dropped over the top of a nearby stone and oozed along the grass like a limbed snake before disappearing behind the nearby private crypt of one of Martledge's forgotten landowners. *They have seen the glories of His hand*, he remembered the inscription on the outside of the crypt read, and thought, *That's nothing to what I'm seeing*.

They were at the old grave now. Van Hewson wrestled the bag from Booth, opened and upturned it, and unceremoniously dropped the contents into the hole. As Booth, a confused look on his face, began to pray over the bones, van Hewson took a spade and started to throw earth into the yawning mouth at his feet. Over Booth's shoulder, he saw Dent emerge from behind the crypt and begin to slink towards them, face long and pale in the moonlight, smile ever-present, but his eyes were nothing but blackness—black pools that might have gone on forever, burning and cold and endless—and he shovelled faster as Booth came to the end of the prayer. The last fragment of bone vanished under earth, and van Hewson breathed a sigh of relief. It was done.

Only, if they'd done it, why was Dent still slipping towards them, body naked and thin and smooth like an eel's but white, bone-and-dust white? Van Hewson couldn't speak, couldn't breathe, as the dead thing grasped Booth from behind.

Booth didn't cry out. Instead, he made a kind of tired, strangled gasp as Dent's face rose up from behind him, the pale hands locked around his throat. Was this what he'd wanted all the time—to get revenge on the people who'd woken him? Because the look on his, on *its*, face was triumphant, eyes blazing and mouth open and still grinning, a rictus wrench that twisted his face unnaturally about. Van Hewson ran, abandoning Booth and running to where the labourer's tools were piled against the church's rear wall. Somewhere in the pile, he knew, were hammers and long, heavy iron spikes used to repair the fence when it broke. Scrabbling through them, as Booth made a lesser, more terrible sound from behind him, he found the hammer and a spike and started back across the grass to the grave.

Dent was on top of Booth now, in an embrace that was almost a lover's, curling around the man. He ignored van Hewson, thank God, so busy was he with Booth. It gave van Hewson time to push the stone at the head of the dead man's grave. Already made unstable by twice having the earth at its feet dug up, the stone wobbled, shifted and then fell, creating a lid over the bones. *No coffin*, thought van Hewson, *no coffin but a stone lid*, and then he was trying to hammer the spike into the stone as Dent finished with Booth and turned towards him.

At the first blow, the spike skidded off the stone and Dent's smile widened into a grin, but with the second blow van Hewson drove the heavy pole into the stone and sent chips up about his head. The stone cracked as he hit it a third time, sparks flying from the spike's head and giving the scene a nightmare light for the briefest moment—Dent stretching out towards him, fingers longer than they should be, tongue drooling from his mouth, skin gleaming and wretched—and then he hit a fourth time, and the spike was driven though the stone and into the earth beneath, where the bones lay waiting.

Dent stopped, staring at van Hewson, then started to dwindle away, slipping back into the shadows around him, his paleness becoming nothing more than moonlight. His grin fell back to its more usual half-smile and, as he vanished, van Hewson was sure the dead man mouthed something at him. Van Hewson took a few seconds, the scene processing through his mind, before realising what the dead man had said.

Dent had said, *Thank you.*

Van Hewson slumped over Dent's fractured, impaled grave, and waited for the sun to come. It started to rain, a summer storm, and bones emerged from the earth like new, tender shoots.

ROSALIE PARKER

HOLIDAY READING

ROSALIE PARKER co-runs the award-winning independent UK publisher Tartarus Press with R.B. Russell. Her three collections of short stories are *The Old Knowledge and Other Strange Tales*, *Damage*, *Sparks from the Fire* and *Through the Storm*.

With Russell, she co-edited the 1995 anthology *Tales from Tartarus*, and her solo anthologies include five volumes of the World Fantasy Award-winning *Strange Tales* series. and the celebratory volume *Strange Tales: Tartarus Press at 30*. Her stories have appeared in *Best New Horror*, *Shadows and Tall Trees*, *Black Static* and *Best British Horror*.

"'Holiday Reading' was written after a visit to Ilkley second-hand book fair," recalls the author, "although I came away empty-handed, on that, and so many other occasions."

THE BOOK FAIR was held in the town every August, when many locals were away. Nevertheless, it attracted a good-sized crowd of literature-loving customers augmented by visitors to the town looking for something to do. Most of the latter were perplexed by the antiquarian and collectable modern editions on offer. There was hardly a paperback in sight, Callum noticed as he strolled through the fair, fascinated despite himself. What kind of person bought second-hand books on traction engines, or keeping geese? Even the fiction was mostly by authors unknown to him. It seemed that book collectors were a whole new, previously unsuspected subset of humanity.

He picked a luridly-covered volume at random from the shelf in front of him. It was *The Haunted Abbey* by Mrs. Ashley Galbraith. The blurb was breathless:

Adela Everingham, recovering from a broken engagement, arrives at Aunt Celia's cottage in the country. Exploring the ruins of nearby Sakeby Abbey, Adela meets tall, sardonic soldier Captain Paul Repton, who tells her the story of the ghostly monk that haunts the Abbey. Later, Adela comes across handsome local solicitor Mark Frampton, who intimates that things at the Abbey are not all they seem. In a thrilling climax, Adela must choose between the two explanations of the mystery, and the two men who profess to love her.

Callum looked inside the front of the book for the price. It was £35.00, far too high for an impulse purchase. He put it back on the shelf and made his way outside. It seemed bright and busy on the street after the hushed gloom of the book fair. He leant against the façade of the town hall, watching the passers-by. It was all very well taking an enforced break, but what the devil was he to find to do?

The town was small, with an historic castle, prison and abbey, the first two of which he had visited on the first day of his holiday. He had also gone into some of the charity shops on the high street in search of reading matter, but it seemed that his lassitude made it impossible to find anything that appealed to him, not even amongst the contemporary detective fiction that he usually read. Decisions had become a problem, and his inability to make them the reason why his boss had ordered him to get away from everything for a couple of weeks.

"Everything" included Tessa, who was already showing some signs of impatience with his condition. Doctor Piper had assured him that he had in all probability been working too hard (the Leicester contract had been signed just in time to save the company) and concurred with his boss that he needed a complete change of scene. Tessa had hoped he would take her to Barbados, but he chose instead on a whim to come away on his own to this Northern town without even a car to get about in. The hotel was very comfortable, but small, with few facilities. He did not feel like staying in his room watching television, and Doctor Piper had warned him about drinking too much alcohol. That left walking around the town, or taking a train or bus to attractions further afield.

Callum bought himself a cup of coffee at a café. Sitting outside at a table on the pavement he contemplated the rest of his day. There was always the abbey, he supposed, smiling as he remembered *The Haunted Abbey*. Surely every monastic ruin in the country must have its putative ghost.

The abbey was beyond the town to the west, and Callum decided to walk there. It was hot: the midday sun blazed down—he had bought a bottle of water and sipped from it frequently. The abbey ruins lay in an idyllic spot near the river and as Callum drew closer he could see that they were impressive—the church seemed to survive almost to roof height. He bought a guidebook from the kiosk and thoroughly explored the site: there were rare survivals such as the coloured, glazed floor tiles in the church and an almost complete perpendicular window in the refectory. The abbey was constructed of handsome, locally quarried sandstone. There were few other people about, only a family, with two toddlers in a bulky pushchair, and a young woman, who seemed to be on her own. Callum could not help but notice her. Good-looking in a waif-like way, she trailed around listlessly, seemingly only half-awake, apparently following in his footsteps, although he noticed that she did not have the guidebook. As he was looking at the floor tiles in the church, she appeared beside him. He glanced at her face and to his dismay saw that she had been crying.

"Is there anything I can do?" he asked diffidently

"I very much doubt it," she said, "unless you have a magic wand." Her voice was low and musical. She took a handkerchief from her blouse pocket and dabbed at her eyes. They were green, Callum noticed, and her hair red. He had never seen such pale, translucent skin.

"I'm afraid I'm not a magician, but I am a good listener," Callum said, putting on his most cheerful voice. "The ruins are rather melancholy, aren't they? But romantic, all the same. Are you on holiday?"

"I've been here many times," she said. "Sometimes I find a sympathetic friend."

"Well I hope that I am that," said Callum.

"I am Gwendoline."

"Callum," said Callum.

Gwendoline had stopped crying.

"Shall we walk together?" she asked.

They strolled somewhat randomly among the ruins. Occasionally, he pointed out a feature. She smiled wanly.

"You seem to know a great deal about the abbey," she said.

"I've read the guidebook."

"There are some things it doesn't include."

Callum laughed. "I suppose there has to be a ghost."

"Yes. Of course. It's of a young woman from the town who was the secret lover of one of the monks. She took to pagan practices and he, in a fit of horror at what she had become, killed her and buried her outside the abbey grounds. She is said to appear only to male visitors."

"I'd better watch out then!"

"Don't worry, I'll protect you."

They had wandered into the monks' dormitory.

"Are you a Christian, Callum?"

"I was a choirboy at school, but that was a long time ago."

"But you enjoy visiting old monasteries?"

"They were such impressive buildings in their day, and must have seemed quite alien to the local people."

"The religion of the monks would have been equally foreign."

Gwendoline reached down and picked a piece of tall grass. She shredded the seed-head between her fingers.

"Are you feeling better?" he asked.

"A little," she answered, glancing up at him with a flash of a smile.

She sat down on the grass. Callum sank down beside her. She put her arms around his shoulders and nuzzled into his neck. He felt the sharp nip of her teeth. Instinctively he leaned away from her.

"What's the matter?" she asked. "I thought you liked me?"

"I do. It's...oh I don't know!" He put his fingers to the trickle of blood that ran down his neck. "You've broken the skin!"

"I got a bit carried away. I like you, Callum. I want you now. Why should we wait? You don't have to buy me expensive meals."

Callum was aware that he must seem somewhat priggish. "I have a girlfriend at home."

"She doesn't need to know about me. I don't mind."

Gwendoline put her hand on the back of Callum's head. She looked into his eyes. "Besides, you taste nice."

Callum felt his resistance crumble. He leaned forward and allowed her to kiss him.

Later that afternoon Callum awoke. They had walked to the corner of the field behind the ruins and laid down under the hedge. Gwendoline had gone while he was asleep—there was no trace of her. He put his fingers to his neck. The blood was no longer flowing, but he could feel the slight puckering of the wound. Feeling rather foolish now the heat of passion was over, he stood up, brushed himself down and walked back to the abbey. There was no one around: even the kiosk was empty. He began the long trudge to the town.

Callum realised that he had no idea how to find Gwendoline. They had not exchanged phone numbers and she hadn't left a note. Presumably she preferred it that way. He would have liked to see her again—get to know her better. She was an interesting girl and he had enjoyed making love to her, though the truth was that she had made most of the running.

Once he got back to the hotel he was exhausted, and it was all he could do to keep awake for dinner. He ate heartily, however, and felt better. One of the other guests, a woman called April, joined him in the bar afterwards. She, too, was staying at the hotel on her own. Her husband was away on a business trip in the US and she was taking the opportunity to have a short holiday. "It's good not to be in each other's pockets all the time," she said.

Callum found himself telling her about the reasons for his own enforced break. She was very sympathetic. "Burnout is a terrible thing. Taking a holiday is the best way to deal with it. And this is a good hotel, very discreet." She smiled at him. His eyes were drawn to the red of her lips. He fought against a sudden impulse to lean over and lick them.

He mentioned that he had been to visit the abbey and she laughed. "You know it's meant to be haunted?"

"So I understand."

"It's a story put about to warn people off. After dark, the abbey is a notorious... trysting place."

"How do you know all this?"

April laughed. "I have my sources."

Callum found April very easy to talk to. She asked him about himself and he felt no need to hold back. She was a good-looking woman, immaculately made-up and dressed. It was difficult to guess her age. She mentioned that she did not have any children. It seemed to be the one thing she struggled with.

"We have plenty of room, but it seems that George can't have them. He won't consider adoption, and all the other stuff didn't work." She sighed.

"You haven't considered a donor?" asked Callum. "Wouldn't that be the easiest way?"

"George thinks he might be able to father a child one day, despite what the doctors tell him. He doesn't want to raise someone else's brat."

"You could get pregnant and tell him it was his."

April shook her head. "What a dastardly thing to do, though, Callum."

"Oh, I don't know."

She eyed him speculatively. "You're not offering, are you?"

Callum had drunk several gin and tonics. "Maybe I am." They were alone in the bar. He kissed her neck, then took the tender skin between his teeth.

"Easy," she said.

He took April's hand and allowed her to lead him up to her room.

In the morning Callum found himself back in his own room, although he had no memory of how he had got there. He did remember making love to April, though. At one point she had asked him not to be so rough, though he was sure he had restricted himself to only a few playful nips. The warm taste of her lingered in his mouth. She had thanked him profusely after he had promised never to contact her again. He found it intriguing that even now it was possible that she was carrying his child.

Despite having made love to two women in one day, something that he could not remember having happened before, Callum was filled with an unaccustomed longing. He walked the streets of the town, newly aware of possibilities both obvious and more nebulous.

As he passed the town hall he could see from the posters that the book fair had reached its last day. Inside it was as cool and dim as ever. *The Haunted Abbey* was no longer on its shelf. Instead there were some new pulp titles, *Curse of the Rotten Scoundrel* and *Loud Sings Her Blood*. The stall holder saw him looking at the books.

"You'll not go wrong there," he said.

Callum walked back out into the sunlight, carrying his parcel. A blonde girl was waiting by the door, clutching a bag of books from the fair. He could smell the heady ripeness of her above the mustiness of the old volumes. Just as he caught her eye she smiled at him—he was sure he could hear the blood singing in her veins. He sauntered over.

The break seemed to be doing Callum the world of good.

GRAHAM MASTERTON

RESONANT EVIL

G RAHAM MASTERTON is mainly recognised for his horror novels, but he has also been a prolific writer of thrillers, disaster novels and historical epics, as well as one of the world's most influential series of sex instruction books.

He became a newspaper reporter at the age of seventeen and was appointed editor of *Penthouse* magazine at only twenty-four. His first horror novel, *The Manitou*, was filmed with Tony Curtis playing the lead, and three of his short horror stories were filmed by Tony Scott for *The Hunger* TV series.

Four years ago Masterton turned his hand to crime novels and *White Bones*, set in Cork, in Ireland, was a Kindle phenomenon, selling over 100,000 copies in a month. This has been followed by ten more best-selling crime novels featuring Detective Superintendent Katie Maguire, the latest of which is *The Last Drop of Blood*.

In 2019 he was given a Lifetime Achievement Award by the Horror Writers Association. His latest novel is *The House of 100 Whispers*, to be followed by *The Children God Forgot*. He is a frequent visitor to Poland, where *The Manitou* was the first Western horror novel published after the fall of Communism.

"Ever since I first read about synesthesia, I have wondered how much of what we believe to be 'supernatural' is in fact nothing more than a function of our own brains," explains the author. "Although there are many different manifestations of synesthesia, it basically describes the stimulation of one or more of our senses by another, such as having a metallic taste in our mouths when we hear a hammer banging on an anvil.

"The first recorded instance was in 1690, when the Oxford University philosopher John Locke found a blind man who swore that every time he heard a trumpet, he could see the colour scarlet. In a castle near Wrocław, in Poland, I talked to a guide who swore that whenever she heard singing she could see hooded figures walking across the courtyard.

"Myself, I have always believed in the possibility that ghosts are real, not supernatural at all, and that we simply don't yet understand the science of their existence. We didn't know about the existence of viruses until 1892 and didn't have the means to see them until 1931, and in earlier centuries we thought plagues were caused by demons. Even today, though, I could easily be convinced that COVID-19 came not from Wuhan, but from Hell."

M ARTIN DREW INTO the curb and turned off the engine. "There," he said. "Tell me that isn't perfect."

Serena looked at the white two-storey house with its patchy front lawn and its overgrown ninebark bushes and its peeling window-frames. Six or seven of the uprights in the veranda rail were missing, which gave the house a gap-toothed appearance; and the shutters of one of the upstairs windows were hanging askew.

"You didn't say it was a fixer-upper," she said. "How much are they asking for it?"

"Five-nine-nine. It's a steal. It has five bedrooms, two-and-a-half bathrooms, and a totally private yard with a view of Little Pond if you stand on a step-ladder."

"I don't know. It looks like a whole lot of work. And I won't be getting any more agile, will I?"

"Just take a look inside," Martin coaxed her. "I promise you, you're going to love it."

"Well, okay," said Serena, reluctantly. Martin climbed out of the car and walked around to open the door for her. Although she was six months' pregnant, she was still quite skinny, except for her baby bump. Her long blonde hair was tied back with a pale blue scarf, and she was wearing a pale blue smock and tight black leggings. Her blue denim sandals had five-inch wedges, but Martin didn't mind because he was seven inches taller than she was, lean and dark-haired and gangling, more like a basketball player than a neuro-scientist.

They walked up the path together and climbed the steps. Martin took out the key that the realtors had given him and unlocked the faded green front door. A corroded brass knocker was hanging on it, in the shape of a snarling wolf's head.

"Maybe I should knock first. You know—in case there are any ghosts still inside. I wouldn't want to startle them."

"Don't you go scaring me," said Serena. "The house looks creepy enough as it is."

"Don't worry," Martin told her. "Ghosts are all in the mind. Trust me. I'm a professional."

He pushed open the door and its hinges made a thick grating sound, as if they hadn't been oiled for years. "Do you know who used to live here before? Vincent Grayling. How about that for serendipity?"

Serena peered into the hall. It was dark and airless, because all of the shutters in the house were closed, and it was panelled in brown-varnished oak. She stepped inside, her sandals crunching on the gritty oak floor. On the left-hand side of the hallway there was a steep colonial staircase, which led up to a galleried landing. Some of the risers were rotten and needed replacing, and four or five of the banisters were missing, like the veranda outside. A huge crystal chandelier was suspended from the ceiling, trailing cobwebs like rags.

She sniffed. "It smells like nobody's lived here for *years*."

"They haven't. Vincent Grayling died in 1957. The realtors told me that the house remained in his family, but none of them wanted to live here so they rented it until it got too run-down. They wanted to sell it, but they couldn't agree on which member of the family was supposed to get the biggest share of the proceeds. It's only come onto the market now because the last-but-one of them has gone to meet his Maker."

On their right, a wide doorway led into a living-room. Although it was so gloomy in there, they could make out a worn-out brown leather couch, two mismatched armchairs with stretch nylon covers, a "contemporary" coffee table shaped like an artist's palette and a standard lamp with a broken shade.

"You don't want to live here just because it was Vincent Grayling's house, do you?" asked Serena. "I mean—sweetheart—have you worked out how much it's going to cost us to remodel? Not to mention all new furniture."

"All right," said Martin, "I confess. Vincent Grayling is one of my great heroes. But look what we'd be getting for the money. There's a much smaller house further down the street and it's nearly eight hundred."

"I always thought that Vincent Grayling was some kind of a nutball," said Serena, as she followed Martin along the hallway to the kitchen. "Didn't he do some experiment when he spoiled the taste of people's food just by showing them horrible pictures while they ate?"

"That was one of his experiments, yes. And most of his research was pretty far out, I have to admit. But he did some incredible work on synesthesia. That's when you stimulate one sense, like for instance *hearing*, and it affects another sense, like *taste*. He discovered that some people, whenever they hear a telephone ringing, taste salt on their tongues."

"How about smell?" said Serena. "I'm looking at this kitchen and I can definitely smell drains."

The kitchen was still fitted in 1950s-style, with green Formica worktops and a cream Westinghouse gas range, and wall cupboards with frosted glass windows. The faucet was dripping monotonously into the sink, and all those years of dripping had stained the sink several shades of brown.

Serena pulled open the dome-topped Frigidaire. On the middle shelf there was a single Tupperware container with something black and speckled inside it. She looked at Martin and Martin could see that she was almost about to tell him that she wouldn't move into this house if the entire MIT tug-of-war team tried to drag her into it.

"First thing we'll do is, we'll rip out this kitchen," he promised her. "We'll put in one of those fancy American Range ovens with a banquet burner broiler, or whatever it's called. And a fridge you could fit a family of Inuits into."

"Hmm," she said.

"Come on upstairs," he said, taking hold of her hand. "You ain't seen nothing yet."

They gingerly climbed up the half-dilapidated staircase, until they reached the landing. "Can't you imagine it?" he asked her. "Your guests are waiting for you downstairs in the hallway, and *ta-da!* you appear right here, dressed up like Scarlett O'Hara. Slowly you descend the stairs, the chandelier shining on your diamond necklace..."

"What diamond necklace?"

"The diamond necklace I'm going to buy you when they make me head of my department."

"Do I really have to wait that long? I won't be able to dress up like Scarlett O'Hara when I'm eighty-five years old."

He gave her a playful slap on the bottom. "Oh ye of little faith. Now, just take a look at this...the master bedroom!"

He opened the door. The master bedroom was enormous, dominated by a huge four-poster bed with carved oak pillars and dusty orange drapes. In the centre of the opposite wall there was a pair of French windows, covered by shutters, so that the afternoon sunlight shone onto the floor in narrow parallel bars. Martin crossed over to the windows, pulled back the bolts which secured them, and then forced open the shutters.

Outside, a balcony overlooked the yard, which was crowded with blossoming cherry trees. Beyond the cherry trees they could see Little Pond, blue and sparkling, with two rowboats tied together in the middle of it, and children swimming.

Serena came out onto the balcony and stood there for a while, with her eyes half-closed. The warm wind blew a few stray blonde hairs across her forehead.

"Well?" asked Martin.

"You've convinced me," she smiled.

They looked into all of the other four bedrooms. Three of them were quite small, and empty, without even a bed in them, but the fourth was almost as large as the master bedroom, and it had obviously been used as a study. The walls were lined with bookshelves, although there were no books on them now, apart from a dog-eared telephone directory and a residents' association newsletter. In the worn beige carpet there two rectangular indentations with a dark scuffed patch in between them, where a desk had once stood. A dusty black telephone with a rotary dial had been left on the windowsill.

At the far end of the study there was a red-brick fireplace, and in the alcoves on either side of the chimney-breast, oak-fronted closets had been built. Martin went over and tried to open them, but they were both locked, and neither of them had keys.

"This would make a fantastic den for you," said Serena. She peered through the shutters to see what was outside. "There's a girl next door, washing her car. She has thick glasses and a *very* large ass. I think I can trust you in here."

"Does that mean you want us to buy it?"

Serena reached up and put her arms around his neck and gave him a kiss. "I think you've persuaded me, yes. Let's go talk to the realtors, shall we?"

It was seven more weeks before the paperwork was completed and they were able to move in. By now the air was feeling sharper every morning and the trees all around Little Pond were beginning to turn rusty-coloured.

Because their baby was expected in less than two weeks, Serena's sister Emma came to help them move, although Serena was blooming. Her hair was shiny and her skin glowed and Martin had never seen her so happy. They were going to have a girl, and they had chosen the name Sylvia Martina.

"Just because we're naming her after you, Martin, that doesn't mean I want her to be a neuroscientist," Serena had told him. "I want her to be a singing star."

"What *we* want her to be is irrelevant," Martin had replied. "My mom wanted me to go into the grocery business, like my dad. Can you imagine me in an apron, slicing salami?"

"Actually, I just want little Sylvia to be healthy," Serena had said, resting her head against his shoulder. "I don't care what she does, so long as nobody ever hurts her."

On the third day, the sky was dark grey and it was raining hard, which made the trees rattle. Serena and Emma were cleaning the kitchen together, and Martin was waiting for a house-clearance company to take away the living-room furniture, which was out on the front veranda now, looking old and worn-out and sorry for itself.

He stood on the veranda watching the rain for a while. The truckers were over an hour late now and he wondered if they were coming at all. He went back inside. Serena and Emma were singing some Rihanna song in the kitchen, out of key, and laughing together, so he decided to leave them to it. He climbed the stairs to the study. All his books were up there now, in eleven cardboard boxes, and he could make a start unpacking them.

His desk was there, too, although it looked distinctly out of place in a colonial room like this because it was made of chrome and smoked glass. He would have to see if he could find an antique one, with brass handles and an embossed leather top.

He went across to the closets beside the fireplace. He had asked the realtors if anybody in the Grayling family had keys for them, but there had been no response. The Graylings had never taken an interest in the house, except as an investment, and they probably didn't even know that these closets existed, let alone where their keys might be.

He took out his Swiss army knife, opened out the longest blade, and slid it down the crack at the side of the left-hand door. He could feel the metal tongue of the lock, and he wiggled his knife from side to side to see if he could dislodge it from its keeper. It held firm, and so he gave up. He didn't want to damage the colonial oak beading.

In a last attempt to open the door, he opened out the corkscrew and inserted it into the keyhole. He jiggled it, and twisted it, but the door still remained firmly locked. He took out the corkscrew and gave the door a frustrated thump with his fist. As he turned away, the lock softly clicked and the door opened up, almost as if somebody had very gently pushed it from the inside.

He stood and stared at it. *No,* he told himself, *you're a neurobiologist, you're an associate professor in Brain and Cognitive Sciences at MIT. You do not believe in ghosts, or any kind of paranormal activity. Ghosts aren't supernatural, they're synaptic. Like you told Serena, they're all in the mind.*

Cautiously, he swung the door open wider. Inside, there were three shelves. The top shelf held half-a-dozen black hard-backed notebooks. On the centre shelf stood a portable record player from the late 1950s, cream and brown, an RCA Victor High Fidelity autochange. On the bottom shelf there was a large cardboard box, with a lid, marked: *S-Disks #5–#31.*

Martin tried to lift the box out of the closet, but it was so heavy that he had to drag it. When he opened the lid he found that it was full of long-playing vinyl records, all in brown-paper sleeves. He picked out the first one and slid it out of its sleeve. On the white paper label in the middle there was scrawly purple handwriting: *Lavender, recorded D Lab, 77 Massachusetts Avenue, 08/13/54.*

Lavender? thought Martin. What the hell did that mean, *lavender?* How do you record lavender?

He lifted out the next record. *Smoke, recorded D Lab, 77 Massachusetts Avenue, 08/21/54.* Then, *Lightning flash, 0.03 sec, recorded 76 Oliver Road, Belmont, 08/23/54.*

Each successive record had a similar notation on its label. There were *Moving Shadows, Apples, Faces, Snow, Cold Fingers* and *Child.*

He stood up and took down the notebooks. On the front of each of them was a white label with the same scrawly handwriting. The first one read: *Experiments in Synesthesia, 1954–55. Vincent D. Grayling, PhD.* When he opened it, and read Vincent Grayling's hand-written introduction, he began to understand what he had found.

I am working toward the stimulation of one sense through the stimulation of another. My first experiments are with hearing. I have successfully used sound recordings to evoke smells, visions and various physical sensations, such as the feeling of being stroked, touched, prickled, and even burned.

I am firmly convinced that there is almost no limit to what the human mind can be persuaded to perceive through the manipulation of the various senses. We are already aware that music can dramatically sway our emotions. Sad songs can make us cry. Martial music can make us feel aggressive. But this is only scratching the surface. I believe that we can create an alternative "reality" through sensory stimulation—a "reality" so convincing that a subject will not be able to distinguish between "real" and actuality.

In the same way that a pilot can feel on flight simulator that he is actually flying, we can allow people to experience "real" events, such as walking through a scenic garden and smelling the flowers, or swimming in the ocean, or making love, or even meeting relatives or loved ones who have died.

Vincent Grayling's explanation of how he had managed to conjure up "real" sensations by the use of sound recordings went on for page after page. Martin sat at his desk, fascinated. It was hard to believe that nobody at MIT had made any effort to find out what had happened to Vincent Grayling's notebooks and records after he had died. Martin had read that he had been a difficult man to get on with, and that his arrogance and overwhelming self-belief had antagonised many of his associate professors. Even today, though, his work on synesthesia was cutting-edge, and had limitless potential for psychiatric therapy and who knew what other possibilities? Maybe troops could be trained by thinking that they were fighting in Afghanistan, when they were simply sitting in a laboratory with earphones on. Maybe surgeons could separate conjoined twins before they actually made an incision. Maybe widows could meet their dead husbands again, and talk to them as if they were still alive.

He turned the next page and found a black-and-white photograph had been tucked into the margin. It showed a stocky man in a wide-shouldered grey suit, standing in the back yard, with the cherry trees behind him, although it must have been winter or early spring, because their branches were bare. He had black, slicked-back hair and a large, pale face, with near-together eyes and a heavy chin. Martin recognised him immediately as Vincent Grayling.

When he looked at the photograph more closely, he saw that there was a blurry white figure between the trees. It looked as if a child had been running past, just as the shutter was opened. It was impossible to tell if it was a boy or a girl, but Vincent Grayling didn't appear to be aware of it. He was staring straight at the camera as if he resented having his photograph taken at all.

Martin turned the photograph over. On the back was written: *Vera, 01/16/55*. Not *Vincent* or *Me* as he would have expected, but *Vera*. Maybe that blurry figure between the trees was Vera, whoever Vera might have been.

Martin took the record player out of the closet and placed it on his desk. He plugged it in and turned the ON knob and it immediately came to life. Its autochange arm dropped a non-existent record onto the turntable with a complicated clicking noise.

"Martin!" called Emma, from downstairs. "Your lunch is ready! Hot dogs!"

"Thanks, Emma!" he called back. "Just give me a couple of minutes, okay?"

"Don't be long! You don't want cold dogs!"

Martin took out the first record, *Lavender*, and laid it on the turntable. He carefully lowered the stylus onto it, and then turned up the volume. There were a few moments of hissing, and then he heard a very soft whispering sound, almost inaudible. The whispering went on and on, like somebody trying to say something confidentially in his ear, yet too close and too breathy for him to be able to make out what it was.

After about twenty seconds, the whispering was punctuated by an intermittent buzzing, which reminded him of the noise that a faulty fluorescent light makes just before it flickers off for good. These two noises went on and on, with the whispering rising and falling from time to time, and the intervals between the buzzing noises varying in duration, but that was all.

"Martin? Are you coming or not?" called Emma.

"Okay, sure!" said Martin, and reached across his desk to switch off the record player. As he did so, however, he was suddenly aware of a strong smell of lavender, as aromatic as if he had found himself standing right in the middle of a lavender field.

He breathed out, and then breathed in again, deeply, just to make sure that he wasn't mistaken, or that he was deluding himself. But there was no question about it—he could smell lavender. Not only that, everything in the study seemed to have a lavender-coloured tinge to it, as if he were wearing sunglasses with purple lenses.

"*Vincent*," he said, under his breath. "*I don't know how you found out how to do this, but you were a genius.*"

He lifted the *Lavender* record off the turntable and took out the next record, *Moving Shadows*.

"Martin!" shouted Serena. "If you don't come down now I'm going to give your wieners to the cat!"

He placed the record carefully on his desk and went downstairs, swinging himself on the banisters to avoid the rotten risers.

"We don't *have* a cat," he said, as he came into the kitchen. Serena and Emma were already sitting at the table, eating their hot dogs with coleslaw and curly fries.

"I know. But we will one day, and I was going to freeze your wieners until we do."

"You women," he complained. "You're such sadists." But before he sat down, he leaned over Serena and waved his hand under her nose. "Here—" he said. "Can you smell anything?"

She breathed in deeply. "I smell *something*, yes . . . but I'm not sure what." She breathed in again, and then she said, "It's not your after-shave, is it? At least I hope not. Why? What have you been doing?"

"I'll tell you later," he told her. "I managed to open one of the closets in the study, and there was a whole lot of Vincent Grayling's

notebooks and records in it. I should take them all in to the department, I guess. Well, I probably will, but I want to go through them
first."

Serena breathed in yet again, closing her eyes for a moment.
Then she said, "That smell...I think I know what it is."

"Go on, then," said Martin. "Have a guess."

"It's like when you first open a pack of ground beef from the
supermarket."

"What do you mean?"

"It's like blood."

That night, after Emma had gone home to Watertown and Serena
had retired to bed early, Martin went back to the study. He propped
up the photograph of Vincent Grayling against the side of the record
player, so that he could look at it while he opened his laptop and
checked him out on Wikipedia.

Vincent Grayling, born October 17, 1908, died December 12,
1957. Assistant professor at the Department of Brain and
Cognitive Science at Massachusetts Institute of Technology,
1934–1957.

Grayling was a neuroscientist specializing in various forms
of synesthesia, a condition in which senses are linked together,
so that the stimulation of one sensory or cognitive pathway
automatically stimulates a second or even a third pathway.

He married Joan Bannerman, the youngest daughter of
Professor Himphrey Bannerman, in 1928. They had one
daughter, Vera Joan, born 1931, who was fatally injured in a
traffic accident at the age of six, while Vincent Grayling was
driving.

Martin looked across at the photograph. Vincent Grayling had
written *Vera, 01/16/55* on the back of it, and yet the blurred image
between the trees couldn't be Vera—at least not the same Vera. If she
had died when she was six, his daughter had been killed in 1937,
which was eighteen years earlier.

Martin read on:

Joan Grayling died in 1952 of ovarian cancer. After her death Professor Grayling became extremely reclusive, although he published several papers on synesthesia, notably "Cognitive and Perceptual Processes in Congenital and Adventitious Synesthetes." None of these papers was very well received, because research into synesthesia had been more or less abandoned by the scientific community, and after 1955 he submitted no more.

He was found in his study, having bled to death from a fatal wound to his carotid artery. There was some bruising to his body, and one of his shirtsleeves was torn, but because the study was locked from the inside, with the key still in the door, the Middlesex county medical examiner decided that he had taken his own life.

Martin closed his laptop and sat back. He wondered if he ought to try listening to the *Lavender* record again. He couldn't understand why Serena had said that he had smelled of blood after he had come downstairs, when he was quite sure that he had still been carrying the lingering scent of lavender. Maybe—with Sylvia's birth so imminent—her sense of smell had been thrown out of whack by her raging hormones. He was much more keen to put on the second record, *Moving Shadows*, and find out what happened when he listened to that.

He was just about to put the record on when he heard Serena calling him. He went along the landing to the master bedroom and opened the door.

"Are you going to be long?" she asked him.

He crossed the bedroom and bent over to give her a kiss on the forehead. "Only a half-hour or so. I'd like to listen to one more record, that's all."

"It's just that I feel strange in this house."

"Strange—like how?"

"I feel like we're not alone. That there's other people here."

"Of course there's other people here. There's Sylvia."

Serena slapped the pillow. "I don't mean Sylvia, stupid. I feel like there's other people walking around the house."

"Really? Have you seen them? Have you heard them? Have any of them left their dirty coffee mugs in the sink?"

"No, of course not. It's a feeling, that's all. I'm probably letting my imagination run away with me. I've never lived in an old house like this before. I'll get used to it."

"Okay, darling," he told her, and kissed her again. "Why don't you try to get some sleep? You've done a lot today, cleaning up the kitchen and everything. I don't want you going into labour before you're due."

"I don't think there's any chance of that, Martin. I feel like I'm going to be pregnant forever."

Martin left the bedroom door ajar in case she wanted to call out to him again, and he left the study door open, too. He sat down at his desk, lowered the *Moving Shadows* record onto the turntable, and started to play it.

After the initial hiss of the stylus, he heard a rustling sound, like a breeze, blowing through trees. It went on and on for almost a minute before it was joined by some awkward, sporadic tinkling. It could have been a wind-chime, or somebody stirring a glass of Russian tea. Then both rustling and tinkling were punctuated by deep, distant, reverberating groans. The groans didn't necessarily sound human. They could have been caused by anything, like pit-props under tremendous strain, or dying animals calling out to each other across a swamp.

After the fourth or fifth groan, Martin glimpsed something out of the corner of his eye—a dark shadow that flickered across the open doorway, so quickly that he couldn't be sure that he had seen it at all. He stared at the doorway intently, waiting for it to reappear, but even though the rustling and the tinkling and the groaning continued, it seemed as if one fleeting shadow was the only illusion that this record was going to evoke.

He thought of playing the record over again, and he was just about to lift up the tone arm when he saw another shadow, halfway along the landing this time, as if it had just come up the stairs. It was very dim and indistinct, and it rippled like the shadow of somebody walking past a picket fence. But it was definitely the shadow of a person, and it was making its way towards the half-open bedroom door.

"Hey!" shouted Martin. "Hey, you! *Stop!*"

He pushed back his chair and hurried along the landing. All the same, the shadow reached the bedroom door a split-second before he did, and stepped into it, without any hesitation at all. It was only a shadow, though. The door was still only half-ajar, and no human being could have walked through it without pushing it open wider.

Martin burst into the bedroom. Serena had already switched on her bedside lamp and was sitting up, wide-eyed.

"What?" she said. "Who were you shouting at?"

Martin looked around. There was nobody else in the room.

"*Martin*," Serena repeated. "Who were you shouting at?"

Martin circled around the room and even looked behind the drapes. All he could see was the sparkling lights of the neighbouring streets of Belmont and, less than a half-mile away, the red-and-white river of traffic on the Concord Turnpike.

He opened the doors of the built-in closets but all he found in there was their clothes, hanging up, and their neatly-folded sweaters and socks.

"Martin, you're scaring me now! What are you looking for?"

"Nothing," he said. "It's okay. It was just like an optical illusion, that's all."

"What kind of optical illusion? Jesus, you haven't been smoking any of that skunk again, have you?"

"Of course not. I only tried that under laboratory conditions, for that neuropsychology programme."

"Well, it made you all jumpy, like you are now."

"I haven't been smoking skunk, Serena, okay? Even if I wanted to, I don't have any. It was a visual aberration, that's all. Like a mirage."

"A *mirage*? This isn't the Sahara, Martin, in the middle of the day. This is nine o'clock at night. Indoors. In Massachusetts."

"I'm fine. I'm okay. I promise you."

"Well, come to bed. You're freaking me out. Next thing I know, I'm going to start having contractions."

Martin set aside the *Moving Shadows* record for the time being, but over the next few days he tried out several of the others, such as *Apples, Snow, Cold Fingers, Lightning* and *Faces*.

Some sounds stimulated his other senses much more than others. *Apples*, for instance, gave him a strong taste of Tremlett's Bitter apples in his mouth, and he could even smell apples, too. With *Snow*, however, he could feel only the faintest of chills, as if he were standing in front of an open fridge, and he could see nothing more than a pale reflected light in the window of his study. When he looked outside, there was no snow in the yard, although the grass appeared whitish, as if an early frost had settled on it.

Lightning was more spectacular, especially when he played it in the evening. The record was a mixture of creaking and crackling, and after about thirty seconds Martin began to see static electricity crawling across his desk and around the window-frame like sparkling centipedes. Outside, over Little Pond, he could see branches of lightning flickering behind the trees, although he could hear no thunder, and the evening was completely calm.

Cold Fingers was the first record that actually made him jump. It started with a light scampering sound, like a small rodent running, and then the scampering was accompanied by the shrill, sharp ringing of a bell. Immediately, Martin felt somebody drawing their chilly fingertips lightly across his cheek, even though there was nobody there. As the record continued, he felt it again and again. He stood up, knocking his chair over, and stumbled back across the room, holding up both hands to shield his face, but the chilly fingertips kept stroking him, faster and faster—not only his cheeks but his forehead and his ears and the back of his neck, even his lips. It was like being fondled by a dead but urgent lover.

He crossed over to his desk, still with one hand held up in front of his face, and pushed the record player so that the stylus scratched sideways across the record and stopped it.

"Martin?" called Serena, from the hallway. "What's all that banging?"

"Sorry!" he called back. "I'm re-arranging my study, that's all!"

He slid the *Cold Fingers* record back into its sleeve. He felt guilty that he hadn't told Serena what he was really doing. After all, he had first met her when she was a student in the department of cognitive neuroscience, and she was quite capable of understanding Vincent Grayling's research into synesthesia. For several reasons, though, he wanted to find out more about the true psychological effects of these records before he shared them with anybody, especially Serena. They were exciting, but he was concerned by the way in which they manipulated his senses so easily, making him see shadows where there were no shadows, and lightning where there was no lightning, and feel as if he were being intimately touched by somebody when he was alone. Serena was just about to give birth, and the last thing he wanted to do was mess with her mind.

He put on *Faces*. The sound of this record was quite different from the others. It was a jumble of hundreds of human voices, talking so quickly and indistinctly that it was impossible to make out what they were saying. He sat hunched at his desk, listening to them intently, but for over two minutes he didn't see anything, or smell anything, or feel that there was anybody else in the room. Maybe this was one record that wouldn't stimulate any of his other senses, and it would be interesting to know why.

He stood up and walked around the room, still listening. The voices made him feel as if he were surrounded by a huge crowd, still babbling away to each other, but a crowd which was completely ignoring him. Maybe that was the point of the record: to make him feel isolated, as if nobody cared about him.

It was only when he turned back towards his desk that he realised how wrong he was. *Faces* meant exactly that—faces. On the left-hand closet door, where he had found the records, he saw two faces, both of them in bas-relief, as if they had been carved out of the wooden door itself.

Martin stopped where he was and stared at them. One face was on about the same level as his own, a man's face, and even though it was fashioned out of wide-grained oak, he recognised it imme-diately as Vincent Grayling. Those near-together eyes, that heavy jaw, that suspicious, pugnacious pout.

Below Vincent Grayling's face, and slightly to his right, as if she were standing next to him, was the face of a young girl. She was quite plain, with a long nose and thin lips, but then she looked as if she were still too young for her features to have developed.

Martin thought: *Vincent Grayling and Vera. That's who these faces belong to. I can see them. I can actually see them, the way they must have appeared when they were alive. Not ghosts, not supernatural appari-tions, but images created by stimulating my sense of hearing, and through my sense of hearing, my sight.*

He raised his hand towards Vincent Grayling's face, wondering if he ought to touch it—or, if he did, if he would actually feel anything. As he did so, however, a voice blurted out from all of the other voices. It was distorted, and some words were muffled and incom-prehensible, but he could understand most of what it was saying.

"*Can you hear me? I said, can you hear me? I have to bring her back. It was my fault. I was* (incoherent) *and I should have known better. I can bring her back. I can. It's only a question of* (incoherent). *If I should fail, what future do I have? I will have lost everything. Joan, Vera. Everything.*"

Martin stared at Vincent Grayling's face on the closet door. Although he assumed that it was Vincent Grayling's voice that he could hear above the hubbub of other voices, the lips on the wooden face stayed motionless, and the eyes showed no sign of movement. Martin reached out again to touch him, but as he did so the record came to an end, and the tone arm lifted, and the face immediately melted away, leaving nothing but the flat closet door. The little girl's face disappeared, too.

"*I should have known better.*" What had Vincent Grayling meant by that? Martin would have to listen to the record again, more care-fully, to find out exactly what he had said. Maybe he had blamed himself for his daughter's death. Maybe he had been driving under the influence of drink or drugs or even the mind-distorting influ-ence of his own research.

It sounded to Martin as if he had been attempting to use synesthesia to bring Vera back to life. Not physically, that was impossible, but by stimulating his own senses so that he could see her and feel her and talk to her. Maybe the photograph of *Vera, 01/16/55* showed that synesthesia could evoke an image that could not only be perceived by people's neural pathways but by light-sensitive film. After all, if invisible voices could be recorded, why not invisible people?

He went downstairs. Serena was sitting in the living-room, watching a repeat of *Party Line with the Hearty Boys*. He sat down next to her, put his arm around her and kissed her.

"Thinking of opening your own restaurant?" he asked her, nodding towards the TV.

"I think I'll have enough on my plate once Sylvia's born. I just want some ideas for when your parents come round."

They sat in silence for a while, watching Dan and Steve make a three-cheese spaghetti. Then Serena said, "There's something on your mind, Martin. I can tell."

"It's nothing. Well, it's not *nothing*, but it's nothing for you to worry about. It's only that I've been listening to Vincent Grayling's records, and he really was on to something. It *works*, sweetheart. Synesthesia actually works. Before I hand over any of his research to MIT, I want to find out how far he actually went with it. I may even be able to take it further, who knows?"

"If it worked, why didn't he win a Nobel Prize for Neuroscience? Or a Hartmann Prize, or whatever they had in those days? Not even his own department took him seriously. Come on, Martin, he was the archetypal mad professor, and you know it."

Martin was about to come back at her, and tell her about the taste of apples, and the flashes of lightning, and the wooden faces on the closet door. Maybe if she hadn't been so close to giving birth he would have done, but he didn't want to argue with her, and he didn't want to upset her. Right now she needed him to be very normal and very dependable. The most important thing in their lives was Sylvia Martina, whose feet were churning under Serena's smock as relentlessly as the paddles of an old-fashioned washing-machine.

Martin reached across and stroked Serena's hair, which was shining in the afternoon sunlight. He wished he could think of words that meant *I love you, but a thousand times more than anybody else ever could.*

Sylvia Martina was born a day late at the Bain Birthing Center at Mount Auburn Hospital. She weighed 7 lbs 2 ozs and she was blue-eyed and fair-haired and when she was born showers of red-and-yellow leaves flew upwards past the fifth-floor window of the maternity unit and rattled against the glass as if to welcome her.

On the third day they took her home to Oliver Road, and placed her in the crib in their bedroom. She would soon have a room of her own, but at the moment it was brown-wallpapered and bare, and it would have to be decorated first.

Sylvia was a good baby, docile as well as pretty, and she hardly ever cried. A week after she was born, Martin came quietly into the bedroom at seven o'clock in the evening to find both Sylvia and Serena asleep. For the first time in his life, he knew what it was to feel blessed.

He went across and kissed Serena's cheek, and then he switched off her bedside lamp and left the bedroom, although he left the door a few inches open so that it wouldn't be totally dark.

He went into his study and poured himself a glass of Jack Daniel's. He hadn't listened to any of Vincent Grayling's records since Sylvia had been born, all except for *Lavender* which he had played again while Sylvia was asleep and Serena was taking a bath, just to make sure that he couldn't detect any hint of blood. He had inhaled deeply while it was playing, and all he had smelled was lavender, *lavandula angustifolia.*

This time he put on *Child*, and at the same time he leafed through Vincent Grayling's notebooks until he found a heading for *CHILD*, hand-written in capitals followed by several pages of Grayling's scrawling purple script. The handwriting on these pages was even more untidy than he had used for previous notes, with wild loops and fierce downstrokes, as if he had been angry or upset when he wrote it.

Martin lowered the tone arm onto *Child* and the first thing he heard was breathing. It was quick, and panicky, like the breathing of a small child fighting for air. It went on and on for more than three minutes before it was eventually joined by a very low grumbling sound, so deep that it was almost below the range of Martin's hearing—more like an earth tremor than a noise. His whiskey glass started to rattle against the side of the Jack Daniel's bottle, and all the pencils and ball-pens that he kept in a white china mug on his desk began to jump up and down as if they were trying to escape.

The grumbling continued, drowning out the breathing altogether, although Martin couldn't be sure that the breathing hadn't stopped. Then, suddenly, there was a scalp-prickling howl. It was a man, no question about it, but a man howling in such agony that he could have been mistaken for a dog crushed under a truck.

On the opposite side of the study, next to the bookshelves, a shadowy figure materialised—the figure of a man, dressed in grey. His features were indistinct, but Martin could see that his mouth was stretched open wide, as if it were him who was howling. He was making his way towards the door, in a flickering motion, one image of him after another, a succession of grey shadowy men like a very early motion picture.

He reached the door. Although it was open already, Martin felt that it wouldn't have mattered if it had been closed, he still would have gone through it. He went out onto the landing, and as he did so the howling twisted itself into a cry of "*Vera! Vera! My dear little Vera!*"

Martin got up from his chair and went after him. He was just in time to see him enter the master bedroom, without opening the door any wider than it was already.

"*Vera! Oh, God, Vera! You've come back to me! My little Vera!*"

Martin pushed open the bedroom door and switched on the overhead light. Serena was already sitting up in bed, looking bewildered.

"Martin, what's—*Martin*! Who's that! Martin, what *is* that! Martin, *get it away from Sylvia!*"

This time, the figure hadn't vanished when it had entered the bedroom, but was standing by the side of Sylvia's crib, looking down at her. He was half-transparent. His face and hands were dark grey and his eyes were white, like a photographic negative, but at the same time Martin could clearly see that it was Vincent Grayling.

"*Vera,*" he said. "*My wonderful little Vera.*"

Martin could hear his voice quite distinctly, even though it wasn't coming out of his mouth, but playing on the record in his study.

"*We thought you were gone, my darling one, but here you are again, alive and well.*"

"Martin, get him away!" screamed Serena, pushing back the covers and climbing out of bed. "Don't let him touch her!"

Martin seized Vincent Grayling by the shoulders and tried to twist him away from the crib, but he was jolted by an electrical shock that threw him back against the wall, jarring his spine. He lurched forwards, snatching at Vincent Grayling's sleeve, but another electrical shock froze all of the feeling in his leg-muscles, and he dropped onto his knees on the floor.

Vincent Grayling reached out for Sylvia. "*Come to Daddy, my darling. I never thought to see you again.*"

But he wasn't quick enough. Serena bounded across the bedroom floor and snatched Sylvia out of the crib before he even had the chance to pull back her blankets. Then she ran for the door, gasping, "Martin! Help me! Stop him!"

As Vincent Grayling flickered past him, one still image after another, Martin pitched himself sideways and tried to trip him up by grasping his ankle, but again he was stunned by a thrilling electrical shock.

Serena ran out onto the landing with Sylvia clutched tightly in her arms. The animated images of Vincent Grayling pursued her, only three or four feet behind, and as he did so the record in the study produced an eerie whining noise, as if Vincent Grayling were deliberately trying to panic her.

Martin reached the bedroom door just as Serena was starting to hurry down the staircase. Vincent Grayling was almost close enough to catch at her nightdress.

"*Serena!*" Martin shouted. "*Watch out for the stairs!*"

He didn't know if she had heard him or not, but she continued to run down the stairs as fast as she could. A third of the way down, they collapsed under her feet, cracking and groaning and then noisily crashing as the risers broke and the treads were ripped in sequence away from the wall.

Serena dropped into the space below the stairs, still holding Sylvia close. She didn't scream. She didn't utter a sound. In her nightdress she looked like an angel falling, until she was impaled by a capped-off gas pipe that ran vertically up through the floor from the basement. She was stopped with a jolt, her arms and legs flapping upwards, and blood spurted out of her lips. She dropped Sylvia somewhere into the darkness and Sylvia didn't make a sound, either, not that Martin could hear.

The figure of Vincent Grayling turned around and stared at him with his white negative eyes. Martin had the feeling that he was about to say something. He thought he heard something like a croak of anguish. But then the record in his study abruptly came to an end, and Vincent Grayling vanished, and all Martin could hear was *hissss-clikkk! hissss-clikkk! hissss-clikkk!*

Shivering with shock, he climbed down the staircase, clinging to the balustrade. He looked down at Serena and it was clear that she was dead. Her bare feet were ten inches clear of the floor below her. She was wearing a bib of blood on the front of her nightdress and her pale blue eyes were staring at nothing at all.

He found Sylvia lying in a cardboard box full of spare electrical plugs and adapters. Her eyes were open too; and she, too, was staring at nothing at all.

It was not until three weeks after the funerals that Martin found the strength to go back into his study and take the *Child* record off the turntable. He sat at his desk, holding it in both hands, and his overwhelming urge was to bend it backwards and forwards until it snapped in half.

But he needed to understand why an apparition of Vincent Grayling had appeared that evening, and why he had seemed to believe that Sylvia was Vera. Surely Vera had lived until she was six years old. She hadn't been a baby.

He took out Vincent Grayling's notebook again and started to read. Gradually, as he deciphered the scrawly purple handwriting, he began to realise what had happened, and why Vincent Grayling was a greater neuroscientist than any of his colleagues had been prepared to believe. Greater even than Marks or Cytowic or Patterson or Heidel.

Vincent Grayling had found out how to stimulate his own senses through sound—so that different noises could lead him to see, hear, touch and taste things that didn't actually exist. When somebody said "blue", he could not only *taste* ink in his mouth, he could *see* and *touch* a bottle of ink, and even *spill* it, even though to any other observer it would make no mark. He had not only been able to see Vera when he played sounds that stimulated his senses into thinking of Vera, he had been able to hold her and kiss her and talk to her. To him, but to him only, she became real.

Because Vera had never survived until she was six years old. Vera had died in her crib when she was only three weeks old.

I cannot begin to describe the grief of losing her so soon, my little darling. I thought of her constantly, of what she could have done, of what she could have been, of what a happy life she could have led. I saw her dancing through fields full of daisies. I saw her sitting at her desk, her tongue protruding, carefully copying the letters of the alphabet, her blonde hair shining in the light through the classroom window.

That was when I decided that I would use synesthesia to bring her back to me, and at least allow me to witness the life that was taken away from her, if nobody else.

Martin sat back. The following pages were filled with Vincent Grayling's acoustic formulae, and how he had tuned various instruments and artefacts to produce the evocative sounds that would stimulate his senses into bringing his Vera back to him.

He succeeded. The notebooks that followed were full of descriptions of how he had been able to produce a virtual Vera who could grow, and learn to dress herself, and dance, and even have conversations with him.

The blow had come in January 1937, when Vincent Grayling had been driving into Cambridge one icy morning and crashed his Dodge Business Coupe into the rear of a garbage truck. He had suffered no serious physical injuries, but he had struck his head on the steering-wheel and been concussed, and when he had recovered from his concussion he had found that his synesthestic sensitivity had been severely impaired.

He could no longer stimulate his senses to recreate Vera, not as fully as he had been able to, before the accident. He could glimpse her running through the trees, he could hear her laughing, but that was all.

He tried for twenty years to bring her back the way she was. "*I need to hold her in my arms, if only once, if only for a moment.*" But his sensory perception was damaged forever, and on December 12, 1957, in despair, he locked his study door and prepared to take his own life.

What he had failed to realise was that he had left *himself* on his records, his own longing, his own grief, all immortalised in vinyl. Just as Vincent Grayling had been able to bring Vera back to life, Martin's senses had been stimulated into bringing Vincent Grayling back to life.

Martin stayed in the house on Oliver Road for the next five years. He wrote numerous papers on various forms of synesthesia, such as grapheme synesthesia, in which letters and numbers appear to some people to have colours; and chromesthesia, in which music and other noises can produce the effect of waves, spots or even fireworks, and lexical-gustatory synesthesia, in which words have distinctive tastes, like honey, or rust, or green.

However, he kept his most advanced research to himself—his continuation of the work that had been started by Vincent Grayling. He hated Vincent Grayling with a dark, bitter rage that would never diminish as long as he lived, but his records and notebooks were the only way in which he could bring back something of what had been taken away from him.

He was writing up the results of his latest acoustic experiment when there was a tapping at his study door.

"What is it?" he asked.

A blonde-haired girl of five years old came into the room, wearing a pink knitted sweater and red OshKosh dungarees. Her hair was tied up with two red ribbons.

"*Dadd-ee,*" she said coyly, "can we go out to the park, and have a slide on my sledge?"

Martin pushed his chair back and the little girl climbed onto his knee. "Not today, sweetheart," he told her. "The roads are real icy, and we don't want history repeating itself."

"What does that mean?"

Martin shook his head. "You really don't want to know, believe me."

At that moment, a voice called from downstairs, "Sylvia? Are you bothering Daddy again?"

"No, Mommy!" the little girl called back. Then she turned to Martin and said, "I'm not bothering you, am I, Daddy?"

"No, of course you're not. Not at all."

She frowned at him seriously and touched his left cheek with her fingertip. "If I'm not bothering you, then why are you crying?"

MICHAEL CHISLETT

REDRIFF

MICHAEL CHISLETT has had his stories published for nearly thirty years in various journals and anthologies, including *Ghosts & Scholars*, *Supernatural Tales*, and volumes from Sidereal Press and the Oxford University Press. Sarob Press has published two collections of his work, *In the City of Ghosts* and *Where Shadows Gather*. The first of these won the Dracula Society's Children of the Night Award for Best Collection in 2016. His work has also been published in translation in both Mexico and Japan, and the author names his literary influences as, amongst others, Fritz Leiber, M.R. James, Arthur Machen and Clark Ashton Smith.

'Redriff' is the fourth story of his to be published in *Best New Horror* and, as Chislett explains: "It is one of a series of tales featuring the misadventures of a group of occultists, all of which have appeared in David Longhorn's magazine *Supernatural Tales*. Amongst other things, I am currently working on one featuring Mr. Neckinger, purveyor of mandrake root to the trade. Most of my stories are set in locales that I know, and those who are familiar with the more arcane byways of London may well recognise them..."

REDRIFF GAVE NO credit to ghosts. He believed instead, that what are named as phantoms were not the returned dead, but emanations from a host of invisible beings, always capricious, and usually inimical to mankind, who surround us like a kind of spiritual dark matter. They would seek to cross the threshold, and that, if we knew how to recognise these trespassers into our world, then measures might be taken against such intrusions. Or if one were so inclined, to make use of them. But, that did not mean that he was not haunted.

The first message that he received was in the mundane surround-ings of a London bus. On picking up one of the give-away papers that littered the upper deck, Redriff was surprised to see, written on the front page in red felt-tipped pen, these words:

HAVE YOU READ SINISTRARI'S BOOK

He had. *De Daemonialitate et Incubi et Succubi.* That is, if it were the same Sinistrari, and Redriff knew of no other. *Of Sex with Demons,* the book's given English title. Such arcana was an interest of his, for he had been a member of a society, a loose sodality, which delved into such matters. Though lately, after some distressing occurrences to a number of his fellow seekers, as they liked to term themselves, he had withdrawn somewhat from those activities.

Redriff turned the pages of the news sheet, to see if any other interesting writing was on them, but there was nothing. He studied the words again. Could it be only coincidence? He doubted that; to find a reference to so obscure a text, in such a place and such a way, showed intent. He had just boarded the bus and the paper was already on the seat where he sat. Was it deliberately placed there, as a joke or a warning to him? But those whom he had dealt with lacked humour, or gave warnings. He thought then of Mardyke. The witch had a whimsical sense of fun. Though where she was now, it was unlikely that she would be out and able to perform such japes. But, there were certain ways that might be utilised.

He looked carefully around the bus as it made a slow way across Waterloo Bridge and saw nothing untoward. He considered tearing the paper and taking the message with him, to study later. But Redriff had an aversion to accepting found things, especially those with writing on them. He would remember the words, and in his library at home was Sinistrari's book and he might read it again with renewed interest.

That evening, after finding the volume at the back of a cupboard full of such arcana, Redriff settled down to read. It was the Abney Scrope translation and so, not to be trusted as a correct text. Scrope had been a man who had allowed his own particular and peculiar crotchets colour his work. Some words struck him as he read.

Incubi and succubi do not obey exorcists, have no dread of exorcism, and show no reverence for holy things, at the approach of which they are not in the least affronted.

Redriff had once encountered what might be classed as a succubus. He was equivocal about that experience. But such adventures, if indulged in too frequently, could lead to consequences, dependencies, and he was a little too old now, a bit wiser, nor desperate enough to seek that dubious, though stimulating, companionship again. But might it want to resume the old, familiar relationship?

Finding the message, for that was what Redriff suspected it to be, was curious, and he did not believe in coincidence. Best to keep an eye out, for other such cryptic communications. What it meant was a matter for conjecture. He would think on it.

Every few weeks he travelled to a station on the southern end of the Northern Line. There was always a notice board by the ticket barrier, which carried a cheering homily, written in chalk to encourage commuters. Redriff read these, thinking that a member of staff was having a sarcastic laugh by putting out such wisdom as CONSIDER YOUR GLASS HALF-FULL RATHER THAN HALF-EMPTY.

He cast his eye on the board as he passed through the electric gate and read written there:

WHAT LEADS TO LONDON AND OUT AGAIN, YET STAYS?

A riddle? Unusual! And there was no answer after it. Redriff looked closely at the writing, red chalk that had been scrawled over another, earlier message. A conundrum, to be thought on?

"The road," was the opinion of Neckinger whom he visited. "For all roads lead to London, and they stay."

"But, they go out again," Redriff argued.

"Out is a different road to the road in," was the reply.

In an echo of this exchange, when he returned to the station, Redriff looked at the notice board again, to see that someone had chalked an answer, so that it now read thus:

WHAT LEADS TO LONDON AND OUT AGAIN, YET STAYS?
THE DIFFERENT ROADS

Another coincidence? One could see too much in little things, make a lot of what was nothing. But...then again...

On the tube he picked up the evening give-away sheet and flicked casually through its pages. There was something about a female "celebrity", whom he had never heard of, and, at the top of the page, over a picture of the dishevelled wench being carried out of a night club in a tired and emotional condition, was written, again in that red felt-tip pen, these words:

IS THIS NOT A DISGRACE? A WOMAN TO GIVE BIRTH TO
A PUPPY!

Redriff raised his eyebrows slightly and read. There was nothing about pregnancies, natural or otherwise. No knowing references to, Caprice, for that was the name of the celeb, being a dog-lover. This he did tear neatly across the page, fold, and put into his pocket. If any other such writings came his way, when collected they might form a coherent narrative. Though such sendings rarely did. For their source, whatever that might be, by its very nature, was not exactly, as we understand it, structured.

When, later, Redriff examined the scrap of paper, he found that the writing had faded to an unreadable smear of red.

Redriff now scanned whatever free paper he found on public transport for more writings, but found nothing. Though, when again at that Northern Line station, he did look on the board, to see the usual platitude scrawled there. However, on returning some hours later, he was surprised to see written, in red letters over where the previous maxim had been rubbed out, these interesting words, which he took the trouble to transcribe in a notebook that he carried with him:

THE MENTAL CITY, GOLGONOOZA, IS A PRODUCT OF
THE MIND. THE INTERIOR LONDON, FROM THE
ROOT, "GOLGOS", A SKULL. FOR THIS CITY'S EXIS-
TENCE IS IN THE HUMAN BRAIN AND THUS CANNOT
BE CHARTED

This was interesting. Was the writer a Blakean? Redriff approached one of the station staff, and politely enquired as to whom it was that wrote these messages.

"I find reading such simple wisdom inspiring," Redriff lied with a smile. "And I would like to thank him, personally."

"Well," answered the fellow honestly, "I personally think they're a load of crap. I actually don't know who does them. It's shift-work mate, so I don't know a half of the staff, and we do other stations too. Write a letter to the head office," he suggested and walked over to look at the writing, shook his head, and turned the board around so that its back was towards Redriff. "Sick of looking at them," the railwayman muttered and wandered off about his business.

Redriff saw that other words had been written on the back of the board, and he went to read:

THE CITY IS NOT WHAT IT SEEMS, THOUGH IT IS NOT
ANYTHING ELSE EITHER

Curiouser and curiouser, he reflected, and wrote this down too. It was most unlike what was usually there. He would make enquiries, the next time at this station.

However, before he could do that, Redriff found yet another of what he now thought of as, "communications". The where or what they emanated from, or their purpose, baffled him. It was a conundrum.

He was walking through the tunnel beneath Waterloo Station, from the South Bank to Lower Marsh, to visit a record shop there. Redriff was thinking of Blake, who had lived nearby, as he glanced at the graffiti-covered walls of the vaults, which had once held the famous Necropolis line. It had been given over to street artists, to daub as they will. There were a number of admirers of such work standing in groups, obviously appreciating the bright Fauvist colours, the tags and slogans. Redriff was not amongst them, he knew what he liked in art, and it was not this. Also the smell of the aerosol spray cans used to spray the runes on the walls was offensive. He had reached the end of the tunnel, and ascended the slope to the sunny street, where he saw written on the paving other odd words, in the same red letters:

NO MATTER WHERE YOU GO, YOU NEVER FIND THE
WAY OUT OF THE LABYRINTH

Redriff contemplated this. The floor of the tunnel had been clear of the spray-can art, sticky on the trainers he supposed. There were various dark ways to the sides of the place that seemed to be occupied—coffee shops and art galleries had notices inviting passers-by to enter. He was not tempted, knowing that there was a network of vaults and shafts beneath the whole of that part of London. He had even explored some of them, though not precisely here, and with one wise about these underground places as guide.

He took out his notebook and transcribed the words into it. Had these "communications" actually emanated from himself? There were many possibilities, and Redriff had some knowledge of how the mind can create such mysterious "anomalies". Or were they from some others, not exactly human? That was a more worrying possibility.

After an hour browsing amongst the classical records and chatting with the shop's proprietor, Redriff went back to look again at the writing, which, as he had half-expected, had gone. Leaving only a smear of red upon the ground where it had been erased. Was there a correspondence between the colour of the writing and his assumed name? It was an interesting, if given the rubbing out of the words, disturbing point.

Redriff examined the words that he had written down in his notebook, to see if there was any correspondence between them, a narrative that might be formed. But could find none. They had all been hand-written, that was one definite thing, by something as yet unseen. It was one firm conjecture. He expected that if he received similar "communications", they would take the same general form. Then he received the text message on his mobile phone:

THEY SAY THAT SHE BROKE FROGS

The only person who had the number was Redriff's financial adviser at his bank. Hardly the sort to send such things. Though who knew what was about on the æther? He had heard tell of odd messages coming through on even the most secure systems. You could only protect oneself to a certain extent.

IT WAS SHORTLY AFTER THIS THAT THE DOG WENT MAD

. . . was the second text that he received, a few days later, on another phone, one used for different purposes. Only a few, very trusted folk, had access to this number. They were also not likely to send such things. He thought of the cryptic message of the woman giving birth to a puppy. Had it something to do with that?

Except for his meetings with Neckinger, he had not lately had contact with certain people, those left from a small circle of students of what might be termed "arcana". There had been a number of unfortunate endings to some of them. Haggerston's death. Mardyke's incarceration in the asylum for the criminally insane, though they did not call such establishments that these days. Her attempted decapitation of Shadwell had taken behavioural problems a little too far. The sudden disappearance of Lant. Redriff detected a pattern.

He had been considering contacting Morden, who was sensible about such things, to get his opinion, when purely serendipitously Redriff encountered him in the Euston Road.

Morden stood on the pavement outside of the British Library, and Redriff observed how he seemed wary and watchful, looking carefully all about him. There was a definite nervousness to his demeanour, which was a thing that he had never seen in the fellow before. In fact, the man visibly started as, coming from behind, Redriff called his name.

"Morden! How wags the world with you?"

"Redriff!" he cried out, turning to him. "It is you, isn't it?"

"None other. The one, the only. How goes it?"

Morden looked carefully at Redriff for a long moment, then smiled, seemingly reassured. "Well, it is actually you then? Been a while. I was going to contact you, oddly enough."

"And I you. Coincidence? Or is there no such thing, but only objective chance?"

Morden smiled briefly, and took another long look down the street towards Kings Cross, then turned his head quickly in the other direction, as if by this movement he could catch someone who might be sneaking up upon him.

"Any news of Lant's whereabouts?" said Redriff, observing the man's nervous movements. Something was up with him.

"Oh, him. I did hear that he was hiding in Exeter. There is no one in his apartment."

"Well, now that Mardyke is safely incarcerated, he won't have to hide from that witch. And poor old Shad, has he recovered from his ordeal at her hands?"

"Ordeal! He probably enjoyed it. Did you see the images posted on the Internet?"

The incident had occurred during a pagan rite at a "sacred well", in Greenwich Park. Shadwell, dressed in a white robe and with a long blond wig on his head, had handed the sickle that he carried to Mardyke, who promptly swung the sharpened weapon at him. At first it seemed that Shad had been agreeable to this, actually arranged it with the witch, for he had assumed a kneeling posture and lifted the wig to expose his neck. But, when the blade bit into his flesh, second thoughts arose. Not so with Mardyke, who, with considerable brio, continued to attempt what she later admitted was to be a ritual decapitation. The woman became vexed with the fellow for his sudden withdrawal from what would have been a beautiful ceremony.

None of the assembled "New Agers" had attempted to stop this. Most were too busy filming it on digital cameras. Indeed, some did try to hold the now-protesting Shadwell down in order to aid the decapitating as one of the company, a toothless harridan who frequented such events, pranced around the circle that they had formed whilst beating a ritual drum and chanting. The urban shamaness, for so she had styled herself, came a bit too close to the swinging sickle, which punctured her drum, and a dispute arose between her and Mardyke. Which probably saved Shad from permanent injury, even death, for he managed to flee, bleeding badly, and with the sickle-wielding witch and some of the more militant pagans, angry at his unsporting disruption of their rite, in pursuit.

"They certainly had a fun afternoon," said Redriff. "I think it a shame of Shad to have had second thoughts. The man was always unreliable. He might have become the head in the well, and we could have consulted him about things."

"Bran's head," muttered Morden, and turned suddenly to look again towards that station, "is said to be buried at Kings Cross."

"Are you expecting someone?" asked Redriff, curious about this behaviour.

"Expecting! Why do you ask? Who might I be expecting?"

"I don't know, which is why I am asking you," Redriff answered, reasonably. "You do, if you don't mind me saying this, seem a bit on edge."

"Yes! That is exactly it. I am on the edge. The abyss you know. It has stared back at me, so to speak. And spoken too, come to that."

"What did it say?" Redriff asked, facetiously. He thought that Morden, like others of his calling—poor old Haggerston was a horrible example—was losing it. The man had always seemed so, well, solid: a chap with bottom, so to speak.

"A warning to the curious. That, in plain language is what I was given." His voice dropped as though he talked to himself. "But, I fear that the warning came too late for me. I have to go. I am expected." Abruptly, he began to walk away, hurrying across the Euston Road. "I'll call you, if I can."

Redriff watched with interest as Morden dodged between the moving traffic. Then, after a moment, followed, keeping somewhat back and behind people on the busy pavement. His quarry crossed the road again and he, in turn, did the same. The man was walking very fast, almost at a run, before turning into Eversholt Street, and Redriff thought to have lost him. But, on proceeding down a little way, he saw him standing on the corner of Phoenix Road and looking very agitated indeed. For a woman had appeared, seemingly from out of nowhere, to catch him in her arms.

A lovers' tryst? Not right to spy on that. But he was, as ever, curious, so crossed over the road to stand at the bus stop opposite, partially concealing himself amongst others there waiting for transport.

At first Redriff had thought it a woman who had hold of Morden, but then, he was not so sure. It was a very humid day, noon actually, and there was a heat haze, traffic fumes. These things can affect the atmosphere and what we think to see, he knew, and there were ever odd folk about in Camden. The figure was peculiar, black and thin. Elongated. This person seemed to be swiftly binding Morden in what appeared to be a net or web of some kind, that the fellow was making no attempt to extricate himself from. There was the unpleasant suggestion of the arachnid: too many arms, which appeared to be weaving about the fellow, in thin, securing tendrils. It reminded Redriff of a statue of the goddess Kali, which had impressed him when, as a child—he had seen it on display at the Horniman Museum. Strange how such images are retained in the mind, to become, it might be, demons of them.

Morden and his companion wavered in the polluted, miasmic haze   of
city heat, losing their contours, as if they were melting into one. Then a bus travelling north stopped in the traffic before him, hiding

them from Redriff for a few moments, and when the vehicle at last moved, they were gone. He quickly crossed Eversholt Street, to look down Phoenix Road, to see the odd couple heading in the direction of St. Pancras Station. But it was too far away to properly tell or follow, even if he had wanted to. Pursuit might not be either wise or welcome, by one or the other of them, for there was the impression that the fellow was being compelled by this company. Indeed, actually being carried by the dark spider-like, scuttling figure.

Later that day, Redriff tried to phone Morden. A recorded voice informed him that the number was no longer recognised, then immediately after he received another text message, with no sender's name of course to return it:

THE EATER OF FLOWERS, DESTROYER OF MEN.
A WOMAN SHARP AS THORN

This one did disturb him, and Redriff thought again of Kali. Similar avatars of that archetype. He would have to be careful, monitor the situation. He was not now in contact with any, besides Neckinger, of his old circle that had gathered around Lant, "The Sceptical Occultist", as he had styled himself. The man was off that scene. He might not be so sceptical now. Haggerston, who had thought that his shadow had been eaten, was dead, frozen to death in St. Nicholas' churchyard in Deptford. Mardyke incarcerated. Shadwell had, so it seemed, become religious and retired to a monastery after his encounter with the pagans and the sickle-wielding witch. The man was an idiot anyway. There was now only Neckinger and he left, and so he made the journey on the Northern Line to meet with that fellow.

He examined the notice board when leaving the station, but there was just the usual homily. Redriff did not feel like smiling so that the whole world joined with him in the grin.

Redriff sat in the cool shade of Neckinger's garden. The man nurtured some unusual growths there. He had knowledge of herbs and plants, the surprising uses that the most common weeds might be put to, and made a decent living selling online to a specialised market.

"I am," he admitted, "the UK's leading supplier of organic mandrake root."

"Nurtured and cultivated in the old, traditional way?" Redriff asked.

Neckinger smiled and said, "You would be surprised at just who some of my customers are."

Redriff did not ask, though he did want to know, if there had been any truth in the rumour that Neckinger and Mardyke had once attempted to create the Alrune, and what the result had been. But, such things, if not volunteered, were best not enquired about.

"There have been," ventured Redriff, as they sat together in the shade, "a number of odd...well...messages, they might be." He took a sip of the lemonade that Neckinger had thoughtfully provided and studied the half-wild garden, for trees and bushes flourished all around its edges. The curious, if looking over the high fence, would see little. But there was a plan to it, one not readily discernible, though most certainly there.

"You did mention the board at the station. I do look, but always see the usual banalities." Neckinger raised the cool glass jug of lemonade and replenished both his and Redriff's glasses.

"I have written some of the things down," said Redriff, and opened the notebook on the table. "Been looking for a pattern but, I cannot yet, perceive one."

He had already told of the encounter with Morden and his unsettling companion. What he had seen going on between them? The man had disappeared. Or was not answering texts, which was much the same.

"They sound to me," responded Neckinger thoughtfully, after Redriff had read out what was written in the notebook, "like those inconsequential messages that are received at spiritualist séances. Which usually mean nothing to those there, but might be of import to their senders. I don't know what to make of them. That last one, the 'Eater of Flowers', I am sure I have heard that appellation before, but cannot recall just where."

"Me too," agreed Redriff. "It is like something just at the edge of consciousness, waiting to be woken."

"Best not roused. That dog went mad once! I use the animal for digging up mandrakes. They do go mad and are useless for anything else after. And the breaking frogs! They are very useful in a garden for keeping down insects. I rather like them actually. Certainly would never harm one."

"What do you do with the dogs," enquired Redriff, "after they have gone... barking... in a manner of speaking?"

"I leave them tied-up outside of Battersea Dogs Home, with a note explaining that I cannot afford to keep them, being a poor person. They get the best of attention there. Better than a human being in the same situation would."

"Any suggestions as to what I might do, if the messages continue?"

"I would not be concerned too much about the messages. But, if the sender comes, then you should worry. But those like us have always sought strange company, is that not so Redriff?"

On considering the company that he had seen with Morden at Euston, Redriff thought that he would not care to be in with it. He remembered the succubus. That was enough for him. His interest in such things drew the line at risking his personal safety. Poor old Haggerston being the horrible example of taking such intercourse too far. Mardyke's incarceration, for the attempted decapitation of Shadwell. Lant's withdrawal. Of all their circle, only the sleek and prosperous Neckinger thrived. Gardening was said to have a good effect on folk. Though, given what the man grew there, the nurture certain growths needed, "good" was questionable. He doubted that it was Battersea where the no-longer-useful canines went, after going three stops past Upton Park.

After taking his leave of Neckinger, who had kindly pressed on him *gratis* a mandrake root with a booklet on raising the plant too, Redriff made his way back to the tube station. There were the same words written on the blackboard as when he had arrived there, no messages either were on the news-sheets. He was expecting something, though unsure of just what.

Redriff got off at London Bridge station—he had decided not to go straight home. It was the third Thursday of the month, and there was the regular meeting of Occultists in the Pub, at a local hostelry. The talks could be, if not instructive, then entertaining. A lecture to be given by a librarian of his acquaintance, a woman surprisingly learned about matters arcane. An hour there would take his mind off things. Being a little early for the start, he took a walk by the Thames through Bankside.

The heat had not abated. Redriff carried his light, linen jacket over his shoulder as he walked slowly through the throng. They were mostly young folk, on school visits from Europe. Italians by the sound and look of them. He had a preference for the Latin sort of woman. Very brief shorts seemed their favoured mode of attire, and he appreciated a long, lithe and well-tanned, female leg. For a moment he recalled his stimulating encounters with the succubus. But then a woman caught his eye, walking just a little way in front of him. Something about the severely-cropped hair, the look of the ageing punk rocker. It was familiar.

She entered into the maw of the surprisingly dark tunnel beneath Southwark Bridge and he lost sight of her. His intent had been to walk as far as the Globe Theatre, then make his way back. It was the crowds, the heat, Redriff told himself, that made him retrace his steps. He looked behind him, several times, to see if anything or anyone, who might possibly had scented his interest, was reciprocating.

Reflected in the dark-glass front of an office building, others walked beside him. Shadowy, uncomfortably close companions that, as he turned slightly the better to see, became one with his reflection in the mirroring glass. This monochrome mirror-world reflected an alternative, negative sun, which diminished to a darker point that was sucking his shade in. Those he saw for a moment distressingly resembled that which had been with Morden. Redriff felt a jolt of panic, but it must only be an optical illusion—a *Fata Morgana*, a mirage caused by this infernal heat. London seemed to have become a liquid, melting city in its grip. And of course, the sun was now beginning its descent into night, way to the west.

The meeting was entertaining, "occultism-lite" as he thought. Ms.

Hand's knowledge of necromancy and related arts was second to none. Redriff had had some acquaintance with her in the past, they knew people incommon. After the lecture, he congratulated the librarian on her presentation. It was a shame that a room above a busy pub in central London was not the place for a practical demonstration of the Endoric rites so graphically described.

"Gosh," said the librarian, "I do hope that my little talk has not encouraged the suggestible among the audience to go out digging around in cemeteries. Bloody hard work, I can tell you, as well as being illegal; and it's no use if the corpse has been embalmed. You can do it just as well on the Internet these days, anyway."

"You are not a traditionalist about these things, then?" asked Redriff.

"Crikey! No. You have to move with the times. It is very romantic, if rather mucky, doing all of that midnight graveyard stuff. But give me a computer screen and the right code word and well...it is amazing just what can be raised. A word to the wise—certain entities are no easier to control. Demons are all over the Internet, have their own websites. You can have Mephistopheles as a Facebook pal now, and don't have to sign a pact in blood. Just pay your Internet provider."

"People don't realise," Redriff agreed, though he rather thought that the librarian was being facetious—one never knew with her. "If you are on Facebook then your soul is already gone. I do get some very odd messages coming through."

"Aetheric peramental entities Redriff. They are coming into their own with the new technology. You knew where you were with the old rites. I'll say that for them. The romance of the witchcraft," she sighed. "I do miss it in a way. The midnight coven, the Goat of Mendes and the Black Man, the sacrifices. The dressing-up Gothic."

"Did you hear about the incident at Greenwich, the attempted decapitation?"

"I am sorry that I did not go. That Mardyke! She does rather go to extremes about these things. But then, I understand that the prospective decapitee—the sacrifice—was, at first, willing. That's the thing that I have found about your sacrificial volunteer, when it gets to the point. A sickle wasn't it? They do tend to have second thoughts. I am in favour of administering a soporific to them before-hand. More humane that way too, and she should have used an axe—much more efficient for decapitations."

"It's a funny thing," said Redriff, thoughtfully, "but I took a stroll down Bankside before coming here tonight and, walking a bit ahead of me and entering the tunnel beneath Southwark Bridge . . . well . . . I was sure that I saw Mardyke."

"She was probably going to the Globe. The Scottish play is on there, and she likes the witches, of course."

"The woman is incarcerated, I believe."

"Hard to keep a girl with her transvection skills in custody. They dropped the charges. That's what I heard anyway."

"Oh," said Redriff.

Someone else engaged Ms. Hand's attention, so Redriff did not have a chance to speak with the librarian more about these send-ings. There was another one, later that evening, when on his way home from the station. He stopped short, seeing these words sprayed upon the metal blinds pulled down over the window of a local barber's shop:

UNWELCOME TO OUR TRYST IN THE DARK. MY
THUMBS PRICK UPON CONSEQUENCE

Redriff remembered those similar lines in the Scottish play. Had that witch Mardyke been going to see it? He did then feel a sort of odd, sympathetic tingle in his thumbs. Was something wicked coming his way? A coincidence perhaps? He had not noticed these rather ominous words when passing by yesterday evening, and the next morning, when going out before the opening of the shop, they were gone, leaving just a smear of red on the metal blind.

Had Mardyke anything to do with this? Perhaps she too was receiving them? Of his old circle, there was only Neckinger, and he had claimed not to have received anything similar. There was no reason for him to deny it, if he had. Redriff had no desire to contact the witch, having always tried to keep her at arm's length, whilst still keeping good relations with her. This, given Mardyke's little ways, could be difficult. She had certainly been a bad influence on Haggerston and Shadwell. There was also the poltergeist phenomena, which seemed to accompany the woman wherever she went. He had not actually witnessed the transvection, though there had been reliable witnesses.

Things in the past, to do with his interests, could have roused certain *energies*, which might in turn have taken note of him. Redriff had drawn away from such activities, but there always remained a residue, and those disturbed by such inquisitiveness were unlikely to forget. He and the others had left what might be called "openings" to such, and he knew how difficult it was to close a door within himself that was susceptible to their intrusion.

As long as there was nothing physical, he should not worry. But the mental thing was another matter, and there was the recollection of what had been with Morden. Had the fellow attracted some form of succubi? Why had he dropped, or been taken, out of sight?

Not so Mardyke, for the woman—or one very much like her— had begun to make an appearance in very different places. There seemed to be a proliferation of women with bad haircuts and grungy punk demeanour all over London. On being confronted by two of them outside of his local supermarket, who aggressively demanded spare change from him, Redriff thought that they might be doppelgängers of the witch. Or was he just noticing something that had been there before?

A few afternoons later, Redriff noticed a lone figure walking just ahead of him down the wide, monotonous, shadeless street. Clothed all over in black, and hard to tell if man or woman, for the appearance was androgynous from the back. Then it was not there. Suddenly switched off, to leave a sort of person-shaped tear in the world that for a long and unnerving moment stood before him, as if inviting his scrutiny, or even entry, into a place of darkness. His recollection of what had been reflected in the office window at Bankside was still vivid. It was not far to his flat and he hurried across the road to it, and there stood at his window to view the world outside.

It was now at that time of late afternoon, when the colours become deeper but less vibrant than full day, as things begin to retreat into themselves as they await the approaching dusk. It was perfectly clear to see though and, even though Redriff's eyesight was very good, he was uncertain of just what he saw on the pavement opposite.

That person-shaped absence—a missing piece in the jigsaw of reality. Like things seen at the blaze of noon, when the sun is in one's eyes and all becomes scintillate black in the dazzle of its rays. Then, in an instant, a piece of that horrible darkness sprang over the road and up towards where Redriff stood watching.

He gasped and stepped back, for the glass of his window was occulted by absence, before this slid slowly down it to reveal that evening had swiftly fallen. In a second it might have been, or had there been some hiatus in time, caused by the shock of seeing this phenomena?

Redriff took a deep breath and fought down a feeling of panic. He had known of such things before, "emanations" they might be called, even witnessed manifestations. Though never had they been like this, or—which was worrying—directed at him in particular. Had his interest in such phenomena been taken too far, and an opening made for these intruders to enter? He could not help but think of those others in that sodality, poor old Haggerston and what had happened to him.

It had been impressed upon him by Lant that such things could not really hurt one, unless they were allowed to. They might feel a certain resentment towards trespassers into their plane. But what could they do, physically, to those that had mastered them? So said the magician. But where was the sceptical occultist now? No one seemed to know.

Carefully he approached and looked out of the now-clear window. There was no sign of a missing piece of the world on the pavement opposite. Indeed, just normal human activity, as people walked there in the early evening. Nor was there any residue of the dark ectoplasmic it might have been, blankness that had covered the glass.

Had Lant been right in his claims about the ineffectuality of the manifestations? They being unable to do anything physical—merely give a fright and not harming, unless one was weak-minded and suggestible? He did not consider himself to be of that number, but it was best to be careful.

Then Redriff saw, gradually appearing, reflected in the glass of the window, a blank, black, featureless face next to his. Indeed, it was emanating from his body in a stream of dark, viscous material that swiftly grew to take the semblance of a human form.

He stood frozen as tentacle-like arms, seemingly birthed from within himself, enclosed him in an embrace. The blackly shining face was close to his, and there was a sucking movement where a mouth should rightfully be, which sought his to give a long, damp and clingingly horrid kiss. It was not that his soul was sucked out, but that whatever that insubstantial thing was had been poured back into him.

Redriff remained for a time unable to move until, hearing a whispering in the room, managed to turn and see the company with him.

At first they had all seemed featureless, as what had embraced him. Black and shiny, clothed all over in glistening eel-like flesh. Despite this outward change, he soon recognised them—Haggerston and Morden. And, most horribly, was that himself too? They spoke, to tell truths about their situation that he found understandably distressing. Slimy hands reached down to help him to stand with them, as his surroundings began to change from a comfortable suburban living room to what might be a very interior place—one that Redriff had really never been out of, as now what had been within was brought forth into the world.

NICHOLAS ROYLE

THE BLINK

NICHOLAS ROYLE is the author of three short story collections—*Mortality, Ornithology* and *The Dummy and Other Uncanny Stories*—and seven novels, from *Counterparts* to *First Novel*. He is series editor of *Best British Short Stories* and a Reader in Creative Writing at the Manchester Writing School at Manchester Metropolitan University, where he is also head judge of the Manchester Fiction Prize.

Nightjar Press, which he founded to publish signed, limited-edition short stories in chapbook format, celebrated its Tenth Anniversary in 2019. A new collection, *London Gothic*, due to have been published by Confingo Publishing in spring 2020, was delayed by the Coronavirus outbreak. The same publisher plans two more collections in subsequent years.

"The inspiration for the story was a news item about a similar incident that occurred in a BBC drama," recalls Royle, "which got me thinking."

"For the writing of the story I applied a simple constraint to the process: all the scenes had to be the same length. Applying constraints can have a liberating effect when, for whatever reason, it might have become more difficult to write, or complete, short stories."

∞

I'M HAVING A drink with Gina Hamilton in a hotel bar in Manchester.

"This place has changed," she says.

"You haven't," I say. "You look as gorgeous as ever."

When she smiles she reveals her front teeth, one of which leans slightly back and the other slightly forward.

"I hope you don't mind me coming to see you," she says.

I refill her glass. "I can honestly say I've never minded you coming to see me."

She smiles, then looks away; the smile vanishes.

"I had to get out of London," she says. "I couldn't go out. Wherever I went, they were after me."

I look into my wine glass. "You have to admit, it was pretty funny."

"I can't understand why nobody saw it," she says.

"Plenty of people have seen it. It went viral."

"I mean before it went out. You know what I mean. The editor, the director. God, even the bloody critics."

"Maybe one of them did. Imagine you're a TV critic and you see that. What would you do? E-mail the programme-makers in the vain hope they can fix it before it goes out or write it up and hope it stays in? It's good copy."

Gina had always wanted to be an actress—and I do mean actress. This was when not only were you *allowed* to use the word, but it was the word you were *supposed* to use. If you were a girl—and I do mean girl—and you said you wanted to be an actor, people would have, as Gina once put it, looked at you funny. Hers was the first hand to go up at school when volunteers were sought for the end-of-year production. At university she was so busy at Dramsoc she narrowly avoided being kicked off her course for poor attendance. I was studying journalism, Gina English, so we wouldn't even have met had we not been in the same hall. I used to leave my door open and I'd see her walking past, nose in a book. I asked what was so good that she couldn't put it down. It was a play script, covered in highlighter. I said I'd go and see it if she let me know when and where. She did and here we are, thirty years later.

If, in the past couple of decades, I've seen more of Gina on TV than in the flesh, that's mostly a reflection of how her career took off. If she was filming in the north she would let me know—sometimes—and we would have a drink and a catch-up. When my on-off relationship with a Chorlton psychotherapist was off—and sometimes, if I'm honest, when I wasn't sure if it was on or off—Gina and I might allow the evening to be extended into the night.

"It's also good publicity," I say, upending the bottle over Gina's glass. "Shall I get us another? I'll get another."

I go to the bar. As I'm waiting I fiddle with a pack of breath mints and watch someone enter the bar. I'm not sure if it's a man or a woman. My attention is drawn to the figure's awkward progress towards the bar. I'm going to go with female, even while no doubt breaking a dozen social codes by wanting to nail down gender. She moves like she's already drunk—I'll be surprised if they serve her—or has had to learn to walk again after a stroke. There's a deliberateness about the placing of her feet. Even the swing of her arms looks practised.

"That's just £29.00, sir."

I turn back to the bar and look at the young man behind it placing an opened bottle of white wine on the counter.

"Just?" I say and pop a mint into my mouth.

"You ordered the Sauvignon, sir. The house is only nineteen."

"Only?"

He looks at me blankly.

"Contactless?" I say.

I take the bottle of wine back to our table and notice that Gina is looking at the new arrival with an expression approaching alarm.

"Shit," she says.

The thing was that Gina *was* making fewer appearances on TV whether I realised it or not. The offers weren't drying up but the gaps between parts were getting longer. I blame the effects of the ageing process on me for my not realising this, time seeming to pass more quickly, meaning that I telescoped six months into as many weeks, and the reason for the lengthening gaps should have been obvious to me.

Apparently I'm unusual in finding middle-aged women more interesting to look at and, yes, more attractive. Most people—most men?—prefer to look at younger women in films and TV dramas where the part is a middle-aged woman, or should be. So either the part is written for a younger woman or it's written for a middle-aged woman and a younger woman is found to play it. Either way, it gets harder for middle-aged "female actors" to find parts, so, hoping for regular work, maybe Gina and other actresses started going for parts they might not otherwise have gone for.

The Academy of Motion Picture Arts and Sciences still gives awards to the Best Actress in a Leading Role and the Best Actress in a Supporting Role, but for how much longer? What about Princess Grace of Monaco, who won an Oscar in 1955? Must we call her Prince Grace of Monaco? What about Princess Diana? Princess Anne? The rap artist known as Actress, and Princess Michael of Kent?

I'm pouring her a glass of wine, but Gina has an elbow on the table and a hand in front of her face.

"She's seen me," she says. "I know she has."

"Who has?"

"Woman at the bar who's just come in. She's one of them."

"That's what we used to say, isn't it, 'one of them', or what our parents used to say? What do we say now? LGBT."

"LGBTQ," she says with a half-smile.

"LGBTQQ," I say.

Gina looks at me from under her shielding hand. "LGBTQQI."

"Hmm." I narrow my eyes and purse my lips. "LGBTQQIS."

"S?"

"Straight. Apparently. So my friend Tony told me yesterday."

"Is your friend Tony slightly homophobic?"

"Well, he was sitting next to his husband when he told me, so I doubt it."

"Oh God, look, she's on her mobile." Gina is looking over my shoulder.

"So?"

"She'll be rounding up all her mates." Gina knocks back the rest of her wine.

"That's thirty quid a bottle," I say.

It did go viral, but let me remind you. Gina had a part in a crime drama. ITV, post-watershed, I forget the name of it, but aren't they all essentially the same, especially on ITV? The body of a woman is found, usually a young woman, as discussed. Crime scene tape. Flashing blue lights. SoCos in white suits. A white tent. SIO, distinctive in some way—we'll get to know her in a short scene at home later. Bluff pathologist—seen it all. Rookie policewoman, maybe.

Gina turns up half an hour in. She's a witness. Her character is barely sketched in—good job, nice husband, couple of kids—and then she's killed in an RTA that is probably not an accident. She's on the slab in the morgue, just lying there while the SIO and the pathologist exchange a few lines of dialogue across her legs. She's covered up, for modesty, but her face is exposed and she blinks.

How come, as Gina says, no one saw it? No one on set, no one looking at the rushes. The editor doesn't see it later. The director doesn't see it. No one sees it who is connected with the production. Unbelievable.

Yet thousands of viewers see it. Social media goes crazy. People take the piss, because it's funny. But then it gets serious, when the aggrieved voices make themselves heard and their owners start mobilising, and it's not so funny any more and Gina gets out of town.

Gina's hands grip the sides of the table and she starts to lever herself up, but then I'm aware of movement behind me. The woman from the bar draws level.

"Excuse me," she says in a harsh, cracked voice.

Gina sits back down, her features flat with resignation.

"Do you mind if I ask," the woman says, "are you Gina Hamilton?" The skin of her face, lit by the candle on our table, is papery. There's the faint scent of Listerine on the air that briefly masks an underlying smell of soap, formaldehyde and the flowers of those invasive Himalayan plants that grow by the river.

Gina looks up, raises her eyebrows.

"Would you like to sit down?" I ask the woman, who ignores me. They don't so much like sitting down; standing, walking and lying down are more their thing. Lying down I get. I'm not so sure about the standing and walking, and wonder if it might not be a bit of PR. Gina looks at me.

I'm aware of shapes passing by outside the windows, then a group appears at the entrance to the bar, their white faces turning this way and that like searchlights. One of them points in our direction and they start to move across the room, bumping into tables, causing eyerolls and tuts among drinkers. It's like the remake of *Night of the Living Dead* that Mike Leigh always promised he wouldn't do.

Their first campaign revolved around extras. Bodies on battlefields or at crime scenes. Corpses in the morgue, toes with labels sticking out of sheets, having assumed no previous active role in the drama. Only dead actors should play these parts, they said, and their campaign, aggressively mounted, quickly gained momentum. A live actor playing such a part very soon became the equivalent of a white actor blacking up.

Until Gina's blink, a live actor playing a live part who then dies and, crucially, enjoys a certain amount of screen time dead had been a grey area. Dead actors argued they should play the part, either in a switch at the point of death, which would require body-doubling or lots of expensive make-up, or right from the start. Live actors maintained that that was ridiculous: the dead couldn't convincingly play the living, while the living could easily handle lying still.

The blink changed all that.

"It's our *Philadelphia*," said the dead, referring to Tom Hanks' portrayal of gay lawyer with AIDS Andrew Beckett, a part that, it was argued by some, should have been played by a gay actor.

Good luck finding an openly gay actor in Hollywood in 1993.

"Do you think it was right?" the woman asks Gina. "Do you think you were the right actor for that role? I don't think so. We don't think so." Having been leaning forward to deliver her rebuke to Gina, she now straightens up at the waist and takes a half-step back as if to become one with the mob that has gathered around her.

For all the potency of George Romero's images of shambling hordes, they were, as we now know, a guess. The dead are not especially sociable. They don't hang out together and the living tend not to encounter them in groups. The effect of being this close to a large group of them now begins to show on Gina's face, which wears an expression of mild disgust. She gets to her feet and moves sideways around the table, so that it forms a barrier between her and them. Feeling at a strange disadvantage remaining seated, I also get up, but from the wrong side of my chair, so that I end up standing with the group looking across the table at Gina. She looks at me, it seems to me, accusingly. I suck on the last of my mint and feel myself shrugging back at her.

JOHN LANGAN

THE DEEP SEA SWELL

J OHN LANGAN's most recent book is a collection of stories,
Children of the Fang and Other Genealogies. He lives in New
York's Mid-Hudson Valley with his wife, younger son, and an office
full of books which are slowly multiplying.

"'The Deep Sea Swell' is rooted in the single trip my wife and I
took to see an old college friend of hers in Shetland the winter after
we were married," he explains. "Although we spent only a few days
on Shetland and its surrounding islands, the visit played a role in the
composition of my first novel, which drew its title from the name of
an abandoned house just outside Lerwick, and also this story, whose
account of a ferry ride back to Scotland during a winter storm at sea
is closer to fact than I wish were the case.

"Some of its other details are drawn from my stay on Shetland,
too. There's at least one more story inspired by that trip waiting to be
written. Funny, the things that stay with us."

"It may be that the gulfs will wash us down"
—Alfred, Lord Tennyson 'Ulysses'

I F SHE HADN'T argued with the man, Susan thinks, they could
have been in a first-class cabin, instead of down here, at the

193

bottom of the bloody ferry. The floor tilts forwards. There's a great swooshing sound, the sensation of plunging down a steep slope, the briefest of pauses, and a tremendous *bang*! that rattles the ship's hull. Slowly, the floor levels, then tilts backwards. The swooshing returns, accompanied now by the feeling of being on a roller-coaster as it climbs a sheer set of tracks. Somewhere near, somewhere inside the ferry, Susan hears the steady drone of a motor. The sweet stink of fuel (diesel?) swirls near the floor, below the bunk on which she's lying. On the bunk above, her husband snores intermittently. The Dramamine they took an hour ago knocked Alan out, the lucky bastard; whereas all it did for Susan was sand the edges off the dizziness and nausea, freeing her mind to run through every disaster-at-sea movie she's seen, from *Titanic* to *The Poseidon Adventure* to that cheesy horror film, what was it called, *Leviathan*? Something like that.

The sail up from Aberdeen wasn't this bad, not nearly. She'd never been on a ferry like this before. The nearest thing had been the ship they'd taken out to Martha's Vineyard on their honeymoon, which was maybe half the size of this one? Less than that? This was a proper ocean-going vessel, built to cross the roughly two hundred nautical miles between the north-east of Scotland and the Shetlands, which, as Alan delighted in saying, lay closer to Norway than they did the UK. There was something romantic about travelling by ship, she'd thought, a notion of taking your time, enjoying the journey as well as the destination. They spent much of the journey in bed, trying to work out the mechanics of sex on a surface that was rising and falling with the sea. She was "Sexy Susan", the sailor's friend; he was "Able Alan", always up for adventure.

That was in the first-class cabin to which they'd been upgraded after she passed one of the ship's crew a twenty-pound note. She'd been quite pleased with the luxury, which consisted primarily of a room done in 1970s-era panelling and set high enough in the ship to have its own window, but less so once they'd been in Lerwick for a day and Alan's university friend, Giorgio, informed her that, as long as there were cabins available, the ferry staff were supposed to upgrade passengers free of charge. "They pocket the money, you know," Giorgio said, which had let the air out of her self-satisfaction, and left her determined not to be taken advantage of again. In turn, this led to her challenging the crew member who requested twenty quid for a boost to first class lodgings on the return voyage. (Possibly, it was the same man: several of the staff appeared related, cousins or even brothers—short, broad fellows wearing grey sweater-vests under their blue blazers and over their shirt-and-ties, their faces red, their curly hair black yielding to grey.) "You know," Susan said, "one of my friends in Lerwick told me an upgrade to first class is supposed to be no charge."

"Did they?" the man said, raising his bushy eyebrows as if to indicate his surprise at such a statement.

"Yeah," she said, nodding.

"Well..." The man smiled, shrugging and spreading his hands.

"My friend said you guys keep the money."

Whatever warmth was in the man's performance chilled. "It's twenty pounds," he said.

Which was how they descended she isn't certain how many flights of stairs to the corridor that brought them here, to a narrow room with bare white walls and a pair of economy-sized bunk-beds in it. "Think of it this way," Alan said, "we're experiencing the full range of travel options."

Those options included a mid-winter storm, whose centre lay somewhere to the east, but which had stirred the North Sea to a tumult. They climbed to the dining area, but already, Alan was queasy and opted for a cup of tea and a packet of digestive biscuits, leaving Susan to order a Coke and the fish and chips, which she ate half of before a sudden squall of nausea caused her to set down her knife and fork and not pick them up again. The two of them tried sitting in the large padded chairs positioned in front of the wall of windows that looked out over the ferry's stern, but night had fallen hours ago, with the heavy blackness of early January at a northern latitude. All that was visible was an expanse of blackness with a cluster of orange lights twinkling in the far distance that Alan thought was an oil rig. Although the sea was more sound than sight, the rise and fall of those lights added a visual dimension to the ferry's see-sawing movement. "Next time Giorgio wants to see us," Alan said, "we'll fly." It was an extravagant promise: the tickets from Edinburgh weren't too far shy of what it had cost them to cross the Atlantic from Newark.

"Or he can take the ferry," Susan said.

Not long after, they descended the stairs to their cabin a second time. Gazing out the windows wasn't doing anything for him, Alan said, and Susan agreed. The more she stared at it, the more uneasy the dark outside—its sheer thoroughness—made her, until she could feel panic nipping at the edges of her mind. "It's as if we're already at the bottom of the sea," she said.

"Whoa," Alan said, "touch wood," knocking the chair's armrest. "Although," he added, "it's pretty deep, here. I imagine it's calm, down there."

"You just have to go through the whole drowning thing," Susan said.

"Will you *stop*?" Alan said, rapping the armrest again.

"You and your superstitions."

"The middle of the ocean is not the place to test them."

She supposed he had a point.

In the cabin, they dry-swallowed the Dramamine tablets Susan had in her bag and climbed into their bunks. Alan sang, "Yo-ho, blow the man down, yo-ho, blow the man down."

"Now who's tempting fate?" she said.

"It's only a song," he said, his words slurring as the pill tugged him into unconsciousness.

"Remember that when we're saying hi to King Neptune."

"Hey..." he began. The rest of his reply disappeared into a mumble.

Despite herself, Susan knocked on the cabin wall. It wasn't wood, but it was the best she had.

The next hour passed with stomach-churning monotony. The ferry rose and fell, rose and fell. Alan snored, snorted, went back to snoring. The distant engine churned steadily. In the corridor outside the cabin, a little girl's voice asked a question Susan couldn't decipher. The ocean rushed along the hull. A woman, likely the girl's mother, said they were just going for a wee lie down. The smell of fuel made Susan's nostrils bristle. Someone laughed as they passed the cabin. The ship slid down into a pause that lasted a second too long, as if the waves were weighing whether to let the vessel continue its descent, all the way down. A woman, the same one from before, said she was just going to the toilet. The sea smacked the ship like a giant's hand, *bang!*

In an odd sort of way, Susan has thought, this trip has been all about the ocean, salt water threading its way through her and Alan's winter vacation like a recurring theme in a longer piece of music. The flight across the north Atlantic was only the second time she had traversed the ocean, and she spent the daylight hours of the voyage gazing out the scuffed and scratched window beside her seat at the corrugated grey expanse visible through the gaps in the clouds below. Alan's parents' house in North Queensferry was one of a half-dozen on a cul-de-sac set on a high bluff overlooking the stretch where the Forth River merged with the North Sea. The sea was a constant companion as they drove their tiny rental up Scotland's east coast, stopping for an early lunch at an Indian place outside St. Andrew's, a wander around the ruins at Stonehaven, and then a couple of days in Aberdeen, revisiting Alan's university haunts and a few of his friends who had settled in the city. With one of those friends and his partner, they walked a rocky beach washed by the waves they would ride to Shetland, where Alan's friend Giorgio ran a small chip shop overlooking Lerwick harbour.

Once they were ashore on Shetland, however, something about the sea changed—or, to be more accurate, something about her perception of it shifted. The afternoon of their arrival, Giorgio took them for a quick jaunt to a spot where the land on either side of them shrank towards the road, until they were between a pair of narrow beaches onto which water splashed in long foaming rolls. "On that side," Giorgio said, pointing right, "is the North Sea. On this side," pointing left, "is the Atlantic." No matter where they went, it seemed, salt water was visible. When she mentioned this to Giorgio, trying to keep her tone light, carefree, he nodded and said, "Aye, someone told me once you're never more than three miles from open water on Shetland." No doubt the landscape of the island, low hills bare of trees, contributed to the sensation, but she began to feel horribly exposed, surrounded by the ocean, which, if you thought about it, could rise and wash over the place without much effort at all.

Nor did the stories Giorgio liked to tell help matters. An amateur historian of the Shetlands and their surrounds, he possessed a seemingly endless supply of narratives about the islands. In the majority of them, the sea figured prominently. They would begin with a bold, almost ridiculous assertion. "You know," he would say over drinks at one of the pubs, "Shetland was part of the actual Atlantis." Then, as she and Alan coughed their beers, he would raise his hands and say, "No, I'm not talking about that Disney rubbish. I mean Doggerland. You've heard of it, yeah? No? Ten, eleven thousand years ago, during the last ice age, all the seas were lower. The water was bound up in the glaciers, right? From Shetland down to Orkney and Scotland, over to Europe, was dry land. You could walk across the North Sea, the English Channel, and folk did. There was a whole civilisation spread across the place. As the ice started to melt, though, the sea crept closer. Some of the archaeologists think it was a process of years, decades, and that the people living there had plenty of time to pack their things and leave. I've heard others say it was more catastrophic, an ice-dam broke and sent hundreds of millions of gallons of water rushing through all this low-lying land. That's where your story of Atlantis comes from."

Another afternoon, as they were sitting in Giorgio's car on a local (smaller) ferry from the main island to the neighbouring island of Yell, Giorgio said, "When you were coming up, did you notice there was a point the sea went all choppy—I mean, worse than what you'd been used to?"

Susan and Alan exchanged glances. Had they? "Maybe," Alan said.

"Aye, that was you passing Fair Isle," Giorgio said. "The sea behaves funny there, has to do with currents or some such. You know there was a fellow drowned out there? This was during my granddad's time. It was a man from away down in Edinburgh, a professor—

from Edinburgh University, must have been. He was an anthro-
pologist, studied the prehistoric sites in the north of Scotland, the
Orkneys, up Shetland way. This chap took an interest in Fair Isle—
in the ocean floor off the island. Something had washed up on one
of the island's beaches, and it found its way into this professor's
hands. I'm not sure what it was, but it got the man all worked up.
He decided he needed to have a look under the water next to the
island. This was none of your scuba diving; this was one of those
suits with the big round helmet and the hose up to a boat on the
surface. Fellow hired a couple of locals out of Aberdeen to man the
boat and mind the air pump, and another pair of lads from Fair
Isle to help them. The lot of them took the boat to the spot the
professor had calculated was the best bet to search for more of whatever it was brought him there in the first place. Over the side he
went. This was what you'd call a low-tech rig, no diver's telephone.
Well. Maybe an hour into the professor's dive, a storm blew in. The
sky went dark, the wind rose, and the next anyone knew, the rain
was bucketing down, the waves spilling over the sides. It's no fun
to be in a big ship when the weather turns against you, and this
boat was far from big. At first, the lads thought they could ride out
the storm. I gather they gave it their best, but it wasn't long before
they realised that this was not a workable plan. The sea was heaving,
and none of them had the experience to maintain their position in
these conditions. They tried to contact the professor—there was no
telephone, right, but they had this system of bells he'd set up for
basic communication. One bell on the boat, and a tiny one in the
helmet. I'm not sure exactly how it worked. Morse Code, I'm
guessing—had to be. Anyway, as things went from bad to worse
topside, the crew was signalling the professor, *SOS, come back*. If
he heard them, he didn't answer. Now the boat was riding waves
halfway to vertical. Water was foaming onto the deck from every
side. It was all the lads could do to keep from being swept overboard. And still no response from the professor. Funny, the things
you'll do in a crisis. One of the crew grabbed a hatchet and, *chop*,
cut the diving suit's air hose. That was the end for the professor.
You have to hope he found whatever he was looking for."

Susan said, "That's terrible. What happened to the crew?"

"Oh," Giorgio said, "they made it back safely. Went straight to the police and confessed everything. Only problem was, each man said he was the one had picked up the hatchet, and nothing anyone could threaten or promise would persuade any of them to change his story. In the end, none of them was charged, and the professor's death was ruled an accident. The body was never recovered."

Still a third time, as they were treating Giorgio to dinner at a nice restaurant in a small hotel located on the shore of a slender inlet, he set down his salad fork and said, "There's a ghost in this hotel, you know, right in this very room. A woman dressed in a long dark-green dress and a short jacket, with a little hat. Like the style women wore at the beginning of the last century. She sits at one of the tables over there." He pointed to an alcove at the other end of the dining area. "It's always after the last customer has left, and one of the staff is cleaning up. I used to date a lassie had seen her on two separate occasions. The first time, she ran out of the room as if the Devil himself was clutching at her heels with his pointy nails. The second time, Colleen (that was the lassie's name) stayed put. She said the woman stood, turned around, and walked to the door. Her face was in shadow, that was the way Colleen described it. She couldn't manage a good look at her. She said the woman passed through the door, the way you hear ghosts doing. Colleen ran to the door and opened it. Although it was late, this was during the summer, so there was plenty of light for her to watch the woman cross the lawn to the water and keep going, out into it until she was gone, submerged, hat and all. No one knows who she is, or was. Another drowning victim, right? Sometimes I wonder, though: what if we have it backwards? What I'm trying to say is, instead of someone who used to live on land returning to it, maybe it's someone, or something, whose home is the water coming up to have a look and see what all the fuss is about."

"Really?" Susan said.

"No," Giorgio said, "I'm just speaking out my arse. Still, the ocean is deep and dark and full of secrets, right? Isn't there a saying to the effect that we know more about outer space than we do the bottom of the sea?"

"I don't know," Alan said, "sounds good, though."

"Aye, so it does," Giorgio said.

Between Giorgio's stories, and the omnipresent water rolling to the horizon, Susan found herself revising her opinions of life beside the ocean. Since she and Alan had met at a mutual friend's house in Bourne, on the mainland side of the Cape Cod canal, Susan had declared it her fondest wish to return to the area to buy a house overlooking the ocean. It was a favourite fantasy, one she indulged by scrolling through online real-estate listings. That such houses were out of their price range by a factor of several hundred per cent was of no real concern. Alan was doing well enough at his architecture firm to make the daily commute to Manhattan worthwhile, and the director of Penrose College's art museum was sufficiently pleased with her performance to hire Susan full-time. They saved what they could, and eventually, they would be in a position to afford a place in Bourne, or further out on the actual Cape, in Orleans or even Wellfleet. In the meantime, they had their friend's house to return to. Her dream was in part a declaration of loyalty to the place where she and Alan had so improbably found one another. But she also fancied the Cape an appropriate symbol for the relationship they had discovered, a place of fundamentals, land and sea and sky. Not once had it occurred to her that part of the reason she could appreciate the Bay at Scusset Beach was because the entire continent was behind her, thousands of miles of mountains and hills, cities and plains. Even way out on the end of the Cape, in Provincetown, there was the sense of being connected to something larger, a solid mass of land. Five days on Shetland, and she had learned that being on the margin between sand and water was a different thing from being surrounded by the ocean. Giorgio diagnosed what she described to him as island fever. "It's not for everyone, living up here," he said. "The sea..." He shrugged, as if the word was explanation enough.

Bang! As if making Giorgio's point, the water smacks the hull directly outside her bunk, from the sound of it. The metal groans, a loud complaint that lasts an ominous length of time. Susan stares at the wall next to her. The dread she's been managing since they sailed into the storm surges within her. Her heart breaks into a full gallop. Should she wake Alan, grab their bags, head for the upper decks, closer to the lifeboats? She doesn't know. She can't draw enough air into her lungs. The edges of her vision darken. She's burning up. The panic attack isn't the first she's had, but it's without doubt the worst. She can't keep lying down; she's suffocating. She throws off her blanket, sits up as the ferry begins another slide down down down . . . She grips the edge of her bunk, braces her feet against the floor. *Bang!* The ship protests, asking how much more of this abuse it's expected to take. Susan has to get out of here. She grabs Alan's bunk, uses it to haul herself to standing. On the other side of the hull, water swooshes as the floor tilts back. She crosses to the door in four lurching steps, opens it, and exits the cabin.

The corridor outside the room is empty, the rest of the cabin doors shut. No sign of the little girl and her mother, the laughing passer-by. Susan isn't so distracted she can't think, *Well, good for them.* One hand on the wall, she turns left, towards the stairs. The ferry levels, tips, lunges. The wool socks she's wearing slide on the floor. She flattens on the wall. *Bang!* The impact shudders through her. While the ship tilts to climb the next swell, she scuttles along the wall as fast as her feet and hands will move her, which isn't as fast as she'd like, but it occupies her while the ferry slides up and then down. *Bang!* By the time the ship has summited the following waves, Susan has reached the doorway to the stairs. *Alan*, a distant part of her mind objects, *what about Alan?* She plunges into the stairwell.

It's like trying to play some demented fun-house game, climbing the stairs as they rock this way, then that. Although each stair is covered in studs to aid traction, they benefit her socks little, and she clings to the guard-rail with both hands. The acoustics of the space make it sound as if the water streaming past the ship is filling the stairwell, while each *bang!* shivers all the stairs at once. She manages four flights, two decks, before she has to abandon the stair-well.

As she emerges into a corridor more or less the same as the one she left, the lights dim, then brighten, then go out. "Oh, come on," she says. With a click, emergency lights pop on at either end of the corridor. "Thank you." She backs against the wall to her left and slides down it until she's sitting. Her heart is still racing, but the short excursion she's taken has left her exhausted. Maybe it's the Dramamine having more effect, too. If it weren't for her pulse jackhammering, she'd swear she would pass out right here. She places her hands on the floor to either side of her to help with the ferry's relentless rocking, which feels as if it's grown worse. *We must be close to Fair Isle*, she thinks. *Isn't that the place Giorgio said the sea was especially rough?*

Another *bang!* and a horrible smell floods her nostrils. She claps her hand over her mouth. For an instant, she wonders if a sewage pipe has broken under the waves' pounding, only to reject the idea. This is not the pungent stink of shit. It's the reek of a beach—of a North Atlantic beach at low tide, a medley of decaying flesh and baking plant matter. Tears blur her eyes. At the same time, the temperature in the corridor drops, heat escaping as if out a hole in the ferry's side. The cold that swirls into its place is thick, gelid. There's something else, a note in the atmosphere that reminds her of nothing so much as the worst arguments she and Alan have had, when hostility foams and froths between them. Malice washes over her. She swallows, shakes her head.

To her left, movement on the floor draws her eye. An eel, long and skinny, slides away from her. It isn't an eel: it's a length of hose, dun-coloured, the end closest to her ragged, vomiting water as it moves. That's the source of the awful smell, the cracked and peeling hose that's being dragged towards and through the doorway at the far end of the corridor, making a sound halfway between a hiss and a breath. She can't see what's on the other side of the threshold; the emergency lights cast a veil of brightness her vision cannot pierce.

Even were she not schooled in hundreds of horror films, Susan would know that following the foul-smelling hose to whatever is dragging it would be a bad idea. In fact, she has no intention of hanging around this location one second longer than is necessary. She pushes to her feet, and staggers up the corridor to the exit to the stairs.

Up or down? She opts to climb. It's slow going. The stairs are like an enormous metronome. She loses her footing twice, has to clutch the railing to keep from tumbling down. Her heart is still pounding, her skin burning, but she isn't sure if it's from the panic attack continuing or her brush with what was standing beyond the lights at the other end of the corridor. *Or both*, she thinks, one of her favourite rhetorical sayings returning to haunt her: *Why does it have to be either/or? Why can't it be both/and?* When the water smacks the hull, the *bang!* echoes through the stairwell like thunder. The best Susan can do is two flights of stairs, and then she stumbles out the doorway to the next deck. The motion of the ship combines with her slick footing to send her into the wall opposite; she catches most of the impact with her arms, but the force drops her to one knee.

At least the lights are working properly on this level. That revelation, however, is accompanied by another: the terrible smell permeates the air here, too, and with it are the same cold and the same impression of overwhelming malevolence. A noise equal parts a breath and a hiss jerks her head up, to watch a peeling and cracked hose snaking along the floor. *How...?* The thing drawing the hose towards it halts the thought. Susan has the impression of a figure the approximate size and shape of a man, its hide studded with barnacles, strung with seaweed, a single round eye staring out of its misshapen head. Hatred rolls off it in waves. Before her mind can process what she's looking at, she's back in the stairwell, her legs propelled not so much by fear as by some deeper impulse, something that precedes and pre-empts rational thought. (*How...?*) The same response sends her down the stairs, flight after flight, until she's back where she started, at the deck where Alan lies slumbering on his bunk in their cabin. *Alan:* for the first time in what feels an eternity, she thinks of her husband as more than a name. What if he woke to find her missing? What if he went in search of her, and encountered whatever is stalking the hallways? Fear for him runs down her spine like ice water. She staggers across the tilting floor into the corridor.

The monster is waiting for her. It swipes at her with oversized hands, and would probably have her if her feet didn't slip and dump her on her ass. The pain registers dimly; she's already scooting backwards, her attempted escape hindered by the floor tilting her towards the monster. It leans to grab her legs, spilling a rain of tiny green crabs onto them. Susan jerks her legs back, avoiding the thing's grasp, and slaps at the crabs scrambling over her pyjamas. She twists onto her stomach, crawls for the stairwell. The ferry levels, and she pushes to her feet. Stiff-legged as Frankenstein's monster, the thing lurches after her. The floor slopes forwards. Struggling not to lose control of her balance, she slides on the soles of her socks, as if ice-skating. The monster's feet clatter behind her. She's almost at the stairwell. The sea pounds the ferry, *bang!* The monster reaches, catches her left arm, and swings her in a long arc all the way around it into the wall. She tries to get her right arm up to protect her head, but she still sees a brilliant flash of white, feels the impact rattle her teeth. The monster releases her arm, steps in close, catches her by the shoulders. She's spun to face it, pressed against the wall by heavy hands.

This close, the stench brings her to the verge of fainting. Arctic cold envelops her, extinguishing the remaining heat the panic attack kindled in her skin. She twists from side to side, trying to loosen the thing's hold on her, but its grip is unbreakable. Its eye flashes. Malice batters her, its ferocity utter, unrelenting. She turns her head from the thing, closes her eyes—

—and she is somewhere else, a place mostly dark, here and there dim, an expanse of bare mud ornamented with rocks. Shadowy forms, each the size of a large dog, float languidly in the air, and she sees that they're fish, which means she's underwater, from the look of things, somewhere deep. In front of her and to the right, maybe twenty yards away, a light spreads a yellow cone through the murk. It's a large flashlight, carried in one hand by a figure wearing a diving suit, rounded helmet and all. Its air hose rising behind it, its heavy boots raising clouds of mud, it trudges towards a low heap of rocks. Long,

rectangular, the rocks have a consistency of size and shape that gives them the appearance of having been carved into their present forms. When the flashlight's beam illuminates designs grooved into their surfaces, Susan understands that she's looking at an archaeological site, that she's watching the protagonist of Giorgio's Fair Isle diver story as he sees the object of his expedition. (Which means...) His flashlight ranges over the stones, picking out symbols she doesn't recognise, concentric circles, a triangle with rounded corners, a crescent like a smile. Other characters are obscured by mud and algae. The arrangement of the stones suggests that they've fallen over onto one another. Before one of them, the diver stops, directs the flashlight to a spot immediately in front of him. Something flashes in the mud. Slowly, ponderously, the diver kneels, reaching down with his free hand. He brushes away a layer of mud, and as he does, sends a small white object tumbling up from its resting-place. It's a wonder that he's able to catch it, but catch it he does, and holds it up for view. Susan is too far away to see his discovery in much detail. It's circular, the diameter of a saucer, composed of a white material that shines in the flashlight beam. The diver turns it over, examines the other side, then slides it into a bag hung down his chest. He rises and continues towards the piled stones. As he draws closer to them, his flashlight seeks out the gaps between the rectangles. What it reveals quickens his pace. At the pile, he bends forwards, bringing his helmet as close as he can manage to one of the larger spaces between them, holding the flashlight beside his helmet. He slides his other hand into the gap. Whatever he's after resists his efforts. He withdraws the flashlight and turns to the side, to extend his reach. He doesn't see the slender white hand shoot out from the space and grab his arm. By the time he's aware of the contact, the hand has pressed his arm further down into the gap, where the space narrows, wedging it there. The diver pulls back, but his arm is stuck fast. The hand retreats amidst the stones. The diver releases his flashlight, which is looped to his wrist, and attempts to use that hand to pull the other free. It's no use. He pulls; he pushes. He shakes his trapped hand with such fury, Susan can imagine his screams ringing in his helmet. He stops, lets go of his hand and turns as best he can to look behind him. Undulating like a sea serpent, the

*air hose to his suit descends the water, bubbles venting from its torn
end as it falls. Frantically, the diver flails at the back of his suit, where
the hose attaches, but he can't manoeuvre his arm to it. Even if he
could grab hold of the hose, it's hard to see what good that would do
him. The same thought appears to occur to the diver, who surrenders
his attempt. As the hose snakes across the mud, he turns again to the
stone heap, sagging against it, his helmet coming to rest above the
space that has trapped him. If he isn't dead already, he will be soon.
The white hand steals from between the stones and trails its fingers
across his faceplate, almost lovingly—*

Susan recoils from the sight, and confronts the monster holding
her, which, she sees, is no monster, but the diving suit in which
Giorgio's professor met his watery end. The barnacles, the seaweed,
the tiny green crabs scuttling across it, are the yield of decades
beneath the water, as are the dents that have misshapen the helmet,
the cracks that spider-web the face-plate's glass. It has looped the
hose around itself like a bandoleer. She can't say if there's anything
left of the suit's former inhabitant, though she doubts it. What has
remained is his anger, his rage at having made the find of his career,
of his life, and then been abandoned to death. Contained in the
suit, that fury, burning with the blinding flame of an underwater
welder's torch, has sustained it, has maintained its integrity long
after time, salt water, and the ministrations of a thousand ocean
creatures should have dissolved it.

It is terrifying; she has to escape it. She drives the heel of her
right palm into the face-plate, hears a chorus of snaps. The helmet
draws back, as if surprised. She strikes again, missing the face-plate,
hitting the metal beside it with a hollow *bong*. A surge of hatred
blasts her. When she tries to hit the thing a third time, it releases
her left shoulder to swat her hand away. It catches her by the throat
and squeezes. Never mind that she was years from birth when the
professor drowned, that she hasn't the slightest connection to this
tragedy. She is here now, the accident of her presence as good a
reason for the thing's hostility as any. Fingers thick and cold dig
into her neck. She grabs its hand, searching to pry open its grip. It
is inhumanly strong. She cannot breathe. Her vision contracts.

Somewhere distant, the sea strikes the ferry's hull, *bang!* She lets go of the hand, opts for another round of blows, punching the suit's shoulders, chest, striking the hose wound around it, searching for a last-second vulnerability. Her knuckles tear on barnacles, slip on seaweed, rebound from the hose wrapping it. *Oh, Alan,* she thinks. Her arms feel incredibly heavy. She can't have much time left. *Goddamn it,* she thinks, *Goddamn it,* the curse summoning a last surge of strength. Muscles screaming for oxygen, she punches as hard and fast as she can: *One-two-three-four.*

With a crack, her right fist connects with an object that breaks under its impact. There's a burst of something between them, a soundless explosion. The hands at her neck and shoulder fall away. Gasping for air, Susan collapses into the wall, her fists still out in a trembling attempt at a guard. The diver steps away from her, its hands pushing aside the hose, searching through the seaweed decorating its chest, to a woven bag hung from its neck. Within the bag, the shards of a white disk slide against one another. The damage to the bag's contents confirmed, the diver's hands drop to its sides. The cold is bleeding from the air, taking with it the awful smell. The figure retreats another pace. Its malevolence gutters and puffs out. Susan has the impression of something behind the suit, retreating at great speed through the wall, out of the ship, an impossible distance. On slightly unsteady legs, the diver lumbers to the exit and proceeds into the stairwell. Its heavy boots clank on the metal stairs.

Susan feels no desire to follow. With a kind of visionary certainty, she knows that the diver is going to continue its climb until it reaches a level that admits to the ferry's exterior. If enough of the force that animated it remains, it will walk to a bulwark, lean forwards, and allow the weight of its helmet to carry it over into the heaving waves. If not, one or the other of the crewmembers will come across an astonishing discovery, the remains of an old diving suit, apparently washed onto the ferry by the storm. Perhaps they'll examine the contents of the bag around its neck, perhaps the professor will receive his recognition yet. Or perhaps not.

For the moment, all Susan wants to do is to return to the cabin where she hopes she will find her husband fast asleep. There's still a long way to go and the storm has not abated. In the morning, Alan will ask her why she's wearing gloves and a scarf. She'll say that she'll tell him once they're back at his parents', safely removed from the sea, and all its marvels and horrors.

For Fiona

CHRISTOPHER HARMAN

SISTERS RISE

CHRISTOPHER HARMAN is a former librarian who currently
lives in Preston, Lancashire. His recent stories have appeared in
Rustblind and *Silverbright, Shadows and Tall Trees*, Paul Finch's *Terror
Tales* anthology series, two volumes of *The Ghosts and Scholars Book
of Shadows* and *The Ghosts and Scholars Book of Mazes*. Previous
tales have also appeared in *The Year's Best Fantasy and Horror* and
Best New Horror, while *The Heaven Tree and Other Stories* is a
collection of his work published by Sarob Press.

"On a recent holiday in Orkney I had been fascinated by the eerie
enigmatic standing stones at Stenness," explains the author. "Closer
to home, in Cumbria, is the famous stone circle known as 'Long Meg
and her Daughters'. I tried to tie in ancient stones with something
allied to the numerous Lancashire legends involving magic and
witchcraft. The end result is the following tale, which first appeared
in the *Ghosts and Scholars Book of Folk Horror*."

AT THE SUDDEN babble of children's voices entering the Centre,
Rodney looked up from the images of Bowland farms on the
laptop. "Call Rodney!" called out Dan who must have entered with
the class. Then it was like a black-and-white courtroom drama. "Call

Rodney," called out Sue from the corner shop. "Call Rodney," called out Val as her mop slapped. All very good-natured, and Rodney smiled from his low-slung chair inside the maze of maps of Bowland. He'd been dubbed "Useful Rodney" by Dan and he'd liked that, ready as he was to turn his hand to fence-repair, manning the shop, guiding groups, litter-picking—but everyone knew local history was his thing.

He took the laptop to the office, locked it inside, and put on his amenable public face. He liked imparting local history information almost as much as gathering it.

He stepped out in front of the kids, all clutching bark rubbings.

"Here's your man, Miss," Dan said, lingering. The teacher approached Rodney with a chilly smile.

"Ann Allan. St. Margery's in town. Mr. Leavett says you can talk to the children about Tall Maud."

Tall herself, slender, elegant and aloof of expression. She clutched the thin strap of her large, expensive-looking shoulder bag with one hand and extended her other hand for him to shake. Dan's teeth were clamped in his grin. He was craggy-faced, old enough to be her dad and clearly smitten.

"Certainly can," Rodney said. "And can take you there too if you've got transport."

Miss Allan told him the school minibus was outside. Rodney said Sisters Rise was on farm property, but the Bowland Visitors Centre had an arrangement with the owner of the land.

"Oh, Marjorie's Farm, yes, we're going there this afternoon for the petting zoo." She took a stoical breath and called out "Gather round!"

Dan wagged a finger at the children. "You have to behave yourself up there or Tall Maud'll come down on you like a ton of bricks."

Rodney enjoyed the blank-faced reaction.

The children were herded into the café first for their mid-morning break.

"Rather you than me," Sue said, tidying the leaflet stand.

"They're receptive at that age," Rodney said.

"No, I meant going up the Rise. Not been up since I was a kid myself."

Even before the tragedy, Rodney had heard paid staff and volunteers at the Centre express a similar dislike for the place. Most, being local, had known the stories since childhood. As an incomer from twenty miles away, Rodney could take or leave the creepy reputation of Sisters Rise, but he loved its remoteness and dizzyingly long vista of history.

"Safety in numbers," Rodney said, humouring her.

She sucked in her cheeks. "Tell that to the young man's family."

Rodney nodded solemnly at the floor, conceding her point. The young man had been one of a group celebrating the summer solstice last year. He'd wandered off by himself and, in a freak accident, impaled himself on a lethally sharp horizontal tree branch. The inquest stated there were drugs in his system. Not much blood, staff at the Centre heard on the grapevine.

Rodney read yesterday's newspaper until the children were queuing at the main doors.

In the front passenger seat of the minibus he gave directions between vividly green fields and flowery meadows. Hedges burgeoned into copses here and there. Whenever the children's chatter and squabbles reached a peak, Miss Allan quelled the commotion with a bored-toned reprimand into the rear-view mirror. There were distractions—an orange bull, a drooping scarecrow. Sheep had their heads down while their lambs gambolled. When a couple of girls begged to stop by several small woolly heads poking through a five bar gate, Miss Allan said they might see some at the farm later. Rodney confirmed they would and said he was hearing them all day long lately, with living next door to the farm buildings. Miss Allan muttered that it would "drive me mad".

Rodney unlocked the first tubular steel gate. On the other side, in an almost imperceptible gradient, was a rough farm track. The children grew quieter as Sisters Rise rose up ahead. The hill had a wandering collar of trees with a couple of breaks showing sections of the long flat summit.

They'd risen maybe fifty feet over the fields when Rodney got out to unlock the second and final gate and swing it inwards. The trees weren't massive and not yet in full leaf this early in spring.

Scrub oak and ash mostly, growth curtailed due to the relatively exposed position, or so Dan said.

Miss Allan drove through and Rodney swung the gate shut. Back in the minibus he directed her to a point where the rough track divided, one part dipping to return down into the fields, the left-hand continuing around the hill. He directed her to park on a small area of ash and dirt and everyone got out. There was a wide gap between the trees into which the children ran, chattering and laughing.

"Slow down," Miss Allan instructed needlessly. As they burst onto the top they slowed as Rodney predicted, and two or three stopped. Tall Maud did that to people.

She was towards the far end of the long hill which was a flattish length about the dimensions of a football pitch bordered by bands of trees, mostly rooted a yard or so down the sides. Rough grass was marked by shallow furrows and depressions here and there.

The children walked silently to within three yards of the brutal irregular block of sandstone, ten feet tall and the width of three men at its thickest. Investigators had been undecided if grooves and hollows were the remains of designs long since weathered away. Rodney sometimes saw a hip or a shoulder, a depression like an eye socket, but more often he saw an undifferentiated imposing piece of rock thought to have been transported from the Pennines or Westmorland, embedded here and probably innocent of chisel and hammer.

He faced the children, Maud at his back. A high priest might have stood in this same spot. He felt like a go-between—and Maud needed one. She needed some kind of explanation—more than one. It was like having a piece of the cold moon behind him right now.

"Hands up if you know who this is?" It amused him the way the tone came back. Once a teacher, always a teacher, now minus the bolshy teens, the targets, the headaches, the head teacher the biggest headache of all, out to get him and succeeding with the help of Rodney's heart murmur. Minus the money too, but he was managing.

He chose from the copse of raised hands. The boy nearly got the answer right.

"Yes, but she's *Tall* Maud—and you can see why." Heads craning past him, necks cricked back to take in Maud's height. "And why is she special?" Whispers, eager raised hands: everyone knew the answer. He chose.

"She's a witch."

He smiled indulgently. Everyone preferred the witch stuff of virtually yesterday to the theories of what might have actually happened here millennia ago. "She does look rather witch-like doesn't she." Always different features in the rock, dependent on the time of day, angle of sunlight, ambient light, passing clouds. He pointed out the vaguest hint of uneven shoulders, a suggestion of robes over a long-boned frame.

"Not just any witch, but the most powerful one. She came up here with her sisters and they cooked up all kinds of mischief and wickedness. Maud was the worst though. She could even change the weather. One time she brought on a storm that ruined the harvest. The local people were so sick and tired of her they called on a travelling wizard to help them and one day, when the witches were all gathered up here in a great circle, he turned them all to stone." Patting Maud's flank chilled his hand to the bone.

"They say she's never forgiven local people for what happened. A long time ago a farm labourer thought he saw her crouching down to stare into his kitchen window. Others say they can feel the vibrations as Tall Maud comes to life and stamps around the hill. Some people say they can hear the spirits of the sisters whispering angrily to each other on the wind. Listen..."

The children did so, wide-eyed, and turned to the band of trees behind them to the right, where a light breeze hissed through foliage.

"Where are the other sisters?" A boy had his hand raised.

"Hundreds of years ago the landowner at the time was fed up with his workers getting spooked by the stones, so he ordered them to be knocked down. When there was only Tall Maud left, a great wind came up and the men got frightened. They never came back for Maud. But—before you start getting worried about witches, you must remember that the tales came about because people didn't know why the stones were here at all. We know more now. In fact, the stones were brought here thousands of years ago from mountainous areas like..."

Miss Allan had sidled up to him. "Could we get them to stand where..." Looking across the hill she made a vague circle with her phone. He got her drift, thought it a good idea he could initiate himself with future groups.

He explained there were no definite indications of where the stones had stood but, judging from the position of Maud towards the head of the open space, they were likely to have been arranged in a rough oval. He said there were eleven sisters including Maud. Ten children giggled and acted-up as they spaced themselves out, with help from the adults. In Rodney's narrowed eyes a moment of stunted shapes, clothing hard as statuary. He blinked, and colours and smiling faces were back. A kid on one leg, another making outstretched zombie arms, one who'd been a boulder was tying his shoelace.

Miss Allan called out, "Keep still as..." She held her phone at arm's length and stared into the screen. "Stone." They were but for a breeze rippling their clothing. She pressed a button, took a couple more pictures and looked at the sky.

A surprise, the vast nose of darker cloud from the north east. Miss Allan told them to get out their exercise books and make notes and drawings for their projects or stories, adding they'd got twenty minutes. Rodney thought there might be rain before they'd elapsed.

The children wandered back to Maud. Some sketched, others pressed paper to her flanks and shaded with crayon. That contact always gave Rodney a slight *frisson*, though the worshippers were long gone and the nameless nature deity had never been. It was an inert block of stone, and nobody was left to be offended at the sacrilege.

Miss Allan swiped leftwards on her phone screen. She noticed him looking and flushed.

"So. Tall Maud changed the weather before they could get at her?" She spread two fingers on the tiny screen and cupped her chin in consideration.

"Very much doubt it."

"Go that girl, I say."

Rodney wandered over to the children around Maud. He brought a finger up close, traced the vaguest hint of two short curving parallel lines an inch apart. Maybe an accident of geology, maybe not.

"Can you see this? It looks like part of an eye. It could be a symbol that you see in a lot of standing stones where people believed in nature spirits. They may have brought offerings so that the spirits would ensure their crops grew and there were animals to hunt and eat."

Miss Allan came up and looked at their work.

"What are those trees over there?" a boy asked, pointing off to the left.

No different from trees in similar bands around the top except these were the ones that had, as in a beautifully arranged film-edit, stirred in a breeze when he'd referred to the spirits of the sisters angrily whispering.

"Should be easy to find out after the tree man gave you all those tips this morning," she said. Rodney wasn't certain the boy had been thinking about species... but *the tree-man*. He looked forward to passing that on to Dan.

As soon as the boy headed off with his clipboard towards the trees that intrigued him, others were asking if they could follow. Miss Allan agreed with a slight roll of her eyes and with instructions not to go out of sight. "You've got ten minutes," she called out.

She sighed. "Maud's history all a sudden." Suppressing a yawn, she made a toothless beak of her mouth. "A park bench up here would be good."

Rodney laughed. "It can get busy in the summer. I've already suggested ditching the gates and installing a turnstile. Marjorie said she'd run it by English Heritage."

A tune got Miss Allan answering her phone. Rodney wandered from break to break in the trees to look at the views. The air was still. Silence, all the children close together and engrossed in their work amidst the trees. Five minutes gone and he was looking at distant Pendle Hill. A sharp tug of the grey-shaded air was unexpected. A cry, and he whirled, traced it to the small figures within the agitated trees.

He jogged heavily, his face shaking. Miss Allan was some way behind on the long grass the wind was combing in all directions. A dash of rain in his face, another. Sheets of paper flapped in the gloom of the trees, children running out onto the hilltop, pinching collars, squinting, clutching clipboards to their chests. Open mouths in stunned faces.

"Come on. To the minibus," Miss Allan called out, counting heads. In the dust-storm of last winter's leaves the trees looked spiky, barbaric, more ancient than Tall Maud. Miss Allan was telling them not to run and Rodney spread his arms to emphasise the point as they raced by him. Air rushed by him in the opposite direction, cold, stony-scented as if from Tall Maud herself.

He felt a shadow of stone-cold greyness until they were all in the minibus.

The shivering children looked small and waif-like, any cheek and mischief long gone from their faces. Another head count and to Rodney's huge relief all were present. His heart still thundered.

"The wind took mine," a small girl complained.

"And mine." A chorus of voices, complaint mixed with amazement that a strong breeze could behave in such a way. Too much screen-time and not enough time outdoors, Rodney suspected. But it was unsettling that they'd somehow lost all their work.

Calm again outside, the muzzle of dark cloud dissolving into the surrounding grey. Miss Allan started the engine and her knuckles were white on the steering wheel as she did a three-point turn.

"Took what?" she said.

"Our bark rubbings."

"Never mind, you got plenty of those this morning."

A mumbled discussion before a boy turned spokesman. "These had faces."

Miss Allan turned her head in Rodney's direction, her frown deep, her smile crooked. This one was for him, and it was a difficult one.

"Trees with faces? Never heard of that." A chuckle grated out of him while anger stiffened in his chest. Had some vandal, or some extreme tree-hugger type, carved into bark?

"No," a girl complained. "They only showed on paper."

"Ugly, monster faces," a boy said.

His companions giggled nervously. Rodney twisted around in his seat and saw why. A boy was pulling a face to illustrate the point just made. It robbed Rodney of thought and word, his frozen expression eliciting a new round of giggles that petered out.

They drove in silence. Rodney rationalised that the bleakness of the hill presided over by Tall Maud had turned impressionable heads. Hysteria as one imagination fed others. Direct supervision by the teacher would have quelled that but she'd been too busy on her phone. A pity the children failed to keep hold of the sheets. Physical evidence would have destroyed fanciful notions.

He said as much when they were back in the Visitors Centre. Miss Allan shrugged and thanked him for the trip. "Looks like they've got over the experience." The children were chattering as they ate in the café.

"And I can post you some stuff on nature spirits to take their minds off witches if you like."

"If you could." She was looking out through the tall smoked windows. "Sunny now. Typical."

"Might go up there again. If I find their sheets, I could send them too." He smiled. Useful Rodney. "They'll see bark, not..."

A boom of pastoral orchestral music from the tiny auditorium where a film on Bowland was on a loop and next on the agenda for the children.

"There's really no need," she said with a head shake and slight wrinkle of her nose.

He ate lunch at home and worked on short pieces of history for the new display boards coming in soon. The weather was staying fine. The intense flurry of air might not have sent the sheets far in that fastness of tree and bush. The class was due at Marjorie's Farm mid-afternoon. There was time.

From his cottage the Rise was half the distance it was from the Visitors Centre. He walked along farm tracks, field-side ditches, negotiated two stiles, two gates, the gradually rising gradient telling in his legs and heart, but the cool movement of air and a bottle of fizzy water sustaining him. The bright sun hid deep shadows in the interrupted band of trees around the upper reaches of the Rise.

He entered onto the summit. The trees were like an audience before Tall Maud, as dominated by her as all the standing stones must have been. As he headed to where the children had got scared, Tall Maud weighed down darkly in his eye-corner.

Stunted trees, but tough and hardy looking. Spikiness of limbs was offset to a degree by vines and creeper, hanging like perished rags. He was surprised how quickly he came upon a sheet of paper. It was at the base of an oak tree. He picked it up. Shading by the rapid application of red crayon on paper held against bark showed deep fissures. He squinted, rotated the sheet, held it horizontally before his eyes for any chance and hideous alignment an impressionable child might have found. No, nothing.

A rustling. He traced it to another sheet, walking in tiny increments on its corners before the slight breeze that made dead leaves bob and whisper. Another bark rubbing. A finer texture, maybe rowan. Not the merest hint of a face. He found another sheet and another. In all the irregularities in the general pattern of bark, an isolated feature might resemble anything from an eye socket, to a lip, to a brow, as anyone might expect, but nothing was remotely suggestive of an entire face.

More sheets within the space of nine or ten trees until he had ten in all. Ten children in the group, so maybe he'd found every one. A good thing if he had, as a dankness in the air was feeling for his bones.

He emerged onto the top and Tall Maud startled him. Her position hadn't shifted in thousands of years and hadn't in the past few minutes either. That she was more face-on to him was because he must have exited at a point farther along the space she dominated. He sensed her directly at his back until he was at a point in the tree-break from where he judged she'd be out of sight had he turned.

Twenty minutes later, roofs of the farm buildings floated on hawthorn blossom. Children's voices came to him. How would they react to getting their sheets back?

A fork in the path—on the right towards his white-washed cottage, left to the farm's main gate set in high walls.

The minibus was parked in the yard. Miss Allan was talking to Marjorie who was even taller, big-boned in Wellington boots, scarf, jeans. Children were gathered at the slatted gate into the cowshed. Off to the left, three girls were with a young woman feeding a lamb from a bottle.

He was about to call out, but his voice stopped in his throat. The sheets pressed into the heart-side of his chest like a layer of cold flesh. Miss Allan and Marjorie were having a chuckle about something. He wanted to be rid of the bark rubbings, but would he look too pathetically keen to please? Laughing now, Miss Allan rocking back on her heels at something Marjorie said. Then there was what sounded like amusement from the pig-pen, a sudden squealing like wheezing, choking laughter. From elsewhere a piping bleat was like the vocal equivalent of a sneer. It was the lamb, looking past the petting hands towards him. Nobody else did. He side-stepped out of sight and returned to his cottage.

He didn't want to think about the bark rubbings. In his upstairs study he shoved them into the drawer of his desk and tried to work. It made sense to choose Marjorie's Farm for one of the display boards. Since moving into the cottage he'd gathered a collection of ephemera on the subject, with Marjorie's approval. He tipped it out from the box-file onto his desk. The earliest record of the farm—Windacre Farm long before its re-naming—dated from 1480. It was partially rebuilt in 1790, and a letter from the same year caught his eye. It was from J.J. Emsworth, builders' merchant, outlining costs of clearance of Sisters Rise and new barn and wall construction. A terse concluding sentence: *Would advise against use of stones from the Rise in walls and new barn due to labour costs of removing.*

He'd forgotten that. He'd no documentation to prove the advice had been taken. If Marjorie's predecessor at the time had permitted use of the stones as supplementary building materials, it would have demonstrated an admirable lack of superstition.

Something else: a photocopy of a letter from a Doctor Trawlings in Chipping to Mr. Eric Barrow, Windacre Farm, 13th November 1851:

…have recommended your fellow, Alfred Allbright, to Superintendent Masters at Whittingham Hospital owing to the impairment of his wits. His ravings concerning the Rise continue and the grave disquiet this has caused in the locality cannot be underestimated. However, the removal and resettlement of Allbright's family to their parish of origin in distant Hornby is a bleak prospect. I hope the Justices of the Peace will take these unusual circumstances into consideration.

At the noise of a vehicle engine, Rodney was up from his chair in time to see the school minibus passing before his front gate on the first leg of their journey back to Preston. He should have handed over the sheets while he had the chance, then they wouldn't be a problem any more. Not for him, anyway. But problem? What was he thinking? Bark rubbings—nothing more. Feminine laughter and the lamb's derisive bleat echoed around the inside of his head for a moment.

He worked on. Later he examined his own photographs of Marjorie's Farm. These mostly dated from the 1960s and were no more suitable than the ones he'd seen on the Centre's laptop. In the window the sky was light but the sun low. Behind the nearer outbuildings the farmhouse was a dark pile. It was getting too late to take new pictures.

There was a dense rural blackness outside when he went to bed. When he awoke later, 3:46 in vivid green on his digital alarm was the only light. Not a glitch in his body clock he realised, hearing the rumble from across the landing. From his study.

He waited, his fists gripping the duvet. The rumble again. Didn't the drawers moving on the rollers in his desk make that sound?

In dense blackness he went to stand at his bedroom door. He pleaded inwardly for the intruder to give up on the study, descend the stairs, leave. No confrontation would be the best outcome for both parties. He waited, scared, and the silence went on. Had the sound been a vehicle at the farm—even at this hour? He was becoming convinced his study was empty.

Minutes passed, nine, ten on the digital clock, before he left the room. He crossed the landing and switched on the light. No sound from the study. He drew down the handle. Pushing the door inwards drew him into the dark. He jabbed at the light-switch to his right in a surge of panic.

The first thing he noticed was the six-inch gap in the top drawer. He must have left that gap—the evidence was before him. The familiar rumble as he pulled it further open, then to the limit.

Nothing in the drawer other than stationery, but the sheets hadn't gone far. They were on the floor around the edge of the room. Not quite evenly spaced, but looking as if placed there. He went to the door, jerked it out from the wall. Nobody had hidden behind it and he breathed out loudly.

Thinking, he was avoiding looking down at the sheets. There was a hands-width gap in the sash-window; a slither of air must have somehow sucked out the papers from the drawer and scattered them, the skirting board the limit to their escape. He wouldn't look directly at scribbled darknesses in the sheets. Because he knew. He knew what he'd see. But he *had* to look.

Faces, as insistent now as they had previously been elusive. Grotesque spacings and configurations of bosses, blotches, wrinkles, furrows—but these were undeniably faces. Looking at him the way eyes in paintings did. But these wouldn't for any longer.

He snatched the sheets up from the floor. With them grasped in one hand, he closed the window with the other. In a back room he had a firebox for deeds, financial and other important documents. He locked the sheets inside. Locked the door.

Artificial lighting? The hour? His initial fright making him as susceptible as the children? In bed he stared till sleep took him, took him too often to the Rise, he recalled at breakfast the next morning. He went to the back room. He had to steel himself to unlock the firebox and look at the sheets. Yes, the same flaws and irregularities as he'd seen last night, but not remotely reminiscent of any face, let alone the grossly distorted ones of nightmare, fixing him with baleful stares. He covered his mouth, his shoulders shook, a cough of laughter at himself. But should he post them to Miss Allan? If a level-headed adult such as himself should see what wasn't there, might the children again?

As he was thinking, his phone rang. It was Miss Allan. *Speak of the devil.*

"Sorry to bother you. Got your number from the Centre. Any luck finding those sheets? Parents have been complaining their kids were having nightmares last night. It might do the kids good to see those bark rubbings are just that and nothing more."

He tried to speak evenly. "So sorry to hear about that. Looks like Tall Maud still has the power to unsettle..."

"...I think we're talking tree-bark here. I take it you've not found anything?" Her voice had cut into his ear.

"Not had a chance to get up there yet." His lie sounded like one. Was he as transparent to her as a guilty child? "Certainly see what I can do. If the worse comes to the worst maybe the class could come back and see the trees for what they are?"

After a few seconds of silence Miss Allan responded with, "Probably not," in a rueful tone that made Rodney wonder how bad the nightmares had been.

Gemma Haversgill of Parks and Amenities was waiting in the meeting room at the Centre. She was trouser-suited and diaphanously-scarfed. Rodney loaded the memory stick onto her laptop and talked through the words and images he had in mind for the display boards. As he clicked past a picture of Tall Maud without comment, she asked if he'd done anything on Sisters Rise. He said, "Not yet". It wasn't his finger on the touch-pad that brought Tall Maud back.

"Looking old."

"She is. Thousands of years."

"No, I meant the photograph."

A hint of deterioration, colours of sky and grass lurid. Maybe from an old Kodak print? Perhaps she was right. She said Phil in Publicity was coming to photograph the meadows and woods around the Centre. She suggested Rodney take him to Sisters Rise to get some new pictures of Tall Maud with himself in shot to give scale.

"I suppose I've got time," Rodney said, not sounding overly enthusiastic and not looking at her, scratching his head and moving on through words and pictures.

When Phil arrived he wanted to take photos nearby first, but Rodney was in no mood to wait.

"Now's better. It'll be clouding over later," he said.

As he drove he was irritated by Phil's constant fiddling with his camera. His saving grace was not being the chatty type.

Rodney parked just below the tree-line then led the way. Both were silent. Phil had his camera tripod perched on his shoulder. As Tall Maud came into sight, Rodney stumbled on a hummock but kept his footing. He felt like an approaching minion on the long walk towards her. Phil checked his light monitor without a care.

With Tall Maud immediately before them, Phil asked Rodney to stand by her. Phil set up the tripod and was ages composing the picture as Rodney tried to smooth the tension from his face. He felt uncomfortable at the prospect of his image sharing the same space with Maud. Phil was no help; he'd be useless at weddings.

After posing twice more, Rodney said "Done with me?"

"Yep," Phil said, looking around for other shots.

Rodney walked away. A sly glance towards the offending band of trees and he froze. Not a child, but someone, gone as he stared.

Past the first trees there was hardly less sunshine, but he shivered in a cellar-like chill. He stalked between the trees. No faces in the bark this time either, but it was a shock—the tree-hole that seemed like a part of one.

Like a mouth, as big as his head. A silent scream, or silent laughter with a thickening around the lower perimeter like a lip. He stepped closer, looked inside. About a foot down was a rough ledge with a cluster of twigs and other rotted vegetation, maybe the remains of a nest.

A crack, like a breaking bone. He looked up. Before him, trees. Behind, someone, not attempting a stealthy approach. He sucked in damp air, swung around.

Marjorie bit back a smile. "Sorry. Did I startle you? Think I was you-know-who?"

"Yes you did and no, I didn't think that." Now both of them could smile openly.

Marjorie's coat falling straight to her knees was open on a woollen sweater with a pebble-dash pattern. A bag depended from her right hand, a long almost cylindrical affair, grey-pink-white in colour. Rodney's smile faded.

"Oh," she said, holding up the bag which wasn't a bag at all. Her fist clasped the hind legs of a dead lamb. "Fox must have got him and brought him up here. Found by Maud."

A pause, then more shared jolliness. "Sorry again!" Marjorie said. "I meant *next* to Maud. Someone walking here dropped by the farm to let me know."

"That's a shame," Rodney said. The lamb looked intact, so whatever had attacked hadn't eaten.

He realised he owed her an explanation for his being here within the trees. Maybe she already guessed. He explained his mission with Phil, adding, "Don't know if the teacher mentioned what happened here yesterday?"

She'd been nodding before he'd finished. "Yes, during the petting-zoo session."

Made you laugh did it? Rodney wondered. "It was a vicious little wind. Not much hope of finding anything."

Marjorie shook her head with affectionate exasperation. "This place!"

After some inconsequential talk she said, "Well, good luck." Remembering she must be referring to the sheets, Rodney made a good-humoured gesture of despair and she left. After a decent interval he followed.

Phil was waiting at the opposite end of the top from Maud. No sign of Marjorie.

Later that afternoon, from his study, Rodney watched a few white clouds drift across the blue sky over Sisters Rise. The tree bole wouldn't shift from his mind. A black hole, silently screaming ancient pain and resentment.

Work settled his mind, and there was no point straining to exclude Tall Maud from his piece about Marjorie's Farm.

Marjorie's Farm feels as much a part of the landscape as the fields, the walls, even the Maud Stone itself. Though it is a mere stripling of five centuries or so, parts may be vastly older. There is a possibility that broken-up stones of the circle on Sisters Rise were used in the construction of the barn and in field walls thereabouts. From the sublime to the mundane you might say.

A better writer wouldn't, he thought. And weren't all stone building materials "vastly older"? He added some more about diversification at the farm, produce sold at farmers' markets, the petting zoo.

He wondered if he'd left it too late for photographs as he stood behind the gate. With the sun on its descent behind the farm buildings, the dirty grey-yellow of the stonework of the barn and cowshed was darkening. He felt a chill movement of air. Felix the dog came running, his barks lessening as he recognised Rodney, and allowed his head to be stroked through the metal cross-pieces. Rodney lifted the latch and made space to squeeze through.

No answer to his knock on the farmhouse door. Head low, Felix nudged at a weed. "Marjorie abandoned you?" Rodney said.

No cows in the shed. They must be out in the pasture, and a plaintive bellow confirmed it. No feed in the troughs.

A sifting sound, almost a hissing. He went next door and stood before the great opening into the barn. Bales of hay-feed towered in the darkness. In the rough stone wall at the back, intense low sunlight filled chinks where the mortar had fallen away. A stone-cold draught came from them at his face, made the surfaces of hay-bales flicker. He backed a few paces, aimed and clicked the shutter of his camera.

He retreated to a mid-point of the yard where he photographed the farmhouse with its tilted chimneys and kinked roofline, the cow shed, the whole barn. He wasn't Phil, but he was sure his own pictures would suffice. He'd run them by Marjorie when he next saw her. He was certain Gemma would okay them in her dour manner.

Back in his study he downloaded the photos onto his computer. In the window, the Bowland fells were leaden heaps under the dark ink stains spreading up from the east. By contrast the Rise's green top was vivid, individual trees tricked out in the deepening sunlight.

A little fanfare sounded. The seven photographs attached to Phil's e-mail Rodney copied and then duplicated in an app called PhotoAdapt. If Phil cottoned on to his tinkering he might be professionally offended, but Gemma would have the last say.

He clicked through the photographs quickly. The fine detail of Tall Maud made the screen seem like a series of windows framing her. A chill swept through him as he stood on the other side of the window in three pictures, Tall Maud in touching distance. He used the special setting and grass ate his image to nothing in each picture. If Gemma complained at his absence she could go up the Rise with Phil herself.

He opened up his own pictures of the farm. A little too dark in the back-lighting from the sun. Filling the screen with the interior barn shot, he sat forward. A dud. Blackness filling the wide doorway. With an adjustment of the light/dark setting the interior greyed. Hay-bales in towers to left and right, between them towards the left where the floor met the back stone wall, a blackness stubbornly remained in place. It was narrow as a ladder but crooked, dividing and sub-dividing into thinner lengths that reached towards the ceiling.

That wasn't a tree. He'd seen into the barn on previous occasions. Not unthinkable that a tree should grow in a barn, but there simply wasn't one present. It wasn't some outlandish farming implement propped there either. Nor the shadow of one, and he recalled the light being too dim for any deep shadow to be cast. Was it a streak of discoloration, maybe the remains of some dark internal cladding on the stone—or tar even, caught better by the camera than his eye at the time? His mind and eye scurried like a farm rat until he deleted the picture. Deletion from the recycle bin rendered it irrecoverable in the hard drive. Not so easy to delete from his memory. Going back to the barn in the morning would resolve the matter. He told himself that.

Tonight was covered. Ed Hill of Central Lancashire Nature Group was giving a talk at the Centre with slides on the geology of Bowland. In the intervening time Rodney watched TV until the barking dug into his consciousness. From his upstairs study he looked obliquely through the glass.

Nearer outbuildings obscured the farmyard, but there was a bloom thrown-up from the security lights attached to the buildings. The frantic barking of Felix went on. If Marjorie was trying to placate him, she was failing.

He went downstairs, unease like a stone in his guts. Still the barking. Maybe it was time to make himself useful and check nothing was untoward.

The barking ceased abruptly before he got to the gate. It was padlocked, as always, this late in the evening. Yellowish illumination from the security lights bathed the entire yard. Felix didn't come running. The black opening into the kennel revealed nothing of the dog, who Rodney assumed must be deeper inside.

A clatter off to his right. From the shadows of huts, a fodder silo, an old plough and other rusted equipment, somebody rose. A powerful light was shone into his eyes. More alarming was the shotgun, the wooden stock clamped under the figure's armpit. Rodney let out a gasp. Marjorie.

"It's not loaded but intruders don't know that." She advanced and her face took on more of the security lighting. Strong bones, the light and maybe foundation make-up gave her skin a uniform yellowish grain. He was struck by how unafraid she looked.

"Maybe it should be," he said. Thefts of livestock, machinery, engine oil, were in the news these days.

"I don't think there's anybody lurking. Thought I heard a noise in the cowshed but found nothing. I've checked everywhere else." With so many dark and cluttered corners around the place, that seemed unlikely to Rodney.

"I heard the dog."

"Could have been a rat or fox got him going." She seemed to be taking this too easily.

"I could hang around for ten minutes if you like." Useful Rodney.

She nodded. "Could you?" adding that she didn't have the key to the padlock so could he climb over the gate?

Walking with her across the yard Rodney said, "Hang on", and detoured towards the barn. He stood before the black maw of the opening. She stopped behind him. "I've checked here."

"Could you..." He gestured for her to shine the torch.

A shadow on the rough stones of the back wall, his own cast by the torch. Nothing grew there and never had. No bizarre and lengthy item of farm equipment. No brachiated streak of oil or tar. His camera must have been at fault.

"Come on, let's get inside. I'll make you a drink," she said.

As they passed by the cowshed, Rodney's head jerked up at a shadow against a lit curtained window upstairs in the farmhouse. Marjorie's shoulders rose and dropped as she sighed massively.

"That's my sister. Went to pick her up from Preston Station this afternoon. Don't mention this if you see her. Here for rest and recuperation. She's enough on her plate. Her husband's an idiot." She averted her face, lifted her palms as if to close off any question on the matter Rodney might have had in mind. He nodded judiciously, and wondered why learning that Marjorie had a sister and that she was here should feel such a revelation.

Once behind the locked and barred front door, she took him through to the back of the house and into a large chilly room with a high ceiling. Stone walls were undressed and stone flags were mostly left uncovered by a couple of rough-textured rugs. A massive stone hearth had a wooden screen before it with a marquetry upland landscape depicting a low hill with stone walls extending away from it like tentacles.

She invited him to sit, and the sofa gave under him with a wheezy crackle like dense dry heather. She towered over him, her head dark against the ceiling light. "I'll just see how she's getting on."

She went back the way they'd come. Rodney heard steps resounding on stone flags, a moment later boxy impacts rising.

Silence. A big house, and anyone's guess how many barriers of wood, plaster and stone separated him from Marjorie and her sister. Silence continued in the passing minutes.

No books or magazines here to distract him. No TV. If work allowed Marjorie any time for relaxation, maybe it wasn't spent in here.

He waited. Understandable her sister coming first, but the minutes multiplied.

He suppressed the thought that the pair of them had been deliberately silenced. Just inconsiderate of Marjorie to forget him, especially considering he'd put himself out on her behalf. Make his own drink? How would she react? He wasn't assertive enough for that kind of gesture. The wait no longer tolerable, he went back through the house until he found the stairway. He called up, "Marjorie? Everything okay?"

No reply. Not hearing him—and he couldn't hear them. Climbing remedied that. Arriving on the landing, he tried to position the muffled voices.

A passage leading off from the landing was lined with white-painted doors. He traced the sounds to a door that by contrast was a single sheet of unvarnished wood. Light underneath. Why the closed door, as if they suspected he might come up the stairs just to eavesdrop? Thick wood deadened the voices. He couldn't distinguish one of them sounding miserable or anguished. In fact, he couldn't distinguish any particular quality to the voices, or even that there were just two. They were like voices on a blustery wind.

Their owners were near, though. A motion of shadows under the door suggested more than one, as if a muted gathering was taking place. More than one light source must be the reason for that, mustn't it?

Standing perplexed wasn't going to resolve the issue. He raised his hand, and it was absurd the courage it took to knock. "Marjorie," he said. His breathy voice wouldn't have been heard, and he felt obscurely relieved until he thought he heard a heavy step inside the room. Another, not so much heard as felt through the floorboards— and nearer.

He had been heard. A new intensity in the voices, though not a whit clearer. The heavy step again. And again. He thought of a piece of massively heavy furniture being moved on its front or back corners.

Suddenly, up and down and to left and right, the wood of the door was everywhere in his vision. The grain was like cured leathery skin. Two knotholes, horribly close, stared into his soul.

He turned, fled. He was at the top of the stairs as a creak was like an axed tree falling. A massive cold draught, arboreal scented, pushed him to the ground floor.

Through the heart of the groaning squeaking house he ran. He unsealed the front door, went out into the yard, running, clambering over the gate, running…

He got his car keys from the cottage, sat in his car. He pressed his key into the ignition, didn't turn it. His body trembled, faces in his swirling thoughts, but one thought he grasped at.

While they were in the house they couldn't be on the Rise. Fear was tempered by his conviction that those pieces of paper must hold the key, if any such existed. Those scribbling children had awakened and released the things from the trees. The trees would get them back again. Useful Rodney? By God, he'd be useful all right.

Back into the cottage. Up the stairs to the back room, into the firebox. He took out the bark rubbings and fetched matches from the kitchen. Back to his car. He sifted through the sheets. Faces, ghastly, hateful, angry and vastly old—and was that fear at what he intended to do? Was the essence of those things in the farmhouse here in the bark rubbings? And at his mercy? He'd bet on it.

A fizzing in his blood and brain, fear and exhilaration interlaced as the car bumped along the track, headlights spinning out lengths of stone wall towards the Rise. His mind was razor-sharp now, it had to be. In the rear-view mirror his teeth were bared in his grin.

Each of the gates screeched when he swung it open. Each time the waiting car engine's hum was like that of someone anxiously seeking distraction. Soon there was a steepening gradient, and not long after the lower reach of the hill was visible in the headlights. The front of the car tipped up, and he saw splayed roots and tree trunks with darkness between them like doorways open on darkened rooms.

He parked. Grabbing the torch from the glove compartment, he was out and running into the tree-break. He felt adrenaline—not fear, all that was left behind with Marjorie and those she'd been keeping company with in the bedroom.

He emerged on to the bare top of the Rise.

Back-lit by the moon, which was bright and smoking in swathes of wispy cloud, Tall Maud was hunched and towering, edges softened by the light fanning out around them.

No need for torchlight, not yet anyway. He kept left, hugging the border of trees and scrubby underbrush until he was roughly at the point he had last entered in daylight.

A few yards into the trees he felt shielded from Tall Maud, though from the unexpected depth of the darkness he knew cloud had thickened over the moon. He trod slowly, looking for that hole in the tree, little method in his aiming of the torch-beam this way and that. A withering inside him. He'd presumed too much. Here was no place to be, any more than in that tainted farmhouse. He'd go back to his car and think again.

He was about to when the moon dropped a great limb of light down to spotlight the tree with the bole like a toothless screaming mouth, or a wound. There, yes. He took a single step, and it was magnified into a massive impact that shook the hill. But he'd no time to consider that. He ran to the tree, shone the torch inside. Yes, where better?

He took out the sheets from his inner pocket, thrust them down into the hollow to rest on the rotted, twiggy, makeshift ledge. Now to turn them to smoke.

His fingers trembled, but the first match caught and flared. He dropped it precisely, and it landed on the top-sheet corner. Flame licked across the paper and the face's hideousness increased a thousandfold. Fire burrowed down into the others, paper and faces curling and shrinking, crackling like the faintest laughter.

Rodney stepped back. The shifting light of the flames made the perimeter of the bole uncertain, like a minimal shaping of words. Suddenly the flames were gone. Blackness in the bole, spreading out around it as the moon rolled in thickening veils and was gone. A dense darkness. He whipped the beam of his torch to all sides. Wait, what had that been? Only more trees.

He'd done what he'd set out to do. Bowland was his again.

He flashed the torch in the direction he thought he'd come. He tried to regulate his breaths.

A face, an ancient face in a tree-trunk, three wrinkles in bark making for eyes and a mouth—shocking to see. He took two paces, and the swing of his torch froze on another face. So different, but just as bizarre and pitiless in its chance arrangement of crooked lines and fissures. Moving the torch beam again, it landed on a beetling brow over a pinched cluster of features. Another direction, and it lit a vertical mouth of outrage as long as the bone in his forearm. And there were more faces. They hadn't been apparent to him in daylight, but he was a child this night and in the mood to see terrors after his upset in the farmhouse. Eye and brain must be doing the fashioning, helped by weathering and natural deformities, torchlight etching details and shadows in the wood. Answers to be clung to as he felt a huge, dull beat.

Again, and the earth shivered, sending a tickling sensation up his legs so that he almost giggled. Looking for the direction of its source, he saw that the trees with faces were evenly spread around him, branches extending horizontally to link like bony arms.

But one way was empty. It led back onto the bare hilltop, where another immense impact shivered the Rise. His shaking hand dropped the torch, but he didn't need it to light her approach. The moon did that.

He turned from her and continued turning within the circle of terrible faces and quivering arms. He felt his future shrinking to wood or stone. A splinter of comfort in the seconds before she arrived, that the reaching sisters would get him first.

RAMSEY CAMPBELL

The Run of the Town

R AMSEY CAMPBELL is described by the *Oxford Companion to English Literature* as "Britain's most respected living horror writer". He has been given more awards than any other writer in the field, including the Grand Master Award of the World Horror Convention, the Lifetime Achievement Award of the Horror Writers Association, the Living Legend Award of the International Horror Guild, and the World Fantasy Lifetime Achievement Award. In 2015 he was made an Honorary Fellow of Liverpool John Moores University for outstanding services to literature.

Among his more recent novels are *The Wise Friend, Somebody's Voice* and his "Brichester Mythos" trilogy, *The Searching Dead, Born to the Dark* and *The Way of the Worm*, while *By the Light of My Skull* is a recent short story collection, along with a two-volume retrospective round-up, *Phantasmagorical Stories*.

His novels *The Nameless, Pact of the Fathers* and *The Influence* have been filmed in Spain, where a television series based on *The Nameless* is in development. He is the President of the Society of Fantastic Films.

As Campbell explains: "My crumbling brain suggests that the seed of the story was simply the sounds during a country walk (that activity people used to enjoy in the days before the apocalypse) of people calling their dogs. It occurred to me that the names might grow strange and ominous, and what would that portend? I think some runners passed us as well as I began to reflect on possibilities, and the story caught them too."

CRAMP WAKENED PLATER before dawn. He sprawled out of bed and lurched stiff-legged around the hotel room, ending up at the window. As he gripped the sill so hard his nails bent while he stretched out his leg in the hope of diminishing the pain, he glimpsed activity in the distance. Beyond ranks of grey roofs descending a hill a park was dimly lit by streetlamps. The pale glow outlined a statue at the junction of several paths, and when he strained his eyes Plater made out joggers in the park. Perhaps they were keeping fit for the hilly streets, though he would have thought the streets themselves might keep them trim. The cramp had subsided to a dull ache, and he limped back to bed.

He hadn't planned to spend the night away from home. Helping Carol unload her belongings at the university—such a carload that it had left no space for her mother—had taken hours longer than he'd anticipated. On the drive home he'd met a downpour so relentless that he could see no more than a few yards ahead. Though the fog of spray failed to slow the traffic, several accidents did, and once he was reduced to crawling little more than a mile in an hour he'd followed an exit sign he could scarcely read. He'd left the rain and the daylight behind by the time he found the hotel at the edge of Chalmerston, a small steep grey Derbyshire town. He didn't think he'd seen the name on the motorway sign, but just then he couldn't have imagined a more welcome sight than the hotel car park.

A twinge of cramp roused him from dozing. A blob of sunlight mushroomed in the clotted greyish sky above the jagged horizon. Plater used the shower, which suffered from an intermittent chilly stutter, and took the lift down to the basement. As he collected items from the breakfast buffet—enough to last him all the way home without a break—several greying couples bade him a muted

English morning. He was back in his room when he thought of walking before driving, not least to work out the last persistent trace of cramp. He brushed his teeth with the flimsy instrument the hotel provided, and was crossing the lobby when the hotel receptionist, a squat broad long-faced man, halted him with a frown. "Leaving us already?"

"Just going for a walk first." Plater felt sufficiently accused to add "I'll settle up now if you like."

"No call for that. We've got you written down." The man tapped the computer screen in front of him, which emitted a pinched clink. "Not here for the chase, then," he said.

"I can't say I am."

The man raised his head, which seemed both to lengthen his face and intensify his disapproval. "You're one of them who'd like it stopped, are you?"

"I might if I knew what it was. If we're talking about hunting, surely that's banned."

"We leave the wild life to itself round here. It can't help what it gets up to, not like you and me."

"Then I'm honestly lost. What were you thinking I should know?"

"You've got a way with words and no mistake." The frown squeezed the comment dry of any trace of praise. "Best thing might be," the receptionist said, "the world forgets about us."

"You aren't still talking about you and me."

"I'm talking about history some interfering buggers want to do away with."

"I hope you don't think I'm one of those. I've just dropped off my daughter who's studying history."

"I'd not like to say what I think. The way they teach history these days..." With a breath fierce enough to do duty as an observation the receptionist said "Tradition, that's what they want to get rid of."

"I really don't think that's altogether the case. Will you have met many lecturers yourself?"

"Meddlers." Apparently to clarify, the man said "The ones who want to try and take away our character."

Plater had to assume "Of your town."

"It's been three hundred years and more, and the town's getting on for that too. That's when they started mining far side of the hill."

"And before that..." When the man didn't answer, Plater said "What was more than three hundred years back?"

"The real chase, and if you ask me it did none of them much harm. If they hadn't lived round here they might have come off a lot worse." The man's head jerked as though he'd wakened from a reverie. "Any road," he said, "you'll be wanting your walk."

Plater might have enquired further if the phone on the counter hadn't rung. As he made for the street the glass door crept aside for him. On his way downhill he had to step into the road to avoid an aproned butcher who was hauling out an awning with a hook. Otherwise the street was deserted except for a large whitish dog that fell to all fours from nosing in a bin and fled along an alley at Plater's approach. Ahead he saw the river to which the streets led down both sides of the valley—water that the sky turned a grey like the colour of sluggishness—but he was heading for the park.

Or was it a park? Perhaps it once had been. When he located the entrance, having followed a hedge twice his height and so impenetrably tangled that it wasn't much less solid than a wall, he found the gates were padlocked. Through the rusty iron bars, which were as spiky as the hedge, he saw that the place must have been abandoned quite a while ago, since the weedy grass between the trees had grown taller than him. Nevertheless the area was still in use, perhaps only by intruders. The tracks he'd mistaken for ordinary paths last night had been forced through the vegetation, to judge by the only one leading away from the entrance—from a gap in the hedge beside the lichened pillar that supported the left-hand gate.

The gap was barely wide enough for him to sidle through. Perhaps children had originally made it, breaking off the twigs that were strewn outside the hedge, and the joggers he'd seen were sufficiently thin to fit. He clenched himself to slimness so as not to be scratched by the thorns, because he was interested in visiting what he'd seen from the hotel window, not to mention the large house that his vantage point had hidden. Encountering so many students yesterday had left him feeling old and unadventurous. Once he would have been eager to explore a place like this, and he could think of no reason not to feel that way still.

Whoever had trampled the grass seemed to have been in no hurry to arrive at the house, for the sodden brownish path took quite a devious route among the trees. Well before he reached the statue Plater crossed several other tracks, which wandered maze-like out of sight through the grass. They appeared to converge on the statue, which was encircled by a wider patch of trodden vegetation. He was close to the weathered figure before he noticed that it and its companions had their backs to him.

They faced the house, where planks were nailed across the lofty front door and every visible window was boarded up. The eroded statues bristled with wads of moss, and the central figure's face had sloughed away like fungus. The features of both of the heads on which its hands rested had fallen off as well, and Plater couldn't imagine what expressions they might have borne as the pair of figures stooped forward. No doubt the stance was meant to acknowledge the touch of their benefactor, however much they resembled runners awaiting the start of a race. Having searched in vain for names—not even the main figure was identified—Plater made for the house.

Five windows flanked each side of the pillared porch, and a solitary trampled path led to the nearest left-hand window, from which a board had been wrenched loose. The pane was smashed as well, and through the gap he could just distinguish a room so large that the muffled sunlight fell short of most of it. As his eyes adjusted to the dimness he saw an indistinct reflection of the statue in a mirror across the room. The gap between the boards was so narrow that it would take somebody thinner than him to clamber through, and in any case that seemed more foolhardy than adventurous. Instead he leaned against a scaly flaking pillar of the porch and used his phone to search for Chalmerston.

It had been a miners' town until the industry exploded into conflict in the 1980s. After the mine was shut down, Chalmerston had become a centre for walkers in the countryside. The Wikipedia entry made no mention of any kind of chase, and Plater wondered if whoever the receptionist had accused of trying to end the tradition could have edited the article. As a breeze made the broken pane whistle, a sound so thin it might have been issuing between teeth, he tried looking up Chalmerston Chase. It was an annual event, a May Day run through the town, all the way from the top to the bottom and up the other side. May Day was nearly a week hence, but Plater didn't know if he would have enjoyed the spectacle of competitors exerting themselves so much. Apparently the event was called Chalmer's Chase, and as Plater searched for further information he tried to ignore the attenuated whistling, which sounded as though it was inside the house. There was indeed a campaign to end the tradition, not least because former miners from nearby towns thought it offensive to celebrate a workers' holiday with an event based on the exploitation of their counterparts centuries ago. By now Plater was certain that somebody was whistling between their teeth and calling in a low voice to a dog. How had people been exploited round here in the past? Another online reference established that the event had originally been known as Charmer's Chase, named for a bygone dignitary and landowner, Justice Charmer—quite possibly, Plater thought, the former owner of the ruined mansion. Had Justice been his name or his calling or both? Supposedly he'd pardoned local criminals so long as they took an oath to guard his property—"to chase away the inquisitive", though the reason was left undefined. Between toothy whistles the man somewhere nearby was still calling the dog, which was presumably able to hear even such a low voice. In fact, there must be more than one, though would anybody give dogs such names except as a joke? "Walker... Hunt... Hill..." A final online link questioned the view of Charmer as benevolent, suggesting that he contrived to find too many of the tenants of the farms and cottages on his land guilty of some offence in order to increase the patrol, and that he'd hold them to their vow even once they'd reached an age that seemed unreasonable if not positively unnatural. If this or any other aspect of his behaviour had eventually provoked a reaction, it seemed to be nowhere on the record, much like the end of Justice Charmer. Perhaps the voice was distant, not muffled, and could its owner be calling his employees to a job? "Hall...Wood...Stone..." The words needn't even be the names of people; perhaps they related to some renovation of the house, and the reiterated whistle might be an inadvertent mannerism. Plater's wanderings online had just prompted a random thought—that charmer was another word for wizard—when the phone twitched in his hand.

The bell was as shrill as the whistling. He had an irrational fancy that he'd attracted the call with his online search, even when he read the caller's name. As he raised the phone to speak it said "Pater."

The word threw him so much that he demanded "What are you saying?"

"Only teasing, dad. My roommate calls hers that. I was only calling to say thank you for being—"

He had to believe he'd misheard Carol's last word. "Being dad, you said."

"What else would I have? You're not driving, are you? You sound a bit distracted."

"I will be. Driving, that's to say. The traffic was so wretched I stayed somewhere overnight."

"Then don't let me stop you getting back to mum. Have a good run and I'll call you when you're free."

As Plater put away his mobile he heard the whistle and the voice. He found it even harder to determine how far away the fellow was, though he seemed to be calling for a painter. Despite his eagerness to set off for home, Plater went back to the broken window. The only figure to be seen was the reflection in the mirror, and it occurred to him that the statue might have been situated so that the owner of the house could see his own image from any of the front rooms. Leafy shadows on the statue lent restless movements to the dim discoloured shape across the room. A trick of light or of perspective obscured its companions, so that Plater might have imagined that the outstretched hands were resting on emptiness—in fact, that they were lifted higher and extended further than the ones behind him. He swung around to see that there were no shadows on the statue, just patches of moss. He hadn't time or any wish to think why he made at some speed for the path to the gates.

He could still hear the man calling out names. Perhaps one of them was Painter, not anybody's job after all. Even once the statue was behind him Plater could still hear the low voice. When he reached the track through the grass the sounds of his progress began to blot out the calls, until the rustling around him grew so insistent that he could have imagined he wasn't alone. No doubt a wind was responsible for this and for keeping the voice after him. Of course only vegetation was on the move along the paths he crossed, and he focussed his attention on the gates. While easing himself through the hedge he noticed once again that all the snapped-off twigs lay outside the grounds of the mansion, as if the gap had been forced open from within.

His cramp had threatened to return on the path, and his leg kept giving a reminiscent twitch as he tramped uphill. Nearby somebody was whistling, a practice that a fast food chain had brought back into fashion, though this whistler stopped at one note. More shops were open, and one that bore a tobacconist's vintage sign exhibited a placard for the CHALMERSTON CHAMPION, declaring that this year's chase would go ahead. He'd left it well behind when he heard somebody selling the paper, unless they were announcing a delivery of one. It wasn't in this street; a backwards glance showed him no sign of the paper. The shout had made his leg jerk, at the mercy of a nerve, and he did his best to limber it up as he climbed to the hotel.

He was regaining his breath when the receptionist came out of the office behind the counter. "Had your run, have you?"

"I wouldn't call. It that." Once he could utter an uninterrupted sentence Plater said "I think I found where your chase began."

Perhaps the man was as exhausted as Plater felt, since he seemed to need to sit down. "Where are you saying?"

"The big old ruin near the river. That's Charmer's statue down there, isn't it? I couldn't see its name."

"Who said you could go in there? It's all locked up."

"Someone was jogging there last night, or maybe they were practising for your event."

The receptionist stared as though suppressing a response. "Thought you didn't want to stir things up."

"I'm not sure how you think I—"

"The lot that want to stop it did," the receptionist said and turned to the computer.

As the man muttered at the screen Plater caught his own name. "I'm sorry, what did you say to me?"

"I'm saying you've got your stay with us to pay for."

"I was about to. I just hadn't heard you ask."

The receptionist scrutinised the credit card at such length that Plater could have thought he was going to read out the name. When the machine protruded a paper tongue the man tore it off and enfolded the card in it so thoroughly that the act looked almost ritualistic. "Hope you find your way," he said and retreated into the office.

Plater was at the glass door, though apparently not close enough to trigger the mechanism, when he thought he heard his name. His leg gave an inadvertent jerk before he realised he must have over-heard something else. It was surely too early for anyone to be asking for a chaser in the bar. No doubt the voice was in the breakfast room; he'd sounded subterranean, the man ordering a plate of what-ever it had been. Plater lurched at the door, which crept aside at last, and limped to his car.

He leaned on the roof and flexed his leg while he called Dorothy. He'd spoken to her last night, but now she wasn't at home. The message she'd recorded years ago promised that one of them would call back later. A trick of the connection emphasised their last name and her final word. "Just Sam," he said, "setting off right now," and lowered himself into the car.

A pointer opposite the exit from the car park sent him down-hill. He turned left at the first cross street, since there was no entry to the right-hand stretch. He meant to turn uphill as soon as he could, returning to the road that had brought him to Chalmerston. The street he reached was one- way too, and he had to drive down-hill until a right turn led him back to the street he'd started from. When he crossed it, a series of one-way streets that might almost have been a mirror image of the route he'd just followed took him to the junction where he'd turned left in the first place.

The way out of town must be further downhill. As he drove past the tobacconist's he thought he heard the call about the paper once again, and his leg gave an involuntary twitch. He could only turn left at the next crossroads, where the opposite street didn't admit traffic. The route led downwards and then right, crossing the street that contained the hotel before directing him through another series of grey stone terraces, so similar to those he'd already encountered that it felt like a repetition. It certainly resembled his previous route, given how it contrived to bring him back to the junction nearest the hotel.

He swung the car downhill at once, with a screech of brakes piercing enough for a whistle. Somewhere nearby a teacher was announcing playtime at a school, though Plater would have thought they'd use a bell. There was only one more crossroads, and the noise of the brakes made his leg twitch. Yet again he could only turn left, but the one-way street at the end of the terrace of grey houses descended straight to the foot of the hill—to the road alongside the grounds of the ruined mansion.

A pointer—he could have imagined that he was hearing the word, though surely only in his head—sent him past the mansion. Presumably there was a sports field on the far side of town, since somebody beyond the hedge was exhorting people to play to win, though Plater missed the last word. His leg jerked and the brakes whined high as he turned uphill, having found a street that would admit the car. He was almost prepared to find himself back at the highest junction, in which case he meant to park wherever he could and ask for directions at the hotel. But when the route forced him to follow a street across the slope, it returned him to the road closest to the mansion.

How distracted had he let himself become? Why hadn't he thought of using the map? When he brought up the town on his phone, however, it showed no trace of the one-way system. This only helped the streets to put him in mind of a maze—of the paths through the grass—and staring at the image made parts of it appear to darken, not least some of the letters spelling the town: a, l, e, r, t ... Plater meant to be, though he was troubled by the notion that they could form other words: alter, later. He dropped the phone on the seat next to him and drove down to the lowest road, passing the unseen mansion before he took another uphill route. Unrelieved ranks of grey stone houses shut him in and sent him right, and right again. When he reached a crossroads he was desperate to believe he hadn't previously met it, but there was the mansion again, lying in wait at the bottom of the hill.

The streets weren't deserted. There were people he could ask. One was labouring downhill towards him: a woman with a toddler in a pushchair and a small girl beside them. It was plain that rotundity ran in the family, and the woman and the girl might have been striving not to jog, proceeding at a slowness meant to counteract the effect of the slope. Plater lowered his window as the plodding party came abreast of him. "Excuse me, which way for the motorway?"

The woman's voice was as dull as her sluggish blink. "Way for?"

"Wafer," the girl said to her little brother, so low that Plater might have mistaken the word.

"Which way to it, I'm asking."

"Way to?"

Plater felt not much less confused than she appeared to be. He was disconcerted by observing that the toddler had a chewed plastic whistle in his mouth. Carol would never have had such an item at that age; they were too easily swallowed. "Wafer," the girl murmured, or a similar word.

Was she playing a game, perhaps a local one? "The way out," Plater told the woman while he tried to quell the jerking of his leg. "The way out of town."

"Outer," the girl muttered, if not something else, as her mother said "How did you get in?"

"On the road that comes to the hotel at the top."

"Better go the other way, then."

"Other," the girl mumbled—at least, Plater thought he heard that— and the toddler's face puffed up as he blew the whistle with unexpected strength.

The sound felt as if it was penetrating Plater's body, and made his foot jerk on the accelerator. "Thanks," he said and was driving downhill almost before he could choose to do so. The woman might have helped, however perfunctory her advice had been. If he must leave Chalmerston by the far side, at least he would be escaping the town. Once he reached the open countryside there would be signs to show him the way home.

He turned right when the clawed hedge rose above him, and drove past the mansion it hid. It ended at a junction, one branch of which led behind the building to a bridge across the river, while on this side of the water both roads climbed the hill. He could see how they became entangled in the one-way system, but the road beyond the bridge led straight to the top and over the hill. He swung the car onto the bridge at once.

A waterfowl emitted a piercing note as he passed over, a noise he found difficult to put out of his head. He tried switching on the radio, which brought him a local station; certainly the man sounded local. Was he saying he would pray for someone or, surely likelier, announcing a record he was about to play for a listener? No doubt the whistle was the start of the track, but it made Plater's leg twitch, and he turned the radio off. He needed to concentrate, because the hill was so steep that he could imagine the grey houses toppling down it like dominoes—so steep that he had to change to a lower gear. No wonder some people at the top were descending at such a speed, several of them on both pavements. They would be joggers, however helplessly precipitous their progress looked—in fact, so haphazard and beyond their control that they were spilling off the pavements into the road. Couldn't they see his car, or did they expect him to accommodate them? Admittedly they had the street to themselves; everybody else must be staying inside the houses or out of the way elsewhere. The runners were racing towards him faster than the car was climbing, and he could have thought they were unaware of him, especially since their heads were lowered, which went with their crouching stance. There were at least a dozen of them, and as Plater changed to second gear they spread across the road, blocking his way entirely despite how thin they all were. He leaned on the horn, and they lifted their heads in unison, revealing far too much.

They were already close enough for him to see that their clothes were ragged and discoloured, but so was the rest of them, not least their faces: the frayed gaping lips, the eyes like blobs of dried mud. Now he saw that they were mouthing in chorus, "play too" or a name or both. They were almost upon him, and he thought of driving straight through them, but the car was still losing impetus. He swerved with a screech of brakes that might have covered up another high sound and sent the car speeding off the main road.

He'd thought he was driving into a side street, but it was no more than an alley. In fact, the high blank walls on both sides were closing in, and he wasn't halfway to the next street when they began to scrape the housing of the wing mirrors. As he fumbled to lower the window beside him so that he could drag the mirror against the car, he glimpsed figures swarming into the alley behind him. The alley was growing narrower still, and if he drove much further he would simply jam the bonnet between the walls. In a panic that swept away most of his thoughts he opened the door while he still could—at the entrance to another alley—and fled downhill.

The mansion rose towards him as though it had all the time in the world. He would have dodged aside if he could, but the alley led straight down without a break in either wall. Plater felt as if the jerking of his leg was compelling him to jog faster. Echoes of his footsteps, shrill as whistling, boxed him in. He heard scrabbling and scrawny thuds behind him as pursuers made their various ways past or over the car. The slope seemed to be forcing him into a crouch that brought his head low, and he was so intent on not glancing back that he only belatedly noticed the figure that was waiting for him. He would have liked to think it was a statue, because surely only stone could make the costume so indistinguishable from its wearer and from the lichen that blotched the crumbling form. But when it pressed Plater's head down, its hand was colder than stone.

ALISON LITTLEWOOD

THE MARVELLOUS TALKING MACHINE

A LISON LITTLEWOOD's latest novel, *Mistletoe*, is a seasonal ghost story with glimpses into the Victorian era. Her first book, *A Cold Season*, was selected for the Richard and Judy Book Club and described as "perfect reading for a dark winter's night". Other titles include *A Cold Silence, Path of Needles, The Unquiet House, Zombie Apocalypse!: Acapulcalypse Now, The Hidden People* and *The Crow Garden*.

Her short stories have been selected for a number of "Year's Best" anthologies, and published in her collections *Quieter Paths* and *Five Feathered Tales*. She has won the Shirley Jackson Award for Short Fiction.

"I've come across many oddities in the course of my research into Victorian times," reveals the author, "and the Euphonia talking machine was one that stuck in my mind and wouldn't leave. It originally featured in the opening chapters of my novel *The Crow Garden*, but ended up on the cutting-room floor. It didn't belong there, but the Euphonia eventually found a new home in this story.

"Joseph Faber did indeed demonstrate his talking machine at the Egyptian Hall in 1846, although Tom Thumb's appearance was actually two years earlier. The other characters in the story, including Faber's sister, are fictional, though the audience's reaction to the Euphonia was a matter of record. One theatre manager of the day,

John Hollingshead, said: 'Never probably, before or since, has the National Anthem been so sung. Sadder and wiser I, and the few visitors, crept slowly from the place, leaving the Professor with his one and only treasure—his child of infinite labour and unmeasurable sorrow."'

I T IS ACROSS a distance of many years that I remember the events of 1846, and yet it might have been yesterday that I first heard the voice that haunts my dreams. It is not the words that have troubled me so, ever since I was a boy; it is the way they were spoken—and the fact of their emerging from no human throat.

I was twelve when I first heard of the inventor Professor Joseph Faber. Now my hair is grey, and yet inwardly I feel much the same. I still remember my father's theatre, the magnificence of its halls; the sense of never knowing what wonders would pass before my eyes; the idea that perhaps, truly, they were not entirely of this world.

My father set me to work early, not because we were in need of funds, but because I begged him to release me from the tyranny of slate and desk. For what were schoolrooms to me, when life itself— and such life—passed daily before my eyes at the Egyptian Hall?

The edifice itself was a curiosity to behold. Part of the row of mansions lining Piccadilly, it was yet a thing apart; for its gargantuan figures, winged globes and lotus motifs would be better suited to an ancient tomb of Egypt than the heart of London. The mysteries continued within. Vast pillars suggested the great avenue at Karnak, while indecipherable hieroglyphics adorned every surface. Its everchanging displays were equally entrancing, having included extraordinary statuary, dioramic views, historical artefacts—including Napoleon's coach—and indeed human entertainments; we had hosted a family of Laplanders offering sleigh-rides, the Anatomic Vivante or Living Skeleton, and a mermaid—this last, alas, sadly pretend.

Indeed, it might be said that I was accustomed to wonders, and yet, when faced with something more remarkable still, I longed only to turn my face away. But I was not alone in that, for Joseph Faber's was one of our most poorly received attractions.

My first sight of the man was not promising. He was a hunched fellow, wearing a frock-coat with too few buttons, and those dulled with time. His beard was untrimmed, his shoes smeared with street-dirt and his features were unprepossessing; his eyes, which were dull likewise, looked askance when he was addressed, even by me, a mere child.

He gave his name softly and with a slight German accent. It was only when he directed the placement of his boxes and crates that his expression became sharp, even mercurial in his assiduousness. I showed him to the chamber wherein his display would appear and he glared about before closing its door in my face, presumably to prepare himself. Later, my father sent me to offer any assistance he may require. I knocked and a voice responded with some phrase that I had no doubt meant "Go away".

I did not go away, however, for I was young and curious; or perhaps it was stupidity that made me press my ear to the door and listen.

He was constructing something: that was certain. I decided I must ask my father what it was, for I had been much distracted by the imminent arrival of General Tom Thumb, a fellow celebrated for his diminutive stature and comic scenes, and had paid little attention when he had told me of it. I knew only that it was some kind of machine, and so it seemed, for I detected the sound of wood being slotted into place and the clearer sound of metal striking metal. But it was Faber's mutterings that interested me the most.

It did not sound as if he were talking to himself. He would murmur in a low voice and then pause so that I could sense him listening before giving some reply. It sounded as if he were engaged in conversation with someone I could not quite hear.

Suddenly my ear stung as my father cuffed it. He told me to step sharp and see about the scenery flats in the main theatre, in tones so loud that Faber, shut up in his room, must surely have heard.

And so I left him in there, alone yet not alone, speaking to whoever would listen; and to prepare for his performance that evening, whatever that may be.

I stared down at the handbill. THE MARVELLOUS TALKING MACHINE, it proclaimed. I had wasted no time, after dressing the stage for the hilarious capers of Tom Thumb, in obtaining a copy from the ticket-seller.

So here was the answer to the sounds I'd heard coming from Professor Faber's room. The bill informed me that not only could his machine speak, but that a full explanation would be given of the means by which the words and sentences were uttered. It said that visitors may examine every part of his Euphonia—that was what he named it—not only demonstrating a wonder of science, but providing a fund of amusement to young and old alike.

All at once, I understood. Examination notwithstanding, it was clear to me that Faber was a cheat; for of course he must have some accomplice who would be concealed within this "wondrous" machine and speak on its behalf. It had been done before. Almost a hundred years ago, Kempelen's chess-playing Turk was heralded as the most magnificent automaton of its age, until it was discovered that its contests were won by a mere human hiding within its base. Thus it was made plain: it was a feat of wonder for a machine to mimic a man, but a matter of imposture and derision for a man to mimic a machine.

I could not confront Faber or reveal him as a fraud, however, for were we not his hosts, and party to all that passed? Yet I was determined to see for myself how the trick was done, and I confess I longed to lay eyes on whatever little creature may be concealed so cunningly. For, of course, it occurred to me that he or she may prove even tinier than Tom Thumb himself.

My disappointment may only be imagined when my father asked me to sort through a heap of mouldering costumes, to put some aside for repair, others for disassembling and yet others for the ragman. I knew I would never finish in time to take my seat for the start of Faber's demonstration, and it being held in a somewhat small chamber, I could not then disturb those who had paid their shilling by making my entrance.

Still, as the time came for it to end, I could not resist waiting in the passage to glimpse what I may when the doors opened. This time, I could more distinctly make out the sounds from within. People called out in turn, the audience I supposed, and something answered, though in tones the like of which I had never encountered. The voice was flat and dead and empty, and it made me shudder, and then the first notes of music sounded, and the awful voice began to sing. It was the National Anthem, but emotionless and dry, as if the life was missing, or perhaps the soul; as if the voice progressed from the very heart of a tomb. But of course this must be Faber's Talking Machine, his Euphonia, and I grasped the reason at once. For he could not wish it to sound human; if it did, all would guess at its true nature and his imposture would be discovered. It must perforce sound like something long dead—indeed, like something that had never lived. And yet I could not quite shake the chill as I pressed my eye to the keyhole.

But the door suddenly shook and swung open. I started back; a gentleman stood there, with commodious whiskers and a gloriously shining top hat. He gave me a disdainful look before leading the exodus from the room, and I made a hasty bow, gesturing towards the exit as if I'd come especially to point the way.

All the ladies and gentlemen filed past me, and as they went, I realised something odd about them. Usually, our patrons left smiling and laughing, exclaiming over what they had seen. But these did not smile; they did not laugh. They were entirely silent as they moved towards the cabs and carriages that awaited. There was no light in their faces; the only emotion emanating from them was dismay.

I looked away from them and saw Faber, his skin pallid, his eyes as lightless as the rest—and fixed upon mine.

I mouthed an apology, catching a glimpse of the contraption behind him: a wooden frame, through which I could see the back of the stage; an arrangement of keys and levers and bellows; and, affixed to its front, a human face. It was in the form of a woman— or rather, a girl—with reddened lips and gleaming ringlets, but with a cold and empty expression. It unnerved me to look upon it, and I knew in that instant there was nowhere for anyone to hide, even if they were half the size of Tom Thumb.

Faber stepped towards me and I turned and closed the door between us. I did not leave, however, but leaned heavily against the wall. Thankfully, he did not follow; after a time I heard shuffling sounds and the scraping of wood against the floor.

Then I heard a soft call of "Good night".

I froze, thinking he called out to me, then the light that crept from under the door was extinguished and I was left in near-darkness. Faber was to sleep in the chamber, then, with his machine. Whatever his trick, it seemed I would not discover it that evening.

The next day, I asked my father what he knew of the strange inventor who remained ensconced within our chamber. In response, he pulled a face.

"His takings are underwhelming," he said.

I opened my mouth to enquire further and found myself unsure what it was I sought. However, he went on regardless.

"He's a scientist, not a performer, and a mad one at that. This isn't his first talking machine, did you know? He burned the first one."

"Why did he do that, Papa? Didn't it work?"

He looked as if he'd like to spit. "Who knows? Drove himself maniacal with it, I reckon. It's clever—more than clever, some would say—but people don't like it all the same. There's some asked for their money back."

"It really speaks, then, his machine?"

My father affirmed that it did, and I remained silent, musing on that. It seemed intolerably sad to waste such an effort, if the professor really had somehow made the thing work. But perhaps his first attempt had failed?

I did not realise that I had voiced my feelings until my father replied. "Sad, you say? There's worse things, boy. Sleeps in the same room with it, he does. Insists he can't leave it by itself. It's not good for a man to become so obsessed—mark that. And—"

"Yes, Papa?"

He hesitated before he spoke and when he did it was with reluctance, as if it were something better left unsaid. "It's just—I did hear tell he gave that machine his dead sister's face."

I recoiled, thinking for an instant he meant it was made from flesh and blood; but of course it could not be so. I remembered the Euphonia's visage, her bow lips, her pretty ringlets—her lifeless eyes. And it came to me of a sudden that "euphonious" meant pleasant, honeyed, bell-like; agreeable. How could Faber give his deathly sounding machine such a name—and such a face, one that was dear to him? But of course, he could not have meant it to sound as it did. Perhaps that was why he had been driven mad, why he burned his first machine; he must have realised the gulf between what he hoped to achieve and reality. And yet, if his machine could truly speak, he was responsible for a miracle—was he not?

That evening, I witnessed the miracle for myself.

I did not know if Faber saw me as I scuttled inside and took a seat at the back of the room. I did not see him, only his machine, its pale face and shining hair standing out from the shadows. The edges of the room were dimly lit, though the stage was bright with gaslights, hissing and sputtering and highlighting each strut and lever and key—making it abundantly clear to all that no one could be concealed within. Those lights would not be lowered, not for this performance. Everyone could see as much as they wished.

Faber stepped forward. In a halting voice, he begged the liberty of introducing us, one and all, to his Marvellous Talking Machine, his Euphonia. His voice softened when he spoke its name, and he looked upon the immobile face with something like affection. I saw that he had hung a white dress beneath it for this performance; a dress that hung limp and empty almost to the floor, swinging slightly in some unseen draught. The hem, I noticed, was a little frayed, and I wondered where he had come by it. Had this, too, been his sister's?

Faber took his seat at the instrument as at a pianoforte, stretching his hands from his sleeves like a great proficient before placing them above a set of ivory keys.

A noise like a great intake of breath filled the room. It was the only sound; no one moved or spoke. Then the Euphonia opened her mouth. Slowly, so slowly, she said, with a slight German accent, "Please excuse my slow pronunciation. Good evening, ladies and gentlemen... It is a lovely day... It is a rainy day."

I realised I was leaning forwards in my seat. Despite the ordinariness of the words, I was repulsed; fascinated. Her lips moved like human lips. Her tongue lolled within her mouth like a human's. She breathed like a human, and yet no one could mistake her voice for a human voice.

I think my feelings were shared, for it was only when she ceased speaking that those around me began to move again as people do, shifting in their seats, rubbing their lips. No one applauded, however. No one cheered.

I looked at Faber, whose mouth was compressed into an unhappy line, his brows drawn down.

He invited the audience to provide words for his machine to copy. One soul, braver than the rest, bid her say, "*Buona sera*".

No doubt he intended it for some trick, but say the words she did, though slowly, sounding each syllable as if she were learning his language. Another called out a line from *The Taming of the Shrew*. She could pass no comment upon it, only copy his words. Another demanded something about the fineness of the summer and this she spoke too, all with the same languor, although sunshine and warmth seemed a long way from this accursed chamber.

Then Faber demonstrated how, with the turn of a screw, the Euphonia could whisper. This was even worse. In this way, she gave out the words of a hymn, though such a horror of a hymn I'd never heard. Still, I could not take my eyes from her empty gaze until I became sensible that someone else was watching, someone standing at the back of the stage.

It was a girl, almost concealed by the curtain. Her hair was shining, her dress white, her face pale. I did not look at her directly but even from the corner of my eye, I could see that her lips were moving. Was this Faber's accomplice after all? I turned my head to better focus on her, and I saw that no one was there. It was only a fold in the curtain, nothing more, and I shook my head. I told myself I was unsettled by the dreadful voice and the dismal man operating it. Little wonder he had burned his first effort—would that he had burned the second!

Then everyone around me rose from their seats, and I realised it was time to inspect the machine. I did not wish to go closer, yet I followed, not wishing to remain alone either, and in the jostling of the crowd I found myself standing directly before the Euphonia's face.

Close to, it appeared more lifeless than ever, more like a doll, and I wondered that I could have imagined it to be made of flesh. And Faber explained its workings: the replicated throat and vocal organs made of reeds, whistles, resonators, shutters and baffles, and then he showed how the bellows drove air through it all, and the Euphonia opened her lips and let out a long exhalation. I started away. It felt like breath on my cheek, but cold—cold as the grave.

I turned and, hidden amidst the bustle, I slipped from the room. I had heard the Euphonia speak. I had no wish, now, to hear her sing.

I could not keep away, however, for after the crowds had dispersed, I returned to that little room. I did not know what drew me there, only that I had been unable to cast it from my thoughts. Perhaps it was pity for poor mad Professor Faber. I expected to find him lost in despair at the horror induced by the thing he loved, but no; even from the passage I could hear voices and the clanking of keys.

Quietly, I opened the door and slipped inside. He was seated once more at his infernal machine. He had not seen me enter, for his head was lowered as he played upon it. The Euphonia's mouth gaped and twisted. She was singing after all, but not 'God Save the Queen' or any such thing. I had not heard its like before, but I guessed this must be some German nursery-song, perhaps even a lullaby.

My gaze went to the place by the curtain where I had imagined seeing a young girl. With those sepulchral tones resounding all about me, I could almost believe I had truly glimpsed the spirit of his dead sister.

Faber suddenly let out a cry of despair and slumped across his machine, folding his arms before his face.

And yet—I can see it still—his machine sang on. Her lips continued to move; her eyes still gazed blankly at me, holding me there until her song was done.

Slowly, Faber began to unwind his arms and lift his head. I did not wait to see his sorrow, or whatever message his expression might hold. I grasped for the door again, pulled it open and I fled.

That was many years ago. Faber left us soon afterwards, saying he had an opportunity with Barnum in America, and yet success was never his. I heard sometime later that he had destroyed his beloved Euphonia once more; and he too had then perished, by his own hand. It seemed plain to me, upon receiving the news, that they must always have risen or fallen together.

And could I believe that his was only a machine—that the glimpsed figure was an illusion conjured by my overwrought imagination? Sometimes, perhaps. But more often it seemed to me that he created not a Talking Machine, but a vessel; and that something immeasurably distant yet always close to him had come to reside within it.

I have thought upon it more than ever after my wife, Mary, died. Like Faber, we had no children. My father died long before; I was the last of my line. I was grown old and was alone, and lonely. Mary went before me into the dark, and I wondered: what would I not do to bring her back, to have my dear wife speak to me again?

The question would have signified nothing, of course, if it were not for the parcel addressed to me that arrived at the Egyptian Hall, years after Faber's death, but not long after my wife's.

The writing within was in a tongue strange to me, yet I saw its purpose at once. For there were plans and diagrams within: plans with levers and keys and shutters and baffles, and an empty space where a face should be.

Some unknown beneficiary of the professor must have sorted through his sad possessions at last—yet it seemed almost meant to be. It appeared that Faber had not been able to entirely destroy his life's work, but had decided to pass it on, to let some other man decide whether it should live or die. The only name he had bethought himself to write on the stained, torn envelope containing all his wisdom was mine.

And I began to dream of it, that awful, dry, dead voice whispering as I slept. Would it be worth the cost, I wondered, to have my wife speak, but in such a voice—dead—soulless? But perhaps, I told myself, it needn't be so. I pored over the plans with increasing avidity. Could not the arrangement of baffles be improved upon a little? And the whistles and resonators could surely be of finer make than had been available to Faber. If I followed the plans carefully, exactly, yet made my own little improvements here and there, surely the vessel would be perfect. I would hear her the way she was in life, her honeyed tones, her bell-like laughter...

I could only pray it would be so. It took many more months of hearing that voice, of wondering, but eventually I could resist its call no longer. I had the papers translated piecemeal, so that none but I would learn their whole secret. And I started to build, creating lungs, glottis, vocal cords, tongue, lips. I laboured long in closed rooms, my beard becoming unkempt, my clothes as stained as Faber's had been. It consumed me, this thing, and yet still I hoped.

Now it is nearing completion. With his footsteps carved into the earth before me, I have achieved what cost Faber many years of torment. Soon it will be time to take my place at the machine and see what emerges from its waiting lips.

The time has come to try my creation. I sit at its keys, regretting the arrangement that has Mary's face turned outward, so that I cannot see it. I wonder what expression might be revealed upon it? But it is of no matter. If my wife returns to me, I will know. I will feel her presence.

I place my hands so that they are just resting on the ivories, and I fill her artificial lungs with air. She takes a breath. We are ready.

I touch my fingers to the keys, and in answer she begins to speak. I press and press and her vowels turn into words that become sentences, and still I cannot stop, though I want to; with my whole heart, I want to. But my fingers betray me. They keep pressing, performing their dance, and I do not know what drives them; perhaps it is horror. Perhaps it is only that I wish, so very badly, that it is not true...

The voice speaks with a German accent. It is unmistakable, even in its hoarse whisper. And there is so little life in it that I can almost convince myself I am wrong, but as it speaks to me, I know: the voice is not a woman's, but a man's. It is Faber's voice I hear.

I sense a presence, though not hers, not the one I longed for so badly. I can picture the dishevelled, hunched figure standing at my back, watching me with narrowed eyes. I feel his sorrow, his yearning, his unfathomable despair, and still, I play. I make my machine whisper. I make it sing, but even then, the truth does not change.

I press my hands to the keys more firmly than ever. I am driven onward by something—madness, perhaps; yes, it is likely that. And yet there is fascination too, with the terrible miracle that is before me. Most of all, I realise it is fear. For what would happen if I ceased giving it these words—my words? The thing might not stop speaking. It might keep opening its lips—and what might I hear then?

I keep feeding it, and as I do, I feel my own humanity slipping from me. I do not mourn it as it goes. I think of Faber shutting himself in a room, setting fire to his machine, to himself. I can almost sense the flames that await me, that are waiting to consume us both.

JAMES WADE

WHO'S GOT THE BUTTON?

JAMES WADE (1930–83) was an American writer and poet who, following his army service, settled in South Korea, where he wrote widely on music for a variety of periodicals. His symphonic and chamber music has been performed in many countries, and he completed an opera based on Richard E. Kim's best-selling novel of the Korean War, *The Martyred*.

He wrote a regular column for *The Korea Times* ('Scouting in the City' as by "Alf Racketts"), which from time to time included reviews of genre books and films. A collection of Wade's poetry, *Early Voyagers,* was published by Hollym Corp, Seoul, in 1969. The full extent of the author's musical compositions and non-fiction pieces may never be known.

His genre fiction, however, was published by such noted editors as August Derleth, Ramsey Campbell, David A. Sutton, Stuart David Schiff and Herbert Van Thal. Wade's short stories ranged from supernatural tales from the mid-West, to weird tales set in Korea and works based on H.P. Lovecraft's "Cthulhu Mythos".

From the late 1960s to the early '80s, his fiction and poetry appeared in such magazines and anthologies as *The Arkham Collector, HPL, Whispers, Fantasy Crosswinds, Fantasy Crossroads, Tales of the Cthulhu Mythos, The Eleventh Pan Book of Horror Stories,*

Dark Things, Weirdbook, New Writings in Horror and the Supernatural, New Terrors and *The New Lovecraft Circle*.

James Wade missed out on a collection of his work appearing in the mid-1970s because Arkham House did not wish to use reprints of stories which had already appeared in their previous anthologies and, at the time, the author had not accumulated enough new material to otherwise fill the book.

In 1979, Fritz Leiber wrote the Foreword to a collection of Wade's supernatural fiction, which was later cancelled by Lancaster-Miller publishers. Finally, in 2018, Shadow Publishing issued *Such Things May Be: Collected Writings*, edited by Edward P. Berglund. It is the most complete book of Wade's writings to ever appear, containing all the proposed material for the earlier collections, along with many more pieces of non-fiction and poetry and Leiber's Foreword.

As James Wade readily acknowledged, his stories "…were written to entertain, to be entertaining, and—I think the phrase is Lovecraft's—to 'crystallise a mood'." The posthumous short, sharp shock that follows certainly achieves all of those things…

R ALPH ELIOT BEGAN descending the stairs two at a time, then thought better of it and settled for a less perilous scurry, the rhythm of which had to be interrupted and re-established at every landing. The apartment elevator was still broken, he was already late for work, and scuttling down twelve flights of steps would make him even later.

Worse yet, perhaps, there was something in the back of his mind, some foreboding that he couldn't quite bring into focus, something to do with the new baby, Helen, who was sick again and whimpering miserably when he left the apartment.

He was late, of course, because of the unutterable confusion in the apartment; baby Helen crying, the new nursemaid inexplicably absent. Alice not feeling well enough to cope since the difficult childbirth, and little Ralphy always underfoot and asking questions.

It was perfectly natural for a nearly-four-year-old to ask interminable questions, Eliot realised. Even the bland, fake-innocent malice the child sometimes showed when he knew his questions irritated was a phase of exploring the reality and personalities around him, he supposed.

Eliot was not so sure about Ralphy's recent mistreatment of the cat, Tigger; he hoped that was a phase, too, and would pass soon— along with the boy's manifest resentment of his new sister.

The child had been especially annoying this morning while Eliot was rushing to get dressed in the crowded bedroom with the whimpering baby's crib always in the way.

"What's this, Daddy?" Ralphy asked, burrowing into the back of a bureau drawer crammed with odds and ends.

"That? Where did you get it? It's a button-hook. I thought it was lost years ago."

"What's a button-hook, Daddy?"

"It's something people used to use to tie-up their shoes, a long time ago, before shoes had laces."

"Who put it here, then?"

"Your mother. It's your mother's, and it was her mother's before that, when they used to have shoes with buttons."

"Why is it in the drawer, Daddy?"

Eliot was trying to fasten his tie; his reflection flickered in the wavery mirror above the dresser and he cursed under his breath.

"It's there because your mother can't bear to throw anything away, not even a button, much less a button-hook that's been in the family for years."

Where was Alice, anyway? He would have to leave right away or lose his job. He heard the water running in the bathroom and realised it had been going for the last ten minutes. Alice chose the oddest times to wash out under-things!

Ralphy was examining the small, shiny metal hook with methodical attention.

"How does it work, Daddy?"

"Well, you just push the hook in behind the button and pull it through the hole. See!"

He knelt, undid a button on the child's blouse and, fumbling in his haste, re-buttoned it with the hook. It was sharper than he expected, nearly catching in the cloth. "You button it this way, and then you can unbutton it with the hook, too. Like this."

(Where was that idiot nursemaid, anyway?)

Eliot stood up.

"I've got to go, Ralphy. It's late, and I don't hear the elevator running this morning."

"Why won't the elevator run?"

"Well, they haven't fixed it yet. It's still stuck, just like it was last night."

He struggled into his coat and groped for his briefcase.

"Is the elevator sick too, like Helen?"

"Yes, it's sick—it's broken."

"Will the doctor come?"

"Some men will come and open up the motor and look inside. Yes, it's almost like a doctor coming."

He took his hat from the closet. "You be a good boy, now, and don't touch anything while Mommy is in the bathroom. And don't hurt Tigger today."

He was edging toward the bedroom door when Ralphy, standing beside the baby's crib and peering in, asked one last question.

"What's this Daddy?"

Now, four flights down. Ralph Eliot suddenly paused in his frantic scurry to work. His mind finally made the connection it had rejected, and he turned rushing back up the stairs two at a time with an urgency even more frantic than that which had goaded his descent.

Above, little Helen's cries had become screams—piercing, agonised shrieks that were suddenly and ominously cut off.

He remembered his answer to his son's last question:

"That's the baby's belly-button, Ralphy."

RIO YOUERS

THE TYPEWRITER

R IO YOUERS is the author of the novels *Westlake Soul, Halcyon* and *Lola on Fire*. His 2017 thriller, *The Forgotten Girl*, was a finalist for Canada's Arthur Ellis Award for Best Crime Novel. He is the writer of IDW's *Sleeping Beauties*, a comic-book series based on the best-selling novel by Stephen King and Owen King.

"I firmly believe that we live on, to some small degree, in the things we leave behind," says Youers. "That an inanimate object— something as innocuous as a pocket-watch, or a wallet—can harbour its owner's good (or evil) energy.

"That got me thinking about serial killers and their possessions: Jeffrey Dahmer's glasses, Ted Bundy's hairbrush, Jack the Ripper's fountain pen. I recall taking this one step further: imagining one particular murderer as an old man, hunched over a typewriter, writing his memoirs. Just think of the wicked energy that typewriter would have absorbed! The image was so stark and wonderful that I just had to do something with it.

"Thus, 'The Typewriter' came to life—written on a laptop, I hasten to add, and with (mostly) good energy."

Thursday, January 16th, 1964

S O FRIGHTFULLY COLD outside. Watkins says it's going to snow overnight, and Watkins is usually right about such things. He has uncanny knowledge. Ask him about the Purley contract and he'll chase his tail like a dog. Ask him about dowsing or the healing properties of certain minerals and he'll talk for hours. A most peculiar individual.

I told the children to expect snow, and how their little faces glowed. Patricia danced up and down the hallway, and Christopher has already set aside his coat and gloves. They won't sleep tonight, I'm sure. It warms me to see them so full of glee. After tea, Christopher asked if he could put a log on the fire and I permitted him, watching as he removed the guard from the hearth and gently laid the log amongst the flames. He gave it a couple of manly prods with the poker, then replaced the guard and turned to me with an expression of boundless pride. We then sat as a family and talked for a full hour, mostly nonsense, but with a measure of love and understanding I so miss when I'm not with them...and sometimes when I am. It was a precious moment, and it didn't matter that the windows rattled in their draughty way, or that the chimney sometimes howled and made the single log hiss as if it were alive.

At eight o'clock we sent the children to their beds, and Evelyn and I curled in front of the fire, she with her head on my shoulder, me with my fingers in her hair. I smiled and watched the flames, listening to the window rattle, believing myself the luckiest man alive.

Friday, January 17th, 1964

A strange day, all told. Watkins was right about the snow. My goodness! I woke to a different world, with everything draped in a white so clean it hurt your eyes to look at it. When I left for work, Christopher and Patricia were playing in the front garden, their noses red and their gloves wet from snowballing.

There were no buses running, so I had to walk, and thus arrived late. I wasn't the only one, of course, so Drummond couldn't reprimand me, although I could tell he wanted to. I appeased him by completing the Worthington contract ahead of schedule, and starting on Blackwell-Wright. I occasionally glanced up at our single office window, watching the snow fall, sometimes in dusty swirls, often in delicate clusters. The drifts were knee-deep by the time I collected my wages and left. Still no buses, so I walked with my coat tugged close and my scarf wrapped about my face. I trudged down the Old Kent Road, desperately cold and bleak, until I passed Temple's Bric-à-Brac, where the light spilled onto the pavement in a most inviting fashion. I was drawn to look at the window display and saw there an item that immediately took my fancy: an old typewriter, an Oliver No. 6, with a ridge of dust along its platen and its green paint in places scorched away as if it had been recovered from a fire. The price tag propped between the second and third row of keys read: £1/5s. Rather pricey for a thing so neglected. Nevertheless, it had a distinct appeal, like a mongrel dog or a worn pair of slippers, and I was moved to enquire within.

The shop itself is quite fabulous: a cornucopia of wondrous arte-facts in various states of disrepair. Muskets spotted with corrosion, gramophones with tarnished horns, spinning tops that have lost the will to whistle. Temple himself is equally threadbare, a chameleon amongst his wares, to the point that I thought the shop empty when I first entered, and in calling his name was startled to see him rise from the camouflage of a cluttered desk.

"Temple, my good man," I said as he shuffled towards me. "The typewriter in the window... what can you tell me about it?"

"One pound, five shillings," he replied.

"Yes, I can see the price tag," I said. "But does the machine work? It looks in questionable condition."

Temple shrugged his dusty shoulders. "It's not meant to work, is it? It's an antique. A display piece."

"A display piece?" I barked, aghast. "Where would you display such a monstrosity? Other than in your window?"

"Obviously, it needs to be restored." Temple took a packet of Embassy Regal from his shirt-pocket, but didn't offer me one. He lit the fag with a box of matches plucked from a nearby table of oddments and blew his smoke into the air above us. "Think of it as a project. You clean it up, replace a few parts, tighten some screws, and Bob's your uncle. Display in pride of place or sell to a collector. You might even make a few nicker."

The idea had appeal. Not for fiscal gain, but to take a thing so untended and make it kind on the eye. It seemed the opposite of what we do with our lives—everything being worn to nothing: our possessions, our bodies, our state of mind. Here was an opportunity to reverse the process.

Temple, as I have mentioned, is a dishevelled individual. His skull consists of three teeth, brown as ale and unkindly spaced. His left eye is perpetually closed. It works fine, to the best of my knowledge, but he keeps it screwed shut, regardless. This gives him the appearance of a pirate, which makes bartering with him easier.

"I'll give you fifteen shillings," I offered.

Temple blew a string of smoke into the air, which bloomed like a peacock's tail. "You saw the price tag." He cracked an unsightly grin. "I'll take a pound even."

"Codswallop," I said. "Seventeen shillings. I'll not go higher."

"Nineteen," he said. "And six."

"Eighteen," I countered brashly. "And not a penny more."

He considered in histrionic fashion, rubbing his chin and shaking his head, and then agreed with a greasy handshake. I subtracted the total from my wage packet of £15.00, and then left with the typewriter—a deceptively heavy beast—in my arms.

It made the walk home longer, and harder.

I could write several pages more in regard to Evelyn's reaction to my purchase, but suffice it to say that she was not best pleased, and the atmosphere in the house tonight was decidedly icier than that of yesterday. Indeed, it was less frosty outside, standing next to the snowman built lovingly by my children. At one point his carrot nose fell off, and I popped it back into place, thinking, with a wry smile, that I had better get used to restoring things.

Sunday, January 19th, 1964

The typewriter is in the shed, sitting on my workbench. It is an ugly little thing, and I can see why Evelyn does not want it in the house.

It smells dreadful too. A sickly, back-of-the-throat stench I can only liken to a dead puppy I once discovered in a drift of fallen leaves. Yes...the typewriter smells like a dead puppy.

But not for long. I shall strip it and clean its individual components with cotton-buds, fine brushes and turpentine. Broken parts will be either fixed or replaced. Once reassembled, I dare say it will be fine enough for a museum.

Wednesday, January 22nd, 1964

Spent the entire evening in the shed with my typewriter—or what used to be my typewriter, but is now a sprawl of levers, wheels, bars, and various other pieces I have no name for. Had a blanket wrapped around me, but still so cold, my fingers numb as I painstakingly cleaned each piece. Got about 1/8th of them done. Will continue tomorrow.

Monday, January 27th, 1964

Repainted the typewriter's body today. Found the exact shade of olive green in a model shop. It took me hours to sand away the old paint and scorch marks, and I used a spray gun to apply the new coat evenly. I must say, it looks rather splendid.

Wednesday, January 29th, 1964

An altercation this evening. Evelyn says I am spending far too much time in the shed with my typewriter, to which I replied that a working man is entitled to his small pleasures, and I would not be in the shed at all if the machine were permitted in the house. Voices were raised and the children wept. Evelyn dashed to the bedroom and locked the door. I could hear her crying into the pillows, the foolish woman, so removed to the shed where I lovingly polished the type bars F through to U.

Thursday, January 30th, 1964

On the way home I bought some carnations from Cheeky Dave's stall and presented them to Evelyn. It softened the edges, somewhat. By the time we'd finished tea, she could look me in the eye again. She even managed a smile. We then gathered about the fire and listened to the wireless. Patricia showed me her new dance. An imperfect tap dance, of sorts, but then she is only eight. Christopher showed me the book he had borrowed from the library: an illustrated abridgement of *Treasure Island*. He turned to a picture of Long John Silver, and this made me think of Temple, which in turn made me think of the typewriter. Suddenly I yearned to be in the shed, cleaning ink from the type bars and listening to the comforting click of the ribbon spools. I even stood up, quite distracted from Christopher's enthusiasm, and took two steps towards the door. Then I stopped. That I would rather be in a cold shed than spend time with my wonderful family filled me with shame. I dropped to one knee, pulled my children close, and whispered that I loved them.

As deep as my obsession with the typewriter runs, it will not come between me and my family. When convenient, I shall tinker. Until then, I shall not.

Speaking of tinkering... Evelyn waits for me in bed as I write this. Her eyes reflect the shaded lamp and her smile is so alluring.

Tonight I shall go to bed with my pyjama bottoms off.

Saturday, February 1st, 1964

Ordered: 1 x carriage release lever, 1 x backspace lever, 1 x replacement rubber for platen, 1 x space bar, 1 x shift key, 1 x type guide, 2 x paper guides, 4 x type bars (G, O, T, M), 6 x face keys (B, E, H, O, R, W), 1 x ribbon, 1 x bell.

I spent all day looking around specialist shops in London. Evelyn was in a foul mood when I returned home.

Sunday, March 22nd, 1964

It is done. After more than two months of fastidious cleaning, fiddling, adjusting, and waiting for parts, the typewriter is now in working order. Not quite as polished as I had hoped, but a vast improvement on the eyesore I brought home from Temple's Bric-à-Brac. Even Evelyn stated that I did a splendid job and has allowed me to bring it into the house (although a whiff of dead puppy remains; try as I have, I simply cannot eradicate it). I set it on a table in the back room, where we keep all manner of items too cumbersome to transfer to the loft: the children's old cot, a wardrobe with a cracked mirror in the door, Auntie Mabel's mangle, which we inherited after a rather unfortunate mishap. I must admit to a wonderful feeling of achievement, to have breathed new life into something so fractured... so pitiable. I wonder if heart surgeons feel the same way after a successful operation. Needless to say, I was as happy as a sandboy this evening, singing along to the BBC Light Programme, dancing with Patricia, and play-wrestling with Christopher on the living room floor.

"You're in good spirits, Arthur," Evelyn remarked. "Perhaps we should get you to fix some things around the house."

To which I laughed, twirled her in my arms, and planted a kiss on her lips.

Later, with the children in bed and Evelyn listening to her favourite show, I retired to the back room with a sheaf of foolscap, thinking I would compose a brief poem on my restored machine, one pertinent to my good mood. I pulled a chair to the table and sat for a moment, admiring my handiwork, and then fed a sheet of paper into the carriage. Before beginning, I thought I should test the quality of each letter, but no sooner had I set my fingers upon the keys than a dire sensation gripped me. It was like nothing I'd felt before, and I lost all sense of myself. My fingers rattled upon the keys with a will of their own. I heard the type bars strike the page and the carriage judder to the left. With a gasp I pulled—yes, pulled: an act of force—my hands from the key-top and stood up quickly. The chair toppled over, but I barely noticed; my attention was on the page. Whereas I had intended to type, `The quick brown fox jumps over the lazy dog`, what I had actually typed was, `Kill the harlot. Cut her in half.`

I took a quick, sharp breath, then pulled the page from the carriage and crumpled it in my hands. I was shocked beyond measure, and my heart raced in my chest. I cast a distrustful eye upon the typewriter and stepped away from it, but not before catching my reflection in the cracked mirror on the wardrobe door. I'm sure it was a device of the mirror's imperfection, but I was certain I saw two reflections: my own, and that of a distorted figure looming not behind, but *within* me, like a blurred photograph.

I hurried from the back room, disposed of the offensive sheet of paper (I pushed it to the bottom of the dustbin, where Evelyn would not find it), then washed my hands and joined my wife in the living room.

She was too absorbed in her show to notice my strained smile.

Monday, March 23rd, 1964

Couldn't concentrate at work today. Thinking about the typewriter, more particularly about the odd sensation that overcame me, and the words—those shocking words—that had jumped unbidden across the page.

I returned home subdued and confused. Evelyn asked what was wrong and I told her only half the truth—that I'd had a long and stressful day. The lamb chops and mint sauce cheered me up a little, although the mashed potatoes were cold and lumpy.

Avoided the back room, but felt the typewriter calling to me.

This is all very disturbing.

Tuesday, March 24th, 1964

Called in sick today after a night of terrible dreams. In the most vivid of them I stood in the living room with a human kidney in my hands. The wireless played, not the BBC Light Programme, but a melody of clicks, clacks and bells. I turned to the fire, then laid the kidney gently amongst the flames. It hissed and sizzled. I gave it a couple of prods with the poker, then turned around, my chest swelling with pride.

I awoke in a dishevelled state, dripping with perspiration, my heart pounding in my chest.

I think I'm coming down with something.

Friday, March 27th, 1964

Feverish for... I don't know how long. Days? Yes, days. In bed writing this. The room is spinning and the sheets smell of sickness. I can barely read my own writing. Think I'll sleep for a while.

Monday, March 30th, 1964

The fever continues and every sound hurts. I need a shave. I'm a whiskery chap. Like a sailor. No, like a pirate. Arrrrggh! Did you hear that the quick brown fox jumped over the dead puppy? What a terrible smell. Arrrrrrrgggggghhh!

Tuesday, April 14th, 1964

It is illogical to fear an inanimate object (unless the object happens to   be a Nazi V-1 Doodlebug, as my dear grandmother discovered—God rest her soul). After three weeks of avoiding the typewriter, I decided to confront it, having attributed the previous aberration to the fledgling stages of my illness.

And so, after tea, I entered the back room and found the typewriter as I had left it, sitting on the table, its U-shaped type bars resembling the wings of an insect about to take flight. I pulled up a seat and wiped sweat from my brow, then grabbed a sheet of foolscap and rolled it into position.

I placed my fingers on the key-top and typed, `Cut their juglars very quiet with a razer and use an ax to lop off their fucken limbs.`

So, nothing to worry about, then. And all the letters in fine working order.

Jolly good.

`Wednesday, April 22nd, 1964`

`Writing diary entry on typewriter for first time. Why not, eh? Will cut out her kidne and snip off her fingurs and staple it into the diary proper.`

`Rather a long day at work. Drummond still giving me flack for taking two weeks off sick, but I had a doctor's note so I don't know what his problem is I'll kil him too cut his fucken throat the toad.`

`The family was in fine form tonight. Jollity all around. Nothing I lik more than to watch someon bleed.`

`Sausage, egg and chips for tea.`

Thursday, April 23rd, 1964

Wrote a poem tonight on my typewriter. A rather beautiful piece, reminiscent of Coleridge. I may try to get it published.

Friday, April 24th, 1964

My reflection in the cracked mirror is a peculiar thing. The defect runs directly down the middle of my face. On one side I appear quite normal. On the other I am distorted. My mouth is twisted, my eye dripping, and the air around me is dank with shadow. However, when I move away from the table upon which the typewriter sits, my reflection snaps back into something more familiar. It is simply me again, on both sides of the crack. A handsome devil, it has to be said.

Saturday, May 9th, 1964

Received a rather stern rejection from *Ambit* magazine, requesting I never sully their slush pile with my filth again. A perplexing response.

Sunday, May 10th, 1964

Another quarrel with Evelyn. Been happening a lot of late. She suggests that I haven't been myself, and that our relationship is fractured. I of course told her that she was being downright silly, but I wonder...

She is sleeping now. I have spent the last twenty minutes or so standing by her bedside, staring at her. Moonlight spills through the window and her skin seems so pale, and so breakable. I think how vulnerable her eyes are, and how soft her lips. It amazes me how easily she would shatter.

We are such fragile creatures.

Wednesday, May 20th, 1964

Tried my hand at some traditional Japanese haiku. I have stapled one into the diary:

```
Slyce the bitch open
```

```
Krimson petals stane the floor
Her eyes close slowly.
```

Will submit to *Ambit*. Reject that, you buggers!

Tuesday, June 23rd, 1964

The last month or so has been extremely trying. Diary entries have been sporadic, at best, but I'll try to cover the important things here.

I'll begin by saying that Evelyn has threatened to take the children and leave. She has called my behaviour damnable and believes I need psychiatric help. She doesn't like my beard either. She says it makes me look like a Russian. The beard (which I think looks rather dashing) is a problem that can be solved with a pair of scissors and a sharp razor. I am more concerned with other issues.

Namely, the typewriter.

I began to suspect a deviance about the little machine, something—dare I say it?—*paranormal*. Not simply because of the dead-puppy smell, or my deformed reflection when I'm typing. There is a disquieting presence about it...a dismalness to the clacking of the keys and the peal of the tiny bell, and I believe some small measure of it has leaked into me. And so I hastened to the one man who would know about such things: Watkins. I cornered him on his lunch break. He was eating marmalade sandwiches, like Paddington Bear, and reading a book on radiesthesia.

"Watkins," I said. "I need your expertise."

"The Purley contract?" he enquired worriedly.

"No," I said. "Something even more inexplicable."

He raised an eyebrow.

"Is it possible," I began, "for a non-living object to be spiritually possessed?"

"You mean like a house?"

"No," I replied. "Something smaller."

"A packet of fags?"

"Don't be an imbecile."

"Well, what do you mean, Arthur? Spit it out."

I told him about the typewriter. I thought, prior to our conversation, that I would share only the relevant details, but found myself divulging everything, from the dead-puppy smell to the fact that my wife now sleeps in a separate bed. He listened, munching his marmalade sandwiches, nodding occasionally, and when I finished he took a pen from a pot on his desk and wrote down the name and telephone number of someone who could help.

"Kingsley Pringle?" I asked, eyeing the piece of paper suspiciously. "Is this a psychiatrist, Watkins? Do you think I'm bananas?"

"Not at all," he said. "Pringle is the most renowned psychometrist in the UK, and luckily for you, he's right here in Bermondsey."

"Psychometrist?" I said.

Watkins nodded. "It is believed that all things—be they animal, vegetable, or mineral—have a unique vibratory signature. The psychometrist, through touch, is able to channel this energy and divine aspects of the subject's history. For instance, he or she might touch an item of clothing and be able to tell you to whom it belonged. Pringle is particularly remarkable, and has several times been employed by Scotland Yard. He has touched murder victims, weapons, etcetera, and provided the police with vital information."

"Fascinating," I said.

"Quite," Watkins agreed. A blob of marmalade dripped onto his tie. "Take your typewriter to Pringle, and he'll be able to tell you more about it than you probably want to know."

I thanked Watkins, went to my own desk, and called the number at once. Pringle answered. Our conversation was brisk. I told him about the typewriter and made an appointment for the following evening.

Pringle lives in a gloomy block of flats on The Grange. I took the bus to Tower Bridge Road (feeling somewhat odd with the typewriter perched on my lap) and walked from there. He lives on the top floor, of course, which meant I had to lug the beast up four flights of stairs. I was out of breath when I reached his door.

"Clayworth?"

"A pleasure to meet you, Mr. Pringle."

"Come in," he said.

I had expected a bright, fox-faced man in wire-framed spectacles, but Pringle was a dour-looking oldster with a plumage of silver hair and dandruff on his shoulders. He asked for payment of one pound up front, then led me to a room furnished only with a table and chair. At his request, I set the typewriter on the table and stepped back.

"An Oliver No. 6," he said, looking at it carefully, but not touching.

"Yes," I replied. "It was in terrible con—"

"Shh." He waved one porky digit in the air. "Don't tell me anything."

I bit my lip and nodded mutely.

"Partially restored."

I wasn't sure if it was a question or not, so remained silent.

"1909, I believe."

I shrugged.

"And an ugly mite, if ever there was one."

"It has a certain charm," I said, having become used to defending the typewriter. Evelyn calls it the cockroach, and has begged me to get rid of it. But I cannot bring myself to discard something I worked so hard to restore. With my hands I made it comely (to my eye, at least), working in a cold shed to bring it to life. It feels like a part of me.

"Charm," Pringle repeated. He shook his head and took a seat at the table. "Now, I ask that you remain quiet, Clayworth. I require absolute silence when scrying."

"Scrying?"

"Shh." The porky digit again.

I have since learned that Pringle has "scried" over a thousand objects, many of them with huge degrees of success. Smaller objects he places against his forehead. Those too heavy to lift are touched with hand position aligned with certain celestial energies. His usual reaction is a light fluttering of the eyelids and perhaps a few mumbled phrases. Then he will break contact and reveal what he has learned.

On this occasion, he assumed the position, placed his hands on either side of the typewriter, and immediately started to tremble—and quite violently too, as if several thousand volts of electricity were passing through his body. I, of course, thought this a normal aspect of the scrying process, along with the frothing at the corners of his mouth, so simply stood and watched, silently, as requested. However, I suspected something was awry when I smelled his silver plumage burning and noticed blood trickling from his ears.

"I say... Pringle?"

Pringle shrieked. He pulled his hands from the machine and flew backwards in his chair, spilling to the floor in a most ungainly manner.

"My dear man," I said. "Is this quite normal?"

"Evil," he said, holding his head. Tears sparkled in the corners of his eyes. "I've never known such evil. And it's restless... looking for—"

"What are you talking about?" I took a step backwards.

"Blood... screaming."

I shook my head. The sight of Pringle so distressed, and the smell of his burning hair, was extremely unsettling.

"Go," he pleaded, waving at the door. "And take that infernal machine with you."

"Go?" I asked, gathering the typewriter to my chest. "But I gave you a pound."

Pringle drew a long breath that sounded like the wind rattling my windows. Tendrils of smoke rippled from his scalp.

"What do you mean by evil?" I asked. "I shan't leave without answers."

The psychometrist regarded me with his small, wet eyes. "That typewriter belonged to Emory Grist. That's all I can tell you. Now please... leave!"

That name, Emory Grist, was familiar to me. I pondered it on the bus ride home, but couldn't place it—one of those annoying tip-of-the-tongue things. Evelyn would know, but she was sleeping by the time I arrived home, so I didn't disturb her. I waited until the following day at work and asked Watkins.

"Leather Apron strikes again," Watkins said.

"What do you mean?" I asked.

"That was the headline in the *Evening Standard*," Watkins said. "April of 1910, I believe. Emory Grist killed six women in Whitechapel in the space of three weeks. Cut their throats in two places, from left to right, and disembowelled them too. The similarities to Leather Apron—also known as Jack the Ripper—were so remarkable that many people believed Grist and the Ripper were one and the same."

My heart dropped in my chest. I shook my head and took a deep breath.

"Grist killed himself in a house fire as the police were closing in," Watkins continued. "To this day nobody knows if he truly was the Ripper."

"House fire," I said vaguely, recalling the scorch-marks on the typewriter's body.

"Then there were the letters," Watkins said.

"The letters?"

"From Hell." Watkins grinned and rubbed his chin. "In 1888, someone purporting to be Jack the Ripper sent a letter to the head of the Whitechapel Vigilance Committee. The communication was badly misspelled—deliberately, some scholars believe—and accompanied by a portion of human kidney. The address in the top corner read simply, 'From Hell'. Twenty-two years later, Emory Grist did something eerily similar. The only notable differences were that his letters were sent to Scotland Yard, and they weren't hand-written...they were typed."

Watkins made typing gestures with his fingers.

"Of course," I said, feeling woozy.

"Which reminds me," Watkins said. "What did old Pringle say about your—" And then his mouth closed with a little snap and his eyebrows knitted neatly in the middle of his forehead. I could almost hear the proverbial penny drop.

I walked away from his desk and avoided him for the rest of the day.

Returning home that evening, I brimmed with resolve to jettison the typewriter. My plan was to put it in a sack and throw it in the Thames. However, when I walked into the back room and laid my hands on the machine, I had a sudden change of heart. I found myself caressing its key-top and platen. Same the following evening, and the evening after that. Much as I knew I should, I just couldn't bring myself to part with it.

It would appear that it has quite a hold on me.

Wednesday, June 24th, 1964

So many bad dreams. *Click-clack-ding! Click-clack-ding!* Last night was the worst yet, and the violent imagery still pours through my head. Far too disturbing to commit to paper. I'll keep it in my head and hope it fades.

Thursday, June 25th, 1964

Drummond has requested I shave. And bathe. He insists my shabby-genteel image is not appropriate for the workplace. I imagined plunging my dividers into his left eye. *Ding!*

Monday, June 29th, 1964

I stopped at Temple's Bric-à-Brac on the way home, fully intending to ask if he would take the typewriter off my hands. He could have it for free, if he was willing to come and collect it.

I couldn't do it, though. I stammered like a moron and Temple looked at me through one eye, but the offer wouldn't spill from my lips. Instead I purchased a ceremonial Japanese samurai sword. The blade is a little rusty, but I'm sure it'll sharpen nicely.

Tuesday, June 30th, 1964

Many tears tonight. Not from me, but from Evelyn and the children. They are all sleeping now and their bags are packed. They leave for Liverpool tomorrow.

The window rattles, but the sound of the whetstone along the blade is very comforting.

```
                         Wenzday 1st Juli 1964
I mad some poetry for a whil and lookd in mirror
and saw the crack. Then I got my samri sord and
went upstares and there was Evelyn sleping in
the bed like an angel. I thoht I could kep her
```

and stop her from leeving if I cut her into peeses and put her in a nise littel box. Then the windo ratteld a sound like clik and clack and clik and Evelyn waked up and saw me and screemed. I tryed to cut her in half with the sord. I think I cut somethin bekuase there was some blood but not much and Evelyn throw the lamp at me the fucken bitch. She run from the bedroom and down the landin and I chayse her with my sord. She gos to kiddys bedroom and slams the door and bloks it with somethin I think a chare. I could here them all cryin and screeming. I try to brake down the door and evn used my nise sord but I couldnt brake it. I needed somethin hevvy so went downstares and got my typewryter which I luv. I carry it back upstares and use it on the door wam and bam and crak and yes the door brake open but wen I lok inside the windo is open and Evelyn the fucken bitch is gone and tak the kiddles with her. I think she gos to Livrpol but she left her bags. Mayb she come bak. The windos still rattel and I lik the way they go clik and clak and ding.

Friday, July 3rd, 1964

The police are looking for me. My picture adorns the *Evening Standard*, along with a warning that I am extremely danjerous and not to be approached. I think they will be looking for some time, though. I have effected a disguise by shaving my hed bald and trimming my beard into a neat goatee. I look very different from the man I used to be.

I feel different, two.

I write this—my final dire entry—from the Ten Bells in Whitechapel. It is late, and the pub is crowded with merrymakers. Some rabblesome men, and a bounty of young women—pale and frajile, all.

So many shadows outside. So many places untouched by street-light.

I think I'll linger here a whil, with my samri sord conceeled inside my long koat. I rather like these crooked streets. It feels like hell.

In fact, it feels lik coming home.

KEN MACKENZIE

THE KEEPERS OF THE LIGHTHOUSE

KEN MACKENZIE works as a senior software engineer for a large German telecommunications subsidiary. After dark, he is more celebrated as the cantankerous typesetter at the Swan River Press in Dublin.

Originally from Teesside, the "posh" end of the North East of England, he lives with his wife in Milton Keynes. Their three beautiful, talented children have long-since flown the nest (thank heavens).

"This story came pretty much fully-formed," he remembers. "My wife was away for a weekend visiting relatives, so the world was my oyster. I'd wanted to write a Christmas ghost story as a chapbook for friends and enemies—something brooding and atmospheric, but with an unusual setting. A lighthouse popped into my head and then everything literally fell into place. I wrote a synopsis of the tale over a bottle of Beaujolais.

"When my wife returned, she read it through and made some brilliant, important changes. After she'd expunged the gratuitous sex scenes that had crept in, we were pretty much there. All that remained was for me to knock out the story and spend many painful weeks re-writing and tinkering incessantly with the minutiae of the prose.

"As a professional programmer, old habits die hard . . ."

∽

A THICK SEA fog had rolled in from the Atlantic. Reynolds watched with growing interest as a rowing boat inched its way towards the rock, pitching and rolling against the incoming tide. In the boat, he noted, were two figures: one, whom he recognised as Mr. Cartwright, had the oars and rowed with great skill; the other, his head over the gunwale, retched violently into the sea.

"Ahoy—below there!" Reynolds called from the top of the lighthouse. But his voice, muffled by the dense fog, failed to carry and it drifted unheard on the wind.

When the boat reached the wooden jetty that clung to the rock like a limpet, the oarsman climbed out and secured it fast with a rope. His companion, struggling to maintain his balance in the swaying craft, gingerly clambered onto the deck, his unsuitable footwear causing him to slip and slide on the sodden planks. The two men stood and looked about them. In the gloom, the lighthouse towered over them like an unassailable colossus, bleak and alien and replete with foreboding.

It stood in the middle of the ocean on an outcrop of black rock. To the east, tall cliffs rose from the craggy Sutherland shoreline, a wall that obscured the view of the mainland. To the west, the grey Atlantic unfurled as far as the horizon like a soiled winding-sheet.

As they made their way across the seaweed-slippery rocks, Reynolds observed that the stranger carried a sailor's sack. Mr. Cartwright lugged a crate of provisions.

When the two men reached the lighthouse, Reynolds had already descended from the catwalk and was already waiting for them in the galley. They dumped what they were carrying and Mr. Cartwright proceeded to light a fire.

Maitland was not impressed with what he saw. The galley had an overpowering musty odour about it. The plaster on the walls was powdery and crumbling and it fell away in places. A large kitchen table dominated the centre of the room. Under the galley window hung a stained, deep sink with a single tap. An ancient, blackened cooking stove stood to one side of it.

Reynolds had grown accustomed to the place over time. He no longer noticed the dankness and the discomfort. Upstairs, a cluster of spartan cells served as sleeping-quarters, each furnished with a camp-bed, a rickety chair and a wardrobe from the middle of the last century. They were draughty and uncomfortable, but Reynolds, fortunately, didn't feel the cold.

"Not what you were used to in the chokey, eh?" said Mr. Cartwright. "It'll soon feel like home-from-home!"

As they sat at the table drinking tea, Mr. Cartwright said: "I must remind you, Mr. Maitland—don't get complacent during your time here. The sea today is fairly calm. But you'd be advised not to venture out when the weather gets up. It can be treacherous on the rocks and we've lost many a keeper that way over the years."

Maitland, who was a stocky, powerful man in his early forties, grunted: "Understood, Mr. Cartwright."

He was dressed in ill-fitting, hand-me-down clothes, as if they'd been thrust upon him in haste. His chin was unshaven and his hair unkempt and it looked to Reynolds as if he'd been on the road for a number of days. Reynolds instinctively sensed that he should be on his guard with this man.

Mr. Cartwright, on the other hand, was a short, rotund man with small hands and fat fingers. His head was shiny and bald with wispy patches of red hair at the sides and back. He was clean-shaven apart from a small toothbrush moustache on his upper lip.

Reynolds, who had taken a shining to Mr. Cartwright at their first meeting, put him in his mid-fifties. He wore a fawn-coloured mackintosh over a navy blazer and grey Oxford bags. A bright red tie on a neatly-pressed check shirt added a splash of flamboyance to his appearance. His feet were shod with a pair of black, well-worn boots with thick, rubber soles. To Reynolds, Mr. Cartwright was a grey, unremarkable man who was gradually fading from sight as the years tumbled past. There was an air of neglect about him, like that of a man who had once enjoyed, but long-since surrendered, a devoted spouse.

"As you know, I'll be your superior for the duration of your stay here," said Mr. Cartwright. "Any problems, you let me know toot-sweet.

"And no fraternising with the natives—it's been a long war and they're weary and a bit fractious, especially if you start sniffing around their womenfolk. They'll take no prisoners."

There was a pause as the message sunk in. Then Mr. Cartwright slapped his knees and jumped to his feet: "Right-o, inspection time!"

He pulled a clipboard from his khaki haversack. A pencil dangled by a piece of string and as they made their way through the lighthouse, he ticked off items from a list. Sometimes he would pause, a frown on his face, and scribble a short note.

"Just making sure everything's ship-shape," he said with a grin. "Don't want you to be uncomfortable here or start making complaints. Far too much paperwork involved!"

When they reached the lantern-room at the top of the lighthouse, Mr. Cartwright pointed towards the giant mirrored lenses with his pencil.

"You won't need to worry about this lot, you'll be glad to hear," he said. "The lantern is to remain unlit for the duration. If the coastie sees it beaming across the ocean, he'll shoot on sight on the assumption that the Hun has landed and is signalling to his mates out at sea that it's party-time."

He grinned once more and nodded through the window to the horizon.

"There's also one of our destroyers somewhere out there," he said. "It patrols the shipping lanes from the Orkneys down to the Clyde. Its commander has a wee red book with the gunnery co-ordinates of every lighthouse within range, from the Kirkwall sweetie shop down to Celtic Park. You can't see *it*, but *it* can see you. Orders are that any lighthouse is to be shelled if the lamp is lit without authorisation—no questions asked, no quarter given. So Jerry will be blown to high heaven before he lights his last fag.

"Which reminds me—your main job here is to keep watch. You'll spend most of your days scouring the sea. There are some powerful naval binoculars in the cupboard over there. We want you to sweep the oceans and log anything you notice in yon big green logbook.

"At the moment, we're short of experienced keepers, but there'll be one along in a few days to see what you're up to. He's the captain of the ship, so to speak—I'm just a lackey in the Ministry; a pawn of the prison board. Bottom of the food-chain, but still above all you jailbirds! It's my job to help you *reformed characters* do your bit for the war effort and hopefully keep you on the straight-and-narrow.

"Now, any questions?" asked Mr. Cartwright.

"I thought lighthouses were painted white?" said Maitland. "This one's a dirty brown colour."

"Camouflage," replied Mr. Cartwright. "Don't you know there's a war on?" Then he grinned. "I can see that where you've come from you'd probably be none-the-wiser."

Maitland looked at his superior without expression.

Once the inspection tour was over, they made their way down the long, spiral staircase to the rusting, cast-iron entrance door at the base of the lighthouse.

"Remember," said Mr. Cartwright, "take care when the weather turns. Choose the times well when you must go to the mainland—the calmness of the sea today is about as good as it gets. Never, ever trust the sea," he warned.

"What happened to the last crew?" said Maitland.

"There was only one man—we're a bit stretched, as you know," said Mr. Cartwright. "The head keeper looked in on him every few days. Then, after a month, the young man went missing. When the keeper next visited, he looked high and low for him. Said that the place was like the *Marie Celeste*—cup of tea on the galley table, slice of toast half-eaten. It looked as if the man had simply vanished."

Reynolds whistled low under his breath. Maitland's eyes widened and he looked in Reynolds' direction.

"The procurator fiscal recorded that he'd probably been taken by a rogue wave whilst gallivanting on the rocks, but I reckon he did a runner. Couldn't hack the solitude, I suppose. Can't blame him. He was a conscientious objector, too—so hunting him down has hardly been a priority, what with the war and everything. He's still missing.

"Aye, this is no life for a young man. Once the cabin fever takes hold, they get restless. Like jail, but without the *bonhomie*," he laughed. "They miss having a dram with their mates; they miss family, sweethearts, a smile from a pretty face in the street."

There was a lull in Mr. Cartwright's monologue as the men pondered the mystery. Then he dragged open the heavy entrance door and turned to Maitland.

"But you don't look like a conchie to me, Mr. Maitland, if I'm honest," he said, frowning. "You look like a villain."

Maitland said nothing, but Reynolds noticed a whitening of his knuckles.

"Just keep your nose clean and I'll help you as much as I can," said Mr. Cartwright.

"I'll not go back inside," said Maitland. "It'll send me right doolally."

"Oh, well—cheerio, then. Take care," said Mr. Cartwright. As he made to leave, he stopped.

"Ach, I have to take a photo of you before I go," he said. "It's for the prison board, to prove you've actually made it here. It won't take a moment. If we do it out on the rock, we can get the lighthouse in the frame as well—a wee souvenir of your holiday here. They like documentary proof at the Ministry. It means they can cover their arses if anything goes wrong."

He fished a leather case from his haversack and led them towards the landing jetty. A small colony of guillemots burst into the sky from their shelter amongst the rocks. They soared high into the cold December air, squawking in rage at the intrusion. Maitland started in alarm.

Mr. Cartwright held his arm aloft and peered into the tiny glass viewfinder of the box-brownie. When he was happy with the composition, he shouted: "Say cheese!" and pressed the shutter button.

"One more for the King and we're done!" he called, winding the spool for a second shot. Maitland and Reynolds stood looking at him grimly. He repeated the action, then yelled: "All done!"

Without a word, Reynolds and Maitland turned and clambered back over the rocks to the lighthouse.

Mr. Cartwright fastened the camera back into its brown leather case and returned it to his bag. Like a ghost, he turned on his heel and strode along the jetty to the little boat. He cast off, manoeuvred the boat and headed back to the beach. Reynolds observed him from the rock. A strong current carried the boat effortlessly over the waves to the shore.

Maitland stood half-naked in the galley. When Reynolds passed the open door on his way upstairs, he had automatically turned his head to look into the room. He saw Maitland leaning with both hands on the sides of the sink in front of a woman's compact mirror. Maitland had balanced the mirror on a shelf above the sink, his safety razor in a bowl to one side. He seemed to be mouthing silently at his own reflection, as if in conversation with someone. Reynolds, out of embarrassment, stood behind the door-jamb. He tapped lightly on the frame.

"Is everything okay, Mr. Maitland?" he said, a nervous whisper.

Maitland froze instantly. He stared straight into the mirror, his shoulders trembling.

Taken aback by the bizarre nature of Maitland's reaction, Reynolds swept past the galley doorway and dashed up the stairs to the lantern-room. He stopped to take in huge gulps of air only when he reached the halfway point of his climb.

Here, the walls of the lighthouse were as thick as trees. Years of neglect meant that much of the original rendering had fallen away, exposing the bare inner-lining of lattice and brickwork. This too had started to crumble in places, partly from the constant dampness and partly from the incessant battering of the ocean and the stinging rain.

The towering column of the lighthouse echoed with the *drip-drip-drip* of water. It seeped from hidden fissures high in the building. To Reynolds, it seemed that every porthole was rusted and every window-frame rotten and leaking.

More worrying was the loud creaking and groaning sounds of the iron spiral staircase under his weight. The framework had originally been secured to the curved inner wall, but in some places its fixing bolts had been wrenched away completely, and the wall and the staircase had separated.

As he neared the top of the staircase, Reynolds paused and listened to the violent slamming of a door far below.

There was no discourse to be had with Maitland. Reynolds was tempted to strike up conversation on several occasions, but he was afraid that Maitland might react unpleasantly to the intrusion. He was an anxious sort of a man, jittery like a bird.

He put the reticence down to the fact that a man who's been banged up for a stretch learns to rub along quite happily without conversation—indeed, he knew this well enough from his own experience.

Yet still he felt that there was some other reason for Maitland's hostility—something just under the surface that was much darker; a secret that Reynolds had no desire to unearth. Even Mr. Cartwright had expressed doubts that Maitland was a *bona fide* conchie. Well, he—John Oliver Reynolds—would make sure their paths crossed as infrequently as possible. Maitland would do a runner soon enough, he was certain, leaving him in peace once more.

So Reynolds spent his time in the lantern-room, out of sight, pretending that he was the sole occupant of the lighthouse. The only sign that Maitland was still alive came from the smells of cooking that drifted upstairs. Maitland lived on root vegetables and fish—the former he usually boiled to within an inch of its life, the latter he grilled. Years of rationing had meant that meat, eggs and almost everything else were scarce. In this part of the country, remote as it was, the only food in abundance was fish. The shipping routes had mostly been blocked by the enemy so that what was available was grown and fished locally. And this far north, the harsh climate and poor soil made for limited fare.

Reynolds spent most of his days on the catwalk at the top of the lighthouse. He took pleasure in watching the sea, marvelling at the way it changed almost hourly. He used the hefty binoculars to observe the sea-birds as they swooped and dived for fish, squabbling cantankerously. Occasionally, a fishing-boat chugged past in the near distance and he'd wave and shout wildly to the men on deck. But they never returned his greeting. The wind was raw at this time of year but the sun was often bright, so visibility to the horizon was excellent. He never felt the cold.

All the while, Maitland remained firmly hidden away in his room, deep in the bowels of the lighthouse.

The head keeper had still not turned up. Reynolds knew that he was kept busy doing the rounds of all the lighthouses in his charge and that he would get to theirs soon enough. He'd grown used to the solitude, and Maitland wouldn't trouble him if he kept out of his way.

It was in the early hours of the morning that Reynolds heard the noises. He was on the staircase when he heard Maitland's voice in conversation, the low drone of his distinctive Yorkshire accent. For a moment, Reynolds was alarmed that there was someone else in the lighthouse. He had not heard the tell-tale creak and groan of the iron entrance door as it was opened; nor had he spotted any boat approaching the jetty. So to whom was Maitland talking?

He leaned his ear into the stairwell. Maybe Maitland was just mad, he reflected. He strained to listen—it became clear that there was only a single voice in the conversation. In an instant, Maitland started shouting, as if an argument had broken out.

Reynolds crept down the stairs to the galley kitchen. It was empty. As he approached Maitland's room, the racket grew louder and louder. Who on earth was he talking to? The argument continued, but Maitland's speech was slurred and it was impossible to make out what he was saying.

Reynolds rapped sharply three times on the door. The racket ceased abruptly. He could hear Maitland breathing hard on the other side of the door. In the tense silence, Reynolds whispered: "Is everything okay, Mr. Maitland?"

There came an awful, forlorn wail from within the room. It was followed by a loud crash as an object was thrown at the door. Reynolds recoiled in fright and fled back up the stairs.

The following morning, Reynolds stood on the staircase looking out of a porthole towards the mainland. Far below, he spotted Maitland in the rowing boat. He was making his way to the shore. It was obvious that Maitland was not a competent oarsman, for he flapped and slapped the oars against the strong current, making more splash than progress.

At first Reynolds was intrigued as to why Maitland was on the water. Then he felt relief at the prospect of being alone for a while without the brooding presence of the strange man. Maybe the bastard would drown on the way back.

With Maitland ashore, Reynolds decided to have a snoop in the man's quarters. He knocked lightly on the door before turning the handle and squinting into the gloom.

The room had been turned upside-down and it looked as if a brawl had taken place. The bed had been wrenched away from the wall and the bedclothes were strewn across the floor. A chair had been broken apart and Reynolds trod on shards of broken glass from the water jug that had presumably been flung at the door the night before. As Maitland's possessions were few, and there was little else to see, Reynolds left the room and had a scout around the galley. The galley was in order.

The weather was fine that morning and Reynolds was determined to take advantage of Maitland's absence. He spent the day outside the lighthouse, exploring the rocks, watching the gulls go about their business.

In the afternoon, as the sun weakened, Reynolds spotted the rowing boat making its way across the channel. The sea was placid and Maitland rowed with comparative ease this time. Reynolds returned to the lighthouse before Maitland reached the rocks. He went back up to the lantern-room out of Maitland's way. He walked around the catwalk and leaned over the balustrade. A stiff northerly wind was whipping up off the sea.

Maitland tethered the boat to the jetty and stood for a moment looking around, as if making sure the coast was clear. He gathered up the box of provisions from the boat and made his ungainly way over the rocks. Reynolds heard the door below as it was heaved open. He'd spotted that the box contained a bottle of whisky.

∽

Reynolds swiftly descended the stairs to the galley after he caught the sound of Maitland filling a bath. He was curious to see what else Maitland had brought back from the mainland.

On the galley table stood a small bowl that contained two eggs. Reynolds was surprised to see them. They were like gold and could only be obtained if one was on very friendly terms with the supplier. Reynolds imagined that, unless he'd stolen them, Maitland had met up with a local woman and that maybe she'd given the eggs to him as a token of affection.

A piece of paper lay next to the bowl of eggs. Reynolds picked it up. It was a telegraph from Mr. Cartwright, scribbled in pencil. Reynolds read the stark message:

+++ Ullapool shelled last night. Head keeper killed.
Arranging replacement. Terrible business. +++end+++

Reynolds assumed that the telegram had been sent to the local shop on the mainland. It had presumably been handed to Maitland when he'd bought the provisions.

Next to the telegram was the opened bottle of whisky. Maitland had started drinking early. Reynolds was not looking forward to the night ahead if Maitland got drunk.

But, as the evening wore on, Reynolds was relieved that Maitland had drunk himself into a stupor. He heard Maitland stumble eventually to his room, and Reynolds heard only snoring for the rest of the night.

Reynolds squinted far out to sea. From the top of the lighthouse, the diminutive, white wave crests flickered like tiny lights on the ocean below. He could see for miles in almost every direction. The elevation made him dizzy and he closed his eyes, reaching out to grip the balustrade that encircled the catwalk. The wind blustered wildly— but not strong enough to blow him onto the rocks.

As the morning wore on, Reynolds discovered that Maitland had disappeared. He looked for him in the quarters and outside on the rocks, but there was no sign of the man. Then he noticed that the rowing boat had gone. Reynolds sat brooding on the cat-walk.

Maitland returned unexpectedly after a couple of hours. Reynolds, who didn't envisage his return until much later in the day, especially if he had a woman on the go, noticed that his face bore scratch-marks. There was also blood on his shirt. He looked as if he'd been in a fight.

But what disturbed Reynolds the most was the look of bewildered panic on Maitland's face. What had happened? What had he been up to?

He heard Maitland enter the lighthouse and slam the door shut. Something had happened.

Reynolds decided to stay out of Maitland's way.

It was early evening when Reynolds made his way down the stairs to the galley. A veil of darkness shrouded the sea and the cliffs on the shore, and only the stars and a thin, quarter-moon provided any sort of illumination.

An enforced blackout was in effect even in this remote landscape, the more so given that the Germans had shelled targets along the coast.

Reynolds tiptoed to the door of the galley. He heard the sound of Maitland's voice. This time, Maitland was not shouting or railing against someone or some unseen thing. He appeared to be pleading to someone, begging forgiveness for some transgression.

Reynolds held his breath and peeped into the room. Maitland had his back to the door. At the opposite end of the galley table, a white figure sat motionless on a chair. Reynolds recoiled in alarm.

When he looked again, he breathed a little easier. It looked like Maitland had placed a mop against the chair and covered it with a bed-sheet. The effect was of a pantomime ghost sitting motionless in the chair.

Maitland was in tears. His arms were outstretched across the table, beseeching the white figure in his heavy North Riding accent.

"I panicked. You shouldn't have squirmed around like that," said Maitland. "I only meant to calm you. I'm sorry. But you went crazy, screaming and fighting. I was afraid someone might come—I'd be right up shit-creek."

His tone darkened. Another long pause.

"I went for help when I saw the blood. There wasn't a soul around on the farm, so I started for the village. Then I spotted the farmer, far across the ravine, heading back to the farm. I knew he'd find you and then you'd be all right."

There was silence for a minute or so. Maitland had buried his head in his hands. From time to time, his anger flared up again, but it soon subsided and he was back to seeking forgiveness for his misdeed.

"I'm sorry," he said finally. "I can't go back inside again."

The bottle of whisky was empty.

The sun disappeared in the gathering clouds as the morning began. A hard frost still encrusted the lighthouse with a lustrous sheen. From his position on high, leaning against the balustrade, Reynolds watched as a small motor launch navigated its way along the coast towards the lighthouse. It weaved a jagged path as it followed the channels that hugged the near-shore, avoiding the treacherous, hidden rock formations that would tear the hulk and sink it in seconds if it collided with them.

The vessel was difficult to make out as it was still some distance away, but it looked as if it contained three uniformed men. They must be patrolling this part of the coast, thought Reynolds, in the aftermath of the recent shelling.

Despite the blustery wind, Reynolds caught the sound of someone mounting the stairs of the lighthouse. Alarmed, he turned round to face the little landing area that served as the entrance to the lantern-room.

In the reflection of the mirrored lenses, a head popped up. It was Maitland's. The rest of his body remained out of sight. He looked about him, getting his bearings before climbing further into the lantern-room.

Reynolds watched Maitland's reflection in the glass as it turned towards him. For a brief second or two, Maitland looked directly at him.

"Is everything okay, Mr. Maitland?" called Reynolds, unable to take his eyes off the man.

Without warning, Maitland's face creased and he let out a loud wail. His head disappeared from view and the disturbed man fled back down the stairs, his boots clattering loudly on the steps, half-stumbling, half-falling.

Reynolds' hands shook uncontrollably. Maitland was completely unpredictable and unstable—he'd lost his marbles, that was for sure, but this latest episode was something new and more worrying. Reynolds made up his mind to take a sharp knife from the galley when Maitland was locked in his room—just as a precaution.

His attention was drawn back to the chugging of the motor launch as it tacked closer to the lighthouse. Abruptly, the boat's engine cut out. It sat there, bobbing on the waves, waiting. Reynolds spotted the rifles that the uniformed occupants held in readiness.

Reynolds made his way around the catwalk to the shore side. From his vantage point, he spotted a convoy of cars and vans that were stationed on the beach. A group of men, both police and military, had assembled on the sand. Amongst them he saw Mr. Cartwright, who stood out in his fawn mac.

A second motor launch was already in the channel, making its way towards the lighthouse. Reynolds could see that its occupants were also armed. One of them carried a crowbar. When the boat reached the jetty, Reynolds leaned further over the balustrade to get a better view of the rocks at the foot of the lighthouse.

The men tipped out of the motor launch and made their way quickly over the rocks like ants. With the crowbar, one of them jemmied open the door. As one body, they stormed into the lighthouse and disappeared from sight. Reynolds rushed back around the catwalk to the lantern-room doorway.

From far below came the sound of a fracas. Men were shouting and there came a clattering of boots on the iron staircase as they clambered upwards. Reynolds began to panic. He heard a deafening gunshot and a scream of pain. He backed out onto the catwalk.

The clanging footsteps grew louder as they approached the lantern-room. Suddenly, the head of Maitland popped up. Terror-stricken, he climbed into the lantern-room, clasping his left arm. It streamed with blood where he'd taken a bullet. He peered down the stairwell. He listened for a moment or two then scurried around the lantern-room, hither and thither, clearly panicked and disorientated. He froze when he spotted Reynolds on the catwalk and both men looked at each other in silent terror.

Then Maitland screamed: "It's you! It was you!"

He lunged forward to attack Reynolds. As he did so, his foot caught in the doorjamb and he tripped, losing his balance. He tried to grab hold of Reynolds' jacket but his attempt failed. His face displayed a curious expression of confusion and horror. He regained his balance momentarily but was then pitched clean over the balustrade. He made no sound as he fell through the air, apart from a singular *crump* as his body dashed onto the sharp, angular rocks at the base of the lighthouse.

Reynolds stood for a moment in a state of shock.

Then at the top of the staircase, the head of a young policeman appeared. It swivelled left and right and up and down, anticipating an attack of some kind. Cautiously, the rest of the policeman's figure appeared until he stood at full height in the lantern-room. He stood in wonderment before the massive lens, momentarily distracted by its magnificence. But then he quickly re-gathered his senses. He gripped a pistol with both hands, creeping out onto the catwalk, stooping cautiously, the gun held at eye level. He inched his way around the catwalk until he'd completed a full circle of the light-house. Breathing hard, he stepped back into the lantern-room and leaned down into the stairwell.

"All clear!" he called.

Cartwright frowned at the pile of papers in his in-tray. The attack on the local girl and the incident at the lighthouse had given him an enormous amount of paperwork to complete. He had enough work to do without having to clear up the mess left by a lunatic.

There was a tap on the door to his office and a young woman appeared with a cup of tea and an envelope.

"Thought you might need a cuppa," she said with a broad smile.

"Perfect timing, Avril," he replied.

"Your photos arrived. Do you want me to send them on to the Ministry?" she asked.

"Seems little point, now," he said.

She opened the envelope and scrutinised the two images, her brow furrowed.

"It's funny," she said, "but I was sure you told me there was only one man keeping the lighthouse."

"That's right," said Cartwright, holding his hand out for the photographs. "Maitland was his name—a rough sort. I knew he'd be trouble the moment I clapped eyes on him."

"Who's the other man, then?" she said.

Cartwright looked at the first of the black-and-white images. On the rocks, about fifty yards in front of the lighthouse, stood Maitland. He looked directly into the lens. At the entrance to the lighthouse there appeared to be another figure. The camera's shallow depth-of-field and its distance from the figure meant that it was out of focus and difficult to make out.

The second photograph, taken from the same position, showed a similar scene. This time, however, Maitland had turned his head to look over his shoulder, as if something had caught his attention. To his left, some ten yards behind him, stood the figure. It appeared to be gesticulating wildly, a blurred, flapping motion, frozen in a single frame.

Cartwright peered more closely at the photograph.

"Why—that's Reynolds," he said. "That's the youngster who vanished."

TRACY FAHEY

THE HUNGRY GRASS

TRACY FAHEY is an Irish writer of Gothic fiction. In 2017, her debut collection *The Unheimlich Manoeuvre* was short-listed for a British Fantasy Award for Best Collection. Her first novel, *The Girl in the Fort*, was released that same year by Fox Spirit Books. Her second collection, the folk horror *New Music for Old Rituals* was published the following year by Black Shuck Books.

In 2020, the Sinister Horror Company released an updated third edition of her debut collection—*The Unheimlich Manoeuvre Deluxe Edition*, with an accompanying mini-collection of new material, *Unheimlich Manoeuvres in the Dark*.

Fahey's short fiction has been published in more than thirty American, British, Australian and Irish anthologies, including *Supernatural Tales, Nightscript V, Uncertainties III, The Fiends in the Furrows II: More Tales of Folk Horror* and *Women in Horror Anthology: Volume II*, and she is compiling her third collection, *I Spit Myself Out*.

She holds a PhD on the Gothic in visual arts, and her non-fiction writing has been published in edited collections and journals. She has been awarded residencies in Ireland and Greece.

"Ireland's folklore is a reservoir of horror," observes the author. "In this case I've delved into the dark seam of Famine folklore. The Great Famine of 1845–47 caused a drop in population of two million people. From this dark time only a few supernatural tales emerge—

a theory is that some events are too horrific for fictional echos, but the 'Hungry Grass' story is one of these.

"It relates to flattened yellow-green patches of grass where it's believed that starving people lay down and died, bellies full of grass. Legend has it than when you stand on these patches, you can't find your way out . . ."

I T'S THE LAST hill that does it. I hurl the backpack onto the flattened, yellowish grass in front of the old Famine cottage, not caring if I break everything in it. My breath is coming in tearing snorts, and there is sweat everywhere—under my arms, down my back, trickling down my damp neck.

I hate you. My fists clench, white-knuckled, in front of me. *I hate you.* I pull up my T-shirt, not caring if any ramblers in this blighted landscape see me, and roughly wipe my face, feeling the heat of my cheeks through the thin, damp fabric. *I hate you.*

It was Maebh's idea, of course. Fit, athletic Maebh who can't conceive of anyone being unable to walk more than a couple of miles. She organised this whole hiking trip. And it's driving me crazy. Her stringy legs in expensive hiking boots stride ahead of me, her backpack shifting easily on her shoulders like it's made of candyfloss. Behind her, always behind her, is me. I pound on, all chunky legs and red face, my rucksack lumpish as a coal-sack, sweat collecting in my eyebrows till it runs, salty and stinging into my eyes. It's only the first day and already she's stopped calling me on.

I drink deep out of the warm, plastic bottle of water. The stale liquid gushes sweet down my scorched throat. The faded grass is warm under my thighs. I touch the velvety blades and remember the old stories of the Hungry Grass. According to my mother, the 'Hungry Grass' was the local name for those flat patches of green-yellow grass, in memory of the terrible 19th-century Famine where starving people, bellies full of grass, lay down and died by the road-side.

I lean back against the warm stone as a flurry of birds flit by the old ruined cottage. I close my eyes and see them pass, dim shapes fluttering against in the pink shade of my eyelids. I don't know if it's the rest, the water, the heat or the cawing of the crows, but I feel something shift deep inside me; suddenly, impossibly, my mood has started to lift. I stretch out on the flat rock and think about Maebh and our long, tangled relationship.

We've loved and fought each other since childhood. Until that last summer before university, and then shockingly, it was ten years later and we'd lost touch. I'm not surprised she wanted to meet-up, I'd often thought about it too. But I still can't believe she chose these fields for us to meet again in.

I close my eyes and draw in deep breaths, just like my therapist taught me, three deep breaths to drive away the bad thoughts. *One.* A pheasant bursts straight out of the grass beside me into a heavy, stumbling flight. *Two.* I feel a breeze shift and flow around me. *Three.* I close my eyes and inhale the smell of hot grass and moss. I keep my eyes closed. The sun goes in, and the pink glow of my eyelids darkens to a dull red.

I open my eyes. It's cold and damp and I'm shivering hard, my muscles spasming in the chill air. I can't see anything but a white swirling fog, soft and treacherous. I scramble up, my feet slipping against the slick grass. I feel around me but my tracksuit top and rucksack are gone. *They must be somewhere*, I think rationally, and start to pat the wet grass. Nothing. My thin vest is drenched, I can't stop shivering. I need to get out of this pocket of mist and find Maebh. I walk forward into the whiteness. There's nothing but soft, wet cloud pushing against me, and no matter how far I go—carefully, carefully—hands stretched in front of me, I can't find its perimeters. The damp grass squeaks beneath my boots, dark and slippery. I'm filled with a bright, hard panic, solid as a rock in my chest.

"Maebh!" I call, hopelessly. "Maebh!"

There's no reply. I continue to walk, hands still raised, feet hesitant. I expect at any moment to hit another rock, stumble against a tree. But I don't. My feet skid onwards, as I slip slowly down the grassy hollow.

"Rebecca?" It's soft as a breath in my ear. My heart hammers hard in my chest.

"Re-becca?" There it is again, this time drawn out, almost sing-song.

"Maebh?" I say weakly. But I know it's not. It's a deep voice, a man's voice. I'm suddenly alive with a pure white terror.

"Who is it?" I yell, heart crashing in my throat. "Who is it?"

I blunder about, terrified. *I know who it is.* My feet skid, stutter on rock, stop, and I pitch forward on my hands and knees. The limestone cuts my palms, and the rock bites through the right knee of my jeans. I feel the material split, and pain blossom red-hot in my knee.

"Re-becca?" The soft voice is still there. Still sing-song. It sounds even nearer this time. *I don't want to know who it is.*

I start to cry, lying on the ground, covering my head with my arms. My wet hands clamp over my ears.

Then I hear a shout.

"Rebecca!" It's a different voice—a woman's voice—Maebh's voice!

I choke down my sobs and yell as loud as I can—"Here. Over here!"

"What the hell?" She looms over me, angry, blissfully solid and present. The mist starts to curl away, resolving itself into thin white strands; flimsy, innocent. "I've been looking for you all day. Where have you been?"

"I–I don't know."

"Well you've completely ruined the hike." Her voice is cold and livid. Suddenly I'm angry.

"What the hell possessed you to come here? Here of all places? You know what happened here!" The words pour from me like a torrent, my heart shaking within me with a tremendous pendulum beat. "What made you think coming back would be a good idea?"

Maebh twists her face up, and with a shock I realise she's trying to remember. The very idea she's forgotten gives me a sick, vertiginous feeling.

"What are you talking about Rebecca?" It's the honest puzzlement in her face that destroys me. I'm engulfed by a hot sick panic;

I close my eyes, feeling the blood pounding in my face. When I open them, Maebh is looking at me curiously.

"Don't you—don't you...?" My voice falters, stops.

"Don't I *what*?" Now she's getting angry again. She starts to gather up the contents of my spilled bag, throwing the bottle, tracksuit top, wallet back in, a sequence of hard, vicious thuds.

"Don't you *remember*?" My voice is choked. I can see it so clearly, the bright, hard sunshine on the grass, the hill, the rocks, me falling over, and Maebh running on, leaving me behind. Even now, when I close my eyes, I can hear the rough tear of his breath, as he whispers my name, and feel his hard hands as they grab me.

But as Maebh shakes her head dismissively, and bends to pull me up, I know that she has forgotten; that is, if she ever really remembered. That bright summer was the last time we were truly friends. Since then Maebh has continued to run ahead, laughing, ever onward, while I've stayed behind, circling the fields, left behind in the Hungry Grass.

DANIEL McGACHEY

GHOSTLY STUDIES, DR. GRACE, AND THE DIODATI SOCIETY

DANIEL McGACHEY's stories have appeared in the *Black Book of Horror, BHF Book of Horror Stories* and *MX Book of New Sherlock Holmes Stories* series, and aired as instalments of Jim French Productions' long-running *Imagination Theatre* radio series.

Dark Regions Press published his collections *They That Dwell in Dark Places* and *Sherlock Holmes: The Impossible Cases*. His most recent collection of ghost stories, *By No Mortal Hand*, appeared from Sarob Press in 2018.

McGachey is a regular contributor of reviews, features, fiction and illustrations to *Ghosts & Scholars*. He is currently engaged in developing a supernatural audio project, and in researching and transcribing more of the neglected supernatural tales of H.S. Grace.

As he explains: "This piece was written as a preface to a pair of short stories credited to Dr. H.S. Grace that were included in my Sarob Press collection, *By No Mortal Hand*. My interest in exhuming this obscure author's work began over a decade ago, when I was writing 'The Travelling Companion', a story following the unlucky purchaser of a book of ghost stories that was, itself, haunted, and whose author had hidden some additional contents within its pages.

"Although I've since written several prequels and sequels to M.R. James' ghost stories—via Rosemary Pardoe's *Ghosts & Scholars* magazine and Haunted Library imprint—at the time the prospect of attempting to write extracts from unknown stories by James himself seemed far too daunting, and, besides, James' biography was too well-known to leave room for the necessary mystery surrounding my haunted book's author. So, casting around for a contemporary of James who had abruptly given up writing ghost stories and then fallen into obscurity led to H.S. Grace.

"I've long been fascinated by half-forgotten or dimly-remembered stories, books, films and shows, and by pursuing the career of a fringe participant in the ghost story movement of the early 20th century, I've found myself peering through the cracks at a shadow development of the horror field in the decades that followed, and beginning to trace a parallel history of the genre in the UK."

W HEN I CHOSE to include the long out-of-print ghost story 'An Unwise Purchase' by Dr. Herbert Sidney Grace in my first collection (*They That Dwell in Dark Places*; Dark Regions Press, 2009), my stated hope was that it would, in some small way, act as a tribute to the author, as well as bring his name back before the public following decades of obscurity. The few scant paragraphs of biography appended to the tale were necessarily brief, with mentions of his dates of birth and death—1863–1935—his academic background and scholarly works and, of course, his three collections of ghost stories—*A Ghostly Study* (1905), *Further Tales from a Ghostly Study* (1908), and his last verified words on the subject, *Intangible Apparitions & Other More Substantial Terrors*, released in 1910 (all three published by Cadman & DeMauleon)—before touching on speculation concerning a fourth volume (as yet unsubstantiated), and the final retreat into religious pursuits that saw him distance himself from his former, more macabre hobby.

The brevity of these remarks was unavoidable as, Dr. Grace's works having long since fallen out of fashion and eluding the gaze of even the most diligent of anthologists and editors within recent years, tracking down verifiable data on the author was not always an easy task. Of particular value were a number of articles in editions of *The Rhodean: A Rhodes House Ephemeral* published between 1881 and 1885, Ronald Perdew's *Breaking the Silence: A College Librarian Remembers* (St. Montague's Press, 1926), and Eleanor Temple's *St. James's During the War* (with a preface by Gregory Singer; Sadleirs, 1934).

The Grace Estate, comprising a great niece not yet born when the scholar died, provided as much assistance as was possible, often going above and beyond in laying open his surviving documents, and in placing me in contact with the relevant authorities at those august seats of learning where the doctor had spent the greater portion of his life. Again, I am indebted to the assistance of archivists and librarians at those institutes in which he studied and served, and to Miss M.A. Allen, who was kind enough to forward me her own findings, including transcripts of several of the ghost stories, uncovered by her own researches into Dr. Grace's more scholarly works.

Thus has much about H.S. Grace's early schooling and his latter-day calling to religious studies been learnt. Of the ghost stories, aside from the texts themselves, for which I could rely on my own hard-won copies of the original collections, and some brief recollections and anecdotes in the autobiographies of a number of his peers, it appeared as if Dr. Grace had succeeded in all but burying every trace.

Therefore, my other, unstated reason for invoking Grace in print after almost a century was in hope that it might prompt some reader somewhere to blow the dust off a stack of old letters in the attic, or to prise open the pages of an ancient journal left behind in a half-forgotten legacy. Some suggestions were forthcoming for further reading, pointing to yet more biographical accounts by contemporaries of the writer, all of these leads useful and very welcome. But by far the most intriguing pointer came with a vague recollection of a small-press magazine—a dedicated H.S. Grace fanzine, no less— a correspondent had browsed, and subsequently regretted not purchasing, in a now-defunct fantasy-themed bookshop in the early 1980s. The writer recalled that the cover bore "*a striking black-and-*

white illustration of a creature emerging from a shadow on a wall", that there was a mixture of articles and fiction within, and that the title, drawing on those of the first two H.S. Grace collections, was *Ghostly Studies*. Further details were in short supply, and chances of locating copies—if there were more editions than that one reported sighting suggested—were slim, but vigilance sometimes pays off, even if it can take six-and-a-half years to do so.

Earlier this year a single copy of *Ghostly Studies'* first, and apparently only, edition appeared for sale online, in notably fine condition for what is essentially a photocopied A5 publication produced in 1980. It was not cheap, but neither was it something I could afford to miss, and it was purchased without hesitation. Any elation at the addition of this rarity to my Dr. Grace collection was tempered by the fact that it was only through the death of a much-respected bibliophile and the gradual auctioning off of his collection that it came onto the market, though perhaps there is some comfort to be gained in the knowledge that this item was to find a new home with a recipient who prizes it highly.

As per the initial description, the cover portrays the shambling denizen of some other realm that creeps from a stain in the wallpaper in Professor Tewkes' college study in Grace's 1905 tale 'Mistress Amber's Journal', while within are three new stories in tribute to Grace's style—'The Door in the Wall' (bearing no obvious relation to the identically-titled H.G. Wells tale) by Faye Slater, 'An Unspoiled View of the Sea' by Austin Patrick, and 'Wraith's Veil' by Hogan Best, each of these illustrated, like the cover, by T.J. Groome. Non-fiction includes 'Grace Notes' by Jonathan Daniels, listing the dates of issue of Grace's books, both supernatural and scholarly, plus dates, where known, of composition of the individual ghost stories, and a few fleeting reprint appearances in anthologies and other publications—without which I would have remained unaware of several appearances in *The Satyr Book of Ghost Stories* series (edited by Desmond Vanderlour; Satyr Books, 1974–79), and an abridged text serialisation of 'In a Distant Vista' in "The Chilling Mystery Paper for Girls" (also dubbed by a squeamish tabloid press "The Ninepenny Nightmare" in an effort to stir up ghosts of the horror comics scare of the 1950s) *Enchanted* (Issues 154–166; World-Wide Distribution, May–August1979).

The publisher is listed at the base of the contents page as "The Diodati Society Redux", and for information on the original Diodati Society, and its importance in the story-telling career of H.S. Grace, one need only to turn to the issue's main article, penned by the 'zine's editor, Nicola Franklyn, entitled 'Dr. Grace and the Singular Society of Supernatural Storytellers'. As a source for major biographical information on Grace and of his closest contemporaries, as well as for seeding a number of valuable avenues for further investigation and verification, this essay alone made the purchase an invaluable investment.

University societies are neither new nor uncommon, of course, and such was true even during Herbert Grace's tenure at Rhodes House. We need only think of The Disobligers' Society, The Panopticon Club or The Chitchat Society, for examples of groups devoted to the art of discussion, deliberation, oration and narration enfolding a wide and varied selection of subjects, or more narrowly-focussed groups, such as the Spook Story Society, whose specialism needs little clarification.

Of a similar ilk to the latter, and formed in 1891 in celebration of the 75th anniversary of the conception of *Frankenstein; or, The Modern Prometheus*, was The Diodati Society, its name deriving from the Villa Diodati, the mansion near Lake Geneva where Lord Byron, John Polidori, Percy Bysshe Shelley, and his young bride Mary Shelley famously spent part of the rain-drenched summer of 1816 engaged in a contest to create the most frightening or fantastical ghost stories they could conjure from their own imaginings. Amidst fragments by Byron and Shelley, Polidori would produce the forerunner of the modern vampire novel with his own *The Vampyre*, while Mary Shelley was reportedly driven by a dream to create her tale of blasphemous anatomical experimentation that has inspired, provoked, and been imitated ever since on the page, the stage, in sound, and on the large and small screens.

The Society's members would take turns in acting as host, and the peripatetic group would gather in different locations for each of their bi-monthly "conjurations", dependant on the tastes, whims, or sheer theatricality of the incumbent host. Most frequently, these were simply held by lantern-light and firelight's-flicker in the studies and sitting-rooms of the respective hosts, but excursions were made on special occasions—invariably those meetings scheduled around Hallowe'en and Christmas—to premises as diverse as a storage vault beneath the college museum, an abandoned theatre, a private library in a neighbouring country house, the family chapel of the same house, an art gallery whose carved exhibits were shrouded for the night beneath white draperies, a supposedly haunted room above a tavern, and—aptly enough given the society's inspiration in Mary Shelley's famous novel—the anatomy rooms of the University's Medical faculty. The sessions would last from late night until dawn, with each location designated "Villa Diodati Proxy" for the duration.

H.S. Grace, although not a founder, was to prove an enthusiastic member on joining some six years into the Society's life, and he entered wholeheartedly into the ghoulish festivities. At that time the membership included the botanist N.S. Sydney, best remembered amongst ghost story aficionados as the author of *The Spider Plant and Other Macabre Stories* (Bertrands, 1923); Dr. (later Reverend) Campbell Fitzgerald, whose single collection of ghost stories *Midnight Whispers* (Purgis & Valentine, 1920) would be released posthumously; Matthew Ellis Cox, the noted anthologist who prepared that same volume of his late friend's work, and C.P. Bellward, the future MP for Oldmire and Greymarsh and a keen part-time psychical researcher until his death in 1947.

In a letter of December 1902, quoted at length in an unfinished biography of his father by Campbell Fitzgerald, Jr., details were given of a Society gathering, apparently typical but of particular note for being that conjuration held in the anatomy lecture hall of Rhodes:

Inevitably, given the setting, the majority of our narratives had the air of the dissecting room, mortuary or charnel house to them. Proceedings commenced with a grisly little squib by M.E.C. in which a purportedly 'eye-catching' apparition in surgical garb proves to live up to its billing with quite an alarming degree of literalness. Cox, with a showman's touch, fixed the beam of his dark lantern upon a particularly apt pair of specimens which glared back at the assembly from within the glass jar where they floated in suspension.

Following this display of pawky grotesquery my attempts to restore a degree of chill to the atmosphere were moderately successful, as I gave vent to the legend of the doctor whose cures for any ill brought those symptoms crashing back upon himself and who, to reverse his decline, discovered immortality through murder. I was especially gratified by the reception afforded a denouement conjured up only as I'd walked to the meeting under the gathering gloom; a nasty little twist in which the doctor, his manifold crimes having been brought to light, is duly executed, whereupon those slain by his hand awake to find themselves imprisoned within their graves.

Then came H.S. Grace's turn in the chair, with a story concerning the fortunes of an arrogant young buck going by the unlikely name of Dr. Peacock. You will imagine, dear sister, how I fought to suppress a grin as I saw how set was my old college classmate on delivering a good-natured, but thoroughly well-deserved, ribbing in a none-too veiled reference to my former, less respectable ways that had earned me that soubriquet. Perhaps this biased me, but I thought it Grace's best by a long-chalk, if only narrowly pipping the one from two years ago about the scheming uncle and the ghastly manikin awaiting a soul to power its movements [presumably an early version of 'The Stolen Animus', which was to feature in Grace's first volume some three years later] *for malevolent glee.*

Campbell Fitzgerald, Sr. was a near contemporary of H.S. Grace at St. Montague's, having arrived there two years before following his expulsion from a more prominent institute for unspecified acts of "high-handed tomfoolery". That his early years were marked out by an arrogant and superior attitude he made no secret, and several of his own stories, notably 'The Shrilling Mask' and 'In the Blink of the Medusa's Eye', feature the dreadful consequences of such hubris. One feature of his own youthful streak of overconfidence manifested as a daredevil approach to exploration and breaking boundaries, and Dr. Grace's *The Lost and Forgotten Buildings of Greymarsh* (St. Montague's Press, 1912) would carry the dedication:

> To 'The Peacock' C.F., for foraging the paths only visible due to his plumage wafting like a flag above the tangled overgrowth, thus laying trails others would one day follow.

Fitzgerald's son would later speculate that the reckless streak never really faded, and may have spurred his father's decision to enlist as an Army Chaplain during the Great War, despite having been married a little less than a year at the time, and unknowingly due to become a father. In a move which has seen inevitable, if facile, comparisons to Ambrose Bierce's disappearance during the Revolutionary War in Mexico, Fitzgerald marched directly into the arena of battle and was never seen again. His last recorded words, spoken as a thick mist enveloped the trench in which the survivors of his platoon were blockaded, came in the form of an instruction to his "chaps" to hang back till he investigated what he believed to be "a clear passage out of this sordid bloody mess". His body was never recovered, and one theory put forward was that in the poor visibility he had mistaken a hole blasted in the trench-wall for a clear tunnel, which had then caved in, burying him completely. In a macabre mirror to this disappearance, Campbell Fitzgerald, Jr. would also go missing in 1954 while *en route* to St. Montague's to further his researches for his study of his father and his fellow Diodatists.

The Diodati Society itself had disappeared from view several years before the outbreak of war, at approximately the time when Grace chose a new path of spiritual enlightenment over the raising of literary spirits. Nevertheless, even in its brief span of existence, it could claim a rightful part in the origins of some dozen or more books of ghost stories, a handful of novels, and many more individual stories besides that saw print in the pages of magazines, journals and anthologies.

An insert slip still intact between the pages of that edition of *Ghostly Studies* stated that if enough stories and articles of a sufficient quality were forthcoming then a second issue would appear in the near future, with a Post Office Box number provided for submissions and sales enquiries. Whether on a whim or out of desperation, the price of a stamp and envelope seemed a worthwhile sacrifice in attempting to make contact with the former editor and founding member of the Diodati Society Redux.

While P.O. Box 169 no longer exists—indeed with the Post Office that housed it in 1980 now a mobile-phone emporium—any mail sent to that address is still forwarded on, as I was informed in the reply sent to the e-mail address included in my tentative enquiry. This response also contained links to the online archives of *The Oldmire Examiner*, as well as to several national newspapers that carried the story. The first of these, dated September 16th 1986, is headlined FEARS GROW FOR MISSING AUTHOR, while a number of follow-ups in the weeks following repeat the initial article's description of Nicola Franklyn, and pleas for information from family, friends, and co-workers in the office where she was an accounts manager, and from a fiancé concerned about her mental well-being.

The e-mail's sender, Nicola Franklyn's younger sister, Penny, expressed natural curiosity as to why anyone should attempt contacting such an outdated address, though my inclusion of that Grace story in my earlier book served to satisfy any equally natural suspicions concerning my motive in writing. With her kind permission, I can share some details brought to light during our subsequent correspondence.

The mail re-direction had been maintained by Nicola and Penny's mother, Janice, to keep alive the—admittedly slim—hopes that anyone contacting it might provide some clue leading to Nicola's whereabouts. Following Janice's passing in 2015, Penny had kept the re-direction service renewed as a link to her mother and her sister. The contents of the P.O. Box had been thoroughly checked by the police at the time of the disappearance, before being returned to Nicola's next of kin. Some of these items dated back half-a-dozen years, and prominent among them were the results of that request for *Ghostly Studies* submissions, including a number of short stories and artwork pieces of variable quality, a speculative feature tying in rumours of that unconfirmed fourth volume of ghost stories to a notorious and now long-extinct family whose ancestral home formed part of the foundations of St. Montague's, and an article detailing the behind-the-scenes travails of Alex Llewellyn-Kent's 1975 adaptation of Grace's 'The Shrieking in the Cloisters' for that director's troubled late-night horror anthology series *The Witching Hour*. Scanned copies of these pieces, and several more, are now in my safekeeping.

There were other, less explicable items of mail found on opening the box, including several envelopes whose contents consisted of entirely blank sheets, and a large quantity of flakes of what was discovered to be a very brittle and crumbling paper.

One particular piece, however, although dated some weeks before Nicola Franklyn's vanishing, seems eerily to prefigure aspects of the case, and these similarities caused significant speculation among the investigating officers. Despite their concerted efforts, their analysis led to no tangible conclusion and the item was returned to the family at a later date. Acting as an updating of themes most clearly evident in Grace's 'In a Distant Vista', 'The Scholar's Chair' and 'The Painted Path'—those of objects through which, or places in which, spheres other than our own may be glimpsed, or even, if not careful, touched—this brief, unsigned story was evidently a belated submission for that never-to-see-print second edition of *Ghostly Studies*, and is headed simply 'The Underpass':

The quickest way home, though you consciously avoid admitting as much until you are already on its inexorable path, is through the underpass. Normally you go out of your way to avoid it, especially after dark, but you're beyond tired, the rain is heavy and chillingly cold, and nobody is liable to be hanging about down there in this weather. Nobody in their right mind, anyway. (You silently, sarcastically thank yourself for that cheering thought.) Damn it all; striding quickly, though not so quick as to appear nervous or frightened, you march through deepening puddles into the concrete tunnel beneath the tangled junction's busy lanes.

You allow yourself to drop the aggressively confident swagger as you see that the tunnel is empty. None of the usual gangs of kids that hang around in the entrance whispering nastily and jeering and leering at anyone with the nerve to walk through their gathering. Though they've left their traces, marking their territory with their leavings. Empty lager cans most of them are too young to have bought for themselves and disintegrating cigarette butts swim in the gathering rainwater. Perhaps the downpour will wash away the smell of teenaged body-odour and cheap perfume and stale smoke? You doubt it. Instead it just smells damp, like an unheated house left vacant too long, or a cavern whose limits lie much deeper than this man-made burrow.

The only sounds are the echoes of your footsteps in the narrow space, and the faltering buzz of the broken strip-lights that flicker like enclosed lightning overhead-- not quite in sequence, so the underpass never falls into absolute darkness, but pulsing as if to separate and distinct heartbeats. You pause, considering. Even if it suddenly fell totally dark, you'd make the last glimmerings of the overcast dusk at the end of the passage in a matter of seconds at a run, but still the constantly shifting illumination disorientates you, making that far end of the tunnel seem to recede and then return, recede, then return.

As the light dims ahead of you, a shape seems to emerge about halfway along the tunnel. You are alone down here, aren't you? You force your feet onwards, trying not to stop in your tracks, not to turn tail, desperate not to show alarm as you peer ahead at the stooped form pressed back against the wall as if in a rudimentary effort to conceal itself. There are no alcoves or hollows for anyone to hide in, you're sure, so there are no shady corners for anything to loom out of. And as your eyes adjust, you see that it's only the dark outline of some faded piece of graffiti. A crude blur that might have once been an attempt at a figure, the detail lost amidst an overlaid scrawl of obscenities. You've seen this--well, if not this exact daub, then many others like it --every time you've ventured through here, though you'd never paused long enough to pay it more than glancing notice. You walk on by, resisting the urge to run your hand across the concrete surface to reassure yourself that it's really only paint.

The bzzzz-bzzzzz-bzzzzzzzz of the faulty lighting seems louder now the overhead traffic's rumble has faded. Its persistence puts you in mind of the drone of some insect, something huge, much vaster than any native species of these isles. Something white flits by your face, the draught of wings brushing your cheek. A waft of damp air, a smell of wet earth and dry dust. Startled, you turn, watching its flight. Too large for any moth, too white for a bat. Something nocturnal, at any rate. Something that doesn't venture out into the light. It disappears into the diminishing concrete corridor behind you, its pallor leaving an after-image seared on your retinas.

But that surely isn't right? You can't have walked so far that you can no longer see where you entered? Another trick of the unreliable light!

There, a sliver of grey from a sky turned the colour of old stones. You turn, striding onwards, actually looking forward to being out in the rain and the biting wind again. The end is in sight (another sarcastic thank you for the choice of words), just a few more yards now.

Just a few more yards.

Just a few...

You can no longer recall when you lost all sight of the end of the tunnel. Those few more yards must have extended into miles by now. Was it when you'd turned too quickly at a whispering rustle from the gloom and lost your bearings, unable to tell the thickening murk from the dank walls? When you'd pressed ahead, pushing through what felt like a drapery of cobwebs that prickled against your skin and left you brushing flakes of concrete dust and brittle old paint from your clothing and hair? It may have been when you finally noticed that the ground beneath your faltering feet had started to dip. First a gradual incline, but one which rapidly assumed a steeper angle, taking you ever downwards.

That dank subterranean smell had grown stronger with every step further you descended. Of course you had turned, retraced your movements, trying to locate the entrance of the underpass and the familiar world above. After an hour, perhaps two, of this determined plodding, the conviction that the tunnel was leading you in a circle, taking you back onto your original downward path as once more the ground sloped away under your feet, had reached an unbearable level of despair. There, now, proof that you have passed this way before--that jumbled mass of coiling limbs that on first passing you had mistaken for the roots of some ancient tree forcing itself through fissures in the wall, until they had shivered convulsively as if sensing your approach.

Just a few more yards. It's either a mantra or a scream.

The walls, ceiling and floor haven't been concrete for many hours now, though the solid rock is peculiarly smooth and rounded. The pulsating light now comes from some natural luminescence in the rock itself, meaning that the still persistent bzzzzz-bzzzzz must be caused by those bone-coloured things that rustle and flap overhead.

You no longer have to resist any urge to touch the paintings that still adorn the walls around you, you don't even want to make contact with your eyes. That underground space you entered hours, even days before may have been built to human design, but these nightmare images, far older than you will allow yourself to imagine, can only be attempted portraits of the architects of this deeper, darker space. And whatever they were-- whatever they still are--they bear no relation to anything remotely approaching humanity.

As Nicola Franklyn's last confirmed sighting was a blurred but unmistakable image captured on CCTV footage as she entered the underpass in Oldmire Newtown Centre, with no subsequent footage from the camera on the other side to show her, or anyone else, exiting the subway, the coincidental parallels between her disappearance and the fate of the unnamed subject—in essence the reader—of this tale are both inescapable and unnerving.

Penny Franklyn remains unconvinced that these similarities are merely an unhappy coincidence. Her sister had long-abandoned her interest in publishing ghost stories following a short but serious illness while researching the works of Grace and his fellow Society members. For the five years leading up to her vanishment she had divided her time between work and an ever-expanding manuscript bearing the title *Apports, Apparitions, Transference and Parallel Biblio-Archeology*. This huge and, it must be said, frequently incomprehensible document has defied many efforts at analysis by people infinitely more expert than me, and is rendered all the more indecipherable by the crumbling of many of the pages—the fragments bearing a resemblance to that powdery residue found littering the bottom of P.O. Box 169—this inexplicable damage leaving frequent gaps that make it impossible to tell if the manuscript was ever completed. And, though I claim no special expertise in the idiosyncrasies of 1980s typewriters, as her sister suggests, the typescript on the extant pages does appear to bear some distinct similarities to that seen in 'The Underpass'.

There are two quotations on the title page of Nicola Franklyn's incomplete *magnum opus*, both serving to prove that she was not quite as finished with Dr. Grace and the Diodati Society as she may have led her close associates to believe. The first derives from Campbell Fitzgerald's 1912 story, his last-known completed supernatural tale, 'Passing Beyond All Knowledge':

> "There is knowledge that may be gained yet does not belong. Not to man, nor to his world," insisted the whisperer among the shadows. "And for everything that is taken out of the dark, something else must go back in its place. Something equal, though not necessarily the same..."

Whatever happened to the editor of *Ghostly Studies*, wherever she may have gone and for whatever reason, it seems apt to close with the second quotation, drawing on H.S. Grace's prefatory remarks concerning the story 'In a Distant Vista' in his 'Author's Introduction' to *Further Tales from a Ghostly Study* (1908). To Dr. Grace, and to Campbell Fitzgerald Senior and Junior, to the Diodatists, and most especially to Nicola Franklyn, let it stand as a tribute, and to others—perhaps—as a note of caution:

> There may yet endure places, lonely, thin spots bordering even the most brightly sunlit of byways, where the darkness presses

in, and where it would serve us well to avoid peering too intently at that which may be glimpsed glimmering, or lurking, beyond, lest it lure us or jolt us from the path and set us wandering endlessly into the night.

DAMIEN ANGELICA WALTERS

It Never Looks Like Drowning

D AMIEN ANGELICA WALTERS is the author of the novels
Paper Tigers and *The Dead Girls Club*, while her Bram Stoker
Award-nominated short fiction has been collected in *Sing Me Your
Scars* and *Cry Your Way Home* and reprinted in *Best Horror of the
Year*, *The Year's Best Dark Fantasy & Horror* and *The Year's Best
Weird Fiction*. Walters' stories have appeared in various anthologies
and magazines, including *Autumn Cthulhu*, *The Madness of Dr.
Caligari*, *Cassilda's Song*, *Nightmare Magazine* and *Black Static*. She
lives in Maryland with her husband and two rescued pit bulls.

"I adore British crime dramas," she admits, "and love when they
feature the angry seaside, with all the steep, treacherous cliffs, grey
sky and furious waves. For 'It Never Looks Like Drowning', I wanted
to capture that clouded, unforgiving feel as a mirror to the main
character's grief and guilt. I think it set a perfect backdrop for a tale
of loss, and feel the story would have had far less impact had I set it
anywhere else."

T HE COASTLINE HERE, all craggy, plunging cliffs and white-
whipped froth, would never fly back home. They'd ugly it up with
metal barricades and huge warning signs that inevitably wouldn't
deter the driven or the thrill-seekers or eager candidates for the

Darwin Awards. They'd build a theme park nearby with expensive day-passes, kiddie rides and roller coasters, and a massive parking lot. Souvenirs and sunburns. Or, Bree thought, tipping her chin towards the clouded sky, maybe not so much the latter.

Easier for her to think about things like that. About rubbish and nonsense. Easier than thinking about the arrangements she was here to finalise. Easier than thinking about her sister.

She stared out—not down—at the grey-green water, the waves crashing on the rocks a cudgel to her heart. Once again, she was sweeping in to tidy a mess Mikayla left behind. But this time, Bree didn't have to be afraid. Nothing could hurt her. A pinch of relief nestled in her breastbone and felt the worst sort of betrayal. It wasn't even a fair thought; it had been years since she'd been at risk. She touched the small scar above her right eyebrow. No one's fault. She'd been young and had gotten too close, hadn't fully grasped the inherent danger.

"Bree, come away from there, please?"

Mark, her boyfriend of three years, stood twenty feet away, his face as white as the foam below. She wanted to tell him she was fine, she wasn't that close to the edge, but she wasn't and she was, so she stepped back until his shoulders let go of their tension.

He took her in his arms, and while a curious numbness had fallen over her as soon as they'd landed at Heathrow, she still welcomed his touch. A hundred yards from the cliff sat Lavender House, the reason her sister had come to England in the first place. A bequest from a great-aunt neither knew in life. A six-bedroom behemoth with a peaked roof, widow's walk and a wide porch. A little run-down, but nothing a bit of money and time couldn't fix. *A bed and breakfast, Bree, can't you just see it?*

They'd flipped a coin to see who'd come to see if it was viable, never mind that they had plenty of pictures and reports from an agent. The toss was really only a formality. Bree wouldn't have been able to come for several more months because of work, and Mikayla wanted to start yesterday, the way she always did with everything.

Bree's bosses were far more understanding with respect to a death in the family.

"The realtor is coming this afternoon, right?" Mark said against the top of her head.

"Uh-huh, but they're called estate agents here."

He laughed. "Same difference. Are you hungry? Want me to make some breakfast? If I can figure out how to work the stove anyway."

She nodded. He offered to take care of the dishes after, something she gladly accepted. She wandered through the first floor of the house, catching glimpses of her sister everywhere—four wavy streaks in the dust atop the mahogany buffet in the dining area, the half-open curtains in the parlour, books pulled halfway from the library's shelves. And in the bedroom upstairs, her clothes, her hairbrush with long blonde strands still caught in the bristles, her open suitcase. Her prescription bottles.

They'd arrived at the house late last night, leaving their luggage in the foyer and taking the only suitable space. She'd had a brief moment to breathe in her sister on pillow and duvet—funny how they always chose the same side of the bed, the one furthest from the door—and then she was out for the count.

She hadn't noticed that everything was mussed in a way that said police, not Mikayla. Bree had spoken to the Detective Inspector a few times on the phone. He'd seemed kind and patient, but there'd been no point in arguing or causing a fuss. Not even when they called off the search for a body. They'd seen the medication, had known what it was for. A few other phone calls had revealed her history, the other attempts. The investigation was finished, the inquest done. The official story: suicide. Mikayla, another statistic in a long line of the same, all driven to the edge by shadows they couldn't escape.

And lest there'd be any doubt, she'd left a note.

Perched on the edge of the bed, she opened that note now, left at the house by DI Lewis. He'd read it over the phone, but seeing her sister's words, her handwriting, sent a shudder through her.

Dear Bree:
   I can't do it anymore. I'm tired of fighting them, tired of every-thing. It hurts too much.

I'm sorry.
M.

Them. No one else would understand what she'd really meant. They'd make their own assumptions. And they'd be wrong.

Bree had killed Mikayla's first shadow before she started kindergarten. It was small and easily squished to ruin beneath a light-up sneaker, a thought that now struck her as almost funny. But only almost.

They'd been playing in the backyard. Mikayla suddenly bent over, whimpering and pulling at her hair, her clothes. As Bree opened her mouth to call for their mother, Mikayla started coughing deep in her chest, and a small darkness slipped from her lips, like a short ribbon of charcoal-coloured bile. Without thought, Bree stomped one small foot. The thump of her sole, a small wet squish, and only a dark smudge remained, similar to the guts of an insect. And it was done. They looked at each other with wide eyes, Mikayla no longer crying. The roles were set in that instant. Whenever Mikayla felt one trying to emerge, she would find Bree and tug her hand. Bath or basement, yard or crawl space, anywhere at all. With each passing year, the shadows grew larger and larger, but Bree was always at the ready. Shoes, a rolled newspaper, a baseball bat. Whatever it took to destroy them. Until a few months after Mikayla's thirteenth birthday, when she stopped sicking them up.

"I can't," she told Bree. "I feel them in me, and I try and try but they won't come out."

Syrup of ipecac, a finger shoved down the throat, nothing they tried worked.

"It'll be okay," Bree promised. What else could she say? But even at fifteen, she sensed her words were lies. Sensed Mikayla knew it, too.

From that point on, Mikayla changed. She jumped at nothing, shrank from things unseen, withdrew tightly into herself, and stayed in her bedroom with headphones turned to the highest volume. And all the doctors and the pills in the world couldn't fix her. And neither could Bree. No matter how many nights she crept into her sister's room, trying in vain to help her vomit. To make her better.

No one knew the truth except for the girls and their mother, and she took off not long after she carried in a pile of laundry and saw what they were doing. They'd managed to keep it a secret from their father until his death the previous year.

Bree folded the note and tucked it away. Over the years, Mikayla had tried pills, a knife to her wrists, and once Bree caught her carefully reading the label on a bottle of drain-cleaner. Mikayla was always as strong as she *could* be. The shadows were stronger. But a few years ago, everything had seemed to get better. Maybe it was the right combination of meds, maybe it had all finally run its course. Or maybe she'd simply gotten better at hiding the darkness from her sister.

The door chimes rang, a melody Bree felt she should recognise but didn't. The estate agent was already familiar with the place, didn't need anything other than a few signatures.

"How long will you be staying?" the agent asked as she was placing the documents in her satchel.

"Not long," Bree said. "We'll be leaving as soon as I finish all . . . this."

Sorrow danced across the agent's face and Bree extended a hand, wanting her gone. Soon enough, she was on her way, with the reminder that it might take quite a bit of time before they—*she*—found an interested buyer, because of cliff erosion. "Sad to say, it's the whole coastline," she said.

Mark was in the library, tucked in a leather chair. He started to rise when she entered, but she stayed him with a hand.

"I'm going for a walk," she said.

"Do you . . . "

"No. I won't be long, just need to clear my head a bit."

She went back to the cliff's edge, back to the water, and this time, she looked down. Five hundred feet or near enough. All that force, all that relentless energy. All those jagged rocks concealed and then revealed, like a softly draping cowl across a woman's décolletage. How bad must it have been for Mikayla to jump? "Fuck you," she muttered to the water, her words swallowed by the crash and hiss.

The pale sun vanished behind a cloud, turning the grey day even darker, the water murky and mottled. Bree shivered in the chill, grimacing. And to think that this was spring.

Mark was still in the library when she returned. She pretended the walk had been more beneficial than it really had been, and he accepted her words as fact. She suspected it only a polite fiction on his part as well, but it was appreciated. The last thing she needed was to be picked apart and dissected for weak spots.

She fell asleep to the rhythmic pounding of the surf and woke in the middle of the night to the same. For a few moments, her fingers clutched at the sheets, but the disorientation ebbed. She rolled on her side, Mark's steady breathing a comfort. A gust of wind rattled the eaves. The light from the bathroom across the hall didn't penetrate the corners of the room, making it seem so much smaller than it really was.

A strange sound, oddly liquid and wavery, came from somewhere in the distance. She bolted upright, one hand reaching for Mark's shoulder, fingers a hair's breadth from his skin, head cocked to the side. The house creaked and groaned as it settled deeper into its bones. The waves pounded the cliff. *Pull yourself together*, she told herself as she sank into the too-soft mattress. Still, though, she rubbed away goosebumps as she listened to the house, and the sun was lightening the edges of the window when she finally fell asleep.

Mark had coffee ready when she came downstairs. On the counter near the stove, there were several canisters of tea that must've belonged to the great-aunt, because neither she nor Mikayla cared for it. She was halfway through her coffee when she shoved away from the table, crossed the room, and one by one upended the containers into the trash can, leaves spilling with a soft patter. After only a moment's consideration, the canisters went in as well.

When she returned to her chair, Mark cleared his throat. "What was that for?"

"I have to start somewhere, don't I?" With straightened arms, she rubbed her hands together under the table.

"I guess so." He gave her a half-smile. "Did you sleep okay?"

"Of course not," she said, her words sharper than she intended. "How could I?"

He poured another cup of coffee at the counter and she wrapped her arms under his, pressed her cheek between his shoulder blades. "I'm sorry."

"If it makes you feel better, I didn't sleep well either. This house...way too old and noisy."

Bree laughed softly against his back. "Very much so."

"What do you want to do today?"

She swallowed hard before answering. "I want to pack Mikayla's things."

"Do you want some help?"

She shook her head. "No, but when I'm done, could you arrange to have them shipped home?"

"Of course."

"In case I forget, thank you. For everything, but mostly for being here."

He gave her hands a squeeze. "Where else would I be?"

She finished her second cup of coffee and had a third, but when that was finished, she couldn't delay any further. The staircase seemed narrower. Back in the bedroom, the walls loomed closer, the ceiling lower, the floor ready to pull her under. She fisted her hands and took long, deep breaths.

Mikayla's medication took a trip down the toilet, requiring multiple flushes. Her clothes were folded into neat piles, her shoes tucked into plastic bags. A thriller with a dog-eared page remained on the nightstand. The sight of that folded edge, of knowing her sister would never know the answer to the mystery within, brought forth a fresh wash of tears. Subtle movement registered in the corner of Bree's eye and she wiped her sorrow away with a forearm. "Yes?"

No answer.

She turned to find the space as empty as it had been. There was something muted—a footfall?—from the hallway.

"Mark?" she said, her voice shrill.

Again, no answer.

The hall was empty. So, too, the staircase and the rooms at the front of the house. Mark was in the kitchen, sending a text message, steam from a fresh cup of coffee curling in the air.

"Everything okay?" he asked, his brow creased.

"Were you upstairs a minute ago?"

"No, why?"

"I thought I heard someone." She rubbed her upper arms. "Just more house noise, I guess."

His face softened. His tone, too. "If it's too much, I can pack everything."

"No, it's fine. Honestly, I'm almost done. She didn't bring that much." Tears burned but she blinked them away and returned to the second floor. When she finished, save for a stack of papers with sketches and snippets of what first appeared to be poetry, she gave everything over to Mark and he left to find packing materials and a post office.

The house seemed darker, more closed-off when she was alone and she wandered through, pressing fingers and palms to walls and furniture. The sensation of being watched settled on her shoulders, a shawl of unease. In the library, Mark hadn't touched the books Mikayla had pulled halfway out. Now, Bree went through and tucked them in until their spines aligned with their neighbours, even though she was only going to have to pull them out again to box them up. She'd just fixed a copy of *Alice's Adventures in Wonderland* when from deep in the house, a noise. A laugh?

She froze in place, fingers spread, lips parted. It wasn't Mark's laugh; not his genuinely happy, nor his to humour you, nor his intoxicated revelry laugh. Maybe it wasn't a laugh at all. The spell in her limbs broke and she moved, whisper-soft and feather fall-slow, to the door, keeping just inside but craning her neck to listen.

"Mark?" she called, wincing at how loud her voice seemed, and yet how small when compared to the house. She gnawed a cuticle. "Mikayla?" Her voice broke in the middle. She pinched the bridge of her nose. Knuckled her upper lip.

With a grunt, she returned to the shelves. A bookseller the agent had recommended was coming tomorrow to look for first or early editions, the rest to be donated to a local library—another agent suggestion. The day after, a dealer in antiquities was coming to look at the furniture. Once those things were taken care of, a service was coming in to survey the house to give an estimate for a deep cleaning, and she had a meeting with a local couple who'd be caretaking the house until it sold.

And then? Home, to take care of Mikayla's apartment.

She left the library and visited the unoccupied bedrooms. Bedframes without mattresses, dressers adorned with dusty picture frames containing black and white histories of someone else's life, wardrobes with neatly folded blankets and, in the smallest at the very end of the hall, a satin gown the colour of the Caribbean. A mirror stood in the corner and she held the dress in front of her, swaying from side to side, the hem sliding along the floor with a gentle susurration.

She stopped moving. The dress stilled. The whisper continued.

Whirling around, she left the gown in a puddle on the wood. Mark's name lodged in her throat, a dry-swallowed pill. One step, then another, on wooden feet of apprehension and fear. And the sound... Fabric on wood or water running over a stone. Soft, but pervasive. Moving further away, albeit slowly.

The front door opened with a bang. "I'm back!"

She yelped and ran down the steps, skin slipping on the treads, hand holding tight to the railing to keep from tumbling to the bottom. She ran into his arms without stopping and burst into tears.

"What's wrong?"

"I just, I heard—" More tears and then laughter as embarrassment washed over her. "My mind was playing tricks on me and—" More laughter, and was there an edge of the hysterical? She thought there might be.

He pulled her close, kissed her forehead and held her tight, and when his arms finally loosened, she felt better. Mostly.

They finished the day by boxing all the knick-knacks and photographs and wiping dust from the flat surfaces. Evening baths for both left a grey halo of grime on the porcelain tub. A storm rolled in just before they turned in, filling the house with the rage of the wind and ocean. Mark fell asleep quickly, but Bree tossed and turned. A gust of wind shook the window shutters and she flopped on her side, facing the interior wall.

The light in the bathroom flickered once, twice, and went out. Bree held her breath and closed her eyes. Silly, perhaps. Darkness reigned there, too. Slowly, she slitted her lids open. Lightning strobed the room, bright enough to reveal someone in the doorway.

She sat up with a yelp, spine jamming hard against the bed-frame, shaking Mark awake at the same time.

"Huh?" he said, voice thick with sleep.

"Someone's here," she hissed, her fingers talons.

The lightning flashed again. The entry was empty.

"They were standing right there. Watching us."

Mark thumped out of bed and she tried to pull him back, but her fingers touched air instead. She pawed for the light-pull on the bedside lamp; the yellow glow went on at the same time Mark stepped out. She slid from the bed to follow.

He turned on the overhead in the hallway and they went room to room, closing each door once they'd finished checking. The tension in Bree's shoulders lessened a bit with each one, but when they took the stairs to the first floor, her muscles tightened again. They made a slow circuit, turning on lights until the place was daylight bright, double-checking all the locks. They ended in the kitchen, which was as empty as everywhere else. Outside, the lightning and thunder spaced further and further apart and the wind ceased its howling.

"I swear I thought I saw someone," Bree said, her voice small.

"It's okay," he said. "Are *you* okay?"

She shook her head, her words too tangled to emerge.

They stood in the kitchen, arms wrapped round each other, until finally he said, "Let's go back to bed."

"I doubt I'll be able to sleep," she said.

But, eventually, she did.

They slept in, and Bree had just finished dressing when the

bookseller, a thin woman with long, white hair and Doc Martens, arrived. The woman worked quickly, creating multiple piles in the library, and when she finished, she took several boxes with her and left a cheque. Bree and Mark loaded the rest of the books into the rental car and followed the agent's directions to the library. Afterwards, they had dinner in town at a small restaurant with dark-panelled walls and dim lighting, and by the time they got back to the house they were yawning fiercely.

Still, though, before they turned in, Mark walked through the house and made certain everything was secure. Bree knew it was for her benefit and loved him even more for it. They fell asleep curled together in the bed, like two snails sharing the same shell, the light from the bathroom peeking in.

But Bree woke in darkness. No storm, no wind. She reached for Mark but withdrew her hand and exhaled through her nose. The light bulb probably burned out. No reason to wake him. No reason to be alarmed. She snuggled closer, his body warm against hers. In the distance, the soft conversation of the ocean. Drawing closer, growing louder.

And louder still.

Too loud.

Sitting, she fumbled on the bedside lamp. The ceiling was too close, too low. She slid down until she was flat. It wasn't the ceiling. Above, darkness stretched from end to end, a foot lower than the plaster it concealed. It moved and shifted, pulsing slowly, the rhythmic, liquid noise accompanying each movement.

She elbowed Mark. "Wake up," she said, barely moving her lips.

"What?"

"Shhh. Look up. No, don't sit, just look."

"What the—"

But she knew, oh yes, she knew. Mikayla might have gone over the cliff, but she'd left something behind. Not intentionally, no. Her sister would never do that to her. The shadows, rats deserting a sinking ship. Too large for a shoe or even a baseball bat. Had they been waiting for this moment for years? Planning for it?

Mark slowly scooted to the edge of the bed, pulling her with him.

Together, they slipped onto the floor, attention focussed overhead. The pulse, the hum, continued. They scuttled towards the door and the darkness descended another foot. Bree moaned against flatlined lips.

Inch by inch, they closed the distance between bed and exit and Mark had one hand on the jamb when the shadows dropped yet again. He shoved her out and quickly followed.

"Go, go," he shouted, yanking her up.

In the hallway, their feet tattooed the wood with fear and fury. Around them, more shadows began to peel off the walls. Strangely-shaped with many limbs, creeping inexorably towards them on floor and baseboard with that terrible wet, slippery murmur.

"Hurry, hurry, hurry," Bree urged.

Their passage on the staircase was marked with a series of erratic thumps. When they reached the bottom, they raced towards the door. Through the foyer and then out; a pinch of sunrise on the horizon pinking the sky. As the door slammed shut, the inhuman hum silenced and relief pricked the edges of her mind. Then it returned.

She didn't want to look, to know, but she couldn't *not*. Shadows were melting from the windows, charcoal veils spilling down the sides and pooling on the ground.

Bree and Mark ran towards the car. Movement to her right. A long shadow speared through the grass with the sound of wheat caught in a strong wind, and she pushed Mark to the left to avoid it. The shadow split in two, piercing the green between their feet. Cutting them off from each other. Cutting *her* off from the car.

She shrieked and stumbled to her knees, her fingertips scant inches from the murk. Mark reached for her, but the shadow widened, forcing him away from her. Forcing her back, too.

And back and back.

Pebbles dug into her arches, the tips of her toes. Mark's arm was still extended, mouth contorted in horror, panic rendering his gaze wild as he scanned in all directions for a way to reach her that no longer existed. The darkness pushed. She moved. Heading towards the cliff's edge, being *herded* towards the edge.

"What do you want from me!" she shrieked through her tears.

She'd always thought they lacked intelligence, acting on something akin to instinct. But this didn't feel like instinct. This felt intentional. This felt personal. The realisation was acid on her tongue.

"You can't do this," she sobbed. "I'm sorry! I'm sorry!"

She took mincing, baby steps. The darkness surged, forcing her to hasten her pace. Mark was too far away to help, but she screamed for him nonetheless, screamed until her throat burned and her voice rasped.

The shadows continued their slow and steady advance. Behind and below, the sea crashed against the rocks again and again and again.

MICHAEL MARSHALL SMITH

THE WINDOW OF ERICH ZANN

Michael Marshall Smith is a novelist and screenwriter. Under this name he has published more than ninety short stories, and five novels—*Only Forward, Spares, One of Us* and *The Servants*—winning the Philip K. Dick, International Horror Guild and August Derleth awards, along with the Prix Bob Morane in France. He is the only author to have won the British Fantasy Award for Best Short Fiction four times. In 2017 he published *Hannah Green and her Unfeasibly Mundane Existence*, and the collection *The Best of Michael Marshall Smith* was recently published by Subterranean Press.

Writing as "Michael Marshall", he has published seven international best-selling thrillers, including *The Straw Men* series, *The Intruders* (made into a BBC America series starring John Simm and Mira Sorvino) and *Killer Move*. His most recent novel under this name is *We Are Here*. Now, additionally writing as "Michael Rutger", he has published the adventure thrillers *The Anomaly* and its sequel, *The Possession*.

He is currently co-writing and executive-producing development of *The Straw Men* for television. He is also Creative Consultant to The Blank Corporation, Neil Gaiman's production company in Los Angeles, and involved in the development of multiple TV shows, including *Neverwhere* and *American Gods*.

He lives in Santa Cruz, California, with his wife, son, and three cats.

As the author reveals: "This story came about in the way I like best—the collision of discovering a fascinating true fact about a place I know (and a fact that most seem unaware of), together with a request for a story that seemed almost designed to show how the idea could best be written.

"Though San Francisco is a very young city by European standards, the layers of history are still there (and at times, what with earthquakes and fires, it's been a pretty turbulent one) and to find out that elements of its past are still there, provocatively buried beneath streets which people walk along every day, was a tale waiting to be written.

"Since writing it, I've made a point of going and standing on certain points in the city, so in a way this piece of fiction has changed its reality for me…"

S HE ARRIVED, LIKE so many, on a Greyhound bus.

Also as with many, she had little clue where to go, no idea how to find a home. Until the moment when she first glimpsed the iconic Golden Gate Bridge looming in the sun-warmed fog, it hadn't properly occurred to her that this was going to be an issue. Sure, she'd need somewhere to sleep, and wash, but the city would provide, right? Everything she needed was waiting there for her, for *them*— manifest destiny reinvented for the first generation to realise they were a generation, a harbour from which to set off for parts unknown.

Not every person on the bus was on that journey. Some were leading regular lives. Coming back from visiting family. Going to the city to look for work. But history tends to forget that majority who are merely keeping on keeping on, and one in five believed they were going on to something bigger and better, travelling inexorably toward some higher place—ignoring the fact that in reality many of them were also moving *away*. Leaving behind old places, old people, old lives, casting them off like old clothes, skins that chaffed and constrained. Most who arrived in San Francisco that year were barely old enough to have given old lives a chance, but all knew they were ready for something new. Something different.

That this was their time.

And so Marion clamped down on the tension in her guts, telling herself it was unworthy of this great adventure, that worrying about where she was going to sleep was precisely the style of petty bourgeois bullshit she'd left Illinois to escape. Nonetheless, she was relieved when the girl next to her—a petite and serious-looking girl from South Dakota, wearing what Marion guessed was her grandfather's waistcoat (over otherwise very straight clothes) in an attempt to look fashionably old-timey, a single layer of hippie on top of a hometown girl—turned nervously to her.

Her name was Katie, and she'd climbed onto the bus late the previous evening, in Montana. It had been pretty full, with many seats taken up with people crashed out full-length, and the girl had stood in the aisle, looking apprehensive.

Marion moved along her seat and smiled up at her. "There's room next to me."

Katie sat gratefully. The two girls had talked a little since, though Marion spent much of the night looking at the darkness out the window. Katie had slept, or read.

"Do you have somewhere to stay tonight?"

"No," Marion admitted. She had enough money for maybe three nights in a cheap hotel, five if it was *really* cheap. After that she'd be putting herself in the hands of fate.

"So what are you going to do?"

Marion shrugged, glad of the chance to appear unfazed, cool, and finding that—for a moment at least—it made her feel that way too. "I don't know. Ask around, I guess?"

"Can we do it together? Look for a place?"

"Sure," Marion said, and smiled. She was aware this would make it harder, but she could tell that Katie needed reassurance, and a temporary friend.

"Don't worry about a thing," a voice said from behind.

Marion and Katie turned cautiously. A girl with a huge frizz of red hair was leaning toward them, elbows on the back of their seat. "My cousin," she said. "Been here a month, got a place. He says there's space for me. If we scrunch up small, there's space for three, right? I'm Cindy, by the way."

"Are you sure?"

The girl grinned, broad and crooked, the grin of a girl who was sure about pretty much everything. "My mom's annoying as hell, but I don't think she'd lie to me about my actual *name*."

Marion laughed. "About the house, she means."

"That too. Done deal. And it's right in Haight. You've heard of Haight, yes?"

Of course they had. Haight-Ashbury, the well-spring of everything that was going on in the city—of the whole world—and the epicentre of cool. Marion nodded, her stomach relaxing. See? The world was on her side.

She was inevitable.

Forty minutes later the three girls got off the bus together, brave new spirits arriving in the promised land.

Five weeks later Marion moved out of the house. It was a Sunday, and she left in the late morning and tried to find Katie and Cindy before she went. Though she was tired and hungover, she was dogged, and eventually located Cindy under some guy in one of the bedrooms. Both were passed out, as were the six other people spread around the room. Thirty seconds of poking in the side from Marion resulted in the redhead eventually opening her eyes, one more slowly than the other.

"I'm leaving," Marion said. "Catch you soon, okay?"

Cindy looked at her without apparent recognition, blinked, and then passed out again.

Katie was nowhere to be found. The girl had steered clear of anything stronger than pot since the disaster at the end of the first week, so Marion thought she was most likely fine, and at her waitressing job. Katie's shit was pretty much together.

On the way out Marion passed the kitchen. She preferred to pass this room whenever possible, on the grounds that it was safer than actually going in. The place was a health hazard, as she knew to both her cost, and benefit.

Everybody was super-enthusiastic about experimenting with new ways of cooking—on very limited budgets, people who until recently had relied upon their moms to fill their plates, and who therefore had only vague and idealistic ideas of how you turned raw ingredients into something edible—but much less good about clearing up the mess afterward. That'd be too square, too obsessed with appearances, too much the way their appallingly unhip parents did things. And so the sink was piled precariously high with dirty plates, and the cold, murky water a minefield of silverware, while the counters, floor and parts of the walls were encrusted with multiple layers of grime and spilled remnants of food.

Marion estimated that she'd lost seven pounds in weight since arriving in Frisco. Katie was holding steady, because she got one square meal a day where she worked and could actually cook a little, too. Marion had long-ago clocked the fact that Katie's timid request that they find a berth together on that first day had been not a sign of weakness but indicative of a quiet, focussed ability to judge the best way of achieving what she needed. Meanwhile, a diet of sex and drugs seemed to be suiting Cindy just fine.

There was a guy in the kitchen. At first Marion didn't realise who it was, because everybody looked pretty similar. Denim. Layers of shirts and waistcoats. Long hair. When he turned toward the door, she saw it was Dylan.

"Hey," he said. His voice was a croak, his eyes bloodshot. He peered at her face for a long moment, then at her backpack. "You, you've, like, got your bag."

"Right. I'm leaving."

"Cool. I mean, why?"

Dylan was Cindy's cousin. The guy who'd opened the door when they arrived, already majestically high, and said sure, come join the party, step right in and pull up a joint. Which was basically how it had gone on—a tidal, day-after-day party, under the influence of one thing or another, or more often several things at the same time.

On that first night, and for the next week or so, it had seemed utterly exotic and far out and exactly what they'd come to the city for. Everybody was talking non-stop about the Revolution, and what they could do to help set the old ways on fire. Planning meetings for anti-war protests. Impromptu jam sessions, where an inability to play an instrument was no barrier. Long—freakin' endless—discussions about how to get the message of what was happening from here out into the world at large. It was only as the second week wore on and the effects of consecutive hangovers began to take their toll, that Marion began to get a clearer fix on her situation.

The house—though a tall, narrow, and dilapidated Victorian of approximately the same style—was not in the Haight district after all, but fifteen minutes uphill walk away in a neighbourhood that was far less happening and much more scary, especially at night. Each room looked like some other entire house had been upended into it: an ever-evolving chaos of guitars, art materials, half-finished canvasses—some of which had been used multiple times, shadows of earlier terrible paintings dimly visible under the current image— stained mattresses, dirty clothes, fliers and posters, discarded take-out food containers, and a screen-printing contraption that a number of very stoned people had tried to fix several times and so was destined to never work again.

And people.

God, yes, people.

When Marion and Katie arrived, there were already at least four sleeping to a room. Every day, though people came and went, that average had increased. Generally, newcomers knew at least one person in the house, or had met someone before. It had been getting up in the small hours to take a pee—and don't even try to imagine what the bathroom was like—to find a complete stranger passed out in there, his penis hanging flaccidly out of his pants, that made up Marion's mind to leave. This was not the scene she'd come to be a part of. There was somewhere better, and she was the girl to find it.

"You know there's some half-naked dude in the john?"

"I just talked to him. He's okay."

"So who is he?"

"I have literally no idea."

He beamed. Marion liked Dylan, she really did. Though apparently incapable of turning down any intoxicant that was passed in front of him, he seemed solid in the core. Or relatively so. Some of the others... not so much. A few, not even a little bit. There were people who'd brought darkness with them, or an emptiness so deep and profound it was somehow even worse. She needed to spend longer in the city before unconditional acceptance of others was going to play for her, and preferably do it somewhere that didn't smell of burned lentils and armpits. She knew there were houses where the cool/chaos balance was better. She needed to find one of those.

Dylan took a gulp of coffee, and winced. "So where are you going?"

"Met a guy in City Lights yesterday. He said he knew somewhere I could stay. Less crowded."

Dylan raised an eyebrow. "Hot guy?"

She laughed. "No. Old."

"They're the worst."

"Not this one. Or, I don't think. He seems cool. If it's a problem I'll bail."

"Cindy will be bummed you've gone."

Marion wasn't too sure about that. The primary message she'd been getting from the other girl in the last couple weeks was that she felt Marion wasn't letting her hair down hard or fast or often enough, and that she was bordering on being officially uncool. "Tell her I'll see her soon."

"But you're coming Tuesday afternoon, right?"

The event half the house had been preparing for. "Of course. And look, also tell Katie I'll drop by in the next couple days, okay? Tell her especially."

"You got it."

Marion was pretty sure he'd have forgotten by the time she left the house, but she thanked him and walked out the door into the sunshine on a mission.

He'd said he'd meet her in the bookstore at five-thirty, but at nearly seven o'clock she was still in the poetry room upstairs, waiting. Wondering, too, if she'd made a mistake. It wasn't unrecoverable: if the guy failed to turn up, she could simply hike back to the house and say it didn't work out and people would shrug and pass a joint and that would be that.

But she didn't want to. It would feel dumb.

It would be a big fail.

So she stayed there, as the day faded outside, watching people cooing over the books, explaining poems to each other, necking, hanging out. After a while the lights began to look strange to her, a souvenir of the disaster in the first week. After three days in the house she'd gone with Katie and Cindy to a big happening in the park—somewhat reluctantly, because though she totally wanted to go, her stomach had been feeling weird since breakfast. It was crowded and sunny and loud and fun, and The Dead played a set, and there had been buckets of Kool-Aid and friendly people encouraging newcomers to quench their thirst, and maybe some of the drinkers had known what they were getting into, but not all of them.

Sure as hell not Marion and Katie, and that's why Marion had reason to be thankful for the unsanitary conditions of the kitchen of the house. It turned out her stomach gripes were the harbinger of a violent food poisoning episode that suddenly had her vomiting into the bushes—purging her body of a large portion of the LSD before it had time to kick in.

Katie had not been so lucky. She'd spent the next eight hours on a roller coaster of alternating laugh-out-loud euphoria and catastrophic paranoia, including a long episode where she'd been convinced that the wide grass of the park was in fact a part of the bay. She'd infected Marion with this vision, and the two of them spent a period of unknown duration clinging to each other, trembling, convinced they were on an invisible raft slowly spiralling around a cove, while everybody else danced and sang and ran in circles.

Eventually Marion (who'd only been suffering about 20% of the effects, but was still intermittently barfing), managed to get the two of them back to the house, where someone far more experienced managed to plane them back toward normality with a regimen of herb teas, chocolate, and pot.

Marion and Katie decided the next morning that the doors of their perception were quite wide enough already, and had steered the hell clear of LSD ever since. There were times when Marion still felt affected, though that had to be an illusion, surely. It'd been a month now. But certain types of light still looked strange to her, as if the glow existed between her and the object causing it, rather than in the lamp or bulb itself. And once in a while she heard...

She could hear it now, in fact.

Music.

A faint single line of notes, which—though she assumed it was something she'd heard in the park that afternoon, and had become locked in her head—was unlike anything she'd heard before. Different to what she'd normally think of as music, in fact—though a lot of local musicians liked to explore those kind of sounds, to show how liberated they were from outdated conceptions of melodic yadda yadda yadda.

This was a little louder than she'd heard it before—so much so that she turned in her seat to look out of the window, expecting to see some guy with a flute (she thought that was probably what it was, though she wasn't sure, maybe a piccolo or something) busking on the sidewalk.

Fog had begun to roll in. The Broadway/Columbus crossroads was pretty crowded—this borderland between Chinatown and North Beach had become a Mecca for both real hippies and buses of tourists come to gawp at them—but there was nobody obviously playing.

After a moment, however, she spotted something (or someone) else, and got up and hurried down, out of the store.

The man was standing on the corner.

Short, half-bald, rather stooped and overweight. His nose was large, the skin of his face liberally sprinkled with moles, some disconcertingly large. Though his clothes looked as though they had once been well-tailored, they were now somewhat shabby. Not at all a hot guy, bottom line.

"Hey," Marion said, diffidently, as she approached. "I thought you weren't coming."

"Aha," he said. His voice was soft, with the trace of an accent. "There you are."

"You said to meet inside. At five-thirty."

"I'm sorry," he said. "It was hard today. I couldn't finish in time."

"Finish what?"

He shook his head. "It's done. Come. Follow me."

Twenty minutes later he suddenly stopped walking. Marion had been getting more and more confused—they were heading away from the places where people actually lived, the kind of people she knew anyhow—but for an older guy he walked super-fast, a relentless beetling motion that covered the ground quickly. She asked at one point if they could take a streetcar instead, but he just shook his head again.

"Why are we here?"

They were standing in front of a tall, weathered building in the Financial District, on a narrow side street at the corner of California and Battery. The structures here were tall, constructed of stone or sometimes brick, making the alleyway feel like a canyon. There was a sense of heavy permanence to the area, despite the excavations they'd passed farther up Market, part of the process of installing the new BART/Muni system. Everything in sight seemed to be either a bank or business, apart from a battered neon sign on the opposite corner for something called YUGGOTH, wreathed in the fog coming in more and more thickly from the bay.

The old man didn't answer. Instead he stood looking at her, head cocked to the side, his sharp blue eyes narrowed, as he'd been doing when Marion first noticed him, in City Lights on the previous afternoon. "Do you see me?" he'd asked then.

She'd frowned. "Well, yeah."

He nodded, and somehow from there they'd got to how she came to be in the city, and where she was living, and its insufficiency. He'd made the offer of somewhere to stay, and her initial reaction had been to laugh—she'd been hit on at least three times a day since she'd been there, though you weren't supposed to see it that way because everybody (or the guys, mainly) were framing rampant promiscuity as "generosity of spirit", something they were all supposed to have.

Cindy had discovered enormous generosity within herself, very quickly. The very first night, in fact. Katie was having no truck with the whole concept—you can take the girl out of the prairie, but extracting the prairie from the girl is a whole other thing. Marion was adopting a wait-and-see policy and trying to be open about it, but she was damned sure this elderly, foreign-looking guy, wasn't going to break the dam.

She realised he wasn't looking salacious, however, or hopeful or even desperate. More thoughtful, even a little sad. Sometimes you'd see that in older guys—an awareness of how undignified and gross their lingering drives were making them appear—but it didn't seem to be that either. If anything he looked paternal, and not in a weird way.

So she'd agreed.

The building they were now standing in front of looked even more ancient than the others around it. Battered, stained, stoic. As the old man got out keys, Marion noticed the name PENTIMENTO chiselled into the stone above the door.

"Italian?" she asked.

"I believe so."

He opened the door and they stepped into a cramped vestibule. The old man flicked a switch and a pale, dusty bulb illuminated the space. Scuffed-up floorboards, stone walls. In the corner, rusted ironwork in front of a tiny elevator.

"Doesn't work, I'm afraid," he said, indicating the narrow steps which led from the other side.

Six flights later, she was glad to see they'd reached the top of the building. There had been no windows on the ascent—just another old bulb on each landing. Then finally this upper space, with a single wooden door.

"This is it," the old man said, as he unlocked it. "Now, don't get your hopes up. It was the caretaker's place."

The other side lay a room, perhaps ten feet wide and twenty long. It was bare, with dusty grey floorboards and peeling wallpaper that looked old. They were up in the roof, and so the ceiling bore sharply inward on one side, revealing beams. A single bed had been pushed into the corner. A small table. One chair. A small area on the right-hand side evidently designed to serve as a kitchenette, with a hotplate. There was a narrow doorway open next to it. Beyond was a tiny room with a toilet and a shower-stall, both of which looked like they had not been used in twenty years. Overall, it felt like a cabin below-decks on an old wooden ship.

In truth, it would have been a pretty depressing place, were it not for one thing. Marion walked straight toward it.

"Wow," she said. "That's cool."

The old man stayed where he was, back by the door to the stairs. "I suppose so. There are two conditions. The first is that you bring nobody else up here. *Ever.* This cannot become another flophouse filled with free spirits and freeloaders."

"Works for me," Marion said. "That's exactly the scene I'm bailing out of."

"The second is that on Tuesday evenings I need this space myself. Not for long—a couple of hours. Between eight and ten. I require you to be elsewhere during that time."

"Sure thing."

"That's all."

"And you really don't want me to pay anything?"

He shook his head, handed her a pair of keys, and turned away. She said thank you to his back, and he raised a hand in return as he started down the stairs.

As the sound of his footsteps receded, Marion closed the door and took stock. Sure it was dusty and smelled weird, and the ceiling made it feel kind of cramped, and in general it was a long way from nice, but listen...

It was silent.

Nobody talking. Nobody playing the guitar badly. Nobody snoring. Nobody... just *nobody*.

She smiled, then wandered back down to the room's biggest and most redeeming feature. A window. *The* window, in fact. It was the only one, but it was large. Circular, with different coloured panes divided by spokes that came out from the centre: the panes broken up into further sections by a tracery of leading. What they called a "rose window", in a church. She dimly remembered from child-hood—there'd been such a feature in the chapel back home—that they were usually placed at the western aspect, and wondered if this was the case here. Maybe.

She stood for a while and looked out, across the rooftops, at the city lights that stretched toward Nob Hill and beyond. Without real-ising she was doing it, after a few minutes she slipped the pack off her back and set it gently on the floor, continuing to stare through the multicoloured glass as night fell.

She followed the people as they marched, and after a while they were all singing and shouting, and if you've never been part of a crowd like that, a swell of humanity all driven by the same cause and dreaming the same dream then you simply don't know how it feels. You can't know what it's like to become a part of something that blurs every individual into one, all their single candles turning for a bright and shining afternoon into a sea of infinite light—a light that each one of them believes will be enough to illuminate the universe in ways it has never been before.

They strode along the streets together, chanting the same slogans, waving at the straights and squares standing mired on the sidewalks, as they frowned confused at the free spirits in their midst—and as they progressed toward Haight, more and more people started to join them at the back, and from the sides, impulsively throwing off the shackles of their lives and swelling this tide of humanity into a fleet of souls too powerful to resist.

People sang, and played instruments, weaving together one enor-mous song. Guitars, flutes, drums. And after a while Marion realised she could hear something else, too—a high, keening melody played on a single violin.

The thing she'd been hearing for days now, and that spoke to her, sang in a way that was dark but direct and true. It took all this noise and joy and condensed it to a single note.

She turned her head back and forth, tried to see where it was coming from, but there was no sign. By then the crowd around her was so loud that it sounded as if the tune was coming from between her own ears, and so she forgot about it and rhythmically punched the air with her fist like all the others.

And they marched on.

That evening she ate sitting at the little table. The meal consisted of two vegetable egg rolls from a place she'd found five minutes' walk away, all she convinced herself she could afford. It wasn't impossible to find casual work in the city. She'd washed dishes. Waited tables. A few nights of bar work before they found out she'd lied about her age and was only eighteen. What was tougher was keeping your position. Hardly anyone was offering stable employment, because they knew there were countless other girls and boys out there desperate to earn a little cash, and they didn't trust hippies to be reliable. Most people got hired by the day, or even the hour. The only person Marion knew with an actual job was Katie.

After eating she read for a while, a water-damaged copy of *The Naked Ape* that an older guy named Karl, the manager in City Lights, had let her take on permanent loan.

At ten o'clock she went to bed.

Haight-Ashbury. Ground zero. Heaving with humanity. Placards. Chanting. Protest songs. Men and women on soapboxes, all shouting different things, but they were all the same thing at heart, and so it spiralled up into an extraordinary new music, a choral symphony of those who would up-end the universe.

For the next forty minutes, Marion was happier than she had been in her entire life. Happier than on the sporadic days as a young child when her mother remembered she was around, and spent some actual

time with her. Happier than when a little older, and her bedroom
door for once did not open in the middle of the night. Happier even
than when she went to sit alone in her grandmother's yard, away from
everyone. Away from her uncle especially. Happy as only a person
can be when their mind, every molecule of their bodies, their very
soul is in tune with the world around them.

Happy, happy, happy.

She saw Cindy walking by, swigging from a plastic cup, her arm
around some guy, grinning and pumping her fist. She ran over when
she saw Marion and planted a big kiss on her lips before dancing back
away into the crowds. Marion spotted Dylan too, and some of the
others from the house, and for a moment felt a keen stab of loneli-
ness, but convinced herself it didn't matter because, look: here they
all were together again—that all of them would always be together,
preserved in moments like this, when they stood together and changed
the world, fierce insects frozen in the warm amber of history.

They all sang together, and somewhere in the background or deep
inside, that simple un-melody played.

When Marion woke, at first she wondered if she'd heard a noise. She
lay in the narrow bed, listening, before realising it was more likely
the lack of noise that was unusual. For weeks she'd been living
under the kind of conditions they use to soften up political prisoners
prior to interrogation. There was no noise here. There were no
people.

Once she'd realised that was the difference, she turned on her
side and tried to get back to sleep. Soon it felt as if the silence was
pounding in her eardrums, however—so loud it was almost like
tinnitus, a single note, varying in pitch. It compelled you to listen,
to unsuccessfully predict where it was going next, like the strangest
kind of experimental music. She'd heard more than her share of
that over recent weeks (Dylan was an enthusiastic, though
unschooled, bass player), and learned something.

If you could actually play—and a few people in the house could—
then your hands and ears wouldn't let you leave the path. However
much a real musician tried to be random and free, previously-learned

patterns ensnared them. Muscle memory pulled you back to the norm, to the established shipping lanes of melody. You had to be wholly ignorant of the process to play something truly new, and even then a vestige of recognisable rhythm would eventually emerge as utter incompetents bashed clumsily on out-of-tune guitars with only four strings. Humanity, the things we learn without even realising, intervenes and re-gathers. To truly throw the past aside and become new requires both strength and a willingness to throw yourself into the void.

This sound, the sound her ears or brain made without intervention... it sounded like that. After a while it had woken her sufficiently that she sat up. It was only then that she understood what had really roused her.

She got out of bed and walked to the window.

It was light out there. Not like during the day, of course—she checked her watch and found it was a little before 3:00 a.m.—but starkly moonlit, bright enough to flood a multitude of colours into the room. Below that shining level, the buildings all around were wreathed and enveloped in fog.

In the moonlight, everything looked psychedelic.

Marion pulled the chair over to where she could sit and look out. Though she'd spent a while gazing out of the window earlier, she must have been looking at a slightly different angle. Fog, like snow, will make a place look unfamiliar. Presumably that was what was making the angles between the buildings look altered. And presumably it was the fog that was turning the few lights a curdled yellow, almost as if they were running on gas, instead of electricity.

She moved the chair right up close to the window, noticing something. Sounds, from outside. This wasn't the single note thing, but the kind of noise people made. Distant shouting. Not in anger, but workmanlike shouts, the kind you heard when men were engaged in some kind of task.

Then a screeching cry, like a seagull.

Perfectly possible, of course—the building was only a ten-minute walk along Market from the Bay, and the mouldering piers and warehouses there—but combined with the shouts, it reminded her of something. She couldn't work out what it might be.

Now she was close to the window, she could see some of the individual panes in the design were mottled, making the views through them crooked, twisted. They also somehow magnified the effect of the fog, causing it to seem to move more quickly, sinuously, as if with intent. As she panned her gaze slowly down one of the nearest buildings, she noticed tendrils of it feeling their away around some bricked-up windows and then move on, as if seeking some easier mode of entry. Silly, of course, just a night-time thought, but nonetheless she was glad the fog didn't reach up as high as her own window.

She kept bending her head, slowly, looking farther and farther down, then suddenly stopped.

For just a moment the fog had parted, giving her a glimpse right down to street level. But it hadn't been a street she'd seen, or even a sidewalk.

It was water.

She knew from the time before, that first happening in the park, not to drink anything that anybody passed her, however much it looked and smelled innocent, and if they told her it was fruit juice.

But she was hungry, as well as thirsty—and there were cookies and brownies being passed around. And once she'd had a few of those her guard started to slip, and probably she did have a drink, or two, and then there was some guy with tabs and blotters, and Marion was standing with Cindy at that point, and when Marion shook her head and said no, she didn't want any of that scene, no thank you and no way, Cindy rolled her eyes and made fun about how her time in the city wasn't changing Marion at all, she was still the same uptight small-town girl she'd always been, nothing was ever going to help her evolve—and she'd never dance like the rest of them.

The other people with them thought Cindy was joking, just playing around. But Marion looked at her and saw twinkling lights around the girl's eyes, probably only the sun glinting off glitter and make-up but still so bright and sharp, and in their lights she saw every girl in school and high school who'd looked at her the same way, those exact same girls, the girls who've always been there, and realised Cindy was no different even if she floated like an angel with layers of velvet and denim and second-hand silk, even if her skin was clear and shone like milk, even if she walked though this place like a fairy queen. The uniforms change, the times change, but deep inside everybody stays the same.

Marion looked Cindy straight in the eye and took the tab.

And she danced.

"And then I woke up," Marion said. She shrugged and laughed. "Weird, huh?"

"Woke up where?"

"In bed, in the attic. I hadn't gotten up at all. I'd fallen asleep, and just dreamed that I did."

"I had a dream like that once," Katie said. "Where I dreamed I was where I actually was. It was freaky."

They were at a table outside the café next door to City Lights, making a pair of coffees last as long as they could. After a morning trying unsuccessfully to find work, Marion had wound up at the bookstore by default. She'd spent a couple hours reading—the staff were cool about people doing that, and the manager (Karl) positively encouraged it—and then looked up to see Katie standing over her. Katie had played it all "Oh, what a coincidence," but she knew Marion often spent chunks of the afternoon in the store, and the longer they'd sat outside together, the less Marion believed their meeting had been an accident.

"You okay?" she asked eventually, after a pause in the conversation had stretched to a full minute.

Katie took a moment before replying, looking down into her coffee cup. When she looked up, Marion realised how tired the other girl looked. Tired, but resolute.

"I'm fine," she said. "But I'm done."

"Done how?"

"I'm out of here. The city. This whole scene."

Marion felt her stomach turn over. "For real? Why?"

"Because it's bullshit," Katie said. "I mean, not all of it. I get that. There's stuff going down. This is...it's a thing. No doubt. People are going to look back and say wow, far out man. But right now, for most of us, that's not in reach. It's the other side of the window-pane. We can see it, but we can't touch it. There're people who are making a real difference, doing real things, having a real good time. I'm not. Any of those things. And I'm done pretending otherwise."

"So what are you going to do?"

"Go home."

"Doesn't that feel like..."

"Failing? Giving up? Nope." The girl's eyes were hard, thoughtful. "There's a 1% getting things done here. The rest of us are only adding weight. Having 'fun'—except a lot of the time it's really not fun—and hanging around. This city right now is like a hundred thou-sand people jumping in the air at once, and it's great while they're still up, but gravity is strong and at some point the love-bubble's going to burst and they're going to fall back to earth—hard. 'Failing' would be sticking it out until that happens, and finding yourself stranded here afterward. I'm just getting a head-start on the inevitable."

"When are you going?"

"Today. I called my dad last night and told him. He sounded happy, and said cool, and he'd be waiting to give me a hug. He trusted me to make my own decision six weeks ago, and he trusts me again now. Including when I said I might bring a friend back with me."

"A friend? Who?"

"You. If you wanted. You never really talk about what you left back at home. If it wasn't good, and you wanted to leave here, there's a place for you in South Dakota."

Marion looked at her, blinking rapidly. "But why?"

"When I climbed on the bus that got me here, in the middle of the night, everybody else looked away. You smiled right up at me and said, 'There's room next to me.' You're a nice person, and my friend, and always will be."

"Thank you," Marion managed to say, quietly.

"But that's a 'no?'"

Marion realised again how sharp the other girl was, and for a long moment teetered toward a different future. One where she said yes, and travelled with this girl back to the prairies, and they let the world unfold after that. She'd never been to that part of the country, but she imagined herself standing wholesomely in a waving field under a huge sky, smiling, looking into the distance. Maybe wearing a check shirt. The vision was so strong that she almost thought she could smell the wheat around her, but then she realised the smell was fog instead—the fog that was starting to creep up the street toward where they sat. A fog that smelled of the sea and old things, and said she was staying here because it was where she belonged. The fog that was here even when it wasn't. A fog that sounded of something.

"I don't think I'm done here yet," Marion said.

Katie pulled a pen out of her bag and scribbled something on a napkin. She gave it to Marion. "My address back home," she said. "And take care of yourself, okay?"

Marion smiled brightly.

Katie got up and looked down at her before walking off down the street, quickly swallowed up by the sea mist.

It was too early to head back to the place where she now slept. There was nothing else she particularly wanted to do. So Marion wound up back in City Lights, in the basement, scrunched up in a tatty chair in the corner, trying to read some Kerouac. The light wasn't good, and the bulbs in the lamps dotted around the space also seemed to be flickering intermittently. The pages blurred in front of her.

"Now, what's going on here?"

Marion looked up to see Karl, the manager, crouched in front of her. He was heavy-set, paunchy, with chaotic grey hair that wisped up from his temples to make him look like a kindly owl.

"What do you mean?" she asked.

He reached his hand toward her, slowly, giving her plenty of time to understand his intention, and gently ran his thumb over her left cheek, and then the right. She realised both were wet, and she'd been crying, and that's why the light had seemed strange. And because it was the first time in a long while that someone had done something like that, she wound up telling him about her dream too, and that her friend was blowing town, and she wondered whether she maybe should too.

Karl listened and said the right things, and left the right pauses, and let her make up her own mind, and eventually got her laughing about some of the store's more notoriously weird patrons, and by the end of that she felt okay again.

He walked with her up the stairs and told her to go home and get some sleep, and to eat more, she was looking thin.

"Here's a thing, though," he said, before she left.

"What?"

"Your dream. The place where you're living now. You know that area used to be under water, right?"

"Huh?"

"Yeah. I mean, forever ago. But half of the Financial District used to be part of the bay. There was a thing about it a few years back. They found some stuff during an excavation or something. You should look it up."

She stepped out into the evening. It felt cold, and the street-lights looked strange.

Three hours later she was cross-legged on her bed, surrounded by paper. She'd stopped off at the main library on the way back to the building, expecting it to only take a few minutes. Instead she lost an hour of time—and six bucks she absolutely couldn't afford—duplicating several old maps, along with sections from a couple of books.

She was holding two of these now, trying to compare them. The picture in her left hand was an old photo. A daguerreotype taken by a man called William Shaw in 1852, showing a wide panorama of the San Francisco Bay, taken from Rincon Point. The far left of the picture held a few shacks and low buildings, and gave a sense of the area stretching behind. Much more interesting was the way in which, as it panned across this part of the Bay—a shallow portion called the Yerba Buena Cove—the view became at first dotted and then positively cluttered with sailing ships. Some looked ready to roll, as if they could head straight out for pastures new. Others less so, and a few were in advanced states of disrepair. On the far right of the picture, the two closest to the camera had lost their masts and significant chunks of their sides, looking like sad, bedraggled ghosts.

One of the books had informed her that over sixty thousand people arrived in the city in the 1850s, come to try their luck in the Gold Rush. They came on ships like these, and abandoned them in the Bay. Not completely—some had caretakers, men who lived in the gradually declining hulks, much as she now sat alone in this room—but the truth was, almost none of these ships ever sailed the open seas again.

In her other hand she was holding a reproduction of a section of an old map published by a San Francisco company called Britton & Rey, some years later. It showed approximately the same area as the daguerreotype, though looking rather different. Yerba Bueno Cove, which had once stretched from Rincon Point to Clark's Point, had disappeared. It remained indicated as a dotted line on the map, but where once had been water now lay streets, some of the main ones—like Market, California, and Sacramento—clearly following what had used to be the line of the old wharves into the cove.

From reading a history from 1922, pages of which she'd also copied, Marion knew how one view had turned into the other. As the city grew and grew (bolstered by men returning empty-handed from the gold fields), the pressure for land increased, especially that which had coveted Bay access. By scuppering the old ships still languishing there, speculators had been able to make sanctioned land-grabs of small portions of the Cove. The section of land under your sunken ship became yours by right. Some had even towed ships into position before dropping them. They then got busy with dumping sand and debris into water, which in parts had only ever been a few feet deep, and before long the entire cove had disappeared into prime real estate that eventually became the Financial District.

Marion looked more closely at the map and confirmed that half of Battery Street had once been in the cove, and all of California south of Montgomery. This included the point where Battery and California intersected.

Where she was sitting, right now. Or at least, where the foot of this building met the ground six stories below.

And more than that. She reached across to the last bundle of photocopies, and pulled out the portion reproducing a newspaper article from 1963. She found the sketch map and bent over it. As she did so, she noticed a couple of spots of moisture on it. She looked up, and watched as another drop of water gathered and fell from the wooden roof a couple of feet above her head.

It wasn't raining. The fog, perhaps, condensing in sufficient quantities to drip. She kept watching for a moment, but it didn't happen again.

So she went back to her documents.

It was the sound of shouting that woke her this time. Again, not angry shouting. The distant bellows of men working, attracting the attention of others, calling instructions.

She knew now what the sound reminded her of. The noise you hear at a busy harbour, the hubbub of sailors and the men who work the docks. Loading, unloading. Moving cargo to and fro. She got quickly out of bed and went to the window.

The moon was bright once again, but it looked different to the night before. Then it had been almost full. Tonight it was only a sharp sliver. That didn't make much sense, but she immediately forgot about it.

All the other buildings had disappeared.

Though fog billowed below, she could see through it right down to a shallow cove. A few large shapes lurked within it, prows and sterns, and here and there a mast tilted like the charred remnant of a forest fire.

Marion pinched herself. It hurt, as she'd known it would. She grabbed her coat and ran over to the door.

She clattered down the steps as fast as she could, and was breathless by the time she got to the bottom. She yanked the big door open and stuck her head out.

It wasn't there. What she'd seen from above.

Instead she was looking out onto a grimy backstreet, murky in the shadows of the same old buildings. It looked just the same as it had when she'd returned home from the library. All she could hear was the sound of distant traffic.

On the other side of the street, a middle-aged man shambled by, broken by drugs or alcohol. He shouted something incoherent at her.

She closed the door and walked slowly back up the stairs. She went back to the window and stood looking out, even though all she could see now were the buildings everybody else saw. She couldn't hear the far-away shouting any more.

But she could hear something else. Again. Something so faint it could almost have been her imagination. A melody. It sounded as though someone must be standing somewhere nearby, perhaps even on one of the rooftops, playing this composition to himself, or perhaps up toward the stars above.

Then it was later.

Back at the house. The one where she'd lived for over a month. Even more crowded now. Even dirtier than it had been. It smelled like damp wood and sea-water, like rot and decay.

Even louder, too. Different music in every room. Two groups of people who couldn't play, but played nonetheless. And people who danced nonetheless, too, arms flailing, bodies contorting, faces smeared with movement and incoherence.

Marion staggered around for a while, looking for Katie. Her vision was foggy at the edges, and sometimes at the centre too. She got lost in one room for ages, and couldn't find her way out even after she remembered that Katie wouldn't be there or anywhere else in the house. Katie was gone.

It was getting later.

It was getting darker too.

Then she was in the downstairs hallway and somebody gave her another drink. She was very happy again for ten minutes, laughing and laughing, and made it into the living room. But she fell over there and lay on the floor for a while, as people walked and danced around and over her.

She couldn't get up because she couldn't work out which way that was. It seemed like she was lying there on her back for about a thousand years, and then she saw blurry shapes and realised it was Dylan and Cindy, kneeling on either side and leaning over her. She smiled and tried to say hi, but couldn't.

And then the ceiling was coming down to get her, and she was afraid. The ceiling was covered in mould, dripping with salty water, creaking as in a high wind.

"She's having a bad trip," Dylan said, indistinctly.

"There are no bad trips," she heard Cindy say, as the girl pulled at Marion's belt buckle. "Only bad people. We have to help them see the light."

She overslept. When she hauled herself out of bed at 9:30, she felt exhausted. Her calves hurt, as if she'd walked a tremendous distance, though she knew it was probably just because she'd waited for so long in the dead of night, looking out of the window, seeing if it would change. It did not.

She stood under the near-cold of the weak shower for a long time. It smelled weird, rusty, salty. It didn't help much. Her clothes smelled that way too, when she climbed back into them, and she realised it had been a week or more since she'd taken her scant set of outfits to a laundromat. She needed to find one soon.

Late-morning she walked to the café where Katie worked. The owner confirmed that the girl quit the day before. Marion hadn't doubted her friend's resolve. But she'd had to check, and now the city now felt very big. Katie was gone.

After that she walked over to City Lights for want of anything better to do. Karl wasn't there when she arrived, so she sat in a window-seat, watching all the people outside, walking back and forth, feeling her eyelids start to droop. She wondered how many of them had real places to go, real things to do, and how many were just ballast, ships rocking gently up and down on a shallow tide, with no onward voyage charted. It seemed busier out there than normal, a lot of people headed in a particular direction, so maybe so.

She woke at the sound of her own name. It wasn't someone talking directly to her, however.

"Her name's Marion." She recognised Karl's voice, even though he was keeping it low. "She's good people."

Marion opened her eyes. She couldn't see him, and realised he was the other side of the half-wall, near the register.

"Has she ever actually bought a book?"

Marion recognised this voice too. Carol, the older woman who acted as manager when Karl wasn't in.

"Yes," Karl said. *The Naked Ape.* I ... sold it to her. Several weeks ago."

"What an excellent memory you have. She's rather young, though, isn't she?"

"Fuck off, Carol."

"Teenagers don't care about the likes of us, Karl. They're off on their own journey. Isn't that what they like to say? It's true. We're just the lands they leave behind."

"If you say so."

"Well, it's up to you. But even in these enlightened days free love comes with strings attached. Baggage. And to be honest, she smells."

"She does not."

"Not always, I'll admit. But she does today."

There was a little more of the conversation, but Marion didn't listen. She pulled herself upright on the window-seat, feeling dizzy. Hunger. She'd forgotten to eat anything this morning. Last night, too, though then it had been more of a choice, after she'd spent her money on the photocopying. She was about to stand when Karl came through.

"Oh, hi," he said, as though he'd no idea she was in the store. A lie, but a small one, and forgivable. Kind.

"Don't worry," she said. "I'm leaving."

"You don't have to."

She shook her head, though she wasn't sure what she meant. "I only came by to say thanks."

"For what?"

"Yesterday. Cheering me up. And telling me stuff. I looked into it."

"Interesting, huh?"

"You know they're still there?"

"What are?"

"The boats," she said. "They sunk them, then filled in over the top. Easier than taking them away or breaking them up. The boats are still down there, and sometimes contractors find the remains when they're re-digging foundations or fixing pipes. The BART goes right through one. There's a map showing where some of the others are."

"I'd love to see that," he said. "After you'd gone, I found out something else that might interest you. You told me there was a name on the building you're staying in. I thought I'd look it up, see if I could find anything about it."

Marion nodded. Whatever she might think of Carol, one thing was true: Karl was being very thoughtful about Marion. Attentive. "I wondered if it was Italian," she said.

"It is, but it's not a name. Or at least, I couldn't find anybody called *Pentimento* in city history. And you think they'd have had to make at least some mark, to have a building in their name. Wait here a moment."

He darted off toward one of the stacks. Marion stood, feeling woozy. She saw Carol behind the register, making a not-very-fairly subtle job of watching her. Marion held out her hands, fingers wide, to show she wasn't trying to steal anything. Carol looked away. Slowly.

"Here," Karl said, having returned, holding a battered old paperback. "It's an art history term."

Marion looked at the page he was holding open. The word was there, with an explanation: *Pentimento (noun)—A trace of an earlier painting, beneath the top layer of paint on a canvas.* She shrugged.

"Yeah, I know," Karl said. "Can't see why you'd name a building for that. So maybe there *was* someone by that name, and I simply couldn't find them. I did find out a bit more about the building, though. It was owned by some guy called Erich Zann. There wasn't much about him. He seems to have been a musician or something, came over from Europe sometime in the early 1920s. Couldn't find out anything about him since then, I'm afraid, or who owns the building now."

Marion wasn't really listening. She could tell that, at the periphery of her vision, Carol was still keeping an eye on her. "She's right about one thing," she said.

"Who is?" Karl asked, confused.

"The register bitch. Carol. I do smell funny."

"You really don't."

"You can't smell it? You can't smell the sea?"

"No," he said. But Marion thought he was lying.

She left him standing there awkwardly and walked out of the store, flipping the bird at Carol in passing.

Outside, she joined the crowds now concertedly heading in a particular direction, and finally remembered that today was Tuesday, which meant today was the day—the occasion of the big protest in Haight that Dylan and Cindy and the others at the house had been planning for weeks. Marion thought that she might as well see if, for a few hours at least, she could float up and join the people who were doing something real. Whatever that meant.

And that is how she wound up back at the house, where it all happened, and she learned that the new ways are just the same as the old ones, and that we live in the shadows of the very dark and very old things that came even before that.

A period of time that Marion would never be able to get back to, even in her most lucid moments. Impossible to tell how long it lasted. An hour, two, three. Split-second snapshots were all she brought with her out of it, and they were more than enough. They were far too much.

Dylan was so high she suspected he barely knew what he was doing. But he still did it.

And so did the other men. She recognised a few of them. The rest were strangers. Either new in the house since she'd left, or part of the protest. Random guys. And a couple of girls, rubbing themselves in her face.

In every snapshot, the people doing these things to her were laughing or smiling. Most because they were deliciously high and assumed this was all part of some generous and giddy game, Marion giving up what she had, because that's how it worked in this big, new happy world they were making. A wet ritual to the new gods, a way of disappearing inside one another, of them all becoming one.

Others had faces that looked like they were smiling, but in the cracks between their teeth and the dark holes in their eyes you could see the old blackness that pools up there between the stars above our heads, and in their grunts you could hear the animals that wrapped themselves in these human disguises. So many hands, so many fingers, so many other things. Going into her, time and again. Like tentacles.

Marion said no. She said no a hundred times. All she heard in response was the distant noise of men shouting, of miserable cargo being loaded.

And most of all, the sound of Cindy laughing.

And then somehow, some time later, in the dark and alone, she was back outside the building. Outside *Pentimento*. With no memory of how she got out of the house, or away from the people there. No memory of her journey.

She was dressed, more or less. Her face stung from where she'd been hit. Her lips were bruised. She was battered all over, bleeding in places. Every means of entry to her body hurt.

She saw two men in dark suits walking quickly up the street toward her. Cops? Maybe. She should tell them what had just happened. But she didn't want to. She couldn't.

She opened the door and fell in.

Got to her knees and slammed the door shut.

Crawled up the staircase. Maybe there was a loud knocking sound from below. She didn't care and didn't stop crawling. It was a long way and took a long time, but what she could hear from up there kept her going.

The door was ajar on the top floor, and yes, the music was coming from the other side.

She pulled herself to her feet, and lurched in.

The old man stood at the other end of the room, in front of the window, with a violin under his chin. The last unearthly note of his music still hung in the air, like smoke, like fog.

"Oh, child," he said, when he saw her.

"They hurt me," she murmured. There was no reason for him to care, but she had nobody else to tell.

"They will. People always will."

"But why?"

"Because there is no 'us'. There is no 'together'. We are just sheep milling around the same pen. We are all food. Mouthfuls of sustenance for things we cannot see."

"Why?"

"Because they are hungry."

"No—why are *you* here?"

"Every Tuesday," he said. "I told you. Every Tuesday night I must be here, and do this. Some other days and nights I do it somewhere else. There is a schedule. Recently it has been hard, even more of a struggle. That's why I let you stay. I thought perhaps you seeing might help, that another set of eyes through the window would keep what's out there at bay, and our world in place. This layer of it, at least. But you saw through it, didn't you? You saw to the other side."

"I don't know what you mean."

"I think you do. And it's too late to change it now."

He walked over to the table and put his viol in the case lying upon it. "I'm sorry for your pain," he said. "But that is food for them too, and perhaps you have bought us a little time. For that, I thank you."

And with that, he left the room.

An unknowable period of time later, Marion realised that the view had changed outside. She had spent the intervening minutes or hours standing in front of the window, but mired deep inside her head, feeling as though she was running after a musical note, chasing it, trying to catch it—the otherworldly note that the old man had left with her in the attic.

Then she was aware of herself again, and seeing past the fractured reflections of herself in the coloured glass to what lay beyond.

It was different now.

No buildings, only the dark ships and the fog. The shouts of men as they loaded cargo, and as she stared down at the cove she finally glimpsed what they were shoving aboard the rotting hulks—the lines of pale men and women, naked and filthy and tied together with chains.

Not slaves. *Food*.

For the things that live in the star-oceans above.

She turned and limped to the door, and descended the flights of stairs, step by painful step, gripping the handrail to stop herself stumbling and falling, half the fingernails on each hand ripped off in her attempts to pull people off her in the house near Haight that afternoon. The walls of the stairwell seemed to pulse as she passed, as if breathing, the ever-moving intestine of some vast and terrible creature as it digested her, as it digested all of them.

But she kept going down. At the bottom, she tugged the street door open and stepped outside. This time the modern city had not reappeared and the men in the suits were gone.

It was how it should be.

Her feet, which were bare—and had been for her staggering return from the house up near Haight—stood upon wood, not paving stones. The splintered planks of a narrow old wharf. She turned left, knowing what she would see.

She knew, because the sketch map in the article she had upstairs showed the positions of the fossil ships that had never made it back out of Yerba Buena Cove—and so she had known that the remains of one had been buried beneath the foundations of this very building. A ship from Europe.

And there it was. Double-masted, but with no sails. The sides damaged and sliding. A ship called the *Pentimento*.

A gust of wind came rolling down the wharf, turning the fog

into a roiling cloud. She heard a slamming sound behind her. The door to the building closing.

She turned, but the building wasn't there any more, just the sound. It didn't matter. She hadn't brought the key down. There was no turning back now, and that was the way it was.

She staggered instead along the wharf toward the ship, smelling its rotting interior more clearly with every step. A gangplank reached out to a dark, gaping opening in its side.

This was her ship. This was how she could sail away. It was no coincidence that it had lain all these years beneath the building she'd found herself in, to which the city had steered her. It had been waiting for her all this time.

She stepped out onto the gangway, leaving another bloody footstep on the wharf.

Took another step, and then another.

The rotted wood snapped beneath her, and she plunged down into the water.

Marion could swim, but she chose not to. The water was not deep, but she remembered her grandmother telling her once—long, long ago—that you can lose your life in just two inches of water, if you're facing down.

She turned face-down, and listened to the faint melody born on the fog, or from it, as she slowly drowned.

There is one place you can make your own. A place they can't stop you being. It is a land in flux, somewhere you find not with a ship but with your feet, a realm that is yours alone. Unique, defensible through constant movement, created through twists and turns and exhausted footstep after footstep.

If you walk far and long enough you'll find it, and whatever else people do to you, they can't stop you being there. You can be there forever, in your kingdom of one.

Marion did not die that day, though others did that Summer of Love—before, during and after the counterculture bubble burst and all those pretty birds lost the wind beneath their wings, and they came crashing to earth, a city full of offerings to dark forces they'd never understood. *In every era there must be a great sacrifice. There must be blood.*

Some perished in random accidents. Many—like Dylan, seven weeks later—through overdoses. Others survived against the odds, in some cases for a long time. Cindy lived to the age of seventy, leaving a fifty-year trail of broken lives and casual destruction in her wake, as she unwittingly served the Elder Gods that live beyond the last layer that sane humans can see or understand. She never understood this, or cared, and died a peaceful death that she did not deserve.

Marion did not die in those years either, though for much of the time that followed she had no idea who she was.

Others knew her as the crazy lady on the street corner, or the woman in rags standing screaming at the Bay, demanding that the ships come and take her.

Then, when she was a little older, coming up on thirty, as the huddle of filth that spent the day in bushes at the side of the park, talking and whispering to herself.

But every evening she walked, round and round those streets, following a route that made sense only to her, as she was the sole person who knew that her path took her over every single one of the deeply-buried hulks of the ships underground, the vessels that had refused her passage, instead trapping her in the city as a final sacrifice, one whose soul bled for them. Year after year after year.

One scream at a time.

Until one weekend, mid-afternoon, when Marion was nearly forty years old, crouched in a doorway right by the *Pentimento* building, gnawing on a three-day-old pizza crust.

A family of tourists slowed to look as they passed. Twin girls in their early teens winced at the acrid smell coming from the woman on the ground. Their father shook his head, and tried to keep them moving, wishing they hadn't taken this short-cut—sympathetic, but knowing there was nothing that could be done. That every city holds creatures like these, and they belong there, as part of their fabric.

His wife stopped dead in her tracks, however. Despite the thick layers of grime, she could see who lay below.

"*Marion*?" she said.

Marion looked blearily up at her, seeing the handsome, confident woman Katie had become. The girl who'd seen through it all, back then, and survived to come out the other side, not just in one piece, but twice the size.

It broke Marion's heart, the distance, and she tried to turn away.

But Katie was firm, and reached down to take Marion's hand, to pull her to her feet. To yank her back up out of a shallow, turgid Bay that nobody else could see.

"Come with us," she said.

Marion's voice had soured and broken long ago, and was now little more than a rasp. "Where...?"

"To South Dakota," Katie said. "You should have done it then, but you can still do it now."

"But how can I get there?"

"There's room next to me. And it's time to go home."

MARK SAMUELS

POSTERITY

MARK SAMUELS lives in Kings Langley, England. He is the author of six short story collections and of three novels, the latest of which is *Witch-Cult Abbey*. Zagava Books is now in the process of reprinting all his earlier work in deluxe limited editions, and Hippocampus Press has also published a selection of his best horror stories in *The Age of Decayed Futurity* edited by S.T. Joshi.

"This story concerns a real author of strange stories who died in 1981," explains Samuels, "and it shouldn't take the knowledgeable reader very long at all to figure out who it is depicted therein. The so-called 'Institution' described has only a topographical connection to reality, and in all other aspects is entirely imaginary."

> *I should not care to depict myself in my fiction;*
> *except after my death.*
> —Rupert Alderman

FOR SIBYL COURT it was a time-consuming business, but the thing had to be got through—and not only for the sake of her own reputation. Insinuations made against her of bad faith had developed into open accusations of bias; and although she had been

the scholarly trailblazer of posthumous interest in the fiction of
Rupert Alderman, literary anchorite, and had established a firm basis
for his continued relevance, nevertheless the interpretations she had
drawn from his work had recently been challenged by a series of
anecdotal interviews with his few still-surviving contemporaries. It
was vital, therefore, or so Court decided, to uproot such weeds before
they multiplied and contaminated the whole field of Alderman
studies. She did not intend to defend her integrity by public
reiteration, but rather to present unquestionable evidence that her
interpretations were incontrovertible by means of recourse to
primary sources. There was talk of a Penguin Classics Alderman
collection in the pipeline.

It had been a mistake though (so Court conceded to herself as
she thought back to her University College London Press collection of essays published a year ago) to have relied too heavily on
textual analysis. She turned the thought over at several moments
during her train journey on the 1:30 to Gallows Langley from Euston.
The fact that Rupert Alderman had, in the decade immediately after
his death, become a literary poster-boy for a wildly-popular troupe
of black-comedic television personalities was a development that
the author himself could not have dreamt of during a lifetime of
critical neglect and his steady decline into less-than-genteel poverty.
Ironically, some of Court's detractors (mostly anonymous, she noted)
had pointed out that Alderman loathed television and had even
been threatened with court-action for non-payment of a licence fee.
Of course, she thought, his frequent references to ghostly static
interference in his tales belied that urban legend, but it was
surprising how persistent the rumours were that Alderman thought
himself persecuted by TV detector vans (invariably harbouring rapa-
cious, Gestapo-like, officials).

Court looked out of the window and slid her brand-new iPhone
into her large Gucci handbag. From the overhead luggage rack she
retrieved a small, wheeled suitcase.

She had arrived at Gallows Langley.

Stepping out onto the platform, Court gazed up and down, for
she had arranged in advance to be met there. A horrible viaduct,

carrying the M25 traffic over the Gade Valley and the West Coast Mainline, loomed behind her but in the distance, at the end of Platform 4, was a waving figure in a raincoat and hat. She navigated the underpass and was momentarily confused because she was obviously not headed for the station exit towards which the few other disembarking passengers were all making their way.

The stranger advanced to meet her halfway along the platform, obviously aware of her confusion. He was a thin, spidery person in his middle fifties with a wisp of goatee, wearing granny spectacles held together by gaffer tape. Although the (rather battered) trilby hat seemed designed to project a rakish air, a crumpled beige raincoat (somewhat dotted, she noticed, with mould) projected one of seediness. His black shoes were also long overdue a polish.

"You must be Miss Court," he said, with an indeterminate Home Counties accent. "How do you do? I'm Dan Remal."

"Miz Court actually."

"As you please. Welcome to the Institution. I am at your disposal."

He took out a set of keys and beckoned her to follow him along the platform, right up to its end; there a rusty metal gate was unlocked and they gained entrance to a short passageway, also similarly gated at the other end. Above their heads the noise of the traffic rumbling over the M25 viaduct possessed a booming, heartbeat-like, reverberation.

The Institution had been established in 1845 through the generous legacy of a wealthy landowner, Jonas Atkinson, who had bequeathed grounds for the construction of a retired booksellers home on a charitable basis. The original structure, Atkinson House, a Tudor-revival building two storeys high with flanking ornate finials, had been supplemented a century or more after its foundation by a series of red-brick bungalows, and the whole estate was protected from the outside world by a ring-fence of evergreen yew trees. Were it not for the ceaseless rising and falling wave of traffic noise from the motorway and the shuddering roar of high-speed trains hurtling alongside it every few minutes, one might have regarded the place as restful and secluded. As it was, any retired bookseller coming here would, she thought, find it of distinct advantage to her or his peace of mind to be already half-deaf—no, and here she mentally corrected herself: already hearing-impaired.

Rupert Alderman had come to the Institution when in his sixties, towards the conclusion of his life, having been tipped off by a friend who was vacating his own occupancy in the main building. The Institution Committee had recently relaxed their eligibility rules; and a working lifetime of service to the book-trade had become a minimum of one year in the profession. Since Alderman could show evidence of having worked in a bookshop for eighteen months during his twenties, he found that he met the new criteria. Moreover, the rent was somewhat cheaper than the going rate and included the cost of the utility bills. Though not a television licence.

Alderman had willed his copyrights to the Institution, and also his book collection. A few of his papers were scattered in private hands, but the bulk were kept in the private library—admittance for residents and staff only—contained within Atkinson House. The Institution committee also administered Alderman's literary estate. Not very successfully. But it was this private library which would form Court's base of operations during the two weeks in which she would be staying at the Institution and preparing the ground for her defence of the author.

"The guest bungalow is all ready for you," Remal said, passing her two keys. "I'm sure you'll find it comfortable. The small key is for the bungalow. The large one for the railway gate here. I'll give you the library key tomorrow. Can't think where I left it."

"Where can I find you, should I need you?"

"My office is in the Gatehouse Lodge, at the Gallows Hill end of the estate. Just follow the path to the end."

Frankly, Sibyl Court disliked what she already knew of Rupert Alderman as a person. Of course his recondite literary work ("strange tales" as he termed them) was open to multiple interpretations, and was a mine of immeasurable depths for Critical Theory; but lifelong bachelors who were oh-so-English in outlook turned her stomach. She had been too late to have got in on the likes of reviving interest in someone more cosmopolitan and forward-thinking, such as the multi-lingual Veronica Plunkett, with her connections to the lesbian, Suffragette and conscientious-objection movement. She had hoped to turn up a secret, gay love affair in Alderman's past (even the reactionary die-hard Sinclair Xavier could boast one of those) but, thus far, there was only a juvenile unpublished tract of Utopian musings he'd long disavowed, never mentioned in print himself, and which it appeared he'd somehow neglected to destroy. She had put a great deal of emphasis on this tract, claiming it was the key to unlocking his entire subsequent oeuvre, but she did not much relish going over it again in the original manuscript (though it might be clearer than the grubby, almost illegible photocopy posted to her some years ago by the Institution committee).

Rather than plunging at once into her research work in the Atkinson library, she spent the first afternoon and evening after her arrival settling into the guest bungalow and its environs for her two-week stay.

The furniture appeared to have been retained since the 1940s, and though frayed and worn, at least seemed clean. There was a map (framed on one of the walls) of the Institution grounds, from the same decade, which she studied for a few minutes. She did not have a great deal of clutter to unpack, and the residence included all basic amenities like a laundry, cooking utensils and so forth. Indeed, the process of settling in was more psychological than physical. She had later taken a walk around the area before sunset. It further alienated her. Transition from the urban to the rural unnerved her in subtle ways. It was one of the reasons she so infrequently visited her parents in their cottage just inland of Tenby in west Wales. And yet Gallows Langley in Hertfordshire was scarcely either urban or rural: a case not of "either/or" but of "both/and". It brushed the upper north-western tentacle of the Greater London conurbation, but was surrounded by open fields dotted with suspicious-looking sheep and cattle, framed by hedgerows, looked over by gaunt tall trees and scarred with hidden-away country lanes. Villages now in outer London, as they were being swallowed up by redbrick and concrete, must have had a similar borderland quality during urban expansion in the middle of the 19th century.

When she returned to the bungalow, just after dark, she amused herself by listening to an old wireless set left on the one bare shelf of a bookcase otherwise stuffed with yellowing old paperbacks. She had some initial difficulty in tuning the unfamiliar device on long-wave to the BBC World Service. The crackling, buzzing drone of western cosmopolitanism emanating from the speaker soothed her anxiety. She warmed up organic vegetarian soup, accompanied by some gluten-free bread rolls and, feeling replete and lethargic, dozed in the comfortable old armchair with its long-redundant anti-macassar.

She awoke suddenly, sometime after midnight, vaguely aware that she'd had a disturbing dream. She could not remember the details. There was a foul taste in her mouth and a disgusting stench coming from the front of her blouse. Still only half-awake, she tottered into the en-suite bathroom, took off her soiled top and ran it under the hot tap before tossing it idly into the shower cubicle. She stood for a moment, with hands on hips, in her sports bra, gazing at herself in the smeary mirror of the bathroom cabinet. Her under-garment was filthy too. She unfastened it and tossed it into the shower. Snorting at the whole ridiculous situation, she stomped loudly back into the other room, wrapped herself in a towelling dressing-gown, and curled her knees up on the armchair.

She didn't recall having turned off the radio, but must have done so. After that disgusting experience, sleep would be elusive. It must have been something in the local water, or at least in the old kettle she'd used, which had probably not been cleaned in months. It was monstrous. She could have choked to death on her own vomit.

She tried the wireless again; the silence was oppressive. The trains must have stopped running after midnight and even the noise from the nearby M25 viaduct was dulled. The antique radio didn't work, or wouldn't work, for her. Typical man-product. While she was unconsciously chewing her fingernails (a schoolgirl habit she'd weaned herself off a decade earlier) she became aware of the sound of furtive movement from outside the bungalow. It was doubtless a nocturnal animal of some sort. Perhaps that seedy lecher Remal fancied himself, laughably, as a Lothario. No, she couldn't believe it was him. The thing made a snuffling sound, like an animal, one with a partially-blocked snout, and it seemed to be working its way, low down, slowly and deliberately, around the walls of the bungalow.

Fortified by her outrage, Court finally jumped up and flung back the curtains of the side window once the source of the outside disturbance had reached that spot.

The flash of light illuminated the lawn and she saw a curiously humped creature, about the size of a large fox, ash-grey in colour, loping awkwardly towards the bush-covered dividing bank at the rear of the bungalow. The thing looked dessicated.

After an instant it was gone.

Although Court had only glimpsed it from behind, the mysterious animal appeared to be deformed in some way, perhaps partially crushed by a motor-vehicle; and she had felt relieved that it had not twisted itself around to gaze back at her.

"Sleep well?" Remal enquired as he accompanied Court to the Atkinson library much later that same morning.

She tried to ignore his intrusive question.

They turned the corner towards the front of Atkinson House and the entrance to the library. The porch overlooked a sloping front lawn that descended gradually to hedges separating the grounds from the railway line.

"Oh dear. I need to get your key for the library. It's in the Lodge. How remiss of me to forget. Please excuse me for a moment—I shan't be long," Remal said.

The sun blazed in the clear blue sky and, from that vantage point, one could see clear across the whole of the Gade Valley: the winter-stripped trees stood out sharply on the distant brow of the hills, and halfway along the expanse of lush green fields and grazing sheep in the middle distance a gaily-painted narrowboat worked its way slowly along the local section of the Grand Union Canal. The craft's tillerman seemed to turn and wave in Court's direction, though he was so far away as to be little more than a human-shaped speck and it was hard to make him out.

After a little while longer Remal returned.

"Marvellous view," he murmured, "don't you think?"

She didn't, and tried to imagine an affordable housing estate with chic European coffee shops and a Waitrose on every corner.

Remal wouldn't understand.

"Only if you like that sort of thing. Look, do you get many wild animals around here?"

"Well, I suppose we do. Foxes, badgers, pheasants. Stray harts once in a while of course. And those bloody grey squirrels."

"Anything unusual?"

"What, like Muntjacs? They originally came from east Asia. You know, barking deer. I understand some local folk even stalk them to keep the numbers down."

Court resolved to look up the details about these creatures later, via the Internet. Perhaps it had been one of those things that had been snuffling around her bungalow in the early hours. There was no reason to think it would necessarily come back; she'd probably scared it off for good.

In the porch outside the library entrance Remal suggested that she try her own key, to ensure it worked, and she fiddled with it awkwardly in the lock before it finally turned and gained admittance for them both.

"Are we likely to be disturbed by any of the other residents?" Court said as they passed across the threshold.

"At this time of day? I doubt it. People threaten to drop in here occasionally, to return loaned books, but it's not used nearly as much as it was twenty or so years ago. You know what pensioners are like: overly firm on details, but generally neglectful."

She didn't know, and didn't much care either.

The interior was pleasant enough, and she was relieved to find it was in a good state of repair. It would be quite comfortable undertaking research here: there were a couple of green leather armchairs to lounge in, and the central table was large enough to accommodate the study of a variety of books at once. Her sinuses protested a little at the room's musty odour, but the offence caused was unavoidable.

The stock was mixed; most of the fiction consisting of either old

Penguin paperbacks or row after row of Folio Society editions and shelved on the south wall. The west wall, divided into two sections by the glass-panelled Victorian entrance door, housed, on one bookcase, biographies and memoirs (few dating to after the 1960s), while its neighbouring bookcase contained royal biographies, botanical, horticultural, and film/television encyclopaedias. The east wall shelved atlases, dictionaries, and all other encyclopaedias. Adjacent to it, next to a mysterious white door with lozenge, frosted-glass panels, stood a pedestal on which the patrician, marble bust of Jonas Atkinson himself surveyed proceedings with blank-eyed intent.

"Carlo Marchetti in case you were wondering," Remal said, presumably thinking she'd be impressed. "In the Classical style. Italian sculptor."

"Where does that other door lead?" she replied.

"Upstairs, to what used to be the old committee room. It's part of number four now; where Alderman lived. And—um—died, of course. Due to his presence we moved the committee room to the Lodge."

Court recalled that he'd died of one or other form of cancer. Apparently, towards the end, blood poured regularly from his nose in a grisly stream. He deserved what he had coming to him, she thought. Alderman had apparently disliked socialism so much that he refused ever to be admitted to a state-funded hospital. Instead he relied on a mumbo-jumbo quack treatment: something like acupuncture, always paid for in cash. Madness. His was a long-standing mania; he hadn't paid a single visit to a dentist since 1948, though his poor finances prohibited the private alternative.

She imagined that he must have made his way downstairs from his domicile to this library on innumerable occasions before his final illness; probably relishing the benefit of his exclusive means of access. Whilst wondering briefly where the committee now held meetings, another thought intruded.

"Can I look up there?" she said, voicing it aloud.

"It's locked. Being renovated. The place is empty."

"Still...I'd like to see..."

"I might try to arrange it. Let's see how far we go first. Here's all the literary material you want. Down here."

Remal waved his hand behind her and she turned her head to follow its direction.

The north wall of the library contained a large fireplace, flanked on one side by an extensive range of titles pertaining to the history of the English book-trade, and its individual publishing houses. It also held the bound records of the Institution committee back to its formation in 1845, when the sixth Earl of Clarendon had laid the building's foundation stone (in the presence—or so it was claimed—not only of Jonas Atkinson, but also of his author friend, Sir Edward Bulwer-Lytton, he of the infamous, much parodied, opening line: "It was a dark and stormy night").

The whole of the other side of the north wall shelved the remains of a series of books that had personally belonged to Rupert Alderman, including first editions of those items he had written himself, as well as half-a-dozen archive boxes on the bottom two shelves, containing his extant literary papers. Court's gaze drifted upwards to eye-level and roved quickly over the gaudy spines of Alderman's book collection; the whole mass of them, seen together, formed a jumbled smear of wretched clichés: the titles an inter-changeable word-jigsaw—*dark, strange, dust, weird, dead, night, ghost, shadow, horror, fear* and *terror*.

The offensive musty smell was at its worst here.

"Well, I'll leave you to it then," Remal murmured. "I'm sure you're eager to get cracking."

She grimaced absently by way of reply.

After spending most of the afternoon taking notes of the contents of the archive boxes (which contained mostly business correspon-dence), briefly detailing the few items of use to her and to be fully mined later for information, Court, by way of variety, turned her attention to the personal copies of Alderman's own books. In his first volume of stories, given the lamentable title of *Hands Across the Darkness*, she was (at first) enthused to discover pencilled-in marginalia written in Alderman's distinctive script. His notes eluci-dated certain key symbolic elements in the text that he had rendered obscure to precise psychological interpretation. Up to now, critics, herself included, had taken Alderman's glib comments about the great value of Sigmund Freud's psychoanalysis at face value. She looked at his entries for the first three tales—'On the Night Train', 'Imperfect Demise', 'Disappearing Act'—and the marginalia seemed more akin to the ramblings of some deranged English aristocrat. He hadn't simply disliked progress; he had positively excoriated it.

To her horror, she realised that these additions, written by Alderman himself, substantiated the rival interpretations of his work she had glibly dismissed as "the vile opportunism of neo-reactionaries jumping on the Alderman bandwagon". She found herself breathing heavily as she turned the pages of *Hands Across the Darkness*, more and more appalled at what she discovered therein.

The hope that he had added all this rubbish years after a senile descent into High Toryism later in life was dashed by his carefully dating each entry as he progressed through the book; and not one such entry was dated more than a month after this edition had first appeared in print. He had seemed to know that, one day, this new information would be disinterred by a persistent researcher. In some of the remarks Alderman actually delighted in the fact that he had deliberately misdirected his audience. He genuinely regarded his "strange stories" as a feudal psychological realm wherein readers were Alderman's servants and he alone exercised his will over them.

Court felt violated. If this marginalia came to the attention of other scholars it would not only stain her own reputation but Alderman would become *persona non grata* in respectable literary circles. Each and every expression of praise for his fiction would have to be qualified with an even more forceful denunciation.

In something close to panic, she quickly went through the other five volumes, piling them up on the table. Although it scarcely seemed possible, the marginalia therein was more egregious than it had been in his first collection. There could be little doubt that Alderman had, with the passing years, become increasingly objectionable despite his purposeful concealment of his intentions.

She looked over her shoulder. No one had entered the library for hours. Remal was no doubt occupied by whatever it was that served to occupy his limited attention. She would not be disturbed, she was sure. Reaching into her Gucci handbag, she rummaged in its depths until she located the small oblong weapon she sought. Her face became a mask of rigid fixity as she carefully rubbed the eraser back and forth across the wide margins of the text, gradually eliminating the pencilled additions Alderman had made. They came off easily. She pursed her lips and blew carefully after each successful deletion, dispersing the tiny black fragments of undiscovered insights.

No storm suddenly blew up, no ominous rumble of thunder manifested itself, and by the time she had completed her labours on the first volume, the sun had dipped below the brow of the hills off to the north-west.

Before Court left the library she found Alderman's notebook—his tract on Utopian musings, labelled 'Neutron X'—in one of the archive boxes and took it back with her to the bungalow. Strictly speaking she should probably have asked permission to do so, but it seemed a mere courtesy. The thing wasn't being removed from the estate, after all. Once she'd eaten something nutritious and settled down for the evening, she decided to go through the notebook and remind herself of the speculations therein that had led her to the conclusions she'd formed when reading the grubby photocopy with which the Institution had formerly supplied her.

Court made herself some brown rice, organic peas and Quorn (flavoured by plenty of low-sodium soy sauce). Scarcely had she begun to consume it however when there commenced a loud thumping on the front door. She jumped a little in surprise, and then rose to investigate. Through the little fish-eye lens of the peephole she saw an official-looking man with a toothbrush moustache standing outside the door. He wore a black uniform of some kind, a peaked military cap and carried a clipboard. She couldn't help noticing he resembled Sir Oswald Mosley, leader of the British Union of Fascists.

She opened the door, making sure the security-chain was on, and spoke to him through the gap.

"Can I help you?"

He stared, glassy-eyed for a moment, and then said, in an unpleasant tone:

"I am an official from the local enforcement division. Do you possess a current television licence for this property?"

"What?"

"Can you prove that you do not watch BBC programmes on your television set? It is necessary I examine your premises."

"What?"

"Are you hard of hearing?"

She slammed the door shut and looked again through the peep-hole. The uniformed man took an envelope out of his pocket and thrust it through the letterbox. Then he turned on his heels and marched off along the path and disappeared into what seemed to be a TV detector van parked outside.

Court picked up the envelope from the doormat, opened it, and found therein a grubby sheet of folded paper with the following scrawled message in pencil, written in huge characters:

WHENEVER AND HOWEVER YOU WATCH OR RECORD LIVE TV, YOUR HOME NEEDS A LICENCE.

The last five words were underlined half a dozen times for additional emphasis.

She screwed the sheet up into a ball and threw it across the room. Then, wishing to ensure the intruder had gone for good, she went over to the front window, drew back the curtains and peered out across the lawns. There was no van there; in fact the whole place looked deserted. She could make out four other bungalows across the way, despite the evening gloom, with no lights on. Even the street-lamps on the estate were dead. Perhaps the committee was economising on electricity; or perhaps the devices had fallen into disrepair.

Then she spotted two ash-grey, fox-sized, humped animals rounding the corner of Atkinson House; the deformed creature that had been snuffling around on all fours the previous night had apparently returned and been joined by another member of the same species. They came up the path and settled down on their haunches to stare at the light emanating from Court's bungalow window. They were too far away for her to make out their faces distinctly, but the features did not appear to be either canine or deer-like, but those of horribly wizened children with snouts, their faces crumpled by desiccation.

She closed the curtains abruptly and, after five minutes or so of pacing back and forth nervously in the room, opened them again.

Both of the creatures had vanished.

She would have to discuss this with Remal in the morning. It was difficult to judge whether the visit of the crazed fascist official or the sight of those creepy, deformed animals was the more disturbing. She felt like an unwilling audience member caught up in a surreal circus act.

Remembering her hastily set-aside evening meal, she returned to it, slowly spooning the now-lukewarm contents of the bowl mechanically into her mouth. When that task was completed, Court thought again of going over the 'Neutron X' notebook, but decided against it. She was not sure she could summon the requisite powers of concentration it demanded.

She instead turned on the wireless, but switched it off almost at once as a familiar voice shouted from the speakers at a deafening volume:

"*Your home needs a licence!*"

Court had made her way up, early the following morning, to the Lodge in order to complain to Remal about the events of the previous night. A haze of mist shrouded the Gade Valley, smothering the noise from the traffic; the watered-down sunshine acted on one's vision like cataracts. As she passed the rear of Atkinson House and the other bungalows, still she encountered no signs of there being any other occupants in residence. The buildings of the Institution began to take on, in her mind, the fake aspect of an exterior film set.

She found the Lodge, as she had been previously advised by Remal, situated right out at the edge of the estate, and it evidently had been constructed not long after Atkinson House itself. Similar to the original structure's design—belonging to the revival-Tudor school of architecture—it was a single-storey building with an entrance-bell operated by pulling on a small rope.

Remal had met her at the door and she'd followed him, via a cluttered corridor full of boxes, into the ramshackle office wherein he occupied himself with whatever business it was that required his attention. The piles of unsorted papers littering almost every surface, the paraffin lanterns hung from low ceiling beams, the partially-melted cathedral candles idly deposited at random on surfaces, a noisily droning desk-top computer that seemed to have been built decades ago with a dusty, useless screen; the overall impression was one of a perverse withdrawal into a chaotic, half-baked tradition-alism. An Edwardian Grandfather clock, standing askew on a warped corner floorboard, made no noise, the hands of its dial stilled. Drained bottles of alcohol, breeding mould, were piled up alongside it in a triangular heap.

Remal invited Court to sit down, but there was nowhere obvious to do so. Her sharp grimace advised him wordlessly of this fact, and he retrieved, from the murky depths of some adjacent junk-room, what looked to be a leftover chair from the Atkinson library.

She offered details about last night: the unaccountable intrusion of the licensing official, what appeared to be the man's voice issuing from the wireless, and she also made reference to the disturbing animals she'd seen. Remal replied with an exclamation first of doubt, then of surprise.

"Really? How extraordinary!" he had said.

"Well," Court finally replied, "what can be done about it?"

"What would you suggest?" he asked, his fingers forming an arch in front of his bespectacled face.

"I suspect someone's having a well-organised practical joke at my expense. I think it constitutes harassment."

"Let me put it this way. Have you thought of wearing straight black skirts and shirts with ties? It would suit you."

"What?"

Her eyes registered sudden defiance in a fixed, icy glare. She didn't quite believe what she'd just heard.

Remal, though, went on as if he had said nothing at all untoward.

"Perhaps I should explain something about our residents."

"Go on," she replied.

"The vast majority are very elderly and infirm. They have developed a tendency to be reclusive. They have also expressed a collective desire not to be disturbed by the busybody tendencies of the outside world. Nowadays young people blindly assert one can't turn back the clock."

"I don't see what that..."

"You, however, are currently only a guest of this Institution. Should you wish to remain for the period necessary to complete your research it is incumbent upon you to display the appropriate respect for the culture we have developed here."

"Of course, that goes without saying, but you haven't..."

"As for the matter of some practical joke being played upon you, I can give you my assurance that I am every bit as mortified by the intrusion of this errant public official as you are. I shall deal with it personally—at once—by telephoning the requisite authority responsible. There is no question of anyone on this estate indulging in a practical joke at your expense. I imagine most of our residents are currently ignorant of your presence here."

"But you still haven't..."

"I cannot account for the voice you think you may have heard on the wireless, but when it comes to any stray wildlife on the estate I am afraid it is something you will have to get used to. I quite appreciate that such creatures might look—at first—frightening to individuals who have been confined entirely to the metropolitan environs."

"Those things weren't..."

"Nature can appear nightmarish in the dark. Do I make myself clear?"

She spent that afternoon in the library, carefully reading through and then erasing all of the marginalia's reactionary rants in the hundreds of pages of the remaining five other first edition volumes of Alderman's strange stories (namely *Mala Fide, Broken Mirrors, Dust to Dust, Trespassers* and *Night Forces*). If the author had really believed the vile nonsense he spouted, rather than his ideas being a symptom of a deranged need to privately express taboo speculations, it was no surprise that he wound up impoverished, isolated and half-forgotten. Anyone harbouring such delusions would inevitably, over the years, find themselves without the support of sane friends, colleagues and associates; especially in the social and professional arena of the Arts. As she worked, her own sense of outrage at his views gradually gave way to the soothing idea that she was, after all, not only doing Alderman—but also literature itself—a great service. If his reputation had been so tarnished that it could not have been salvaged by associates *during his lifetime*, at least, now, she had taken the opportunity presented to her to salvage his *posthumous* reputation—even through a radical act of deliberate omission. He had not been a prolific letter-writer (the archive boxes proved it) and any anecdotal interview "evidence" from his few surviving contemporaries was just that: anecdotal, hence unreliable. Old people overwhelmingly resistant to change, she thought, can't be trusted. Such spurious "evidence" would scarcely count against Alderman in the more enlightened era of universal expertise in Critical Theory.

Having finished her erasures, she replaced the five volumes on the shelf in careful order and decided to turn her attention to the Utopian notebook.

Only after she had been through two of the archive boxes did she remember that she had left it back in her accommodation.

That musty smell around her was becoming oppressive again.

It was getting dark anyway, and clouds had mushroomed in the twilight as a band of low pressure had entered the valley; sheets of buffeting rain splattered uselessly against the panes of the library's long, narrow windows. The ghost of Bulwer-Lytton, she thought, once more showing his long Patrician reach. She laughed at the idea, wriggled into the raincoat she'd slung over a nearby armchair, wrapped a headscarf around her hair, and picked up her handbag.

She moved quickly through the deluge, rounding the corner of

Atkinson House as rapidly as her high-heels would carry her: only to stop short when she saw the TV detector van parked outside the guest bungalow.

So much for Remal's promise earlier in the day of "dealing with the errant public official at once via the telephone".

Court cautiously approached the vehicle from the rear. Its British make, model and registration number plate dated it, she supposed, to the 1970s. On the roof was an aerial of some kind and also, very strangely, what looked like a Tannoy or other form of loudspeaker— the type used in election campaigns. The vehicle was certainly in remarkably well-preserved condition. So, she thought, there was some kind of an elaborate prank at her expense going on after all. She moved slowly and quietly around to the front, trying to peer through the window. There was no one inside. All the doors were locked. Nevertheless, that totalitarian official might still be lurking in the back. She remembered hearing, or reading, something about the whole TV detector van fleet having been a deception: that the vehicles contained no electronic equipment and were there just for show—deployed visibly as a means of instilling fear and doubt in the general populace, so it would be cowed and pay up. She couldn't vouch for the truth of the matter, though.

In any case, she could now get that idiot Remal to see the seriousness of the situation. She walked over to the Lodge, thoroughly soaked through to her skin by the rain, and pulled again and again at the door bell-rope. But either he was out or he refused to answer.

When Court retraced her steps to the guest bungalow, she found that the vehicle had gone. It was not possible to explain how it could have got past her; for there was only one road for traffic passing through the whole estate, with entry and exit possible solely by passing alongside the Gatehouse Lodge.

She walked around the estate in case the van had moved and parked elsewhere. But there was no sign of it.

She gave up searching, desperate to get out of her wet clothes and dry off.

Once inside the guest bungalow, she hastily peeled away the

soaking layers of clothing, dumped them in the laundry basket, and went into the bedroom to find her towelling dressing-gown.

Laid across the bed, and freshly laundered, were a white shirt, a straight black skirt and a tie.

All of her other clothes had been removed.

There was nothing else dry for her to wear.

It was evident that Remal had let himself into the guest bungalow and left those items of clothing there as part of some sick fantasy. There was no telling what he might do next. This was no longer an intimidating joke; this was clearly sexual harassment.

She found it, however, oddly difficult to recall what would be the proper response to this situation. The turmoil in her thoughts seemed to parallel the turmoil of the storm outside, which still raged across the Institution. Forcing herself to think clearly, she remembered the new smart phone in her handbag. She had not touched it since her arrival and this fact now struck her as astonishing, since it had scarcely been out of her sight before then. A wave of momentary panic came over her as she rummaged around for it; visions of the thing having been stolen, not working, or of not being able to get a signal. None of these eventualities pertained however, and she tapped in the number for the emergency services.

If the police thought she was simply overreacting about a pile of clothes she would tell them there was a burglar prowling around the place, right at that moment.

She heard the number ringing, there was a click as if the connection were made, and then an empty pause at the end of the line.

"Police? I need the police. Hello? Police?"

Someone at the other end of the line cleared his throat. And then he spoke, almost in a whisper.

"What is your TV licence reference number?" the disembodied voice said.

And then the iPhone made a loud crackling noise, emitted some sparks, and finally died altogether.

Court tossed the device aside. Immediate flight then, was the only solution.

She glanced around the room. There was no time even to pack her few belongings.

Alderman's 'Neutron X' utopian notebook still rested on the main table. Should she take it with her? It would, after all, be theft. She couldn't decide, and quickly flipped through the pages at random, again feeling a sense of rising panic.

The thing had been scored through, over and over, to the point it was now completely illegible and, in fact, malignantly useless.

She retrieved the still-damp raincoat and headscarf from the laundry basket, put them on and braved, once more, the storm outside.

Court's first instinct was to try the railway gate leading to the passage under the M25 that gave access to a platform on Gallows Langley station. She expected, in advance, it would be locked. But she had a clearly-marked communal key by which to obtain entry and exit. However, she found that the key didn't even fit the lock. She thought of screaming for help, but the sound of the storm, as well as the overhead booming of the motor traffic crossing the huge concrete viaduct, would have drowned out her cries. She glanced along the length of the passageway to the distant platform beyond. There were no passengers waiting there.

What next? She was about to turn back when she realised a train was approaching and, as it entered the station, with a shrill breathy whistle and without slowing down, she saw that it was a steam loco-motive, hauling covered cargo. The driver, an indistinct blur, waved at her as it rapidly passed alongside the passageway.

She watched the train disappear off into the gloomy distance, trailing sodden clouds in its wake.

The only other reasonable means of exit was the path past the Lodge at the far end of the estate. But Remal was probably there, lying in wait.

By now she was soaked through again and the rain showed no signs of abating.

There was nothing for it but to try getting assistance from one of the other bungalows at this end. She knocked at the first four, received no replies, and found all the windows obscured from outside view by thick drapes.

She was approaching the fifth bungalow when one of the humped, ash-grey creatures emerged from behind a series of bushes ahead of her. This time she was much closer to one of them, and the uncanny impression—formerly obtained at a greater distance—that the things possessed a wizened and yet curiously infantile face with a snout was now vividly confirmed. This creature did not, however, take any notice of her, but continued on its path towards the bungalow and, when it had reached its destination, it then reared up on its hind-legs, using its forepaws to drag itself up to a curtained window. It pushed against the glass pane, which swung open, and the monstrosity disappeared inside, over the ledge, before closing the aperture behind itself.

So much for obtaining assistance from the residents, she thought; the very concept as distressing as a sudden hallucinatory fit.

Should she try getting through the border of yew trees? They were surely not impassable.

She recalled the map of the Institution's grounds she'd seen on the wall in the Guest Bungalow.

Behind the bungalows on the east-side there was a raised bank, or ridge, but that obstacle was easily traversed, even were it slippery underfoot in this filthy weather. Beyond, no more than ten yards further back, was the tree barrier.

And beyond the trees was a vast open space of grazing farmland, and freedom.

It had taken ten minutes to get over the ridge and force a way through the holly bushes choking the spaces between the trunks of the yew trees. Her soaked raincoat was torn in places, and the skin on both her hands, and on her face, was bloodied by cuts. Nevertheless, she had forced herself through, only to discover a twelve-foot high fence. The barrier was unscalable. At the apex of each of its metal rods was a spike in the shape of the *fleur-de-lis* motif. She edged along the perimeter for some two dozen or so yards, hoping to find a missing bar and thus a gap she might squeeze through, but in vain, for further progress was halted by a vast thorn bush which had grown on both sides of the fence divide. In the opposite direction, there was a similarly huge thorn-bush, one equally as impassable.

She was left with two options: risk going directly past the Lodge and encountering a lunatic Remal waiting for her, or perhaps, to first try the grounds in front of Atkinson House itself. The sloping front lawn leading down to the railway line was, doubtless, enclosed by a fence too, but it could not have been of the same height, else she would have noticed it before, poking above the hedge. The first option still filled her with alarm; she decided she would rather risk the second. Crossing a busy railway line was certainly dangerous enough, but this one had overhead cables and not a ground third rail. And traversing it would take no more than a few seconds.

Once she had clambered back the way she'd come, Court saw that the TV detector van had reappeared and was parked again outside the guest bungalow. But, as she approached it, the Tannoy blared a familiar refrain:

"Your home needs a licence!"

Suddenly the engine started up, the clutch shifted into low gear, and the vehicle lurched forward, coming straight at her in an attempt to run her over. She managed to dodge it, at the last moment, by flinging herself to one side, but she twisted in doing so and landed awkwardly.

The van spun around sharply on the wet tarmac, careered, mounted a lawn in a wide arc, ploughed through some bushes, and then drove away in the opposite direction, towards the Lodge.

Court found she had turned her left ankle and limped painfully around the corner of Atkinson House, intent on somehow descending the lawn and thereafter getting across the railway line. She must also have pulled a muscle in her back, for she was almost bent over with the effort of walking. The rain had got even heavier, and sheets of icy water now swept relentlessly across the unsheltered spaces of the Institution grounds, as if heralding another Biblical deluge directed at transgressors of the Creator's law.

The lights in the library blazed and, within the porch, the entrance door was wide open. She wondered if Remal were trying to lay a further trap for her. Light also glared through the triple-panelled gable window of the old committee room housed above the library.

A figure moved into sight at the upper window of the gable, framed by the illumination but made blurred and indistinct due to a stream of rainwater pouring down the building's exterior from the roof's flooded guttering. Court tried desperately to discern who it was, and at first was certain it was Remal.

But, even as she stood there, Court felt her eyes were playing tricks on her. The form appeared to undergo a drastic alteration.

No, surely this man was much heavier than the (thin) Remal was; and then, with a somewhat theatrical gesture, the occupant raised his hand and waved.

She moved closer, until she slumped on the steps of the porch outside the library, and stared directly overhead. The man above had flung open the central panel of the window, had leaned forward, and peered down at her through the black-framed eyeglasses that had replaced his granny spectacles.

At last she could recognise that pale, chubby, freshly clean-shaven face.

Rainwater soaked his thick black hair, plastering it across his cheeks. The twin streams of cancerous blood that had poured from his nostrils had dried, and the residue caked both of his thick upper and lower lips.

When he finally smiled a manic grin, he did so to show off the most nightmarish, ruined teeth that Sibyl Court ever saw in a brutally truncated life.

"Come inside and let's get you out of those wet things," he shouted down at her with a disembodied, familiar voice.

Court shrieked repeatedly in response—though the actual noise she heard sounded much more like barking; and accompanied by approaching echoes.

THANA NIVEAU

OCTOBERLAND

THANA NIVEAU is a horror and science fiction writer. She is the author of the short story collections *Octoberland, Unquiet Waters* and *From Hell to Eternity*, as well as the novel *House of Frozen Screams*. Her work has appeared in numerous anthologies, and frequently been reprinted in B*est New Horror*. She has also been short-listed three times for the British Fantasy award.

Niveau is a Halloween bride, sharing her life with fellow writer John Llewellyn Probert in a crumbling Gothic tower filled with arcane books and curiosities. And toy dinosaurs.

"There's a lot in this story that isn't fiction," she admits, "and parts of it were very hard to write. I did grow up in Houston, but there is no such place as Octoberland. (That I know of.) When my brother and I were kids we got season passes every summer to the big theme park––Astroworld. It was one of the best places in the world. All that stuff in the story about role-playing and living in fantasy worlds with my brother? All real. That was how we spent our summers. Like my narrator says, they were the best days of my life.

"There's something so melancholy about derelict amusement parks—places that were once filled with laughter and delighted children, now rusting and rotting. I was heartbroken when, one year I suggested to my brother that we go back to Astroworld, and he told me it had been torn down. And the first time I drove past the enormous vacant lot where it used to be, I felt a real chill. As though a piece of my childhood had been stolen."

"**W**ELCOME HOME, MISS Nolan."
I make myself smile as the man returns my passport and I resist the urge to correct him. I'm not *home*. Houston hasn't been "home" for many years and I can't help but resent the assumption that any American travelling abroad must be glad to be back in the good old US of A. I'm already desperately missing the comforts of my *real* home, back in Brighton.

But I don't say any of that. I just offer him the same weary smile of all passengers coming off a cramped nine-hour flight—the ones who haven't had it easy in First or Business class. I find it harder every time to restrain my annoyance at being asked the same old questions and having to give the same old answers. As though they don't already know every single detail of my life from whatever digital file they've got right in front of them.

"Where have you come from today?"

"The UK."

"And what were you doing over there?"

"I live there."

This occasionally elicits an expression of surprise, the way you'd react if a kid said no to ice cream. Americans have a unique brand of xenophobia, all twisted up in a fervent but woefully naïve hyper-patriotism. Choosing to live outside the US just doesn't compute for a certain type of narrow-minded Yank. For some it's practically treason.

But just as I keep my opinions to myself, so does he.

"Enjoy your stay."

The rental car is a green compact that, like me, is a long way from home––all the way from Oregon. I like the design of the plates: the stately Douglas Fir embossed in the centre matches the rich, deep green of the car. I always feel better with out-of-state plates because it warns other drivers that I'm "not from around these parts". Not that they'll afford me any special courtesy; Houston has the rudest and most aggressive drivers I've ever encountered. Still, my outsider plates act like a warning that I might do something unexpected, like actually drive the posted speed limit, or indicate when I want to change lanes.

The drive from the airport to my parents' house is always harrowing, like entering a war zone. A pick-up truck with ludicrously oversized tyres blares its horn at me as I floor the accelerator to push my way onto the freeway before the entrance ramp comes to an end. He's had plenty of time to see that I want on. It would probably make his day to see me smash into the concrete barrier. He swerves into the next lane so he can speed around me, and he'll probably flip me off as he does.

But I've played this game before. As soon as he pulls alongside me, I brake hard and he sails past, robbing himself of the petty satisfaction of cutting in front of me and forcing me to brake even harder to avoid hitting him. Everything about the encounter is depressingly predictable, right down to the Dixie flag on his back window and the gun-rack mounted inside the cab.

Not for the first time, I marvel at the disparity between the way people act in their cars and out of them. In person, they're the very epitome of "Southern hospitality", but on the road they're like characters in a *Mad Max* film. How do they manage such a violent transition?

It reminds me of that *Star Trek* episode where the inhabitants of an alien planet are peaceful, mindless zombies until the hour of "Festival", when they run amok, attacking and killing each other. Afterwards, the bells chime and they stop instantly and return to their aimless wandering, satisfied with their solution to the problem of hidden aggression.

My brother James and I used to act that out as kids. We'd set a timer and then meander through the house until the timer went off. Then we'd go wild and attack each other. James was two years older and just enough bigger than me that he usually won. But it wasn't about winning with us. Like so many of our childhood games, I'm not really sure *what* it was about.

There were no rules, no limits. One time James convinced me to climb inside the tumble dryer while he turned it on. Another time we dared each other to eat spiders. We would frequently sneak out of the house in the middle of the night to act out stories while our parents slept. One time the police found us playing in the auto salvage yard, where we were taking turns being locked in the trunk of a rusty old gangster car. They chased after us but we were too fast for them. Our escape made us feel invincible.

Someone else honks, jolting me out of my reminiscence, but this time the anger isn't directed at me. A battered pick-up truck is trundling along in the fast lane, loaded down with gardening equipment. It doesn't take much imagination to guess what the guy in the sporty red car behind it is yelling as he overtakes.

It triggers a wistful yearning in me for better times. Kinder times. Times when I didn't feel embarrassed to be from here. Times when I wasn't so afraid of coming back.

Why do you keep coming back?

The voice makes me shudder. James asked me that once and I wasn't able to answer. Duty? Devotion? Guilt? Whatever it was, it wasn't love.

It's different this time. This time it's *your* house.

I sense the darkness gathering like an inner storm and I push it away. Turning my attention to the radio, I fiddle with the buttons, scanning for a station playing something familiar. As usual, the previous driver has cranked the bass up all the way and it takes ages for me to figure out how to adjust it so I can hear a melody.

James could have done it easily. He was always the clever one. "Precocious," they called him. He once took apart all the kitchen gadgets—toaster, blender, coffee-maker—and scattered the parts out across the dining room floor to look at them. Our mother had a fit, but our father told her there was nothing to worry about. Sure enough, everything was back together and working perfectly within a couple of hours.

After a while I manage to find a station for '80s classics and I push the button to set it as a favourite. Morrissey insists that he's human and needs to be loved, and I find myself singing along with him. Houston is always an assault on my memories, not all of it good, but the music of my childhood is soothing. It shouldn't be, but it is. It reminds me of my brother.

Another horn sounds as I change lanes to enter the second freeway of my three-freeway journey. I have no idea what I've done this time, although perhaps the honk wasn't meant for me. Perhaps it wasn't meant for anyone and it's just general road rage. Rage at having to drive endless ribbons of highway to get somewhere. Rage at the price of gas for their enormous SUV. Rage at who knows what. How do they live like this?

American city roads are an eyesore and I'm hounded by billboards advertising everything from Jesus to personal injury lawyers. But one sign makes me smile. SUMMERTIME BLUE, it says, instantly releasing a flood of happy memories. It was the name of a water park where James and I whiled away endless summer days when we were kids, when it seemed like September would never come again and the looming spectre of school was just a bad dream. All we had to do to avoid it was not wake up.

We could lose ourselves for entire days in other worlds, role-playing characters from whatever fictional universe provided our obsession of the moment. We were time-travellers and aliens, secret agents and pirates, warriors, wizards and witches. They were truly the best days of my life.

I remember trying to be a mermaid once at the local public pool. I got James to help me wind an entire roll of aluminium foil around my legs, fashioning a crude tail at my feet. As usual, the pool was packed with screaming children and weary parents trying to get out of the miserable heat, so no one paid any attention to what we were doing.

I hobbled to the edge and let myself fall in with a huge splash. And I sank to the bottom at once, my makeshift tail remaining stubbornly synthetic. I couldn't swim with my legs bound and I remember flailing my arms in helpless desperation for a small eternity before James finally jumped in to save me. Unfortunately, a lifeguard had also spotted my distress and he was the one who pulled me, choking and spluttering, out of the water.

The police were called, our parents were called, and there were strong words exchanged about "unaccompanied minors" and "endangering children". Lots of things James and I didn't understand. Our parents were banned from dumping us at the pool unattended. And since leaving us on our own somewhere for hours was the whole idea, we never saw that pool again.

We showed them though, didn't we, Kelly?

I shake off the voice, wincing at a sudden pain behind my eyes. It feels like a migraine is trying to set in. From all around me I hear the violent staccato sound of metal cranking, as if something is being hoisted. But there's no sign of road construction. No jackhammers or excavators. Just the noise in my head.

I pinch the bridge of my nose and tell myself firmly that there is no pain. Forcing myself to concentrate, I cast my mind back into the past, fishing for happier memories. They are there in abundance, and they all involve my brother.

Oh yes, we showed them all right. They hardly knew us anyway. We lived more in our own made-up worlds than in the real one. And it was wonderful.

We had our own languages. Codes no one could ever break. We could communicate complex ideas with a single word. Or a look. We overheard our mother once saying it creeped her out, that we were like aliens. At the time it filled us with pride.

We renamed everyday objects and annoyed everyone by refusing to call them by their real names. We clambered through the house backward on all fours, looking through our legs at everything upside-down. We closed all the doors in the windowless hallway and took turns pelting each other with rubber balls. We jumped off the roof using garbage bags as parachutes.

My nostalgia is soured by the bumper-to-bumper traffic ahead of me. Lines of cars inch along past the intimidating Houston skyline. It's not rush hour, so there must have been an accident. It seems there's *always* an accident when I come back. I always seem to get stuck in this kind of traffic, crawling along the ugly asphalt roads to reach the little corner of the city where I lived for half my life. The hardest thing about the journey is the memories. Good or bad, it makes no difference: I don't want to see the house again, especially not now that it's empty.

Oh, now's a fine time for guilt, I tell myself. I could have come back to say goodbye. I could have come back more often so their absence wouldn't feel so much like an accusation. But then, who were they to accuse me? They had ruined my life, mine and James'.

Even as a child I had always felt like an outsider, removed from the rest of humanity. So as soon as I came of age I went someplace where I truly was an outsider. I don't belong here any more and everyone knows it. They can sense it. Maybe that's why they're all so hostile towards me.

I trained the Houston drawl out of my voice long ago, but Brits can still tell I'm from this continent, even if they can't place exactly where. I've been in the UK long enough to pick up some British pronunciation and colloquialisms and I often forget to revert to American words when I'm here. I'll say boot and bonnet instead of trunk and hood. *Gare*-idge instead of gar-*razh*. To American ears, I sound vaguely British, but to British ears there's no mistaking where I'm from. My accent is stateless, which feeds the weird sense of isolation. As a kid one of my favourite character quirks was to be mute, and I confess that there have been times in my adult life when I've used the same trick.

The traffic report tells me exactly what I expected to hear. There's been an accident. So I'll be stuck here for a while, creeping along with the rest of the frustrated masses. At least it's autumn. In the sweltering oppressive heat of a humid Houston summer, people start to break down along with their cars.

I have plenty of time to fiddle with the radio, and I'm instantly cheered when I find Oingo Boingo. 'Dead Man's Party' is a Halloween staple. Danny Elfman sings about shiny silver dollars on his eyes and there being room for just one more. My favourite holiday is only days away and if there's one single thing I wish I could Americanise about Britain, it would be Halloween. For Brits it's a sinister night, full of mischief and vandalism, all trick and no treat. But here it's basically a twenty-four-hour costume party.

I need only think of it and I taste candy corn, those little honey-flavoured kernels striped white, yellow and orange. They were my favourite treat of all. Even better, I can smell pumpkin. My fingers recall the feel of the stringy, gooey ropes of seeds inside what would soon be a grinning jack-o'-lantern, the rich texture of the thick orange skin as the knife punched through, carving triangular features. We always toasted the seeds afterwards. I close my eyes for just a moment and imagine them bursting between my teeth.

I remember the cobwebs we covered our house with and the hanged man we suspended from the tree. I remember the plastic bones we scattered in the front yard. And I remember the cold sawdust scent of the fog machine. It's a smell I always associate with Halloween, with autumn, with better times.

The flood of memory makes me smile. James and I loved turning our modest little house into a haunted mansion year after year. And of course we loved choosing our costumes. One year we were ghosts. Another year we were gremlins. And one year we were sent home from school for dressing as matching road-kill. The looks of disgust we got for that idea made it all worthwhile.

I never had any friends as close to me as James. There was no one in the world I'd rather have spent time with. Only rarely did we fight like normal siblings. Most of the time we were inseparable. Other kids at school thought we were weird, but no one dared pick on me. They were afraid of my brother.

But then everything changed. Elementary school was over for James but not for me. He graduated to secondary school, and I felt abandoned. With no big brother to look out for me on the playground, I withdrew completely. I had no friends in my class and I ensured that's how it would stay by going into a shell.

Our parents were called to the school to talk about me like I wasn't there, and they made no secret of their annoyance at having to deal with it. In tones of frustrated helplessness, they explained that James and I had always been like that, always been "a bit odd", but that they were sure we'd eventually grow apart.

Well, they got their wish.

There's another memory hovering just on the edge of my mind. It's so close but I just can't seem to fix on it. The Cure is playing now. 'Fascination Street'. Robert Smith's voice sounds different as he sings that he likes me like that, likes me to scream. He sounds like my brother. And suddenly I have it. The images come rushing back, so intensely I nearly drive into the back of a van. I brake just in time. And I remember.

Octoberland.

It appeared one year in the empty lot behind an abandoned strip-mall within walking distance of our house. We lived off a lonely stretch of I-45, halfway to Galveston, a strange place to build a mall, as it wasn't an area likely to see much exiting traffic. And it didn't. People never stopped for the mall, but they stopped for Octoberland.

It was one of those travelling funfairs, the kind that seem to spring up overnight. We never saw it being assembled or dismantled. It was just *there*. And then it was gone.

It seemed like something from another time, another world. The midway, the carousel, the rides, it was all distinctly offbeat. Everything was painted in shades of black and orange, like Halloween come to life. Even the people who worked there seemed to be from another era. They weren't at all like the relentlessly perky costumed help you saw at major theme parks.

James and I loved that place. And for the two weeks of the year that it existed, we spent every minute we could there. Our parents never trusted it. In a rare display of concern, they told us they didn't think it was safe and offered to drive us all the way across town to Astroworld instead. But we wouldn't be persuaded. Astroworld may have been bigger and better, but Octoberland was the one we loved, the one that spoke to us.

It was less crowded, for a start, and less mainstream. Less juvenile. Even the names of the attractions felt more grown up. Scarier. Edgier. There was the Hangman's Drop. The Deranger. The Agony Booth. The Devil House.

One of my favourites was the Bottomless Pit, which was like a giant hamster wheel on its side. You stood on a circular platform with your back to the curved metal wall as the ride spun and picked up speed, the force pushing you back until you were so well pinned that they could drop the floor out from beneath you, revealing a painted abyss into which you might fall forever. I always screamed when I saw that gaping hole, both terrified and thrilled at the prospect of plunging into it.

Flashing lights jolt me back into the present and at last I reach the site of the accident. A car is straddling the concrete barrier between the freeway and the high occupancy lane, its front half crumpled like an accordion and its windshield smashed. An ambulance and three police cars block the lane and of course everyone has slowed down to gawk. There's something morbid in human nature that makes us feel we're owed a gruesome sight after being kept waiting so long. I'm no different. Like everyone else, I look, but all I see is a pair of athletic shoes at the end of the stretcher being loaded into the ambulance. There is a dark stain on the road.

It's kinder this way. You should never let anything suffer.

I shake my head to banish my father's voice. Of all the things he ever said to me in my life, those are the words whose echo I have never stopped hearing.

Traffic moves swiftly once I'm past the accident and the rest of the drive is uneventful. I hear several songs in a row that I don't recognise and I can't shake the feeling that the radio doesn't want to comfort me any more. I switch it off.

The sky has darkened. Have I really been driving so long? The sunset colours penetrate the city's polluted clouds, turning them shades of rust and blood.

Rusty like the tracks, blood on the wheels...

I remember James dragging me into the Devil House. I was nine and he was eleven. It was late at night, the fair was about to close, and there was no one inside. No one but us. The room swam with shadows and the walls ran with painted blood. Screams and laughter came from everywhere and I felt surrounded by ghosts. I was terrified.

"Come on, Kelly," James said, blocking the doorway with his arm so I couldn't get out. "Don't be a pussy."

I didn't know what that word meant, but I knew it was a bad one. Ever since going to the big school, he'd started using strange words like that. It sounded all wrong coming from him.

"*You're* a pussy," I said, pretending I knew what I was saying.

He just laughed, knowing I didn't. I didn't like the way he looked in the dark. I couldn't see his face, couldn't make out his eyes. I could only see his silhouette. He might be anyone. Or any*thing*. It was like the darkness had changed him.

"Stop it," I murmured, trying to push past him. "It's not funny. You're scaring me."

"You're *supposed* to be scared!"

From somewhere in the Devil House came the evil yowling and shrieking of a cat, the cackling of a witch. It reminded me of the sound effects record we had at home, the one we played at top volume every Halloween while we waited for trick-or-treaters. A few screams and howls later and I realised it was the exact same record. And just like that, the thrill was gone. Something hissed and the room began to fill with smoke. I watched as the white plumes wreathed our feet, indifferent to the effect.

My brother's grin appeared to glow in the dark and I relaxed into the cheesy haunted house clichés. I always needed to be pushed, but once there, I loved wherever I'd been pushed.

Being scared was fun, but in a way it was almost more fun when we were the ones doing the scaring. And on Halloween we lived for it. We waited all year for the chance to put on a horror show for trick-or-treaters. The look on younger kids' faces when we got them to put their hands into bowls of peeled grape eyeballs and cold intestine spaghetti, the music of their screams as one of us would distract them at the front door while the other ran around behind them in the dark to jump out at them when they turned to go. We loved it all.

Abruptly, the sound effects stopped and the fog dissipated in one long final breath, like a dragon sighing. The lights went out with a heavy *clunk* and we were plunged into darkness. A couple of fluorescent yellow skulls still leered at us from one wall, but otherwise we were in total darkness. The park must have closed.

We were silent for several moments, neither of us daring to speak. My heart pounded in my chest. It suddenly felt as though a world of endless possibilities had opened before us like the painted floor of the Bottomless Pit.

After a while we crept to the window and peered out. We saw a few people locking up rides and going about their business before leaving. We heard the roar of car and truck engines as they left the site. And then we were alone. Octoberland was ours.

I'm nearing the exit for the road that will take me to my parents' house. *My* house, I remind myself. The oncoming traffic is dotted with headlights and after some searching, I find the switch for mine. Instead of signalling, I just let the car drift into the far lane. No one is behind me to complain. But when the exit comes up, I don't slow down. I don't even glance over at it. I drive right past it to the next one, the one that leads to the place that's calling to me.

I see the silhouette of the strip-mall in the twilight haze. The few remaining shop-front windows glint like huge red eyes and the headlights splash against the scattering of broken glass in the parking lot. It looks like crystallised blood. The way in is around the back and I guide the car towards it. It almost feels as though I'm not driving at all, that the car is following a track to take me there.

My stomach flutters with a familiar sense of eager anticipation as I reach the entrance. Two giant skeletons loom before me, wreathed in mist. Time has taken its toll on their painted wooden bones and now they are swollen and warped. Their dangling scythes no longer swing as though to slice apart the cars that move between them. I pass through unhindered.

The parking lot is empty and dusted with fallen leaves. Mist gathers above the autumn carpet, a veil the headlights don't quite penetrate. The car drifts to a stop and I shut off the engine and then the headlights. For a moment I just sit there, staring.

All the familiar shapes are there, the angles and curves of the rides, silhouettes against the darkening sky. I haven't been back here since that night. To my left is the Hangman's Drop, its wooden tower no longer seeming as high as it did when I was little. The crossed beams have cracked and broken and, like the skeletons, the whole structure has become warped, sodden with pollution and rain.

It wasn't so much a ride as an experience. You were strapped into a car, your legs dangling, while a booming voice passed sentence for the unnamed crimes you had committed. Then you were hoisted to the top of the gallows to be hanged.

For me the scariest part was the ascent. It was always faster than I was expecting. And no matter how long I held my breath, waiting for it to start, in the end I would always be caught off-guard. My stomach plunged in concert with the memory. I was never quite sure just when the ascent stopped and the free-fall began. There was just enough time to scream before the car reached the bottom and slid into the horizontal curve, coming to rest at the end with a gasp of air brakes. Then it would swing down below the track and we would be righted again, laughing and exhilarated.

From where I am it looks as though the car is stuck at the top of the tower, poised to drop its unwary passengers. I am disquieted by the thought of a prisoner standing on the gallows indefinitely, waiting for the floor to open and the noose to tighten. The prospect of such an agonising wait makes my stomach flutter.

I look away.

The car's engine is still ticking, a curiously urgent sound. It makes me open the door and get out. I stare at the car for a moment, feeling uneasy, as though I'm abandoning a source of shelter. The dark brown bulk of it unnerves me. I'm convinced it was green before, but perhaps that's just a trick of the fading light.

The moon is a curved silver blade in the sky, imparting only a hint of a bluish glow. It makes the trees look cold and icy, their bony fingers turning to claws as they shed their covering of leaves. Even the tree on the licence plate looks barren.

The Devil House stands opposite the Hangman's Drop, a dilap-idated ruin, barely visible through the mist. I close my eyes for a moment and hear screams and laughter, the eerie pipe organ, the creaking doors. But the sounds fade into memory. It was where things began that night, but it's not where I'm drawn now.

Further in, a different ride beckons. My feet carry me deep inside the park, leading me towards the centre. It's the only ride we were never allowed on and the one we were most afraid of. The Death Plunge.

I remember the anticipation every year as James and I made our way to the rattly wooden roller coaster and stood against the sign that showed how tall you had to be. And each year that we weren't tall enough, we came away feeling cheated.

The serpentine loops and sweeps of the ride arch high overhead, dominating the strange skyline, visible from anywhere. The tracks seem to writhe as I draw nearer, urging me on. I feel as though I could close my eyes and the mist would take my hand and guide me there, to the exact spot where we found her. The night Octoberland was ours.

Never let anything suffer.

It's James's voice this time, echoing our father's. I push it away, willing him to say anything else, anything but that.

I clamber over jagged, broken boards and into the high grass at the base of the roller coaster. The moon soars between the slats and I close my eyes, listening. I hear the cranking of the winch as it hauls the train up to the top of the first hill. I hear the creaking of the wood, the squeal of metal, the violent rattle as the cars plunge down, rocketing along the track. I hear the screams of passengers as the coaster follows its course, picking up speed, then losing it, a wild adventure of terror and excitement.

James and I wanted so much to be a part of it, to know what the ride was like. We found out that night.

Above me in the trees, the leaves chatter like teeth.

The girl was lying beside a stretch of track that ran along the ground just after the final big drop. At first I thought she was a doll. But then she moved her head.

I screamed and jumped back, but James was intrigued. Fearless. He kept inching nearer and nearer to her. I followed.

She must have wandered off from her parents and got lost. We crept closer, peering down at her. She looked about six or seven years old, with long stringy blonde hair caked with mud. Her eyes were dull and glazed and she was whining softly, a low keening sound that had probably been full-throated crying only moments before. She didn't seem to notice us, not even once we were right beside her.

I looked at James and he looked at me. Neither of us knew what to do. She smelled foul, and as we crept closer we realised why. Her leg was wedged under the edge of the tracks, twisted at a hideous angle. A jagged shard of bone was sticking out. There were streaks of dried blood all over the lower half of her and she had soiled herself. That was what finally made it seem real to me.

The smell. The blood. It had only been a year, but I remembered the squirrel like it was yesterday. I remembered our father. Most of all I remembered the stone and the sound it made as it struck the soft fur, shattering the tiny bones within.

The squirrel had fallen onto the driveway from someplace high in the trees. Its belly had split open and a tiny red coil of guts was spilling out. I'd cried out in horror while James had just knelt down to peer more closely at it, feeling sympathy, but not the deep, wrenching anguish I did.

"Poor thing," our father said.

It was rare for him to be there, rare for him to be with *us*. I could never remember why we weren't alone when we found it. In later years I accused him of having set the whole thing up, to get even with us for having our own life, one we never shared with him or our mother.

The three of us watched as the injured squirrel shuddered and twitched its legs, uttering pathetic little squeaks of pain.

"It's suffering."

Then, as James and I watched, he bent down and prised a large edging stone from the flowerbed. At my gasp of horror he said, "It's kinder this way. You should never let anything suffer."

A part of me understood while another part raged at the idea. He was right, of course. Even at that age I *knew* he was right. But I never forgave him for not telling me to look away.

The little girl's eyes were exactly like the squirrel's, frenzied and hopeless. She was barely even aware of us. Death was close. We could feel it as surely as we could feel the autumn chill. Even if we left now, if we ran all the way home and called 911, the ambulance would never reach her in time. And even if we tried, we'd have to leave her here to do it, leave her all by herself, dying horribly.

It never even occurred to us to split up.

We stood there for long moments, staring at her, each of us thinking the same thing, reliving the same memory. The night was still and calm, the only sound the girl's raspy breaths. Deep in my cowardly little heart I urged James to do it, just end it, put her out of her misery. I turned away, hoping that when I looked back, he would have done it.

I don't remember him saying a word. He just took my hand and looked at me, and then he pointed up at the tracks. A strange sort of calm settled over me and I nodded. Together we took hold of the girl's arms. She gave a strangled little moan and shuddered in our grasp, but she was beyond screaming from the pain. As gently as we could, we moved her so that her body was lying across the tracks. Then we made our way up to the boarding platform of the roller coaster.

It only took James a minute to figure out how to turn the power on and start the ride. The train began inching forward at once, dragged towards the lift hill by a chain running underneath. We clambered into the front car as it began its ascent, pulling the bar down across our laps. After that it was out of our hands.

I am standing there before I know it, looking down at the tracks. I can almost see her bloodstained yellow dress, like a drift of autumn leaves. That was how she looked to us when the train went roaring down that final hill. Just a splash of bright colour in the shadows. Then the train struck her, a horrible jolting impact we hadn't expected, and our car leapt up off the track. We'd been screaming since the coaster began the plunge, and we continued to scream as the derailed cars lurched to the side, throwing us free.

The memory reawakens the pain and my hand moves instinctively to my leg, which I broke in the fall. I'd been thrown against the wooden supports. They said I was lucky not to have broken my neck, lucky not to have been killed.

James had landed in a clump of bushes, escaping with only minor bruises and scratches. But no one ever told him he had been lucky.

I crouch down in the grass and run my hand over the rusted

steel of the track. Flakes come away on my fingers, staining them deep red.

We couldn't let her suffer.

It was hours before anyone came, before we were found. My broken leg felt like a thing separate from me, an animal eating me alive. From where I lay, I could see the overturned front car of the train. Blood dripped slowly from its wheels, falling like liquid leaves into the grass. I wondered if some of it was mine.

I was delirious with the pain but James wouldn't leave me to go and get help and I didn't want him to. I couldn't bear the thought of lying there in the dark, all alone, and someone finding me and dragging me onto the tracks.

Some time later there were flashing lights and sirens, police and paramedics, our frightened parents, and the blurring of chaos as whatever I was given for the pain began to take hold. Suddenly I realised James wasn't there with me and I started screaming. All I could see in my mind was the mangled wreck of the dead girl, a crushed autumn leaf in a pool of blood. A paramedic tried to reassure me, telling me my brother was with the policemen, but I kept calling his name until someone brought him back to me. And just before I slipped into unconsciousness, he leaned down to whisper in my ear.

I told them it was me. Just me.

I rub my hands together, spreading the rust stains over my palms as his voice echoes in my memory.

The girl had died instantly. And something inside us had died with her.

Once all the facts came to light, everyone looked at us differently. Expressions hardened towards my brother, while softening with intolerable pity towards me. There were so many strangers circling us now like vultures. Doctors and counsellors and social workers. We overheard discussions about "removing us from the home" and "long-term psychological damage". One phrase was familiar: "unhealthy obsession". That one had been applied to us and anything we cared about for as long as we could remember.

In hushed tones, these concerned people told our parents that James had dangerous personality traits, that he was something called a "sociopath". About me they only made noises of sympathy. They said I was a victim, that I'd been under his influence. I didn't understand what was going on, and at the time I wasn't sure James did either.

When they questioned us separately, I stuck to the story James had told me, that he was the one who had done it. They didn't even ask why I'd gone along with him. They just assumed I'd had no choice. He'd made me go in the Devil House, after all. He'd once locked me in the tumble dryer. And there was that incident a couple of years earlier when he'd tried to drown me in the pool. No one listened when I tried to tell them that had been *my* idea.

I was lucky, they insisted. Lucky to be alive. It wasn't until they took my brother away and locked him up that I understood what they'd really meant by that.

I never forgave my parents for letting it happen. I never forgave any of them. I wasn't allowed to see James for almost a full year. It wasn't until they finally accepted that my despair wasn't going to magically go away that they relented and began arranging supervised visits. But neither of us would ever be the same again. How could we?

By tacit agreement, we stuck to James' version of events, the version where I'd had nothing to do with what happened at Octoberland. It probably wouldn't have made any difference to admit that I'd been just as guilty. But the same cowardly part of me that had simply willed James to put her out of her misery in the first place allowed me to keep silent.

And as the years passed, and we grew up, that silence stretched between us like a noose. I kept waiting for the drop, for my neck to snap. It never came.

I can't remember when I stopped visiting, or when I stopped writing. There are no words to describe the rotting away of a relationship like ours. We faded from each other's lives like ghosts.

I hadn't come back for our parents' funerals, a joint affair since they were in the same car when it happened. Houston traffic.

Someone in a hurry. I can't recall the facts. But the letter telling me the house was mine had only been addressed to me, the sole remaining heir.

A flurry of dead leaves drifts down on me from high above. They fall on the ground at my feet, covering the area of the track where two children had once killed a little girl. I'm uncertain which role I'm meant to play now. I don't know if I should board the roller coaster one last time. I close my eyes and listen for my brother's voice, but the only sound I hear is the rustle of leaves. It sounds like the ticking of a clock. It sounds *expectant.*

He's been waiting here for me all these years. He doesn't have to speak for me to know what he wants. I don't belong on the ride with him.

A feeling of calm settles over me as I remove my jacket, fold it and set it aside. Then I ease myself back and lie down on the tracks. After a while I hear the grinding of the winch as the train begins its long slow climb up the first hill. I look up at the cold ocean of stars as I wait for the roar and clatter, the screech of metal, and I wonder if I will scream. I should. I owe him that much.

(for my brother)

REGGIE OLIVER

PORSON'S PIECE

R EGGIE OLIVER is an actor, director, playwright and award-winning author of fiction. Published work includes six plays, three novels, an illustrated children's book, eight volumes of short stories, including *Mrs Midnight* (winner of the Children of the Night Award for best work of supernatural fiction), and the biography of Stella Gibbons, *Out of the Woodshed*.

His stories have appeared in over eighty anthologies, and three "selected" collections of his stories have been published: *Dramas from the Depths: The Selected Stories (and Other Diversions)* (Centipede Press, 2010), *Shadow Plays* (Egaeus Press, 2012) and *The Sea of Blood* (Dark Regions Press, 2015). Most recently published is a ninth collection of "strange" stories, *A Maze for the Minotaur*, from Tartarus Press.

Oliver's short story 'Flowers of the Sea' was included in the *Folio Book of Horror Stories* (The Folio Society, 2018) amongst such classic luminaries of the genre as Edgar Allan Poe, H.P. Lovecraft and M.R. James. He is also an illustrator, and has recently contributed artwork to books by Anna Taborska and Robert Shearman.

"I met the philosopher Sir Alfred ('Freddie') Ayer when I was at Oxford in the 1970s," recalls the author, "finding him charming and delightful company; and I also went to his lectures. He was a staunch atheist—very much the Richard Dawkins of his day—but towards the end of his life, while undergoing an operation, he had an experience which, temporarily, made him revise his convictions (or lack of them).

"I have always been fascinated by this incident, as I have with stories from the area where I live, near Saxmundham in Suffolk, of people seeing the spirits of the dead dancing in a particular field on summer evenings. No explanation: but the legend persists, thus proving yet again that there are more things in Heaven and Earth than are dreamt of in your—or Sir Freddie Ayer's—philosophy."

I CAN'T REMEMBER exactly when I first had the idea for *Last Thoughts* but it rapidly became an obsession with me. Originally it was going to be called *Philosophical Conclusions*, though, when I submitted the proposal to the Commissioning Editor of Radio Documentaries, she said that sounded too ponderous and academic. Reluctantly I have to agree, but at the time I thought it was symptomatic of the BBC's relentless urge to "dumb down". Naturally, I did not use that expression to her. Even to mention such a phrase as "dumbing down" at the BBC is to invite the accusation of "elitism": another anathema of the Corporation, volubly opposed, yet covertly practised.

The "concept", to use our jargon, was for a series of half-hour programmes in which prominent but now retired academic philosophers, nearing the end of their earthly existence, were asked to give their final verdicts on Life, Death, God, whatever, and to say whether in old age their views had been modified or matured. One of the reasons my proposal had found favour was that I had already sounded out two very distinguished philosophers, Dame Felicity Regan and Professor Garstang, and obtained their provisional agreement to feature on the programme. There was, however, one person whom I really wanted to include, but who proved more elusive: Sir Bernard Wilkes.

When I had been at Oxford thirty years before, "Bernie" Wilkes was the man. He was head of the leading school of "Rational

Positivist" philosophy which held sway then, and, for all I know, still does. He was a brilliant lecturer and tutor, and, though he did have a reputation as a womaniser, that was something that was less frowned upon then than it is now. In those days, affairs, even with students young enough to be your daughter, were condoned, provided that one did not persist in unwanted advances and maintained discretion. Sir Bernard kept to both these unwritten rules— I was going to say "religiously", but that, given his radical opposition to all things theological, would be inappropriate.

Male students of my acquaintance always expressed envious astonishment at the way he managed to "pull" some of the most glamorous women in Oxford. I was not personally drawn to him in that way, which was just as well because I was not the type of young woman he would be drawn to, but I could understand his attraction.

In appearance he was not immediately prepossessing, being rather short and having a large nose, but he was full of animation. Someone once described him as "a cross between a rodent and a firefly" which, strangely, does rather sum him up. His brown, somewhat prominent eyes, glittered with genial mischief. Most importantly of all, it was quite obvious that he actually *liked* women, not simply for their sexual possibilities, but for their company. At dinners and drinks parties, he would be talking to them in preference to any man, however distinguished. Once he was a guest at a philosophical dinner at my college, and, during the sherry stage, I happened to find myself talking to him, one to one. For the brief duration of our exchange he somehow managed to convey to me that he thought I was the cleverest and most delightful person in the room. Such charm and grace excuses much and is not easily forgotten.

However, I would not like it to be thought that it was some sort of unfinished emotional business that made me so anxious to seek out Sir Bernard. No. Let me make that quite clear. But Wilkes had, somehow, symbolised for me the freedom and intellectual openness of Oxford during a significant period in my young life.

Enquiries at his old college yielded the information that Sir Bernard had left Oxford five years ago and his forwarding address either could not or would not be supplied. Surely, I thought, it could not be that hard to track down such a prominent figure? Yet it was. In the end I had help from an unexpected quarter.

I happened to mention to Dame Felicity Regan that I was looking for him, and though I expected a sympathetic ear, which I received, I did not anticipate any actual assistance. Dame Felicity and Sir Bernard had had many public run-ins over the years, mainly because Dame Felicity is a Roman Catholic and Sir Bernard was of the view that any kind of religious belief was inconsistent with serious philosophical activity. However, it turned out that behind-the-scenes the two had got on reasonably well, at least in later years.

"When Bernie got married for the third time about ten years ago now," Dame Felicity told me over the phone, "he was transformed. Alison Kentley, her name was, a graduate D. Phil student he was mentoring, and yonks younger than him, of course, but she suited him and they were very much in love. He stopped his philandering altogether: they were amazingly happy. Alison was a remarkable person in many ways: even brought about a certain rapprochement between me and Bernie. *Not* what I expected. Then something terrible happened. Alison died very suddenly from a brain aneurysm. She was only thirty-five. Bernie was devastated. He felt he'd been offered the top prize in the lottery of life only to have it cruelly and unjustly snatched away from him. I don't think I've ever seen a man (or woman) so angry. I don't mean blowing his top, that sort of thing, but just deeply, permanently enraged. *Out*raged might be the *mot juste*. And of course the terrible thing was, you see, that there was no one he could be angry *with*. He couldn't be angry with God of course because he didn't believe in one. There are times when that is the whole point of there being a God: to have someone to be angry with. Not *at* you understand—that would be foolish—but *with*."

I failed to understand the distinction, but I trusted Dame Felicity to mean something by it. "So what happened?" I asked.

"He couldn't stand Oxford any longer after that, and he'd been such a sociable bird in his day. He was past the retiring age anyway, so he just withdrew altogether, making it as difficult as possible for anyone to get in touch. He bought a little house in the Cotswolds and has gone to live there, allowing only a few trusted people to know where he is, I being one of them for some reason. Since then he's made no public appearances, published nothing, never answers the few invitations that manage to reach him... I'm telling you all this because I think it's time he stopped being a recluse and you might just be the person to bring him back." And without any further discussion, she gave me Sir Bernard's telephone number. That is Dame Felicity for you.

Sir Bernard was now in his early eighties, but his voice on the telephone was just as I remembered it from lectures thirty years before. And the delivery was the same: faultlessly articulated, but headlong and hurrying towards the end of each sentence, as if he had already worked out what he was going to say in the next and was impatient to get to it.

He listened without interrupting to my pitch about the programme, there was a pause, and he asked me who else was going to be featured. I mentioned Garstang and Dame Felicity.

"Hmm." He seemed unimpressed. "I suppose it was *she* who gave you this number?"

"Yes."

"Hmm."

He then interrogated me closely about my work at the BBC, my marital status (single), my career at Oxford. From this conversation I caught a tiny whisper of the old charm. I did not feel invaded because he seemed genuinely interested in me as a person.

"Well," he said at the end of it, "you'd better come down and see me. Come for lunch. But don't bring any of your recording equipment. I haven't decided to do this thing yet." And he then gave me detailed instructions as to how to find his house: evidently news of the Sat Nav had not reached him. His final words were: "You'll find me rather remote."

I could not decide whether a reference to his location, his psychological state, or a humorous allusion to both was intended. I chose not to laugh in case that might offend him and said I was looking forward to seeing him.

"Hmm!" And he rang off.

Lovers of irony will I suppose be amused by the fact that Sir Bernard lived in a house called The Old Rectory, in a village which went by the name of Bourton Monachorum, not far from Stow-on-the-Wold. Sir Bernard was a man who paid very little attention to his surroundings, so I am not sure that he was much bothered by the ecclesiastical connections. When I had asked him on the telephone about the name, he said he understood that there had been a Benedictine Priory at Bourton before the Dissolution, hence the "Monachorum". "There are some ruins somewhere in the village, I believe," he said casually. "Haven't seen them myself."

I arrived by car on a May morning, shortly after a rainstorm. Everything was young and green and glistening. The village of Bourton stood on a slope of the Cotswold Ridge, with the Rectory on the lower edge of it, close to the church. It was a fine old 17th century house of Cotswold stone standing in its own grounds, and I wondered if Sir Bernard had chosen it, not simply for its comparative remoteness, but also because its architecture, in miniature, was akin to a typical Oxford college.

The approach was up a gravel drive between trees which partially obscured the house. Despite the fact that the sun was now out and the trees were in their early summer panoply of fresh young green, the overall effect was slightly lowering. Had you not known, you might have guessed at a reclusive occupant.

The door was opened by a large, middle-aged woman with a Gloucestershire accent whose "Come in, we have been expecting you" contained just a hint of menace.

"Sir Bernard is in the sitting room. I am Mrs. Jacks. I come in and do for him most days." She appeared to be anxious to establish that theirs was a respectable professional relationship. I nodded to confirm I understood. From somewhere I heard the sound of classical music. It was mid-18th century, faintly familiar but I could not quite place it.

"Sir Bernard likes his music," said Mrs. Jacks, as if she were talking about a teenage son with an addiction to Heavy Metal. She ushered me into the sitting room with the words: "She's arrived, Sir Bernard. Shall I get the lunch on?"

"Yes. Thank you, Mrs. Jacks. Thank you so much."

A little smile and a nod from the hitherto unsmiling Mrs. Jacks was enough to tell me that even she had fallen under his spell. She left the room.

"How nice to meet you again after all these years, Jane." I had told him in our telephone conversation of our previous brief encounter. "Would you mind awfully turning the music off for me. The far left black button in the thing on the sideboard." He pointed and I obeyed. "Thank you. Gluck's *Orfeo*," he added.

I had already guessed because, before I had switched it off, I heard the opening bars of 'Che farò senza Euridice?'.

Sir Bernard Wilkes was much as I remembered him, though smaller than in my imagination, and of course much lined and with white hair. The liveliness was still apparent, though, and—I don't think this was merely because of what Dame Felicity had told me— I saw sadness in the eyes. He was sitting in a comfortable bucket swivel armchair of a classic 1960s design. The room was entirely equipped with modernist furnishings which, though attractive and of high quality in themselves, looked curiously out of place in a 17th-century, oak-panelled parlour. The few pictures were mostly nondescript prints of Oxford, but above the fireplace was a large framed black and white photograph, a head and shoulders portrait of a woman in her thirties. She was laughing, and the effect was immediately captivating. Behind her loomed the out-of-focus form of the Radcliffe Camera.

"Yes. That's Alison," said Sir Bernard, noticing that my eye had been drawn to it. After that he made no further reference to her, but he talked abundantly. Once he had started, the flow was unstoppable, and it went on through lunch, at which he ate very little and drank next to nothing, though an excellent Pouilly Fumé was on offer for my benefit. It was not that he monopolised the conversation—he was constantly asking me questions and soliciting my views—but his need to communicate was strong, at times, it seemed to me, almost desperate. He kept to topics outside himself:

politics, the arts, the latest developments in science and ideas, and rarely made any reference to his present situation. He was a lonely man refusing to admit to his own loneliness.

Briefly we discussed the programme we were going to make. I outlined some of the questions I would ask him and he raised no objections to them, even nodded his approval occasionally. That was what I had come for, so by the end of the meal, I felt that my task was done and I was ready to take my leave. But as we were finishing our coffee, Sir Bernard suddenly said:

"I thought we might have a walk after lunch. I nearly always do. Keeps me going. Exercise, you know."

He looked at me eagerly and I thought it impolitic to refuse.

"They tell me the countryside round here is very—" He searched for a word and finally lighted on: "—picturesque." It was typical of his intellectual austerity that he would not commit himself to an aesthetic judgement of his own.

We were in the hall, while he put on a cap, and chose a walking stick from the umbrella stand, when Mrs. Jacks emerged from her kitchen domain. Sir Bernard seemed startled by her appearance, even nervous.

"Just going for a walk, Mrs. Jacks," he said. "Showing Jane here a bit of your countryside. Delicious lunch by the way. Delicious."

Mrs. Jacks frowned. "Now Sir Bernard, you won't be taking her down by—"

"No, no, no! Not to worry. We'll be fine. Won't be long. Cup of tea when we get back. Come along, Jane!" And with that we were out of the door before Mrs. Jacks could respond.

Once out of the sphere of Mrs. Jacks' influence, Sir Bernard relaxed a little. We went down the drive then up the winding main street of the village, flanked by ancient stone houses with cottage gardens that were beginning to come into bloom. Sir Bernard did not walk fast, but he walked steadily, and seemed undaunted by the slope. It was an impressive performance for a man in his eighties.

"Picturesque, you see," he said gesturing, but not looking, at the houses to his left and right. We said little until we had almost reached the top of the village, when he indicated a footpath to our left with his stick.

"This is where we turn off," he said. "We will come back to the Rectory by a different route."

The footpath, much overgrown, passed between two dry-stone walls that encircled village gardens. Sir Bernard, plodding ahead of me, began to hum. It sounded like one of the dances of the Blessed Spirits from 'Orfeo', but he stopped abruptly when we came to a narrow sunken lane that crossed the end of the footpath at a right angle. Pointing to his left, Sir Bernard said: "We go down this way."

The path was of beaten earth and, because of the rain we had had that morning, somewhat slippery and treacherous in parts. Was this what Mrs. Jacks had tried to warm him against?

The lane, gouged out of the surrounding landscape and quite steeply sloping, was fringed on both sides by trees. To our left were the back garden walls of cottages we had passed on our way up; to our right we caught glimpses of fields beyond the oaks and beaches that spread their dappled shade over the path. The air was close and still. A few insects hummed, but no birds sang. Despite the sun above, I felt a certain oppression in the atmosphere, but Sir Bernard did not appear to be so affected.

"This path is called Churchyard Lane. When the villagers died, they were traditionally brought down this way to enter the grave-yard on the south side of the church. I don't think it still happens."

Having delivered this piece of information, Sir Bernard proceeded on his way, stopping only when he came to a gap in the fringe of trees. Through it there was a view up a gentle slope of sunlit meadow. The grass was long and uncropped, and wild flowers such as poppies, buttercups, and cornflowers abounded. Sir Bernard pointed at it with his stick without himself looking at it.

"That field there is called Porson's Piece," he said. I wondered why my attention had been drawn to this pleasant but unremark-able stretch of land. "Nobody knows who it belongs to. Generally thought to be some sort of common land, but the name implies it was once owned by someone, presumably called Porson; though that could be a corruption of 'parson'. In which case it could belong to the Church—or indeed to me, I suppose, since I own the Rectory." He gave a short laugh. Still he did not look at the field, but examined my face as I did. "Occasionally a local farmer grazes his cattle on it, but rarely in the summer months. Mostly it's left alone. Hence the wild flowers, as you can see." He paused. I nodded. "Butterflies later on in the summer. Interesting local feature. Well, onwards, onwards!" And without turning to look at Porson's Piece he began to move on down Churchyard Lane. I was beginning to be troubled by his behaviour.

We had come almost to the bottom of the lane when Sir Bernard started to talk again.

"As you may have gathered, I am not usually very susceptible to scenery. It was once said of me that when I thought of New York, I would picture in my head a sign with the words NEW YORK written on it, and that images of the Empire State Building, Central Park, Statue of Liberty, so on, so on, which apparently occur to most people when they think of that city, were entirely absent from my mind. That is of course quite untrue. I have never said any such thing. It is a myth, but like many myths—*some* myths—there is an element of truth in it. I tend not to think in visual images, more in—" He paused for a moment in his headlong delivery. "—concepts, I suppose. The visual arts, painting, sculpture, so on, even architecture, don't mean very much to me. Music on the other hand... That is why it is so strange that... Tell me, what is it that *you* think in mainly? Images? Sounds? Concepts? Algebraic equations? Is that a meaningful question to ask?"

"I don't know. I suppose I just think in—thoughts."

"Aha! Ha! Very good answer. But tautologous of course. What I mean is, how do your thoughts appear to you? Are they—" We had somehow arrived back in front of the drive of The Old Rectory. Sir Bernard nodded and smiled at me, reassured by the familiarity of his surroundings. "Ah! Home again. A cup of tea?"

Mrs. Jacks stared at us searchingly when we entered the Rectory, and, after she had brought us tea in the sitting room, Sir Bernard waited for some moments upon her leaving the room before he began to talk.

"I wonder... When I showed you Porson's Piece, on our walk, did you see anything—unusual there?"

"No. Just a meadow with some rather nice wild flowers."

"Yes. Yes... Nothing—else?"

"Nothing. Why?"

"Well, no reason really, but... It is rather odd. I'd been doing that walk down Churchyard Lane for some time—the one we did—and then, a couple of weeks ago, I was passing Porson's Piece when I saw something. It was still light, but getting towards evening, and there were people in the meadow, and they were dancing. Interesting, I suppose, but only slightly unusual except for two odd things. The first was that they were all in white. I mean everything—clothes, shoes, even their skin and hair. It was all the same white you see. But they were perfectly solid, as far as I could judge: I mean not translucent or transparent. Not like ghosts, you understand. Of course ghosts don't exist, but what I mean is, not like ghosts are imagined by some to be like." He paused, seemingly exhausted by his narrative efforts.

"And the other odd thing?"

"Ah, yes. This was even stranger, I suppose. They made no sound. No sound at all. There were these lines of them all holding hands and they wound round each other, moving quite slowly through the grass and the flowers. But in the middle of them was this man who looked as if he were playing a fiddle, and he was all in white too and his fiddle was also white—bow and everything—but the instrument made no sound at all. I must have watched it all for about a couple of minutes, possibly longer, but not much. Somehow I didn't like it. I didn't like it at all. I thought it must be some kind of—joke; I don't know... But a nasty joke, if it was. Well, when I got back I naturally asked Mrs. Jacks about the dancers in Porson's Piece and she gave me a strange look and said that nobody went dancing in Porson's Piece. And then she said I should not go down Churchyard Lane again, and when I asked why, she wouldn't answer, but a few days later she gave me this book. Now where is it?" He scrabbled among the papers on his desk until he found a small leather-bound book which he tossed over to me. "You'll find the relevant passage on page 165."

The book, entitled *Ramblings in Old Gloucestershire*, had been written by a clergyman towards the end of the 19th century. The passage on page 165 had been heavily underscored in pencil, presumably by Sir Bernard.

In the picturesque village of Bourton Monachorum there is reputed to be a piece of land where, on summer afternoons and evenings, the Dead dance. This pleasant legend states that they are the spirits of those who have not been buried in hallowed ground and who are not good enough to enter Heaven, nor yet wicked enough to be cast into the flames of eternal torment. The worthy old beldame who told me this story would not reveal the precise location of the meadow, "for," said she, "them as sees the dancers are not long for this world, but them as both sees and hears them will perish at the coming of the next new moon after they hears them." It is a commonly held belief in these parts, but I have encountered it nowhere else in the county.

"All nonsense, of course!" said Sir Bernard as soon as I had finished reading. "I suppose it must have been some sort of hallucination on my part. And somewhere or other in a book or whatever at some time in the past I had picked up that old legend and it had lodged in my subconscious only to emerge later on. That is the only rational explanation." After a long hesitation he added: "But the thing is, I've seen those dancers a couple of time since in Porson's Piece."

"But not heard them?"

"No. No! Not heard, thank—thankfully. It is all quite absurd, but what is really—*annoying*, you might say, is that it should happen in this way. I am perfectly aware that certain people—especially at the beginning and end of their lives—have what are called 'religious' or 'spiritual' experiences. The great William James, as you know, wrote a book about it, *The Varieties of Religious Experience*. And I am prepared to concede, with James, that these experiences, though not of course real in any... real sense, have a certain value—'cash value' as William James liked to put it. That is, they offer consolation, reassurance, freedom from fear of death, so on, so on. And if I had had such an experience, akin, say, to those described by

Wordsworth in *Tintern Abbey* or *The Prelude*—oceanic feelings of oneness with an Eternal Being, or whatever—I would have been prepared to accept it as part of some kind of evolutionary process connected with old-age. And appropriate to my intellect. But *this*! I mean, it's a folk legend of some kind. It's so ridiculous! So trivial! Dancing dead people? I mean, really!"

"Do you think you should see a psychiatrist about it?"

"No, no, no! Never had any time for shrinks. Psychology is a pseudo-science, posited on a mind-body duality which is totally invalid."

"Perhaps you should simply take Mrs. Jacks' advice and not go down Churchyard Lane any more."

"Maybe... Maybe... But why should I give in to this nonsense? It would be as if I believed it. Well, there we are! I expect you want to be on your way. Perhaps talking it out with you has cured me. Isn't 'the talking cure' all the rage these days in shrink circles? Maybe it's done the trick."

Soon after that, I left, having fixed a date for recording an interview with him at The Old Rectory.

Three weeks later I came to record my interview. It was now June and high summer. At Sir Bernard's insistence we sat outside on the front lawn to do our talk. It suited me as it provided the opportunity for one of those classic introductions, so beloved of radio presenters:

I am sitting here in a beautiful garden somewhere in Gloucestershire. The sun is shining: it is a perfect English summer day and with me is Sir Bernard Wilkes, Grand Old Man of British philosophy, and founder of the influential and controversial Rational Positivist school of thinking...

As a matter of fact, it was not a particularly beautiful garden, just a well-mown lawn fringed by a few desultory bushes and trees. There were no flowers or exotic plants as Sir Bernard's interest in horticulture was minimal. However, I was able to obtain a "wild-track" of a few birds twittering which supplied the requisite aural atmosphere for our discussion.

Sir Bernard seemed relaxed, but perhaps a little subdued. When he talked he was as fluent as ever, but his eloquent paragraphs were interspersed by quite long pauses in which he did not look as if he were engaged in concentrated thought. He stared around the garden, apparently listening for something. Occasionally he would look towards the house where, once, I saw Mrs. Jacks staring anxiously out at us from the dining-room window.

When I asked Sir Bernard about his achievements he said: "Of course I got a lot of things wrong, as one does. Most things, perhaps. I never really, to my satisfaction, sorted out the Verification Principle, for example. But I think the spirit of Rational Positivism was the right one. Has one been influential? Impossible to tell. Maybe one has moved philosophical thinking a few inches in the appropriate direction, I don't know..." I don't believe his modesty was assumed.

Finally I had the courage to ask him: "Sir Bernard, you are now in your eighties, and nearing the end of your life. How do you, as a philosopher, view the prospect of death?"

There was a longer pause than usual, during which Sir Bernard gave a slight start when a blackbird suddenly began to sing quite close by. I was to keep most of that pause in when I edited the recording.

"Death?" he said finally. "Death? Well, of course, death doesn't exist. It is a concept, like God, which is frequently used, but has no real meaning, because it is simply an absence, a non-existence. There is *dying*, a process with which we are all familiar, and one may fear, or be apprehensive about that process. But death itself? There is, quite literally, nothing to fear."

"*No rational being can fear a thing he will not feel.*"

"Exactly."

"But doesn't Larkin in the same poem say that it is precisely this absence of feeling that we *do* fear, whether it is rational to do so or not?"

"Ah, well! Larkin was a poet, not a philosopher, you see!" He laughed. "A very good one, so I'm told. Didn't he also say: 'What will survive of us is love'? An admirable sentiment, a nice expression of feeling, but hardly—hardly verifiable in the philosophical sense."

I had to press him: "But have you had no experiences recently that have made you revise the idea that death is simply a cut-off point?"

Sir Bernard shot me an angry glance. I thought for a moment he was going to terminate the interview and storm off in disgust at my impertinence, but he stayed seated. He turned his face upwards to the sky and stared long at the cloudless blue.

Finally he spoke, dreamily at first, then gathering momentum in his old familiar manner. "Well... one has experiences of course. Strange experiences of all kinds, which are not to be discounted. No experience is invalid, only the interpretation placed upon it. For example, an alcoholic in the condition known as *delirium tremens* may say to you: 'I saw a pink rat'. And he would be telling the truth, but you must not infer from that that there *are* such things as pink rats, only that some alcoholics *see* pink rats. Thus the validity of all sense experiences is conditional upon the meaning one gives it. Or one does not give it. To put a metaphysical gloss on some sense experience is to rob it of its true meaning, which may simply be that one has had that experience. If philosophy has any purpose, it must be as much to strip experience of any false significance rather than to confer it. To apply, as it were, Occam's razor to the cheek of circumstance and scrape away the stubble of superstition."

After that Sir Bernard fell silent. He knew better than to try to add to this peroration. A stillness followed, untouched by so much as the trill of a bird or the hum of an insect. The sunlit garden was serene. Then Sir Bernard started violently.

"What was that?"

"What?"

"Did you hear that just now? I thought I heard music. Solo violin. Bit like a Paganini 'Caprice' or something."

"I can't say I did."

"Must have been Mrs. Jacks indoors playing one of my CDs. Yes, that must be it. Well, are you finished with me?"

I congratulated him on an excellent interview. I stayed a while after that because Sir Bernard seemed reluctant to let me go, but eventually I told him I must leave because I did not want to drive back to London in the dark. As I was going, I found myself for a moment alone with Mrs. Jacks in the hall.

"Mrs. Jacks," I said, "while we were doing the interview in the garden, did you play any of Sir Bernard's music on the CD player?"

Mrs. Jacks looked shocked. "Oh, no! I wouldn't do that! Mind you, I like a good hymn—I'm Strict Baptist, you see—but I don't go in for all that music."

As I drove away from the Old Rectory that evening, Sir Bernard stood on the drive waving my car goodbye, with Mrs. Jacks at his side towering over him. It was the last time I saw him alive, and he looked strangely forlorn.

A few weeks later I was working on the programme in one of the editing suites at the BBC when I had a call on my mobile from Dame Felicity Regan. She told me that Sir Bernard had died quite suddenly the previous afternoon. He had had a heart seizure while walking in Churchyard Lane.

"There is going to be a grand memorial service at Oxford in a few weeks time, of course, but I think you ought to come to the funeral proper," she said. "It's going to be a cremation in Cheltenham. I don't really approve of cremations, as you know, being R.C., but that's what he wanted apparently. There won't be many there, but I think he would have wanted *you* to put in an appearance. The last time I talked to him on the phone, only a couple of nights before he died, he spoke about you with some affection." She waited for my reaction, which was an astonished silence. "I know. I was surprised too."

The service at the crematorium was as dismal as I had expected it to be. The officiating clergyman had not known Sir Bernard, and was obviously embarrassed about conducting the funeral of a notorious atheist. After the committal, we, that is Dame Felicity, half a dozen assorted Oxford dons, and a distant cousin of the deceased, drove the twenty or so miles back to Bourton Monachorum where Mrs. Jacks had tea, sherry, and sandwiches waiting for us. At the wake I did not feel much like talking, and I quickly felt very superfluous when the dons got into a huddle to plan the splendours of the Oxford memorial service.

It was another fine summer day, if a little blowy. I went out onto the empty lawn; then, feeling the need to put even more distance between myself and the academics, I wandered down the drive and into Churchyard Lane. I wanted to be still and remember Sir Bernard, but a restlessness kept me on the move. I began to walk up Churchyard Lane.

Presently I found myself at the gap in the line of trees, which marked the spot from which Porson's Piece could be seen. The sun was beginning to decline into the west, sending slanted golden rays across the meadow, now strewn with wild flowers: purple vetch and willow herb, comfrey, campion, and blood-red poppies. They waved and glittered in the breeze.

Then at the very top of the field something white appeared, which moved quicker than anything caught by the wind. It seemed to bob up and down, appearing above the tops of the grass and then vanishing again, finally resolving itself into a chain of white objects that rose and fell in an undulating motion. It began to come closer, and I could see now that it was a line of dancers all in white.

The dancers wove their serpentine way down the field towards the sunken lane. They were, as Sir Bernard had described, white, dead white all over and perfectly solid in appearance, except that the evening mist, which wreathed the grass of the field, sometimes obscured their feet. There was nothing overtly threatening about these figures—they seemed too absorbed in their own convoluted movements to threaten anyone—but their sheer strangeness terrified me. I felt my heart banging in my chest, and because the world was silent and the tread of their feet made no sound, the noise of the heartbeat and the rush of blood through veins and ventricles filled my ears. I could not move from where I stood, and they were weaving their way towards me, chains of men and women in white, holding hands, dancing down the meadow. As they came closer, I began to distinguish their clothes and their features. They were all different: they belonged to no one period or type; only the same dead whiteness of their garments and exposed skin gave them a dreadful uniformity. At the end of one of the lines of dancers one man, I noticed, was stumbling slightly, evidently not as used to the steps as the rest. This line began to make a wide sweep around the field, folding the other dancers into closer concentric circles, until the stumbling end man came down the slight incline towards me where I stood in the lane.

The man had his back to me at first, but the line of dancers he was holding on to swung him round so that I saw him full-face, and so close I could almost have reached out to touch him. It was Sir Bernard, all white, even his eyes, which stared at me blankly like the eyes of a marble statue. He extended his free arm and gestured to me, as if inviting me to join him. He opened his mouth to cry out, but no voice could be heard, and a moment later he was pulled away, stumbling into the lines of souls as they swayed in endless circles around each other.

I thought I heard the scrape of a fiddle. I was probably mistaken. I almost certainly was, but I could take no chances. Covering my ears, I ran headlong down Churchyard Lane back to the Old Rectory, as the men and women of Porson's Piece danced on through the twilight.

BRIAN HODGE

HE SINGS OF SALT AND WORMWOOD

BRIAN HODGE is the author of thirteen novels, more than 130 short stories and novellas, and five collections. His most recent works include the novel *The Immaculate Void* and the collection *Skidding Into Oblivion*, companion volumes of cosmic horror, neither of which are even available anymore. He doubts there will be much more.

"For me," explains Hodge, "ideas often arise out of a swirl of things I've been exploring or have experienced or blundered across, that end up getting hopelessly entangled. This one began to coalesce six months after I'd shredded a knee. I was healed enough for a sorely needed getaway, so we spent a week seaside, on the Oregon coast.

"Far up the beach, barely visible from our cliff-top B&B, stood a desolate-looking observation platform that I dubbed 'Neptune's Throne'. We were lured down to visit it several times, and got some nicely atmospheric photos. As well, during a visit to the aquarium in Newport, I learned about shipworms, and quickly found I regarded them with equal parts repugnance and fascination.

"Shortly after we were home, I went through a spell where, without trying, I kept running across the exploits of surfing legend Laird Hamilton.

"Sooner or later, I can take a hint."

～

I T WAS EVERYTHING about the sea that had always unnerved him, waiting at the bottom in one cold, disintegrating hulk.

Not two minutes earlier, Danny was in another world, the world above the waves, the world of air and land and the hot, dry feel of the summer sun. His wetsuit snug as a second skin, he sat on the cuddy boat's transom long enough to Velcro a lanyard around his ankle, binding him to a safety-line with ninety feet of slack. He cinched tight his goggles, round and insectoid, then slipped over the stern. Bobbing in sync with the hull, he sucked wind and huffed it out, cycling a few times before filling from the bottom up: belly, lower chest, upper chest, like trying to cram a stuffed suitcase with more, and a little more on top of that.

In the boat, against the lone cloud in the sky, Kimo held a stop-watch with his thumb on the trigger. "Ready."

Danny squeezed in one last sip of air and plunged headfirst, like a seal, full-body undulations propelling him down, with the safety-line trailing after. The swim fins helped. He'd not been blessed with big feet. They never made fun in Hawaii, but guys always made fun here on the mainland. *Hey Danny, with those dainty little Asian paws of yours, how do you manage to even stay up on a surfboard?* Maybe they didn't mean anything by it. Or maybe they did, trying to get inside his head, psyche him out. *Small feet, small...yeah.* He converted it to fuel, that much more drive to bring home a trophy, another spon-sorship.

But all that was a world away. He was in the blue world now, a gradient of cerulean to indigo yawning beneath him, where the farther down you went, the more the topside laws unravelled.

Until he'd first experienced the shift for himself back in the spring, he had always believed the same as everyone else he brought it up with: that free-diving was a non-stop struggle against your own buoyancy, fighting the lift of the air heaved into your lungs.

Another misconception dies hard. It was like that for only the first forty or so feet down.

Make it that far, to what they called the Doorway to the Deep, and there came a transition he had yet to stop regarding with wonder. Buoyancy was neutralised, the weight of the water bearing down nullifying your tendency to rise to the surface. No more struggle, the fight was won. The sea had you then, a downward pull he could feel tugging on his shoulders and skull.

He held his arms along his sides, aqua-dynamic, and continued to descend, effortlessly now, like a skydiver bulleting in free-fall. The trickiest part had been learning how to equalise the pressure on his ears, in his sinuses, and turn back the pain.

The deeper he sank, the more the pressure became like the slow tightening of a fist that would never relax. It had taken some re-framing of the changes it made, seeing them as comforting rather than distressing. *This is what happens down here. This is normal, another version of normal.* No big deal, just the mammalian dive reflex: shifts of physiology so distinct, so foreign out of the water, so automatic in it, they could recalibrate a lifetime of thinking after a dive or two. *Maybe we really do belong here.*

Despite the exertion, his heart rate slowed. Even before the threshold forty feet down, his lungs were already compressed to half their normal size. At sixty, they were reduced to a third. If he were acclimated enough to go that far, at three hundred feet his lungs would be no bigger than baseballs.

Here, though, a couple miles out to sea, over a shelf of land jutting from the central Oregon coast, the bottom cut him off at a depth of seventy-six. Almost there, he tucked into a ball and flipped head over tail, to finish dropping flippers first. He touched down with a gentle bounce that stirred the silt, amid a sparse garden of kelp and seaweed that swayed in the current, and all was so very quiet, like awakening to a dream world of slow time and profound tranquillity. The need to breathe remained on some far horizon. The pressure was a cocoon, a presence as welcoming as a hug.

All this time he'd been lying to himself. Thinking he knew some-thing about the ocean, and why—because he'd grown up on an island? Because he'd first stepped onto a surfboard when he was seven and had hardly stepped off since? That was how you fooled yourself into believing you truly understood the sea when all you'd ever done on a board was scratch the water's surface.

Above, the day was clear, bright and sunny. Down here, the sun still found him but was filtered to a murky twilight, as if the fog of morning and blue of evening had joined, to wrap around and welcome him home.

It took slow moments to take shape: a mass off to his left, a ragged, edgeless hill rising from the sea floor. Danny moved towards it in fin-encumbered hops, a feeling maybe like walking on the moon. He hadn't gotten close enough to satisfy his curiosity before his tether to the surface ran out of slack.

The dumbest thing in the world would be to strip the lanyard from his ankle. He did it anyway, fearing if he didn't get close enough for a look now, he might never find this spot again. He left the safety-line behind, and was truly diving free.

The mass was no longer edgeless, and no hill. A hill wouldn't have two masts, jutting down from one side to dig into the sea floor. A hill wouldn't have rectangular openings, nor broken windows, metal railings, cleats still wrapped with decaying rope. It was some-body's lost sailing yacht, a fifty-footer at minimum, resting on its starboard side. The build was old school, lots of wood where most buyers would've been content with aluminium and fibreglass. Now it was an ecosystem, submerged long enough to have sagged into itself and crusted over with rot and life.

The cold found him through his wetsuit and went for his marrow. Shipwrecks had always bothered him, even from the safety of pictures. Planes lost at sea, too, and sunken cars, and houses and timber groves in valleys flooded to make new lakes.

It was more than the tragedies and calamities they told of. It was their status, things perfectly normal in the topside world, aliens now, lost and alone where they were never meant to be. They were a rebuttal: *You're lying to yourself, you know. It's the hypoxia talking. You think you belong? This isn't your element at all.*

Regardless, the wreck drew him, until he was close enough to touch it.

Everything down here is so much better suited to belong than you. Here, all you are is a resource.

Breathing? Soon. The pent-up need, he now understood, wasn't driven by a lack of oxygen. The body had no sensors for that. An amazing oversight. Nobody would ever design an oxygen-powered machine that way on purpose.

Down here, you're food. All you have to do is wait.

Instead, the clawing need to breathe came from a build-up of carbon dioxide, and you could hack that to a degree. He let a poof of stale air slip his lips and it bought him a little more time. He squatted and gripped the yacht's tilted gunwale, to shove off it and launch his ascent... but to his surprise, it gave way with a muffled crunch and a cloud of debris, crumbs and shards of rotten wood drifting loose.

It was what was inside that really gave him a jolt.

The cross-section of wood appeared tunnelled, the burrows full of soft, pale bodies—worms, they looked like, some as short and thin as matches, others the size of a finger, one as plump as a cigar.

Danny vented more CO_2, this time not meaning to, a sound of disgust burping loose. And he'd been down too long, his vision starting to close around the edges, with the height of a seven-story building left to swim. He pushed off the bottom and kicked towards the beckoning daylight.

If your vision began turning to a haze they called the pink cloud, that was when you really had to worry. What came next was a blackout, and he feared it was moments away—the resetting of the clock to a final countdown. You could drift unconscious for a couple minutes, no harm done, your larynx automatically closing like a valve to keep the water out. Up top, they would know before it opened again, if they were paying attention. You just had to trust your team, they'd realise you were in trouble, haul you up by your safety line...

Oh. Right. Shit.

He kicked harder.

Which came first then—the movement out in front of him, or the movement he felt *through* him?

Through, probably. Yeah, go with that. His insides felt stirred, quivering as if he'd hugged a vibrator. Right away he knew what it was, he'd felt the same thing from dolphins—echolocation, a ping of sonar developed over millions of years of evolution, so advanced it made the Navy's best look like a toy.

But this was no dolphin. If a dolphin was a whisper, what he'd felt was a bark.

He lowered his gaze from the beacon of the sun and back to the deep-blue haze. Twenty, thirty yards out, it was dimly visible, a darker bulk against the murk, a slick, bulbous head and a body stretching too far back into the gloom to make out. With his vision closing down, Danny could barely see it anyway, and only for a moment before it faded into a wash of pink.

He heard a muffled thump and the sensation enveloped him again.

If you're lucky and you know it clap your hands...whatever was out there could've obliterated him without trying. Sperm whales? Loudest animals on earth. Their clicks could be so loud they couldn't even exist in the air as sound. They could blow out your eardrums, maybe kill you as surely as the concussive blast of a bomb.

Lucky. It was only scanning, giving him a sonogram.

Kicking again, with legs starting to feel like tingling rubber, nearly blind now, he rose towards a total eclipse of the sun. A few feet from the surface he spewed a gush of bubbles to empty his aching lungs, then with a titanic whoosh broke through into the glorious air.

"You stupid motherfucker!" Kimo was peering down from the boat as if he were looking at a ghost. Things started going clear again, even the sweat spraying from Kimo's shaved head as he whipped the lanyard at the end of the rope, like shaking a leash at a naughty dog. "What is this? What the fuck is this!"

My bad...? Didn't quite cut it under the circumstances, did it?

"What, almost drowning once this year wasn't enough for you, you thought you'd find another way?"

Treading water, Danny peeled off his goggles and flipped his hair back from his face to splat against his shoulders. "Sorry, man. I needed more than ninety feet."

"But you stopped moving." Kimo jabbed a finger towards the sonar screen. "It still makes you dumb as a rock, but if you'd kept moving, you wouldn't have sent me from zero to panic mode, hauling this up and you're not on the end of it anymore." He flung the safety line to the deck. "I was two seconds from going in after you."

"But I started moving again. Obviously. You didn't see that?"

"While giving myself ninety feet of rope burns? No! I don't multi-task."

The man had been looking out for him for years, one displaced Hawaiian to another, and his anger was so pure, so righteous, so Kimo, Danny couldn't help but laugh. It was the right thing at the right time—same as below, the body knowing what to do, and doing it.

"I was fine. Really." He took Kimo's hand and clambered over the side into the boat, then tapped the sonar. "How about the whale? Did you see the whale?"

For a moment, Kimo could only blink. Translation: *Good going, asshole. Now you made me miss an entire whale, too.* "You saw a whale?"

"Just for a second or two. My vision was going, so..."

"Are you sure you weren't hallucinating?"

"I felt him check me out. I didn't hallucinate that." He turned a clumsy 360 to scan the waves for a breach but saw nothing. "How long was I down?"

"I think you were around two-forty-five, two-fifty when I went for the line. I don't even know where the watch landed."

Danny plopped onto the transom and wriggled out of his fins. "So I had to break three minutes, easy." Nothing impressive by competition standards. Competitive free-divers could rack up depths and times that were off the chain. But those people were all about the numbers, the endurance, not about merging with the sea. "A new personal best and I don't even know what it is."

He tossed his fins aside, then spotted the stopwatch beside their cooler of water bottles. He snatched it up and held it towards Kimo's face, back to normal brown after all that furious brick red.

"Check it," Danny said. "Six-thirty-four and counting."

Kimo rolled his eyes. "That'll look good on your tombstone. *'Still holding my breath, bitches'.*"

"Shipworms. That's all you saw when the wood came apart," Gail told him that afternoon. "They're called shipworms."

Danny didn't know whether to be fascinated or appalled. A whale, he could wrap his brain around that. Those aquatic grubs were something new.

"Shipworms. That's actually a thing?"

"For someone who's eaten as many waves as you have, your sense of maritime history really is lacking." She gave him a peck on the cheek, as if to say she loved him anyway. "Yeah, they're a thing. In the age of sailing ships, before steel hulls, they were a big, bad, serious thing. Termites of the sea, is the best way to describe them. If they weren't busy eating shipwrecks, they were causing them. Or chewing through wharves, piers, anything like that. Waiting for a nice juicy log to drift by, to turn into a floating condo."

Your home is your food—pretty much the definition of a parasite. Like taking a gander around this cliff-top cottage and thinking, hey, break me off a piece of that wall, I'm feeling peckish. What am I in the mood for? The green room, the blue room? Something in the line of a honey-gold breakfast nook? Yum.

"But they're not actually worms. They're mollusks. Like long, skinny oysters. They've got little shells on the front, that's how they burrow in." She perked up. "If you dive that wreck again, bring up a few. They're supposed to taste like clams."

"That's a bucket of nope, right there." His stomach did barrel rolls at the thought. "How do you know this? You don't even sail."

This was the distinction between them. For all her astonishing symbiosis with the sea, Gail hardly ever got out on it. That was his department. Gail was perfectly happy being its next-door neighbour.

She crossed her arms and, with a cockeyed grin, withered him with a glance. He knew how to translate that look: *Come with me, you fool.*

With a swirl of her skirt, she led him out of the cottage and across the stone path to the outbuilding—her workshop, bright and airy and open to clear out the smell of varnish. Its walls were the colour of sea-foam, its windows faced a panoramic view of the Pacific, and it was always, always, full of driftwood. Most of the pieces were still raw, just as they had been harvested from the beach. The rest were in various stages of processing and transformation.

Every chunk she brought in was its own starter kit, anything from simple projects like necklace racks to elaborate constructions like lamp-stands and chandeliers, that she sold through galleries from Portland to Santa Barbara. Last year, she'd taken hundreds of seemingly useless fragments and, where anyone else might have seen only kindling, turned them into a mosaic of a whimsical octopus, with spiral seashells for eyes.

Gail snatched up a sun-bleached branch the length of his arm, peppered with perforations as if someone had used it for target practice.

"After almost twenty years of seeing me do this, you've never wondered where these holes come from?"

"I guess I thought it was weathering." By her sceptical look, she wasn't buying it. "Okay, I guess I never thought about it at all."

She gave him one of those shakes of her head, playful but dismissive, that left him feeling she had so much more wisdom that he did, baked-in from birth. "If it doesn't eat the surfboard out from under you, it doesn't exist, right?"

"Pretty much," he conceded.

As a rule, ignorance was no virtue, but if you gave too much thought to the sea, and everything with teeth that called it home, you'd never venture out to meet it.

Maybe that was why she stayed on shore.

They grilled on the patio that evening, marinated tempeh and vegetables, and as they usually did unless the rain had other ideas, carried their plates out to the wrought-iron table on the little redwood deck, so they could eat beneath the sky, facing the sea. The cottage was one of a haphazard nest of six, perched near the edge of a two-hundred-foot cliff overlooking the beach and breakers below.

Bellies full, they kicked their feet up on the brick retaining wall around the fire-pit and passed the evening's joint back and forth.

Danny wanted to say he liked it better living at the condo in Santa Monica and Gail liked it better here, but that wasn't true. Santa Monica was only more convenient. He liked it better here, too. Time passed differently here, the days longer, the seasons more pronounced. On the luckiest nights he might awaken to the faraway squeal of a passing whale—humpback, he supposed, the only kind he was aware of whose songs carried above water. He would roll over to find that Gail was already up, her silhouette framed by the bedroom window, where she sat as still as stone and listened for as long as it would last. They never got that in Santa Monica.

Although she was never farther away from him than she was in those minutes, lost inside a trance, and there was little he could do to get her back but wait.

Anyway. Out with it. He'd been meaning to bring it up for months. Now felt as right as ever.

"I'm going to have to find a business to go into. Or invent." Telling the water but for Gail's ears. "Got any suggestions?"

She looked more concerned with diagnosing causes. "Is it the . . . ?"

Fear? That wasn't it, but it made sense she would go there. They'd had to give the topic a couple of airings after his wipe-out this spring at Prevelly Park.

The bigger the wave, the more ways a ride could go wrong. Miscalculations, human error, the never predictable hydraulics of any given wave—however it happened, things went wrong. While you went shooting through the tube, the board got sucked up the wall of water curling over behind you. Or the wave rose up while the bottom dropped out, and you got slammed into the impact zone. You were no longer riding the wave. It was riding you, maybe grinding you into the sand and rocks to really teach you a lesson.

He knew of no greater helplessness than that. Being held under by the first wave was terror enough. It you were still down when the next one came crashing in, you felt exponentially worse, battered and exhausted and desperate to breathe. Still hadn't surfaced before a third one came along? That was when it seemed as though the ocean had made up its unfathomable mind: it wasn't letting go.

He'd known a couple guys who hadn't come up alive. But he had. No idea how, but after a three-wave hold-down at Prevelly Park, he had. *The ocean doesn't want me today . . .* it was as good an explanation as any.

But one day, it might. It was the reason he'd taken up free-diving. To extend his breath-holding duration. To get comfortable with being under the water a long time, because as a surfer, *under* was the last place anyone wanted to be. And it had helped. He felt recalibrated, more at peace with *under* than ever.

So no. This had nothing to do with fear.

"It's worse," he said. "It's the calendar. And the numbers."

Gail had been holding back a toke, and lost it with a hacking laugh. "I thought it would be at least another twenty years before maybe I'd hear you make a concession there." She fixed him with a hazy leer. "Who are you, foul thing that crawled from the sea, and give me back my Danny."

Which version? He was developing a nostalgic longing for the Danny Yukimura who seemed incapable of thinking about consequences.

Gail rubbed his arm. "It's just another birthday, but with a zero. Don't you know? Forty is the new eighteen, I think is what it's down to."

"That only helps if eighteen is the new as-yet-unborn." He took the joint, made it smoulder, handed it back. "It's the rankings. In the top thirty in the world, I've had a good run, but I've never gotten higher than twenty-two, and now I'm right back on that edge. The only place to go is down. That's how this goes. Especially now."

It was the times—thrilling to be around to witness them, but shitty when you were a casualty because you couldn't keep up. People were out there doing amazing things, unthinkable things, feats that had been considered impossible.

"There's something changing in the world . . ."

He traced it back to when Laird Hamilton had caught the Millennium Wave, in Teahup'po. Until then, nobody had ridden a sixty-foot wave. Nobody. It wasn't merely the height; it was the length, the girth, the colossal magnitude. Even Hamilton hadn't been planning on it. He got towed into the wave, then it rose a behemoth. As the tube collapsed behind him, everybody watching thought he was dead, until he came shooting up out of the spray.

A thing like that did something magical. It opened a doorway to unknown realms of potential. Eighty-footers? Ninety? Guys were riding them now.

It wasn't only surfers, either. Skateboarders, skiers, snowboarders—super-humans were popping up everywhere. Somebody does something that blows minds around the globe and everyone says, *damn, dude, that record's gonna stand for years*, then it doesn't even stand a season.

Something in the air, maybe. Something in the water.

He loved seeing it unfold in the world. It was a beautiful time to be alive. But it wasn't his arena anymore. He couldn't compete with that. Go big or go home? He *was* home. He just had no idea what to do next.

"So you launch your own line of boards. Or gear. Or both," Gail said. "Or you open up the Danny Yukimura School of Surfing, and turn into one of those cute old guys with the long white hair and wispy beard, but still a badass, and wait for people to come to you. Because they will."

He wanted to believe. Gail made it easy to believe.

Even if he still ached for more, and had no idea what it was.

Before the dawn, even before coffee, they made their way along the stairs that zigzagged down a cleft in the land from cliff-top to sea-level. The wooden steps were perpetually damp, even in summer, crowded over by trees so that the sun never reached them.

They nearly always had the shore to themselves when beach-walking this early, sharing it with at most a neighbour from above, out with a dog and a stick.

He knew of no place where dawn was more different from dusk than here, with the sun on the other side of the continent behind a 200-foot wall of rock and earth. Here, dawns were gradual and grey, a time of mist and fog. This morning the wind was up, sending ribbons of fine, dry sand skimming over the damp-packed plains of the beach. The surf rolled and pounded behind a veil, as if the sand were of one world and the water of another, and every sunrise it took the proper spell to bring them back together.

They wouldn't be going home empty-handed. They never did. The only variable was what Gail would find, and how long it would take after she shucked his hand and went on the hunt.

He'd never met anyone more suited to spend her life seaside. Not merely to live here, but thrive. She smelled of the sea, tasted of it. Even the ocean knew its own. The sea had recognised this about her as soon as Gail arrived for good, a couple years before they'd met.

She had grown up Midwestern, landlocked in every direction, but the farthest shores had always called her, from as early a time as she could remember. A week after her eighteenth birthday she made the 1500-mile trek west, one-way this time. A week after that, one morning's beach-walk set her up for years, when she came upon what appeared to be a peculiar yellowish rock, stone-like yet waxy, embedded in the sand.

Right away, she'd known it for what it really was: ambergris, a solidified lump of secretions from the belly of a sperm whale, nearly three pounds of it. No substance on earth was more prized by the makers of perfume, especially in France. It was illegal to sell in the States, though, so one impromptu trip to Canada later, she returned three pounds lighter, $140,000 heavier, and after making the down-payment on the cottage, had hardly left the ocean's side ever since.

Such a find had to be more than dumb luck. Gail had taken it not merely as a welcome, but as a blessing. *You're where you belong now. This is your home. It's always been your home. You just had to find your way back.*

The sea never stopped giving to her. Danny had never seen anything like it, the sheer reliability of it. Some days the swells didn't want to be surfed, and you had to accept that. But Gail and her walks along the shore, harvesting the ocean's cast-offs? She always came back with something, and the desire to see what she could make of it. Send her out beach-combing with ten other people, and there was a good chance she'd come back with more treasure than everyone else combined. He imagined salt-encrusted nymphs out in the surf, working on her behalf: *Look alive, mateys, it's her again! Heave to!*

This morning, the farther north they walked, the lighter the dawn became, as ahead of them, Neptune's Throne took shape out of the grey haze.

Neptune's Throne was all he'd ever heard anyone call it. It was an observation platform for surfers to watch the incoming, but whoever had built it hadn't made it particularly convenient. It was four solid, tree-trunk pillars driven deep into the sand, braced with crossbeams and supporting a planked deck just above head height. No steps. If you wanted to clamber onto it, you had to have either the upper body strength to pull yourself up, or friends to push you from below.

It had a back, like a gargantuan chair—a windbreak, he assumed, blocking what the cliffs didn't—two of the trunks joined above the platform with an X, which in turn supported a row of ragged planks that were shortest on the outside and rose to an imperial peak in the middle.

The deck was usually thatched, and at first glance the bristly edges gave it the look of something that belonged somewhere tropical. Kimo recalled more of Hawaii than he did, and said the thing reminded him of rough-hewn structures he'd seen in places tourists didn't get to: burial platforms, and shrines where fishermen laid offerings to the gods of the sea before heading out, or after rowing back in with their catch.

Keep looking at it, though, and the tropical impression faded, darkened. Danny wasn't sure why. Maybe it was the way the two front trunks topped out with the flared stumps of long-gone limbs as thick as the trunks themselves. Neither appeared shaped by hand, only weathered, yet each had the look of a skull that faced the sea, like the bones of a pair of malformed whales.

Who had first built the thing, and when—questions no one could answer. If their neighbour Felicia was to be believed, Neptune's Throne was older than he was, and her as well. Felicia had lived atop the cliff for fifty years, and claimed the structure was there when she and her husband moved in. Claimed, as well, she'd seen a photo dated decades earlier, from the time of the Great Depression, and it was standing then, too. Meaning none of today's throne could have been the original wood—it was too well maintained to have withstood over eighty years of weathering. But in the years he and Gail had been dividing their time between here and Santa Monica, he'd never seen anyone repair it... only use it.

When they passed by, Gail patted one of the grey-weathered anchor posts as if it were the leg of a friendly elephant. He lingered, fingertips tracing the little holes along the wood. He knew what they were now, but wasn't pleased about that, as if there were a chance he could probe far enough inside to find a tangle of worms that had learned how to live outside the sea.

In their present direction, north, they were nearing their terminus, where a point of land fit for a lighthouse curved around from the right and speared out into the waves. At the base of the wall ran a stream fed by tributaries that trickled down the hillsides, then joined and cut ever-changing channels in the sand before emptying into the sea.

It was here she found it, a still-wet chunk of driftwood the size of a truncated log, mired in the sand of a delta that might not be there tomorrow morning, erased by the tide and re-cut somewhere else.

Gail knelt. She scraped off sand and picked away rags of seaweed. "You want to do the honours, my strong guy?"

Danny wrestled it free of the beach's hold and stood it on end. It was lighter than it looked, would be lighter still after it dried. Regardless, he didn't relish the thought of lugging it two hundred feet up slick wooden stairs.

"Wow," she said after she'd had a longer look. "If I didn't know better, and maybe I don't, I'd say this was something that had already been carved."

They traded places, Gail holding it up while he stepped back for a view. She was right. It had a suggestion of form—human, or maybe he was biased that way. Still, working with the contours and curves of what remained, he could discern legs, pressed together and thickening into hips. A waist and sloping shoulders. A head. It would be unrecognisable without a head.

"The figurehead off a ship's prow, maybe?" He recalled yesterday's yacht, being gnawed to slivers on the ocean floor. Maybe not that boat in particular; a stray chunk of someone else's bad luck. The ocean was forever digesting the remains of bad luck and coughing up the pieces.

"A lot of figureheads were big-breasted women. Traditionally speaking." Beside it, Gail went ramrod-straight and perked up her chest, comparing. "If I squint just right, I can make out a couple of boobs." She looked him in the eye, squinty. "And if you say, 'But what about the wood,' I will murder you in your sleep."

She had him call heads or tails, then they took their places at either end and began to shuffle the thing home.

Two days later she found another one washed up half a mile to the south, longer by a few inches, but shaped almost identically. Two half-rotted figureheads on the same beach at the same time? Not likely. By now he was leaning towards dismissing it as a case of pareidolia, the tendency to see ships in clouds, the man in the moon, and Jesus on a burnt tortilla. Or making a face out of two holes, a bump, and a line.

Even so, lugging them home felt like carrying corpses, complete with grave-worms. The sodden outer wood sloughed and squished in his uncertain grip. Halfway up the cliff with the second one, his fingers broke through as if piercing a crust, and pulped an embedded shipworm as thick as a sausage. He nearly dropped the log and went down with it. The stairs were damp underfoot and slick with wet flora—treacherous for carrying this kind of load.

When Gail found the third one a few days later, he had no idea what to make of it. If pareidolia was simple pattern recognition, okay then, what sort of pattern was this? On the surface it seemed the same old relationship Gail had always had with the sea and the generosity of its tides. But it had never given her the same exact thing time after time. If it was going to do that, why not be *really* generous, and keep lobbing more lumps of ambergris at her.

She first left her finds outside on heavy racks to dry in the July sun, turning them every few hours like hot dogs on a grill. Then she moved them into her workshop, lined against one wall, standing in a row.

They'd turned pale now that they were dry, bleached by the elements and time. With the muck wiped off and the water-bloat gone, finer details emerged. The pieces all tapered and thickened the same way, with dual concavities that suggested eyes, and a nub that suggested a nose, and a crack against the grain for a mouth. They were just humanoid enough that Danny didn't like turning his back on them, as if they were shells that would break open and release some worse form gestating inside.

"Gotta be a simple explanation," Kimo told him on the boat while out on another free-diving trip. "Maybe they're something that fell off a cargo ship, some shipment of carvings that weren't very good to begin with. Or there's some asshole out here who lives on a boat, thinks he's an artist, more money than talent, and dumps his mistakes overboard when nothing turns out the way he wants. Whatever they were, now that they're washing up, they look that much worse."

"Incompetent artists," Danny said. "Really? That's your explanation."

"If you had a better one, you wouldn't have asked me what I thought."

Point taken. But the wobble in this theory was that nothing about any of these pieces appeared to have been carved. Danny had looked, and closely. No evidence of chisels, rasps, scrapers, drawknives. They showed no obvious signs of hand-tooling at all. Even the ends looked broken, not sawed. What was the likelihood that someone who couldn't turn out a carving that looked more than vaguely human was, nevertheless, skilled enough to keep everything smooth, free of facets.

"Erosion. Wear," Kimo said. "You ever see a jagged stone in a riverbed? Not me. Pick any rock, you don't know how it looked when it went in. You're just getting what's left."

And when Gail found another—number four, but who was counting?—Danny wasn't even surprised. Well, yes, he was. Not by the find, but by the irritation he felt at the news. How many of these things did she need, anyway? Just because they washed up, did that obligate her to accept every single one, bring them *all* home?

It wasn't like him to be resentful. But analyse it anyway. Things hadn't merely come easily for Gail. They came effortlessly. The ocean gave and never ran out. All she had to do was show up and take possession.

He'd been lucky to be able to make a decent living doing something he loved. But it had never come easily. It had taken thousands of hours of wave time to hone his skills. It had taken near-drownings, lacerations from coral, jellyfish stings, reef-rash, a staph infection, various sprains, two separate concussions when the board smacked him in the head . . . and that was before factoring in every competitor on the tours breathing down his neck, eager to take his ranking and sponsorships for themselves.

Worst of all, it was life with an expiration date. He couldn't keep doing it forever, and he was nearly there. He could feel the downward pull as surely as he felt it during a dive, after entering the Doorway to the Deep.

Gail, though, went on as ever, bringing up trinkets as though she were being wooed by the sea. The same sea that she claimed to love, but wouldn't go out on, not even with him.

As she began to spend more hours in her workshop than ever, he wondered if it was karmic payback. If this was what it had been like for her over two decades, forced to share him with a passion that consumed him, sent him around the world to wherever the waves were at their biggest and baddest: from Mavericks to Waimea Bay, from Tavarua to Padang Padang. Maybe that was the part that hadn't come easily for her.

But by the time the fifth figure turned up, even Gail seemed past taking any joy in it. Something about this was not right. It had never been quite right.

"This feels like a cat sometimes, bringing you its kills," she confessed in the workshop one evening. At the bank of windows, the sun dropped boiling-red into the cauldron of the sea. "It loves you. But it's love on a whole different wavelength."

He had no idea what to say to that. Along the north wall, the carvings seemed to be daring him to try. He was beginning to hate them. Whatever secret they knew, they weren't telling.

At the centre of the shop, a rectangular worktable, as stout and sturdy as a stage, held half a dozen pieces of driftwood in various stages of transformation—sculptures and a bonsai planter—none of which had progressed in three days. All Gail did now was come out and sit with them, seemingly stymied by the new arrivals that were piling up. As if they'd come to tell her that her work was at an end.

Her methods hadn't changed in all the time he'd loved her, across nineteen years of being together, seventeen of marriage. Each piece of driftwood she harvested merited its own staring contest, a still, silent interrogation during which she divined what it wanted to be, needed to be, in its new and resurrected life.

But these? These unblinking humanoids? Gail was treating them as if they were complete already, in no need of refinement. They didn't seem to be going anywhere. Like her, they were home.

"You know, we've done the seaside thing for more than half our lives," he said. "If I'll be retiring soon anyway, maybe we should give mountains a try."

She almost laughed. "Lie awake at night listening for elk? I don't know if that would work or not."

She turned at the window and faced the rolling waters. He followed her gaze in case there was something to see, but if there was, only Gail could see it.

"Did you ever hear about the 52-hertz whale?" she said.

He hadn't.

"It's the saddest thing ever. Researchers have been picking it up on hydrophones for years. It's only ever been heard, never seen." She was still facing the window, as if telling the ocean, and he was just around to eavesdrop. "This whale, this one single whale, that sings at a higher frequency than all the others. Fifty-two hertz. All the usual suspects—blue whales, fin whales, like that—they're down around fifteen or twenty or thirty. So nobody even knows what kind of whale this is. All they know is that it just keeps roaming the Pacific, calling out, singing its song, and nothing else is answering."

She turned her back to the window, facing him again.

"Better keep your mountains. I don't think I could handle that with an elk. They'll come right up in your front yard."

He left her to it—all of it, the worm-eaten pieces of wood and the stalled magic she wielded over them—and traded the workshop for twilight. Out here on the grass, the fifth refugee carving remained wedged in its drying rack. Horizontal, it looked helpless. As he stepped closer, Danny wondered how she would react if he dragged it towards the setting sun and threw it off the cliff.

He hadn't given this one a second look since it was cleaned off, and mostly dry. What would've been the point? They were all the same, more or less.

Except this one... wasn't.

He dared to touch it, to run his hand over what had been obscured before, and was still barely visible: a faint impression scored around it, near the bottom end, like the groove on a finger after taking off a wedding ring, tattooed with a trace of rust.

No way, he thought. This whole time, assuming these had started out as ordinary logs, when they were nothing of the sort. *No way.*

The great thing about Kimo was that there was almost nothing he wouldn't drop at a moment's notice to take his boat out. He'd saved the GPS co-ordinates of the sunken yacht, so even after three weeks it was easy to find again. Once Danny was in the water, Kimo waved the coil of rope before tossing it over the side.

"I'm giving you a longer leash, so leave it on. If you touch the lanyard this time I'm going to break your arm."

"Yes, Mom." Danny huffed wind to saturate himself, filled up, locked it in, then ducked and plunged.

By now he'd traded his frogman flippers for a monofin. Kimo called it his mermaid ass. It fitted over both feet and forced his legs to move together, scything the water like a whale's flukes to turbocharge each kick. It made the hardest part of the dive easier, if no faster; he could equalise the pressure in his head only so quickly. But it took less energy to power downwards, dolphin-kicking, and to manoeuvre around once he got below neutral buoyancy, and that was what mattered.

Seventy-six feet down, the wreck waited in the hushed indigo haze, still tipped onto its starboard side with its mast jutting down into the ooze. And if the boat still unnerved him, helpless, disintegrating in a grave of silt and mud, it was at least familiar now. He knew it was pointless to check the prow for a figurehead but felt compelled to do it anyway, and of course there was no evidence of one ever having been there.

He turned onto his side and swam parallel to the sea floor, really mermaiding it now, cruising the length of the deck from bow to stern, inspecting the damage and the rot. He was gliding back the opposite way when it struck him: he'd been so focussed on the small details that he had missed the big obvious one right in front of him.

He'd been looking for a hole ripped in the deck, or a broken stump, evidence of a missing mast. He'd been looking over what remained for signs of mast hoops, iron reinforcements especially, that might have chafed a groove of rust and wear around the bottom of its mast in the push and pull of the currents.

And they were there.

It was only when he took in the big picture that he realised: three weeks ago the wreck had *two* masts, angled down towards the sediment. Now there was only one, the foremast.

There appeared to have been three, total. Masts detached from wrecked ships, sure, it happened. *But where were they now?* No telling how long the rearward mizzen had been gone. But within the past twenty-two days, the main mast shouldn't have gotten far.

Shouldn't. But had.

He feared he could guess where thirty-plus feet of them might have ended up. Where, but not how. There was no *how* he could imagine. There was no how he *wanted* to imagine. There was only his quickening heart and the hunger to breathe and the air above the waves.

He surfaced and plunged, surfaced and plunged again, like a pearl diver looking for a prize too big to be misplaced. He widened his search to the limits of his safety-line, and still it wasn't enough. Looking out towards deeper waters, beyond the spot where he'd caught that glimpse of the whale emerging through the dim blue, he saw how the sea floor sloped away, and that down the incline, some indistinct patch of shadow waited. A trick of light would waver. This didn't waver.

"We need to move," he told Kimo the next time he surfaced. "Forty or fifty yards that way."

Never thought he'd see Kimo balk at piloting the boat. "Dude. You've had a month of downtime since the Corona Open. Is this really how you want to spend your final days of it, instead of getting your mind on the Billabong Pro?"

Treading water, spitting salt: "Yeah. It is. It helps. Everything helps."

"What's so special about fifty yards that way?"

"Because I'm ready for it."

Kimo made the move, grumbling, but insisted on doing a sonar reading of the bottom. Ninety-four feet—Danny had never dived that far. Not a huge leap from last week's new personal best of eighty-three, but still, it meant more pressure and another twenty-two feet of round-trip. This was not insignificant.

He went anyway. Deeper, bluer, colder, darker. He relaxed into the squeeze, welcoming it like an embrace.

From above and to the side, he couldn't yet tell what was waiting below. Submerged another eighteen feet lower than the yacht, even less light reached his target zone. But it was more than that. The water looked cloudier here, too. As his vision acclimated to the gloom, he could make out what appeared to be a slab on the sea floor, three times the width of a car, furred with growth and set in the midst of a forest of bull kelp. Their stalks swayed with the currents, their fronds wavering like pennants in a breeze.

The further he sank and the closer he drifted, the less natural the slab looked, like a mound of sand and mud and stones scraped into a heap and packed together with intent. For no reason he wanted to explore, its flatness and order—its look of *purpose*—

reminded him of the worktable in Gail's shop. Again he was overcome with the uneasy sense of facing something out of place, lost from above and drowned without pity.

Because rising from the mound was a grove of logs, eight of them, seemingly jammed into the muck to hold them in place. Their tops were ragged, splintered, a sight that nearly locked his mind. He could imagine no force in the sea that could take a ship's mast and break it up this orderly way, or would even want to.

Around each piece, a thrashing cloud of motion churned and blurred the water. By now he knew a shipworm on sight. Even at their most normal they still filled him with loathing, but he didn't think they were supposed to behave like this, hundreds of them visible, like hagfish burrowed into the side of a decomposing whale. They streamed over the wood with the furious energy of a feeding frenzy.

The dread crept in cold, from the outer dark. This was something no one was meant to see. Ever. A hiker would feel this way, stumbling across the half-eaten carcass of a mule deer, then smelling the musk and carrion scent of the returning grizzly.

Danny flicked his fin to drift close enough to see the hard little shells on the worms' heads, scouring the wood, shaping it as surely as rasps and chisels and lathes.

He recognised the human form gnawed free from the lengths of mast. Anyone would.

He knew their contours. He'd lugged their predecessors up from the beach five times already.

And amongst the three that appeared farthest along, he recognised the face taking shape out of the grain. He had loved it for the past nineteen years.

Danny tried to will the sight away as an illusion born of low light and a brain hungry for oxygen. But it wouldn't resolve into anything else. He pinched off a half-dozen of the worms, fat and lashing, and flung them to the silt so he could caress his hand along the fresh-carved visage. Even blind, in the dark of an infinite abyss, he would know that cheekbone, that nose, that jaw-line, that hollow at the throat.

Already, the worms he'd dropped were wriggling back up to her face, to dig back in and resume their task. Mindless, they seemed to obey a directive he couldn't begin to fathom. But if something out here was capable of snapping a ship's mast into pieces like a pencil, then maybe it followed that it had workers, drones subjugated by the kind of group-mind that turned a school of fish in perfect unison.

There was no *why* he wanted to imagine, either.

Five above, eight down here, and who knew how many more might be drifting unfinished somewhere between. In revulsion, in the grip of something he felt but couldn't name, he gave the foremost effigy a shove to send it toppling back, pulling free of the muck and thunking into another behind it, then a third gave way, a slow chain reaction that disturbed the silt, but the worms not at all.

Abruptly, his legs were yanked from beneath him and he was upside-down again, moving up and away, something reeling him in like a fish. He nearly panicked and lost the breath locked inside, until the tug on his ankle made sense. Kimo being Kimo again. He couldn't right himself under the tension, never enough slack to turn around. Rather than flail at the end of the rope, he relaxed and let it happen, until he broke the surface spewing bubbles and foam, and breathed with a violent gasp, once more a creature of land and air.

Kimo peered down from the boat as if expecting to see him floating motionless. Huh. Must have set another personal best without even realising.

"How long?" Danny said. Normal. He had to act normal.

"Seven minutes."

Seven? Whoa. He would never have guessed.

"I had to pull the plug. And yet ... you're fine."

"You sound disappointed about that."

"No. That part's good." Kimo shook his head—never again, never again. "You need to find somebody else to take you out for this, brother. All you do is scare the shit out of me."

Poor Kimo. Danny felt genuinely bad for him. Bad for them both.

Because it wouldn't have helped one bit to tell Kimo that, no, he wasn't fine. He hadn't come up fine at all.

Worse, he couldn't tell Gail, either. How was he supposed to convey a thing like this? *They're you. They're supposed to be you.* He couldn't even be sure how she would react—if she'd find it flattering, the best thing since ambergris, or if the balance would tip and this weird synergy between her and the sea would finally leave her spooked.

Once she picked up on the obvious, that something was bothering him, his only option was to lie. Had a bad dive. Burst a blood vessel in my nose. It happens.

All he could do was look ahead. Try to get her away for two weeks, inject some time and distance to break this encroaching spell, and leave whatever carvings might wash up next for someone else to find.

"Why don't you come with me to Tahiti, for the Billabong? It's been years."

"I know. But I should stay. I don't have the kind of work I can take with me."

She was hardly doing the work now. "It'll still be here when you get back. You might even get some new ideas there to bring home."

"Like tiki carvings? I went through my tiki phase years ago."

Oh. Right. She had.

He packed and planned and tried his best to make it sound enticing: seeing the Pacific from another side would do them good. This could be the last time he went there as a competitor. None of it seemed to quite get through.

"I know. I just like it here. There's something about here. Some people go their whole lives looking for the place they should be. I found my *here* a long time ago."

Even before she'd found him—Gail was too kind to say so, but it had to have crossed her mind. He was one more gift the sea had given her, the one thing it was most capable of taking back. That worried her. It had all along.

I love you. You've always been my anchor, she would tell him. *But it scares me what could happen if the anchor-chain ever broke.*

In that way of sounds, unusual enough to penetrate, familiar enough to not alarm, it wove its way into his dreams before teasing him awake. The dream dissolved at once, so he lay in the dark with the only thing left: the far, reverberant squeal of a whale rolling in across the water and floating up through the open window.

"Listen," he whispered, and reached over to give Gail a gentle shake. But her side of the bed was empty, a sure sign she was listening already.

She wasn't at the window, wasn't in the kitchen, wasn't in the bathroom or front room. He knew the feel of a house emptied of any other heartbeat than his own. Danny yanked on enough clothing to call himself decent, a T-shirt and shorts that felt backwards, then stumbled outside, but she wasn't on the deck, either.

The night was as bright as nights got... all moon and no clouds, and the sea a glittering expanse of silver-white and blue-black. It was the world. It was their entire world.

Braced against the redwood deck, he peered down at the beach. After a moment, his fingers gripped the rail with the same steadying ferocity as his toes gripped a surfboard. He felt every bit as much in motion, shooting through a rolling barrel that collapsed behind him.

From up here, he was so accustomed to the sight of Neptune's Throne that the high-backed platform was as familiar a fixture of the landscape as the ridge on which they lived. But now... now its shape was different, wrong. He couldn't see what, exactly, only that some hulking form occupied it, bulbous and enormous, wet enough and slick enough to catch the moonlight with an iridescent gleam.

To his left, a form no bigger than a person, traversed towards it, small and dark against the pale sands.

He heard it again, rebounding from the cliffs—the same high, rolling squall that had brought him awake, the forlorn cry he'd always taken for a passing whale, roaming the endless waters and calling out for what or who might answer.

Danny sprinted for the beach stairs, the zigzag flights up which he'd helped lug a lifetime's worth of the sea's gifts, clueless, never imagining what it might have wanted, or expected in return.

Pounding down the steps he was as good as blind, the moonlight trapped above the canopy of leaves that crowded up and over. Although he held the rail, heedless of the splinters he picked up along the way, he went tumbling before he knew what happened, something damp and slick skidding beneath his bare foot.

His leg torqued one way while the rest of him torqued another. If pain glowed, his knee could have lit the night. No wave had ever flung him more violently than this, than gravity and his own momentum. He juddered down the stairs, sometimes on his hip, sometimes on his rump, every hardwood step another bruise. When he thudded to a stop he had two flights left to go, and scooted the rest of the way on his ass.

Down on the beach he tried to stand but his knee wasn't having it. He tumbled to the sand, still warm from the day's sun. He crawled, striving to see through the pink haze of pain, first making out the moon-etched lines of the cliffs ahead, then below them, the suggestion of some lesser mountain that rose up and slouched back towards the sea.

Danny crawled until he found a line of dimples in the sand, footprints, unbroken and resolute. He followed them, dragging his useless leg behind him, hearing nothing but the wheeze of his breath and the crash and retreat of the waves.

He crawled until the pillars and planks of Neptune's Throne loomed above him, empty now, but darkened with water and draped with robes of seaweed, the air around it rich with a heavy musk of brine. The sand before it was churned to wet clumps and crooked furrows, as if between here and the water's edge the beach had been ploughed by some dragging thing, bristling with appendages, that had tried to walk but was never meant to move on land.

Alongside the disturbance, the line of her steps turned, veering towards the water. He followed these too, scrambling on both elbows and one good knee, until they were no longer dimples but true footprints pressed into the wet sand, heel and arch and five small toes.

He scurried ahead, frantic now, as step by step the prints began to change, the impression left by each toe deepening, as though dug by a hooked and spiny claw, with a growth of webbing in between. He followed them to the foaming lip of the sea, where he lost them, her last footprints erased as the water washed across and smoothed the sand blank again.

Still, he floundered onwards as the waves battered him head-on, stopping only when he was slapped across the face and shoulder by something solid, heavy as a wet blanket, that clung like a caul. Sputtering, he peeled it away, and when after the longest moments of his life he accepted what the tattered thing was, he had no idea what to do with it. He couldn't bring himself to pitch it away, couldn't think of any reason to keep holding on.

If Gail didn't need her skin anymore, then where on land or sea was it supposed to go?

Out past the breakers, beneath the moon, a gleaming bulbous dome submerged with an elephantine skronk that he felt ripple through the waves and shudder through the sand.

Then he was alone.

He knew the feel of a shore emptied of any other heartbeat than his own.

He retreated far enough to keep from choking, then rolled onto his back to face the stars, exhausted and sweating from the pain. The water surged in and out for a thousand cycles, and a thousand more.

In time he wondered which of the ligaments in his knee were in shreds. ACL, PCL, LCL, MCL...any and all. He surely had a motherfucker of a hamstring tear, as well. Whatever the damage, his career was done even sooner than expected.

By the time Danny was ready to move again, the sky had lightened to a formless grey. Fog had crept in across the waters, and with it a stinging drizzle of rain. His knee was swollen double and he couldn't bend his leg, but nothing much hurt by default anymore.

There was dawn enough for him to spy a familiar shape stranded in the channels where the sea met the freshwater stream from the cliffs. He made for it, mocking thing that it was...as complete a carving as he'd seen, even farther along than the ones sunk amid the kelp beds. Or maybe this was one of them, finished along the way.

He knew its shape, knew the face, the hands folded as if in prayer. But he knew nothing of the depicted changes wrought upon the rest of her: the thin, frilled slits at either side of her throat; the fins along each forearm and lower leg. But he did know, and had all along, that she'd smelled of the sea, and tasted of it, too, and that the ocean and its gods recognised their own.

Gail must have known, as well, somewhere inside. Must have cherished the sea even while living in fear that if she ever went out on it, she might not come back. It would never stop wanting her.

He had to admit that this carving—all of them—appeared to have been made with love. But love, as Gail had said, on a whole different wavelength.

He rolled the effigy back out into the surf, fighting the wishes of the waves, the most gruelling task he'd ever done. But it was still a log at heart. It floated. The first twenty yards from shore were the hardest, the next hundred a little easier. He clung to this new Gail until he could no longer push off the sandy bottom, then threw his good leg over and across, straddling it like a surfboard and paddling out to sea.

In time, the roar of the breakers faded behind him, until he was left with the quieter slop and splash of a calmer sea, as the dim sun rose over his shoulders and began to burn the fog away.

He paddled as far as he could, until he thought he might have just five more good, strong minutes left inside. The ocean yawned deep and dark beneath. He could still breathe, but with one leg, could he kick hard enough to overcome the air in his lungs? Could he reach that threshold that changed everything? He had to believe he could. Forty feet. He only had to make it another forty feet.

Two days ago, he'd spent seven minutes under, and it went like nothing. There had to be meaning in that. Super-humans were popping up everywhere, remember. Something in the air, something in the water. A beautiful time to be alive.

He rolled off the log and made the plunge.

He would find Gail again, or he wouldn't.
He, too, was ready for another way of life, or he wasn't.
The ocean would accept him. Or it wouldn't.
He could still be a part of it either way.

CAITLÍN R. KIERNAN

VIRGINIA STORY

C AITLÍN R. KIERNAN is a two-time recipient of both the World
Fantasy and World Horror awards, and has been nominated for
the Nebula, Shirley Jackson, Mythopoeic and British Fantasy awards.
Their critically acclaimed novels include *The Red Tree* and *The
Drowning Girl: A Memoir*, and their short fiction has been collected
in multiple collections, including *The Ape's Wife and Other Stories,
Dear Sweet Filthy World, The Dinosaur Tourist* and *The Very Best of
Caitlín R. Kiernan.*

Kiernan is also a vertebrate palaeontologist and is currently a
research associate at the McWane Science Center in Birmingham,
Alabama. Their accomplishments in that field include the discovery
and description of a new mosasaur, *Selmasaurus russelli*, studies on
mosasaur biostratigraphy, the discovery and description of the first
velociraptorinae dinosaur from the south-eastern United States, and,
mostly recently, co-authoring the description of a new fossil sea
turtle, *Asmodochelys parhami.*

"'Virginia Story' was inspired by one of my many long drives
between Alabama and Rhode Island," reveals the author.
"Specifically, a trip I made in the late winter of 2018. In the dead of
night the highway through the Appalachians becomes a surreal,
haunted place. It's easy to glimpse things at the side of the road that
aren't there. Rest stops and gas stations are oases of brilliance in the

wilderness of forest and rock and towns that have become all but ghost towns.

"This was, without a doubt, the best story I wrote in 2018, which, by the way, happened to be the same year I gave up on New England—a Southerner can only be cold and wet just so long—and moved back to Birmingam."

I'M SOMEWHERE WELL south and west of Roanoke, and I admit that I haven't been paying attention to the road signs. Driving since before dawn, since Baldwin County, Alabama, and here it is almost midnight now, and the wheels on the wet interstate sound like sleep. The rubber-on-asphalt drone is as surely a siren as any mermaid ever was, as any winged maiden luring sailors to their doom with pretty songs of paradise and pussy. I rub my eyes, rubbing back the sleep demons, and squint at oncoming headlights and reflective highway signs and at the pitchy Appalachian night. I turn the radio up a little louder, wondering when and how the rock station out of Knoxville became a country music station out of Richmond. I fish the last can of Red Bull from the cooler, pop the top, and grimace at the syrupy taste like carbonated SweeTarts. I'm thinking about maybe taking the next exit and getting a motel room when I see the tall girl walking along in the breakdown lane. She doesn't strike me as a hitchhiker, because she doesn't appear to be making any effort to get anyone to stop for her. She's just walking, head down, arms crossed. I pull over, anyway, because maybe she ran out of gas or had a flat or a broken fan belt or a leaky, busted radiator. Maybe she doesn't have a phone to call for a tow truck, or maybe her phone ran out of juice, or she can't get a signal. I pull over a little ways ahead of her, let the engine idle, and wait for her to catch up to me. After a moment or two she appears in the rear-view mirror, painted red and bloody in the brake lights. She pauses and stares at the car, and I think, just for a second, that she's going to back away, that she might even bolt. But then she steps around the rear-fender and raps on the passenger-side window with her knuckles, and I turn the radio down again, reach over and roll down the glass. Her hair's wet, so I know that she's been walking since sometime before the rain stopped, even if I can't clearly recall how long ago that was. An hour, half-an-hour? I ask if she needs a ride, and she frowns and glances back the way she's come, as if there's anything to see but darkness and the headlights of oncoming traffic. "Yeah," she says. "I guess I do, don't I?" She wants to know if I'm going as far as Harrisonburg, and I tell her that I'm going a lot farther than that, all the way to New York. "I only need to get to Harrisonburg," she says. "I don't need to go to New York." I tell her I can drop her off, no problem. She opens the door, but then hesitates, still gazing back down the wide asphalt ribbon of I-81. It's a rainy October night in the mountains, but she's only wearing a T-shirt and a hoodie and jeans. I ask her if she isn't cold, if she isn't half-frozen, and she shrugs and turns to face me again. The girl stares at me for what likely only seems like a long time before she slowly shakes her head and answers no, no she's fine, but thanks for stopping and am I sure it's no bother, taking her to Harrisonburg. "It's right there on the way," I reply, and she gets into the car. She brings the smell of the rain with her, and the smell of cigarettes and sweat. She fastens her seat belt, and that's when I realise that she isn't wearing any shoes, and that's also when I see that she's missing two fingers off her left hand, the middle and ring fingers. I switch on the heater, and she pulls the door shut and locks it. "I'm really not all that cold," she says, but then holds her hands up to the heat vent and rubs them together for warmth. Her remaining eight fingers are long and slender. Her nails are short and painted some dark colour, a very deep shade of red or maybe black or dark blue. Maybe purple. It's impossible to tell in the soft green glow from the dashboard. I check the rear-view mirror again, then put the car into gear and pull back out onto the interstate. "I'm Hannah," she tells me. I reply, "Nice to meet you, Hannah. I'm Margaret, but people usually call me Meg," and then I wonder immediately why I didn't simply tell her to call me Meg in the first place, why I bothered with Margaret at all. "Where you from, Meg?" she asks, and I ask if she means where was I born or where do I live, and she says that if they're different places, she guesses she means the latter. "I was born in Mobile," I tell her, "but I live in Manhattan. I've lived there almost nine years now." She asks if I was visiting home, if that's where I'm on my way back from, and I say yeah, it is. "I've never been to New York," she says. "I've never been to Mobile, either. Hell, most time it seems I've hardly been outta Wythe County, Virginia." Hannah stops rubbing her hands together and sits back, watching the night rushing past outside the car. She tells me she's sorry if she's getting the upholstery wet, and I tell her not to worry about it, and that if I had anything at all to give her to dry off with, I would. "I'm fine," she says. "The rain doesn't bother me, not usually." I tell her that my coat's in the backseat, if she's cold, and she repeats that she isn't. That she's fine, really. "Did you break down back there?" I ask, and she says no, she was just walking. I start to say something about her being barefoot, barefoot without a coat in October in the rain, but instead I say, "You weren't planning on walking all the way to Harrisonburg, I hope," and she says no, no she didn't guess that she had planned on that. "I have a sister," she says, "in Harrisonburg. I haven't seen her in a while." And then Hannah asks me what I do in New York City. I tell her that I teach at City College. She asks what I teach, and I tell her I'm an English lit professor. "So poems and Shakespeare and stuff," she says and almost smiles. "You don't want to hear about all that," I tell her, mostly because I don't want to talk about all that. I don't want to explain to her that I'm only adjunct faculty, and that I'll almost certainly be out of work in another six months or so, and then who knows what the fuck happens next, how maybe I'll be moving back to Mobile. How maybe I'll be waiting tables. "I wasn't ever any good at school," she tells me. "But I do like poetry." And then, despite myself, I say, "I don't teach poetry. I teach literary theory. The history of literary theory, actually." She says oh, well, she's doesn't know anything about that, and I tell her it's okay, neither does anyone else. "What's it like, New York City?" she asks. I don't reply right away. There's a semi truck coming up fast behind me, and I wait until it has roared and rumbled past my car and is a good fifty yards ahead of us before I answer her. I hate those trucks.

I have since before I learned to drive. Few things make me more nervous than being passed by a semi, especially on a rainy night, especially on wet roads. "It's very crowded," I say, finally. "And expensive. And loud." Hannah says that she's never actually been to a city, but that she's never wanted to, either. "I'd miss the mountains," she says. "I'd miss the trees." She asks if I like living in New York, and I tell her no, not really, so she asks why I moved there, all the way from Mobile, Alabama. "Well, when I was in high school, I thought I had to move away, far away, or I'd never amount to anything. And Manhattan seemed like exactly the sort of faraway place that one moves away to in order to amount to something. Manhattan or Boston or Chicago. Someplace like that. But I should have settled for Atlanta. If nothing else, I'd have saved a small fortune on gas." She asks if I ever think about going back home for good, and I tell her yeah, I think about that a lot, more and more it seems. She starts telling me about how she used to believe that she wanted to be a veterinarian, because her grandfather had been a veterinarian, the sort that looks after farm animals—cows and horses and pigs and such. I listen and try to guess how old she is, but I'm lousy at that sort of thing. She could be as young as nineteen or twenty, or she could be a lot older. There's something worn about her face that seems at odds with her eyes and her voice. "Problem is," she says, "I never really got along with animals, especially not with horses. I like them, but they don't much care for me. So, that kinda got in the way. And I wasn't any good at math or science neither, and apparently you need math and science to be a vet, so there was that, too." It's started raining again, and I switch on the windshield wipers. I glance at the clock and see that it's a quarter past twelve and I wonder how long it's going to take to make Harrisonburg, how much the rain will slow me down if it gets bad again. I'm already regretting picking the girl up. If I hadn't, I could have stopped somewhere and slept for a while, had a hot shower and breakfast, instead of enduring two or three hours of awkward small talk with a stranger. Should'a, could'a, would'a. I'm trying to think of something else to say, considering turning the radio back on, when Hannah says, "I don't mind you're a lesbian, by the way. I want you to know that."

For a moment, I'm a little too flustered to reply, and before I can get unflustered, she adds, "I saw your bumper sticker when you stopped for me back there. The rainbow bumper sticker, I mean. And I want you to know it doesn't matter to me, and that I didn't vote for him. I didn't vote for her, either. But I didn't vote for him. Just about everyone else I know did, but not me. Truth is, I didn't vote for anyone. I probably should have, but I didn't." And I'm still trying to think what to say, when Hannah asks, "Do you have a girlfriend in New York City?" Not anymore, I tell her. We pass a sign that lets me know its another seventy-two miles to Roanoke, and I begin wondering if maybe I could convincingly fake engine trouble, get off at the next exit with a motel, and let Hannah find someone else to drive her to Harrisonburg. "I don't mean to pry," she says, and then she brushes a few stray strands of damp hair from her eyes with the hand that has only three fingers. "I know it's hard, being different. I ain't queer, but I know what that's like. Anyway, I didn't mean to make you uncomfortable. People say I talk too much. People say I ask too many questions." I tell her not to worry about it, and that if I minded people knowing that I'm a lesbian, I probably wouldn't have put the sticker on my car. That's not what I'm thinking, but that's what I tell her. "I went to school with a gay girl," Hannah says. "Everyone said it was because she was too fat and none of the boys would want to go with her, and so she might as well like girls. But I know that was just folks being hateful. It amazes me how hateful folks can be. Sometimes, I think it's like in the Bible, when Lot couldn't find even ten good men in all of Sodom. Sometimes, I think that if I tried I couldn't find ten good people in the whole damn world, much less in Wythe County." I don't know what to say to that, so I wind up saying something insipid like how maybe people aren't as bad as you think, at least not all of them, maybe not even most of them—something like that—and Hannah gives me a tired, sort of pitying glance. It's the way you'd look at a kid who's still got a lot of suffering to do before they finally learn just how hard the world can be, and it makes me feel foolish, and it makes me wish all over again that I hadn't picked her up. She turns her head and stares out the windshield at the cold rain peppering the glass and the metronomic sweep of the wipers. "It's actually a pretty fucked up story, Lot and Sodom and all," she says, sort of (but not quite) changing the subject. I ask if she means because of Lot's wife being turned into a pillar of salt, and she says no, not that. Well, sure that, but not only because of that. "I mean how when the men of Sodom come to Lot's door and demand that he turn over the three strangers—the three angels who have come to warn him that God's going to destroy the city—how Lot offers up his two girls to try and make them go away. Lot knows perfectly well that the men at his door want to rape the strangers, and he's saying, no, you can't have them, but you *can* have my two virgin daughters and do with them whatever you please. And *this*, mind you, is the one good man that God could find in all of Sodom and all of Gomorrah." I tell her that I'd never heard that part of it, and I half-wonder if maybe she's making it up, but she tells me, "It's right there in the Book of Genesis. Anyone can see for themselves, but you won't hear it too often in the Sunday school lessons." And then she adds, with a faint air of authority, "I had an uncle who was a Pentecostal preacher, an uncle on my daddy's side." And who am I to argue. I haven't picked up a Bible since high school, and that was more years ago than I like to think about. "So, did Lot give the men his daughters?" I ask, and Hannah says no, no he didn't. "The angels blinded the men at Lot's door. And that was the end of that." Then she asks if I have a cigarette, and I tell her no, I don't smoke. "I know I should give it up," she says. "I know I never should have started to begin with, and I should give it up. I swear, it feels like just about everything I enjoy is bound to kill me, sooner or later." She folds down the sun visor and stares at her face reflected dimly in the little mirror. I start to tell her she can switch on the interior lights, so she can see better, when she sighs loudly and folds the visor up again. Hannah sits back and watches the rain. "I know you want to ask about my fingers," she says. "It's okay. You really don't need to pretend like you don't, like you aren't sitting there thinking about them, like you haven't even noticed they're missing." And she holds out her left hand, but I keep my eyes on the road. "To tell you the truth," I say, "I didn't figure it was any of my business." I can hear a faint tremble in my voice, but I'm not sure if that's because I'm embarrassed that Hannah has dared to call out my morbid curiosity, that she's perceptive enough to see it, or if it's because I'm angry that she's acting so presumptuous. "Hardly anyone ever comes right out and asks, but everyone wants to know," she says. "It's only natural, ain't it, wanting to know what happened when you see something like somebody missing two fingers?" The rain's coming down hard enough now that, even set on high, the wipers are having a hard time keeping up, and the water drums loudly on the windshield and the roof of the car. I know that if it doesn't slack off soon, I'll have to pull over again and wait it out, and I silently curse the sky and the night and whatever misguided bit of charity made me stop for the woman sitting next to me. "It's not like I'm ashamed of my hand," she says. "I hope that's not what you think, that I'm ashamed of it." I tell her no, that's not what I was thinking. That's not what I was thinking at all, and I sound defensive and hate myself for sounding defensive. "I just didn't think it was any of my business," I say again, and it comes out even less convincing than the first time I said it. "No, Meg, that's not it. You're just worried what I'd think of you if you were to ask, worried maybe it would make me uncomfortable and so I'd think less of you for having noticed my hand and for sitting there turning it over and over in your head, trying to imagine what it was took my fingers off. I know that's what it is, so you don't have to pretend. I don't think less of you. It's only human." I glance at her and see that she's watching me now and that she's still holding up her left hand. And I should just own up to my curiosity and agree with her, admit that she's right and that I'm no different from anyone else. But, for whatever reason, I don't want to give in and give her that satisfaction. And maybe she's right and it is because I want to believe I'm somehow above such things, that I'm too sensitive or conscientious or enlightened or what the fuck ever to have such a base reaction to another person's misfortune. Maybe it's exactly that. "I don't mind telling you," she says, and she lowers her arm, letting the diminished hand rest in her lap. And I want to say, *Honest to fuck, I'm a lot more worried about running off the road in this rain or getting sideswiped by a tractor-trailer truck than I am worried whatever it was happened to your hand.* But I don't. Instead, I tell her, "When I was a kid, I had a cousin lost a finger fixing a lawnmower." I'm not sure why. Maybe since it seems she's determined to tell me how she lost her fingers, me telling her about my cousin and the lawnmower amounts to some sort of fair trade. Tit for tat, an eye for an eye, a finger for a finger. I don't know. "Is that so?" she asks me, at least pretending to sound interested, and I nod and watch the road. "I guess he was lucky," I say, "that he didn't lose his whole hand." And Hannah says, "Some people are like that, just born lucky." Then she's quiet for a while, watching the rain and the dark, and I'm almost ready to believe that she's decided not to tell me how she lost her fingers after all, when she says, "I dropped out of school after tenth grade and married this guy who'd just come back from Iraq. Jimmy. Jim. Jim Byrd. I'd known him before he was deployed. We'd been friends a long time, and when he came back, well…he came back like a lot of guys come back. And I suppose I had it in my head how I was going to take care of him, save him, do something good with my life by being there for him after what he'd gone through. I was young. I still believed people could do that, save other people. I guess I was idealistic." We pass a sign that informs me there's still seventy-five miles left to go until Roanoke, and right after the mileage sign there's a doe crumpled in the gravel and weeds at the side of the interstate. The way its head's bent back, the way its skull is resting between its shoulder blades, I know the deer's neck is broken. It jumped out into the traffic, someone hit it—probably one of the semis barrelling along in the rain—and the impact broke the animal's neck. Its dead eyes are open wide, staring nowhere, waiting for a thoughtful crow or vulture to come along and peck them out. I try to put the sight out of my mind and concentrate on the road and Hannah's story. In the twelve hours or so since leaving Mobile, I've probably seen a dozen deer lying twisted and broken at the side of the road, at least a dozen, in various stages of dismemberment and decay. What's one more. "So it's not like he went to jail for it," Hannah says, "but he still couldn't hold down a job." I realise that I've missed something she's said, but I'm not about to ask her to repeat herself. "He got a pretty good job at the PepsiCo Gatorade plant, but that didn't last long at all. By then, he'd mostly traded the whiskey for meth. He swore it helped with the nightmares, but I always knew that was bullshit. Meth and oxy and I don't know what the hell else all he was taking." Hannah pauses and wipes at the condensation that's formed on the passenger-side window, rubbing at it with the heel of her good hand, but not doing much more than smearing the water around and around. She gives up and wipes her wet hand on her jeans. "After he got fired, he saw someone at the VA about the nightmares," she says, "but all the goddamn doctor did was put him on more drugs that made him even crazier. I should have left him, I guess. My momma tried to get me to leave him, and I should have listened. But I've always been better at talking than listening. Maybe that's one reason I couldn't really help Jimmy. Maybe he needed someone to listen more than he needed anything. Anyway, it wasn't too long after all that, after him getting fired, that he started in dreaming about wolves. Whatever else he'd been dreaming about before, the desert and his buddies getting blown up and little kids with bombs strapped to their chests—you know, war shit—well, those dreams stopped and it was just the wolves from then on." Another semi passes us, even though I'm doing the speed limit. "Wolves?" I ask, without actually having intended to say anything at all, and "Yeah," Hannah replies. "Wolves in the sand. And not just regular wolves, he said, but werewolves. He said the wolves were really women who'd lost babies in the fighting, and at night they became wolves and hunted American soldiers." I say, "I don't even think there are wolves in Iraq," and Hannah shrugs and tells me she wouldn't know and, besides, it's not like bad dreams have to make sense. She says, "It got so that's all he would talk about, when he talked, which he was doing less and less. I tried to talk about, well, just about anything else, but he'd always start in again on the wolves in the sand. Jimmy said that even when he was awake he could hear them. He said that they didn't howl like real wolves do, that instead they prayed and sang Muslim holy songs and called out the names of the men they were hunting. He'd say, 'God gave the wolves our names. The wolves were the instruments of God's vengeance.' Crazy shit like that. But I didn't leave him. Jesus, where the fuck was I even gonna go? Move back in with my momma and father-in-law? No thank you." Hannah stops talking long enough to cough and clear her throat, and I glance at the clock. It's almost a quarter past one. Hearing Hannah's story and seeing the dead deer, somehow the two have worked together to jog loose a memory of another rainy night, almost four years ago now, the night I saw a coyote in Central Park. It had never occurred to me that there could be coyotes in the park, or anywhere else in Manhattan. But there it was, regardless. I was taking a taxi back downtown from a dinner party in Harlem and the coyote dashed out in front of the cab somewhere along East Drive. It seemed painfully thin to me, and in the headlights, its eyes flashed red-gold. The cabbie cursed in Hindi, honked his horn, and the animal immediately vanished into the trees and underbrush. There had been something in the coyote's mouth, something small and limp and torn. Beside me, Hannah yawns and rubs at her eyes, and then she says, "Fuck, I feel like I haven't slept in a week." And then she rubs her eyes again. I'm pretty sure that Hannah's eyes are blue, a very pale blue, but in the dimness of the car, it's hard to be sure. I want to say that she doesn't have to tell me any more. Sitting there, I feel like I've been forced somehow into the role of voyeur, and it's making me a little angry and embarrassed. I've always been a private person, rarely sharing more than I have to, sometimes to the detriment of relationships with friends and lovers and family members. I'm starting to resent the way that Hannah has made me a captive audience to her personal tragedies and those of the man she married. I want to change the subject, and I'm trying to figure out how to do that tactfully, when she stops rubbing her eyes and continues. "One night," she says, "Jimmy came home from—shit, I don't know where he got off to most days, and I didn't really want to know. I rarely bothered to ask. But he was high as a kite and scared half to death. I don't think I'd ever seen anyone half as scared as he was that night. He told me the wolves had found him, that they'd followed him home, that they were waiting outside the house, waiting until we went to sleep." Hannah looks down at her hands lying in her lap, and then she covers her incomplete left hand with her whole right. "I was trying to get him to settle down, because he was starting to scare the shit out of me, too. I'd sort of gotten used to his being crazy and the things he'd say, but that night—it was a summer night, a night in July—he'd been so much worse than he'd ever been before. So, I'd been trying to get him to calm down, but that only made things worse. He hit me. He'd never done that before. I always swore I'd never stay with any man who hit me, and I never had. He slapped me hard enough to knock one of my front teeth loose. He didn't knock it out, but he knocked it loose. I tripped over a chair and wound up on the kitchen floor, and I was sitting there on the linoleum, with my ears ringing, trying to clear my head, when he told me that he knew what I was, that he'd known all along." She pauses, still looking down at her hands. She clears her throat again, then stares out the windshield at the rain. Despite myself, I ask her, "What did he mean by that, that he knew what you were," and Hannah laughs. It's a soft, dry, papery sort of a laugh. Brittle. Thin. It makes me wish I had kept my mouth shut. It makes me wish all over again that I hadn't stopped to pick her up, that I'd minded my own business, rather than trying to play the Good Samaritan. "He said he knew how I was one of the werewolves. That's what he meant, Meg. And then he went into the bedroom and got one of his hunting knives and came back to the kitchen with it. I think I told him he was crazy and that I was going to call the police if he didn't stop. If he didn't settle down. But Jimmy said he knew what I was, and he said what's more he could prove it." I realise that the rain's slacked off a little, and I switch the wipers back onto low. "Prove it how?" I ask her, and she replies, "Jimmy said there was a way, because even when the werewolves were women they still wore their fur on the inside. He said if you cut one of them open when they were pretending to be a woman, that's how you could be sure the woman was really a wolf. That's why he'd gotten his hunting knife out. He said he'd start with my hands, if I wouldn't admit to it, if I wouldn't own up to being one of the monsters that had followed him all the way back from overseas to get even for all the murdered children." And that's when I finally tell her I don't want to hear any more. That's when I ask her to please stop. And she does, and she apologises. She says, "I shouldn't ought to have started in on that. I know I shouldn't have. I hope I haven't upset you, not after you were good enough to stop and give me a ride." I tell her it's okay, that I'm not upset, but that I just don't want to hear any more. She asks if it's all right with me if she turns the radio on, and I say sure, go ahead. I don't mind. There's a Hank Williams, Jr. song on the country station out of Richmond, and she turns it up loud enough that I can't hear the rain anymore. After that, we don't really talk. I drive, and she listens to the radio. She dozes off somewhere after we pass the exit for Newbern, and I let her sleep. I glance at her, from time to time, wondering if the story I didn't let her finish is true or if it's nothing but a tale she's concocted to hide some far more ordinary explanation for what had happened to her hand. I wonder—if it *is* true—what happened to Jimmy, and why he didn't hurt her worse than he did. Maybe it was because he cut off those two fingers and saw there was only flesh and bone and blood, and he wasn't so out of his mind that it wasn't sufficient to stop him. I wonder if he's in prison or a mental hospital somewhere. But I decide it's easier not knowing for sure. I can live with the uncertainty, and, anyway, I suspect it's more likely Hannah lost her fingers in a car accident or to an infection from an untended cut or to just about anything but a husband who'd decided she was a vengeful Iraqi werewolf. It's just a little after 1:30 a.m. when we make it to Harrisonburg. I leave the interstate and pull up to the pumps at a Shell station. Hannah wakes up when I cut the engine, and she sits staring out at the bright glare of the LED lights shining down from the gas station's canopy. She asks if this is Harrisonburg, and I tell her yeah, that we're there, and she gets out and stands by the front of the car while I fill the tank. It's long since stopped raining, but the night is cold and damp, and she stomps her feet and rubs her hands up and down her bare arms. She's starting to shiver. I return the nozzle to the pump, screw the cap back down tight, and then I ask her if she's going to be okay, if she needs me to take her somewhere in town before I get back on the highway. "Thanks, but I can find a phone and call my sister," she says. "My sister's expecting me." I ask if there's anything else she needs, and I know that I'm feeling guilty for not having let her finish her story, for having interrupted her and cut her off like I did. Hannah tells me she's fine, and she thanks me for the ride, and she says that it was nice to meet me. "If I ever make it up to New York City," she says, and she smiles sleepily. "Sure," I say. "I'd be glad to show you the sights." And then she turns and walks away, heading for Shell's convenience store. She holds up her good right hand, shielding her eyes from the lights, and I think how I probably should have offered her my coat again. But I don't call her back. I wait until she's inside, and then I get back into my car and drive away. I make it a little ways past Wilkes-Barre, Pennsylvania, before sunrise, before I'm finally forced to admit that I'm too tired to safely go any further and decide to stop for breakfast. It's rainy again and foggy, and the overcast morning sky is the cold blue-grey colour of mould. Exiting the interstate, an animal darts out in front of my car, and I very nearly hit it. It might have only been a dog. It's hard to be sure, and I have no idea if there are coyotes in northern Pennsylvania. I'm pretty sure there haven't been any wolves for a very long time. But its startled eyes are bright in the headlights, shining like the sun off copper, like twin dabs of molten gold.

PETER BELL

THE VIRGIN MARY WELL

PETER BELL's second contribution to this volume of *Best New Horror* also comes from his Sarob Press collection, *Revenants & Maledictions: Ten Tales of the Uncanny*, the contents of which were mostly inspired by real places where the author had felt a nuance of what the Germans' call Unheimlich.

"'The Virgin Mary Well' draws upon the Isle of Man's profuse fairy lore and the presence, amidst lush eerie glens, of the many wells sacred to spirits long predating Christianity," he explains. "When I was a boy, it was still the custom to greet the fairies politely when crossing the bridge at Ballasalla."

Pulsis hinc phantasmaticis collusionibus
ac diabolicis insidiis
—Hope's *Holy Wells of England*

CURIOUSLY, THE WELL was identified on the one-inch map but not the two-and-a-half. The one-inch had belonged to his uncle, and possibly dated back to the 1930s. The other he had purchased only recently, part of a new "tourist series". One might have expected the newer map to be more accurate—but perhaps ancient wells were no longer deemed of interest to today's tourist; the new map preferred sporting features, with a smiling portrait on the cover of a cycling celebrity. Even his uncle's map was only of limited help, as it spread the words "Virgin Mary Well" across half an inch of page with no indication of its precise location: it could be anywhere in half-a-mile of woodland, hill and river meadow.

Norman was spending the week with his twelve-year-old daughter, Alice, at a holiday cottage at Ballasalla on the Isle of Man. The school vacations were the only chance he had to be with her. He was not sure it was proving a success. Alice, a quiet child given to self-absorption and bookish pursuits, was not the most enthusiastic walker. Admittedly, the humid August heat—rank and stifling in the woods, harsh and baking in the fields—was hardly suitable for their expedition that day.

They stood in a meadow of baled hay, its earthy odour heavy on the air. The field was encircled on three sides by a sharply-curving stream, an oxbow lake in the making, as he recalled from school lessons long ago; possibly, in high floods, it became such. Alice did not appear impressed at this exhibition of text-book geography.

Norman had rather hoped she might be inspired on this, their last day, by the prospect of discovering the well.

"Is it a wishing well?" she enquired

"That depends on what you wish for!" he declared brightly. "It's a Holy Well—Holy Wells are supposed to do good! Healing—that sort of thing!"

"Miracles, you mean?"

"Yes, I suppose that's one way of putting it. But some of these wells have water that does natural good—and so people said it was holy."

"I've heard horrible things live in wells on the Isle of Man," said Alice, unimpressed.

"Like what?" he asked.

"There's a goblin called the Glashtyn, a shape-shifter... And there's the Lhiannan-shee, a well-guardian—it means 'the Fairy Sweetheart'. A beautiful lady—but she's very dangerous."

"Where did you hear that?" he asked. His daughter's erudition sometimes surprised him.

"Oh, it's in a book at Molly's," she replied glibly. "I'll show it you later, if you like?"

Molly Quirk's Tea-room was situated in the old station at St. John's, where the Peel and Ramsey branches formerly divided from the Douglas line on the disused railway. The only remnant of a system once connecting the whole island was now the southern track to Port Erin, a bone-shaking ride behind a stuttering, smoking tank engine, patronised now only by hardier tourists and steam-railway enthusiasts. Molly's was popular with Alice because it contained a small bookshop.

"*All* wells have guardians," she affirmed, grimly.

"But *good* guardians," her father protested. "This one *must* be good, because it's dedicated to the Virgin Mary."

Alice pulled a face.

"Mrs. McManus at school says that anyone who worships the Virgin Mary is a heathen—she's a pagan goddess, really."

Norman had presumed that education enlightened children.

"That's only because Mrs. McManus is a Presbyterian. We should *respect* other religions, even if we don't agree with them."

Hot and bothered, they sat upon the bank and quaffed of their rapidly depleted water. On the far bank, wooded slopes plunged and crowded. Only a yellowing of the birches, a russet touch in the sycamores, broke the ubiquitous green gloom, presaging autumn's imminence. Here, where the sluggish stream turned on itself, was a stagnant creek choked with water lilies, marsh marigolds and a thicket of bulrushes. Insects skimmed the languid surface; a dipper darted back and forth; willows bowed as if to drink. It was a beguiling scene. Here, fauns might dance, Naiads step from the glistening waters, a hornéd figure play upon his pipes. A sudden, splashing commotion—squabbling mallards—startled them.

"Well, Alice!" he declared, eyeing her brooding countenance, "do you think we might see the Piper here, like in *The Wind in the Willows*? And young Portly, the otter?"

It was, in fact, the one episode in the book he loathed.

Alice regarded him, red-faced, a strand of sandy hair dangling over her perspiring brow.

"The Piper piped at the *Gates of Dawn*," she corrected. "Not on a horrible hot afternoon!...Where *is* this stupid well? I want to go to Molly's."

Norman looked over to the woody slopes. The Well must be over there on the other bank. Somehow, they had crossed without noticing to the wrong side of the stream. Though not wide, the stream was insufficiently narrow to jump and of a marshy, immeasurable depth. It had gone noon. The sultriness deterred further exploration.

"Okay," he replied. "Let's call it a day."

Wearily, they retraced their steps.

With every footstep the heat seemed to strengthen. A heavy gloom had surreptitiously possessed the sky; all lay in the grip of a terrible stillness. Only the flies were active, flitting from the dark water, surging over dried cowpats, buzzing round their heads. There were midges, too, insidiously itching. Thunder rumbled, and sporadic drops of rain began to fall, foretelling a downpour. Alice marched ahead in sombre silence.

Their path back up the hill felt harder and longer than before. Norman noticed that the stream ran through a steep declivity on the fringes of the wood, before descending to the meadows. When they reached the lane where they had left the car, the mystery of their unintended crossing of the stream was solved: it tumbled underneath the road through a narrow chasm. Shading trees and shrubs overhung the tiny bridge's parapet, almost wholly concealed. Its voice burbled in the depths, gentle with a strange melancholy, mingling with the *drip-drip-drip* of the overarching verdure. Such deep gorges were known on the island as "Fairy Glens"; some were reputed to be impenetrable, associated with all manner of weird legend and superstition. Peering over the parapet into its moss-girt abyss, where the waters chattered and chuckled invisibly beneath the ferns, one could easily imagine why.

They reached the car, running, just as the heavens opened, sheltering until the rain had eased, eating their packed lunch. Norman consulted his maps; confirming that the wood they had seen from the riverbank was that beside which they were now parked. Stag-headed firs and a monkey puzzle loomed above the canopy—the kind of grand trees the Victorians planted on their domains. Indeed, the maps suggested the presence in the wood of a substantial property. No doubt the well was on its land. The clearing where they were, he noticed, was the beginning of an abandoned, overgrown drive, a nettle-infested track that led between a pair of gateless sandstone pillars, almost hidden by ivy and bindweed.

The torrent ceased as suddenly as it had arrived. The skies were breaking, great shafts of sunlight sparkling through rents in the towering, silvery cloudbanks in Sistine Chapel splendour. Southward, the emerald slopes of South Barrule were emerging from the vapours. Norman opened the car door and made to step outside.

"Hey! I thought we were going to Molly's!"

"And so we are," he reassured, "but let's take a quick look down this track—five minutes! It might lead to the well."

"Huh! Five minutes!" grumbled Alice, following him nevertheless.

The track entered a glade of tall beeches, their silvery-wet boles shining in the sun. Soon, they were descending, plunging amidst rhododendrons that all but blocked the derelict path, edged with the remains of ornamental balustrades. At intervals, stone steps led down to side-paths, overwhelmed by briars. They crossed an arched bridge over a brook that fed the parent stream, which they could hear rushing and splashing deep within the woods. Eventually, they reached an open space—at least it had been before the shrubs encroached—an old formal garden, where shattered, lichen-clad statues lay recumbent beside tilting pedestals, or peered, hollow-eyed and gaunt-faced, from the shrubberies. Blue hydrangeas and bright orange clumps of montbretia thrived amid the desolation, sole survivors of the glory of the ancient days. Before them loomed a ruin that looked as if it had sprung from the pages of Mrs. Radcliffe. To a degree, the structure was intact, its façade still standing, though the roof had buckled, the windows gaped, and a lone chimney-stack lurched at a perilous angle. All in all, the impression was of a place abandoned to a slow, ineluctable decay.

"Five minutes are up!" announced Alice.

It was frustrating. Another half-hour or so, Norman thought, might well yield the secret site of the well. On the other hand, one could blunder around all day in this reverted wilderness; the cliché of the needle-in-the-haystack occurred to him.

And Alice was becoming impatient, arms akimbo, an angry expression on her face.

Suddenly, Alice stopped. They were at a little bridge, where an enticing side-track led further into the wood.

"Look!" she murmured. "Over there. I can see someone—a girl."

In a shady dell overtopped by slender birches, shimmering in the dancing sunbeams, they beheld a figure—a girl in her teens or early twenties. Her sandy hair blended with the glinting birches, as if painted into the scene by an artist seeking a figure for perspective in a romantic, bucolic landscape. In the dappled light, there was about her something ethereal, as one might expect of a spirit of the woods—Norman recalled W.H. Hudson's *Green Mansions*. The vapours of the fallen rain, the dripping, lambent foliage, the percolation of the sunlight, lent to the scene a touch of the fey.

"What do you think she's doing?" whispered Alice.

The girl was standing with her back to them, motionless but for a faint trembling. She wore a long, nondescript brown coat. Her hair hung loose over her shoulders, her head was bowed. She had, Norman thought, a disconsolate air, as of one weighed down with grief, perhaps seeking Nature's solace. He felt reluctant to disturb her. Equally, and it was difficult to say why, he felt a strong disinclination for their presence to be noticed. It was as if he beheld a scene that, by rights, he had no business to be beholding; and, yet, on any sensible analysis, there was hardly anything remarkable about someone meditating in a wood.

"I think she's crying," hissed Alice. "She looks so sad."

"No, no, Alice," he whispered, taking her hand. "That's not crying you can hear. It's only the sound of the stream—you know, as the poet says, the babbling brook?"

Silently, they departed, picking their wary way. Soon they were beyond sight of the dell.

Five minutes had lengthened to half-an-hour.

"Molly," he asked, "have you ever heard of a well round here called the Virgin Mary Well?"

He was sitting in the tea-room, eating a delicious home-made scone, while Alice browsed the bookshop.

Molly regarded him for a moment, slightly bemused. "Yes," she replied in her gently lilting Manx accent. "Now—it's a long time since I've heard anybody asking about that well..."

There was sufficient hesitation in her response to convey the impression that she had not so much struggled to recall a forgotten place, as pondered, and rejected, outright denial.

"Why do you ask?"

Norman spoke about the confusion of the maps, and their searching for it on their walk; he gave only an edited account of their explorations, nor did he mention the melancholy maid. He was loath to admit trespass in a community which closely guarded its privacy. There was restricted access on the island, and there were few rights of way over the countryside, unlike the English National Parks.

"Can anyone go there?" he asked.

Her reply confirmed his suspicions.

"Oh, no!" said Molly, "it's private. You need to speak to Mr. Farrer—it's on his land."

"Mr. Farrer?" he queried.

"Yes, he lives at White Lodge—you've just missed him, as a matter of fact."

A burly, bad-tempered man, attired in the Barbour outfit of the gentleman farmer, had rudely brushed past them as they stepped into the tea-room. It was not an encouraging prospect.

"It's part of the old Cronk-y-Voddy Estate," Molly continued, "it was divided up after the war. The well's on his side. He lives with his two daughters in one of the lodges."

So that explained the girl in the woods. "Cronk-y-Voddy?" he said.

"Yes," replied Molly, "Cronk-y-Voddy Hall has quite a history. It was built—oh, it must be nearly two hundred years ago. Then it was owned by a shipping merchant. The family had a lot of bad luck; it was not a happy place. In the war the Manx government took it over as a prisoner-of-war camp—their contribution to the war effort."

Molly's tone hardened to disapproval

"Italians! And they had the time of their lives—much better than fighting. They were allowed to *mingle*." She invested the word with such vitriol, Norman thought it best to enquire no further, dismissing it as an islander's parochial contempt for foreigners.

"Then, at the end of the war when they heard they had lost, they ran amok. Tore the place down! Started a fire! Smashed it up! That lovely old hall, it was gutted. Its tapestries, its paintings, its books—everything! The ruins are still there."

Norman managed to stop himself admitting they had been and seen them. "Fancy, after all this time!" he remarked.

"Oh, yes," said Molly, "there's a superstition here that a ruined house of ill-repute mustn't be demolished. You have to let it fall down of its own accord. Otherwise, you're colluding with the Devil's work."

Nowhere, he reflected, had they encountered such a wealth of superstition as on the island. Mrs. Kneen, whose farm cottage they were staying in, appeared to organise her life around a complicated set of arcane regulations, which he and Alice were meant to respect; including a solemn adjuration, each time they went out, that on passing the "Fairy Bridge" near Ballasalla they must declare "Good morning, fairies!" or other suitable greeting for the time of day. It had long been a source of amusement for he and Alice to cry out such affirmation, albeit in a manner which, if indeed the *Ferryshin* did hear, was more likely to invite reprobation than good fortune. Tradition here died hard—as in the case of the Manx parliament, the Tynwald, introduced by the Norsemen, presided over by a caste of authoritarian, robed figures, the Deemsters. Prominently displayed over Mrs. Kneen's fireplace was a portrait of her father, imperiously adorned in ruby silk and ermine, in his revered capacity as First Deemster of Man.

Molly bustled off to rinse the cups.

"Found it!" cried Alice, coming in from the shop. "The book I told you about!"

She clasped a large, colourful volume: *The Lore & Legend of Ellan Vannin* by Mrs. Irene McGlynn, President of the Ballymona Local History Society.

The book, published by a local printer, appeared too learned for a child, yet of a garish presentation with somewhat juvenile illustrations, purporting to represent the pantheon of strange creatures inhabiting the Isle of Man. The name W.B. Yeats caught his attention: there were several quotations, and the nature of Mrs. McGlynn's "research" became evident, being in the nature of a magpie-like assemblage of anecdotes culled from the usual sources: Professor John Rhŷs, A.E. Waite, Lewis Spence, and Evans Wentz's classic *The Fairy Faith in Celtic Countries.*

The *Ferryshin* assumed a bewildering variety of guises, inhabiting the vicinity of creeks, gullies, ponds, lakes, streams, swamps and wells, invariably performing some nefarious or spiteful purpose, or else offering good fortune on strictly contingent terms that, alas, few humans were smart enough to meet. Alice read out to him a passage: *"The tall well-guardian, usually feminine, was prone to emerge visibly and haunt a human being, therein partaking of the nature of the Lhiannan-shee."*

"Gosh! We've just been talking about you!" said Molly—ever a worrying welcome—when, one fine October morning later that year, Norman and Alice returned to the tea-room.

The old platforms were still draped in vermilion bandannas of nasturtium despite the lateness of the season. Again, they were staying at Mrs. Kneen's, and had duly paid their respects to the fickle guardians of the bridge. A visit to Molly Quirk's was *de rigeur* on this, their first day back since the summer. It was Alice's half-term.

Each time Norman met his daughter he noted how much she had changed since the previous vacation; this time, he thought, particularly so. She looked taller, lither, indeed quite graceful; and, with a

new pair of stylish spectacles, quite the scholar. This time there was
little need for persuasion regarding her interest in what he imagined
would have been the forgotten matter of the well. It appeared Mrs.
McGlynn's book had set a hare running, and Alice had developed
an curiosity concerning things antiquarian. Thus, when he hinted
they might renew their search, he was pleasantly surprised at her
enthusiasm. That it might involve trespass seemed to attract rather
than deter her.

"Don't mention anything to Molly," he had warned, as they
approached her café.

Yet it had been Molly who raised the subject.

Alice had vanished into the shop.

"Yes, I was just saying to my friend here," said Molly. "That's why
your name came up—you were asking last time about The Virgin
Mary Well? Here, have a look at this!"

"They've found it again," announced the middle-aged woman in
smart outdoor clothes finishing her tea, introduced as Mrs.
Dinwoodie. She handed him the parish news.

The paper contained an account of an excavation in September
on the Cronk-y-Voddy Estate by the Department of Archaeology
at Queens University, Belfast. The purpose had been to trace the
layout of a water system deployed at the Hall during the last war.
The excess number of residents—prisoners, guards, and estate-
workers—had proved too much for the existing supply from the
River Dhoo. Water diviners were hired to locate an ancient well.
The Virgin Mary Well, lost to local knowledge, was duly found.
Despite an unfavourable site and some awkwardness about the
gradient and flow, an ingenious network of pipes and pumps had
been installed to divert its waters to the Hall. Following the latter's
demise, the well had fallen back into oblivion, reclaimed by rampant
nature. The archaeologists had not only salvaged the old pipe system,
but found and cleared the old well. *The water system*, wrote the
project director, *afforded a telling insight into the technical ingenuity
induced by war, that regrettably disperses in complacent peacetime.*
Generous thanks were accorded to the landowner, Mr. John Farrer,
without whose generous support this exciting excavation would not

have been possible. It was a lot of fuss about old water-pipes, Norman reflected, but he was not an archaeologist.

More fascinating was the well. It struck him that, as the dig appeared on-going, two more wandering around the site was unlikely to provoke accusations of trespass. No doubt a generous sum had been paid to Mr. Farrer; the Barbour-clad gentleman they had brushed with had not looked the type averse to mercenary gain.

"Amazing!" Norman remarked. "So, the work's not finished?"

Molly looked at Mrs. Dinwoodie, and Mrs. Dinwoodie looked back at Molly.

"Oh, no," said Mrs. Dinwoodie, "I think not."

She did not sound sure. Her accent was Manx, but with a distinct timbre of English public school.

"Well," said Molly, pouring the coffee, "they're hoping to proceed— but I'm not sure it was ever a good idea."

Norman had the impression they knew more than they were saying.

At that moment Alice returned.

"Now, what is it you've got there, Alice?" Molly asked, glad he thought to change the topic.

Alice displayed her book, another by Irene McGlynn, equally flamboyant: *Manx Glens, Mystery and Mayhem.*

His daughter must have overheard their conversation.

"The Virgin Mary Well's in this book—about it being lost... Do you think it's where we saw the girl crying? Oh!..." She put her hand over her mouth.

Molly, evidently, had not heard, busy prattling to Mrs. Dinwoodie. But Mrs. Dinwoodie, who was standing, buttoning her coat, appeared to pause and stare at Alice.

They stayed a while longer, exchanging pleasantries with Molly, catching up on local gossip.

"Excuse me!" a voice called as they stepped out of the old station. It was Mrs. Dinwoodie; surprisingly, she was still there, seated in a green Range Rover. She beckoned them over. "I hope you don't mind me intruding," she said. "It was something your little girl said."

Alice's expression at this epithet was of one chafed. But she was soon in harmony with Mrs. Dinwoodie's tune.

Mrs. Dinwoodie asked her to describe the girl they had espied in Cronk-y-Voddy Woods.

"She had sandy hair," said Alice, "same length as mine, loose round her shoulders. Slim—like me. Young, but older than me. She was wearing a long brown coat."

Norman marvelled at his daughter's memory. When Mrs. Dinwoodie turned to him, as if for elaboration, he merely shrugged.

"Oh, yes," Alice added, "and she was crying."

She caught her father's eye: "And it was *not* the babbling brook!"

"Crying?" said Mrs. Dinwoodie, as if this fact were especially significant, then nodded sagely.

Then she questioned Alice extensively as to where precisely the girl had been seen.

"Hmm," she observed, as Alice gave directions worthy of a guide-book. "That's certainly Mr. Farrer's land. Think yourself lucky he didn't see you! A terrible man!"

Norman was beginning to wonder what all the mystery was all about.

"Oh!" he said dismissively, "it was probably one of Farrer's daughters."

Mrs. Dinwoodie shook her head.

"No, couldn't be. Farrer married late; his wife was twenty years younger. Divorced, of course—that kind of thing never lasts. No, his girls are little more than toddlers."

"Then who could it be?" he asked.

"A good question," Mrs. Dinwoodie replied briskly. What came next surprised him. "Look," she said, "how would you like to visit the well?... Hop in the car, I'll take you!"

Alice's eyes were all agog, and Norman readily fell in with a quest he had so long cherished.

"What about Farrer?" he asked, as the car drew away.

"Don't worry about him!" replied Mrs. Dinwoodie, "he's not home at present. I'm his neighbour; we own different halves of Cronk-y-Voddy woods; he's White Lodge, I'm Red Lodge. There's no fence, just a tangle of woodland. I'll take you down—you can see the well quite clearly now the archaeologists have been. Then we'll have a cup of tea in my house, okay?

Red Lodge was situated on the edge of the woods, a quarter-mile further on from the Hall's main entrance, where they had begun their act of summer trespass. The former gamekeeper's cottage rested tranquil in a golden glade of beech, backed by black pines. Their guide led them down a steep slope into the trees, glimmering in autumn glory, rendered more ethereal by a faint October mistiness.

The track plunged steeply over rough ground. Norman wished he was wearing Mrs. Dinwoodie's robust boots, as she tramped energetically ahead into the forest. At first, the aspect was wholly unfamiliar. It was Alice who noticed the gaunt silhouette of the ruined mansion, which they were approaching from a different direction to last time. The bright autumn sunshine shone through the skeleton of Cronk-y-Voddy Hall. The scene became more recognisable as they proceeded.

"That's where we saw her!" Alice suddenly cried.

They were on the cusp of a deep dell beneath glistening birches, peering down into it instead of viewing it from below. On the far side, the depredations of the archaeologists were all too evident: trenches and spoil-heaps following a zigzag route towards the Hall, a plethora of abandoned equipment and sections of the excavated water-pipe. They crossed the frontier into Farrer-land, stepping down through golden bracken and the rustling remains of last year's foxgloves, into the mysterious maiden's dell.

"You're absolutely sure this is where you saw her, Alice?" asked Mrs. Dinwoodie.

"Yes," Alice replied, "over there!"

They stepped through fading ferns into the dell. From the midst of the earth bubbled a spring, falling into a deep, black pool. The water gushed loudly, its churning spate glinting silver in the sunlight. The surrounding verdure had been stripped away, exposing a stone parapet around the edge, and an upright slab with a worn inscription.

All three gazed in silence.

It was a haunting, elegiac scene, touched with an eerie melancholy. The bubbling waters warbled with a strange timbre, now shrill, now low, now rising in plaintive crescendo, suffused, like a keening voice, with an ineffable pathos. Yet it was, withal, a terrible place, where the waters flowed from nothingness to nothingness, like the stream of time itself, plunging ineluctably towards the grim iniquity of oblivion.

It was Mrs. Dinwoodie who broke the spell.

"It is as I thought," she sighed, as if to herself. "Now I know I am not seeing things."

"Is she a ghost?" enquired Alice, wide-eyed.

"No, I don't think so, Alice," replied Mrs. Dinwoodie. "Just someone who shouldn't be here, that's all... I just wanted to make sure this was where you saw her. Now, come on! Tea-time!"

"So, what do you think of the Virgin Mary Well?" asked Mrs. Dinwoodie as they made their way back through the woods.

Norman voiced his thanks and expressed his fascination. Mrs. Dinwoodie expanded on the topic of Manx wells, which were numerous.

Alice was running on ahead, beating down last summer's foxgloves with a stick.

When she was out of earshot, Mrs. Dinwoodie turned to him: "We must have a word in private."

Norman regarded her, nonplussed.

"I'm not sure I want your daughter to hear what I have to say," she added.

"Oh, Alice is pretty thick-skinned!" he declared.

"Nevertheless..." Mrs. Dinwoodie spoke with finality.

A stratagem was devised, once tea had been served. Mrs. Dinwoodie possessed a frisky Jack Russell, Tipsy. Alice required no persuading to take the friendly dog upon its walk.

"Make sure you don't let her off the lead," she warned, "and don't go back into the woods. There's a good path round the other way; Tipsy will show you, it's her usual walk."

More tea was brewed, and Mrs. Dinwoodie told her tale.

"You know the history of Cronk-y-Voddy Hall?"

Norman summarised what Molly had told him.

"Yes," Mrs. Dinwoodie continued, "they had more freedom than you might expect. I suppose they thought it'd be hard to escape on an island. Some of them worked the estate: forestry and so on. You know about the fire and wrecking the house? What's less well known is that three of them, ringleaders they said, were shot.

"During the war my grandmother worked at the Hall. Towards the end, a sixteen-year-old girl came to work there. She got involved with one of the prisoners. They took to courting—if I might be so polite—secretly in the woods. I need not elaborate. In those days on the Isle of Man, to bear an illegitimate child was no trivial matter. So, the full force of our antediluvian customs fell upon the poor girl. She had to perform the penance prescribed by the Deemsters for such heinous sinners. She was required each Sunday to stand at the altar rail in a white sheet facing the congregation, though denied communion. Baptism was withheld until fostering was in place. Meanwhile, she had to perform all motherly duties, during which, of course, the bond was nurtured, making the eventual loss all the harder. It was made worse by the fact that the father, for whom she cherished a naïve love, imagining a future together after the war, was amongst those shot.

"Well, you can imagine the strain. One night, she disappeared, together with the baby. She was found wandering these woods—without the baby. It was suspected she had made away with the child. In the end, she confessed, though who knows what persuasion was applied—because she gave two conflicting accounts. At first, she said she had taken her child to the Virgin Mary Well for the baptism denied by the Church. There is a tradition that wells dedicated to the Virgin are effective for the baptism of illegitimate children—the obverse of a more sinister superstition that wells were used by the Fairy Folk to bless into their own world stolen, unbaptised infants. The baby, she said, had accidentally fallen into the well, but no body was found. But then she admitted she had left the baby beside the well overnight, which some say is required by the Virgin; and when she returned it was not her baby but a changeling, brown-skinned and deformed. It so filled her with terror that she threw the baby into the well and ran away.

"Of course, this led to criminal proceedings, and it was argued she was in sound mind when she perpetrated the crime. But this was rapidly overtaken by events. Somehow she escaped, and made her way back to the wood. They found her weeping at the well."

Norman yawned inwardly—*Alas poor ghost.* "So, she threw herself in and drowned?" he concluded.

Mrs. Dinwoodie looked vexed.

"No!" she responded shortly, "that might have been a blessing!... When they found her, she bore the expression of an imbecile and seemed not to know who she was. She passed the rest of her short life in a home for the incurably insane. Those who saw her said she was no longer the same person; that, as they say on the island about those who lose their wits, she had 'gone with the Lhiannan-shee.'"

Norman was at a loss what to say. Alice was familiar with far worse than Mrs. Dinwoodie's melodrama.

"So, does Molly know about all this?" he asked.

"Oh, yes," replied Mrs. Dinwoodie. "Margaret Quirk—that was the poor girl's name. She was Molly's elder sister."

She reached into a bureau and produced a photograph album, skimming through the sepia prints, showing him a group photograph on the platform of St. John's station, where a tiny locomotive billowed smoke; it showed a family outing. The small child in the foreground he recognised as Molly; behind, hands resting on her shoulders, was a smiling teenager, tall and slender, radiant with all the gladness of youth...

A shiver passed over Norman.

It was the very girl they had seen beside the well—before tribulation had bowed her.

"Understandably, Molly never speaks of it," continued Mrs. Dinwoodie. "I've never told her what I've seen. Nor must you. You're the only one I have told... It has been good to share it with someone... and to know I'm not going out of my mind..."

Norman was not sure quite how to respond; he did not believe in ghosts.

"How often have you... seen this girl?"

"Once, many years ago," she sighed, "when I was a child... and again, more recently—since they came and cleared the well."

"And, have the archaeologists... seen anything?"

Mrs. Dinwoodie paused.

"I really shouldn't be telling you this," she responded slowly, "it affects people other than me. It's all been hushed-up until they work out... well, what they think they've found. When they unearthed the sections of the old pipeline, they discovered bones inside—in fact, an almost complete skeleton of a baby... or so they surmised. It had curious deformities. The two girls on the dig who discovered it, students, were so horrified they downed tools and left right away. I heard that one of them, previous to the discovery, had voiced disquiet about that part of the woods, and claimed to have seen a ghostly figure crouching at the well.

"It's a wicked place. There were tales my grandmother told. We were never allowed near—in those days there was a fence. Mr. Farrer, who only arrived a few years ago, took it down, saying we'd annexed some of his territory. I advised him against the dig, but he never listens. I had hoped it was lost for good."

"Yet it's a Holy Well?" Norman mused. "The Virgin Mary Well. And you say it's wicked?"

Mrs. Dinwoodie smiled.

"A 19th century convention! They did it all the time to repel evil spirits—rename them Holy Wells, and perform some ceremony or other... Did you not see the Latin inscription at the well?"

Norman neither knew Latin, nor had he read the words.

"*Pulsis hinc phantasmaticis collusionibus ac diabolicis insidiis.* Do you know what that means? *Begone from this place spectres who collude with the Devil's snares*—or words to that effect. It's a banishing spell, an exorcism; they're not unusual. Its old name is *Chibber ny Ferrishyn*—the Fairy Well. But there's a still more ancient name: *Chibber yn Garey Dhoo*—Well of the Dark Wasteland."

They were disturbed by barking, sharp and agitated. Outside the window was the Jack Russell—but she was on her own; soon bounding into the house, seeking her mistress, growling.

"Something's troubling her," Mrs. Dinwoodie declared. "She's off the leash!... Where's Alice?"

There was no sign of his daughter, though they called her name many times.

"There's Tipsy's lead!" Mrs. Dinwoodie exclaimed, indicating a branch, where it had snagged, at the edge of the woods.

They rushed down the rough track through the trees, fleet as panicking gazelles, scrambling over tree roots and through the brambles, until they found themselves at the dell.

Norman breathed a sigh of relief.

There was Alice. She was standing with her back to them, gazing into the black, bubbling depths beneath the flickering, gilded glory of the birches. The misty sunlit vapours lent the scene a diaphanous unreality, and for a moment her figure coalesced in his mind with the vision of the strange girl in the woods. Slowly, she turned. Lean and lithe and languorous, she began to walk towards them.

"Holy Mother of God!" gasped Mrs. Dinwoodie.

Proudly, yet slightly sadly, Norman watched as his daughter approached, thinking again, as when he had met her at school, how much Alice was growing up. Yet, as she drew near, a disquietude possessed him, and the true import of Mrs. Dinwoodie's epithet became clear, for his daughter appeared, in some sinister way, transformed.

STEPHEN JONES & KIM NEWMAN

NECROLOGY: 2018

L ONG BEFORE COVID-19 spread its tentacles of death around the world, we were already losing far too many creative people who had made significant contributions to our field (or left their mark on popular culture and music in other, often fascinating, ways). Depressingly, 2018 was another record year for significant deaths in the genre. Along with a number of major authors and artists, we also saw the passing of several prominent science fiction legends and, once again, far too many good friends and colleagues...

AUTHORS/ARTISTS/COMPOSERS

Fred Bass, the owner of New York City's iconic Strand Bookstore, died of congestive heart failure on January 3, aged 89. The store was founded in 1927 by Bass' father with an investment of $600 (half of it borrowed). The store now stocks some 2.5 million titles and is the last survivor on a stretch of 4th Avenue, between 8th Street and 14th Street, that was known in the mid-20th century as "Book Row" and was home to more than thirty used bookstores. Bass left $25 million to his heirs in his will.

British-born author **Adrian Barnes**, whose novel *Nod* (2012) was nominated for the Arthur C. Clarke Award, died in Canada of an aggressive brain tumor on January 5, aged 54. His surreal second novel, *Satan à la Mode* (2015), was illustrated by Yuliya Kashapova.

British screenwriter **David Sherwin**[-White], who scripted the anarchic Lindsay Anderson films *If....*, *O Lucky Man!* and *Britannia Hospital*, died of sepsis on January 8, aged 75. He also worked (uncredited) on the script for *Venom* (1981). Sherwin's memoir, *Going Mad in Hollywood: And Life with Lindsay Anderson*, was published in 1996.

American comics editor **William "Bill" Harris**, who worked for Gold Key and King Comics in the 1960s, died the same day, aged 84. One of Harris' titles was Lee Falk's *The Phantom*, which he also scripted.

British TV scriptwriter **David Fisher** died on January 10, aged 88. Between 1978–80 he scripted the Tom Baker-era *Doctor Who* serials 'The Stones of Blood', 'The Androids of Tara', 'City of Death' (credited as "David Agnew" with Douglas Adams and Graham Williams), 'The Creature from the Pit' and 'The Leisure Hive', also novelising the last two. Fisher also wrote 'Guardian of the Abyss' for *Hammer House of Horror* and 'The Corvini Inheritance' and 'The Late Nancy Irving' for *Hammer House of Mystery and Suspense* (aka *Fox Mystery Theater*).

British-born journalist **John Francis Lane**, who was the Rome correspondent for *Films and Filming* magazine from its first issue in 1954 until the early 1980s, died in Italy on January 15, aged 89. Lane subsequently became a correspondent for *Screen International*. As an actor, he had small roles in a number of films, including *The Witch's Curse* (as "Francis Lane") and Fellini's *8½*.

British theatre writer and director **Bob Carlton**, who created the 1980s stage musical *Return to the Forbidden Planet*, died on January 18, aged 67. The show later transferred to London's West End and won the Olivier Award for Best New Musical in 1990.

American author **Julius Lester**, whose novels include *Time's Memory* and the YA fantasy *Cupid*, died the same day, aged 78. He also had a story in the 1982 anthology *Best-loved Folktales of the World*.

American music composer **John [Leonard] Morris** died on

January 21, aged 91. His many credits include the Mel Brooks movies *Young Frankenstein*, *High Anxiety* and *Spaceballs*, along with *The Adventure of Sherlock Holmes' Smarter Brother*, *Doctor Franken*, *The Elephant Man*, *The Electric Grandmother*, *The Doctor and the Devils*, *Clue*, *Haunted Honeymoon* and *Second Sight*.

American feminist fantasy and SF author, poet, critic, scholar and social commentator **Ursula K. Le Guin** (Ursula Kroeber) died on January 22, aged 88. In a career that spanned more than fifty years, she won five Hugo Awards, six Nebula Awards, a World Fantasy Life Achievement Award, the SFWA Grand Master Award and the Medal for Distinguished Contribution to American Letters. Le Guin began publishing science fiction in 1962, and her best-selling novels include *The Left Hand of Darkness*, *The Lathe of Heaven* (filmed in 1980 and 2002), *The Dispossesed* and *A Wizard of Earthsea* (plus many other titles in the series, which was adapted into a Japanese *anime* and a Sci Fi channel mini-series). Her short fiction has been collected in such books as *The Wind's Twelve Quarters*, *Buffalo Girls and Other Animal Presences*, *A Fisherman of the Inland Sea*, *Changing Planes* and two volumes of *The Unreal and the Real: Selected Stories*. Non-fiction publications include *From Elfland to Poughkeepsie*, *The Language of the Night*, *Dancing at the End of the World*, *The Wave in the Mind* and *No Time to Spare: Thinking About What Matters*, and Le Guin also edited the anthologies *Interfaces* and *Edges* (both with Virginia Kidd) and *The Norton Book of Science Fiction: North American Science Fiction 1960–1990* (with Brian Attebery).

American horror writer **Jack Ketchum** (Dallas William Mayr, aka "Jerzy Livingston"), blurbed by Stephen King as "the scariest guy in America" and "quite simply, one of the best in the business", died on January 24, aged 71. He had been battling cancer for some years. His often visceral novels include *Off Season*, *Hide and Seek*, *The Girl Next Door*, *Offspring*, *Road Kill*, *Stranglehold*, *Ladies' Night*, *The Lost*, *Red*, *The Woman* and *The Secret Life of Souls* (the latter two both with Lucky McKee), while his short fiction was collected in *The Exit at Toledo Blade Boulevard*, *Broken on the Wheel of Sex*, *Peaceable Kingdom* and *Gorilla in My Room*. He edited the 2006 anthology *Absinthe* with Tim Lebbon, and the movies *The Lost*, *The*

Girl Next Door, *Red*, *Offspring* and *The Woman* were all based on his work (with Ketchum scripting the last two). The winner of three HWA Bram Stoker Awards for his fiction, he was named World Horror Convention Grand Master in 2011 and received the Bram Stoker Award for Life Achievement in 2015.

Mark E. (Edward) **Smith**, the lead singer and songwriter with the British post-punk band the Fall, died of lung cancer the same day, aged 60. A fan of Arthur Machen, H.P. Lovecraft and M.R. James, Smith's lyrics often featured references to supernatural fiction, and his songs 'Hip Priest' and 'High Tension Line' could be heard in *The Silence of the Lambs* (1991) and a 2009 episode of TV's *Being Human*, respectively.

American poet **Wade Wellman** (Manly Wade Wellman, Jr.), who is credited with co-writing with his father Manly Wade Wellman the stories that were collected in *Sherlock Holmes's War of the Worlds* (1975), died on January 25. He was in his early eighties. Wellman's poetry appeared in such publications as *The Howard Collector*, *The Arkham Collector*, *Galaxy Magazine*, *Coven 13*, *Weirdbook* and the Arkham House anthology *Fire and Sleet and Candlelight*.

David Dean Oberhelman, a Professor of Library Service at the Edmon Low Library at Oklahoma State University, died after a short illness the same day, aged 52. For many years, he was the Mythopoeic Society's administrator for the Mythopoeic Fantasy and Mythopoeic Scholarship awards.

American gaming artist **William** [Todd] **O'Connor**, who worked on *Dungeons & Dragons* and *Magic: The Gathering*, along with other role-playing games, died on January 31, aged 47. He also did book covers, video games and concept art. O'Connor wrote a number of how-to books, including *Dracopedia: A Guide to Drawing the Dragons of the World* and *Dracopedia Legends: An Artist's Guide to Drawing Dragons of Folklore*.

American comic book writer and editor **Don J. Arneson** died on February 1, aged 82. In the early 1960s he went to work at Dell Comics and soon found himself promoted to editor-in-chief. With little or no budget for writers, "Don" Arneson soon started scripting the comics himself, including the superhero versions of Frankenstein,

Dracula and the Werewolf. While at Dell, Arneson and artist Tony Tallarico are credited with creating the first American comic book to star a black protagonist, although *Lobo*, about the eponymous gunslinger in the Old West, only lasted for two issues. He also began moonlighting for other companies, such as Charlton (on *Ghostly Tales*, sometimes as "Norm DiPluhm"), Tower and Gold Key/Western Publishing (where he scripted issues *Dark Shdows* and *Grimm's Ghost Stories*). Arneson left Dell around the end of the 1960s and later worked on some of DC's ghost titles.

American comics writer **Michael** [Lawrence] **Fleisher** died of complications from Alzheimer's disease on February 2, aged 75. He wrote three volumes of *The Encyclopedia of Comic Book Heroes* (1976–78, with five further volumes planned) and began working for DC Comics in the early 1970s as Joe Orlando's assistant editor, writing such titles as *Secrets of Sinister House, House of Mystery, House of Secrets, The Witching Hour, Phantom Stranger* and *Forbidden Tales of Dark Mansion*, often in collaboration with other writers. After scripting the Steve Ditko-created series *Shade, the Changing Man* (1977–78) and contributing to the Batman mythos, Fleisher was promoted to editor at DC, where he controversially revived the 1940s character "The Spectre" in *Adventure Comics* with artist Jim Apro. He also took over "Jonah Hex" in *Weird Western Tales* and, later, in the character's own self-titled comic. He also worked for Atlas/Seaboard (*The Grim Ghost, Morlock* and *Weird Suspense featuring The Tarantula*), Marvel Comics (*Ghost Rider, Man-Thing, Savage Sword of Conan* and *Star Trek*), Warren Publishing (*Creepy, Eerie* and *Vampirella*) and *2000AD* ('Rogue Trooper'). In response to a typically outspoken interview with Harlan Ellison in a 1979 issue of *The Comics Journal*, Fleisher filed a $2 million libel suit against both the author and the publisher over his novel *Chasing Hairy*, which he subsequently lost. Paul Levitz, the former president of DC Comics, described him as "One of the most professional writers of his time".

American-born author **David F.** (Francis) **Case** died after a short illness in London on February 3, aged 80. The author of an estimated 300 books or more under various pseudonyms, he was a regular contributor (with reprints) to the legendary *Pan Book of Horror Stories* during the early 1970s, and his stories were collected in *The Cell: Three Tales of Terror* (aka *The Cell and Other Tales of Horror*), *Fengriffen and Other Stories*, *Brotherly Love & Other Tales of Faith and Knowledge*, *Pelican Cay and Other Disquieting Tales*, *Masters of the Weird Tale: David Case*, *Fengriffen & Other Gothic Tales* and *The Cell & Transmorphic Tales*. Case's novels include *Beast of Shame* (as "Don Holliday"), *Wolf Tracks* and *The Third Grave*, published by Arkham House. His short stories 'Fengriffin' and 'The Hunter' were filmed as, respectively, *—And Now the Screaming Starts!* (starring Peter Cushing) and *Scream of the Wolf*. Case was a Guest of Honour at the 2010 World Horror Convention held in Brighton, England, and his story 'Jimmy' appeared in *Best New Horror* #11.

British video game designer **Hugh Hancock** died of a heart attack on February 5, aged 40. With Anthony Bailey he coined the term "machinima" (a combination of "machine" and "cinema") to describe ultra-realistic computer graphics and animation. In 1999 Hancock co-founded Strange Company with Gordon McDonald to develop VR games and, in 2000, the Machinima.com online hub. Strange Company released its first feature-length film, *BloodSpell*, in fourteen episodes in 2006.

American author and lecturer **John Anthony West** died on February 6, aged 85. During the 1960s he published short stories in *Shock: The Magazine of Terrifying Tales* and *The Magazine of Fantasy and Science Fiction*, and he later contributed to *Omni* and the anthology *A Shocking Thing* edited by Damon Knight. In 1961 he published the collection *Call Out the Malicia: Short Stories*, and he also wrote a number of non-fiction books about Ancient Egypt.

American book cover artist **Robert Bonfils** died on February 8, aged 95. During the 1960s, he was reportedly producing around fifty covers every month, mostly for sex-novel paperbacks from such publishers as Playtime Books, Nightstand Books and Earl Kemp's Greenleaf Classics. Some of his best-known covers are for Edward D. Wood, Jr.'s *Orgy of the Dead*, the movie tie-in for *Queen of Blood*, and the *Terror Tales*, *Dr. Death* and *The Phantom Detective* pulp reprint paperbacks. Bonfils left the book industry in the 1970s to paint for galleries.

48-year-old Icelandic composer **Jóhann Jóhannsson** was found dead from cardiac failure in his apartment in Berlin, Germany, on February 9. He suffered from "melancholia" and the unofficial cause of death was a fatal combination of prescription medication and cocaine. His music credits include *Arrival* and *Mandy*. Jóhannsson also co-wrote and directed the experimental film *Last and First Men*, inspired by the 1930 SF novel by Olaf Stapleton and narrated by Tilda Swinton. It premiered at the Berlin International Film Festival in 2020.

American crime and mystery author **Bill Crider** (Allen Billy Crider), who edited the 1970s and '80s magazine *Paperback Quarterly*, died of cancer on February 12, aged 76. Under the pseudonym "Jack MacLane" he published the Zebra horror novels *Keepers of the Beast*, *Blood Dreams*, *Goodnight Moom*, *Just Before Dark* and *Rest in Piece*, while *A Vampire Named Fred* and *Mike Gonzo and the UFO Terror* were aimed at younger readers and appeared under his own name. His short fiction was published in various anthologies compiled by Joe R. Lansdale, Martin H. Greenberg, Edward E. Kramer and other editors lacking a middle initial. Following his death, The Bill Crider Prize for Short Fiction in the Mystery Genre was created by Bouchercon.

Prolific American author **Victor** [Woodward] **Milán** died of complications from pneumonia and cancer on February 13, aged 63. He started publishing in 1979, and his novels include *The Cybernetic Samurai*, *The Cybernetic Shogun*, *Runespear* (with Melinda M. Snodgrass), *CLD: Collective Landing Detachment* and "The Dinosaur Lords" trilogy, along with numerous tie-ins. Milán published under various pseudonyms, such as "James Axler" (the "Deathlands" and "Outlanders" novels), "Richard Austin" (the "Guardians" series), "Alex Archer" (the "Rogue Angel" series), "S.L. Hunter" (the "Steele" books) and "Robert Baron" (the "Stormrider" trilogy); plus he also wrote books in the "Battletech", "Forgotten Realms", *Star Trek*, "Tokugawa", "War of Powers" (with Robert E. Vardeman) and "Wild Cards" universes.

American animator, character designer and storyboard artist **Bud Luckey** (Edward Everett Luckey) died after a long illness on February 24, aged 83. Mentored by Disney animation veteran Art Babbitt, he worked on *The Mouse and His Child* (based on the novel by Russell Hoban), *The Secret of NIMH*, the short *Betty Boop's Hollywood Mystery*, *A Bug's Life*, *Monsters Inc.* and TV's *Sesame Street*. He was also credited with coming up with the cowboy design for "Woody" in *Toy Story*. Luckey also voiced the character of "Chuckles" the Clown in the *Toy Story* series, "Rick Dicker" in *The Incredibles*, and "Eeyore" in the 2011 revival of *Winnie the Pooh* on film and TV.

American film and television writer **Paul** [James] **De Meo**, who co-created CBS-TV's *The Flash* (1990–91) with writing partner Danny Bilson, died on February 26, aged 64. De Meo and Billson started out writing smarter-than-usual movies for Charles Band's Full Moon Entertainment with *Trancers*, *Zone Troopers*, *Eliminators*, *Pulse Pounders* and *Arena*, before going on to script *The Rocketeer* (based on Dave Stevens' comic book), create the TV series *The Sentinel* and *Viper*, and writing a number of video games, including several featuring James Bond. They also wrote the 2006 DC Comics series *The Flash: Fastest Man Alive*.

American comics artist **Bill Lignante** (William Gaetano Lignante) died on February 27, aged 92. Starting in 1961, he illustrated Lee Falk's *The Phantom* in comic books and newspaper strips, and for sixteen years he was a layout artist on such Hanna-Barbera cartoon series as *Jonny Quest*, *The Batman/Superman Hour*, *Scooby Doo Where Are You!*, *The New Scooby-Doo Movies*, *The Scooby-Doo/Dynomutt Hour* and *Challenge of the Superfriends*.

American author, historian and classical music expert **William R.** ("Bill") **Trotter** [Jr.] died of pancreatic cancer on February 28, aged 74. He published novels, history books and computer guides, and during the 1980s and '90s his fiction was published in such magazines as *Fantasy Book*, *Night Cry* and *Deathrealm*, and the anthologies *The Darkest Thirst: A Vampire Anthology*, *Dark Terrors 5* and *Song of Cthulhu: Tales of the Spheres Beyond Sound*. Trotter's horror novel *Warrener's Beastie: A Tale of the Deep* appeared from Carroll & Graf in 2006.

French author and editor **Daniel Walther** died on March 3, aged 77. His short fiction is collected in a number of volumes, including *Requiem pour demain, Les quatre saisons de la nuit* and *Les mandibules et les dents*. Walther also authored such novels as *L'épouvante, La pugnace révolution de Phagor, La marée purulente, Tigre, Morbidezza, Inc.* and the heroic fantasy "Le Livre de Swa" trilogy, and he edited the anthologies *Les soleils noirs d'arcadie* and *Le livre d'or de la Science-Fiction: Science-Fiction allemande: Etrangers à Utopolis*.

88-year-old Swedish SF fan **Lars-Olov Strandberg**, who was one of the founding members of the Scandinavian Society of Science Fiction in 1959 and Forodrim, the Stockholm Tolkien Society, ten years later, died the same day. He had suffered a severe stroke five weeks earlier. In 2005, Strandberg was a Guest of Honour at Interaction, the World Science Fiction Convention in Glasgow, Scotland.

British author **Clive [James] Sinclair** died on March 5, aged 70. His short fiction appeared in *The First Orbit Book of Horror Stories* and was collected in *Bedbugs*. He also published the novels *Blood Libels* and *Augustus Rex*.

Australian writer, editor, critic, academic and historian **Peter [Douglas] Nicholls** died on March 6, aged 78. He had been diagnosed with Parkinson's disease in 2000. He conceived, and was general editor of, the Hugo Award-winning first version of *The Encyclopedia of Science Fiction: An Illustrated A to Z* in 1979, with John Clute as associate editor, and he continued to be involved in later editions. While living in the UK, Nicholls was the first administrator of the Science Fiction Foundation (1971–77) and co-edited *Foundation: The Review of Science Fiction* from 1974–78. His other books include *Science Fiction at Large: A Collection of Essays, by Various Hands, About the Interface Between Science Fiction and Reality, The Science in Science Fiction* (with David Langford and Brian M. Stableford) and *Fantastic Cinema: An Illustrated Survey*. He won a SFRA Pilgrim Award in 1980 and an Eaton Award in 1995.

American writer, poet and artist **Stanley C. Sargent** died after a long illness the same day, aged 67. His Lovecraftian horror fiction appeared in *Crypt of Cthulhu, Talebones, Cthulhu Codex, Nightscapes, Strange Tales of Mystery and Terror* and *Tales Out of Innsmouth:*

New Stories of the Children of Dagon, and was collected in *Ancient Exhumations* and *The Taint of Lovecraft* from Mythos Books. Sargent's artwork appeared on the covers of such magazines as *Crypt of Cthulhu, Al-Azif* and *Cthulhu Codex*.

Professor **Peter Hutchings**, a senior lecturer in Film Studies at Northumbria University, Newcastle Upon Tyne, died on March 7. His books include the studies *Hammer and Beyond: The British Horror Film* (1993), *The Horror Film* (2004) and *Historical Dictionary of Horror Cinema* (2008).

American SF and mystery author **Kate Wilhelm** (Katie Gertrude Meredith) died of respiratory failure on March 8, aged 89. Her first genre short story appeared in *Fantastic* in 1956, and her fiction was subsequently collected in *The Mile-Long Spaceship, The Downstairs Room and Other Speculative Fiction, The Infinity Box: A Collection of Speculative Fiction, Somerset Dreams and Other Fictions, Children of the Wind: Five Novellas, And the Angels Sing* and *The Bird Cage*, amongst other titles. Wilhelm's novels include *The Clone* and *The Year of the Cloud* (both with Theodore L. Thomas), *More Bitter Than Death, The Nevermore Affair, The Killer Thing, Where the Sweet Birds Sang, Juniper Time, Welcome Chaos, The Good Children* and *Skeletons*. She also edited *Nebula Award Stories 9* and *Clarion SF*. Her story 'Andover and the Android' was adapted for a 1965 episode of the BBC's *Out of the Unknown*, while the 1990 movie *The Lookalike* was based on her short story. A winner of four Nebula Awards and two Hugos, Wilhelm helped run the Milford Science Fiction Writers' Conference and was instrumental in creating the Clarion Writer's Workshop in 1968. Her second husband was writer and editor Damon Knight (1922–2002). Her story 'The Day of the Sharks' appeared in *Best New Horror* #4.

65-year-old American SF and mystery writer **Mary Rosenblum** (Mary Freeman) was killed when the small plane she was piloting crashed on March 11. She began publishing SF in 1990 in *Pulphouse*, and some of her short stories are collected in *Synthesis & Other Virtual Realities* and *Water Rites*. Her novels include the Compton Cook Award-winning *The Drylands, Chimera, The Stone Garden* and *Horizons*.

Karen Anderson (June Millichamp Kruse), who collaborated with her husband Poul on a number of fantasy novels, including "The Last Viking" trilogy (*The Golden Horn, The Road of the Sea Horse* and *The Sign of the Raven*) and the "King of Ys" series (*Roma Mater, Gallicenae, Dahut* and *The Dog and the Wolf*) in the 1980s, died on March 18, aged 85. A long-time SF fan, poet and illustrator, she began publishing SF in 1958, and her other activities included prize-winning costuming and filk singing. In 2010 she received the LSAFS Forry Award for Life Achievement in SF. Her husband died in 2001.

Prolific American author and folk music expert **David** [Fredrick] **Bischoff** died of complications from liver disease on March 19, aged 66. His first story, 'The Sky's an Oyster, the Stars Are Pearls' appeared in March 1975 in *Perry Rhodan 66: The Horror*, and he went on to write numerous short stories and novels, often under various pseudonyms. His own novels include *The Seeker* (with Christopher Lampton), a YA version of *The Phantom of the Opera, The Selkie* and *The Judas Cross* (both with Charles Sheffield), *Madala, The Crunch Bunch, Philip K. Dick High, The H.P. Lovecraft Institute, J.R.R. Tolkien University* and *Jack London Star Warrior*, along with movie and TV tie-ins to *WarGames, The Manhattan Project, The Blob* (1988), *Hackers, Aliens, Gremlins, The Crow, Farscape, Space Precinct, Star Trek: The Next Generation* and *SeaQuest DSV*. Bischoff also contributed to such book series as "A Personal Demon" (as "Michael F.X. Milhaus"), "Bill the Galactic Hero", "Daniel M. Pinkwater's Melvinge of the Megaverse", "Dr. Dimension" (with John DeChancie), "Dragonstar" (with Thomas F. Monteleone), "Mutants Amok" (as "Mark Grant"), "Nightworld", "Star Fall", "Star Hounds", "The UFO Conspiracy" and "Time Machine". He edited the magazine *Stardate* (1985–86, with Ted White), along with the anthologies *Quest* and *Strange Encounters*. Some of Biscoff's short fiction was collected in *Tripping the Dark Fantastic*, while his Nebula Award-nominated short story 'Tin Woodman' (written with Dennis R. Bailey) was later adapted into a 1990 episode of TV's *Star Trek: The Next Generation*.

British-born author, computer programmer and web designer **Tony Plank** died in Australia of complications from a stroke on

March 21, aged 81. He had a number of short stories published in such Australian magazines and anthologies as *Antipodean SF*, *Harbinger: Australian Magazine of Speculative Fiction, Agog! Fantastic Fiction: 29 Tales of Fantasy Imagination and Wonder* and *Daikaiju! 2: Revenge of the Giant Monsters*. A novel, *Rovid Moves*, was published under the byline "Anthony Plank".

Scottish author **Philip** [Ballantyne] **Kerr** died in London of cancer on March 23, aged 62. Best known for his series of "Bernard Gunther" historical PI novels, some of which featured fantasy elements, he also published such genre books as *A Philosophical Investigation*, *Gridiron* (aka *The Grid*), *Esau, Hitler's Peace, Prayer* and *The Most Frightening Story Ever Told*. As "P.B. Kerr" he wrote seven volumes in the YA "Children of the Lamp" series (optioned by Steven Spielberg), along with the science fiction novel *One Small Step*.

American artist **Martin G. Cameron**, who contributed a number of illustrations to *Analog* during the late 1980s and early '90s, died in his sleep on March 26. "Bucky" Cameron also created motion graphics for the LucasArts game universe.

American author and journalist **William Prochnau**, whose 1983 techno-thriller *Trinity's Child* was filmed as *By Dawn's Early Light* (1990), died on March 28, aged 80.

Livia Gollancz, the former governing director of Victor Gollancz Ltd., died on May 29, aged 97. She succeeded her father as CEO of the family-owned British publishing company after he died in 1967, and continued in the role until her retirement in 1990. It was sold to Houghton Mifflin in 1989, then to Cassell three years later, before being acquired by Hachette in 1996, where it now continues as a SF and fantasy imprint.

French SF and fantasy author **Hugues Douriaux**, best known for his "Les démoniaques de Kallioh" and "Les chronicles de Vonia" series of erotic novels, amongst others, from Fleuve Noir editions, died in March, aged 71. He was a dental surgeon in real life.

Acclaimed American scriptwriter and producer **Steven Bochco**, who created such hit police procedural TV series as *Hill Street Blues*, *L.A. Law* and *NYPD Blue*, died of complications from leukaemia on April 1, aged 74. His other credits include the movies *Silent*

Running, Riding with Death, Vampire (1979) and *NYPD 2069*, such TV series as *The Invisible Man* (1975–76), *Gemini Man* (1976) and *Turnabout* (1977), and an episode of *The Twilight Zone* (1986).

American writer **Joe Poyer** (Joseph John Poyer, Jr.) died on April 3, aged 78. During the late 1960s a number of his short stories appeared in *Analog*, and he also published the novels *Operation Malacca*, *North Cape*, *Tunnel War* and *Vengeance 10*.

British author **Elsa Wallace** died on April 7. She grew up in Central Africa before moving to London in 1969. Her novel *Merle*, a novella *A Short History of Lord Hyaena*, and the collections *Kissyface and Others*, *Ghosts and Gargoyles* and *The Monkey Mirror* were all published by the LGBT collective Paradise Press. Wallace also had a story published in the M.R. James tribute anthology *The Ghosts & Scholars Book of Shadows Volume 2*.

TV scriptwriter and actor **Russell** [Louis] **Bates**, a member of the Native American Kiowa Tribe of Oklahoma, died on April 9, aged 76. A student of writer Gene L. Coon, his credits include episodes of *Star Trek: The Animated Series* (for which he won Emmy and Peabody awards with David Wise) and the pilot for *The Secrets of Isis*. He also contributed, apparently uncredited, to *The Ghost and Mrs. Muir*, *The Six Million Dollar Man*, *Kolchak: The Night Stalker* and the original *Battlestar Galactica*. Bates' short fiction appeared during the 1970s in such magazines and anthologies as *Amazing Science Fiction*, *The Magazine of Fantasy and Science Fiction*, *Urania*, *Fantastic*, *Infinity Two* and *Infinity Five*, *Clarion II* and *Star Trek: The New Voyages 2*. He also had several reviews published in *Delap's F&SF Review*.

Sometimes controversial Australian photographic artist **Polixeni Papapetrou** died of breast cancer on April 11, aged 57. Her fairy-tale-like images were surreal, eerie and whimsical, and often featured costumed or masked children. Papapetrou's work included re-imaginings of Lewis Carroll's photographs of Alice Liddell and pictures taken at Hanging Rock.

American TV and radio broadcaster [Raymond] **Reid Collins** died on April 19, aged 88. Between 1978–84 he had four stories published in *The Magazine of Fantasy & Science Fiction*.

American artist **Alice Provensen** (Alice Rose Twitchell) who, together with her husband Martin (1916–87), illustrated more than forty children's books, died on April 23, aged 99. She worked at the Walter Lantz Studio before going on to collaborate with her husband on such books as *The Iliad and the Odyssey*, *The Golden Treasury of Myths and Legends*, *Aesop's Fables* and *The Provensen Book of Fairy Tales*.

Susan Ann Protter died after a long illness on April 26, aged 78. Becoming one of New York's first independent literary agents in the 1970s, her clients included Rudy Rucker, Terry Bisson, Michael D. Weaver, David Hartwell and Kathryn Cramer.

British scriptwriter **Trevor** [Robert] **Preston** died on April 29, aged 79. He had been suffering with cancer and acute arthritis. Preston wrote the 1967 ITV series *The Lion, the Witch and the Wardrobe*, created *Ace of Wands* (1970–72), and scripted episodes of *Shadows*, *Dramarama* and *The Secret Adventures of Jules Verne*, along with the controversial 1972 movie *Night Child* (aka *What the Peeper Saw*), the 1976 TV movie of Roald Dahl's *James and the Giant Peach*, and the offbeat snooker musical *Billy the Kid and the Green Baize Vampire*.

Marvel Comics staff letterer, ocassional logo designer and cover artist **Jim Novak** (James R. Novak) also died in April. He began working for the company in 1975 on *Marvel Spotlight*, and by the mid-1980s had become production manager. Novak contributed to many of Marvel's superhero titles, along with *Star Wars* (for which he redesigned the logo) and *Conan the Barbarian*. He also worked for such companies as Dark Horse, BOOM!, Image, Dynamite and IDW.

Prolific Malayali author **Kottayam Pushpanath** (Pushpanathan Pillai) died on May 2, aged 80. He was apparently grief-stricken about the death of his elder son three weeks earlier. Pushpanath reportedly wrote more than 300 novels in the crime, horror, science fiction and other genres, including *The Death Room of Pharaoh*, *The Daughter of Dracula*, *Lucifer*, *Dracula's Coat*, *Operation Space Rocket*, *Devil*, *Dracula in Asia*, *The Fort of Dracula*, *Dinosaurs*, *Death Rays*, *Hotel Psycho* and *Bermuda Triangle*. He also translated Bram Stoker's *Dracula* into the Malayalam language.

Best-selling American pseudoscientific author **Brad Steiger** (Eugene E. Olson), who wrote about UFOs, alien abductions, visitors from parallel dimensions, Atlantis, and paranormal and conspiracy topics, died on May 6, aged 82. An out-of-the body, near-death experience at the age of 11 changed his perspective on life and, by the mid-1960s, led to him researching and writing about "the unexplained" in such books as *Ghosts Ghouls and Other Peculiar People, Strange Guests, Atlantis Rising, Revelation: The Divine Fire, Conspiracies and Secret Societies: The Complete Dossier, Real Aliens Space Beings and Creatures from Other Worlds, The Werewolf Book: The Encyclopedia of Shape-Shifting Beings, The Zombie Book: The Encyclopedia of the Living Dead* and *Haunted: Malevolent Ghosts Night Terrors and Threatening Phantoms*. Steiger also wrote the nonfiction study *Monsters Maidens & Mayhem: A Pictorial History of Hollywood Film Monsters*, and the novels *Bizarre Honeymoon, The Hypnotist* and *The Chindi*. His short fiction appeared in *Fantastic Stories of Imagination* and the anthologies *Great Science-Fiction, Stories of Ghosts Witches and Demons* and *Reflections of the Future*. Steiger ultimately wrote or co-authored (often with his wife, Sherry Hansen Steiger) more than 170 books, which sold 17 million copies. During the early 1970s, his weekly newspaper column, *The Strange World of Brad Steiger*, was carried in eighty US newspapers and other publications around the world.

American writer, editor and publisher **Adam Parfrey**, the son of character actor Woodrow Parfrey, died on May 10, aged 61. He co-founded Amok Press in 1986 with Kenneth Swezey, where he published his controversial study *Apocalypse Culture*. He then created the Feral House imprint, which issued a number of cutting-edge volumes, including Rudolph Grey's *Nightmare of Ecstasy: The Life and Art of Edward D. Wood, Jr.*, which became the basis of Tim Burton's 1994 biopic about the director. Other Feral House titles include *Apocalypse Culture II*, Stuart Galbraith IV's *Monsters Are Attacking Tokyo! The Incredible World of Japanese Fantasy Films* and Heinrich Hoffman's *Struwwelpeter: Fearful Stories and Vile Pictures to Instruct Good Little Folks*. In 2005 Parfrey launched a second imprint, Process Media, with Jodi Wille, and he also worked on a number of movies, including *Speak of the Devil* (1995) and *Lords of Chaos* (2018).

British-born American publisher **Peter** (Michael) **Mayer**, who went ahead and published Salman Rushdie's *The Satanic Verses* (1988) in the face of numerous death-threats, died of complications from amyloidosis at his home in Manhattan on May 11, aged 82. For fourteen years from the early 1960s he worked at Avon Books in New York, where he became editor-in-chief and publisher. After establishing his own independent imprint, The Overlook Press, in 1971, during the late 1970s he was publisher and president of Pocket Books/Simon & Schuster. In 1978 he became chairman and CEO of Penguin and was credited with turning around the ailing company's fortunes before he returned to The Overlook Press in 1997.

Prolific American TV animation writer **Dean** [Parker] **Stefan** died on May 15, aged 65. He scripted episodes of numerous series, including *Darkwing Duck*, *X-Men: The Animated Series*, *The Mask*, *Extreme Ghostbusters*, *Mummies Alive!*, *Men in Black: The Series*, *Masters of the Universe vs. the Snake Men*, *Dragon Tales* and *Transformers: Rescue Bots*, along with the TV movie *He-Man and the Masters of the Universe: The Beginning*.

German-born Belgian author, poet, essayist and translator **Eddy C.** (Charly) **Bertin** died while on holiday in Crete, on May 19, aged 73. He wrote in Dutch, Flemish, German and English, and his stories appeared in such magazines and anthologies as *Weirdbook*, *Balthus*, *Fantasy Tales*, *Dreams of a Dark Hue*, *Fantasy Macabre*, *The Ninth Pan Book of Horror Stories*, *New Writings in SF-13*, *The Best from the Rest of the World*, *Phantoms of Venice*, *The Second Black Book of Horror*, *Tales Out of Dunwich* and numorous European publications. Bertin's short fiction was collected in several volumes, including the French *Derrière le mur blanc* (1977), but his only English-language collection was *The Whispering Horror* from Shadow Publishing in 2013. He also published the novels *De Kokons van de Nacht* (with Bob van Laerhoven), *De Dertiende Nacht* and *Metro van de Angst* (the latter two for younger readers).

American movie poster designer **Bill Gold** (William Gold) died of complications from Alzheimer's disease on May 20, aged 97. He began working for Warner Bros. in the early 1940s and, over a seven-decade career, he produced more than 2,000 posters for, amongst other titles, *Barbarella*, *The Illustrated Man*, *Dorian Gray* (1970), *No Blade of Grass*, *Diamonds Are Forever*, *A Clockwork Orange*, *High Plains Drifter*, *The Exorcist*, *The Sentinel*, *Twilight's Last Gleaming*, *Exorcist II: The Heretic*, *The Wiz*, *Invasion of the Body Snatchers* (1978), *The Nude Bomb*, *Somewhere in Time*, *The Funhouse*, *Clash of the Titans*, *For Your Eyes Only*, *Firefox*, *Never Say Never Again*, *Splash*, *Pale Rider*, *The Believers* and *F/X2*.

Prize-winning American author **Philip** [Milton] **Roth** died of congestive heart failure on May 22, aged 85. Although best known as the author of such mainstream books as *Goodbye Columbus* and *Portnoy's Complaint*, his 2004 novel *The Plot Against America*—in which Charles Lindbergh became US President in 1940 and signed a peace accord with Adolf Hitler—won the Sidewise Award for Alternate History. Roth's second wife was actress Claire Bloom. He was presented with the National Humanities Medal in 2011 by President Barack Obama.

Newbery Medal-winning American children's author **Richard** (Wayne) **Peck** died after a long battle with cancer on May 24, aged 84. His novels include *The Ghosts Belonged to Me* (filmed by Disney as *Child of Glass* in 1978 and adapted the following year for *Once Upon a Midnight Scary*, hosted by Vincent Price), the Edgar Allan Poe Award-winning *Are You in the House Alone?* (also filmed in 1978), *Ghosts I Have Been*, *Monster Night at Grandma's House*, *The Dreadful Future of Blossom Culp*, *Blossom Culp and the Sleep of Death*, *Voices After Midnight*, *Lost in Cyberspace!*, *The Great Interactive Dream Machine* and *Three Quarters Dead*.

Following a short illness, influential American author and editor **Gardner** [Raymond] **Dozois** died of an overwhelming systemic infection on May 27, aged 70. During his fifty-year career he helped found *Asimov's Science Fiction* in 1976 and was editor-in-chief of the magazine between 1985–2004. He also helped shape the contemporary SF genre with his anthology series *The Year's Best Science Fiction*, which ran for thirty-five volumes. His short fiction (often in collaboration with Jack Dann, Michael Swanwick or his wife Susan Casper) was collected in *The Visible Man, Slow Dancing Through Time, Geodesic Dreams: The Best Short Fiction of Gardner Dozois, Strange Days: Fabulous Journeys with Gardner Dozois, Morning Child and Other Stories* and *When the Great Days Come.* Dozois novels were *Nightmare Blue* (with George Alec Effinger), *Strangers* and *Shadow Twin* (aka *Hunter's Run*, with Daniel Abraham and George R.R. Martin). From 1972 onwards he edited around 150 anthologies, including *Ripper!* (with Susan Casper), *Modern Classics of Fantasy, Dangerous Women* and *Old Mars* (both with George R.R. Martin), *Rogues, The Book of Swords* and *The Book of Magic,* along with *Isaac Asimov's Ghosts, Isaac Asimov's Vampires, Isaac Asimov's Werewolves* and *Isaac Asimov's Halloween* (all with Sheila Williams), and *Sorcerers!, Demons!, Dinosaurs!* and *Little People!* (all with Jack Dann). For a decade he also had a monthly column in *Locus* reviewing short fiction, the first nine years of which were collected in *Sense of Wonder: Short Fiction Reviews 2009–2017.* Dozois won sixteen Hugo Awards, three Nebulas and the World Fantasy Award.

American SF and mystery fan **June** [Konigsberg] **Moffatt** died on May 31, aged 92. With her husband Len (who died in 2010), she was one of the founders of Bouchercon (she chaired three of them). Len and June Moffatt also edited a number of fanzines and were co-Fan Guests of Honour at Loscon (1981) and Bouchercon (1985).

Australian journalist turned prolific TV and movie scriptwriter **Tony Morphett** (Anthony David Morphett) died of a heart attack on June 2, aged 80. His credits include *The Last Wave* (with Peter Weir) and *Dark Age,* along with episodes of TV's *The Evil Touch* ('Dear Beloved Monster') and *Mirror Mirror.* Morphett's 1969 story 'Litterbug' appeared in *The Magazine of Fantasy and Science Fiction* and was reprinted in several anthologies.

American SF fan [Thomas] **Shelby Vick** (aka "ShelVy") died on June 9, aged 89. His early fanzine *Comet* appeared from 1940–41, while *Planetary Stories* was a webzine he published from 2005–17 (and which included his fiction). During the late 1940s and early

'50s Vick had letters published in such pulp magazines as *Startling Stories*, *Super Science Stories*, *Amazing Stories* and *A. Merritt's Fantasy Magazine*, and his artwork appeared in the spring 1953 issues of the fanzine *Destiny*.

American author **Christopher** [Boris] **Stasheff** died on June 10, aged 74. Best known for his long-running "Warlock" series (and various spin-offs), beginning with *The Warlock in Spite of Himself* (1969), his other books include the theatrical "Starship Troupers" trilogy (*A Company of Stars*, *We Open on Venus* and *A Slight Detour*), *Saint Vidicon to the Rescue* and the tie-in *Wing Commander: End Run* (with William R. Forstchen). Stasheff's short fiction is collected in *Mind Out of Time*, and he edited the anthologies *The Crafters*, *Bellsings and Curses* and *The Day the Magic Stopped* (all with Bill Fawcett), *The Gods of War*, *Dragons Eye*, and the "Incomplete Enchanter" series (with L. Sprague de Camp).

British author, poet, artist, editor, reviewer and small press publisher **Steve Sneyd** (Steven Henry Sneyd) died of emphysema on June 13, aged 77. His fiction and poetry appeared in such magazines and anthologies as *Space and Time*, *Fantasy Tales*, *Whispers*, *Back Brain Recluse*, *Dark Dreams*, *Zimri*, *Copper Toadstool*, *Star*Line* and *The Year's Best Horror Stories* series edited by Karl Edward Wagner. Sneyd also published a number of poetry books by himself and others through his Hilltop Press imprint. He was named a Grand Master by the SF Poetry Association in 2015.

Influential, controversial and legendary American writer, editor and raconteur **Harlan** [Jay] **Ellison** died in his sleep on June 28, aged 84. After a variety of jobs, he moved to New York in 1955, where he lived in the same building as Robert Silverberg. After his first SF story was published in 1956, he became a prolific writer of stories and novels (in various genres and under a number of pseudonyms and house names), non-fiction and screenplays. He moved to Chicago to edit *Rogue* magazine in the late 1950s, and he was the creator and editor of the Regency Books imprint from 1961–62. Some of his best short fiction is collected in *Ellison Wonderland*, *I Have No Mouth and I Must Scream*, *Love Ain't Nothing But Sex Misspelled*, *Deathbird Stories*, *Strange Wine*, *Shatterday*, *Stalking the*

Nightmare, Angry Candy and *Slippage*. As an editor, he is best known for the groundbreaking anthologies *Dangerous Visions* (1967) and *Again, Dangerous Visions* (1972), although a planned third volume, *The Last Dangerous Visions*, was compiled but controversially never published. In 1962 Ellison moved to Los Angeles, where he began writing scripts for episodes of such TV shows as *Voyage to the Bottom of the Sea* (disowned as "Cordwainer Bird"), *The Outer Limits* ('Soldier' and 'Demon with a Glass Hand'), *The Alfred Hitchcock Hour*, *The Man from U.N.C.L.E.*, *Star Trek* ('The City on the Edge of Forever'), *Cimarron Strip* ('Knife in the Darkness'), *The Flying Nun* (as "Bird" again), *The Twilight Zone* (Stephen King's 'Gramma'), *The Hunger* (as "Bird"), *The Outer Limits* and *Masters of Science Fiction*. He was briefly the story editor on *The Sixth Sense*, created the 1973–74 series *The Starlost* (as "Bird"), was creative consultant on the 1985–86 revival of *The Twilight Zone* and conceptual consultant on *Babylon 5* and the spin-off movies. Ellison's stories were also adapted for episodes of *Circle of Fear*, *Logan's Run*, *Tales from the Darkside* and *Babylon 5*, along with the movies *A Boy and His Dog* and *Try a Dull Knife*. He won pretty much every award going—including multiple Hugo, Nebula, Writers Guild of America, Edgar Allan Poe and P.E.N. International Silver Pen awards—along with the SFWA Grandmaster and World Fantasy and HWA Bram Stoker Lifetime Achievement awards. Ellison could be curmudgeonly, and he never suffered fools gladly, but he encouraged new writers; anonymously donated to charitable organisations; supported anti-war and human rights causes, and fought against intellectual plagiarism, piracy and copyright infringement. He was married five times. Ellison's stories appeared in *Best New Horror* #2, #5, #6 and #10.

Legendary comics artist **Steve Ditko** (Stephen J. Ditko), who co-created such Marvel characters as "Spider-Man" and "Doctor Strange" with Stan Lee, was found dead in his apartment on June 29, aged 90. It is believed that the notoriously reclusive artist died around two days earlier. Ditko, who began his career working on Atlas Comics' horror titles in 1955, also helped create such classic Spider-Man villains as "Doctor Octopus", "Sandman", "The Lizard" and "Green Goblin". Following a disagreement with Lee (which has never been fully explained), Ditko left Marvel in 1966 and went to work for Charlton, DC Comics and various small independent publishers. He returned to Marvel in 1979, where he worked on such titles as *Machine Man, Micronauts* and *Captain Universe*, and continued to freelance for them into the 1990s. His final creations for the company included the cult favourite "Squirrel Girl" in *Marvel Super-Heroes*, and *Phantom 2040*, based on the cartoon TV series.

American writer, illustrator and indie film-maker **Richard** "Dick" **Siegel** also died in June, aged 63. He wrote the non-fiction books *Alien Creatures* and *Fantastic Planets*, while his SF novel *Alien Plague* was published under the pseudonym "S. Noire". He also contributed articles to *American Cinematographer, Famous Monsters of Filmland* and *Weekly World News*. Siegel worked in various capacities on such movies as *Flesh for the Beast* and *Shadow: Dead Riot* (starring Tony Todd).

Spanish screenwriter, novelist and playwright **Santiago Moncada** died on July 6, aged 90. His many credits include *Macabre* (1969), *Supermen*, Mario Bava's *Hatchet for the Honeymoon*, Eugenio Martín's *The Fourth Victim, Tarzan and the Brown Prince, The Corruption of Chris Miller, The Cauldron of Death, Bell from Hell, The Swamp of the Ravens, Voodoo Black Exorcist, Curse of the Black Cat* and José Ramón Larraz's *Rest in Pieces*. Moncada also came up with the original stories for *Tarzan in the Golden Grotto* and Sergio Martino's *All the Colors of the Dark*.

British composer **Oliver Knussen**, best known for his 1983 opera *Where the Wild Things Are* (with libretto by the book's author, Maurice Sendak), died on July 8, aged 66.

British author and playwright [David] **Clive King** died on July 10, aged 94. His 1963 children's fantasy novel *Stig of the Dump*— about a Stone Age cave-boy discovered living in modern times— has never been out of print, sold more than two million copies, and has twice been adapted for television (in 1981 and 2002). His other books include *The Seashore People*.

French horror author **Claude Seignolle** died on July 13, aged 101. Best known for his 1963 collection *Les malédictions*, which was issued in English as *The Accursed* four years later, his other collections include *Les évangiles du Diable, Histoires maléfiques, Contes macabres, Les loups verts, Histoires étranges* and *The Nightcharmer and Other Tales.*

American book reviewer and collector **Dan Chow** (George Daniel Chow), who reviewed for *Locus* from 1982–92, died on July 17, aged 75.

British playwright and screenwriter **Hugh** [John] **Whitmore** died on July 18, aged 82. He scripted *The Blue Bird* (1976), *Mrs. Amworth* (based on the vampire story by E.F. Benson), *The Haunting of Helen Walker* (based on Henry James' *Turn of the Screw*) and *Jane Eyre* (1996), as well as episodes of *Out of the Unknown* ('Frankenstein Mark 2'), *Late Night Horror* (Robert Aickman's 'The Bells of Hell'), *The Guardians, Dead of Night, BBC Play of the Month* ('Trilby'), *Centre Play* (Edgar Allan Poe's 'William Wilson') and the 1979 mini-series of *Rebecca.*

Japanese screenwriter **Shinobu Hashimoto** died of pneumonia on July 19, aged 100. With Akira Kurosawa, the first screenplay he wrote was for the influential *Rashomon* (1950), and he went on to collaborate with the director on a number of other movies, including *The Seven Samurai, Throne of Blood* and *The Hidden Fortress* (which helped inspire *Star Wars*). Hashimoto's other credits include *The Submersion of Japan* and *Village of Eight Gravestones.*

Spanish movie poster artist **Macario Gómez Quibus** (aka "Mac") died on July 20, aged 92. Amongst his more than 4,000 pieces of film art are Spanish posters for Alfred Hitchcock's *Rebecca* and *Psycho, The Time Machine, Black Sabbath, Dr. Terror's House of Horrors, Un vampiro para dos, Dr. Who and the Daleks, Curse of the Crimson Altar, Night of the Living Dead, The Legend of Hell House, Tales from the Crypt, Asylum, Silent Running, The House That Dripped Blood, The Howling, Vampira, Ravagers, Killer Fish, Cannibal Holocaust, The Fog, Prom Night*, Stephen King's *Silver Bullet*, and Hammer's *Dracula Prince of Darkness* and *Twins of Evil*, along with many others.

"Furry Fandom" artist and writer **Vicky Wyman** died on August 3, aged 65. She had been suffering from severe intestinal cancer. Wyman created the furry sword & sorcery comic book *Xanadu* in

1988, which lasted for six issues. She was the Guest of Honour at ConFurence 2 (1991), ConFurence East 1995 and Anthrocon 1999. In 2013 she also self-published the trilogy of "Raven" novels: *Raven: Journeys of the Sorcerer*, *Raven 2: The Swordman's Apprentice* and *Raven 3: The Wrong Side of the River*.

American computer scientist and SF author **Gerald M. Weinberg** died on August 7, aged 84. He published his first novel, *The Aremac Project*, in 2007, and followed it with *Mistress of Molecules*, *Earth's Endless Effort* and two novellas in the "Stringers" series (*Eyes That Do Not See* and *The Sole Advantage*).

Scottish fantasy and SF writer **Michael Scott Rohan** (aka "Michael Scot") died on August 12, aged 67. He began publishing short fiction in 1973, and his first novel, *Run to the Stars*, appeared a decade later. He is best known for the "Winter of the World" series (*The Anvil of Ice*, *The Forge in the Forest*, *The Hammer of the Sun*, *The Castle of the Winds*, *The Singer and the Sea* and *Shadow of the Seer*), and his other novels include *The Ice King* (aka *Burial Rites*) and *Spell of Empire: The Horns of Tartarus* (both with Allan Scott), the "Spiral" series (*Chase the Morning*, *The Gates of Noon*, *Cloud Castles* and *Maxie's Demon*) and *The Lord of Middle Air*. He mostly gave up writing fiction in 2000, after being disgnosed with an incurable illness, and travelled extensively.

Canadian-Scottish UK publisher **John** [Mackenzie] **Calder**, who was the principal publisher of his friend Samuel Beckett's plays in English, died on August 13, aged 91. He had two stories appear in Michael Moorcock's *New Worlds* magazine, the first of which ('Signals') was reprinted by Judith Merrill in her anthology *England Swings SF* (aka *The Space-Time Journal*).

French TV journalist turned SF author **Jacques Hoven** (Jacques Conia) died on August 14, aged 85. His novels include *Adieu Céred* (1972), *Il était une fois dans l'espace*, *Sombre est l'espace*, *Triplix*, *Robinson du cosmos*, *Les non-humains* and *Une si jolie petite planète*. Hoven also wrote detective, spy and war novels.

British author and painter **Ian Cameron** (Donald Gordon Payne, aka "James Vance Marshall") died on August 22, aged 94. His 1961 novel *The Lost Ones* was filmed by Walt Disney as *The Island at the*

Top of the World (1974). Cameron published a sequel in 1975, *The Mountains at the Bottom of the World*, and his other books include *Star-Raker, Flight of the Bat, Leap in the Dark, Devil Country* and *The White Ship*. He also co-wrote the novels *Counter Force: Beware the Tekrons* and *Counter Force: Find the Tekrons* with George Erskine.

American children's SF author **H.** (Helen) **M.** (Mary) **Hoover** died of cancer the same day, aged 83. Her books include *Children of Morrow* and the sequel, *Treasures of Morrow, The Delikon, The Lost Star, Return to Earth, This Time of Darkness, The Bell Tree, Only Child* and the award-winning *The Winds of Mars*.

Legendary American comics artist **Russ Heath** (Russell Heath, Jr.) died of prostate cancer on August 23, aged 91. He started working for Timely (later Atlas) Comics in 1947, before moving on to EC Comics, DC Comics, Marvel Comics and Warren Publishing. Amongst the numerous titles he contributed to are *Adventures Into Terror, Mystic, Menace, Tales to Hold You Spellbound, Mystery Tales, Tales of Suspense, Strange Tales, Marvel Tales, Uncanny Tales, Journey Into Unknown Worlds, Adventures Into Weird Worlds, Tales of the Unexpected, House of Mystery, House of Secrets, Creepy, Eerie, Vampirella, Curse of the Weird, Weird War, Chamber of Chills, Crypt of Shadows, Dracula Lives!, Vampire Tales, The Haunt of Horror, Savage Sword of Conan, The Son of Satan* and *Clive Barker's Hellraiser*. With writer-editor Robert Kanigher, Heath co-created *The Haunted Tank* and *Sea Devils* for DC, while several of his fighter-jet drawings from *All-American Men at War* were recreated (uncredited) in pop artist Roy Lichtenstein's 1960s oil paintings *Blam* and *Whaam!*. He was inducted into the Will Eisner Comic Book Hall of Fame in 2009.

American artist **Walter Velez** died on August 24, aged 78. He attended the School of Visual Arts in New York City, where one of his teachers was Burne Hogarth. Velez's often humorous art appeared on numerous book covers for almost four decades. Best known for his artwork for Robert Lynn Asprin's long-running "Myth Adventures" and "Thieves' World" series and Craig Shaw Gardner's "The Cineverse Cycle", he contributed covers to *Weird Worlds #2, The Borribles, Lord Darcy, Wild Cards, The Dark is Rising, The Stainless*

Steel Rat Goes to Hell, Isaac Asimov's Halloween and *Betsy the Vampire Queen*, amongst many other titles. Velez also had covers on such periodicals as *Rod Serling's The Twilight Zone Magazine, Amazing Stories* and *The Magazine of Fantasy & Science Fiction*. He also illustrated TSR's *Karameikos: Kingdom of Adventure* and *Glantri: Kingdom of Magic* games, and the *Goosebumps* and *Dune* trading card sets.

British literary agent **Michael Sissons** (Thomas Michael Beswick Sissons) died of complications from melanoma the same day, aged 83. During the early 1960s he edited three excellent reprint anthologies, *In the Dead of Night, Asleep in Armageddon* and *The Masque of the Red Death*. Sissons also helped establish the Association of Authors' Agents in the 1970s.

Pulitzer Prize-winning American writer and producer [Marvin] **Neil Simon** died of complications from pneumonia on August 26, aged 91. Best known for such Broadway plays as *The Odd Couple* and *Barefoot in the Park* (both filmed), he also scripted the 1954 and 1955 TV versions of *Babes in Toyland, A Connecticut Yankee* (1955) and *Murder by Death*.

American short story writer **K.** (Keely) **C.** (Caitlin) **Ball** died of a heart attack on the same day, aged 71. A winner of the Writers of the Future Contest in 2009, her fiction appeared in various anthologies and magazines and was collected in *Snapshots from a Black Hole & Other Oddities* (2012). From 2009–12 Ball published and edited the online SF magazine *10Flash Quarterly*.

American comics artist and colourist **Marie Severin** died on August 29, aged 89. She began her career in the late 1940s, colouring her older brother John's art at EC Comics. After having briefly been at Atlas Comics during the 1950s, she returned to the company—now called Marvel Comics—the following decade. Severin was not only Marvel's head colourist until 1972, but she also began illustrating such titles as *Strange Tales* ('Doctor Strange'), *Chamber of Darkness, Creatures on the Loose, Supernatural Thrillers, Conan the Barbarian, Kull the Conqueror* and *Not Brand Echh*. In the late 1970s she co-created "Spider-Woman" and Howard the Duck's villain "Doctor Bong", while in later years she also worked on projects for

DC Comics and Dark Horse Comics. Severin was inducted into the Will Eisner Hall of Fame in 2001.

American comic book writer **Gary Friedrich** died the same day, aged 75. He had been suffering from Parkinson's disease and near-total hearing loss. He began working for Charlton Comics in the mid-1960s on such titles as 'The Sentinels' in *Peter Canon...Thunderbolt*, 'Blue Beetle' in *Captain Atom*, and *Ghostly Tales*. Friedrich was also scripting Westerns over at Marvel Comics, and in 1967 he took over *Sgt. Fury and His Howling Commandos* from his friend Roy Thomas and went on to write for such series as *Chamber of Darkness*, *The Monster of Frankenstein*, *Monsters on the Prowl*, *Monsters Unleashed*, *Supernatural Thrillers*, *Tower of Shadows* and various superhero titles. He also co-created the characters "Ghost Rider" and "Son of Satan" while at Marvel. At Skywald he wrote for that company's black and white horror comic *Nightmare* and created the character "Hell-Rider", while over at Atlas/Seaboard Comics he wrote about "Son of Dracula" in *Fright* #1 and "Man-Monster" in *Tales of Evil* #3. Friedrich lost a lawsuit against Marvel and others in 2011, claiming his copyright in the character of Ghost Rider had been exploited, but that decision was overturned two years later.

Italian movie poster artist **Silvano "Nano" Campeggi** also died on August 29, aged 95. He created more than 3,000 posters, including those for the Italian release of *Tarzan and the Slave Girl*, *The Invisible Boy*, *The Time Machine* (1960), *Village of the Damned* (1960) and *Dance of the Vampires* (aka *The Fearless Vampire Killers*), to name just a few.

British comics artist **Terry Wiley** died of brain cancer on September 8, aged 56. His pioneering self-published independent comics included the award-winning *More Tales from Sleaze Castle* (aka *Sleaze Castle*) and *Petra Etcetera* during the 1990s. Wiley also lettered *Frankenstein*, *A Christmas Carol*, *Jane Eyre* and other titles for Classical Comics.

Russian-born American children's book illustrator and graphic designer **Vladimir [Victorovich] Radunsky** died in Rome, Italy, on September 11, aged 64. He had been suffering from multiple myeloma for many years. Radunsky illustrated more than thirty books, including *Where the Giant Sleeps* by Mem Fox and *An Edward Lear Alphabet*, and he also created the original cover for Louis Sachar's award-winning YA novel *Holes* (1998).

Welsh parapsychologist and author **Carl** [Lynwood] **Sargent** (aka "Keith Martin") died on September 12, aged 65. In the early 1990s, with Ian Livingstone, he wrote the first four novels in the "Fighting Fantasy" role-playing series "The Zagor Chronicles" (*Firestorm, Darkthrone, Skullcrag* and *Demonlord*). Martin also collaborated with Marc Gascoigne on the "Shadowrun" series (*Streets of Blood, Nosferatu* and *Black Madonna*) and one volume in the "Earthdawn" series (*Shroud of Madness*).

American art and movie critic, **Annette Michelson** (Annette Michelsohn), who published an influential essay on Stanley Kubrick's *2001: A Space Odyssey* in a 1969 issue of *Artforum*, died from complications of dementia on September 17, aged 95.

British academic author **J.** (John) **R.** (Richard) **Hammond** died on September 20, aged 85. He was one of the founders of the H.G. Wells Society in 1960, and wrote a number of non-fiction studies about the author, including *Herbert George Wells: An Annotated Bibliography of His Works, An H.G. Wells Companion: A Guide to the Novels, Romances and Short Stories* and *H.G. Wells' The Time Machine: A Reference Guide*. Hammond also wrote companions to Edgar Allan Poe, George Orwell, Robert Louis Stevenson and James Hilton's *Lost Horizon*. In 1998 he edited *The Complete Stories of H.G. Wells*.

American comics artist **Norm** [Keith] **Breyfogle** died of heart failure on September 24, aged 58. In 2014 he suffered an ischemic cerebrovascular accident that left him partly paralysed and unable to draw professionally. He worked on DC's *Detective Comics, Batman* and *Batman: Shadow of the Bat* from 1987–93, co-creating such villains as "Ventriloquist" and "Ratcatcher" with writers Alan Grant and John Wagner. His other credits include *The Spectre* at DC and issues of *Tales of Terror* for Eclipse Comics, while for Malibu Comics he co-created the superhero title *Prime*.

Spanish comics artist **Carlos** [Sanchez] **Ezquerra**, the co-creator of "Judge Dredd" (with John Wagner) for the British weekly *2000*

AD, died of lung cancer on October 1, aged 70. He also worked on such strips as 'Fiends on the Eastern Front', 'Tharg the Mighty' and Harry Harrison's 'The Stainless Steel Rat' for *2000 AD*, and Wagner and Ezquerra co-created 'Strontium Dog' for companion publication *Starlord*. Other titles that featured the artist's work include *Bloody Mary*, *Preacher* and *Batman: Legends of the Dark Knight*.

Prolific Italian music composer **Stelvio Cipriani** (aka "Steve Powder") died the same day, aged 81. A former jazz painist who studied with Dave Brubeck, his more than 200 film scores include *Luana* (1968), *Whirlpool*, *Sex of the Devil*, Mario Bava's *A Bay of Blood* and *Baron Blood*, *Deviation*, *Night Child* (aka *What the Peeper Saw*), *Evil Eye* (1975), *Frankenstein: Italian Style*, *Vortex*, *Memoria*, *Tentacles*, *The Bermuda Triangle*, *Cave of the Sharks*, *Papaya: Love Goddess of the Cannibals*, *Encounters in the Deep*, *Ring of Darkness*, *The Great Alligator*, *Nightmare City*, *Piranha II: The Spawning*, *Don't Look in the Attic*, *Pieces*, *Beaks: The Movie*, Lucio Fulci's *Voices from Beyond*, and a 2001 version of *She*. Cipriani also scored an episode of the TV series *I giochi del diavolo*, based on a story by H.G. Wells.

American book collector and dealer **David J. Willoughby** died of complications from pancreatic cancer on October 5, aged 67.

Belgium-born American software engineer **Boris Beizer**, who wrote the science fiction novels *Earth Ship and Star Song* and *The Medusa Conspiracy* under the name "Ethan I. Shedley", died in Brussels, Belgium, on October 7, aged 84.

American author **Robert Bausch**, whose 1991 novel *Almighty Me!* was filmed (uncredited) as *Bruce Almighty* (2003), died on October 9, aged 73.

American role-playing games designer and publisher **Greg Stafford** (Francis Gregory Stafford), who founded Chaosium, Inc., died on October 10, aged 70. He created the fantasy world of "Glorantha" and such games as *Elric*, based on the character created by Michael Moorcock. Stafford also founded the fiction line inspired by *Call of Cthulhu* and was a practising shaman.

Influential post-war British film critic and crime writer **Margaret Hinxman** died on October 16, aged 94. She worked as a reviewer for such magazines as *Daily Cinema* and *Picturegoer*, and the national newspapers *Sunday Telegraph* and *Daily Mail*. Hinxman was also a regular interviewer at the National Film Theatre in London.

Italian comic-book artist **Leone Frollo** died on October 17, aged 87. He is best known for his erotic horror titles, such as *Biancaneve*, *Lucifera* and *Yra la vampira*, published by Edifumetto. *L'Arte erotica di Leone Frollo* appeared in 1990 from the Italian fetish imprint Esthetique, while in 2003 Lo Scarabeo issued *Le donna de Leone Frollo*.

American editor and fan **Pat Lupoff** (Patricia Enid Loring) died on October 18, aged 81. With her husband of sixty years, Richard A. Lupoff, and Bhob Stewart, she co-edited the influential SF and comics-orientated fanzine *Xero*, which won a Hugo Award in 1963 (making her only the second woman to win the award). In 2004, the Lupoffs edited *The Best of Xero*, which was a Hugo finalist. Pat Lupoff also worked on a number of other fanzines.

British translator **Anthea Bell** OBE died after a long illness the same day, aged 82. She translated the *Asterix* books (with Derek Hockridge), along with mostly children's titles by Hans Christian Anderson and other authors.

American SF fan and filker **Harold Stein** died of brain cancer on October 26. He was the unofficial sound archivist of the filk-singing community.

Scottish-born Canadian fantasy and SF author **Dave Duncan** (David John Duncan) died of a brain haemorrhage on October 29, following a fall at a restaurant the previous week. He was 85. A former petroleum geologist, he didn't begin writing seriously until he was in his early fifties, and his first novel, *A Rose-Red City*, was published in 1987. The prolific Duncan published the "Rap", "Omar", "The Seventh Sword", "The Years of Longdirk" (as "Ken Hood"), "The Great Game" and many other fantasy series, along with such stand-alone novels as *Shadow*, *West of January*, *The Cursed*, *Pock's World*, *The Eye of Strife* and *Portal of a Thousand Worlds*. He also left fifteen unpublished manuscripts in various stages of completion. Duncan was the founder and honorary lifetime member of SF Canada and was inducted into the Canadian Science Fiction and Fantasy Hall of Fame in 2015.

Hong Kong's most famous writer, Chinese-born **Jin Yong** OBE (Louis Cha Leung-yung), died after a long illness on October 30, aged 94. He was best known for his best-selling *wuxia* ("martial arts and chivalry") novels and newspaper serialisations, which often featured supernatural and mystic elements. Much of Yong's fiction has been adapted into films, TV shows, radio dramas, and video and role-playing games in Asia, and in 1998 he had an asteroid named after him.

Spanish author and editor **Domingo Santos** (Pedro Domingo Mutiño) died on November 2, aged 76. He edited the influential SF magazines *Anticipacion* (1966–67, with Luis Vigil), *Nueva Dimensión* (1968–83, with Sebastián Martínez and Vigil), and *Asimov Ciencia Ficción* (2003–05). As an author, Santos wrote the novel *Gabriel historia un robot*, and his short fiction is collected in *Futuro Imperfecto*, *La soledad de la máquina/Territorio de pesadumbre* (with Rodolfo Martínez), *Crónicas de la Tierra y del espacio: 50 años de ciencia ficción* and *Homenaje*. He also edited the anthologies *Anticipación 6* (again with Luis Vigil), *Antología de novelas de anticipación XIII*, *Lo mejor de la ciencia ficción española* and *Fragmentos del futuro*.

Swedish SF fan and author **Bertil Mårtensson** died on November 4, aged 73. He had been rescued, unconscious, from a fire in his apartment three days earlier and apparently succumbed to smoke inhalation. He co-edited the fanzine *Science Fiction Forum* (with John-Henri Holmberg and Mats Linder), published a number of short stories (in *Antarès*, *New Worlds 7*, *Terra SF: The Year's Best European SF*, *The Penguin World Omnibus of Science Fiction* and elsewhere) and such novels as *Detta är verkligheten* and *Jungfrulig Planet*.

British comic-strip artist **John Allard** died on November 7, aged 90. In 1943, while only fifteen years old, he began assisting artist Stephen P. Dowling on the 'Garth' strip in the *Daily Mirror*, drawing backgrounds and inking. After Dowling retired, Allard illustrated the strip from 1969–71, before relinquishing the role to Frank Bellamy. Allard became one of the strip's writers and also cartoon editor at the newspaper before his retirement in 1993.

Prolific German SF author **Achim Mehnert** died the same day, aged 56. Mehnert was one of the founders of ColoniaCon in 1982, and he published novels in the "Ren Dhark", "Professor Zamorra", "Atlan" and "Perry Rhodan" series.

Jerry [George] **Ohlinger**, the proprietor of the cluttered movie memorabilia store bearing his name in Manhattan, New York, died of pancreatic cancer on November 10, aged 75. Ohlinger opened his first store in 1977, to cash-in on the success of *Star Wars*. In recent years, Jerry Ohlinger's Movie Memorabilia Store at 253 W. 35th Street closed its doors and moved online. As a result of an ongoing legal dispute, the fate of Ohlinger's extensive collection of film memorabilia remained unclear at the time of his death.

American fan and convention-worker **Maurine Dorris**, who co-founded (with Beth Gwinn and Joann Parsons) the World Horror Convention in 1991, died of cancer on November 11. She had fallen and broken her hip twelve days earlier. In 1987 she chaired the 13th World Fantasy Convention in Nashville, Tennessee, and she chaired the first two World Horror Conventions in Nashville. Dorris was a fan Guest of Honor at Con*Stellation III (1984) and at Chattacon XIII (1988), and in 1989 she received the Rebel Award.

Legendary comics editor and publisher **Stan** "The Man" **Lee** (Stanley Martin Lieber) died of cardiac arrest with respiratory failure and congestive heart failure on November 12, aged 95. He joined Timely Comics in 1939 and stayed with the company as a writer and editor when it changed its name to Atlas Comics in the 1950s. When the company became Marvel Comics in the early 1960s, Lee was not only overseeing such horror titles as *Journey Into Mystery*, *Strange Tales*, *Tales of Suspense* and *Tales to Astonish*, but in collaboration with such artists as Jack Kirby and Steve Ditko he created many iconic if often flawed superheroes, like The Fantastic Four, Spider-Man, The Avengers, Daredevil, Dr. Strange, The Incredible Hulk, Iron Man, Nick Fury agent of S.H.I.E.L.D., Thor, The X-Men and numerous others, while also reviving such Golden Age characters as Sub-Mariner and Captain America for a new generation. Often credited as a co-producer, Lee also had cameos in many of the Marvel movies and TV shows, as well as appearing in Larry

Cohen's *The Ambulance, Jugular Wine: A Vampire Odyssey, Citizen Toxie: The Toxic Avenger IV* and *The Adventures of Cinderella's Daughter*. 'Nuff said.

77-year-old American *anime, manga* and anthropomorphic ("furry") fiction fan, collector and writer **Fred Patten** (Frederick Walter Patten) died the same day. He never regained consciousness after being found "non-responsive" at his convalescent facility eleven days earlier. In 2005 he suffered a serious stroke that left him semi-paralysed. Patten edited a number of anthologies, including *Best in Show: Fifteen Years of Outstanding Furry Fiction, Cats and More Cats: Feline Fantasy Fiction* and *Dogs of War*.

British comics artist **Mike Noble**, best remembered for his brightly-coloured artwork, died on November 15, aged 88. He drew such TV tie-in strips as 'Fireball XL5', 'Zero-X', 'Captain Scarlet' and 'Star Trek' for *TV Century 21* and 'Timeslip', 'The Tomorrow People' 'Space: 1999', 'The Man from Atlantis' and 'Worzel Gummidge' in *Look-In*. Noble's other credits include the cover of the 1966 *Fireball XL5 Annual*. He mostly retired from illustrating in the late 1980s, but would still occasionally contribute to various *Thunderbirds* comics during the early 1990s.

Academy Award-winning American author, screenwriter, play-wright and script doctor **William Goldman**, who came up with the famous quote that "Nobody knows anything" in Hollywood, died of complications from colon cancer and pneumonia on November 16, aged 87. He adapted his novels *The Princess Bride* and *Magic* for the screen, and his other screenplays include *The Stepford Wives* (1975), *Memoirs of an Invisible Man, The Ghost and the Darkness* and Stephen King's *Misery, Hearts in Atlantis* and *Dreamcatcher*. As a script doctor, Goldman worked on *Last Action Hero* and King's *Dolores Claiborn*, and he wrote a short-lived Broadway adaptation of *Misery*, which opened in 2015. *Screen Trade: A Personal View of Hollywood and Screenwriting* (1983) was the first of several memoirs he authored.

Cuban-born graphic designer **Pablo Ferro** died of complications from pneumonia in Arizona the same day, aged 83. During the 1950s he began his career working as a penciler on horror comics for Stan Lee at Atlas. Ferro went on to design the titles on many movies, including *Dr. Strangelove or: How I Learned to Stop Worrying and Love the Bomb*, *A Clockwork Orange*, *Amityville 3-D*, *Prince of Darkness*, *Beetlejuice*, *Maniac Cop 2*, *Darkman*, *The Addams Family* (1991), *Addams Family Values*, *Men in Black*, *Doctor Dolittle* (1998), *Psycho* (1998), *Men in Black II*, *The Manchurian Candidate* (2004), *Cthulhu* and *Men in Black 3*. Director Jonathan Demme once described Ferro as "The best designer of film titles in the country today."

British SF writer **Bill Spencer** (William Upton Spencer), who had a number of stories published in John Carnell's *New Worlds Science Fiction* during the early 1960s, also died on November 16, aged 93. A university friend of J.G. Ballard's, his fiction appeared in three volumes of Carnell's *New Writings in S-F* anthologies, and four issues of *Interzone*.

American screenwriter and producer **Gloria** [Pearl] **Katz** died of ovarian cancer on November 25, aged 76. With her husband, William Huyck, she made her movie debut with the cult 1973 horror movie *Messiah of Evil*, and together they went on to work with George Lucas on *Star Wars*, *Howard the Duck*, *Indiana Jones and the Temple of Doom* and *Radioland Murders*.

Japanese *anime* writer **Akira Miyazaki** died the same say, aged 84. His credits include a 1982 adaptation of *The Wizard of Oz* and episodes of such TV series as *The Wonderful Wizard of Oz*, *Grimm Masterpiece Theatre* and *Moomin*.

Stephen [McDannell] **Hillenburg**, who created the award-winning cartoon TV series *SpongeBob SquarePants* for Nickelodeon in 1999, died of ALS (Lou Gehrig's disease) on November 26, aged 57.

68-year-old British magazine editor, writer and poet **Dave Reeder** (David Charles Reeder) died after a long illness on November 28, although reports of his death did not surface for another three months. From 1980–83 he edited the small press magazine *Fantasy Macabre*, and in 1985 he co-founded *Shock Xpress* (with Stephen Jones), which he edited for the first two issues. He also edited the newsstand magazines *Halls of Horror* (1983–84) and *Skeleton Crew* (1990–91). Reeder's fiction and poetry appeared in *Fantasy Tales*, *Eldritch Tales*,

Ghosts & Scholars, Dark Dreams, Dark Horizons, Etchings & Odysseys and *Weirdbook*. He worked for a number of years in Dubai and the United Arab Emirates editing food magazines, before returning to the UK in 2016.

American scriptwriter and producer **John D.** (Donald) F. (Francis) **Black** died on November 29, aged 85. As "Geoffrey Dennis" he co-scripted the 1957 horror movie *The Unearthly* (starring John Carradine), and his other credits include episodes of TV's *Star Trek* (the Hugo-nominated 'The Naked Time'), *Man from Atlantis* and *Star Trek: The Next Generation* (as "Ralph Willis"). Black also produced ten episodes of the original *Star Trek* series, as well as the TV movies *Wonder Woman* (1974) and *The Clone Master*.

American academic and a member of the Science Fiction Research Association (SFRA), **Thomas P. Dunn** died on November 30, aged 78. With Richard D. Erlich he wrote the books *The Mechanical God: Machines in Science Fiction, Clockwork Worlds: Mechanized Environments in SF* and *Clockworks: A Multimedia Bibliography of Works Useful for the Study of the Human/Machine Interface in SF*. Dunn also had articles and reviews published in *Extrapolation* and elsewhere.

British children's comic cartoonist **Terry Bave** died after a short illness on December 6, aged 87. A professional illustrator since the 1950s, he began drawing 'Sammy Shrink' ("The Smallest Boy in the World") for *Wham!* in the 1960s (taking over from David Jenner), and his many others strips include 'Good Guy' in *Buster*, 'Me and My Shadow' and 'Jimmy Jeckle and Master Hyde' in *Whizzer and Chips*, and the ghostly 'Shiver' in *Whoopee!*. He also ghosted 'Grimly Feendish' for Leo Baxendale. Bave retired in 2007 and his illustrated autobiography, *Cartoons and Comic Strips*, appeared in 2013.

Lia Wyler, the award-winning Brazilian translator of J.K. Rowling's "Harry Potter" series, as well as books by Stephen King, Joyce Carol Oates, Margaret Atwood and Arthur Conan Doyle, died on December 11, aged 84.

Nigerian SF writer and poet [Emeka] **Walter Dinjos** died of complications from unmanaged diabetes on December 12, aged 34. His first SF story appeared in 2014, and his African-themed SF and fantasy fiction was published in such magazines as *Space and Time, Beneath Ceaseless Skies, Abyss & Apex, Galaxy's Edge* and *Future Science Fiction Digest,* along with *Writers of the Future Volume 33.*

American horror author and poet **Paul Dale Anderson** died on December 13, aged 74. He had been diagnosed with cancer the previous month. Anderson's short stories were published in such magazines and anthologies as the 1980s *The Arkham Sampler, The Horror Show, Deathrealm, Dark Regions, Weirdbook, Masques III, Hotter Blood: More Tales of Erotic Horror, Shock Rock, Seeds of Fear, Scream, Corruption at the Crossroads* and *What October Brings: A Lovecraftian Celebration of Halloween,* and were collected in *The Devil Made Me Do It!* and *The Devil Made Me Do It Again and Again.* His novels include the "Instruments of Death" series (*Claw Hammer, Daddy's Home, Pickaxe, Icepick, Meat Cleaver, Axes to Grind, Sledgehammer* and *Jackhammer*) and the "Winds" series (*Abandoned, Winds, Darkness* and *Light*).

Italian translator and editor **Giuseppe Lippi** died after a short respiratory illness on December 15, aged 65. He edited runs of the magazines/anthologies *Robot* and *Urania,* and translated the works of such authors as H.P. Lovecraft, Robert E. Howard and Clark Ashton Smith.

Oscar-winning American lyricist **Norman Gimbel**, whose best-known song is the English version of "The Girl from Ipanema", died the same day, aged 91. His songs were heard in Walt Disney's *20,000 Leagues Under the Sea* ('A Whale of a Tale'), *Pufnstuf, The Phantom Tollbooth, The Man in the Santa Claus Suit, The Thief and the Cobbler, A Troll in Central Park* and many other movies and TV shows, and he also wrote the lyrics for the theme to the 1975–79 *Wonder Woman* series.

American SF author and limerick writer **Larry Eisenberg** (Lawrence Eisenberg), whose story 'What Happened to Auguste Claro?' appeared in Harlan Ellison's cutting-edge anthology *Dangerous Visions* (1967), died of complications from acute myeloid leukaemia on Christmas Day, aged 99. Best known for his sequence of humorous stories about "Professor Emmett Duckworth", his short fiction was published in such periodicals as *Fantastic Stories of*

Imagination, Amazing Stories, The Magazine of Fantasy and Science Fiction, If, Venture Science Fiction Magazine, Worlds of If, Vertex: The Magazine of Science Fiction and *Galaxy*, and collected in *The Best Laid Schemes*. Two of Eisenberg's stories adapted for the 1966 BBC-TV series *Out of the Unknown* are now believed to be lost.

American horror author **Billie Sue Mosiman** (Billie Sue Stahl) died on December 26, aged 71. She began publishing fiction in the mid-1980s in such magazines as *The Horror Show, Haunts, The Mage* and *2 AM*, and some of her more than 150 short stories are collected in *Dark Matter* and *Crypt Tales: 9 Scary Stories*. Her novels include *Slice, Deadly Affections, Widow, Pure and Uncut, Stiletto* and "The Vampire Nation" trilogy (*Red Moon Rising, Malachi's Moon* and *Craven Moon*). Mosiman also edited the anthologies *Armageddon* (with David Drake and Martin H. Greenberg) and the Bram Stoker Award-nominated *Fright Mare: Women Write Horror*.

Best-selling American author **Brian** [Francis Wynne] **Garfield**, who wrote the novel the movie *Death Wish* (1974) was based on, died of Parkinson's disease on December 29, aged 79. He also came up with the original story for *The Stepfather* (filmed in 1987 and 2009), while his short story 'Scrimshaw' was adapted for a 1985 episode of *TV's Tales of the Unexpected*.

Cecil Smith, who, as art director of British publisher New English Library in the 1960s and '70s, brought artist Bruce Pennington to the imprint, died on December 31. Smith also worked on some titles for Star Books while employed by NEL.

PERFORMERS/PERSONALITIES

American actor and musician **Jon** [Paul] **Steuer**, who was a regular on the 1990s sitcom *Grace Under Fire*, committed suicide on January 1, aged 33. He appeared in *By Dawn's Early Light* and *Amityville: A New Generation*, plus an episode of TV's *Star Trek: The Next Generation* in which he played Worf's son.

American voice actor **Frank Buxton** (Frank W. Buxton, Jr.), who voiced the 1967 TV cartoon characters "Batfink" and "Hugo-A-Go-

Go", died of heart problems on January 2, aged 87. He directed four episodes of the sitcom *Mork & Mindy*, and also turned up in small roles in the TV movies *Dark Avenger* and *The Diary of Ellen Rimbauer*.

American TV actor **Jerry** [McCord] **Van Dyke**, the younger brother of Dick, died of heart failure on January 5, aged 86. His health had been deteriorating since a car accident two years previously. Jerry Van Dyke turned down *Gilligan's Island* to star in the NBC-TV reincarnation sitcom *My Mother the Car* (1965–66), and he was a regular on *Teen Angel* (1997–98) and *You Wish* (1997–98). He also made guest appearances on numerous TV shows, including *Fantasy Island* (twice) and *The New Addams Family*.

Danish-born actress **Greta Thyssen** (Grethe Karen Thygesen) died of complications from pneumonia on January 6, aged 90. She began her Hollywood career doubling for Marilyn Monroe in *Bus Stop* (1956), and co-starred in *Terror is a Man*, a 1959 Philippines-shot version of H.G. Wells' *The Island of Doctor Moreau*, and the Danish SF movie *Journey to the Seventh Planet* (1962), before her movie career fizzled out in the late 1960s.

American actress **Pat Englund**, who co-starred in the 1951 episode of TV's *Lights Out*, 'The Lost Will of Dr. Rant' (based on M.R. James' 'The Tractate Middoth'), died the same day, aged 92.

American voice actor **Doug Young** (Douglas Hiram Young) died on January 7, aged 98. After working in radio on shows like *Sherlock Holmes* and *The Whistler*, he joined Hanna-Barbera Productions, where he did voices for such TV cartoon shows as *Quick Draw McGraw* (as "Doggie Daddy"), *The Huckleberry Hound Show* (as "Ding A Ling"), *The Flintstones* (as the "Grand Poobah"), *The Yogi Bear Show*, *Jonny Quest* and *A Laurel and Hardy Cartoon*.

Canadian character actor **Donnelly Rhodes** [Henry], who portrayed chief medical officer "Dr. Sherman Cottle" on the reboot of TV's *Battlestar Galactica* (2004–09), died of cancer on January 8, aged 80. In a long career he also appeared in *The 27th Day* (uncredited), *Change of Mind*, *The Neptune Factor*, *Oh Heavenly Dog*, *Big and Hairy*, *Roswell: The Aliens Attack*, *Beyond Loch Ness*, *Riddles of the Sphinx*, *Goblin*, *TRON: Legacy*, *Iron Invader* (aka *Iron*

Golem) and *The 12 Disasters of Christmas*. On TV Rhodes was in episodes of TV's *Mister Ed*, *The Alfred Hitchcock Hour*, *The Girl from U.N.C.L.E.*, *Tarzan* (1967), *The Wild Wild West*, *The Starlost*, *Wonder Woman*, *The Hitchhiker*, *Sliders*, *The X Files*, *The Outer Limits* (1996–97), *Viper*, *The Sentinel*, *The Crow: Stairway to Heaven*, *Millennium*, *The Dead Zone*, *The Collector*, *Smallville*, *Supernatural*, and a 2016 cross-over between *The Flash* and *DC's Legends of Tomorrow* ('Invasion!').

British-born actress **Doreen** [Isabelle] **Tracey**, an original "Mouseketeer" with *The Mickey Mouse Club* (1955–58), died in California of pneumonia and complications from cancer on January 10, aged 74. In 1957, Tracey played the "Patch Work Girl" in musical sequences from the apparently unfinished Disney movie *The Rainbow Road to Oz*, based on characters created by L. Frank Baum. She later became a music publicist and twice posed nude for *Gallery* magazine during the 1970s.

American actress and landscape artist **Julie Van Zandt** (Julie Ann VanZandt) died on January 11, aged 88. She had small roles in *The Couch* (scripted by Robert Bloch) and *Brainstorm* (1965), along with episodes of TV's *Science Fiction Theatre* and *The Twilight Zone*.

British TV comedy character actress **Bella Emberg** (Sybil Dyke) died on January 12, aged 80. She appeared in episodes of *Doomwatch*, *Doctor Who* and *The Tomorrow People*.

Hollywood supporting actress [Bennie] **Jean Porter** died on January 13, aged 95. She made her movie debut in 1936, and appeared in *One Million B.C.* (1940) and *Hellzapoppin'*. She was married to director Edward Dmytryk from 1948 until his death in 1999.

American character actress **Naomi Stevens** died the same day, aged 95. A regular on TV's *The Flying Nun* (1967–70), she also appeared in episodes of *The Twilight Zone*, *The Alfred Hitchcock Hour*, *My Favorite Martian*, *The Man from U.N.C.L.E.*, *Kolchak: The Night Stalker* ('Horror in the Heights') and *Gemini Man*.

French-born British actor **Peter Wyngarde** [Cyril Louis Goldbert] died on January 15, aged 90. Best remembered for playing the flamboyant author/investigator "Jason King" in the TV series *Department S* (1969–70) and the spin-off *Jason King* (1971–72), he appeared in such films as Hammer's *Dick Barton Strikes Back*, *The Innocents* (as the ghostly "Peter Quint") and *Night of the Eagle* (aka *Burn, Witch, Burn*, based on the novel *Conjure Wife* by Fritz Leiber). Wyngarde was also in episodes of TV's *One Step Beyond*, *Out of This World* (hosted by Boris Karloff), *Sherlock Holmes* (1965), *The Avengers* (the notorious 'A Touch of Brimstone'), *The Prisoner* (as a "Number Two") and *The Champions*. In 1975 he was arrested and convicted for an act of "gross indecency" in the toilets of Gloucester Bus Station and, as a result, his acting career never really recovered. He returned to the big screen as the metal-masked "Klytus" in *Flash Gordon* (1980), and also turned up in episodes of *Doctor Who* ('Planet of Fire'), *Hammer House of Mystery and Suspense* and *The Memoirs of Sherlock Holmes*.

American leading man **Bradford Dillman** died of complications from pneumonia on January 16, aged 87. His movie credits include *Monstrosity* (as the uncredited narrator), *The Helicopter Spies*, *Fear No Evil*, *The Mephisto Waltz*, *Escape from the Planet of the Apes*, *Five Desperate Women*, *Revenge!*, *The Resurrection of Zachary Wheeler*, *The Eyes of Charles Sands*, *Moon of the Wolf*, *Last Bride of Salem* (for which he won a Daytime Emmy Award), *Chosen Survivors*, *The Disappearance of Flight 412*, *Bug*, *The Swarm*, *Piranha* (1978), *Covenant* and *Lords of the Deep*. He also appeared in an episode of TV's *The Alfred Hitchcock Hour*, *The Man from U.N.C.L.E.* (with John Carradine), *The Wild Wild West*, *Night Gallery* (H.P. Lovecraft's 'Pickman's Model'), *The Sixth Sense*, *Thriller* (1975), *The Wide World of Mystery*, *Wonder Woman*, *The Incredible Hulk* and *Fantasy Island*. Dillman was married to actress Suzy Parker from 1963 until her death in 2003.

British actor, ballet dancer and choreographer **Simon Shelton** [Barnes], known for voicing the purple "Tinky-Winky" in the BBC-TV children's show *Teletubbies* (1998–2001), died on January 17, aged 52. In its heyday, the programme reached one billion children in more than 120 countries in forty-five languages.

Academy Award-wining American actress **Dorothy Malone** (Mary Maloney), who starred in the TV soap opera *Peyton Place* (1964–68), died on January 19, aged 92. Her movies include *The*

Falcon and the Co-eds (uncredited), *Scared Stiff, Man of a Thousand Faces* (as Lon Chaney's suicidal first wife), *Beach Party, The Day Time Ended, The Being* and *Rest in Pieces*. On TV she appeared in episodes of *Omnibus* ('The Horn Blows at Midnight') and *The Hardy Boys/Nancy Drew Mysteries* ('The House on Possessed Hill').

British character actor **Howard "Lew" Lewis** died in Scotland on January 20, aged 76. He had small roles in *Brazil* and *Quills*.

American character actress **Connie Sawyer** (Rosie Cohen) died on January 21, aged 105. She appeared in *Five Desperate Women, Oh God!* and *It Came from Outer Space II*, along with episodes of TV's *V, Get Smart* (1995) and *Sliders*. She was the oldest working member of the Screen Actors Guild.

American actor **Robert Dowdell** (aka "Bob Dowdell"), who played "Lt. Comdr. Chip Morton" on ABC-TV's *Voyage to the Bottom of the Sea* (1964–68), died on January 23, aged 85. He was also *in City Beneath the Sea, Terror in the Sky, The Initiation* and *Wicked Stepmother*, along with episodes of TV's *Land of the Giants, Buck Rogers in the 25th Century* ('Planet of the Slave Girls'), *V, Max Headroom* and *Freddy's Nightmares*.

35-year-old American actor and musician **Mark [Wayne] Salling**, who was a regular on TV's *Glee* (2009–15), hanged himself at his home in Los Angeles on January 30, a few weeks before his sentencing for possession of child pornography. He also appeared in the horror movies *Children of the Corn: The Gathering* and *The Graveyard*.

American character actor **Louis Zorich** died the same day, aged 93. He was in *Gammera the Invincible, They Might Be Giants, The Changeling* (uncredited), *The Muppets Take Manhattan* and an episode of TV's *The New Avengers*. Zorich was married to actress Olympia Dukakis from 1962 until his death.

Former Hollywood child actress **Ann Gillis** (Alma Mabel Conner) died in England on January 31, aged 90. She made her movie debut in 1934 and her credits include *Postal Inspector* (with Bela Lugosi), *The Time of Their Lives* (with Abbott and Costello) and *2001: A Space Odyssey* (her final film). Gillis also provided the uncredited voice of the adult "Faline" in Walt Disney's *Bambi* (1942). She was married to Scottish actor Richard Fraser from 1952–70.

American character actor **John Bennes** died of lung cancer on February 1, aged 84. He appeared in *Spook!*, *Weekend at Bernie's*, *Black Rainbow*, *Black Magic* (1992), *Children of the Corn II: The Final Sacrifice*, *The Night Flier*, *I Know What You Did Last Summer* and *The Legend of Bagger Vance*, along with episodes of TV's *Adventures of Superman*, *Tales from the Darkside*, *The Young Indiana Jones Chronicles* and *American Gothic*.

British "angry young man" actor **Kenneth Haigh**, who starred in the 1970s TV series *Man at the Top*, died on February 4, aged 86. He appeared in a 1959 NBC-TV version of Agatha Christie's *Ten Little Indians*, *The Hunchback of Notre Dame* (1976) and *Night Train to Murder*, along with episodes of *Alfred Hitchcock Presents* (Stanley Ellin's 'Specialty of the House'), *The Twilight Zone*, *Thriller* ('Hay-Fork and Bill-Hook'), Hammer's *Journey to the Unknown*, *Orson Welles Great Mysteries* and *The Young Indiana Jones Chronicles*. In 2003, Haigh swallowed a chicken bone while eating at a restaurant in London's Soho. His brain was deprived of oxygen, and he spent his last fifteen years in a nursing home.

British-born American actor [Charles] **John Mahoney**, a regular on the TV sitcom *Frasier* from 1993–2004, died of brain disease and lung cancer the same day, aged 77. As a voice actor he worked on *Antz*, *The Iron Giant*, *Atlantis: The Lost Empire* and *Atlantis: Milo's Return*, and he was also in an episode of TV's *3rd Rock from the Sun*.

American character actor and drummer **Mickey Jones** died of complications from diabetes on February 7, aged 76. He was in *Conquest of Earth*, *Starman*, *Total Recall* (1990), *Night Trap*, *It Came from Outer Space II*, *Penny Dreadful*, *Revamped*, *Necrosis* and *World's End*, along with episodes of TV's *Galactica 1980*, *The Incredible Hulk*, *Automan*, *V*, *Misfits of Science*, *ALF*, *Something is Out There*, *Beyond Belief: Fact or Fiction*, *Tracey Takes On . . . End of the World* and *Deadtime Stories*.

Hollywood leading man **John Gavin** (Juan Vincent Apablasa), who co-starred as "Sam Loomis" in Alfred Hitchcock's *Psycho* (1960), died of complications from pneumonia on February 9, aged 86. He was also in *Midnight Lace* (1960), *House of Shadows* and *Jennifer*, along with episodes of TV's *The Alfred Hitchcock Hour* and *Fantasy Island*. In 1978, the actor appeared in a Ohio stage production of *Count Dracula*. Gavin was signed to replace George Lazenby as James Bond in *Diamonds Are Forever* (1971), until the producers convinced Sean Connery to reprise the role. He served as president of the Screen Actors Guild from 1971–73 and was the US Ambassador to Mexico from 1981–86 under President Ronald Reagan.

Emmy Award-winning American character actor **Reg E. Cathy** (Reginald Eurias Cathey), who co-starred in Cinemax's supernatural TV series *Outcast* (2016–17) and Netflix's *Luke Cage* (2018), died of lung cancer the same day, aged 59. His movies include *The Mask*, *Tank Girl*, *Se7en*, *American Psycho* and *Fantastic Four* (2015), and he was also in episodes of TV's *Star Trek: The Next Generation*, *Grimm* (as "Baron Samedi") and *Neon Joe: Werewolf Hunter*.

61-year-old American actress **Jan Maxwell** (Janice Elaine Maxwell) died of neoplastic meningitis complicated by breast cancer on February 11. She was a regular on the 2016 CBS-TV series *BrainDead* and appeared in an episode of *Gotham*.

American singer and actor **Vic Damone** (Vito Rocco Farinola) died the same day, aged 89. He appeared in *Kismet* (1995), the 1965 ABC-TV musical *The Dangerous Christmas of Red Riding Hood* with Liza Minnelli and an episode of *The Hardy Boys/Nancy Drew Mysteries*. The first of his five wives was actress Pier Angeli.

American actress [Johnie] **Louise Latham** died on February 12, aged 95. Her credits include *Sweet Sweet Rachel*, Richard Matheson's *Dying Room Only*, *The Ghosts of Buxley Hall*, *The Philadelphia Experiment* and *The Haunted* (1981), along with episodes of TV's *The Alfred Hitchcock Hour*, *The Invaders*, *The Name of the Game* (Steven Spielberg's 'LA 2017'), *The Sixth Sense*, *The Six Million Dollar Man*, *Highway to Heaven*, *Earth 2* and *The X Files*.

American pop-eyed comedian **Marty Allen** (Morton David Alpern), one half of the comedy team of Allen & Rossi with singer Steve Rossi, died of complications from pneumonia the same day, aged 95. The duo co-starred in the movie *The Last of the Secret Agents?*, and Allen also turned up in episodes of TV's *Rod Serling's Night Gallery* (as Edgar Allan Poe) and *The Monster Squad*.

Mexican actress **Graciela Doring**, who appeared in *El planeta de las mujeres invasoras* (1966) and *Rocambole contra la secta del escorpión* (1967), died on February 14, aged 79.

Italian character actor **Pier Paolo Capponi** died after a long illness on February 15, aged 79. He appeared as policemen in both Dario Argento's *The Cat o' Nine Tails* and Umberto Lenzi's *Seven Blood-Stained Orchids*.

American silent movie child actress **Lassie Lou Ahern**, one of the last surviving members of Hal Roach's "Our Gang" (1923–24), died of complications related to influenza on February 16, aged 97. A protégé of American icon Will Rogers, she had a small, uncredited, role in George Cukor's *Gaslight* (1944).

American hearing-impaired character actress and singer **Nanette Fabray** (Ruby Nanette Bernadette Theresa Fabares, aka "Nanette Fabares") died on February 22, also aged 97. She made her movie debut in 1939 and appeared in *Alice Through the Looking Glass* (1966) and *The Man in the Santa Claus Suit*, along with episodes of TV's *The Girl from U.N.C.L.E.* and *The Munsters Today*.

American child actress and singer **Joy Lane** (Joy Wurgaft), died on February 25, aged 90. During her brief movie career, she appeared (uncredited) in the Laurel and Hardy comedy *Babes in Toyland* (aka *March of the Wooden Soldiers*, 1934).

British TV character actor and jazz singer **Peter Miles** died on February 26, aged 89. His credits include episodes of *Sherlock Holmes* (1968, with Peter Cushing), *Doomwatch*, *Moonbase 3*, three series of *Doctor Who* ('Genesis of the Daleks', 'Invasion of the Dinosaurs' and 'The Salurians'), *Survivors* and *Blakes 7*.

American actor **Sean Garrison** died on March 2, aged 80. He was in episodes of TV's *'Way Out*, *Buck Rogers in the 25th Century*, *The Secret Empire* and *Fantasy Island*.

American actor **David** [Allen] **Ogden Stiers** died of bladder cancer on March 3, aged 75. Best known for playing "Major Charles Winchester" in TV's *M*A*S*H* (1977–83), he made his movie debut as the voice of the "Announcer" in George Lucas' *THX 1138* (1971) and went on to appear in *Oh God!*, *Magic*, *The Bad Seed* (1985), *Creator*, *Perry Mason: The Case of the Sinister Spirit*, *Shadows and*

Fog, Justice League of America (1997, as "J'onn J'onzz", the Martian Manhunter), *The Curse of the Jade Scorpion*, *Lady in the Water* and *Neil Stryker and the Tyrant of Time*. Stiers was also the voice of "Cogsworth", the clock in the animated *Beauty and the Beast* (1991), *Beauty and the Beast: The Enchanted Christmas*, *Belle's Magical World* and *Belle's Tales of Friendship*, and he also worked on many other Disney movies and TV cartoons, including *The Hunchback of Notre Dame* (1996) and *Atlantis: The Lost Empire*. On TV, he appeared in episodes of *ALF*, *The Ray Bradbury Theatre* ('The Pedestrian'), *Star Trek: The Next Generation*, *Poltergeist: The Legacy*, *The Outer Limits* (1999), *Touched by an Angel*, *The Dead Zone* and *Stargate: Atlantis*.

American character actor **Frank Doubleday**, best known for playing "Romero" in John Carpenter's *Escape from New York* (1981), died of complications from aesophegal cancer the same day, aged 73. Usually cast as hoodlums or psychos, he was also in Carpenter's *Assault on Precinct 13*, *Abar*, *Avenging Angel*, *Space Rage*, *Nomads*, *Dollman* and *Shakespeare's Plan 12 from Outer Space*, along with episodes of TV's *Wonder Woman*, *The Incredible Hulk*, *The Greatest American Hero*, *Amazing Stories* and *Beyond Belief: Fact or Fiction*.

Irish character actress **Carmel [Evelyn] McSharry** died in London on March 4, aged 91. Her films include *The Day the Earth Caught Fire*, Hammer's *The Witches* and *The Secret Garden* (1987), as well as episodes of TV's *One Step Beyond*, *Pardon My Genie* and *Goodnight Sweetheart*. She retired from the screen in 1997.

Hollywood dancer and bit-player **Dorothy Barrett** died on March 8, aged 101. She turned up (uncredited) in *The Wizard of Oz* (1939) as an Emerald City manicurist, as well as a number of 1940s movies.

British comedian, actor and self-confessed "sci-fi addict" Sir **Ken** "Doddy" **Dodd** (Kenneth Arthur Dodd) died on March 11, aged 90. He had his own variety series and specials on television during the 1960s and '70s and appeared in the TV movies *Red Riding Hood* (1955) and *Alice in Wonderland* (1999), Kenneth Branagh's *Hamlet* (1996, as "Yorick"), along with a 1987 episode of *Doctor Who*.

German actor **Siegfried Rauch** died of heart failure the same day, aged 85. He was in the Edgar Wallace *krimis* films *The College Girl Murders* and *The Zombie Walks*, as well as *Alien Contamination*.

Argentinian actress and ballerina **Alba Arnova** (Alba Filomena Fossati) died in Italy on March 11, aged 87. She made her movie debut in the 1949 fantasy *Fame and the Devil* starring Mischa Auer and was also in the 1950 Tarzan parody *Tototarzan*.

The world's most famous theoretical physicist, cosmologist, author and Director of Research at the Centre for Theoretical Cosmology, Professor **Stephen** [William] **Hawking** CBE, died on March 14, aged 76. He had suffered from amyotrophic lateral sclerosis (ALS, also known as Lou Gehrig's disease) since the early 1960s. He appeared in an episode of TV's *Star Trek: The Next Generation*, was heard in the cartoon shows *Futurama* and *The Simpsons*, and hosted the 2017 series *Masters of Science Fiction*. His 1988 book, *A Brief History of Time*, was a record-breaking bestseller and Eddie Redmayne portrayed him in the 2014 biopic *The Theory of Everything*.

80-year-old British stand-up comedian and TV quiz show host **Jim Bowen** (Peter Williams), who was in an episode of *Jonathan Creek* ('Ghost's Forge'), died the same day.

American character actor **Beeson Carroll** died on March 15, aged 84. He was in *The Werewolf of Washington*, *The UFO Incident*, *Spacehunter: Adventures in the Forbidden Zone* and *Too Scared to Scream*, along with the TV mini-series *The Dain Curse*, the 1979 pilot *Starstruck*, and an episode of *Monsters*.

American stuntman and stunt co-ordinator [Harry] **Joe Canutt**, the son of legendary stunt performer Yakima Canutt, died on March 16, aged 81. His many credits include Disney's *20,000 Leagues Under the Sea* (1954), *The War Lord*, *Planet of the Apes*, *The Omega Man*, *Soylent Green*, *Earthquake* and *Doc Savage: The Man of Bronze*. He also doubled for Charlton Heston during the classic chariot race in *Ben-Hur* (1959).

Jim (James) **Hendricks**, who created the titular cable TV movie host for *Commander USA's Groovie Movies* on the USA Network (1985–89), died on March 17, aged 69. Hendricks was also featured in the 2006 documentary *American Scary*.

American actress **Sue England** died on March 19, aged 89. She co-starred in *Bomba and the Hidden City* and appeared in episodes of TV's *Space Patrol*, *Shirley Temple's Storybook* and *Voyage to the Bottom of the Sea*.

Norwegian actress **Anna-Lisa** (Anne Lise Ruud) died in Oslo on March 21, aged 84. She was in The Three Stooges comedy *Have Rocket—Will Travel* and *12 to the Moon*, and episodes of TV's *Voyage to the Bottom of the Sea*, *The Girl from U.N.C.L.E.* and *The Man from U.N.C.L.E.*

Three-foot, ten-inch American actress and stuntwoman **Debbie** (Deborah) **Lee Carrington** died on March 24, aged 58. Her credits include *Return of the Jedi*, *The Ewok Adventure*, *Ewoks: The Battle for Endor*, *Invaders from Mars* (1986), *Howard the Duck*, *Captain EO*, *Harry and the Hendersons*, *Spaced Invaders*, *Total Recall* (1990), *Seedpeople*, *Batman Returns*, *Mom and Dad Save the World*, *The High Crusade*, *Men in Black*, *Bride of Chucky*, *Mighty Joe Young* (1998), *The Christmas Secret*, *Scary Movie 3*, *The Polar Express*, *Seed of Chucky*, *Bedtime Stories* and *Curse of Chucky*. On TV she was in the pilot *Earthlings* and episodes of *Amazing Stories*, *Monsters*, *Tales from the Crypt*, *Perversions of Science*, *Buffy the Vampire Slayer*, *The Lone Gunmen* and *Dexter*.

French New Wave cinema star **Stéphane Audran** (Colette Suzanne Jeannine Dacheville) died after a long illness on March 27, aged 85. She was in *Bluebeard* (1963), *Ten Little Indians* (1974), *Night Magic*, Jesús Franco's *Faceless*, *The Spider Labyrinth* and *The Turn of the Screw* (1992). Audran was married to actor Jean-Louis Trintignant (1954–56) and director Claude Chabrol (1964–80), with whom she made twenty-three films.

British character actor and comedian **Bill Maynard** (Walter Frederick George Williams), who appeared in five *Carry On* films, died on March 30 after suffering a fall from his mobility scooter. He was 89. Maynard was also in the 3-D softcore comedy *Four Dimensions of Greta* and episodes of TV's *Orson Welles Great Mysteries*, *Zodiac*, *The Boy with Two Heads*, *Tales of the Unexpected* and *Worzel Gummidge*.

American actress **Susan** [Florence] **Anspach** died of coronary failure on April 2, aged 75. Her credits include Walt Disney's *The Devil and Max Devlin*, *Blue Monkey*, and an episode of TV's *The Hitchhiker*. She was married to *Lost in Space* actor Mark Goddard from 1970–78.

South Korean-born actor **Soon-Tek Oh** (Sun-taek Oh, aka "Soon-Taik Oh"/"Soon-Teck Oh") died of complications from Alzheimer's disease in Los Angeles on April 4, aged 85. He appeared in the movies *Murderers' Row*, *Earth II*, *The Return of Charlie Chan*, the James Bond film *The Man with the Golden Gun* (with Christopher Lee) and *The Final Countdown*. On TV, his credits include episodes of *The Invaders*, *The Wild Wild West*, *Night Gallery*, *Search*, *Kung Fu* ('The Devil's Champion'), *Logan's Run*, *The Greatest American Hero*, *Highlander*, *The Legend of Prince Valiant*, *Time Trax*, *Babylon 5*, *Stargate-SG1*, *Seven Days* and *Touched by an Angel*.

Canadian character actor **Ron White** died of cancer the same day, aged 64. He appeared in the movies *The Evictors*, *Screamers* (1995) and *Shadow Zone: The Undead Express*. On TV, White was in episodes of *Alfred Hitchcock Presents* (1988), *My Secret Identity*, *The Ray Bradbury Theatre*, *Forever Knight*, *The Outer Limits* (1998), *Total Recall 2070*, *Odyssey 5* and *Haven*.

American actor **Tim O'Connor** (Timothy Joseph O'Connor), who played "Dr. Elias Huer" in NBC-TV's *Buck Rogers in the 25th Century* (1979–80), died on April 5, aged 90. He made his uncredited screen debut in the Bowery Boys horror-comedy *Master Minds* (1949), and he was also in *The Devil and Daniel Webster* (1960), *The Groundstar Conspiracy*, *Visions . . .*, *The Stranger*, *Sssssss*, *The Man with the Power*, *The Golden Gate Murders* and *Dreams Awake*. On TV, O'Connor was a regular on *Peyton Place* (1964–68) and turned up in episodes of *'Way Out*, *The Alfred Hitchcock Hour*, *The Twilight Zone*, *The Outer Limits* (Harlan Ellison's 'Soldier'), *Search*, *The Six Million Dollar Man*, *Tales of the Unexpected*, *Wonder Woman*, *Knight Rider*, *Star Trek: The Next Generation* and *The Burning Zone*.

American voice actor and comedian **Chuck** [John Thomas] **McCann** died of congestive heart failure on April 8, aged 83. His vocal credits include such TV series as *Scooby-Doo and Scrappy-Doo*, *Fred and Barney Meet the Shmoo*, *The Plastic Man*

Comedy/Adventure Hour, Captain Caveman and the Teen Angels, Drak Pack (as "Mummy Man"), *Thundarr the Barbarian, Space Stars, Galtar and the Golden Lance, A Pup Named Scooby-Doo, Duck Tales, Attack of the Killer Tomatoes, Toxic Crusaders, Fantastic Four: The Animated Series* (as the voice of "Ben Grimm"/"The Thing"), *The Twisted Tales of Felix the Cat* and *Iron Man*. McCann's live-action performances included appearances in *The Projectionist*, Walt Disney's *Herbie Rides Again, Linda Lovelace for President* (as "Alfredo Fetchuttini"), *Survival* (1976), *C.H.O.M.P.S., Cameron's Closet, Dracula Dead and Loving It* and *They Call Him Sasquatch*, along with episodes of *Far Out Space Nuts* (which he co-created), *Fantasy Island, The Greatest American Hero, Down to Earth, Knight Rider, Tales from the Darkside, Santa Barbara* (as "Kris Kringle"), *Sliders, Sabrina the Teenage Witch, Invasion* and *Beyond Belief: Fact or Fiction*. He also co-scripted an episode of the 1976 series *Monster Squad*, was co-founder (along with Orson Bean) of the Sons of the Desert, an international fan club devoted to the memories of Stan Laurel and Oliver Hardy and, as the voice of "Sonny the Cuckoo Bird" for General Mills' Cocoa Puffs TV commercials, declared that he was "Cuckoo for Cocoa Puffs".

Veteran American actor [Dallas] **Dewey Martin** died on April 9, aged 94. He was in *The Thing from Another World* (1951) and episodes of *The Twilight Zone* and *The Outer Limits*. Martin was married to singer Peggy Lee from 1956–59.

Welsh-born actor **Alex Beckett** committed suicide by hanging on April 12, aged 35. He appeared on TV in episodes of *Cockroaches* and *The Aliens*.

American character actor **R.** (Ronald) **Lee Ermey**, a former Staff Sergeant in the US Marine Corps who was often typecast in military roles, died of complications from pneumonia on April 15, aged 74. He appeared in *Apocalypse Now, Up from the Depths, Demonstone, The Rift, I'm Dangerous Tonight, The Terror Within II, Toy Soldiers, Body Snatchers, Se7en, The Frighteners, The Sender, Megiddo: The Omega Code 2, Willard* (2003), *The Texas Chainsaw Massacre* (2003) and *The Texas Chainsaw Massacre: The Beginning, Solstice* and *The Watch*, along with episodes of TV's *The Adventures of Brisco County*

Jr., *Tales from the Crypt*, *Space: Above and Beyond*, *The X Files* and
Eleventh Hour. Ermey voiced the character of "Sarge" in *Toy Story*
and various sequels and spin-offs, and he was the voice of "Wildcat"
in *Batman: The Brave and the Bold* (2009–11).

South Korean actress **Eun-hie Choi** (Choi Eun-Hee, aka "Son
Hui Chang"), who was kidnapped by North Korea and forced to
work in Kim Jong-Il's film industry, died on April 16, aged 91. She
appeared in a number of movies before being lured to North Korea,
where she starred in the 1985 giant monster movie *Pulgasari* (directed
by her husband, Sang-ok Shin, who had also been kidnapped). The
couple was able to escape while attending a screening of the movie
at a Vienna film festival the following year.

American actress and former child model **Pamela** [Catherine]
Gidley, who played murder victim "Teresa Banks" in the prequel
movie *Twin Peaks: Fire Walk with Me*, died the same day, aged 52.
She was also in *Cherry 2000*, *Disturbed*, *Highway to Hell*, *Aberration*,
The Maze (1997) and *The Little Vampire* (2000), and co-starred in
the TV series *Strange Luck* (1995–96) and *The Pretender* (1997–2000).

American magician-turned-actor **Harry** [Laverne] **Anderson**,
who starred in the sitcom *Night Court* (1984–92), died of a stroke
on April 16, aged 65. His other credits include *The Absent-Minded
Professor* (1988) and *The Absent-Minded Professor: Trading Places*,
Mother Goose Rock 'n' Rhyme, the 1990 TV mini-series of Stephen
King's *It* and *Harvey* (1996), plus episodes of TV's *Tales from the
Darkside*, *Tales from the Crypt* and *Lois & Clark: The New Adventures
of Superman*. Anderson also scripted an episode of *Tales from the
Crypt* ('Séance').

British actor **John** [Edward] **Stride** died on April 20, aged 81.
His screen credits include Roman Polanski's *Macbeth*, *The Omen*
(1976), *The Ice House* and *Oh Heavenly Dog*, while on TV he appeared
in an episode of *Once Upon a Time* ('Frankenstein').

Diminutive American actor and stunt player **Verne** [Jay] **Troyer**,
who was born with a genetic disorder known as achondroplasia
dwarfism, died of suicide from the effects of alcholol intoxication
on April 21, aged 49. Earlier in the year he had undergone treatment for alcoholism. Best known for his role as Dr. Evil's sidekick

"Mini-Me" in the sci-spy spoofs *Austin Powers: The Spy Who Shagged Me* and *Austin Powers in Goldmember*, the 2-feet, 8-inch Troyer also appeared in *Pinocchio's Revenge, Jingle All the Way, Men in Black, Wishmaster, Mighty Joe Young* (1998), *How the Grinch Stole Christmas* (2000), *Harry Potter and the Philosopher's Stone, The Imaginarium of Doctor Parnassus* and *Gnome Alone*, along with episodes of TV's *Young Hercules* and *Sabrina the Teenage Witch*.

Scottish TV actress **Edith MacArthur** MBE died on April 25, aged 92. Her credits include *The Princess and the Pea* (1961) and episodes of *The Omega Factor* and *Sea of Souls*.

Vietnam veteran and multiple amputee **Noble Craig** died on April 26, aged 69. He played the "Snake Man" in *Sssssss* (1973) and turned up in other creature roles in *Poltergeist II: The Other Side, Big Trouble in Little China, The Blob* (1988), *A Nightmare on Elm Street 5: The Dream Child* and *Bride of Re-Animator*.

American actor **Robert Mandan**, who was a regular on the TV sitcom *Soap* (1977–81), died after a long illness on April 29, aged 86. He was also in *The Norliss Tapes, Zapped!*, and episodes of *Circle of Fear, Mr. Merlin, Fantasy Island, Highway to Heaven, Intruders, Star Trek: Deep Space Nine* and *Weird Science*.

American stuntman/actor **Jerry Montgomery**, who worked with Lash LaRue in the 1985 regional movies *The Dark Power* and *Alien Outlaws*, died on April 30, aged 89.

American actor **John Altamura**, who starred in the title role in *The Toxic Avenger Part II* and *The Toxic Avenger Part III: The Last Temptation of Toxie* (both 1989), died of a heart attack on May 4. His age was unknown. Altamura's other credits include the horror movie *Heaven Becomes Hell* the same year.

Canadian-born actress **Margot** [Ruth] **Kidder**, who played "Lois Lane" opposite Christopher Reeve's Man of Steel in *Superman* (1978), *Superman II, Superman III* and *Superman IV: The Quest for Peace*, committed suicide by a self-inflicted drug and alcohol overdose on May 13. She was 69 and had struggled with mental illness for much of her life. Her final wish was that her remains would be devoured by a pack of wolves, but that didn't happen. Kidder was also in Brian De Palma's *Sisters* (aka *Blood Sisters*), *The Suicide Club* (1974),

Bob Clark's *Black Christmas*, *The Reincarnation of Peter Proud*, *The Amityville Horror* (1979), *Beanstalk*, *Shadowzone: My Teacher Ate My Homework*, *The Clown at Midnight*, *Nightmare Man*, *Someone is Watching*, *Death 4 Told*, *The Last Sign* and Rob Zombie's *Halloween II* (2009). On TV, the actress appeared in episodes of *The Hitchhiker*, *Tales from the Crypt*, *The Hunger*, *Touched by an Angel*, *PSI Factor: Chronicles of the Paranormal*, *The Outer Limits* (2000), *The Secret Adventures of Jules Verne*, *Earth: Final Conflict*, *Smallville* and *R.L. Stine's The Haunting Hour*. The second (1979–80) of Kidder's three husbands was actor John Heard.

Iconic 1960s French actress and former model **Janine Reynaud** died of cancer in Texas the same day, aged 87. For Jesús Franco she starred in *Succubus* and, with Rosanna Yanni, as one half of "The Red Lips" detective duo in *Sadist Erotica* and *Kiss Me Monster*. Her other credits include *Ypotron—Final Countdown*, *Castle of the Creeping Flesh* and *The Case of the Scorpion's Tail*. Her first husband was her frequent co-star Michel Lemoine.

American actor **Joseph [Anthony] Campanella** died of complications from Parkinson's disease on May 16, aged 93. He made his uncredited debut in a 1952 episode of *Suspence* (Edgar Allan Poe's 'The Purloined Letter') and went on to appear in *Ben* (the sequel to *Willard*), *Return to Fantasy Island*, *Meteor*, *Hangar 18*, *Earthbound*, *Space Case*, *Dark Dreams*, *Hologram Man*, *The Glow* and *For Heaven's Sake*, along with episodes of *The Wild Wild West*, *The Invaders*, *Captain Nice*, *Rod Serling's Night Gallery*, *The Sixth Sense*, *Superboy*, *Beauty and the Beast*, *Lois & Clark: The New Adventures of Superman*, *Touched by an Angel*, *Early Edition*, *Good vs Evil* and *Star Trek: Voyager*. Campanella was also the voice of the ship's captain in *Silent Running* (1972) and Dr. Curt Connors"/"Lizard" in *Spider-Man: The Animated Series* (1994–97).

Japanese actress **Yuriko Hoshi** (Yuriko Shimizu) died of lung cancer on May 17, aged 74. Her many credits include Toho's *kaiju* movies *Godzilla vs. The Thing*, *Ghidorah the Three-Headed Monster* and *Godzilla vs. Megaguirus*.

Veteran Hollywood actress and singer **Patricia Morison** (Ursula Eileen Patricia Augustus Fraser Morison) died on May 20, aged 103.

She was in the first of Universal's "Inner Sanctum" mysteries, *Calling Dr. Death* (with Lon Chaney, Jr.), and the last of the studio's "Sherlock Holmes" series, *Dressed to Kill* (with Basil Rathbone). Her other credits include *Queen of the Amazons*, *Tarzan and the Huntress*, and an episode of *TV's Matinee Theatre* ('Frankenstein', with Primo Carnera as "The Monster").

American actress **Lois Kelso Hunt**, whose performance as "Mrs. Slater" in the original *The House on Sorority Row* (1983) was dubbed, died of complications from pneumonia the same day, aged 91.

Athletic American leading man **Clint Walker** (Norman Eugene Walker), who starred in the Western TV series *Cheyenne* (1955–62), died of congestive heart failure on May 21, aged 90. He made his uncredited screen debut in the Bowery Boys comedy *Jungle Gents*, and his other movies include *The Ten Commandments* (1956), *Scream of the Wolf* (based on a story by David Case), *Killdozer* (co-scripted by Theodore Sturgeon and based on his novella), *Snowbeast*, *The White Buffalo*, *Deadly Harvest*, *Hysterical* and *The Serpent Warriors*. Walker also voiced "Nick Nitro" in Joe Dante's *Small Soldiers* before retiring from the screen.

Canadian-born American actress, singer and dancer **Allyn Ann McLerie** died the same day, aged 91. She appeared in the 3-*D Phantom of the Rue Morgue* (1954), the TV movie *Fantasies*, and episodes of *Circle of Fear* ('The New House' scripted by Richard Matheson) and *Knight Rider*. Her second husband was actor George Gaynes.

Malaysian-born British character actor [John] **Glynn Edwards**, who was often cast as policemen, died in Scotland on May 23, aged 87. He was in the films *The Blood Beast Terror* (aka *The Vampire-Beast Craves Blood*, with Peter Cushing), *Fragment of Fear* and *Burke & Hare* (1972, as "Hare"). On TV, Edwards played Dave the barman in *Minder* (1979–94) and also appeared in episodes of *The Avengers*, *Journey Into the Unknown*, *Out of the Unknown*, *Thriller* (1973) and *Orson Welles Great Mysteries*. His first wife (1956–68) was actress Yootha Joyce.

Canadian actor **Jeff** [Frederick] **Cooper**, who starred in *Circle of Iron* (aka *The Silent Flute*, with Christopher Lee), died on May 24. His age was unknown. His other credits include *1001 Nights* (1968),

Kalimán, el hombre increíble and *Kalimán en el siniestro mundo de Humanón* (in the title role), *A Knife for the Ladies* and *Jules Verne's Fantastic Balloon Voyage*. On TV Cooper was a regular on *Dallas* (1979–81) and appeared in episodes of *The Alfred Hitchcock Hour, Wonder Woman, Beyond Westworld, The Greatest American Hero, The Powers of Matthew Star* and *Knight Rider*.

Jerry Maren (Gerard Emil Marenghi), the last surviving Munchkin from *The Wizard of Oz* (1939), died of congestive heart failure the same day, aged 98. As a member of the Lollipop Guild that welcomed Judy Garland's Dorothy Gale to Oz, he was the last surviving cast member from the classic musical who wasn't an extra. Maren also appeared (often uncredited) in *Fingers at the Window, Flesh and Fantasy, That's the Spirit, An Angel Comes to Brooklyn, Superman and the Mole-Men, Planet of the Apes* (1968), *Bigfoot* (1970), *The Amazing Captain Nemo, TRON* (1982), *Something Wicked This Way Comes, The Being, It Came Upon the Midnight Clear, House, Spaceballs, The Dreamer of Oz* and *Frankenstein Rising*. A regular of the children's fantasy series *Lidsville* (1971–72), he was also in episodes of TV's *Bewitched, The Wild Wild West, Get Smart, Wizards and Warriors* and *The Twilight Zone* (1986).

American stuntman, stunt co-ordinator and bit-player **Roydon [Elwood] Clark**, who was often a double for James Garner, also died on May 24, aged 90. He performed stunts in *Them!, Conquest of the Planet of the Apes, Battle for the Planet of the Apes, Earthquake, Charlie Chan and the Curse of the Dragon Queen, Escape from New York, The Sword and the Sorcerer, D.A.R.Y.L., Invaders from Mars* (1986), *Jaws: The Revenge, Alien Nation, The 'Burbs, Indiana Jones and the Last Crusade, Ghostbusters II, Not of This World* (1991) and the TV series *Buck Rogers in the 25th Century*.

Curvy American character actress **Gloria LeRoy**, who began her career as a burlesque dancer, died on May 26, aged 86. She appeared in the movies *Miracle on 34th Street* (1973), *Welcome to Arrow Beach, The Strange Possession of Mrs. Oliver, Topper* (1979) and *Dad, the Angel and Me*. On TV, LeRoy was in episodes of *Automan, The Flash* (1991), *Lois & Clark: The New Adventures of Superman, Weird Science, 3rd Rock from the Sun* and *Charmed* (2004).

Tony Award-winning American actor and singer **Russell** [Harold] **Nype** died on May 27, aged 98. He appeared in *One Touch of Venus* (1955) and Larry Cohen's *The Stuff*, along with episodes of TV's *Fantasy Island* and *Murder She Wrote* ('Fire Burn, Cauldron Bubble').

American stunt actor **Johnny Hagner** died on May 31, aged 90. Founder of the Hollywood Stuntmen's Hall of Fame, his credits include the movie and TV series *Voyage to the Bottom of the Sea*, *Mutant*, *Sundown: The Vampire in Retreat* and *Astro*.

American character actor **Bill Phipps** (William Edward Phipps), the voice of "Prince Charming" in Walt Disney's *Cinderella* (1950), died of lung cancer on June 1, aged 96. A prolific actor in Westerns, he also appeared in *Five*, *The War of the Worlds* (1953), *Invaders from Mars* (1953), *The Twonky*, *Cat-Women of the Moon*, *The Snow Creature*, *Lord of the Jungle* and *Space Force*, along with episodes of TV's *Science Fiction Theatre*, *Men Into Space*, *The Twilight Zone*, *Thriller*, *The Alfred Hitchcock Hour*, *The Munsters*, *Batman*, *The Green Hornet*, *The Wild Wild West*, *Cimarron Strip* (Harlan Ellison's 'Knife in the Darkness'), *The Secret Empire*, *Darkroom* (Robert Bloch's 'The Bogeyman Will Get You'), *Tucker's Witch*, *Highway to Heaven*, *Probe* and the short-lived *Time Express* (with Vincent Price). Phipps was also featured in the additional sequences added to the American TV version of Hammer's *The Evil of Frankenstein*, and he narrated the extended TV version of *Dune* (1984).

American TV actress **Georgann Johnson**, who played the villainous "Princess Arura" in *Captain Video and His Video Rangers*, died on June 4, aged 91. She also appeared in episodes *of Tales of Tomorrow* (John W. Campbell's 'The Machine'), *Alfred Hitchcock Presents*, *One Step Beyond*, *Star Trek: The Next Generation*, *Tales from the Crypt* and *Ghost Whisperer*, along with the movies *Looker* and *The Day After*.

The original "Bond girl", British actress **Eunice Gayson** (Eunice Elizabeth Sargaison), died on June 8, aged 90. Not only did she appear as "Sylvia Trench" opposite Sean Connery's 007 in both *Dr. No* (1962) and *From Russia with Love* (1963), but she co-starred with Peter Cushing in Hammer's first horror sequel, *The Revenge* *of Frankenstein* (1958). Gayson also appeared on TV in episodes of *The New Adventures of Charlie Chan* and *The Avengers.*

American TV horror host **Chuck Acri**, who presented the *Acri Creature Feature* along with various monstrous sidekicks in the Illinois and Iowa areas during the 1970s and '80s, died of cancer on June 9. He was 79.

Panamanian-born dancer and bit player **Joanne Genthon** [Eberle] died on June 11, aged 84. She appeared, uncredited, in both Alfred Hitchcock's *Vertigo* and Walt Disney's *Darby O'Gill and the Little People* (as a witch).

American character actor **Robert Alan Browne**, who portrayed "Ralph Statler" in both *Psycho II* (1983) and *Psycho III* (1986), died on June 12, aged 86. He was also in *Frankenstein Meets the Spacemonster* (uncredited), *The Mummy and the Curse of the Jackals* (with John Carradine), *Hysterical, Fleshburn* and *Amityville Horror: The Evil Escapes*, along with episodes of TV's *The Incredible Hulk, The Greatest American Hero, Wizards and Warriors, Misfits of Science* and *Alien Nation.*

British actor **Leslie** [Michael] **Grantham**, best known for playing "Dirty Den" Watts in the BBC soap opera *EastEnders*, died of lung cancer on June 15, aged 71. A former convicted murderer, he was also in *Morons from Outer Space, Deadtime*, and episodes of TV's *Doctor Who* ('Resurrection of the Daleks'), *Woof!, The Uninvited* (which he also executive produced), *Bernard's Watch* and *Urban Gothic.*

Austrian-born leading lady **Maria Rohm** (Helga Grohmann) died of leukaemia in Canada on June 18, aged 72. Her movies include *The Million Eyes of Sumuru, The Vengeance of Fu Manchu* and *The Blood of Fu Manchu* (both with Christopher Lee in the title role), *House of 1,000 Dolls* (with Vincent Price), *Eve, The Girl from Rio, Marquis de Sade's Justine* (with Klaus Kinski), *The Bloody Judge* (aka *Night of the Blood Monster*) and *Count Dracula* (both with Lee again), *Dorian Gray* and *Ten Little Indians* (1974), all for her husband, film producer Harry Alan Towers (who died in 2009). Rohm was also in the 1975 *giallo, The Killer is Not Alone.*

American actress **Deanna Lund**, who co-starred as "Valerie Scott" in Irwin Allen's TV series *Land of the Giants* (1968–70), died of pancreatic cancer on June 22, aged 81. She was also in *Dr. Goldfoot and the Bikini Machine* (as one of Vincent Price's bikini-clad robots), *Sting of Death*, *Dimension 5*, *Superstition 2*, *Elves* and *Transylvania Twist*. On TV, Lund appeared in episodes of *My Brother the Angel*, *Batman*, *Search* and *The Incredible Hulk*.

American character actor **Stanley Anderson** (Stanley Albin Anderson, Jr.) died of brain cancer on June 24, aged 78. He appeared in *RoboCop 3*, *The Lake*, *Armageddon* (as the US President), *Spider-Man* (2002), *S1m0ne* and *Red Dragon*, along with the 1997 TV mini-series *The Shining* and episodes *The X Files* and *Roswell*.

Canadian actor [Laurent] **Daniel Pilon** died after a long illness on June 26, aged 77. His credits include *Malpertuis* (based on the novel by Jean Ray), *The Possession of Virginia*, *Starship Invasions* and *Massarati and the Brain* (both with Christopher Lee), *Plague*, *Scanners III: The Takeover*, *Island of the Dead* and *Lathe of Heaven* (2002). Pilon's TV credits include episodes of *The Hunger*, *Poltergeist: The Legacy*, *All Souls* and *Vampire High*.

Irish character actor **Derrick O'Connor** died of pneumonia in California on June 29, aged 77. He appeared in *Blood on Satan's Claw* (uncredited), *The Final Programme* (aka *The Last Days of Man on Earth*), Terry Gilliams' *Jabberwocky*, *Time Bandits* and *Brazil*, *Hawk the Slayer*, *Deep Rising*, *End of Days*, *Daredevil*, *Pirates of the Caribbean: Dead Man's Chest* and *Unrest*. On TV, O'Connor was in episodes of *Doomwatch*, *Robin Hood* (1986), *Ghosts* (Stephen Volk's 'I'll Be Watching You') and *Carnivàle*.

French-born dancer and Tony Award-winning Broadway actress **Liliane** [Dina] **Montevecchi** died of colon cancer in New York the same day, aged 85. Her movie credits include *The Glass Slipper*, Fritz Lang's *Moonfleet* and *The Living Idol*.

86-year-old American leading man **Tab Hunter** (Arthur Andrew Kelm) died of cardiac arrest caused by a blood clot in his leg on July 8. A gay icon since he came out in his 2005 autobiography *Tab Hunter Confidential: The Making of a Movie Star* (in which he discussed his romance with fellow actor Anthony Perkins), the former screen heartthrob appeared in *Track of the Cat*, *Damn Yankees*, *The*

Golden Arrow, AIP's *City in the Sea* (aka *War-Gods of the Deep*, with Vincent Price), *The Loved One*, *Sweet Kill*, *Pandemonium*, *Cameron's Closet*, *Out of the Dark* and *Grotesque* (with Linda Blair), along with episodes of TV's *Circle of Fear* and *The Six Million Dollar Man*. His recording of the song 'Young Love' topped the charts for six weeks in 1957 and prompted Jack Warner to found Warner Bros. Records.

British stuntman, fight arranger and actor **William Hobbs** (aka "Bill Hobbs"), who played "Hagen" in Hammer's *Captain Kronos: Vampire Hunter* (1974), died on July 10, aged 79. Best known for his inventively staged sword-fights, Hobbs worked on various William Shakespeare productions at the National Theatre at the Old Vic under Laurence Olivier in the 1960s. His other credits include *Macbeth* (1971), *The Adventures of Sherlock Holmes' Younger Brother*, *Flash Gordon* (1980), *Excalibur*, *Brazil*, *Ladyhawke*, *Willow*, *The Avengers* (1998) and *George and the Dragon*, along with episodes of TV's *The Mists of Avalon* and *Game of Thrones*.

Likeable American actor and song composer **Roger** [Lee] **Perry**, who co-starred in *Count Yorga Vampire* (1970) and its sequel *The Return of Count Yorga* (1971), died of prostate cancer on July 12, aged 85. Often cast as doctors, his other movie credits include *Revenge!*, *The Thing with Two Heads* and *Conspiracy of Terror*, along with episodes of TV's *The Alfred Hitchcock Hour*, *The Munsters*, *Star Trek* ('Tomorrow is Yesterday'), *The Invaders*, *The Six Million Dollar Man*, *The Bionic Woman* and *Wonder Woman*. Perry was married to comedienne Jo Anne Worley from 1975–2000.

Dutch-born actor **Robert** [Jacobus Godefridus] **Wolders** died the same day, aged 81. After an uncredited role as a corpse in Federico Fellini's *Juliet of the Spirits*, he appeared in episodes of TV's *The Man from U.N.C.L.E.*, *The Name of the Game* ('The White Birch', with Boris Karloff in his final performance) and *Bewitched*. Wolders was married to Hollywood star Merle Oberon from 1975 until her death in 1979. He then became Audrey Hepburn's companion until her death in 1993, after which he entered into a relationship with Henry Fonda's widow.

Tony Award-winning American musical actor **Gary Beach** died on July 17, aged 70. In 1994 he created the role of "Lumière" in Walt Disney's inaugural Broadway production of *Beauty and the Beast*.

Scottish singer turned character actor **Peter Blake** (John Beattie Dempsey) died on July 21, aged 69. As well as taking over the role of "Frank-N-Furter" in the original stage production of *The Rocky Horror Show* in 1976 (and playing the part more than 1,000 times on tour in the 1990s), his other credits include the obscure "slasher" *Murder on Line One* (aka *Deadline*) and episodes of TV's *Woof!*, *Jonathan Creek* ('The Eyes of Tiresias'), *Dark Realm* and *Lexx*.

American character actress **Elmarie** [Louise] **Wendel**, who played the eccentric "Mrs. Dubcek" in NBC-TVs SF sitcom *3rd Rock from the Sun* (1996–2001), died the same day, aged 89. She was also in *The Immortalizer*, *Rumpelstiltskin* (1995) and episodes of TV's *Knight Rider* and *Weird Science*.

Canadian-born British actress **Carolyn** [Phyllis] **Jones** died on July 25, aged 77. Predominantly a stage and radio actress, she had small roles in *The Devils*, *Goodbye Gemini* and Clive Barker's *Nightbreed*.

Dependable British actor **Bernard Hepton** (Francis Bernard Heptonstall) died on July 27, aged 92. He appeared on TV in episodes of *Out of the Unknown*, *Catweazle*, *Doomwatch*, *Leap in the Dark*, and the 1989 adaptation of Susan Hill's *The Woman in Black* (scripted by Nigel Kneale).

British character actor **Alan Bennion** died the same day, aged 88. He played three different "Ice Warriors" in the *Doctor Who* serials 'The Seeds of Death' (1969), 'The Curse of Peladon' (1972) and 'The Monster of Peladon' (1972), while his other credits include the 1973 movie *Psychomania* (aka *The Death Wheelers*) and episodes of TV's *Sexton Blake* (as "The Scorpion"), *Late Night Horror* (Roald Dahl's 'William and Mary'), *Orson Welles Great Mysteries* (W.W. Jacobs' 'Captain Rogers'), *Thriller* (1974) and *The Return of Sherlock Holmes*.

Hollywood leading lady **Mary Carlisle** (Gwendolyn L. Witter) died on August 1, aged 104. Carlisle made her movie debut in 1923, and she appeared in *Murder in the Private Car*, *One Frightened*

Night, Super-Speed, Beware Spooks! and her final film, PRC's *Dead Men Walk* (1943, with George Zucco and Dwight Frye), before retiring from the screen. In later years she managed an Elizabeth Arden salon in Beverly Hills.

American actor **Ty Henderson**, who starred as "Paul" in the TV series *Space Academy* (1977), died of a heart attack on August 3, aged 64 (although some reports put him in his early seventies). He also appeared in episodes of *Shazam!*, *Tales of the Unexpected* and *Mork and Mindy*.

British actress **Janet** [Elizabeth] **Hargreaves** died on August 4, aged 81. A regular on the TV soap serial *Crossroads* as "Rosemary Hunter" (1973–80), she was also in Hammer's *Frankenstein and the Monster from Hell* and episodes of *The Avengers* and *Doctor Who*.

American TV character actress **Charlotte Rae** [Lubotsky] died of bone cancer on August 5, aged 92. She was in episodes of *'Way Out* and *The Secret World of Alex Mack*, and the movies *Pinocchio* (1968), *Hello Down There* and *The Worst Witch* (1986).

American actor **Robert Dix** (Robert Warren Brimmer), the son of Hollywood star Richard Dix, died of respiratory failure on August 6, aged 83. He appeared in *The Glass Slipper*, *Forbidden Planet*, *Frankenstein's Daughter*, *Las Vegas Strangler*, *Live and Let Die*, *The Werewolf of Woodstock*, and the unreleased *The Last Frankenstein* (filmed in 2016), along with such Al Adamson productions as *Blood of Dracula's Castle*, *Five Bloody Graves* and *Horror of the Blood Monsters* (all with John Carradine).

American supporting actor **Lee Moore** died on August 16, aged 89. Although he began his movie career in 1939, he only appeared in fewer than twenty films, including Joel M. Reed's *Blood Bath* (1975) and *Night of the Zombies*, *Open House* and *Avengers: Endgame* (as the 93-year-old Scott Lang/Ant-Man).

Quirky American actress **Barbara** [Densmoor] **Harris**, who co-starred in Walt Disney Productions' *Freaky Friday* (1976) with Jodie Foster, died of lung cancer on August 21, aged 83. Her other credits include Alfred Hitchcock's final movie, *Family Plot* (1976), *Peggy Sue Got Married* (with John Carradine), *Nice Girls Don't Explode* and an episode of TV's *Alfred Hutchcock Presents*. Harris also co-founded (with Paul Sills, her husband at the time) the improvisational Second City comedy troupe in Chicago and, in 1966, she was nominated for a Tony Award for her performance in the Broadway musical *On a Clear Day You Can See Forever*.

Icelandic actor and comedian **Stefán Karl Stefánsson**, who played "Robbie Rotten" in the children's TV series *LazyTown* (2002–14) and the spin-off *LazyTown Extra* (2008), died of cancer in Los Angeles the same day, aged 43.

British actor, mime artist and choreographer **Lindsay Kemp** died in Italy on August 25, aged 80. He made rare film appearances in Hammer's *The Vampire Lovers*, *The Wicker Man* (1973, with Christopher Lee) and *Jubilee* (1978). Kemp was a mentor to both David Bowie and Kate Bush.

American character actor **Fredd Wayne** (Frederick S. Wiener), best known for his portrayals of Benjamin Franklin on stage and screen, died on August 27, aged 93. On TV he appeared in episodes of *One Step Beyond*, *The Twilight Zone*, *Bewitched*, *Wonder Woman* and *Voyagers!*, and he had small roles in the movies *Seven Days in May*, *Chamber of Horrors* (1966) and *The Phantom of Hollywood*.

49-year-old American actress **Vanessa Marquez**, who was a regular on the TV drama *ER* (1994–97) and appeared in *Maniac Cop 3: Badge of Silence*, was shot to death by police during a routine welfare check at her home on August 30. Marquez reportedly suffered from psychological and other health problems.

Former Hollywood child actress and singer **Gloria Jean** [Schoonover] died of heart failure and pneumonia on August 31, aged 92. As a Universal contract player in the early 1940s, she appeared in *Ghost Catchers* (1944), which also featured Lon Chaney, Jr. When the anthology movie *Flesh and Fantasy* (1943) was considered too long by the studio, Jean's segment was cut and expanded into a separate movie, *Destiny* (1944).

79-year-old British-born American actress **Carole** [Augusta] **Shelley** died of cancer the same day in New York. Her credits include *Alice's Adventures in Wonderland* (1956), *The Boston Strangler*, *Bewitched* (2005, as "Aunt Clara"), and a couple of early *Carry On* films. She also contributed voice work to Walt Disney Productions' *The Aristocats*, *Robin Hood* and *Hercules*, and appeared in an episode of TV's *Monsters*. However, Shelley was much better known as a stage actress, receiving a Tony Award for originating the role of "Mrs. Kendall" in the 1979 Off-Broadway production of *The Elephant Man*. In 2003, the actress also created the role of "Madame Morrible", Elphaba's mentor and later chief adversary, in the original Broadway production of *Wicked*.

American TV soap-opera actress **Susan Brown**, who played "Dr. Gail Baldwin" on both *General Hospital* and *Port Charles*, died of complications from Alzheimer's disease on August 31, aged 86. Brown had small roles in *Fear No Evil* and *The Andromeda Strain* (1971), and she was also in episodes of *The Girl from U.N.C.L.E.*, *It's About Time* and *The Wide World of Mystery* ('Alien Lover').

German-born British actor **Carl Duering** (Gerhard Fuchs aka "Carl Fox Duering") died on September 1, aged 95. His credits include *Escapement* (aka *The Electronic Monster*), *A Clockwork Orange*, *The Boys from Brazil* and *Possession* (1981), along with episodes of TV's *One Step Beyond*, *Tales of Mystery*, *Sherlock Holmes* (1965) and *The Young Indiana Jones Chronicles*.

American character actor [Presley] **Dean Whitworth** died the same day, aged 80. He was in *King Kong Lives*, *The Judas Project*, *Killer!*, *Southern Gothic* and two episodes of TV's *American Gothic*.

British actress **Jacqueline** [Kay] **Pearce**, who co-starred as the sexy but villainous "Supreme Commander Servalan" in the BBC-TV series *Blakes 7* (1978–81) and its subsequent audio spin-offs, died of lung cancer on September 3, aged 74. Her other credits include Hammer's *The Plague of the Zombies* and *The Reptile*, along with episodes of *The Avengers*, *Haunted*, *Dead of Night*, *Leap in the Dark*, *Shadows*, *Doctor Who* ('The Two Doctors'), *Moondial*, *Dark Season*, *The Young Indiana Jones Chronicles* and the animated *Doctor Who: Death Comes to Time*. Both of Pearce's ex-husbands subsequently married actress Felicity Kendal.

American actress **Lydia** [Marie] **Clarke**, who was married to Charlton Heston from 1944 until the actor's death in 2008, died the same day, aged 95. Her small number of film credits include co-starring with Gene Barry in *The Atomic City* (1952), and she was also an uncredited still photographer on her husband's movie *The Omega Man*.

American actor **Bill Daily** (William Edward Daily, Jr.), who co-starred as "Major Roger Healey" in NBC-TV's fantasy sitcom *I Dream of Jeannie* (1965–70), died on September 4, aged 91. He also appeared in episodes of *Bewitched*, *My Mother the Car*, *The Powers of Matthew Star*, *ALF* and *The Munsters Today*, along with *Alligator II: The Mutation*, *Horrorween* (featuring Donald Trump), and the reunion TV movies *I Dream of Jeannie . . . Fifteen Years Later* and *I Still Dream of Jeannie*.

American actor **Christopher** [Kennedy] **Lawford**, the son of "Rat Pack" actor Peter Lawford, died of a heart attack in Canada the same day, aged 63. His credits include *The Suicide Club* (1988), *Spellbinder*, *The 6th Day*, *Terminator 3: Rise of the Machines*, *Slipstream* (2007) and an episode of TV's *Tales from the Crypt*.

Hollywood superstar **Burt Reynolds** (Burton Leon Reynolds, Jr.), named as the consecutively highest-grossing actor in the world from 1978–82, died of a heart attack on September 6, aged 82. He began his career on TV in 1958, and his movies include *Skullduggery*, *Deliverance*, *The Maddening*, *Frankenstein and Me*, *Universal Soldier II: Brothers in Arms* and *Universal Soldier III: Unfinished Business*, *In the Name of the King: A Dungeon Siege Tale* and *Hollow Creek*, along with episodes of *The Twilight Zone* and *The X Files*. Reynolds also directed a number of movies and TV shows, including episodes of *Alfred Hitchcock Presents* (1985) and *Amazing Stories*. His marriages to actresses Judy Carne and Loni Anderson both ended in divorce.

88-year-old British comedic actress **Liz Fraser** (Elizabeth Joan Winch), who appeared in a number of *Carry On* films, died the same day of complications following an operation. She memorably co-starred in the 'The Girl from Auntie' episode of TV's *The Avengers*, along with an episode of *Randall and Hopkirk (Deceased)*.

British character actor **Peter** [Henry] **Benson** died after a short illness on September 6, aged 75. He was in *Cry of the Banshee* (with Vincent Price), *The Shout*, *The Dybbuk* (1980) and *Hawk the Slayer*,

Doctor Who, and the TV mini-series *Maria Marten or Murder in the Red Barn* and *Merlin*.

American character actor **Robert Cleaves**, who was convicted of second-degree murder in 2000 following a road-rage incident, died on September 9, aged 88. He appeared in the movies *Seconds, Project X, Targets, Finian's Rainbow* and *Don't Be Afraid of the Dark* (1973), along with episodes of TV's *Bewitched* and *The Next Step Beyond*.

Canadian-born American actor **Peter Donat** (Pierre Collingwood Donat), who portrayed Agent Mulder's father, William, on *The X Files* (1995–99), died in California of complications from diabetes on September 10, aged 90. His credits include *The Return of Charlie Chan, Mirrors* and *Mazes and Monsters*. On TV, Donat played the time-travelling villain "Mordecai Sahmbi" in *Time Trax* (1993–94) and he appeared in episodes of *The Invisible Man* (1975), *Future Cop, Salvage 1, Voyagers!, The Magical World of Disney* ('Earth Star Voyager'), *Father Dowling Mysteries* ('The Mummy's Curse Mystery') and *The Outer Limits* (1996). He was the nephew of veteran British star Robert Donat.

Husky-voiced British starlet **Fenella [Marion] Fielding** OBE, best remembered as the vampish "Valeria Watt" in *Carry On Screaming!* (1966), died on September 11, following a stroke the month before. She was 90. Fielding had previously appeared in a similar role—as "Morgana Femm"—in the Hammer/William Castle comedy remake of *The Old Dark House* (1963), while her other credits include *Wishbaby*, David McGillivray's *Worst Fears*, and an episode of TV's *The Avengers*. Fielding's uncredited voice can also be heard as the loudspeaker announcer in the 1967 series *The Prisoner*, and it has been suggested that she dubbed the French actress Niké Arrighi in Hammer's *The Devil Rides Out* (aka *The Devil's Bride*, 1968). The actress also narrated an audio version of J.G. Ballard's *Crash* for Savoy.

American stuntman and location manager **Jack N. (Norwood) Young** died on September 12, aged 91. He began his career in the late 1940s, and although he mostly worked on Westerns, he also did stunts on Universal's *Creature from the Black Lagoon* (1953).

Burmese-born British actress **Zienia Merton**, who co-starred as data analyst "Sandra Benes" on ITV's *Space: 1999* (1975–77), died on September 14, aged 72. The exotic-looking actress made her screen debut in the 1962 Children's Film Foundation serial *Masters of Venus*, and her other credits include The Beatles' *Help!* (as the "High Priestess"), *The Chairman*, and episodes of TV's *Doctor Who*, *The Indian Tales of Rudyard Kipling* ('Mark of the Beast'), *Leap in the Dark*, *Hammer House of Mystery and Suspense*, *Chiller* (Stephen Gallagher's adaptation of Peter James' novel *Prophecy*), *Crime Traveller*, *Dinotopia*, *The Sarah Jane Adventures* and *Wizards vs. Aliens*.

Veteran British character actor **Dudley Sutton** died of cancer on September 15, aged 85. A regular on TV's *Lovejoy* (1986–94) as "Tinker", his other credits include Ken Russell's *The Devils*, *Madame Sin* (with Bette Davis), *The Pink Panther Strikes Again*, *No.1 of the Secret Service*, *The Playbirds*, *The Island* (1980), *Brimstone & Treacle*, *Orlando*, *Cockneys vs. Zombies*, Steven Berkoff's *Tell Tale Heart*, *When the Devil Rides Out*, and episodes of *The Avengers*, *Mystery and Imagination* (J. Sheridan Le Fanu's 'Uncle Silas'), *Randall and Hopkirk (Deceased)*, *Thriller* (1975), *Tales of the Unexpected*, *Highlander* and the 2000 revival of *Randall and Hopkirk [Deceased]*. Sutton also portrayed Jack the Ripper in the 2018 short film *Ripper Tour*.

Franco-Egyptian actor **Gamil** [Abubakr] **Ratib** died on September 19, aged 91. His credits include a 1972 TV movie of *L'Atlantide*, *Time Conqueror*, *The Serpent of Death* (aka *Out of Time*) and the TV series *Doors of Fear* (*Abwab El Khouf*).

American pin-up model turned actress **Laurie Mitchell** (Mickey Koren) died on September 20, aged 90. She appeared in Walt Disney's *20,000 Leagues Under the Sea*, Bert I. Gordon's *Attack of the Puppet People*, *Queen of Outer Space* (as the evil "Queen Yllana") and *Missile to the Moon*, along with episodes of *Adventures of Superman*, *The Alfred Hitchcock Hour* and *The Addams Family*. She retired from the screen in the early 1970s.

75-year-old American-born singer and character actor **Al Matthews**, who portrayed "Sergeant Apone" in *Aliens* (1986), was found dead at his home in Spain on September 22. A Vietnam War veteran, his other credits include *The Final Conflict, The Sender, Superman III, The American Way, The Fifth Element* and the James Bond film *Tomorrow Never Dies*. Matthews was also the first black DJ on the BBC's national radio station, Radio 1.

American actor **Archie Valliere** (Richard Valliere) died on September 25, aged 66. He made his movie debut as the Deputy Sheriff in the 1971 film *Zaat* (aka *Blood Waters of Dr. Z*) and appeared in *Jaws 3-D* before becoming a born-again Christian and leaving the industry in the mid-1990s.

American actor **Roger Robinson**, who had a recurring role on TV's *Kojak* (1973–76), died from a heart condition on September 26, aged 78. He was also in *Meteor* and episodes of *The Incredible Hulk* and *Voyagers!*.

British children's TV presenter [Charles] **Geoffrey Hayes** died of pneumonia on September 30, aged 76. Between 1973 and 1992 he presented almost 1,000 episodes of the cult half-hour ITV show *Rainbow* with puppets George, Zippy and Bungle the bear. After the series was cancelled, he ended up stacking shelves in a super-market.

French-Armenian signer and actor **Charles Aznavour** (Shahnour Vaghinag Aznavourian), who recorded more than 1,200 songs and sold over 180 million records, died on October 1, aged 94. His many film roles include Jean Cocteau's *Le testament d'Orphée, Ten Little Indians* (1974) and *The Hatter's Ghost*.

American character actor **Scott Wilson** (William Delano Wilson), who played farm owner "Hershel Green" in the second, third and fourth seasons of AMC's *The Walking Dead* (2011–18), died of leukaemia on October 6, aged 76. He also appeared in *In Cold Blood, Castle Keep, The Ninth Configuration, The Exorcist III, Tall Tale, Judge Dredd* (1995), *Mother* (1995), *The Host* and *The Exorcist III: Legion*, along with episodes of TV's *The Twilight Zone* (1986), *The X Files, Damien* and *The OA*.

Striking American actress **Celeste** [Jeanne] **Yarnall**, who starred as the seductive vampire "Diane LeFanu" in *The Velvet Vampire* (1971), died on October 7, aged 74. The former model's other credits include a small, uncredited role in *The Nutty Professor* (1963*), Around* *the World Under the Sea, Eve* (with Herbert Lom and Christopher Lee), *Beast of Blood, Midnight Kiss, Skinwalker: Curse of the Shaman* and *Unbelievable!!!!!*. On TV Yarnall appeared in episodes of *The Wild Wild West, Bewitched, The Man from U.N.C.L.E., Captain Nice, Star Trek* ('The Apple') and *Land of the Giants*.

American TV actress **Peggy McCay** died the same day, aged 90. She appeared in the TV movies *Good Against Evil, Amityville: The Evil Escapes* and *Alien Nation: The Udara Legacy, UFOria, An Irish Vampire in Hollywood*, and episodes of *The Alfred Hitchcock Hour* (Henry Slesar's 'House Guest' and John Collier's 'The Magic Shop'), *The Girl with Something Extra, Logan's Run* (Harlan Ellison's 'Crypt'), *The Amazing Spider-Man* ('The Kirkwood Haunting'), *The Powers of Matthew Star* and *Highway to Heaven*.

American TV character actor **Lee Delano** died on October 8, aged 86. He turned up in episodes of TV's *Voyage to the Bottom of the Sea, The Man from U.N.C.L.E., Batman, Star Trek* ('A Piece of the Action'), *The Flying Nun, Planet of the Apes, Holmes and Yoyo* and *Small Wonder*. Delano was also in William Castle's *Project X* and Disney's *Splash*.

Italian actor [Enrico] **Venantino Venantini** (aka "Van Tenney"/"Vernon Vernons") died of complications from a fall on October 9, aged 88. He appeared in the 1964 short *Fantasmagorie* starring Edith Scob and such films as *Seven Dead in the Cat's Eye, War of the Robots, The Humanoid, Beast in Space, Cannibals in the Streets* (aka *Cannibal Apocalypse*), *City of the Living Dead, Cannibal Ferox, The New Barbarians* (aka *Warriors of the Wasteland*), *The Exterminators of the Year 3000, Ladyhawke, The Adventures of Hercules* (1985), *Aladdin* (1986), *The Eighteenth Angel, The Return of James Battle* (aka *Atomik Circus*), *The Museum of Wonders, Bloody Sin, Hyde's Secret Nightmare, Phantasmagoria* (the 'My Gift to You' segment) and *House of Ravens*.

British supporting actor **Pat Gorman** (William Patrick Gorman), who was in more than 100 episodes of BBC-TV's *Doctor Who* in a variety of different roles, died the same day, aged 85. He also appeared (often uncredited, playing policemen, soldiers or reporters) in Hammer's *The Curse of the Mummy's Tomb* and *The Mummy's Shroud*,

Trog, The Elephant Man, Venom and *Batman* (1989), along with episodes of TV's *Adam Adamant Lives!, Doomwatch, The Moonstone* (1972), *The New Avengers, Pinocchio* (1978), *The Tomorrow People, Hammer House of Horror, The Nightmare Man, The Day of the Triffids* (1981), *Blakes 7, Hammer House of Mystery and Suspense* and *Dark Season.*

American actress **Diane Jergens** (Dianna Irgens) also died on October 9, aged 83. She was in *Island of Lost Women* and an episode of TV's *The Addams Family.*

Japanese actor **Takanobu Hozumi** (Takanobu Suzuki) died of gall bladder cancer on October 19, aged 97. He appeared in the movie *The X from Outer Space* and episodes of the TV series *Urutora Q* and *Horror Theater Unbalance.* Hozumi also dubbed voices in Japanese releases of the *Back to the Future* films and other titles.

American actress **Diana Sowle** (Diana Mae Laumer) who, during a short screen career, made her film debut as Charlie Bucket's mother in *Willy Wonka & the Chocolate Factory* (1971), died the same day, aged 88.

Chinese actor **Hua Yueh** (Leung Lok Wah, aka "Yueh Hah"/ "Hwa Yuei"/"Hwa Yueh"/"Yue Hwa" and many others) died in Canada on October 20. He was in *The Monkey Goes West, Dragon Swamp, Super Stooges vs the Wonder Women, Black Magic* (1975), *The Web of Death, The Ghost Story, Return of the Dead* and *The Imp.*

Busy American character actor **James Karen** (Jacob Karnofsky) died of cardiac arrest on October 24, aged 94. He made his movie debut in *Frankenstein Meets the Spacemonster* (1965), and his other films include *Hercules in New York, Capricorn One, Topper* (1979), *Poltergeist* (1982), *Time Walker, The Boy Who Loved Trolls, The Return of the Living Dead, Invaders from Mars* (1986), *Return of the Living Dead II, Girlfriend from Hell, The Willies, The Unborn, Future Shock, Congo, Piranha* (1995), *Apt Pupil* (1998), *Mulholland Drive, Trail of the Screaming Forehead, Dark and Stormy Night, Jack and the Beanstalk* (2009), *The Butterfly Room* (with Barbara Steele) and *America's Most Haunted.* The actor's scenes were deleted from *Superman Returns* (2006). On TV, Karen played "Major Wymore" on *The Powers of Matthew Star* (1983) and he appeared in episodes of *The Invisible Man* (1975), *The Bionic Woman, Herbie the Love Bug, Tucker's Witch, Amazing Stories, Highway to Heaven, Touched by an Angel, Dark Skies, NightMan* and *The Nightmare Room*.

American character actor and dancer **Gary [Allen] Cockrell** died on October 26, aged 85. He was in *Tarzan the Magnificent, Gonks Go Beat, The Bedford Incident, Twilight's Last Gleaming* and an episode of TV's *The Alfred Hitchcock Hour*.

Nick Bon Tempi (Dominic Robert Bontempi), who played the left Siamese twin in Bert I. Gordon's *The Magic Sword* (1962), alongside his brother Paul, died on October 27, aged 88.

British stuntman and bit-player **Peter Brace** died on October 29, aged 94. His many credits include Hammer's *Dick Barton Detective, Quatermass 2, The Devil Rides Out* and *Taste the Blood of Dracula*, along with *Gorgo, Dr. No, Captain Sindbad, The Masque of the Red Death* (1964), *Goldfinger, The Black Torment, Circus of Fear* (aka *Psycho-Circus*), *Deadlier Than the Male, Casino Royale* (1967), *You Only Live Twice, Some Girls Do, Tommy, Theatre of Blood* (doubling Vincent Price), *Trial by Combat* (aka *A Dirty Knight's Work*), *Star Wars* (doubling Peter Mayhew's "Chewbacca"), *Flash Gordon* (1980), *Raiders of the Lost Ark, Superman II, Krull, Indiana Jones and the Temple of Doom, Highlander, Willow, Batman* (1989) and *Hands of a Murderer*. On TV, Brace was in episodes of TV's *The Invisible Man* (1958), *The Prisoner, The Avengers, Doctor Who, The New Avengers* and *She-Wolf of London*.

Busy red-haired American character actor **Ken Swofford** (Kenneth Charles Swofford), who was often cast as police captains and other authority figures, died on November 1, aged 85. His movie credits include *The Andromeda Strain* (1971), *Captain America II: Death Too Soon* (with Christopher Lee), *Bridge Across Time* (aka *Terror at London Bridge*, scripted by William F. Nolan), *Hunter's Blood, The Stepford Children* and *Black Roses*. On TV, Swofford appeared in episodes of *The Wild Wild West, The Girl with Something Extra, The Six Million Dollar Man, Battlestar Galactica, The Incredible Hulk, Fantasy Island, Voyagers!, Knight Rider, Max Headroom, Highway to Heaven* and *The Highwayman*.

72-year old deaf American stuntwoman and racing-car driver

Kitty O'Neil died of pneumonia on November 2, having recently suffered a heart attack. On TV, O'Neil doubled for Lindsay Wagner on *The Bionic Woman* (1976–78) and Lynda Carter on TV series *Wonder Woman* (1977–79). She also did stunts on the movies *Foes* and *Damien: Omen II*.

Iconoclastic Hollywood actress **Sondra Locke** (Sandra Louise Smith) died of cardiac arrest on November 3, aged 74. She had been suffering from metastatic breast and bone cancer. Perhaps best known for her high-profile relationship with co-star Clint Eastwood (who she later sued—twice!) during the 1970s and '80s, she appeared in the movies *Willard* (1971), *A Reflection of Fear*, *Death Game* (which she co-scripted, uncredited), *The Shadow of Chikara* and *Ratboy* (which she also directed). On TV, Locke was in episodes of *Night Gallery*, *Planet of the Apes*, *Tales of the Unexpected* and *Amazing Stories*.

American character and voice actor **Joe Medalis** (Joseph G. Medalis) died of Parkinson's disease the same day, aged 76. His live-action credits include *Space Force*, Disney's *The Cat from Outer Space*, *Love at First Bite*, *Meteor*, *Revenge of the Stepford Wives*, *Dead & Buried*, *Looker*, *Endangered Species*, *Deadly Messages*, *From the Dead of Night* and *Cosmic Slop*, along with episodes of such TV shows as *The Next Step Beyond*, *Wonder Woman*, *The Amazing Spider-Man*, *Bigfoot and Wildboy*, *World War III*, *Alfred Hitchcock Presents* (1985), *Amazing Stories*, *3rd Rock from the Sun*, *Sabrina the Teenage Witch* and *Power Rangers Time Force*.

American character actor **James Greene** (James Thomas Nolan) died on November 9, aged 91. He was in *Bug*, *The Spell*, *Ghost Story* (1981) and *Philadelphia Experiment II*, along with episodes of TV's *Max Headroom*, *Star Trek: The Next Generation*, *Alien Nation*, *Quantum Leap*, *The Adventures of Brisco County, Jr.*, *Star Trek: Deep Space Nine*, *Star Trek: Voyager*, *Charmed* and *Miracles*.

Canadian actor **Douglas** [James] **Rain**, who is remembered for voicing the soft-spoken rogue computer "Hal 9000" in Stanley Kubrick's *2001: A Space Odyssey* (1968), died on November 11, aged 90. Rain reprised the role in the sequel, *2010*, and voiced the "Evil Computer" in the Woody Allen sci-fi spoof *Sleeper*.

Polish-born British character actor **John Bluthal** (Isaac Bluthal) died in Australia on November 15. He was 89. Bluthal's credits include *The Mouse on the Moon*, *Carry on Spying*, *Help!* (with The Beatles), *Casino Royale* (1967), *A Ghost of a Chance*, *Digby the Biggest Dog in the World*, *The Flying Sorcerer*, *Superman III*, *The Return of Captain Invincible* (with Christopher Lee), *Labyrinth*, *Leapin' Leprechauns!* and the sequel *Spellbreaker: Secret of the Leprechauns*, *The Fifth Element* and *Dark City*, along with episodes of TV's *The Avengers*, *Super Gran* and *Spirited*. The actor was also the voice of "Commander Wilbur Zero" and other characters on Gerry Anderson's puppet show *Fireball XL5* (1962–63).

Balding British character actor **George A.** (Alphonsus) **Cooper** died on November 16, aged 93. His film credits include Freddie Francis' *The Brain* and *Dracula Has Risen from the Grave* (with Christopher Lee), along with Hammer's *Nightmare* and Amicus' *What Became of Jack and Jill?*. On TV, Cooper was featured in episodes of *Doctor Who*, *The Avengers*, *Sherlock Holmes* (with Peter Cushing as Holmes), *Randall and Hopkirk (Deceased)*, *Doomwatch*, *The Rivals of Sherlock Holmes*, *The New Avengers*, *Shadows* and *Metal Mickey*.

British actor **Andrew Burt** died the same day, aged 73. He starred in the title roles of the TV series *The Legend of King Arthur* (1979) and *Gulliver in Lilliput* (1982), and was in episodes of *Blakes 7*, *Doctor Who* ('Terminus') and *Tales of the Unexpected*.

Canadian character actor **Edward Evanko** died of complications from a stroke on November 18, aged 80. On TV he appeared in episodes of *The Burning Zone*, *The Pretender*, *3rd Rock from the Sun*, *First Wave*, *The New Addams Family*, *So Weird*, *The Outer Limits* (1998 and 2000), *Mysterious Ways* and *Night Visions*. Evanko was also in the movies *K-9000*, *Dark Planet* and *Dead Man's Gun* before being ordained as a Roman Catholic priest in 2005.

British actress **Jennie** (Jennifer) **Stoller** died of cancer the same day, aged 72. She appeared in the 1981 *Sapphire & Steel* TV serial 'Assignment Five: Doctor McDee Must Die', as well as "Helena" in the Royal Shakespeare Company's 1972 stage production of *A Midsummer Night's Dream*, directed by Peter Brook, and "Mrs.

Kendal" in Bernard Pomerance's 1977 production of *The Elephant Man*.

British character actor **Hugh Dickson** died on November 21, aged 91. He appeared in episodes of TV's *Dimensions of Fear, Adam Adamant Lives!, Orson Welles Great Mysteries, Hammer House of Mystery and Suspense, Witchcraft* (1992), *The Infinite Worlds of H.G. Wells* and *Murder Rooms: The Dark Beginnings of Sherlock Holmes* (Stephen Gallagher's 'The Kingdom of Bones'), along with the films *Alice's Adventures in Wonderland* (1956) and *Death Line* (aka *Raw Meat*, with Christopher Lee). On Radio, Dickson played "Elrond" in the BBC radio production of *The Lord of the Rings*.

American model-turned-actress **Michele Carey** (Michele Henson), who co-starred opposite Elvis Presley in *Live a Little, Love a Little* (1968), died the same day, aged 75. Her other credits include AIP's *How to Stuff a Wild Bikini, The Norliss Tapes* (scripted by William F. Nolan), *The Six Million Dollar Man: Wine Women and War, The Legend of the Golden Gun, Death Ray 2000* (and the spin-off series *A Man Called Sloane*) and *The Stay Awake*, along with episodes of TV's *The Man from U.N.C.L.E., The Wild Wild West* (with Victor Buono) and *Man from Atlantis*. In 1973 Carey also starred in the unsold pilot for NBC's ghostly sitcom *Where's Mama*.

Indian-born British character actor **David** [Henry] **Conville** died on November 24, aged 89. He appeared in Hammer's *The Curse of the Werewolf* and *The Evil of Frankenstein*, along with an episode of TV's *Out of the Unknown*.

American magician and actor **Ricky Jay** (Richard Jay Potash), who was a regular on HBO's *Deadwood* (2004), died the same day, aged 72. He appeared in the James Bond film *Tomorrow Never Dies, Mystery Men, Incident at Loch Ness, The Prestige*, and episodes of *The X Files* and *Flashforward*. Jay was also technical consultant on such movies as *The Believers, Wolf, Congo, The Illusionist* and *The Prestige*.

American character actor [Thomas] **Wright** [Thornburg] **King**, who starred as "Ernest P. Duckweather" in the children's TV series *Johnny Jupiter* (1953–54) and co-starred opposite Steve McQueen in the second season of *Wanted: Dead or Alive*, died on November

25, aged 95. King made his debut in an episode of *Captain Video and His Video Rangers* (1949) and he was also in episodes of *Out There*, *Broadway Television Theatre* ('Night Must Fall' and 'Outward Bound'), *The Twilight Zone*, *Voyage to the Bottom of the Sea*, *The Invaders* and *Logan's Run*. His movie credits include *Planet of the Apes* (1968, as "Dr. Galen"), *Finian's Rainbow*, *Invasion of the Bee Girls* and *The Spell*.

British character actor **Peter** [James] **Armitage** MBE died of a heart attack on November 30, aged 79. His credits include TV's two-part *Jack the Ripper* (1988), along with episodes of *Woof!*, Stephen Gallagher's *Chimera*, *The Young Indiana Jones Chronicles* and *The Second Coming*.

American light comedian **Ken Berry** (Kenneth Ronald Berry), who co-starred in the ABC-TV sitcom *F Troop* (1965–67), died on December 1, aged 85. He was also in the movies *Hello Down There* and Disney's *Herbie Rides Again* and *The Cat from Outer Space*. Berry guest-starred on TV's *Small Wonder*, and appeared in seven episodes of *Fantasy Island*. Vincent Price turned up in the 1967 *F Troop* episode, 'V is for Vampire'.

British Guiana-born actor and singer **Thomas Baptiste** (Frederick Eustance Thomas Anthony Baptiste) died on December 6, aged 89. He appeared (uncredited) as the god "Dambala" in the 'Voodoo' segment of *Dr. Terror's House of Horrors* (starring Christopher Lee, Peter Cushing and Michael Gough), and he was also in *Help!*. On TV, Baptiste was a regular on the children's TV series *The Master* (1966).

American actor **Peter Masterson** (Carlos Bee Masterson, Jr.) died on December 18, aged 84. He had been suffering from Parkinson's disease. Masterson's movies include *The Exorcist*, *Man on a Swing*, *The Stepford Wives* (1975) and *Witchfire*. He later became a director and co-wrote the successful Broadway musical and movie *The Best Little Whorehouse in Texas*.

American stuntman and actor **Steve Dash** (Steve Daskawisz) died of complications from diabetes the same day, aged 74. His credits include *Ms. 45*, *Friday the 13th Part 2* (as "Jason Voorhees"), *Alone in the Dark*, *Mr. Hush*, *Emerging Past*, *Hemo* and the kickstarterfunded *Friday the 13th* sequel, *Vengeance*, along with two episodes of TV's *Superboy*.

British-born American actor **Donald Moffat**, who co-starred as the android "Rem" in the CBS-TV series *Logan's Run* (1977–78), died of complications from a stroke on December 20, aged 87. The bushy-eyebrowed performer was also in *The Devil and Miss Sarah*, *The Terminal Man*, *Earthquake*, *Exo-Man*, *Popeye* and John Carpenter's *The Thing*, as well as episodes of TV's *Rod Serling's Night Gallery* (H.P. Lovecraft's 'Pickman's Model') and *The Six Million Dollar Man*.

American tough-guy actor **Frank Adonis** (Frank Testaverde Scioscia) died of kidney failure on December 26, aged 83. He had roles in *Eyes of Laura Mars*, *Wolfen* and *The Woods Have Eyes* (which he co-scripted).

British comedy legend Dame **June** [Rosemary] **Whitfield**, who was the voice of "Nanny Ogg" in the 1997 animated TV series of Terry Pratchett's *Wyrd Sisters*, died the same day, aged 93. The beloved *Carry On* actress also appeared in the 2009 *Doctor Who* Christmas special 'The End of Time' and turned up as "God" in an episode of *You, Me and the Apocalypse*.

American character actor **Herb Ellis** (Herbert Siegel) also died on December 26, aged 97. He often portrayed policemen, doctors and other authority figures in such TV shows as *Alfred Hitchcock Presents*, *My Mother the Car*, *My Favorite Martian*, *Get Smart* and *Bewitched*.

Striking American ballerina and actress **Sono Osato** (aka "Sono Fitzpatrick") died the same day, aged 99. Of mixed ethnic parentage, she appeared on Broadway in *One Touch of Venus* in 1943, then had a few film and TV credits, including the 1959 episode of NBC's *Sunday Showcase*, 'Murder and the Android', written by Alfred Bester..

American actor **Robert** [Charles] **Kerman** (aka "Richard Bolla"/"Richard Balla"/"Martin Spellman" and many others) died of complications from diabetes on December 27, aged 71. He had suffered from health problems for some years. Along with appearing in numerous hardcore porn movies such as *Debbie Does Dallas*, *House of Sin*, *The Devil in Miss Jones Part II* and *Blue Voodoo*, he also had a dual career starring in Ruggero Deodato's *Cannibal Holocaust* and Umberto Lenzi's *Eaten Alive!*, with smaller roles in Lenzi's *Cannibal Ferox*, *The Clairvoyant*, *Night of the Creeps* and Sam Raimi's *Spider-Man* (2002).

Mexican actress and dancer **Rosenda Monteros** (Rosa Méndez Leza), who played "Ustane" in Hammer's *She* (1965), alongside Peter Cushing and Christopher Lee, died on December 29, aged 83 (although some sources claim 86). She also had supporting roles in *The Face of Eve* (aka *Eve*, also with Lee) and *Cauldron of Blood* (with Boris Karloff giving one of his last performances).

Swedish actress **Agneta** [Marie-Anne] **Eckemyr**, who co-starred in Disney's *The Island at the Top of the World*, died of Alzheimer's disease the same day, aged 68.

FILM/TV TECHNICIANS

William Beaudine, Jr., the son of the legendary 1940s horror director, died on January 2, aged 96. After appearing in small roles in some of his father's movies, he went to to become a unit production manager, producer (the 1987 TV movie *The Spirit*) and assistant director (*Safari Drums*, Don Siegel's *Invasion of the Body Snatchers*, and *Queen of Outer Space*).

American movie producer **John Thompson**, head of production at Millennium Films, died of leukaemia on January 9, aged 71. Starting out as a line producer at The Cannon Group, his many credits include *X-Ray*, Luigi Cozzi's *Hercules* and *The Adventures of Hercules*, *The Barbarians*, *Haunted Summer*, *Replicant*, *Mansquito*, *Snakeman* (aka *The Snake King*), *SharkMan* (aka *Hammerhead*), *The Wicker Man* (2006), *Attack of the Gryphon*, *Texas Chainsaw 3D*, *The Legend of Hercules*, *Leatherface* and *Hellboy* (2019). Thompson also came up with the original story for the TV movie *Alien Lockdown* (2004), and he had a supporting role in the Rutger Hauer SF movie *Redline* (1997).

British-born production designer and art director **Terence** [George] **Marsh** died in California of complications from cancer the same day, aged 86. The two-time Academy Award-winner's credits include *Scrooge* (1970), *The Adventures of Sherlock Holmes' Smarter Brother, Magic, Haunted Honeymoon, Spaceballs, The Shawshank Redemption, Fallen* and *The Green Mile*. Marsh also co-scripted *Haunted Honeymoon* (1986) with director and star Gene Wilder, and he had an uncredited cameo in Mel Brooks' *Star Wars* spoof *Spaceballs*.

British independent film writer and director **Omid Nooshin** hanged himself on January 15, aged 43. He had battled with depression for six years. Inspired by *Star Wars* to enter the film industry, Nooshin wrote and directed the segment 'The Patient' in the 1996 anthology film *Virtual Terror*, and he also co-scripted *Kill Switch* (2017).

American movie producer and studio executive **Allison Shearmur** (Allison Ivy Brecker) died of lung cancer on January 19, aged 54. Her credits include the first four *The Hunger Games* films, Disney's *Cinderella* (2015), *Clan of the Cave Bear* (2015), *Pride and Prejudice with Zombies, Rogue One: A Star Wars Story, Power Rangers* (2017) and *Solo: A Star Wars Story*.

American movie producer **Joel Freeman** died of Alzheimer's disease on January 21, aged 95. A production supervisor on *12 to the Moon*, and an assistant director on *Tarzan the Ape Man* (1959) and an episode of TV's *World of the Giants*, he went on to work as a producer on *Finian's Rainbow, Love at First Bite* and *The Kindred*.

Polish-born British make-up designer **Dorka** [Dorota Malgorzata] **Nieradzik** MBE, who was actor Clive Owen's personal make-up artist and hair stylist on a number of films, including *King Arthur, Children of Men* and *Valerian and the City of a Thousand Planets*, died of cancer on February 12, aged 68. She also worked on *The Yellow Wallpaper* (1989) along with episodes of TV's *Doctor Who* (1980–88) and Dennis Potter's *Cold Lazarus*.

American film editor and director **Edward M.** [Meyer] **Abroms** died of heart failure on February 13, aged 82. His editing credits include *Tarzan's Deadly Silence, The Groundstar Conspiracy, You'll Like My Mother, Blue Thunder, Cherry 2000, Nightlife* (1989), *Grave Secrets: The Legend of Hilltop Drive, Street Fighter*, Steven Spielberg's pilot for *Rod Serling's Night Gallery*, and several episodes of TV's *Tarzan* (1966–68). Abroms also directed a number of TV shows, including *Night Gallery* ('Something in the Woodwork', based on the story by R. Chetwynd-Hayes), *The Six Million Dollar Man*, *Man from Atlantis* and *Salvage 1*.

British film director, screenwriter and producer **Lewis Gilbert** CBE died in Monaco on February 23, aged 97. Best known for his James Bond movies *You Only Live Twice*, *The Spy Who Loved Me* and *Moonraker*, his other credits include *Haunted*, the 1995 adaptation of the novel by James Herbert.

American cinematographer **Ralph Woolsey** died the same day, aged 104. He worked on numerous TV series, including *Batman* (1966), while *The Pack* and *Oh God! Book II* are amongst the movies he shot.

American animator **Bud Luckey** (William Everett Luckey) died on February 24, aged 83. He contributed to the character design for *Toy Story*, *A Bug's Life*, *Toy Story 2* and *Monsters Inc.*, and worked as a voice actor on *The Incredibles*, *Toy Story 3* and the 2011 *Winnie the Pooh* (as "Eeyore").

American movie and TV producer **Benjamin Melniker** died on February 26, aged 104. He began his career in 1939 at Metro-Goldwyn-Mayer, but is best known for his connection with DC Comics universe (with Michael Uslan), including credits on Wes Craven's *Swamp Thing*, *The Return of Swamp Thing*, Tim Burton's *Batman* and *Batman Returns*, Joel Schumacher's *Batman Forever* and *Batman & Robin*, *Catwoman*, *Constantine*, Christopher Nolan's *Batman Begins*, *The Dark Knight* and *The Dark Knight Rises*, *Batman vs. Superman: Dawn of Justice*, *The Lego Batman Movie*, *Justice League*, *Teen Titans GO! to the Movies* and the 1990–93 TV series *Swamp Thing*. Melniker also executive produced *Batman: Mask of the Phantasm*, *The Batman vs. Dracula*, *Justice League: Gods and Monsters*, *Batman: The Killing Joke*, *Justice League Dark*, *Scooby-Doo! & Batman: The Brave and the Bold*, *Batman: Gotham by Gaslight* and numerous other direct-to-video animated adventures, along with Frank Miller's live-action version of Will Eisner's *The Spirit* (2008).

American dancer and actor turned TV director **Robert Scheerer** died on March 3, aged 89. His credits include the 1969 version of *Arsenic and Old Lace* (featuring Fred Gwynne as "Jonathan Brewster"), *Poor Devil* (with Christopher Lee as "Lucifer"), *Ants!*, Disney's 1988 remake of *The Absent-Minded Professor* and the sequel *The Absent-Minded Professor: Trading Places*, plus episodes of *The Girl with Something Extra*, *Kolchak: The Night Stalker*, *Star Trek: The Next Generation*, *Star Trek: Deep Space Nine* and *Star Trek: Voyager*.

American documentary film producer **Arnold Kunert** died of cancer on March 14. A long-time admirer of Ray Harryhausen, whom he agented during the 2000s, he won a Saturn Award for his two-disc DVD *Ray Harryhausen: The Early Years Collection*, and his other credits include the 2007 stop-motion short *The Pit and the Pendulum* and the documentaries *The Music of Bernard Herrmann*, *The Harryhausen Legacy* and *Remembering The 7th Voyage of Sinbad*.

Swiss "sexploitation" film producer, screenwriter and director **Erwin C. Dietrich** (aka "Michael Thomas") died on March 15, aged 87. He made seventeen movies with Jesús Franco, including *Jack the Ripper* (1976, with Klaus Kinski), *Die Marquise von Sade*, *Wanda the Wicked Warden* and *Voodoo Passion* (Dietrich also co-scripted the latter two with Franco under the pseudonym "Manfred Gregor"). He also produced Martin Walz's *Killer Condom*.

American TV animator **Fred Crippen**, who created the cartoon series *Roger Ramjet* (1965), died on March 22, aged 90. His other credits include *The ABC Saturday Superstar Movie* ('The Mini-Munsters'), *Yogi's Space Race*, *Galaxy Goof-Ups*, *Adventures of Sonic the Hedgehog*, *Teenage Mutant Ninja Turtles* (1996), *Extreme Ghostbusters*, *Men in Black: The Series*, *Sabrina the Animated Series*, *Monster Mash* (2000) and *Godzilla: The Series* (1999–2001).

Australian producer and director **Gil Brealey** (Gilbert John Brealey) died on April 1, aged 85. He directed the premiere episode of Australia's first science fiction TV series, *The Stranger* (1964), which was aimed at younger viewers.

Japanese *anime* writer and director **Isao Takahata** died of lung cancer on April 5, aged 82. His many films include *Horus: Prince* *of the Sun*, *Grave of the Fireflies* and *The Tale of The Princess Kaguya*, along with two episodes of the TV series *Future Boy Conan*. Together with his friend and fellow animator Hayao Miyazaki, Takahata co-founded Studio Ghibli in 1985.

British puppeteer **Bob Bura** (Robert Barnett Bura), who was inside the monster suit in *Gorgo* (1961), died on April 7, aged 93. He also worked on such TV productions as *The Emperor's Nightingale* (1957), *The Magic Tree* (1960), *Beauty and the Beast* (1961) and *The Dancing Princess* (1962). With his long-time collaborator, John Hardwick, Bura also created the stop-motion animation for such popular children's TV series as *Camberwick Green*, *Trumpton*, *Mary Mungo & Midge* and *The Adventures of Sir Prancelot*.

Czechoslovakian director **Juraj Herz** died on April 8, aged 83. His films include *Cremator*, *Morgiana*, *Beauty and the Beast* (1978), *The Ninth Heart*, *Ferat Vampire* (in which he played "Dracula" in a silent film), *The Frog Prince* (1991) and *Darkness* (2009). As an actor, Herz also appeared in such TV productions as *The Phantom of Operette* (1970) and *Touha Sherlocka Holmese*.

Award-winning Italian director and screenwriter **Vittorio Taviani**, who co-directed the episodic *Kaos* (which features a "werewolf" sequence) with his brother Paolo, died on April 15, aged 88. He had been ill for some time following a car accident several years earlier.

British-born movie director **Michael** [Joseph] **Anderson** died in Canada on April 25, aged 98. After working as an assistant director during the 1940s on such films as the body-swap comedy *Vice Versa* (1948), he went on to direct *1984* (1956), *Around the World in 80 Days* (1956), *The Shoes of the Fisherman*, *Doc Savage The Man of Bronze*, *Logan's Run*, *Orca*, *Dominique* (aka *Dominique is Dead*), *Millennium*, *20,000 Leagues Under the Sea* (1997, with Ben Cross as "Captain Nemo"), *The New Adventures of Pinocchio* and the three-part 1980 TV mini-series of Ray Bradbury's *The Martian Chronicles*.

American director and producer **Jack Regas** died the same day, aged 92. He began his career as a dancer and bit-player in movies in the mid-1940s before going on to direct episodes of such family TV shows as *The Lost Saucer*, *Dr. Shrinker*, *Electra Woman and*

Dyna Girl, Wonderbug, Magic Mongo and *Out of This World*, along with the 1975 TV special of the Broadway musical *It's a Bird... It's a Plane... It's Superman!*.

Italian screenwriter and director **Gianfranco Parolini** (aka "Frank Kramer"/"G.F. Parolini") died on April 26, aged 93. His credits include *Samson, The Fury of Hercules, The Three Avengers, The Three Fantastic Supermen* and *Yeti: Giant of the 20th Century*.

American TV producer **Paul Junger Witt**, best known for such hit shows as *The Partridge Family, Soap* and *The Golden Girls*, died of cancer on April 27, aged 77. He produced the TV movies *Home for the Holidays, A Cold Night's Death* and *Satan's Triangle*, along with the series *Beauty and the Beast* (1987–90 and 2012–16) and *Woops!*. Witt also produced Christopher Nolan's serial killer thriller *Insomnia* (2002).

Academy Award-winning British-born film editor **Anne V. (Voase) Coates** OBE died in Los Angeles on May 8, aged 92. The wife of director Douglas Hickox and mother of Anthony Hickox and James D.R. Hickox, also directors, her credits include *The Legacy, The Elephant Man, Greystoke: The Legend of Tarzan Lord of the Apes, Masters of the Universe, Congo* and *The Golden Compass*. The niece of J. Arthur Rank, Coates also worked on *The Red Shoes* and *The Rocking Horse Winner*, and she co-produced and was the supervising editor on *The Medusa Touch*.

Journeyman American director **Vincent McEveety** died on May 19, aged 88. He directed six episodes (1966–68) of the original *Star Trek* TV series, along with episodes of *The Man from U.N.C.L.E., Kolchak: The Night Stalker, Future Cop, The Fantastic Journey, Buck Rogers in the 25th Century, Herbie the Love Bug* and *The Powers of Matthew Star*. McEveety's movies include Disney's *The Million Dollar Duck, Charley and the Angel, The Strongest Man in the World, Herbie Goes to Monte Carlo, Herbie Goes Bananas* and the uncredited re-shoots of *The Watcher in the Woods* (1980), and he also directed the 1974 TV pilot *Wonder Woman*.

Japanese cinematographer **Tamura Masaki**, whose credits include *The Crazy Family* and *Evil Dead Trap*, died of pneumonia on May 23, aged 79.

Canadian-born special effects illustrator and art director **George Jenson** (aka "George Jensen") died in America on May 25, aged 87. He worked on Disney's *Escape to Witch Mountain*, *Logan's Run*, *Close Encounters of the Third Kind*, *Looker*, *Christine*, *Return of the Jedi*, *2010*, *Red Dawn* (1984), *Dune* (1984), *Big Trouble in Little China*, *Poltergeist II: The Other Side*, *Masters of the Universe*, *Vibes*, *Solar Crisis*, *The Rocketeer*, *Terminator 2: Judgment Day*, *Three Wishes*, *Thinner*, *In Dreams*, *Dr. Dolittle 2*, and episodes of TV's *The Time Tunnel*, *Lost in Space*, *Voyage to the Bottom of the Sea* and *Land of the Giants*. Jenson was also a layout artist for the 1970s cartoon series *My Favorite Martians* and *Star Trek: The Animated Series*.

American TV producer **Tom** (Thomas) **Swale**, whose credits include the 1974–75 series *Land of the Lost*, died on May 29, aged 71. He also scripted the TV movie *Murder in Mind* (1997) and wrote for a number of children's series, including *Space Academy*, *Tarzan and the Super 7*, *Spider-Woman*, *Godzilla* and *Scooby-Doo and Scrappy-Doo*.

British set decorator **Michael** [Dickins] **Ford**, who won an Oscar for his work on *Raiders of the Lost Ark*, died on May 31, aged 89. His other films include *The Empire Strikes Back*, *Return of the Jedi*, *Return to Oz*, *Young Sherlock Holmes*, *The Muppet Christmas Carol*, *Nostradamus* (1994), *GoldenEye* and *Wing Commander*. Ford also worked as a set dresser and art director on the TV series *Star Maidens*, *The New Avengers* and *Space: 1999*.

American TV producer and production manager **Kent** [Baldwin] **McCray**, who often collaborated with Bob Hope and actor Michael Landon, died on June 3, just four days short of his 90th birthday. He began his career working on *Matinee Theatre* ('The Fall of the House of Usher', 1956) and his other credits include Landon's series *Highway to Heaven*.

American business manager and movie producer **Martin** [Leon] **Bregman** died of a cerebral haemorrhage on June 16, aged 92. His films include *Simon*, *Venom* (1981), *The Shadow* (1994), *The Bone Collector* and *The Adventures of Pluto Nash*.

Canadian-born producer and director **Steven H.** [Hilliard] **Stern** died in California on June 27, aged 80. His credits include *The Ghost* of *Flight 401*, Disney's *The Devil and Max Devlin*, *Mazes and Monsters*, *Murder in Space* and *Not Quite Human*, along with episodes of TV's *The Hardy Boys/Nancy Drew Mysteries* ('Mystery of the Hollywood Phantom'), *Logan's Run*, *The Adventures of Sinbad* and *The Crow: Stairway to Heaven*.

British artist and animator **Peter** [Arthur] **Firmin**, who co-created (with the late Oliver Postgate) such animated children's TV shows as *Ivor the Engine*, *The Seal of Neptune*, *Bagpuss*, *Noggin the Nog* and *Clangers*, died after a short illness on July 1, aged 89. Firmin also created the puppet character "Basil Brush".

British stage and screen choreographer Dame **Gillian Lynne** (Gillian Barbara Pyrke) died the same day, aged 92. She began her career as an actress in such TV productions as the BBC's *Beauty and the Beast* (1956) before becoming a choreographer in the early 1960s. Her credits include *Alice in Wonderland* (1985), TV's *The Muppet Show*, and the original stage productions of Andrew Lloyd Webber's *Cats* and *The Phantom of the Opera*. The West End's New London Theatre was renamed in her honour just a few days before her death.

Dutch cinematographer **Robby** (Robert) **Müller** died after a long illness on July 3, aged 78. He worked on *Jonathan*, *Repo Man*, *The Believers*, *The Little Devil* and *Dead Man*, amongst many other films.

American layout and animation artist **Darrell McNeil** died on July 4. He worked on numerous TV series, including *Tarzan and the Super 7*, *Space Stars*, *The Real Ghostbusters*, *Teenage Mutant Ninja Turtles*, *James Bond Jr.* and *Streetfighter: The Animated Series*, along with *Jetsons: The Movie*.

American dancer and choreographer **Alan** [Scott] **Johnson** died on July 7, aged 81. His movie credits include several titles with Mel Brooks, including *Young Frankenstein* (the 'Puttin' On the Ritz' tap-dancing sequence) and *Dracula Dead and Loving It*, along with *The Adventure of Sherlock Holmes' Smarter Brother* and *Neverland* (2003). Johnson also directed the 1986 SF movie *Solarbabies*.

Italian director and screenwriter **Carlo Vanzina** died on July 8, aged 67. His credits include the 1985 *giallo Nothing Underneath* and the time-travel comedies *A spasso nel tempo* and the sequel *A spasso nel tempo—L'aventura continua*.

Academy Award-winning British costume designer **Yvonne [Ann] Blake** died in Spain on July 17, aged 78. She began her career working for Hammer Films on *Never Take Sweets from a Stranger*, *The Terror of the Tongs* and *The Shadow of the Cat*, and her other credits include *Fahrenheit 451* (1966), *Night Watch*, *Superman* (1978), *Superman II*, *Las aventuras de Enrique y Ana*, *Scarab*, *Flesh+Blood*, *Rowing with the Wind*, *What Dreams May Come*, *Presence of Mind* (another adaptation of Henry James' 'The Turn of the Screw') and *Wax*. Blake, who was married to Spanish assistant director Gil Carretero, served as President of the Spanish Academy of Motion Picture Arts and Sciences (2016–2018).

British production designer **Michael Howells** died on July 19, aged 61. He worked on *FairyTale: A True Story*, *Ever After: A Cinderella Story*, *Nanny McPhee* and *Blackwood*.

American animator and director **Jon Schnepp** (Jonathan David Schnepp) died of complications from a stroke the same day, aged 51. He worked on such cartoon series as *Aqua Teen Hunger Force* and *Space Ghost Coast to Coast*, and made the 2015 documentary *The Death of "Superman Lives": What Happened?*.

Emmy Award-winning American sound editor and designer **David Grindstaff**, best known for his iconic work creating the sounds for various devices and tribbles on the original *Star Trek* TV series, died on July 23, aged 87. He also worked on such shows as *Fantasy Island* and *Max Headroom*.

American digital visual effects artist **Jeff Heusser** died the same day, aged 61. His credits include *Kazaam*, *Contact*, *Deep Impact*, *Wing Commander*, *The Adventures of Sharkboy and Lavagirl 3-D*, *Fantastic Four* (2005), *The Fog* (2005), *Æon Flux*, *X-Men: The Last Stand*, *Fantastic 4: Rise of the Silver Surfer*, *The Seeker: The Dark is Rising*, *Alien vs. Predator: Requiem* and *Meet Dave*.

Polish screenwriter and director **Piotr [Andrzej] Szulkin** died on August 5, aged 68. His films include *Oczy uroczne*, *Golem* (1980), *The War of the Worlds: Next Century* (1981), *O-Bi, O-Ba—The End of Civilization* and *Ga, Ga—Chwala bohaterom*.

American cinematographer **Richard H.** (Howard) **Kline** died on August 7, aged 91. Nominated for an Academy Award for his work on *King Kong* (1976), he began his career working as a camera assistant or operator (often uncredited) on such movies as *The Return of the Vampire*, *The Magic Carpet*, *Cannibal Attack*, *It Came from Beneath the Sea*, *Around the World in 80 Days* (1956) and *Bell Book and Candle*. After moving into TV in the early 1960s as a director of photography, Kline went on to shoot *Chamber of Horrors* (1966), *The Boston Strangler*, *The Andromeda Strain*, *Hammersmith is Out*, *Soylent Green*, *Battle for the Planet of the Apes*, *The Terminal Man*, *The Fury*, *Star Trek: The Motion Picture*, *Lovespell*, *All of Me*, *Howard the Duck* and *My Stepmother is an Alien*.

American movie memorabilia collector **Wes Shank** (Walter Shank), who was nicknamed "The Caretaker of the Blob" after he rescued the prop when it was being thrown out, died on August 10, aged 72. A collector since 1960, he also owned props from *Planet of the Apes* and *Forbidden Planet*, amongst other movies, and is credited with locating the censored scenes from the original *King Kong* (1933), which were then incorporated back into all modern prints of the film. In 2009, Shank published *From Silicone to the Silver Screen—Memoirs of The Blob (1958)*.

British casting director **Marilyn** [Elizabeth Florence] **Johnson** died on August 12, aged 74. Her numerous credits include *The Sign of Four* (1983), *Dream Demon*, *Slipstream*, *The Woman in Black* (1989), *20,000 Leagues Under the Sea* (1997), *Doomwatch: Winter Angel*, *Ghostboat*, and episodes of TV's *Worlds Beyond*, *Gormenghast*, *The Secret Adventures of Jules Verne*, *Hex*, *Clone* and *Eternal Law*.

American dancer, choreographer and actress **Miriam Nelson** (Miriam Lois Frankel) died the same day, aged 98. She began her screen career in Hollywood in the mid-1940s before becoming a choreographer on such movies as *Visit to a Small Planet*, *Murderers' Row*, *Buck Rogers in the 25th Century* and *Alice in Wonderland* (1985).

69-year-old American movie and TV producer **Craig Zadan** died of complications from shoulder replacement surgery on August 21. His credits include *Twists of Terror*, *Cinderella* (1997), *Flowers for*

Algernon, Peter Pan Live! and *The Wiz Live!*. Zadan also executive produced the TV series *Veritas: The Quest* and *Drop Dead Diva*.

American movie producer **Andre** [Alvin] **Blay** died on August 24, aged 81. His biggest accomplishment came in the late 1970s, when he convinced the major studios to licence their full-length product to the emerging videocassette market, and in 1982 he became chief executive of Embassy Home Entertainment. After leaving Embassy, he formed Palisades Entertainment Group with Elliott Kastner, and his executive producing credits include John Carpenter's *Prince of Darkness, They Live* and *Village of the Damned* (1995), along with *Brain Damage, Jack's Back, The Blob* (1988) and *Mosquito*.

British production designer **Michael** [Mervyn] **Pickwoad**, best known for his contributions to the revivals of TV's *The Prisoner* (2009) and *Doctor Who* (2010–17), died on August 27, aged 73. The son of actor William Mervyn, he also worked on *Twisted Nerve, The Man Who Haunted Himself, House of Whipcord, The Comeback, A Hitch in Time, Hawk the Slayer, House of Long Shadows, Sword of the Valiant, Jane and the Lost City, Sweeney Todd* (2006), *A Midsummer Night's Dream* (2016) and the TV series *Lost in Austen* and the *Doctor Who* spin-off *Class*.

Hollywood sound engineer and editor **Frank Serafine** died on September 12, aged 65. He was struck by a car and died at the scene of major head and body trauma. Serafine worked on *Star Trek: The Motion Picture, The Fog* (1980), *The Sword and the Sorcerer, TRON, Brainstorm* (1983), *The Day After, New Magic, The Ice Pirates, Star Trek III: The Search for Spock, Ninja III: The Domination, Short Circuit, Poltergeist II: The Other Side, Flight of the Navigator, Manhunter, The Wind, Timestalkers, Pumpkinhead, Short Circuit 2, Meet the Hollowheads, Field of Dreams, Robot Jox, The Hunt for Red October, The Addams Family* (1991), *The Lawnmower Man, Warlock: The Armageddon, Brainstorm* (1994), *Virtuosity, Prince Valiant* (1997), *Orgazmo, P.U.N.K.S., TRON: Legacy, Hoodwinked Too! Hood vs. Evil, VooDoo* and *Defrost: The Virtual Series*.

American movie editor **Pasquale Buba** died of cancer the same day, aged 72. He worked with director George A. Romero on *Knightriders, Creepshow* ('The Lonesome Death of Jordy Verrill' segment), *Day of the Dead, Monkey Shines, Two Evil Eyes* and *The Dark Half*. Buba's other credits include *Effects* (1979), *Stepfather II*, and three episodes of TV's *Tales from the Crypt*.

American-born movie producer **Gary** [Douglas] **Kurtz** died of cancer in London on September 23, aged 78. He got his start working for Roger Corman in the 1960s as a production manager on *Voyage to the Prehistoric Planet* and *Queen of Blood*, and as a sound engineer on *Blood Bath*. Best known for producing the first two *Star Wars* films, his other movies include *The Dark Crystal, Return to Oz, Slipstream, Mickey's Nutcracker* and *The Thief and the Cobbler*.

British animator **Roger Mainwood**, best known for his work on the TV films *The Snowman, When the Wind Blows* and *Father Christmas* (all based on books by Raymond Briggs), died of cancer on September 24, aged 65. His other credits include *Heavy Metal, The Willows in Winter, Faeries* and *The Snowman and the Snowdog*.

American "Claymation" animator and film-maker **Will Vinton** (William Gale Vinton) died after a twelve-year battle with multiple myeloma on October 4, aged 70. He created the "California Raisins" TV commericials and made a number of short films, including the Oscar-winning *Closed Mondays, Rip Van Winkle, The Little Prince, Dinosaur* and *Claymation Comedy of Horrors Show*. Vinton also worked on the visual effects for *Return to Oz, Shadow Play* and Michael Jackson's *Moonwalker*. The Will Vinton Studios in Portland, Oregon, later became Laika.

Hollywood movie producer **Arnold Kopelson** died on October 8, aged 83. His credits include *The Legacy, Warlock* (1989), *Outbreak, Se7en* and *The Devil's Advocate*.

61-year-old American sound recordist and mixer **James M. Emswiller** died on October 11 after falling from a second-storey balcony on the set of *A Beautiful Day in the Neighborhood* starring Tom Hanks. He worked on *Heartstopper, My Bloody Valentine* (2009), *Sorority Row* (2009), *6 Souls, Locke & Key, The Avengers* (2012), *A Resurrection, The Town That Dreaded Sundown* (2014) and the comedy zombie short *Reign of the Dead*.

American movie producer **John G. Stephens** died on October 15, aged 89. He worked on the casting for the 1957 film *Pharaoh's*

Curse before going on to produce the TV movies *Wonder Woman* (1974) and George R.R. Martin's *Doorways*, along with the 1981 season of *Buck Rogers in the 25th Century*.

Veteran British TV producer and director **Pamela Lonsdale** [Tucker], who was instrumental in setting up Cosgrove Hall Films, died on October 16, aged 94. Her credits include the series *The Forgotten Door*, *The Lion the Witch and the Wardrobe* (1967), *Ace of Wands*, *Rainbow*, *The Boy Merlin*, *Stig of the Dump*, *Beauty and the Beast* (1982), *Chocky* and *Chocky's Children* (both based on the novel by John Wyndham), and the anthology shows *Shadows*, *Spooky* and *Dramarama*. Lonsdale is also credited as the editor on the 1983 tie-in anthology of *Spooky*.

British TV producer and scriptwriter **Derrick [George] Sherwin** (aka "David Roberts"/"David Simon"), credited for creating "U.N.I.T." and the "Time Lords" for *Doctor Who*, died on October 17, aged 82. Between 1968 and 1970 he worked on the BBC series, first as a script/story editor, and later as a writer ('The Invasion') and a producer ('The War Games' and 'Spearhead from Space') when the show transitioned from black and white to colour. As an actor, Sherwin appeared in episodes of *The Invisible Man* (1959), *Tales of Mystery* and *Doctor Who*, along with Hammer's *The Vengeance of She*.

American electrical engineer **Earl Bakken** died on October 21, aged 94. Inspired by the laboratory apparatus during a viewing of the 1931 movie *Frankenstein* when he was eight years old, Bakken went on to design a transistorised pacemaker based on a circuit design he found in *Popular Electronics* magazine. Bakken co-founded Medtronic, which is now the world's largest medical equipment manufacturer.

Australian movie producer and director **John D. Lamond** died of Parkinson's disease on October 24, aged 71. His credits include the 1980s films *Nightmares* (aka *Stage Fright*) and *Sky Pirates*.

Hong Kong film producer **Raymond Chow** (Zou Wenhuai), who co-founded Golden Harvest studios in 1970 and made stars out of Bruce Lee and Jackie Chan, died on November 2, aged 91. Best known as the producer of numerous kung-fu movies during the

1970s, amongst his many other credits are *The Bedevilled*, *The Seven Coffins*, *Encounters of the Spooky Kind*, *Megaforce*, *The Dead and the Deadly*, *Zu: Warriors from the Magic Mountain*, *The Seventh Curse*, *Lost Souls* and *Teenage Mutant Ninja Turtles* (1990) and its two sequels.

Canadian-born comics fan **John Rogers**, who was president of the San Diego Comic-Con since 1986, died in California of complications from brain cancer on November 10. He was 57.

Jerry Frankel, a successful New York dress manufacturer who became a producer of Broadway shows, died on November 17, aged 88. Amonst his credits are the 1997 musical *Jekyll & Hyde*, which was later filmed with David Hasselhoff in the dual roles.

Acclaimed British cinematographer turned director **Nicolas [Jack] Roeg** died on November 23, aged 90. He started out working for the camera department on such films as the 1953 short *All Hallowe'en*, *Tarzan's Greatest Adventure* and *Doctor Blood's Coffin*, before shooting *Dr. Crippen* (1963), Roger Corman's *The Masque of the Red Death*, *Fahrenheit 451* (1966) and additional photography on the 1967 *Casino Royale*. Roeg's credits as a director include *Don't Look Now*, *The Man Who Fell to Earth*, *The Witches* (1990), *Cold Heaven*, *Puffball* (aka *Puffball: The Devil's Eyeball*) and an episode of TV's *The Adventures of Young Indiana Jones*. Theresa Russell was the second of Roeg's three actress wives.

Pioneering New Zealand film-maker **Geoff Murphy** (Geoffrey Peter Murphy) died on December 3, aged 80. He worked in all aspects of the film industry, including directing *The Quiet Earth*, *Freejack*, *Fortress 2* and a musical version of Edgar Allan Poe's *Tales of Mystery and Imagination*. Murphy was also second-unit director on Peter Jackson's *The Lord of the Rings* trilogy (2001–03).

Indian film producer and director **Tulsi Ramsay**, a member of the Ramsay film-making dynasty, died after suffering chest pains on December 13, aged 74. Often in collaboration with his brother Shyam Ramsay, his credits include India's most famous vampire movie, *Bandh Darwaza* (1990), along with such other titles as *Darwaza*, *Guest House*, *The Magnificent Guardian*, *The Monster* and the TV series *The Zee Horror Show* (1993–97).

Hollywood actress turned producer and director [Carole] **Penny Marshall** died of complications from diabetes on December 17, aged 75. Her films include the classic body-swap comedy *Big* and *The Preacher's Wife*, and she co-produced the 2005 movie version of *Bewitched*. As an actress, Marshall co-starred with Cindy Williams in the *Happy Days* spin-off TV sitcom *Laverne & Shirley* (1976–83) and related shows, and she was also in an episode of *Good Heavens* and the pilot of *Mork & Mindy* (as "Laverne DeFazio" again), along with the movie *Hocus Pocus*. As a voice actor, her credits include the feature cartoon *Scooby-Doo! and Kiss: Rock and Roll Mystery*.

Philanthropist **Audrey Geisel** (Audrey Grace Florine Stone), the widow of children's author Theodore Geisel (aka "Dr. Seuss"), died on December 19, aged 97. She founded Dr. Seuss Enterprises in 1993 to maintain the Dr. Seuss trademark, and had executive producer credits on the film adaptations *Horton Hears a Who!*, *The Lorax* and *The Grinch* (2018).

British TV producer and director **Bill Sellars** (William Sellers) died the same day, aged 93. He began his career as a production assistant on *A for Andromeda* and made cameo appearances in an episode of that SF serial and its sequel, *The Andromeda Breakthrough*. He directed four episodes of *Doctor Who* (the mostly-lost 'The Celestial Toymaker', 1966), which pitted William Hartnell's time-traveller and his companions against Michael Gough's evil genius.

Spanish screenwriter and director **Jorge Grau** [Solá] died on December 26, aged 88. He began his film career as a second-unit director on such *peplums* as *Goliath Against the Gods* and *The Colossus of Rhodes* before going on to direct *The Legend of Blood Castle* (aka *The Female Butcher*), *The Living Dead at Manchester Morgue* (aka *Let Sleeping Corpses Lie/Don't Open the Window*) and *Violent Blood Bath* (aka *Night Fiend*).

Danish-born animator and jazz musician **Børge Ring** died in the Netherlands on December 27, aged 97. His film credits include *It's the Great Pumpkin Charlie Brown*, *Asterix and Cleopatra* and several sequels, *The Smurfs and the Magic Flute*, *B.C. Rock*, *Heavy Metal* (John Halas' 'So Beautiful and So Dangerous' segment), *Valhalla*, *We're Back! A Dinosaur's Story* and *Momo*.

Controversial British film producer **Roy Skeggs** died on December 29, aged 84. He began his career as an assistant accountant with Douglas Fairbanks Productions in 1956, before moving to Hammer Films in 1963 as a production accountant. He became a production supervisor at Hammer in 1970 and took over the reins of the bankrupt studio (with Brian Lawrence) nine years later. Although he worked on *Twins of Evil, Blood from the Mummy's Tomb, Dr Jekyll & Sister Hyde, Vampire Circus, Dracula A.D. 1972, Straight on Till Morning, Fear in the Night, Demons of the Mind, The Satanic Rites of Dracula, Frankenstein and the Monster from Hell, Captain Kronos: Vampire Hunter* and *To the Devil a Daughter*, after the company went into receivership he found it difficult to get new projects off the ground, despite the Hammer name. He did manage to produce two TV series, *Hammer House of Horror* (1980) and *Hammer House of Mystery and Suspense* (aka *Fox Mystery Theater*, 1984), and he is credited as an associate producer on Ted Newsom's independent documentary *Flesh and Blood: The Hammer Heritage of Horror* (1994).

Hong Kong action director **Ringo Lam** (Lin Lingdong) died the same day, aged 63. His films include *Esprit D'amour, Mad Mission 4: You Never Die Twice* and *Replicant*. Lam also directed the car stunts on *Happy Ghost III*.

Veteran Walt Disney animator and director **Don Lusk** died on December 30, aged 105. His credits with the studio include *Pinocchio, Fantasia, Song of the South, The Adventures of Ichabod and Mr. Toad, Cinderella, Alice in Wonderland, Peter Pan, Sleeping Beauty, One Hundred and One Dalmations, The Sword in the Stone, Mary Poppins, The Jungle Book, The Aristocats, Bedknobs and Broomsticks, Robin Hood, The Little Mermaid* and many other titles. Lusk later freelanced for other studios and moved into television with such titles as *The Man Called Flintstone, Yogi & the Invasion of the Space Bears, Cool World, The Thief and the Cobbler, Captain Planet and the Planeteers, The 13 Ghosts of Scooby-Doo, Challenge of the GoBots, Jonny Quest, Sky Commanders, The Jetsons Meet the Flintstones, Gravedale High, A Pup Named Scooby-Doo, The Addams Family, The Pirates of Dark Water* and a number of *Charlie Brown* TV specials.

USEFUL ADDRESSES

THE FOLLOWING LISTING of organisations, publications, dealers and individuals is designed to present readers and authors with further avenues to explore. Although I can personally recommend many of those listed on the following pages, neither the publisher nor myself can take any responsibility for the services they offer. Please also note that the information below is only a guide and is subject to change without notice.

—The Editor

ORGANISATIONS

Australasian Horror Writers Association (*www.australasian-horror.wordpress.com*) is a non-profit organisation that was formed in 2005 and provides a community and unified voice for Australasian writers of dark fiction, fostering the evolution of the genre within Australia. AHWA is the first point of reference for writers and fans of the dark side of literature in Australia, New Zealand, and the Pacific Islands. It spreads the acceptance and understanding of horror literature to a wider audience, and in doing so gains a greater readership for established and new writers alike. They also publish the magazine *Midnight Echo*, and offer opportunities to be published, mentor programmes, critique services, competitions and giveaways, opportunities to interact with other writers, publishers, artists and other key members of the community, genre news on the Australian scene, and links to horror-related and writing resources. E-mail: australasianhorror@gmail.com

The British Fantasy Society (*www.britishfantasysociety.org*) was founded in 1971 and publishes the *BFS Journal*, featuring articles and reviews, and *BFS Horizons*, which is devoted to fiction and poetry, along with occasional exclusive publications only available to members of the Society. Run by volunteers, the BFS offers an e-newsletter, free entry into the BFS Short Story Competition, free specialist writing workshops, discounted membership of FantasyCon and organised open nights and book launches. For yearly membership see the website for details.

The Horror Writers Association (*www.horror.org*) is a non-profit organisation of writers and publishing professionals around the world, dedicated to promoting dark literature and the interests of those who write it. HWA was formed in the late 1980s and today has more than 1,250 members—making it the oldest and most respected professional organisation for horror writers. One of HWA's missions is to encourage public interest in and foster an appreciation of good horror and dark Fantasy literature. To that end, they offer the public areas of their website, they sponsor or take part in occasional public readings and lectures, they publish a blog and produce other materials for book-sellers and librarians, they facilitate readings and signings by horror writers, and they are dedicated to recognising and promoting diversity in the horror genre. As part of the organisation's core mission, they also sponsor the annual Bram Stoker Awards® for superior achievement in horror literature at the annual StokerCon. E-mail: *hwa@horror.org*

SELECTED SMALL PRESS PUBLISHERS

The Alchemy Press (*www.alchemypress.co.uk*).

American Fantasy Press (*www.americanfantasypress.com*), 919 Tappan Street, Woodstock, Illinois 60098, USA.

BearManor Media (*www.bearmanormedia.com*), PO Box 1129, Duncan, OK 73534-1129, USA.

Black Dog Books (*www.blackdogbooks.net*), 1115 Pine Meadows Ct., Normal, IL 61761-5432, USA. E-mail: *info@blackdogbooks.net*

Black Shuck Books (*www.greatbritishhorror.com/www.blackshuckbooks.co.uk*), "Hillbrow", Northbourne Road, Deal, Kent CT14 0LA, UK.

Borderlands Press (*www.borderlandspress.com*), POB 61, Benson, MD 21018, USA.

Celaeno Press (*www.celaenopress.com*).

Cemetery Dance Publications (*www.cemeterydance.com*), 132-B Industry Lane, Unit #7, Forest Hill, MD 21050, USA. E-mail: *info@cemeterydance.com*

Chthonic Matter (*www.chthonicmatter.wordpress.com*).

The Clive Barker Archive (*www.clivebarkerarchive.com*). E-mail: *philandsarah@clivebarker.info*

Crystal Lake Publishing (*www.crystallakepub.com*).

Dark Ink Books (*www.darkinkbooks.com*).

Dark Moon Books (*www.darkmoonbooks.com*), 3058 Spyglass Ct., Chino Hills, CA 91709, USA.

Earthling Publications (*www.earthlingpub.com*), PO Box 413, Northborough, MA 01532, USA. E-mail: *earthlingpub@yahoo.com*

Edgar Rice Burroughs, Inc. (*www.erbbooks.com*).

Flame Tree Publishing Ltd. (*www.flametreepublishing.com*), 6 Melbray Mews, Fulham, London SW6 3NS, UK.
E-mail: *info@flametreepublishing.com*

Hippocampus Press (*www.hippocampuspress.com*), PO Box 641, New York, NY 10156, USA. E-mail: *info@hippocampuspress.com*

Independent Legions Publishing (*www.independentlegions.com*).
E-mail: *independent.legions@aol.com*
KGHH Publishing (*www.kensingtongorepublishing.com*).

Lycan Valley Press Publications (*www.lycanvalley.com*), 1625 E. 72nd STE 700 PMB 132, Tacoma, Washington 98404, USA.

McFarland & Company, Inc., Publishers (*www.mcfarlandpub.com*), Box 611, Jefferson, NC 28640, USA.

MoonDream Press/Copper Dog Publishing LLC
(*www.copperdogpublishing.com/www.moondreampress.com*), 537 Leader Circle, Louisville, CO 80027, USA.

Nightscape Press (*www.nightscapepress.pub*).

Nightjar Press (*www.nightjarpress.weebly.com*), 63 Ballbrook Court, Wilmslow Road, Manchester M20 3GT, UK.

Night Shade Books (*www.nightshadebooks.com*), 307 West 36th Street, 11th Floor, New York, NY 10018, USA.

Nunkie (*www.nunkie.co.uk/theatre-shows/www.nunkie.co.uk/shop*).

Parallel Universe Publications
(*www.paralleluniversepublications.blogspot.co.uk/*), 130 Union Road, Oswaldtwistle, Lancashire BB5 3DR, UK.

Pigeon Park Press (*www.pigeonparkpress.com*).

Poise and Pen Publishing (*wwwpoiseandpen.com*).

Precipice Books (*www.precipicebooks.com*).

PS Publishing Ltd / Drugstore Indian Press / PS ArtBooks Ltd / Stanza Press / PSi / The Pulps Library / Electric Dreamhouse (*www.pspublishing.co.uk*), Grosvenor House, 1 New Road, Hornsea HU18 1PG, UK. E-mail: *editor@pspublishing.co.uk*

Radiant Crown Publishing (*www.radiantcrownpublishing.com*).

The Refuge Collection (*www.ozhorrorcon.com*).
E-mail: *Dillonstephen@hotmail.com*

Riverdale Avenue Books (*www.riverdaleavebooks.com*), 5676 Riverdale Avenue, Riverdale, NY 10471, USA.

Sarob Press (*www.sarobpress.blogspot.com*), La Blinière, 53250, Neuilly-le-Vendin, France.

Shadow Publishing (*www.shadowpublishing.webeasysite.co.uk/*), Apt. #19 Awdry Court, 15 St. Nicolas Gardens, Birmingham, West Midlands B38 8BH, UK. E-mail: *david.sutton986@btinternet.com*

Shadowridge Press (*www.shadowridgepress.com*).

Storm King Comics (*www.stormkingproductions.com*), 1623 N. Vista Street, Hollywood, CA 90046, USA.

Subterranean Press (*www.subterraneanpress.com*), PO Box 190106, Burton, MI 48519, USA. E-mail: *subpress@gmail.com*

The Swan River Press (*www.swanriverpress.ie*), Dublin, Ireland.
E-mail: *brian@swanriverpress.ie*

Tartarus Press (*www.tartaruspress.com*), Coverley House, Carlton-in-Coverdale, Leyburn, North Yorkshire DL8 4AY, UK. E-mail: *tartarus@pavilion.co.uk*

Telos Publishing (*www.telos.co.uk*), 5A Church Road, Shortlands, Bromley, Kent BR2 0HP, UK.

Things in the Well (*www.thingsinthewell.com*).
E-mail: *news@ozhorrorcon.com*

Ticonderoga Publications (*www.ticonderogapublications.com*), PO Box 29, Greenwood, Western Australia 6924.

TTA Press (*www.ttapress.com*), 5 Martins Lane, Witcham, Ely, Cambs CB6 2LB, UK.

Undertow Publications (*www.undertowbooks.com*) Michael Kelly Editor, 1905 Faylee Crescent, Pickering, ON L1V 2T3, Canada.
E-mail: *undertowbooks@gmail.com*

Unsung Stories (*www.unsungstories.co.uk*), 43 Mornington Road, Chingford, London E4 7DT, UK.

Urbane Publications Ltd. (*www.urbanepublications.com*), Suite 3, Brown Europe House, 33-34 Gleaming Wood Drive, Chatham, Kent ME5 8RZ, UK.

Valancourt Books (*www.valancourtbooks.com*).

Wicked Run Press. E-mail: *wickedrunpress@gmail.com*

Written Backwards (*www.nettirw.com*).

SELECTED MAGAZINES

Ansible is a highly entertaining monthly SF and fantasy newsletter/ gossip column edited by David Langford. It is available free electronically by sending an e-mail to: *ansible-request@dcs.gla.ac.uk* with a subject line reading "subscribe", or you can receive the print version by sending a stamped and addressed envelope to Ansible, 94 London Road, Reading, Berks RG1 5AU, UK. Back issues, links and book lists are also available online.

Black Static (*www.ttapress.com*) is the UK's premier horror fiction magazine, produced bi-monthly by the publishers of *Interzone*. Six- and twelve-issue subscriptions are available, along with a lifetime subscription, from TTA Press, 5 Martins Lane, Witcham, Ely, Cambs CB6 2LB, UK, or from the secure TTA website. E-mail: *andy@ttapress.com*

Classic Images (*www.classicimages.com*) edited by Bob King is a monthly newsprint publication for those who love old movies. Most issues contain material of interest to horror and SF fans, and subscriptions are available. 301 E. 3rd Street, Muscatine, IA 52761, USA. E-mail: *classicimages@classicimages.com*

Disturbed Digest (*www.albanlake.com*), Alban Lake Publishing, PO Box 141, Colo, Iowa 50056-0141, USA. E-mail: *albanlake@yahoo.com*

The Ghastling (*www.theghastling.com*). E-mail: *editor@theghastling.com*

Ghosts & Scholars (*www.pardoes.info/roanddarroll/GS.html*), now published by Mark and Jo Valentine, is a scholarly journal published roughly twice a year. It is dedicated to the classic ghost story and to M.R. James in particular. Two-issue subscriptions are available from Mark and Jo Valentine, Stable Cottage, Priest Bank Road, Kildwick, Keighley, Yorkshire, BD20 9BH, UK.
E-mail: *lostclub@btopenworld.com*

Illustrators (*www.bookpalace.com*) is a beautifully designed and published full-colour periodical devoted to art and artists. The Book Palace, Jubilee House, Bedwardine Road, Crystal Palace, London SE19 3AP, UK. E-mail: *IQ@bookpalace.com*

Locus (*www.locusmag.com*) is the monthly newspaper of the SF/fantasy field (not so much horror these days). Contact Locus Publications, 655 13th St, Suite 100, Oakland, CA 94612, USA. Subscription information with other rates and order forms are also available on the website. E-mail: *locus@locusmag.com*.

The Magazine of Fantasy & Science Fiction (*www.fandsf.com*) has been publishing some of the best imaginative fiction for six decades. Produced bi-monthly, single copies or an annual subscription are available by US cheques or credit card from: Fantasy & Science Fiction, PO Box 3447, Hoboken, NJ 07030, USA, or you can subscribe via the website.

Night Land Quarterly (*www.a-third.com/*), Atelier Third, Room 301, 1-21-24 Takadanobaba, Shinjuku-ku, Tokyo, 169-0075, Japan. E-mail: *makihara@a-third.com*

Occult Detective Quarterly (*www.greydogtales.com/blog/occult-detective-quarterly/odq/*). E-mail: *occultdetectivequarterly@yahoo.com*

Phantasmagoria covers horror, fantasy and science fiction in all media. Copies can be purchased in print form on Amazon or from Forbidden Planet, Belfast, and back issues are also available on Kindle. E-mail: *tkboss@hotmail.com*

Pulp Horror/The Paperback Fanatic (*www.thepaperbackfanatic.com*). Justin Marriott's excellent, if irregular, publications for those who love old and new books. E-mail: *thepaperbackfanatic@sky.com*

Rabbit Hole (*www.harlanellisonbooks.com/shop*) is an informative semi-regular newsletter edited by Jason Davis and issued to members of The Harlan Ellison Recording Collection. You can subscribe via the website or contact The Kilimanjaro Corporation, PO Box 55548, Sherman Oaks, CA 91413-0548, USA.

Rue Morgue (*www.rue-morgue.com*) is a glossy bi-monthly magazine subtitled "Horror in Culture & Entertainment". Each issue is packed with full colour features and reviews of new films, books, comics, music and game releases. Subscriptions are available from: Marrs Media Inc., 1411 Dufferin Street, Toronto, Ontario M6H 4CT, Canada, or by credit card on the website. E-mail: *info@rue-morgue.com*

Space and Time: The Magazine of Fantasy, Horror, and Science Fiction (*www.spaceandtimemagazine.com*) has been publishing speculative fiction for more than five decades—a must-read for true fans of the strange and unusual. Readers will discover the rising stars of genre fiction alongside industry staples like Jessica A. Salmonson, Norman Spinrad, Jack Ketchum and Aliette de Bodard. Published twice a year, single issues and subscriptions are available from the website or from: Space and Time Magazine Subscription Fulfillment, PO Box 214, Independence, MO 64051-1099, USA.

Supernatural Tales (*www.suptales.blogspot.com*) is a fiction magazine edited by David Longhorn, with subscriptions available via PayPal, cheques or non-UK cash. Supernatural Tales, 291 Eastbourne Avenue, Gateshead NE8 4NN, UK. E-mail: *davidlonghorn@hotmail.com*

Weirdbook (*www.wildsidepress.com*) is a PoD revival of the iconic fantasy and horror magazine, edited by Doug Draa and published by Wildside Press LCC, 9710 Traville Gateway Drive, #234, Rockville, MD 20850, USA.

BOOK DEALERS

All Data Lost Books (*www.alldatalostbooks.co.uk*) is an online UK bookstore specialising in the esoteric and strange. They stock a wide selection of horror, occult, witchcraft and science fiction vintage paperbacks.

Cold Tonnage Books (*www.coldtonnage.com*) offers excellent mail order new and used SF/fantasy/horror, art, reference, limited editions etc. Write to: Andy & Angela Richards, Cold Tonnage Books, Poundwater, Farway, Colyton, Devon, EX24 6EG, UK. Credit cards accepted. Tel: +44 (0)1404-871001. E-mail: *andy@coldtonnage.com*

DreamHaven Books & Comics (*www.dreamhavenbooks.com*) is open Tuesday through Saturday and also has a mail-order outlet, offering new and used SF/fantasy/horror/art and illustrated etc. with regular catalogues (both print and E-mail). 2031 E. 38th Street, Minneapolis, MN 55406-3015, USA. Credit cards accepted. Tel: (612) 823-6070. E-mail: *dream@dreamhavenbooks.com*

Fantastic Literature (*www.fantasticliterature.com*) mail order offers the UK's biggest online out-of-print SF/fantasy/horror genre bookshop. Fanzines, pulps and vintage paperbacks as well. Write to: Simon and Laraine Gosden, Fantastic Literature, 35 The Ramparts, Rayleigh, Essex SS6 8PY, UK. Credit cards and Pay Pal accepted. Tel/Fax: +44 (0)1268-747564. E-mail: *simon@fantasticliterature.com*

Hyraxia Books (*www.hyraxia.com*), Toft Cottage, 1 Beverley Road, Hutton Cranswick, East Yorkshire YO25 9PQ, UK. Specialist sellers of rare and collectible modern first editions, including many genre titles. They also buy books. Tel: +44 (0)7557-652-609. E-mail: *shop@hyraxia.com*

The Iliad Bookshop (*www.iliadbooks.com*), 5400 Cahuenga Blvd., North Holly-wood, CA 91601, USA. General bookstore that has a very fine selection of new, used and rare books, with an emphasis on literature and the arts. Tel: (818) 509-2665.

Porcupine Books offers regular catalogues and extensive mail order lists of used fantasy/horror/SF titles via E-mail *brian@porcupine.demon.co.uk* or write to: 37 Coventry Road, Ilford, Essex IG1 4QR, UK. Tel: +44 (0)20 8554-3799.

Terence McVicker Rare Books
(*www.batsoverbooks.com/?page=shop/index*) is a mail-order business offering premium rare and collectible items—many H.P. Lovecraft and Arkham House-related. A weekly e-mail reader features additions, updates and news. E-mail: *info@batsoverbooks.com*

Ygor's Books specialises in out of print science fiction, fantasy and horror titles, including British, signed, speciality press and limited editions. They also buy books, letters and original art in these fields. E-mail: *ygorsbooks@gmail.com*

ONLINE RESOURCES

The Dark (*www.thedarkmagazine.com*) edited by Sean Wallace and Silvia Moreno-Garcia is a free monthly online magazine that is also available for digital download.

Fantastic Fiction (*www.fantasticfiction.co.uk*) features more than 2,000 best-selling author biographies with all their latest books, covers and descriptions.

File 770 (*www.file770.com*) is the Hugo Award-winning online version of Mike Glyer's science fiction fan newzine, reporting on fanzines, SF clubs, conventions, fan funds and fanac. E-mail: *MikeGlyer@cs.com*

Hellnotes (*www.hellnotes.com*) covers news and reviews of the horror genre—horror films, horror novels, horror reviews, writing horror, horror conventions and more.

The Horror Zine (*www.thehorrorzine.com*) is a monthly online magazine edited by Jeani Rector that features fiction, poetry, interviews and reviews. It is also available in a PoD edition and produces its own books.

Locus Online (*www.locusmag.com/news*) is an excellent online source for the latest news and reviews.

Nightmare Magazine (*www.nightmare-magazine.com*) edited by John Joseph Adams is an excellent monthly online site for fiction (both new and reprint), interviews and podcasts.

Pseudopod (*www.pseudopod.org*), the premiere horror fiction podcast, continues to offer a free-to-download, weekly reading of new or classic horror fiction by a variety of voices. The site remains dedicated to paying their authors while providing readings for free and offering the widest variety of audio horror fiction currently available on the net.

Tor.com (*www.tor.com*), publishes new fiction, articles, novel excerpts, artist galleries, reviews and a lot more.

Vault of Evil (*www.vaultofevil.wordpress.com*) is a site dedicated to celebrating the best in British horror with special emphasis on UK anthologies. There is also a lively forum devoted to many different themes at *www.vaultofevil.proboards.com*